# THE YEAR'S 25 FINEST CRIME & MYSTERY STORIES
## Seventh Annual Edition

# THE YEAR'S 25 FINEST CRIME & MYSTERY STORIES

## Seventh Annual Edition

Edited by
Ed Gorman
Martin H. Greenberg

Introduction by Jon L. Breen
With an Overview by Edward D. Hoch

Carroll & Graf Publishers, Inc.
New York

First Carroll & Graf edition 1998

Carroll & Graf Publishers, Inc.
19 West 21st St., Suite 601
New York, NY 10010

Library of Congress Cataloging-in-Publication Data is available

ISBN: 0-7867-0571-X

Manufactured in the United States of America

# PERMISSIONS

# CONTENTS

Introduction                                        xi
    Jon L. Breen

THE KNEELING SOLDIER                                 1
    Jeffrey Deaver

SPEAK NO EVIL                                       17
    Nancy Pickard

SOLO                                                31
    Marcia Muller

PSYCHOFEMMES                                        43
    Melissa Mia Hall

BLOOD BROTHERS                                      67
    Richard T. Chizmar

WAYS TO KILL A CAT                                  79
    Simon Brett

THE HORSESHOE NAIL                                  98
    Bill Pronzini

BIRD OF PARADISE                                   118
    John Harvey

A FRONT ROW SEAT                                   135
    Jan Grape

A LONG AND HAPPY LIFE                              154
    DeLoris Stanton Forbes

NIGHTCRAWLERS                                      165
    John Lutz

REMEMBRANCE                                                 182
　　Carolyn G. Hart

TEA FOR TWO                                                  198
　　M. D. Lake

ON THE PSYCHIATRIST'S COUCH                                  206
　　Reginald Hill

THE EASTER CAT                                               219
　　Bill Crider

CALL ME WALT                                                 232
　　Jerry Sykes

COLD TURKEY                                                  241
　　Carole Nelson Douglas

DEATH CUP                                                    248
　　Joyce Carol Oates

LOVE ME FOR MY YELLOW HAIR ALONE: 32 SHORT
　　FILMS ABOUT MARILYN MONROE                               271
　　Carolyn Wheat

THE CLOCK THAT COUNTS THE DEAD                               287
　　Edward Bryant

TAKE IT AWAY                                                 298
　　Donald E. Westlake

THE MAN WHO BEAT THE SYSTEM                                  306
　　Stuart Kaminsky

KELLER ON THE SPOT                                           323
　　Lawrence Block

THE HOUSE ON THE EDGE                                        340
　　D. A. McGuire

CRIMSON SHADOW                                               381
　　Walter Mosley

1997 Bibliography and Necrology                              391
　　Edward D. Hoch

# THE YEAR'S 25 FINEST CRIME & MYSTERY STORIES
## Seventh Annual Edition

# Introduction
## by Jon L. Breen
# THE MYSTERY IN 1997

Dazzled by the steady stream of good, bad, and indifferent new mystery fiction flowing with dizzying rapidity over the book store and library shelves, most readers probably aren't aware of the sense of crisis felt by many practitioners in the field. Publishers continue to merge, making fewer major markets each year; corporate emphasis on potential bestsellers serves to squeeze out the unspectacular bread-and-butter books in preference to calculated would-be blockbusters; writers who have enjoyed a modicum of longevity and success lose their places on the publishing lists to newer writers who may be no likelier to become new John Grishams or Mary Higgins Clarks but at least haven't proven it yet. As a result of these sad developments, there are more talented, or determined anyway, pros and wannabes than there are slots available in the world of New York bookmaking—for yes, cries the bruised scrivener, that is what mainstream American publishing has become: not nurturing books but making book. For an approximation of what book publishing *used* to be like, a paradise of gentlefolk who would rather read good books than the bottom line, the potential writer must look elsewhere.

Is the above an excessively over-exaggerated hyperbole? Sure—I mean, I hope so—but it provides my excuse for declaring 1997 mystery fiction's Year of the Small Publisher, by which unpatronizing sobriquet I mean everything from semipro fan presses to producers of handsome and expensive limited editions to regional trade publishers in competition with the big New York firms.

Small presses in the mystery field are nothing new. August Derleth's Arkham House, founded to put the works of H. P. Lovecraft into book form, published Derleth's Solar Pons stories and other mystery-related collections under the Mycroft and Moran imprint beginning in the 1940s. In the early 1970s, Colorado book dealers Tom and Enid Schantz published some limited editions, mostly Sherlockian, under the name Aspen House. (The Schantzes have recently reentered the publishing fray, with several handsome reprints of vintage American detective novels as Rue Morgue Press [P.O. Box 4119, Boulder, CO 80306].) Midway in the same decade, Otto Penzler founded Mysterious Press as a specialist in short story collections; the imprint subsequently grew into one of the most prestigious in crime fiction—and now rarely publishes a short story collection. In the 1980s, Meredith Phillips' Perseverance Press produced a number of handsome trade paperback editions of new writers. Before becoming an imprint of Norton, Countryman's Foul Play Press published a succession of originals and reprints, while Academy Chicago, another smaller regional firm, became an increasing presence in the field.

Today there are more smaller publishers on the scene than ever, some of whose products are mentioned later in this article. Douglas G. Greene's Crippen & Landru specializes in short story collections in the manner of (but more prolifically than) the early Mysterious Press. Dennis McMillan, who produced beautiful limited editions and some trade paperbacks of Fredric Brown and other writers in the eighties and early nineties, has reentered the field after a short hiatus.

Regional publishers like Write Way (10555 E. Dartmouth, Ste. 210, Aurora, CO 80014) and Allen A. Knoll (200 West Victoria Street, Santa Barbara, CA 93101) regularly publish a variety of new mystery fiction. The British Do-Not Press, specializing in fiction noir, has an American distributor: Dufour Editions (Chester Springs, PA 19425-0007). Interncontinental (P.O. Box 7242, Fairfax Station, VA 22039), along with its mission to translate all the Dutch author Baantjer's Inspector Dekok novels into English, has published a number of originals by other writers. Gary Lovisi's very prolific Gryphon Publications (P.O. Box 209, Brooklyn, NY 11228-0209) revives lost pulp stories by writers like Howard Browne, while publishing new material ranging from enthusiastically amateur to fully professional in quality.

The products of these smaller specialty publishers are, as one might expect, a mixed bag. But in the past couple of years, they have begun to make a greater impact on the field, among the awards-givers if not on the best-seller lists. In 1997, The Imaginary Press (P.O. Box 509, East Setauket, NY 11733-0509) published a short story collection by K.j.a. Wishnia, *Flat Rate and Other Tales*, introducing Ecuador-born New York cop Filomena Buscarsela, a fresh and energized first person voice. A book-length work about the character, *23 Shades of Black*, quickly followed and gained an Edgar nomination for best first novel. (This marked the second year in a row a small press work was nominated in the category, Margaret Mosely's *Bonita Faye* [Three Forks] having sent first edition collectors scrambling the year before.) Not a nominee but certainly one of the fine American firsts of the year, Charlotte Carter's *Rhode Island Red*, came from Serpent's Tail, a specialty British publisher with an American arm (180 Varick Street, 10th Floor, New York, NY 10014).

Meanwhile, the Robert L. Fish Award for best first short story by an American writer went not to a story from one of the excellent digests fronted by the ghosts of Ellery Queen and Alfred Hitchcock but to Rosalind Roland's "If Thine Eye Offend Thee," from the Sisters in Crime, Los Angeles chapter's original anthology *Murder by Thirteen* (Crown Valley Press, P.O. Box 336, Acton, CA 93510-0336). While some of its companions are hopelessly amateurish, Roland's vigilante wish-fulfillment hits the mark.

In a bizarre crossover between the habits of specialty publishers and trade publishers, Ballantine Books came up with a fresh idea: the signed but virtually unlimited edition. The entire first printings (20,000 copies or so) of books by Jill McGown, Sharyn McCrumb, and Julie Smith came autographed by their authors, an experiment that may have intrigued orthopedists as much as it did collectors.

The increasing visibility of smaller specialty publishers somewhat parallels other relatively recent developments in the entertainment industry: the widening influence of cable and satellite television, lessening the dominance of the big-three networks, and the nineties renaissance of independent film production. Last year, we noted three independent features (*Sling Blade, Fargo,* and *Lone Star*) as potential crime classics, but a surer candidate for cinematic immortality than any of them, this year's Edgar winner, came from a major studio, Warner Brothers. *L.A. Confidential,* adapted by director Curtis Hanson and Brian Helgeland from James Ellroy's 1990 novel, is a spellbinding example of the filmmaker's (and the mystery writer's) art from beginning to end. Few novelists in any genre have been as well served by their screen adapters as Ellroy has here.

# BEST NOVELS OF THE YEAR 1997

Did the products of any of the smaller maverick publishers make my best-of-the-year list? Not this time—the New York majors still dominate—but they're knocking on the door.

Though my reading was sparser than in some years, I found it paradoxically harder than usual to prune my list of favorites to the self-imposed limit of fifteen. Conclusion? It must have been an outstanding year indeed.

K. C. Constantine, *Family Values* (Mysterious). Though retired from his job as Rocksburg, Pennsylvania police chief, Mario Balzic is back on the job as a quasi-official private eye. With his uncanny ear for varying speech patterns, Constantine is the David Mamet of crime fiction.

Lindsey Davis, *Time to Depart* (Mysterious). The seventh adventure for Marcus Didius Falco is among the strongest in the series, notable for its description of the Roman police system along with the usual virtues of humor and plotspinning.

Colin Dexter, *Death is Now My Neighbor* (Crown). In Chief Inspector Morse and Sergeant Lewis, Dexter has created one of the great teams in detective fiction, and he has as much respect for fairly planted clues as any

Golden Age classicist. The reader not only has a chance at solving the murder case but at anticipating the final revelation of Morse's long-secret first name.

P. C. Doherty, *A Tournament of Murders* (St. Martin's). If your heart belongs to the classics, particularly to John Dickson Carr in his swashbuckling historical vein, the third in Doherty's series about Chaucer's Canterbury pilgrims is a must, complete with locked room, dying message, closed circle of suspects, and haunted castle.

John Harvey, *Still Waters* (Holt). Nottingham's jazz-loving Detective Inspector Charlie Resnick is by general consensus one of the outstanding series detectives of the nineties. This superb procedural novel demonstrates why.

P. D. James, *A Certain Justice* (Knopf). The novels about Adam Dalgliesh have often introduced a cast of suspects from a specialized background or occupation; in this case, it's London's law courts. James writes them long, but charges they are padded or bloated generally prove groundless. (*Publisher's Weekly's* review calling this a "locked room" mystery demonstrates how terms with very precise definitions often lose their meanings through misuse.)

Jonathan Kellerman, *The Clinic* (Bantam). Psychologist Alex Delaware seeks the killer of a professor and author of pop psychology. Among the mystery novelists who regularly hit the bestseller lists, some deserve their exalted stature and others do not. Kellerman does.

Margaret Lawrence, *Blood Red Roses* (Avon). The second novel about Colonial Maine midwife Hannah Trevor is nearly as good as its Edgar-nominated predecessor *Hearts and Bones* (1996). Period detail and beauty of language combine with solid plotting to make this one of the best historical mystery series after only two entries.

Anne Perry, *Ashworth Hall* (Fawcett Columbine). In an example of how a historical mystery series can seem *au courant,* this fine entry from the Charlotte and Thomas Pitt series concerns the tensions between Britain and Ireland, which a century later have finally (maybe) been resolved.

Bill Pronzini, *A Wasteland of Strangers* (Walker). The multiple-narrator format is always a challenge, even more so when the author employs as many voices and changes them as often as does Pronzini in this extraordinary small-town mystery, a nominee for both the Edgar and the International Association of Crime Writers, North American Branch's Hammett Prize. It's one of the best from an always professional and often brilliant writer.

Ian Rankin, *Black and Blue* (St. Martin's). Of the contemporary British cops who populate so much of the best detective fiction, Edinburgh's John Rebus must rank in the top half dozen. This Gold Dagger winner and Edgar nominee is long, complex, challenging (especially to one unfamiliar with all the Scottish slang and allusions), and totally enthralling. (British police detectives in fiction are often differentiated by their musical tastes: Resnick and jazz, Morse and classical, Peter Robinson's Alan Banks and opera. Rebus's heart clearly belongs to rock.)

Kate Ross, *The Devil in Music* (Viking). If I were picking the award winners, the fourth novel about Restoration dandy Julian Kestrel might just nose out the Westlake entry (see below) as my top choice for the year. (At least the Agatha voters agreed with me.) It's a masterpiece of devious construction and historical detail, both of which would be empty achievements if the characters didn't spring to vivid life. (Tragically, Ross died early in 1998 at age 41.)

Lisa Scottoline, *Rough Justice* (HarperCollins). This energetic legal thriller, set in snowbound Philadelphia, is a better jury-fixing novel (for its humor, its people, even its believability) than John Grisham's bestseller *The Runaway Jury* (1996).

Donald E. Westlake, *The Ax* (Mysterious). A casualty of corporate downsizing turns to murder in a situation that may remind very long-memoried readers of the works of C. E. Vulliamy, though its dark humor is much more subtle. This one may polarize readers: I found it a noir masterpiece and a high point of its author's career; the Westlake enthusiast closest to me couldn't even finish it.

Carolyn Wheat, *Troubled Waters* (Berkley). In a novel that (for me at least) topped her 1996 Edgar nominee *Mean Streak*, Wheat flashes back to lawyer Cass Jameson's student radical days. Of the many lawyer novelists currently writing, Wheat is far from the top in publicity but near to it in quality.

# SHORT STORIES

Two of the best writers in the field produced single-author short-story collections in lieu of novels last year: Sharyn McCrumb with *Foggy Mountain Breakdown and Other Stories* (Ballantine) and Stephen Saylor with *The House of the Vestals* (St. Martin's), nine stories about Roman sleuth Gordianus the Finder. Amanda Cross's *The Collected Stories* (Ballantine) also gathered nine tales, eight of them about professorial sleuth Kate Fansler. Among the specialists, Crippen & Landru (P.O. Box 9315, Dept. T, Norfolk, VA 23505) brought us the first large collection of Margaret Maron's short stories, *Shoveling Smoke*, plus collections by H. R. F. Keating (*In Kensington Gardens Once*), Michael Gilbert (*The Man Who Hated Banks and Other Mysteries*), and Edward D. Hoch (*The Ripper of Storyville and Other Ben Snow Tales*); while Dennis McMillan (1581 N. Debra Sue Place, Tucson, AZ 85715) collected sixteen of Howard Browne's pulp stories, along with some of the veteran editor/novelist/screenwriter's autobiographical reminiscences, in *Incredible Ink*.

The anthology market also continued strong. Prominent writers fronting original multi-author collections in paperback included Mary Higgins Clark (*The Plot Thickens* [Pocket]), Joan Hess (*Funny Bones* [Signet]), and historical specialists Miriam Grace Monfredo and Sharan Newman (*Crime Through*

*Time* [Berkley]). Also for historical mystery fans, Mike Ashley added to his series of original anthologies with *Historical Whodunnits* and *The Mammoth Book of New Sherlock Holmes Adventures* (both Carroll & Graf). TV sleuth Jessica Fletcher ostensibly compiled *Murder They Wrote* (Boulevard) with the help of flesh-and-blood editors Martin H. Greenberg and Elizabeth Foxwell, who (though uncredited) also put together *Malice Domestic 6* (Pocket), introduced by Anne Perry. Greenberg, along with Ed Gorman and Larry Segriff, added another volume to a long-running series, *Cat Crimes for the Holidays* (Fine). In *The Fatal Frontier* (Carroll & Graf), Gorman and Greenberg combine originals with reprints while exploring the interface between crime and western fiction.

Among the pure reprint anthologies, Otto Penzler and guest editor Robert B. Parker put together *The Best American Mystery Stories 1997* (Houghton, Mifflin); Marilyn Wallace drew on her earlier series of originals for *The Best of Sisters in Crime* (Berkley); and two editors straddled the artificial border between "literary" and genre fiction: Michele Slung with *Murder and Other Acts of Literature* (St. Martin's) and Michael Dibdin with *The Vintage Book of Classic Crime* (Vintage). Cynthia Manson and Kathleen Halligan drew on the seemingly limitless back files of *Ellery Queen's Mystery Magazine* and *Alfred Hitchcock's Mystery Magazine* for *Murder to Music* (Carroll & Graf). Charles G. Waugh and Martin H. Greenberg offered scrambled genres in *Sci Fi Private Eye* (ROC). Another theme anthology from the Greenberg/Gorman team was *Love Kills* (Carroll & Graf). Two similarly titled anthologies, the Gorman-Pronzini-Greenberg *American Pulp* (Carroll & Graf) and Peter Haining's *Pulp Fiction* (Barnes & Noble), ironically drew few of their stories from pulp magazines, drawing more heavily on fifties digests like *Manhunt*.

# REFERENCE BOOKS AND SECONDARY SOURCES

The deserving Edgar winner in the biographical/critical category, Natalie Hevener Kaufman and Carol McGinnis Kay's *"G" is for Grafton: The World of Kinsey Millhone* (Holt), takes an approach that is more Sherlockian than either biographical (at least of Grafton) or critical, cataloging every facet of the fictional sleuth's life and career in a way that will appeal most to very devoted fans.

A secondary source of wider appeal is *Deadly Women: The Woman Mystery Reader's Indispensable Companion* (Carroll & Graf), edited by Jan Grapa, Dean James, and Ellen Nehr, a magazine-style collection of articles, interviews, reading lists, and other good things that no collection of books about mysteries should be without. (Marcia Muller's piece on Margaret Sutton's Judy Bolton series was a highlight for me.) However, parts of the book provoked me to mount a favorite hobby horse: refuting a too-common revisionist history of American women mystery writers that is most bothersome when it forgets or minimizes the works of important earlier writers. Examples follow:

In an interview, Elizabeth Peters states that in 1969, "Male writers had been producing comic mysteries for some time. I guess maybe it was, at that time, a new venture for women."

Peters (pseudonym of Barbara Mertz, who also writes as Barbara Michaels) is not a person to deny credit where it is due and should not be excoriated for one off-the-cuff statement in an interview. But I have two questions: 1) What about Craig Rice, Margaret Scherf, Constance and Gwenyth Little, and Phoebe Atwood Taylor, to name a few American women writers who earlier achieved success writing funny mysteries? (I won't mention Joyce Porter, since by common consent, the British don't count in these arguments.) 2) Were there really so many American *males* not named Westlake producing comic mysteries in the sixties?

Susan Wittig Albert, in the course of making some outlandish generalizations about mystery fiction, disses such pioneering female sleuths as Nurse Sarah Keate (who did *not* play a secondary role to Lance O'Leary in Mignon G. Eberhart's novels) and Miss Marple (if Agatha Christie's sleuth was "modestly non-assertive," how did she solve all those mysteries?) Albert offers no recognition of the existence of writers like Margaret Millar, Dorothy B. Hughes, Dorothy Salisbury Davis, Charlotte Armstrong, and Patricia High-smith, who were not only active in the forties and fifties but *celebrated* as leaders in the field.

To put it simply, from Anna Katharine Green on, women have *always* been prominent in American mystery fiction. I offer this venting not as a wounded male but as an admirer of a long tradition of American women mystery writers whose contribution is denigrated by the rewriting of history. (In fairness, a few articles in *Deadly Women* serve to counter the revisionism, at least by implication, notably Ed Gorman's "Some Women We Should Be Reading," which discusses Millar, Hughes, and Armstrong plus Elisabeth Sanxay Holding and Dolores Hitchens.)

Also of wide appeal to fans was *Crimes of the Scene: A Mystery Guide for the International Traveler* (St. Martin's), by Nina King, with Robin Winks and other specialist contributors identified in the text. What I liked most about this survey of mysteries set outside the U.S.A. and Great Britain was that its annotations are frankly critical rather than just descriptive.

I may have taken too much space venting. For the other secondary sources of the year, see Edward D. Hoch's bibliography.

# SUB-GENRES

Critic's confession: I spent an inordinate amount of my reading time in 1997 gathering entries for the second edition of *Novel Verdicts: A Guide to Courtroom Fiction,* which Scarecrow Press will certainly have received and maybe even published by the time you read this. (Believe me, this is offered as a lame excuse, not a commercial.) Thus, the usual tour of the subgenres will be overbalanced toward the lawyers—a sign of the times, you'll agree. Apart from the Scottoline and Wheat titles in my top fifteen, I can recommend plenty of legal thrillers and courtroom novels.

Most of the first novels I read were by and/or about lawyers. The best of them was D. W. Buffa's *The Defense* (Holt), but Tess Collins's *The Law of Revenge* (Ivy) and Tony Lewis's *Conflict of Interest* (Pineapple) were also strong. Second novelist Bill Blum produced a vastly better book than his first in *The Last Appeal* (Onyx). Among the established series lawyers, William Bernhardt's Ben Kincaid was in good form in the O. J.-inspired *Naked Justice* (Ballantine); Richard Parrish's Joshua Rabb had his best case to date in *Wind and Lies* (Onyx); Richard North Patterson's Tony Lord returned in the very-good-but-way-too-long *Silent Witness* (Knopf); Paul Levine's Jake Lassiter was in strong form in *Flesh and Bones* (Morrow); and Joe L. Hensley's Don Robak made a welcome comeback in *Robak's Witch* (St. Martin's). Also pacing the halls of justice in customary form were Grif Stockley's Gideon Page in *Blind Justice* (Simon & Schuster); Robert K. Tanenbaum's Butch Karp in *Irresistible Impulse* (Dutton); and Sara Gregory's (A. W. Gray's) Sharon Hays in *Public Trust* (Signet).

However, the new lawyer on the block, Billy Bob Holland of Death Smith, Texas, proved a disappointment. Though I've enjoyed a couple of James Lee Burke's Dave Robichaux books, I found his *Cimarron Rose* (Hyperion) the weakest best-novel Edgar winner I've read since Robert B. Parker's *Promised Land* (1977). (To my friends on the Edgar committee: the Hammett Prize selectors also nominated it, so maybe it's me.)

Professional cops in action included Ed McBain's 87th Precinct in *Nocturne* (Warner)—that a series dating back to 1956 should still seem so fresh and vital is a tribute to its author's consummate professionalism; H. R. F. Keating's Inspector Ghote in *Asking Questions* (St. Martin's); Peter Robinson's Alan Banks in *Blood at the Root* (Avon); Jill McGown's Hill and Lloyd in *Verdict Unsafe* (Ballantine); and Richard A. Lupoff's Marvia Plum (a solo effort this time) in *The Radio Red Killer* (St. Martin's).

I don't seem to have read many private eyes in the year just past, but two in reliably solid form were Lawrence Block's Matt Scudder in *Even the Wicked* (Morrow) and Parnell Hall's Stanley Hastings, who serves to lampoon another kind of crime fiction in *Suspense* (Mysterious).

Some of the classical writers filled us in on unusual backgrounds: Tahitian coffee-growing in Aaron Elkins' *Twenty Blue Devils* (Mysterious); wild-west patent medicine selling in the late William L. DeAndrea's *Fatal Elixir* (Walker); the rare book business in Block's *The Burglar in the Library* (Dutton); the furniture trade in Margaret Maron's *Killer Market* (Mysterious); classical music radio in K. K. Beck's *We Interrupt This Broadcast* (Mysterious); and the campaign against land mines in Richard Forrest's *The Pied Piper of Death* (St. Martin's). Most promising new sleuth of the year may be Michael Kurland's 1930s newspaper columnist Alexander Brass in the deliberately Rex Stout-like *Too Soon Dead* (St. Martin's). The book of most surprising quality, coming as it did from a low-profile, small-town library publisher, was Elizabeth Wetzel's *Deadly Arts* (Avalon).

Strong novels in the elastic category of dark suspense included Ed Gorman's *Black River Falls* (Leisure) and Dennis Etchison's *Double Edge* (Dell), yet another take on the fascinating Lizzie Borden case.

And, of course, the Comeback of the Year Award must go to Richard Stark's (Donald E. Westlake's) career crook Parker who resumed his big-capering career in the aptly named *Comeback* (Mysterious). By contrast, a comeback that should have been resisted was Ira Levin's *Son of Rosemary* (Dutton).

# A SENSE OF HISTORY

It was a great year for rediscovering crime fiction's long and illustrious past. Richard Matheson's *Noir: Three Novels of Suspense* (G & G Books, 3601 Skylark Lane SE, Cedar Rapids, IA 52403) gathered the paperback originals *Fury on Sunday* (1953), *Someone is Bleeding* (1953), and *Ride the Nightmare* (1959) in a one-volume limited edition by one of the masters of popular fiction. William March's famous 1954 novel of a murderous child, *The Bad Seed* (Ecco), appeared in a new edition with an introduction by Elaine Showalter. (As a companion piece, see Max Allan Collins's cleverly wrought *Mommy* [Leisure], a novel version of his film sequel to *The Bad Seed*.) Foul Play Press, now an imprint of Norton, revived two vintage Stanley Ellin novels, *House of Cards* (1967) and *Stronghold* (1974). Carroll & Graf offered a new edition of Joel Townsley Rogers' offbeat classic *The Red Right Hand* (1945), introduced by Edward D. Hoch, as well as a first book edition of Rex Stout's first novel, the almost-criminous 1913 magazine serial *Her Forbidden Knight*. Oxford University Press, as part of its recent commitment to mystery anthologies and scholarship, reprinted Robert Barr's famous 1906 collection *The Triumphs of Eugene Valmont*, with an introduction by Stephen Knight. And St. Martin's embarked on a project of reprinting all the novels of Golden

Age icon Ngaio Marsh in the sequence of their American publication, beginning with *A Man Lay Dead* (1934), *Death in Ecstasy* (1936), *Artists in Crime* (1938), and *Death in a White Tie* (1938).

But the biggest reprint news of the year was the Library of America's two-volume collection of fiction noir edited by Robert Polito: *Crime Novels: American Noir of the 1930s and 40s,* comprised of James M. Cain's *The Postman Always Rings Twice* (1934), Horace McCoy's *They Shoot Horses, Don't They?* (1935), Edward Anderson's *Thieves Like Us* (1937), Kenneth Fearing's *The Big Clock* (1946), William Lindsay Gresham's *Nightmare Alley* (1946), Cornell Woolrich's *I Married a Dead Man* (1948); and *Crime Novels: American Noir of the 1950s,* including Patricia Highsmith's *The Talented Mr. Ripley* (1955), Jim Thompson's *The Killer Inside Me* (1952), Charles Willeford's *Pick-up* (1967), David Goodis's *Down There* (1956), and Chester Himes's *The Real Cool Killers* (1959). Before these two volumes, only Raymond Chandler among crime fiction writers had been included in this prestigious series.

# FAREWELLS

It seems the mystery community has had an inordinate amount of mourning to do in recent years, of writers, editors, publishers, critics, and fans. See Ed Hoch's Necrology for the full story of 1997 in this sad regard. But a special good-bye to Don Sandstrom, a discerning critic, a tireless booster of the mystery, and a good friend to countless practitioners and enthusiasts of the genre. Few have been so loved by so many.

# AWARD WINNERS FOR 1997

### EDGAR ALLAN POE AWARDS
### (Mystery Writers of America)

Best novel: James Lee Burke, *Cimarron Rose* (Hyperion)

Best first novel by an American author: Joseph Kanon, *Los Alamos* (Broadway)

Best original paperback: Laura Lippman, *Charm City* (Avon)

Best fact crime book: Richard Firstman and Jamie Talan, *The Death of Innocents* (Bantam)

Best critical/biographical work: Natalie Hevener Kaufman and Carol McGinnis Kay, *"G" is for Grafton: The World of Kinsey Millhone* (Holt)

Best short story: Lawrence Block, "Keller on the Spot" (*Playboy*, November)

Best young adult mystery: Will Hobbs, *Ghost Canoe* (Morrow)

Best juvenile mystery: Barbara Brooks Wallace, *Sparrows in the Scullery* (Atheneum)

Best episode in a television series: "Double Down," story by Richard Sweren and Shimon Wincelberg, teleplay by Ed Zuckerman and Shimon Wincelberg (*Law & Order*/NBC)

Best television feature or miniseries: John Milne, "Blood, Sweat, and Tears" (*Silent Witness*/A&E)

Best motion picture: Curtis Hanson and Brian Helgeland, *L.A. Confidential* (Warner Brothers)

Best play: David Barr, *A Red Death*

Grand master: Barbara Mertz (a.k.a. Elizabeth Peters and Barbara Michaels)

Robert L. Fish award (best first story): Rosalind Roland, "If Thine Eye Offend Thee" (*Murder by 13* [Crown Valley Press])

Ellery Queen award: Hiroshi Hayakawa

Raven: Sylvia Burack

## AGATHA AWARDS
### (Malice Domestic Mystery Convention)

Best novel: Kate Ross, *The Devil in Music* (Viking)

Best first novel: Sujata Massey, *The Salaryman's Wife* (Harper)

Best short story: M. D. Lake, "Tea for Two" (*Funny Bones* [Signet])

Best non-fiction: Willetta L. Heising, *Detecting Men Pocket Guide* (Purple Moon)

# AWARD WINNERS FOR 1996

## ANTHONY AWARDS
### (Bouchercon World Mystery Convention)

Best novel: Michael Connelly, *The Poet* (Little, Brown)

Best first novel: (tie) Dale Furutani, *Death in Little Tokyo* (St. Martin's); and Terris McMahon Grimes, *Somebody Else's Child* (Onyx)

Best paperback original: Terris McMahon Grimes, *Somebody Else's Child* (Onyx)

Best short story: Carolyn Wheat, "Accidents Will Happen" (*Malice Domestic 6* [Pocket])

Best critical or biographical work: Willetta Heising, *Detecting Women 2* (Purple Moon)

Best Fanzine: *The Armchair Detective*

## SHAMUS AWARDS
### (Private Eye Writers of America)

Best novel: Robert Crais, *Sunset Express* (Hyperion)
Best first novel: Carol Lea Benjamin, *This Dog for Hire* (Walker)
Best original paperback novel: Harlan Coben, *Fade Away* (Dell)
Best short story: Lia Matera, "Dead Drunk" (*Guilty as Charged* [Pocket])

## DAGGER AWARDS
### (Crime Writers' Association, Great Britain)

Gold Dagger: Ian Rankin, *Black & Blue* (Orion)
Silver Dagger: Janet Evanovich, *Three to Get Deadly* (Viking)
John Creasey Award (Best First Novel): Paul Johnston, *Body Politic* (Hodder & Stoughton)
Best short story: Reginald Hill, "On the Psychiatrist's Couch" (*Whydunnit: the 1997 CWA Anthology* [Severn])
Best non-fiction: Paul Britton, *The Jigsaw Man* (Bantam)
Diamond Dagger: Colin Dexter

## MACAVITY AWARDS
### (Mystery Readers International)

Best novel: Peter Lovesey, *Bloodhounds* (Mysterious)
Best first novel: Dale Furutani, *Death in Little Tokyo* (St. Martin's)
Best critical/biographical work: Willetta Heising, *Detecting Women 2* (Purple Moon)
Best short story: Carolyn Wheat, "Cruel and Unusual" *Guilty as Charged* (Pocket)

## ARTHUR ELLIS AWARDS
### (Crime Writers of Canada)

Best novel: Peter Robinson, *Innocent Graves*
  Best first novel: C. C. Benison, *Death at Buckingham Palace*
  Best non-fiction: Jean Monet, *The Cassock and the Crown*
  Best short story: Richard K. Bercuson, "Dead Run" (*Storyteller*)
  Best juvenile: Linda Bailey, *How Can a Frozen Detective Stay Hot on the Trail*

It takes a certain kind of author who's willing to delve into the criminal mind, to analyze just how they tick and then use what they have learned in their fiction. Jeffrey Deaver is just such an author. His books *Praying for Sleep* and *The Coffin Dancer* are masterpieces of psychological suspense. In "The Kneeling Soldier" he takes the often-used concept of the stalker, and puts the unique spin on it that only he can.

# The Kneeling Soldier
## JEFFERY DEAVER

"He's out there? Again?"

A dish fell to the tiled kitchen floor and shattered.

"Gwen, go down to the rec room. Now."

"But, Daddy," she whispered, "how *can* he be? They said six months. They promised six months. At least!"

He peered through the curtains, squinting, and his heart sank. "It's him," he sighed. "It's him. Gwen, do what I told you. The rec room. Now." Then he shouted into the dining room, "Doris!"

His wife hurried into the kitchen. "What is it?"

"He's back. Call the police."

"He's back?" the woman muttered in a grim voice.

"Just do it. And Gwen, I don't want him to see you. Go downstairs. I'm not going to tell you again."

Doris lifted the phone and called the sheriff's office. She only had to hit one button; they'd put the number on the speed dialer some months ago.

Ron stepped to the back porch and looked outside.

The hours after dinner, on a cool springtime evening like this, were the most peaceful moments of the year in Locust Grove. The suburb was a comforting thirty-two miles from New York City, on the North Shore of Long Island. Some truly wealthy lived here—new money and some Rockefeller and Morgan hand-me-downs. Then there were the aspiring rich and a few popular artists, some ad agency CEOs. Mostly, though, the village was made up of people like the Ashberrys. Living comfortably in their six-hundred-thousand

1

dollar houses, commuting on the LIRR or driving to their management jobs at publishing or computer companies on Long Island.

This April evening found the dogwoods in bloom and the fragrance of mulch and the first-cut grass of the year filling the misty air. And it found the brooding form of Harle Ebbers crouching in the bushes across the street from Ron Ashberry's house, staring into the bedroom window of sixteen-year-old Gwen.

Oh, dear Lord, Ron thought hopelessly. Not again. It's not starting again . . .

Doris handed the cordless phone to her husband and he asked for Sheriff Hanlon. As he waited to be connected, he inhaled the stale metallic scent of the porch screen he rested his head against. He looked across his yard, forty yards, to the bush that had become a fixture in his daydreams and the focus of his nightmares.

It was a juniper, about six feet long and three feet high, gracing a small municipal park. It was beside this languorous bush that twenty-year-old Harle Ebbers had spent much of the last eight months, in his peculiar crouch, stalking Gwen.

"How'd he get out?" Doris wondered.

"I don't see what good it'll do," Gwen said from the kitchen, panic in her voice. "To call the police. He'll be gone before they get here. He always is."

"Go downstairs!" Ron called. "Don't let him see you."

The thin blond girl, her face as beautiful as Lladro porcelain, backed away. "I'm scared."

Doris, a tall, muscular woman, exuding the confidence of the competitive athlete she'd been in her twenties, put her arm around her daughter. "Don't worry, honey. Your father and I are here. He's not going to hurt you. You hear me?"

The girl nodded uncertainly and vanished down the stairs.

Ron Ashberry kept his gaze coldly fixed on the figure next to the bush.

It was a cruel irony that this tragedy had happened to Gwen.

Conservative by nature, Ron had always been horrified by the neglect he saw on the part of families in the city to which he commuted every day. Absent fathers, crack-addict mothers, guns and gangs, little girls turning to prostitution. He vowed that nothing bad would ever happen to his daughter. His plan was simple: He'd protect Gwen, raise her the right way, teach her good moral values, *family* values—which, thank God, people had started talking about again. He'd keep her close to home, make sure she got good grades, instruct her in everything a cultured young lady needed to learn—from sports to art to ordering in restaurants.

Then, when she turned eighteen, he'd give her freedom. She'd be old enough then to make the correct decisions—about boys, about careers, about money.

She'd go to an Ivy League college and then return to the North Shore for marriage or a career.

This was serious work, hard work, this child rearing. But Ron was finally seeing the results of his efforts. Gwen scored in the 99th percentile in the PSATs. She never talked back to adults, never snuck cigarettes or liquor, never made an issue out of not getting her driver's license. She understood the reasons why he wouldn't let her go into Manhattan with her girlfriends unchaperoned or spend the weekend on Fire Island. And Ron was immensely proud of their relationship.

And so he felt it was utterly unfair that Harle Ebbers picked *his* daughter to stalk.

It had begun last fall. One evening Gwen had been particularly quiet throughout the evening meal. When Ron had asked her to go pick a book out of his library so he could read it aloud, Gwen just stood at the kitchen window, staring outside.

"Gwen, are you listening to me? I asked you to get me a book."

She'd turned and, to his shock, he saw she was crying.

"Honey, I'm sorry," Ron said automatically and stepped forward to put his arm around her. He knew the problem. Several days ago she'd asked if she could take a spring trip to Washington, D.C., with two teachers and six of the girls and boys from her social studies class. Ron had considered letting her go. But then he'd checked out the group and found that two of the girls had discipline problems—they'd been found drinking in a park near the school last summer. He'd told Gwen she couldn't go and she'd seemed disappointed. He assumed this was what troubled her today. "I wish I could let you go, Gwen—" he said.

"Oh no, Daddy, it's not that stupid trip. I don't care about that. It's something else . . ."

She fell into his arms, sobbing. He was filled with his overwhelming parental love. And an unbearable agony for her pain. "What is it, honey? Tell me. You can tell me anything."

She'd glanced out the window.

He followed her gaze and saw, in the park across the street, a figure crouching in the bushes.

"Oh, Daddy, he's following me."

Horrified, Ron led her to the living room, calling out, "Doris, we're having a family conference! Come in here! Now!" He gestured his wife into the room then sat next to Gwen. Put his arm around her. "What is it, baby? Tell us."

Ron preferred that Doris pick up Gwen at school. But occasionally, if his wife was busy, he let Gwen walk home. There were no bad neighborhoods in Locust Grove, certainly not along the trim, manicured route to the high school; the greatest threats were usually aesthetic—a run-down bungalow or a flock of plastic flamingos or herds of plaster Bambis.

Or so Ron had believed.

That night Gwen sat with her hands in her lap, staring at the floor, and explained in a meek voice, "I was walking home today, okay? And there was this guy."

Ron's heart went cold. His hands began to shake and a fiery anger grew inside him.

"Tell us," Doris said. "What happened?"

"Nothing *happened*. Not like that. He just, like, started to talk to me. He's going, 'You're so pretty.' 'You're so beautiful.' 'Where do you live?' "

"Did he know you?"

"I don't think so. He acted all funny. Like he was sort of retarded, you know. Kind of saying things that didn't make sense. I told him you didn't want me to talk to strangers and I ran home."

"Oh, you poor thing." Her mother embraced her.

"I didn't think he followed me. But . . ." She bit her lip. "But that's him."

Ron had jogged toward the bush where he'd seen the young man. He was in a curious pose. It reminded Ron of the green plastic soldiers he used to buy when he was a kid. The kneeling soldier, holding his M1 carbine to his cheek. The boy saw Ron coming and fled.

Ron had called the sheriff's office and found out that they knew all about the boy. Ebbers's parents had moved to Locust Grove a few months before, virtually driven out of Ridgeford, Connecticut, because their son had targeted a young blonde, about Gwen's age, and had begun following her. The boy was of average intelligence but had suffered psychotic episodes when younger. The police hadn't been able to stop him because he'd only hurt one person in all his months of stalking—the girl's brother had attacked him, and Harle had beaten the boy nearly to death. But all charges were dropped on the grounds of self-defense.

The Ebbers family had at last fled the state, hoping to start over fresh.

But the only change was that Harle found himself a new victim.

The boy had fallen into his obsessive vigil: staring into Gwen's classrooms at school and perching beside the juniper bush, keeping his eyes glued to the girl's bedroom.

Ron had tried to get a restraining order but, without any illegal conduct on Harle's part, the magistrate couldn't issue one. The police harassed the young man, rousting him frequently, but he proved surprisingly knowledge-able about his rights and so they gave that up and settled for stepping up their patrols in the neighborhood.

Finally, after Harle had stationed himself beside the juniper bush for six nights straight, Ron stormed into the state Mental Health Department and demanded that something be done. The department implored the boy's par-ents to send him to a private-care hospital for six months. The county would pay ninety percent of the fee. The Ebbers agreed and, under an involuntary commitment order, the boy was taken off to Garden City.

But now he was back, kneeling like a soldier beside the infamous juniper bush, only one week after the ambulance had carted him off.

Finally Sheriff Hanlon came on the line.

"Ron, I was going to call you."

"You *knew* about him?" Ron shouted. "Why the hell didn't you tell us? He's out there right now."

"I just found out about it myself. The boy talked to a shrink at the hospital. Apparently he gave the right answers and they decided to release him. Keeping him any longer on a dicey order like that, there was a risk of liability for the county."

"What about liability for my daughter?" Ron spat out.

"There'll be a hearing in a few weeks, but they can't keep him in the hospital till then. Probably not after the hearing either, the way it's shaking out."

Tonight, as mist settled on the town of Locust Grove, this beautiful spring night, crickets chirped like greaseless gears, and Harle Ebbers was frozen in his familiar kneeling pose, dark eyes searching for a delicate young girl whose father happened to be deciding at that moment that this couldn't go on any longer.

"Look, Ron," the sheriff said sympathetically, "I know it's tough. But—"

Ron slammed the phone into the cradle, nearly tearing it from the wall.

"Honey," Doris began. He ignored her, and as he started for the door she took his arm. She was a strong woman, athletic. But Ron was stronger and he pulled away brusquely, pushed open the screen door, and started across the dewy lawn to the park.

To his surprise, and pleasure, Harle didn't flee. He stood up out of his crouching position and crossed his arms, waiting for Ron to approach.

Ron was athletic too. He played tennis and golf and he swam like a dolphin. One hundred laps a day when the country club pool was open. He was slightly shorter than Harle but, as he gazed at the boy's prominent eyebrows and disturbingly deep-set eyes, he knew in his heart that he could kill the young man. With his bare hands if he had to. All he needed was the slightest provocation.

"Daddy, no!" Gwen screamed from the porch, her voice like a high violin note, resonating through the mist. "Don't get hurt. It's not worth it!"

Ron turned back, hissed to his girl, "Get back inside!"

Harle was waving toward the house, "Gwennie, gwennie, gwennie . . . ," a frightening grin on his face.

Neighbors' lights came on, faces appeared in windows and doorways.

Perfect, Ron thought. He makes the least gesture toward me, and I'll kill him. A dozen witnesses'll back me up.

He stopped two feet from Harle, on whose face the grin had fallen away. "I got sprung. They couldn't make it stick, could they? Make it stick, make it stick, couldn't make it stick. So I. Got. Sprung."

"You listen to me," Ron muttered, fists balling at his side. "You're real close. You know what I mean? I don't care if they arrest me, I don't care if they execute me. You don't leave her alone, I'm going to kill you. Understand?"

"I love my Gwennie, I love her, love her, loveher, loveher, lover, loverloverlover. She loves me, I love her she loves me I love she loves I love she loves shelovesshelovesshelovessssss . . ."

"Come on. Take a swing at me. Come on. Coward! Haven't got the guts to mix it up with a grownup, right? You make me sick."

Harle uncrossed his arms.

Okay, here it comes. . . .

Ron's heart flexed and an ocean crashed in his ears. He could feel the chill adrenaline race through his body like an electric current.

And the boy turned and fled.

*Son of a bitch . . .*

"Come back here!"

He was racing down the street on his lanky legs, disappearing into the misty dusk, Ron close behind him.

For a few blocks.

Athletic, yes, but a forty-three-year-old's body doesn't have the stamina of someone half that age, and after a quarter mile the boy pulled ahead and disappeared.

Winded, his side cramping fiercely from the run, Ron trotted back to the house, climbed into his Lexus. Gasping, he shouted, "Doris. You and Gwen stay here, lock the doors. I'm going to find him."

She protested, but he ignored her and sped out of the drive.

A half-hour later, having cruised throughout the entire neighborhood and finding no sign of the boy, he returned home.

To find his daughter in tears.

Doris and Gwen sat in the living room, the shades down and curtains drawn. Doris held a long kitchen knife in her strong fingers.

"What?" Ron demanded. "What's going on?"

Doris said, "Tell your father."

"Oh, Daddy, I'm sorry. I thought it was best."

"What?" Ron strode forward, dropping onto the couch, gripping his daughter by her shoulders. "Tell me!" he cried.

"He came back," Gwen said. "He was by the bush. And I went out to talk to him."

"You did what? Are you crazy?" Ron shouted, shaking with rage and fear at what might have happened.

He looked at Doris, who said, "I couldn't stop her. I tried, but—"

"I was afraid for you. I was afraid he'd hurt you. I thought maybe I could be nice to him and ask him please just to go away."

Despite his horror, a burst of pride popped inside of Ron Ashberry.

"What happened?" he asked.

"Oh, Daddy, it was terrible."

The feeling of pride faded and he sat back, staring at his daughter's white face. Ron whispered, "Did he touch you?"

"No . . . not yet."

"What do you mean, 'yet'?" Ron barked.

"He said . . ." Her tearful face looked from her father's furious eyes to her mother's determined ones. "He said that when it's the next full moon, that's when women get a certain way because of their, you know, monthly thing. The next full moon, he's going to find me wherever I am . . ." Her face grew red in shame. She swallowed. "I can't say it, Daddy. I can't tell you what he said he'd do."

"My God."

"I got so scared, I ran back to the house."

Her strong-jawed face looking out the window, Doris added, "And he just stood there, staring at us, kind of singing in this sick voice. We locked the doors right away." She nodded at the knife, setting it on the table. "I got that from the kitchen just in case."

*She loves me, I love her she loves me I love she loves I love she loves she loves . . .*

His wife continued, "Then you came back, and when he saw the car lights he ran off. It looked like he was headed toward his folks' house."

Ron grabbed the phone off the wall, hit speed dial.

"This is Ron Ashberry," he said to the police dispatcher.

"Yessir, is it the boy again?" she asked.

"Hanlon. Now."

A pause. "Hold, please."

The sheriff came on the line. "Ron, what the hell's going on tonight? I've had four calls from your neighbors about this thing."

Ron explained about the threats.

"It's still just words, Ron."

"Goddamn it, I don't care about the law! He said the night of the full moon he's going to rape my little girl. What the hell do you people want?"

"When's the full moon?"

"I don't know, how would I know?"

"Hold on a second. I've got an almanac. . . . Here we go. It's next week. We'll have somebody at your house all day. If he makes a move, we'll get him."

"For what? Trespass? And he'll be out in, what, a week?"

"I'm sorry, Ron. It's the law."

"You know what you and your law can do? You can go straight to hell."

"Mr. Ashberry, I've told you before, if you take things into your own hands, you're going to be in serious trouble. Now good night to you."

Ron jammed the phone into the cradle and this time it flew from the wall fixture.

He shouted to Doris, "Stay here. Keep the doors locked."

"Ron, what are you going to do?"

"Daddy, no . . ."

The door slammed so hard a pane cracked and the fissure lines made a perfect spiderweb.

RON PARKED ON THE LAWN, narrowly missing a rusting Camero and a station wagon, lime green except for the front fender, which was the matte color of dried-blood-brown primer.

Pounding on the scabby door, he shouted, "I want to see him. Open up!"

Finally the door swung open and Ron stepped inside. The bungalow was small and it was a mess. Food, dirty plastic plates, beer cans, piles of clothes, magazines, newspapers. A strong animal smell too.

He pushed past the diminutive couple, both wearing jeans and T-shirts. In their late thirties.

"Mr. Ashberry," the man said uneasily, looking at his wife.

"Is your son here?"

"We don't know. Listen, sir, we had nothing to do with him getting out of that hospital. We was all for keeping him there, as I think you know."

"What do you mean you don't know where he is?"

"He comes and goes," his wife said. "Through his bedroom window. Sometimes we don't see him for days."

"Ever try discipline? Ever try a belt? What is it, you think children should walk all over you?"

The father gave a mournful laugh.

His wife said, "Has he done something else?"

As if what he'd done wasn't enough. "Oh, he's just threatening to rape her, that's all."

"Oh, no, no," she clutched her hands together, fingers dirty and bedecked with cheap rings. "But it's just talk," the woman blurted. "It's always just talk, with him."

Ron whirled to face her. Her short black hair was badly in need of a wash; she smelled of sour onions. Her skin, not her breath. "It's gone past the talk stage and I'm not going to put up with it. I want to see him."

They glanced at each other and the father led him down a dark corridor toward one of the two bedrooms. Something—old food, it seemed—crunched under Ron's feet. The man looked over his shoulder, saw his wife standing in the living room, and said, "I'm so sorry for all this, sir. I truly am. I wish I had it in my heart to, you know, make him go away."

"We tried that," Ron said cynically.

"I don't mean a hospital or jail." His voice fell to a whisper. "To go away forever. You know what I mean. I've thought about it some. She has too but she doesn't say it. Being his mother and all. One night I almost done it. When he was asleep." He paused and caressed a crater in the Sheetrock, from a fist, it seemed. "I wasn't strong enough. I wished I was. But I couldn't do it."

His wife joined them and he fell silent. The father knocked timidly on the door and when there was no response he shrugged. "Ain't much we can do. He keeps it locked and won't give us a key."

"Oh, for God's sake." Ron stepped back and slammed his foot into the door.

"No!" the mother cried. "He'll be mad. Don't—"

The door crashed open and Ron stepped inside, flicking on the light. He stopped, astonished.

In contrast to the rest of the house, Harle's room was immaculate. The bed was made and the blankets were taut as a buck private's. The desktop ordered and polished. The rug vacuumed. Bookshelves neat, and all the books were alphabetized.

"He does it himself," Harle's mother said with a splinter of pride. "Cleans up. See, he's not really so bad—"

" 'Not really so bad'? Are you out of your mind? Look at that! Just look!"

On the walls were posters from World War Two movies, Nazi paraphernalia, swastikas, bones. A large bayonet dangled from the desk lamp. A miniature samurai sword sat on a footlocker. One poster was a comic book scene of a man with knives for feet, ripping apart an opponent he was fighting. Blood sprayed in the air.

Three pairs of spit-polished combat boots sat by the bedside. A tape, *The Faces of Death*, sat on the VCR, attached to a spotless television.

Ron reached for the door to the closet.

"No," his mother said firmly. "Not there. He don't let us go in there. We're never supposed to do that!"

The double door too was locked but with one yank Ron ripped the panels open, nearly wrenching them off the hinges.

Gruesome toys, monsters and vampires, characters from horror films fell out. Rubber mock-ups of severed limbs, taxidermied animals, a snake's skeleton, Freddy Krueger posters.

And in the center of the closet floor was the main attraction: an altar dedicated to Gwen Ashberry.

Ron cried out in horror as he dropped to his knees, staring at the frightening tableau. Several photographs of Gwen were pinned to the wall. Harle must have taken them on the days when she walked home from school by herself.

In two of the snapshots she was strolling obliviously along the sidewalk. In the third she was turning and smiling off into the distance. And in the fourth—the one that struck him like a fist—she was bending down to tie her shoe, her short skirt hiked high on her trim legs. This was the photo in the center of the shrine.

*She loves me, I love her she loves me I love she loves I love she loves she loves she loves shelovesshelovessshelovessssss . . .*

On the floor, between two candles, what looked like a white flower, sprouting from a dime-store coffee mug, printed with the name Gwen on it. Ron touched the flower. It was cloth . . . but what exactly? He almost didn't have the courage to lift it from the cup, and when he finally did pull the girl's underpants from the mug all he could do was give a deep moan and clutch the frail garment to his chest. He remembered Doris commenting several months ago that she'd found the outer door to the laundry room open. So, he'd been in the house!

In his fury Ron ripped down the picture of Gwen bending over. Then the others. Shredded them beneath his strong fingers.

"Please, don't do that! No, no!" Harle's mother cried.

"Really, mister!"

"Harle'll be mad. I can't stand it when he gets mad at us."

Ron rose to his feet, flung the cup into a Nazi flag, where it shattered. He pushed past the cowering Ebberses, flung open the front door, and strode out into the street.

"Where are you?" he cried. "Where? You son of a bitch!"

The peaceful dusk in Locust Grove had tipped into peaceful night. Ron saw nothing but faint houselights; he heard nothing but his own voice, dulled by the mist, returning to him from a dozen distant places.

Ron leapt into his car and left long black worms of skid marks as he knocked over garbage cans, streaking into the street.

THREE HOURS LATER, HE RETURNED home.

The bright security lights were on, one of them trained directly at the juniper bush.

"Where've you been?" Doris demanded. "I've called everybody I could think of, trying to find you."

"Driving around, looking for him. Is everything okay?" he asked.

"I thought I heard somebody in the workshed about an hour ago, rummaging around."

"And?"

"I called the police and they came by. Didn't find anything. Might've been a raccoon. The window was open. But the door was locked."

"Gwen?"

"She's upstairs asleep. Did you find him?"

"No, no trace. At least I hope I put the fear of God into him so we'll have a few days' peace." He looked around the house. "Let's make sure everything's locked up anyway."

Ron walked to the front door and opened it, stepping back in shock at the sight of the huge dark form filling the doorway. Gasping, he instinctively drew back his fist.

"Whoa, there, buddy, take it easy."

Sheriff Hanlon stepped forward into the hallway light.

Ron closed his eyes in relief. "You scared me."

"I'll ditto that. Mind if I come in?"

"It's about time you fellows got here," Ron snapped. The sheriff entered, nodding to Doris, who ushered him into the living room. He declined coffee.

Husband and wife looked at the sheriff, a big man in a tan uniform. He sat on the couch and said simply, "Harle Ebbers was found dead about a half-hour ago. He was hit by a train on the LIRR tracks."

Doris gasped. The sheriff nodded grimly. Ron didn't even try to keep the smile off his face. "Praise Him from whom all blessings flow."

The sheriff kept his face emotionless. He looked back to his notebook. "Where've you been for the past three hours, Ron? Since you left the Ebbers house?"

"You went there?" Doris asked.

Ron knitted his fingers together then decided it made him look guilty and unlinked them. "Driving around," he answered. "Looking for Harle. Somebody had to. You weren't."

"And you found him," the sheriff said.

"No, I didn't find him."

"Yessir. Well, somebody sure did. Ron, we've got reports of you threatening that boy tonight. The Clarkes and the Phillipses heard some screaming and looked out. They heard you saying that you didn't care if you got caught, or even executed, you wanted to kill him. And then you took off chasing him down Maple."

"Well, I—"

"And then we got reports that you caused a disturbance at the Ebbers place and fled." He read from his notebook. " 'In a very agitated frame of mind.' "

" 'Agitated frame of mind.' Of *course* I was agitated. He had a pair of my daughter's underwear in this goddamn altar in his closet."

Doris's hand rose to her mouth.

"And I found some pictures of her he'd taken on the way home from school."

"What were you doing at the Ebbers house? Did you break in?"

"No, they let me in."

"Okay, go on."

"There's nothing to go on about. I wanted to talk to him. He wasn't there. So I left."

"And then?"

"I drove around, looking for him. I didn't find him. I came home. Look, Sheriff, I said I'd kill him. Sure. I'll admit it. And if he was running from me and got hit when he was crossing the tracks I'm sorry. If that's, I don't know, negligent homicide, or something, then arrest me for it."

The sheriff's broad face cracked a faint smile. " 'Negligent homicide.' Let me ask you, you read about that somewhere? Hear it on Court TV?"

"What do you mean?"

"Just that it sounded a little rehearsed. Like maybe you'd thought it up before. You threw it at me pretty quick just then."

"Look, don't blame me if he got hit by a train. What the hell're you smiling at?"

"You're good is what I'm smiling at. I think you know that boy was dead before the train came along."

Doris was frowning. Her head swiveled toward her husband.

The sheriff continued. "Somebody crushed his skull with a blunt object—that was the cause of death—and dragged him a few feet to the roadbed. Left him on the tracks. The killer was hoping him getting hit by a train'd cover up the evidence of the blows. But the train wheel only hit his neck. The head was intact enough so the medical examiner could be sure about the cause of death."

"Well," Ron said.

"Do you own an Arnold Palmer model forty-seven golf club? A driving wood?"

A long pause.

"I don't know."

"Do you golf?"

"Yes."

"Do you own golf clubs?"

"I've been buying golf clubs all my life."

"I ask 'cause that was the murder weapon. I'm thinking you beat him to death, left him on the tracks, and threw the club in Hammond Lake. Only you missed and it ended up in the marsh beside the lake, sticking straight up. Took the county troopers all of five minutes to find it."

Doris turned to the sheriff. "No, it wasn't him! Somebody broke into our shed tonight and must've stolen a club. Ron keeps a lot of his old ones there. He must've stolen one. I can prove it—I called your office about it."

"I know that, Mrs. Ashberry. But you said nothing was missing."

"I didn't check the clubs. I didn't think to."

Ron swallowed. "You think I'd be stupid enough to kill that boy after I called the police and after I threatened him in front of witnesses?"

The sheriff said, "People do stupid things when they're upset. And they sometimes do some pretty smart things when they're pretending they're upset."

"Oh, come on, Sheriff. With my own golf club?"

"Which you were planning to send to the bottom of fifty feet of water and another five of mud. By the way, whether it's yours or not, that club's got your fingerprints all over it."

"How did you get my prints?" Ron demanded.

"The Ebbers house. The boy's closet door and a coffee cup you smashed up. Now, Ron, I want to ask you a few more questions."

He looked out the kitchen window. He happened to catch sight of the juniper bush. He said, "I don't think I want to say anything more."

"That's your right."

"And I want to see a lawyer."

"That's your right too, sir. If you could hold out your hands for me, please. We're gonna slip these cuffs on and then take a little ride."

RON ASHBERRY ENTERED THE MONTAUK Men's Correctional Facility as an instant hero. Having avenged his daughter the way he had.

And the day that Gwen gave that interview on Channel 9 the whole wing was in the TV room watching. Ron sat glumly in the back row and listened to her talk with the woman reporter.

"Here was this creep who'd stolen my underwear and'd taken pictures of me on my way home from school and in my swimsuit and everything. I mean, he was, like, a real stalker . . . and the police didn't do anything about it. It was my father who saved me. I'm, like, I'm totally proud of him."

Ron Ashberry heard this and thought just what he'd thought a thousand times since that night in April: I'm glad you're proud of me, baby. Except, except, except . . . I didn't do it. I didn't kill Harle Ebbers.

Just after he'd been arrested, the defense lawyer had suggested that maybe Doris was the killer, though Ron knew she wouldn't have let him take the blame. Besides, friends and neighbors confirmed that she'd been on the phone with them, asking about Ron's whereabouts, at the time of the boy's death. Phone records bore this out too.

Then there was Harle's father. Ron remembered what the man had told him earlier that evening. But Ron's tearing out of the driveway caused such a stir in the Ebbers' neighborhood that several snooping neighbors kept an eye on the house for the rest of the evening and could testify that neither husband nor wife had left the bungalow all night.

Ron had even proposed the theory that the boy had killed himself. He knew

Ron was out to get him and, in his psychotic frame of mind, Harle wanted to retaliate, get back at the Ashberry family. He'd stolen the golf club and wandered to the train track, where he'd beaten himself silly, flung the club toward the lake, and crawled onto the tracks to die. His defense lawyer gave it a shot, but the D.A. and police actually laughed at that one.

And then in a flash, Ron had figured it out.

The brother of the girl in Connecticut! The girl who'd been the previous victim. Ron envisioned the scenario: The young man had come to Locust Grove and had stalked the stalker, seeking revenge both for his sister and for the beating he himself had taken. The brother—afraid that Harle was about to be sent back to the safety of the hospital—decided to act fast and had broken into the nearest workshed he could find to get a weapon, never knowing that Ron had threatened Harle earlier that evening and that he'd become the prime suspect.

The D.A. hadn't listened to that theory either and went forward with the case.

Everyone recommended that Ron take a plea, which he finally did, exhausted with protesting his innocence. There was no trial; the judge accepted the plea and sentenced him to twenty years. He'd be eligible for parole in seven. His secret hope was that the boy in Connecticut would have a change of heart and confess. But until that day Ron Ashberry would be a guest of the people of the state of New York.

Sitting in the TV room, staring at Gwen on the screen, absently playing with the zipper of his orange jumpsuit, Ron was vaguely aware of a nagging thought. What was it?

Something that Gwen had just said to the interviewer.

Wait . . .

*What* pictures of her in her swimsuit?

He sat up.

Ron hadn't found any photos of her in a bathing suit in Harle's closet. And there hadn't been any introduced at trial, since there'd *been* no trial. He'd never heard about any swimsuit pictures. If there were any, how had Gwen known about them?

A terrible thought came to him, so terrible that it was laughable. Though he didn't laugh; he was compelled to consider it—and the other thoughts that sprang up like ugly crabgrass around it: that the only person who'd ever heard Harle threaten Gwen was Gwen herself. That nobody'd ever heard Harle's side of the situation—no one except the psychiatrist in Garden City and, come to think of it, he'd let the boy out. That all the young man had ever said to Ron was that he loved Gwen and she loved him—nothing worse than what any young man with a crush might say.

Ron's thoughts, racing: They'd just been *accepting* Gwen's story about Harle's approaching her on the way home from school eight months ago.

And had been assuming all along that he'd pursued Gwen, that she hadn't encouraged him.

And her underpants . . . ?

Could *she* have given him the panties herself?

Suddenly enraged, Ron leapt to his feet; his chair flew backwards with a loud slam. A guard ambled over and motioned for Ron to pick it up.

As he did, Ron's thoughts raged. Could it actually have happened—what he was now thinking? Was it possible?

Had she been . . . flirting with that psycho all along?

Had she actually posed for him, given him a pair of the underwear?

Why, that little slut!

He'd take her over his knee! He'd ground her so fast . . . She always behaved when he spanked her, and the harder he whipped her the quicker she toed the line. He'd call Doris, insist she take the Ping-Pong paddle to the girl. He'd—

"Yo, Ashberry," the guard grumbled, looking at Ron's purple face as it glared up at the screen. "You can't cool it off, git it on outa here."

Ron slowly turned to him.

And he did cool off. Inhaling deep breaths, he realized he was just being paranoid. Gwen was pure. She was innocence itself. Besides, he told himself, be logical. What possible reason would she have to flirt with someone like Harle Ebbers, to encourage him? Ron had raised her properly. Taught her the right values. *Family* values. She was exactly his vision of what a young woman ought to be.

But thinking of his daughter left him feeling empty, without the heart to continue watching the interview. Ron turned away from the TV and shuffled to the rec room to be by himself.

And so he didn't hear the end of the interview, during which the reporter asked Gwen what she was going to do now. She answered, with a girlish giggle, that she was about to leave for a week in Washington with her teacher and some classmates, a trip she'd been looking forward to for months. Was she going with her boyfriend? the reporter asked. She didn't have one, the girl said coyly. Not yet. But she sure was in the market.

Then the reporter asked about plans after high school. Was she going to college?

No, Gwen didn't believe college was for her. She wanted to do something fun, something that involved travel. She thought she might try her hand at a sport. Golf probably. Over the past several years her father had spent countless hours forcing her to practice her strokes.

"He always said I should learn a proper sport," she explained. "He was quite a taskmaster. But one thing I'll say—I've got a great swing."

"I know it's been hard for you, but I'm sure you're relieved to have that monster out of your life," the reporter offered.

Gwen gave a sudden, curious laugh and turned to the camera as she said, "You have no idea."

The interview ended and the inmates applauded, hooting their congratulations to Ron in the other room; one of theirs was, for a little while at least, a celebrity. But they soon stopped talking about the interview. Baltimore was playing Chicago tonight; money started to change hands and the point spread became the hot subject. Someone called into the rec room to see if Ron wanted to place a bet. But he didn't hear them call his name, or ignored them if he had, and continued to slouch listlessly in a yellow Fiberglas chair, absently flipping through the pages of a three-week-old *People* magazine.

Nancy Pickard is an author who just seems to get busier and busier. Her Jenny Cain mystery series has now reached 10 volumes, the latest being *No Body*. She has also recently turned her hand to editing again, with the anthology *First Ladies*, featuring various presidential wives as detectives, due out in 1999. Of course, we've barely mentioned appearances in anthologies such as *Funny Bones* and *Cat Crimes at the Holidays*. In the following story, she proves that while silence can be golden, it's often deadly as well.

# Speak No Evil
## NANCY PICKARD

We called him the Devil because he killed women at spiritual retreats: convents, mother houses, religious communes. Each victim was slain with an article of her faith: a rosary, in one case; a cross upon a deadly chain; a veil.

I was pulled into the case from an unusual angle when I got a call from an FBI field supervisor in Kansas City.

"Joseph Owen?" he inquired.

When I agreed that was me, he said, "We've got one, Joe."

"When was she killed?" I asked, holding my breath for the answer.

When he said, "Yesterday," I felt both relief and dread, because that was half of the answer I'd been waiting for since June.

"The victim was Lila Susan Pointe," he reported. "P-o-i-n-t-e. Twenty-seven years old. Caucasian. He strangled her with a white silk altar cloth from a chapel on the grounds of a religious retreat called Shekinah: S-h-e-k-i-n-a-h. I don't know what they're all about; it may be a cult. This murder fits the Devil's profile, Joe, except that we've got something nobody else has ever had: an eyewitness."

When I heard that, I pounded my fist on my desk, feeling exultant, like a kid saying, *yes!* It was the other half of the news I'd been waiting to hear.

"Our witness," he said, "is a woman he attacked but didn't kill because other people almost walked up on him. That's the good news, from which you may infer bad. In addition to taking vows of poverty, obedience, and chastity, our witness added a vow of her own. Care to guess which one?"

When I didn't, he said, "Okay, I'll tell you: Our eyewitness took a five-year

17

vow of silence . . . two years ago." His voice combined frustration with irony. "She won't say a goddamn word to any of us. I hear you're good at getting serial killers to chat, Joe. Would you come out and see if you can get her to talk?"

What he meant was that serial killers were my specialty within the FBI. More than two dozen of them had spilled their repellent guts to me. But I had never yet had the chance to talk to one of their victims, since up to now, they'd all been dead. For the first time, I had a live one.

I flew to Kansas City that morning.

FOR THREE YEARS, THE DEVIL had haunted the Midwest, striking seemingly at random, until a former priest within the FBI came to me with a hesitant theory.

"I've noticed," he said, "that the murders always fall on a saint's day associated with the Virgin Mother, or with other saints named Mary."

I would have laughed, because it was absurd, except that I knew the world of serial killers was like a cold, strange planet where each inhabitant lived according to his own weird logic. No doubt this one had an abusive mother named Mary, or Maria, or some damn thing. It was often that simple, and that nuts.

"Has the Devil ever killed in the month of June?" he asked me, and I told him no. "Has he killed in every other month?" he asked me, and I said yes.

"June," he said then, "is the only month in which there is no saint's day for a Mary. July is also an exception because there are two celebrations on the same day, the sixteenth."

It was May when he told me his theory.

He and I waited anxiously through June and, sure enough, no murders were reported. Now, one death and a second attack had been reported for July sixteenth, right on schedule. If the ex-priest was right, I had to make our eyewitness break her vow of silence before July twenty-second, which would be the saint's day of Mary Magdalen.

It was six days away.

Before my flight, I said confidently to my wife, "She'll talk. Under these circumstances, only the devil himself would refuse to cooperate."

BY THAT AFTERNOON, JULY SEVENTEENTH, I was rocking over dirt and gravel in a rental car on a Missouri farm road south of Kansas City. The end of the line turned out to be a parking lot cut into the thick woods and situated in front of a long, low building constructed of redwood planks.

I stretched, working fifteen hundred miles of tension and stiffness out of my muscles. As my nostrils opened to let in more air, I smelled wood smoke. I heard the single human sound of wood being sawed and tasted the dust of a dry summer. Because I was an amateur horticulturist—a hobby I began because I wanted to pull something alive out of the earth, for a change, instead of dead and mutilated bodies—I could identify the trees around me: maples, pin oaks, sycamore, locust, and evergreens, rising to mature heights. Creeping vines filled the spaces between them.

I had a sense of people existing like squirrels, or termites—breathing, smelling, eating, sleeping in trees. In fact, I already had been informed that the members of this community called Shekinah did, indeed, inhabit simple lofts built on stilts among the trees. At the moment, those private cabins were invisible to me; I could see only the headquarters building, which looked like a long, fallen redwood tree. I walked toward it, watching out for poison ivy and snakes, worrying about ticks.

Most signs of the police, sheriff's department, and FBI presence were gone, though very recently they would have been as thick on the ground as leaves. They'd had all the previous day and night and most of this day to gather their evidence, interview people—the ones who would talk—and remove the body. They'd be back, but for now I seemed to be the only investigative authority on the place. That suited me well, because I planned to make friends with this woman, our silent witness. It wouldn't help for her to see me as one more demanding man in an intrusive gang of pushy cops and agents.

Her name, I'd been told, was Sara.

I planned to come on to Sara quietly, respectfully, slowly.

I had it all figured out, down to the crucial moment when I would carefully slip my pen and notepad into my hands. Of course, she would talk to me. How could anyone refuse to talk if saying something would save a life? I marveled at how clumsy the cops who preceded me must have been to prolong her silence. I would put an end to that nonsense. She would talk, for me.

I WAS TAKEN TO A small, plain office occupied by a woman who appeared to be in her seventies. She was white-haired, lean, and tanned brown as a pecan. I thought she looked capable and strong in her commune uniform, which consisted of forest-green trousers and a matching overshirt.

"I'm Joseph Owen," I told her, flashing my FBI identification.

"How do you do, Joseph Owen?" she said, smiling as easily as if nobody had been murdered in her little community. "I am what you might call the director of Shekinah, although my title, my *nom de spirit*, you might say, is Grandmother. They call me the GM when they think I can't hear them." Again she smiled, and her blue eyes twinkled. "If you think you can stand it, I invite you to call me Grandmother, too."

"I'll try," I said, and she laughed at the wry tone in my voice.

I knew her real name; in fact, I knew a fair amount about her and this commune, because I had taken time in Kansas City to copy and study the information a local field agent had put together, and I had all of that, plus copies of the police interviews, in my car. I knew, for instance, that Sara's vow of silence was total, allowing not even the sign language that is traditional with Trappist monks. She didn't write notes. She didn't nod, she didn't shake her head. In no way did she communicate.

"What's Shekinah?" I asked the GM, because the files were vague on that.

"It's a bona-fide religion," she replied, rather quickly.

"That's not what I meant," I said carefully. "But if you're suggesting the government can't make her talk because that would violate her religious freedom, of course you're right. However, I hope you won't fool yourself into thinking the government won't try to force her if they have to. They can make her silence a miserable and expensive experience for all of you."

"They?" she asked, making the point that I was one of them. "I'm afraid I have no talent for misery, Mr. Owen. And I will remind you that we already live under a vow of poverty."

I felt something like heartburn rise under my breastbone when she said all that, refuting my every point. I recognized the discomfort as frustration, not indigestion. Looking at her serene and contented face, I suddenly had the feeling it was going to become a familiar sensation in this case.

THE GM WALKED ME DOWN a forest path that appeared unoccupied by humans until we looked up. Then we could see the lofts among the trees where members of the community lived alone. There was no indoor plumbing in the lofts, no electricity. Not because of their religious beliefs, she told me, but because it was cheaper that way.

"You want to know what we believe, Mr. Owen? We believe in the Ten Commandments, and that's all."

"Which of them forbids her to speak?" I asked.

The Grandmother stopped suddenly on the path and looked back at me. "That was very astute of you," she said, and I felt like a schoolboy who had guessed right on a test and pleased the teacher. "It is the ninth commandment from which Sara draws her will to silence."

I had to search my Sunday school memory to come up with it.

"Thou shalt not bear false witness, right? But nobody's asking her to lie."

"I'm afraid you do not fully understand the commandments, Mr. Owen, at least not as we do. We believe that personality is an illusion, a spider web of lies spun over the truth. We believe the true essence of every person is already perfect, forgiven, and saved. In regard to the ninth commandment, we believe that to say otherwise of any human being is to bear false witness against him."

"Or her," I suggested.

She smiled. "Those distinctions, too, are illusions."

"No original sin?" I asked.

"Only trite and unoriginal ones," she said, gently.

We had arrived at a wooden ladder where a rope hung down.

·"Pull this," she instructed me, "and it will ring the bell in her cabin. Come see me afterwards if you wish."

I stopped her before she could walk away.

"You haven't said a word about the victim, Grandmother."

She stared off into the trees before she looked up at me again.

"Neither have you, Mr. Owen. The difference between us is that in my belief system, Lila Susan is no more dead than you and I are. It's you and the FBI who say she's dead, and who insist on finding her supposed killer. If you believe—really believe—in immortal life, as we do, you understand that no one can ever really die, and so nobody can possibly kill you."

As she walked calmly away and I pulled on the damn rope, I felt the heartburn rise again.

A TRAPDOOR OPENED IN THE floor of the loft above me. I climbed the ladder, ten rungs hand over hand, and entered a Lilliputian chamber. There was a cot with a young woman seated on it, her back propped against the wood wall, her face turned down. There were books stacked against the walls, a basket of what looked like clean underwear under the cot, another basket with eating utensils, a small desk with a straight chair, a neat stack of towels, and a folded green uniform like the one she was wearing. Apart from four tall, ugly green plants in plastic pots, that was all there was in the square little room. Four windows provided cross ventilation; at one of them, the metal tubes of a wind chime clinked in the breeze. I left the trapdoor open and sat beside it, cross-legged in my suit, on her wooden floor.

I felt hot, sweaty, itchy, but she looked cool.

"Sara? My name is Joe—Joseph Owen—and I'm an FBI agent. You must be sick of us by now, and I apologize very much for intruding on your privacy." I paused, carefully feeling my way into her silence. She had glanced up at me long enough for me to see a young, plain face with no makeup. All of the Devil's victims were young, in their twenties or late teens, many of them had brown hair, like hers, and several of them wore their hair pulled back from their face in a long ponytail, as this woman did. After a moment, I started in again. "I'm really sorry about what happened to your friend yesterday, and for what he put you through. We're all glad you survived!"

I let that thought lie between us for a moment while the wind chime played in the window. I was intimate with silence because my own mother had been a profoundly silent woman, except when she exploded in rage at something I—her only child—had done to prick the bubble of her silence. I knew how to wait it out, to coax and manipulate it. Because of my childhood, I hated silence, which was perhaps why I was so adept at getting stubborn people to talk to me.

"Sara, I don't want to frighten you, but the fact is, I'm here to protect you."

Her body made an involuntary movement, and I had a feeling I had startled her, which was what I hoped to do in a sly way. I wanted to pull her off of her calm, silent pedestal, and to prod an exclamation out of her, even if it was only an Oh! or a No! If I could break the dam, force one word out of her compressed mouth, her vow would be irreversibly broken, and then she might as well tell me everything. I wanted to go slow, to win her trust, so she'd do what I wished her to do, but there wasn't much time. I said, "If he thinks you can identify him, you're a threat to him, Sara. So I'm going to stick around to protect you."

That was her chance to indicate in some way that she hadn't seen his face, or that she couldn't really identify him, but she didn't do that. She just sat, not moving or speaking. I resisted an urge to shake her until her teeth rattled and words came tumbling out of her mouth. I wanted to tell her she was a spoiled brat, enjoying the luxury of a silence she could end at any time, but that her friend was not so fortunate. Lila Susan Pointe and the other victims were silent, too, but they would never open their mouths and speak to me.

"I'll be around, Sara," I promised her.

I descended from her loft, pulling the trapdoor shut behind me.

The truth was that she probably wasn't in any danger, because he had never killed between saint's days, and never in the same place on another day. The Devil was probably traveling toward his next victim, or even now stalking and studying her. But Sara didn't know that, and now I had an excuse for snaking my way into her life and her trust.

THE GM OFFERED ME A sleeping bag and a commune uniform when I told her I was Sara's temporary bodyguard. The uniform was even more than I had hoped for; wearing that, I'd soon look as familiar to Sara as any member of her community.

In the GM's office, I said, "What are those ugly plants she grows?"

"They're milkweed, Joseph Owen. I imagine she grows them because they attract monarch butterflies."

Rather stupidly, I asked, "Why does she want to do that?"

The GM smiled. "Who wouldn't? Watch them sometime, Mr. Owen. You'll have the feeling of being in conversation with them. They don't appear to be afraid of us, they hang around as if they want to talk to us, as if they have something really important to tell us."

I tried to keep the cynicism out of my voice. "So she won't talk to people, but she talks to butterflies?"

The GM gently shrugged. "I don't know." She looked meaningfully into my eyes. "Milkweed itself is sensitive to disturbance. You can't jostle them or they'll die, or grow crooked."

"So what are you telling me?" I asked her. "That I shouldn't disturb Sara?"

Instead of answering me, she said, "Are you a reading man?"

"Do you count Clancy?" I asked her. "Koontz, King?"

"Of course." She smiled. "I think people who are readers are more likely to see symbolism where other people just see life."

"So you're saying I'm reading too much into milkweed and butterflies."

"I mean the truth has depth, but no layers."

"What the hell is that supposed to mean?"

The GM smiled at my annoyance. "It means you'll get nowhere by trying to peel the layers off her psyche."

"Jesus Christ!" The profanity exploded from my mouth into the peaceful atmosphere. The entire law enforcement community was seriously annoyed with these people, and I was especially irritated by the sight of the smug old lady standing so serenely in front of me. "There has been a murder. Of one of your own people. And she won't talk, and you talk in goddamn riddles instead of really cooperating. You are selfish, infuriating people."

I was a lot more startled by my outburst than she appeared to be.

"I apologize," I said, and tried to put a rueful, charming smile on my face. "Obviously I am a rude and frustrated man."

She smiled, kindly. "Think nothing of it."

I berated myself all the way back down the path into the woods, where I changed clothes behind a tree and spread out my borrowed sleeping bag to sit on while I waited for Sara to make her first descent from the loft. I was tired, and under time pressure, but that was no excuse. I was going to have to get myself under professional control, or I'd blow it and scare her away.

DAY AFTER DAY I FOLLOWED Sara like her shadow, and every night I slept under her loft, sometimes staring up at the floor of it in utter frustration.

She wouldn't talk; she wouldn't damn talk.

But I talked, chattering like a friendly magpie, sometimes about serial killers in general, sometimes about the Devil in particular, frequently about the heartrending stories of his victims and their families.

And nothing moved her to speak.

On our way to the latrines, with me shuffling behind her in the leaves, I said, "He has already killed a lot of women, Sara. We know his pattern. The next time he will strike is only five days from now."

Her job at the commune was janitorial work, so I grabbed a sponge and scrubbed floors right beside her. While we worked, I said, "I don't know how much you know about serial killers, Sara, but they come in two types: the disorganized kind and the organized kind. Our guy is the latter. He's very organized, very clever, very careful. He scouts out his locations and studies his victims before he makes his attack."

Sitting beside her at the communal dinner table, I whispered, "A place like this, Sara, all he has to do is hide in the woods and watch and wait for his chance."

Going to chapel at sunrise, I said, "We think we know how he gets into some of the places, Sara. He arrives as a repairman, or a deliveryman, which is the only possible way he could worm himself into convents, for instance."

In the evenings, because she didn't object, I climbed her ladder and propped myself on the floor beside a milkweed pot, and I carried on a one-sided conversation with her. "As far as we know, you're the only person who can identify him, Sara. An artist could draw a portrait from your description, but we don't want too much time to go by or you might begin to forget what he looked like. We could broadcast the picture, pass it out to places like this, so they can protect their members. We can find him, Sara, with your description. You can save lives."

Once, I said, "It's you and me and God against the Devil, Sara."

As Monday passed, then Tuesday, Wednesday, Thursday, it became more difficult for me to be gentle and patient with her. I thought she was ridiculous, a fool playing an egotistical, dangerous game with other women's lives.

I ASKED THE GM, "WHY silence?"

Her answer was to hand me a cassette tape, which I took out to the parking lot where I could listen to it privately in my rental car.

The voice that emerged from the car's dashboard was light, girlish, and a little breathless, as if she were nervous, or as if she'd been running and had only stopped long enough to drop a few thoughts into a tape recorder:

"This is Sara," the voice on the tape announced self-consciously. It felt strange to finally hear the voice that went with the silent face I'd been studying so closely. The words tumbled out so fast I had to reverse the tape several times to understand them.

"This is Sara. I've said enough in my life. Way too much. Lots of things that hurt people. Things that make me feel awful, just knowing I said them. I'm good at saying all the wrong things. Mean things. Lies. I talk all the time, too. I lie like a rug, I lie like a whole carpet store! I can't stop it, I don't know how to stop lying, except to stop speaking altogether. I drive people crazy with my talking and lies. They can't trust me, they tell me so. Nobody should ever trust anything I ever say! I'm boring, I'm self-centered, I never listen to anybody, and I know that, and the words keep coming, all the same. I'm sick of the sound of my own voice! I'm going to stop talking, because all I ever do when I open my mouth is lie and hurt people. So, I'm going to start listening. I'm not going to say anything, not anything, unless God puts the words in my mouth. Starting now. Right now. This is the last word. Honest."

The next sound on the tape was her giggling, and then she said once more, and dramatically: "Starting . . . now!"

There was nothing more on the tape.

I sat in the car, thinking the amazing thing was that she'd done it, for two years, so far. Amazing.

In the GM's office, I handed back the tape and said, "So what did she lie about that hurt people so much?"

"It wasn't anything big," the GM told me, "nothing like falsely accusing a man of rape or murder, for instance. Just a constant stream of little lies, gossipy, vicious little fabrications that hurt people's feelings more than anything. She was disliked as a consequence. Now she's quietly accepted everywhere she goes in the community."

"Like a house plant," I said drily. "What does she get out of it?"

"Relief, I think," the GM replied. "She used to steal things, too. Clothing, mostly, which she would wear in front of all of us and claim it was hers. Blatant, outright lies, looking you straight in the face."

"Does she still steal things?"

"No, that stopped soon after she went silent."

"So it's working, her silence?"

"I don't know," the GM admitted. "There's no way for me to know if she has finally learned to tell the truth to herself."

On Saturday, one day before the saint's day for Mary Magdalen, I confronted the GM in her office. "She's lying to herself," I said, "if she thinks she's doing the right thing this time."

"But Mr. Owen, if she talked to you, how would you know she was telling the truth? Have you thought about that? What kind of witness would she make in court, a self-confessed, nearly pathological liar?"

"I don't care what she does in a courtroom." Suddenly, I was angry again and yelling at the old woman. "I just want her to tell me enough to stop him! Don't you get it? He's going to kill another woman . . . tomorrow . . . and another and another after that, unless Sara identifies him. When we catch him, we'll gather other evidence, so we won't even need her for a conviction, but right now, she's got to talk. If she doesn't talk by tomorrow morning, she'll have a lot more than lies on her conscience."

The GM smiled patiently at me, as a grandmother might at a toddler having a tantrum, and she merely said, "Well, she might even lie about his appearance, you know."

I felt like strangling both of them.

I DIDN'T SLEEP THAT NIGHT in my bag under the goddamned loft, because I felt haunted by the ghosts of the other women he'd killed, all of them urging me to *do* something before other women joined their dreadful sorority.

Sunday, July twenty-second, passed in silence, with me dogging Sara's footsteps as usual, but for once I remained as silent as she. That night the telephone brought word of what I feared most: The Devil had struck on schedule, killing a woman at a Buddhist retreat north of San Francisco.

I stalked on stiff legs to Sara's cabin and climbed the ladder, clumsy in my fury and sorrow.

"Well, you've done it," I told her, my voice as cold as the sound of the metal wind chimes. "You've let him kill another one."

I gave her the details, all of them, sparing her nothing.

If she had a reaction, I couldn't see it in the dark cabin where she sat on her cot, her back turned toward me, her face to the wall.

That night, I raged over the phone to the field supervisor.

"I hate these people," I told him. "They don't give a damn about the victims, and I don't give a damn about them."

The supervisor laughed, but it was a cynical sound of understanding, rather than amusement. "So, Joe . . . no more Mr. Nice Guy?"

"Hide and watch," I advised him.

THE NEXT DAY, METHODICALLY, I set about turning the other members of the community against her. I took them aside individually and in little groups under the pretext of interviewing them one more time, and I spoke to them of the suffering of the victims, the heartbreak of the families, and of their own potential for becoming a next victim. I played on their compassion, their fear. I allowed them to get a glimpse of my frustration, of my decent motives, of my anxiety, and of how terrible I felt over my failure to get Sara to talk. By the time I finished with them, I had them looking over their shoulders for fear the Devil was hiding in the woods, watching, waiting, looking them over, winnowing them out, selecting his next victim from among all of them.

One by one, they responded as I hoped they would, in frightened or indignant or sympathetic words. They said, "I'll talk to Sara!" or . . . "Sara has to break her silence!" or . . . "It's not right, what she's doing, it's not holy!" One of them even said to me, "Sara is being selfish and wicked, and I'm going to tell her so."

For the first time, then, I left the commune.

For twenty-four hours I stayed away, luxuriating in a motel while I allowed my poison to do its work.

WHEN I RETURNED, THE GM met me at the headquarters door.

She said, "What have you done, Joseph Owen?"

Instantly, I felt triumphant.

"Is she talking?" I asked.

"No." But the GM looked worried for the first time since I'd met her. "You'd better see her. She's in her cabin."

I hurried down the path, feeling exultant.

At first, when I stepped inside the cabin, I didn't think she was there.

"Sara?" I called, which was silly, because there was hardly anything left in the cabin except her cot. The milkweed pots were gone. The blankets and sheets had been pulled off the cot and pushed under it. The baskets of underwear and eating utensils were gone. So was the stack of towels, and the books.

Dammit! Had she run away from me?

I felt shocked by rage and disappointment.

But then I saw a movement in the jumble of bedclothes under the cot and I realized Sara was wrapped up in them. She had crawled under her cot and covered herself from toe to head in the sheets and blankets.

I heard a muffled sound, and thought at first it was a bird.

Then I realized she was weeping, unable for once to control the sound of her own voice.

My thought was savage: *Good!*

But now I could afford to be gentle, now I could play the good cop once again. I knelt down near her and said softly, "Sara? When you're ready to talk to me, I'll be right here. I won't ever leave you, Sara, not until you're ready for me. I'll be here for you when the time comes."

I slept in her cabin that night, instead of underneath it.

There came a point, however, when my own nature silently called, and I had to descend the ladder to find a john. I took the opportunity to make a fast trip to retrieve the sleeping bag from the GM's office. Sara was going to talk that night, I knew it, and if she didn't, I was going to lock the trapdoor if I had to and keep her a prisoner in her cabin until she did what I wanted her to do.

The GM walked in as I was leaving her office with the bedroll.

Once again her face was unlined, her smile pacific.

"Aren't you worried anymore?" I asked her. "You seemed worried earlier."

"Prayer is a marvelous antidote to worry, Mr. Owen."

"You could probably force me to go away," I told her.

"This is Sara's opportunity for growth," was her calm reply.

"If I were Sara," I said, and I actually laughed, "I think I'd shoot you."

"That, too," said the Grandmother, smiling, "would offer enormous spiritual opportunities for her."

But this time, I was determined to have the last word.

"Your other members don't seem quite as convinced as you are that they're immortal. I get the feeling they're afraid to die."

I was astonished to see tears appear in the GM's blue eyes.

"Thank you, Joseph," she said, "for giving all of us a chance to face our own worst fears."

Damn the woman, she left me speechless, as usual.

I brushed past her, but she surprised me again by putting a hand on my arm to stop me. "Mr. Owen, tell me again about the pattern of organized serial killers, will you?"

I did it quickly, because I was in a hurry to resume my vigil over Sara, so she wouldn't try to escape while I was gone.

"They are methodical, careful, clever," I recited. "They study their victims, who are often very similar to each other, so as to know the best time and means of approach and attack. Frequently, they win their victim's trust by coming on as friendly and sincere, or in need of help. Often, once they have their victims, they hold them prisoner for some time, toying with them, before actually killing them."

"I see," the GM said, and her blue eyes looked brightly into mine. "Are you a good listener, Mr. Owen?"

"Of course," I said, curtly. "That's my business."

"Good," was all she said before releasing me.

I hurried back down the path thinking, what the hell was that all about?

The next saint's day on which the Devil would strike would not come until September, so there was a little time for us, but probably not for me. There was no way the higher-ups would let me stay out in the boonies trying to pressure just one witness. I figured I had only a little more time left before they called me back to my other work. But I would make the most of every minute of the time I had with Sara, if I had to tie her to her cot and show her photographs of the Devil's victims to make her finally talk to me.

It was a hot July, and the air was thick with humidity.

I heard a sound in front of me and realized it was Sara's trapdoor opening.

*No!* I thought, she's not getting out of there, I'm not letting her leave that cabin until she talks!

I ran forward, through the trees, nearing the stilts on which her home was built just as she kicked the ladder away.

Hell! She couldn't defeat me that way, I'd just prop the ladder up again! I slowed my pace, laughing at her for thinking she could keep me away from her.

And then I saw her feet and her legs drop through the hole.

I expected her to drop on down to the ground.

Instead, her legs dangled through the opening; her body knocked against the edges of the hole.

"Sara!"

With a sudden, horrible realization, I comprehended what she had done. I stumbled toward her, yelling her name. Reaching her legs, I embraced them, and lifted them, so that her full weight couldn't fall downward. Above me, through the hole, I saw that she had tied her sheets together, tied one end over the beam in her cabin, and circled the other end around her neck. Then she had jumped through the hole in the floor.

I shouted desperately for help.

Members of the community came running. Two of them got into her cabin through the windows. They untied her and lowered her gently into our waiting arms. We laid her on the ground in the leaves.

"Sara?" I whispered to the still and silent face.

She had tried to hang herself.

Was she still alive?

Had her neck been broken as she fell through the floor?

After a moment, Sara's eyelids quivered and she moaned, the most beautiful sound I had ever heard.

When I was sure she would live, I ran to find the Grandmother.

After that, I simply walked to my rental car and drove away.

My hands trembled on the steering wheel because the Devil was still out there, and I knew him well. I glanced in the rearview mirror and saw a white-faced man. My foot shook on the accelerator as I thought about my reputation for understanding serial killers. Again, I glanced in the mirror. Oh yes, I knew them as well as I knew myself.

I had studied her and stalked her, imprisoned her, tortured her by my presence and my demands, and I had nearly killed her.

And she was only the latest of my victims.

On my flight home, I mentally reviewed the names of the men who were dead because of my investigations, men who were, in many ways, all alike. They'd been killed upon capture, or by the death penalty. They, too, I had stalked and studied, before snatching them and imprisoning them until they were put to death.

I went home to my wife—but then, many organized types of serial killers are married, or have girlfriends. I was no different.

I was no different.

THE DEVIL WAS APPREHENDED WITHIN the year, but I was gone from law enforcement by then, having quit in order to use my law degree in ways that would not tempt me to become what I hated. Somebody had to catch the killers, but it didn't have to be me.

I do a lot of gardening now.

I'm very familiar with milkweed and monarchs.

Three years after I left Shekinah, I received a letter from the Grandmother.

"Dear Joseph Owen," the letter began, in her own unmistakable style. "I thought you would want to know that Sara has recovered beautifully, with no ill effects. She is talking now, rather like a baby with her first words. Her voice sounds rough from lack of use, and she is shy about what she says and to whom she speaks. I do believe she accomplished what she set out to do: to learn to love the truth, and to speak only that, as best she can. The world is, I believe, a sweeter place as a consequence. Frequently I hear her laugh, a welcome and lovely sound to me.

"She told me she desperately wanted to speak to you when you were here, but that she could feel lies building up inside her mouth, and she was terrified that if she spoke she would lead you in such wrong directions you would never catch your killer, and many other women might die. She remained silent to save their lives. Then she tried to kill herself in order to make sure she could not harm you or any woman by speaking the lies that were tempting her.

"Now Sara dreams of the women whom you speak of as being killed, and they talk to her and tell her they are alive in spirit.

"I hope this will comfort you, Joseph Owen."

I threw away the letter, but not in anger.

I've thrown away my scrapbooks, too, the ones I used to keep on the serial killers I helped to stalk, imprison, and kill. Like Sara, I've learned to tell the truth to myself. And so, I no longer allow myself to keep trophies of my victims.

Many authors draw inspiration for their books from their own lives, and Marcia Muller is no exception to that rule. Having recently qualified for her own pilot's license, her series character Sharon McCone has taken to the air as well. McCone makes her latest appearance in *The Cheshire Cat's Eye*. In "Solo" she combines aviation and detection to discover that some flights are better when not taken alone.

# Solo
## MARCIA MULLER

"That's where it happened."

Hy put the Citabria into a gliding turn and we spiraled down to a few hundred feet above Tufa Lake. Its water looked teal blue today; the small islands and gnarled towers of calcified vegetation stood out in gray and taupe relief. A wind from the east riffled the lake's surface. Except for a blackened area on the south side of Plover Island, I saw no sign that a light plane had crashed and burned there.

I turned my head from the window and looked into the forward part of the cockpit; Hy Ripinsky, my best friend and longtime lover, still stared at the scene below, his craggy face set in grim lines. After a few seconds he shook his head and turned his attention back to the controls, putting on full throttle and pulling back on the stick. The small plane rose and angled in for the airport on the lake's northwest shore.

Through our dual headsets Hy said, "Dammit, McCone, I'm a good flight instructor, and Scott Oakley was a good student. There's no reason he should've strayed from the pattern and crashed on his first solo flight."

We were entering that same pattern, on the downwind leg for runway two-seven. I waited till Hy had announced our position to other traffic on the unicom, then said, "No reason, except for the one you've already speculated on: that he deliberately strayed and put the plane into a dive in order to kill himself."

"Looked that way to me. To the NTSB investigators, too."

I was silent as he turned onto final approach, allowing him to concentrate

31

on landing in the strong crosswind. He didn't speak again till we were turning off the runway.

"Ninety percent of flying's mental and emotional—you know that," he said. "And ninety percent of the instructor's job is figuring out where the student's head is at, adapting your teaching methods to the individual. I like to think I've got good instincts along that line, and I noticed absolutely nothing about Scott Oakley that indicated he'd kill himself."

"Tell me about him."

"He was a nice kid, in his early twenties. From this area originally, but went up to Reno to attend the University of Nevada. Things didn't go well for him academically, so he dropped out, went to work as a dealer at one of the casinos. Met a woman, fell in love, got engaged."

He maneuvered the plane between its tie-down chains, shut it down, and got out, then helped me climb from the cramped backseat. Together we secured the chains and began walking toward the small terminal building where his Land Rover and my MG were parked.

"If Oakley lived in Reno, why was he taking flying lessons down here?" I asked. Tufa Lake was a good seventy miles south, in the rugged mountains south of the California border.

"About six, eight months ago his father got sick—inoperable cancer. Scott came home to help his mother care for him. While he was here he figured he'd use the money he was saving on rent to take up flying. There isn't much future in dealing at a casino, and he wanted to get into aviation, build up enough hours to be hired by an airline."

"And other than being a nice kid, he was . . . ?"

"Quiet, serious, very dedicated and purposeful. Set a fast learning pace for himself, even though he couldn't fly as much as he'd've liked, owing to his responsibilities at home. A month ago his father died; he offered to stay on with his mother for a while, but she wouldn't hear of it. Said she knew the separation from his girlfriend had been difficult and she didn't want to prolong it. But he came back down for a lesson each week, and on that last day he'd done three excellent takeoffs and landings. I had full confidence that I could get out of the plane."

"And you noticed nothing emotionally different about him beforehand?"

"Nothing whatsoever. He was quiet and serious, just like always."

We reached the place where our vehicles were parked, and I perched on the rear of the MG. Hy faced me, leaning against his Rover, arms folded across his chest. His eyes were deeply troubled, and lines of discouragement bracketed his mouth.

I knew what he was feeling: He took on few students, as he didn't need the money and his work for the international security firm in which he held a partnership often took him away from his ranch here in the high desert country for weeks at a time. But when he did take someone on, it was because he recognized great potential in the individual—both as a pilot and as a person who would come to love flying as much as he himself did. Scott Oakley's crash—in his full sight as he stood on the tarmac at the airport awaiting his return—had been devastating to him. And it had also aroused a great deal of self-doubt.

I said, "I assume you want me to look into the reason Oakley killed himself."

"If it's something you feel you can take on."

"Of course I can."

"I'll pay you well."

"For God's sake, you don't have to do that!"

"Look, McCone, you don't ask your dentist friend to drill for free. I'm not going to ask you to investigate for free, either."

"Oh, don't worry, Ripinsky. Nothing in life's free. We'll come up with some suitable way for you to compensate me for my labors."

MY OBVIOUS STARTING PLACE WAS Scott Oakley's mother. I called to ask if I could stop by, and set off for her home in Vernon, the small town that hugged the lake's north shore.

It was autumn, the same time of year as when I'd first journeyed here and met Hy. The aspens glowed golden in the hollows of the surrounding hills and above them the sky was a deep blue streaked with high cirrus clouds. In the years that I'd been coming to Tufa Lake, its water level had slowly risen and was gradually beginning to reclaim the dusty, alkali plain that surrounded it—the result of a successful campaign by environmental organizations to stop diversions of its feeder streams to southern California. Avocets, gulls, and other shorebirds had returned to nest on its small islands and feed on the now plentiful brine shrimp.

Strange that Scott Oakley had chosen a place of such burgeoning vitality to end his own life.

JAN OAKLEY WAS YOUNG TO have lost a husband, much less outlived her son—perhaps in her early forties. She had the appearance of a once-active woman whose energy had been sapped by sadness and loss, and small wonder: It had been only two weeks since Scott's crash. As we sat in the living room of her neat white prefab house, she handed me a high-school graduation picture of him; he had been blond, blue-eyed, and freckle-faced, with an endearingly serious expression.

"What do you want to ask me about Scott, Ms. McCone?"

"I'm interested in what kind of a person he was. What his state of mind was before the accident."

"You said on the phone that you're a private investigator and a friend of Hy Ripinsky. Is he trying to prove that Scott committed suicide? Because he didn't, you know. I don't care what Hy or the National Transportation Safety Board people think."

"He doesn't want to prove anything. But Hy needs answers—much as I'm sure you do."

"Answers so he can get himself off the hook as far as responsibility for Scott's death is concerned?"

I remained silent. She was hurting, and entitled to her anger.

After a moment Jan Oakley sighed. "All right, that was unfair. Scott admired Hy; he wouldn't want me to blame him. Ask your questions, Ms. McCone."

I asked much the same things as I had of Hy and received much the same answers, as well as Scott's Reno address and the name of his fiancée. "I never even met her," Mrs. Oakley said regretfully, "and I couldn't reach her to tell her about the accident. She knows by now, of course, but she never even bothered to call."

I'd about written the interview off at that point, but I decided to probe some more on the issue of Scott's state of mind immediately before he left for what was to be his last flying lesson. After my first question, Mrs. Oakley failed to meet my eyes, clearly disturbed.

"I'm sorry to make you relive that day," I said, "but how Scott was feeling is important."

"Yes, I know." For a moment it seemed that she might cry, then she sighed again, more heavily. "He wasn't . . . He was upset when he arrived late the night before."

"Over what?"

"He wouldn't say."

Sometimes instinct warns you when someone isn't telling the whole truth; this was one of those times. "What about the next morning? Did he say then?"

She looked at me, startled. "How did . . . ? All right, yes, he told me. Now I realize I should have stopped him, but he wanted so badly to solo. I thought, One time—what will it matter? All he wanted was to take that little Cessna around the pattern alone one time before he had to give it all up."

"Give up flying? Why?"

"Scott had a physical checkup in Reno the day before. He was diagnosed as having narcolepsy."

"NARCOLEPSY," HY SAID, "THAT'S THE condition when you fall asleep without any warning?"

"Yes. One of my friends suffers from it. She'll get very sleepy, drop off in the middle of a conversation. One time we were flying down to southern California together; the plane was landing, and she just stopped talking, closed her eyes, and slept till we were on the ground."

"Jesus, can't they treat it?"

"Yes, with ephedrine or amphetamine, but it's not always successful."

"And neither the drugs nor the condition would be acceptable to an FAA medical examiner."

"No. Besides, there's an even more potentially dangerous side to it: A high percentage of the people who have narcolepsy also suffer from a condition called cataplexy in which their body muscles become briefly paralyzed in stressful or emotional situations."

"Such as one would experience on a first solo flight." Hy grimaced and signaled for another round of drinks. We were sitting at the bar at Zelda's, the lakeside tavern at the tip of the peninsula on which Vernon was located. The owner, Bob Zelda, gave him a thumbs-up gesture and quickly slid a beer toward him, a white wine toward me.

"You know, McCone, it doesn't compute. How'd Scott pass his student pilot's medical?"

"The condition was only diagnosed the day before you soloed him. And remember, those medicals aren't a complete workup. They check your history and the obvious—blood pressure, sight, hearing. They're not looking for something that may be developing."

"Still doesn't compute. Scott was a good, responsible kid. Went strictly by the letter as far as the regulations were concerned. I can't believe he'd risk soloing when he knew he could nod off at any time."

"Well, he wanted it very badly."

"Christ, why didn't he level with me? I'd've soloed him without getting out of the plane. He could've flown the pattern with absolutely no input from me, but I'd've been there in case. Doesn't count for getting the license, of course, but his mother told you he'd already decided to give it up."

We drank silently for a minute. I watched Hy's face in the mirrored back-bar. He was right: It didn't compute. He needed answers and, now, so did I.

I said, "I'll drive up to Reno tomorrow."

SCOTT'S FORMER APARTMENT WAS IN a newish complex in the hills on the northeast side of Reno, high above the false glitter of the gambling casinos and the tawdry hustle of the Strip. I parked in a windswept graveled area behind it and went knocking on the doors of its immediate neighbors. Only one person was home, and she was house-sitting for the tenant and had never heard of Scott Oakley.

When I started back to my car, a dark-haired man in his mid twenties was getting out of a beat-up Mazda. He started across to the next cluster of apartments, and I followed.

"Help you with something?" he asked, setting down his grocery bag in front of the door to the ground-floor unit and fumbling in his pocket for keys.

"The son of a friend of mine lives here—Scott Oakley. Do you know him?"

"Oh God. You haven't heard?"

"Heard what?" I asked, and proceeded to listen to what I already knew. "That's awful," I said when he finished. "How's Christy holding up?"

"Christy?"

"His fiancée."

"Oh, that must be the redhead."

"She and Scott were engaged; I guess I just assumed they lived together."

"No, the apartment's a studio, too small for more than one person. Actually, I didn't know Scott very well, just to say hello to. But one of the other tenants, his downstairs neighbor, did say that Scott told him he wouldn't be living here long, because he planned to marry some woman who worked at the Lucky Strike down on the Strip."

THE LUCKY STRIKE HAD PRETENSIONS to a gold-rush motif, but basically it wasn't very different from all the other small Nevada casinos: Electronic games and slots beeped and whooped; bored dealers sent cards sailing over green felt to giddy tourists; waitresses who were supposed to be camp followers, clad in skimpy costumes that no self-respecting camp follower would ever have worn, strolled about serving free watery drinks. The bars, where keno numbers continually flashed on lighted screens, bore such names as The Shaft, Pick 'n Shovel, and The Assay Office.

I located the personnel office and learned that Christy Hertz no longer worked at the casino; she'd failed to show up for her evening cocktail-waitressing shift on the day of Scott Oakley's death and had not so much as called in since. The manager wasn't concerned; on the Strip, he said, women change jobs without notice as often as they do their hair color. But once I explained about Scott's death and my concern for Christy, he softened some. He remembered Scott Oakley from when he'd dealt blackjack there, had thought him a fine young man who would someday do better. The manager's sympathy earned me not only Christy's last known address, but the name of one of her friends who would be on duty that evening in The Shaft, as well as the name of a good friend of Scott who was the night bartender in The Assay Office.

As I started out, the manager called after me, "If you see Christy, tell her her job's waiting."

CHRISTY HERTZ'S ADDRESS WAS IN a mobile home park in nearby Sparks. I've always thought of such enclaves as depressing places where older people retreat from the world, but this one was different. There were lots of big trees and planter boxes full of fall marigolds; near the manager's office, a little footbridge led over a man-made stream to a pond where ducks floated. I followed the maze of lanes to Christy's trailer, but no one answered her door. None of the neighbors were around, and the manager's office was closed.

Dead end for now, and the friends didn't come on duty at the Lucky Strike for several hours. So what else could I do here? One thing.

Find a doctor.

YEARS BEFORE, I'D DISCOVERED THAT the key to getting information from anyone was to present myself as a person in a position of authority—and that it was easy to do so without lying. Most people, unless they're paranoid or have something to hide, will cooperate with officials; their motives may range from respect to fear, but the result is the same. I tailored my approach to the situation by first driving to the public library and photocopying the Yellow Pages listings for physicians. Then, in a quiet corner of the stacks there, I went to work with my cell phone.

"My name is Sharon McCone. I'm an investigator looking into the cause of a fatal aviation accident that occurred two weeks ago near Tufa Tower Airport, Mono County, California. The victim was a student pilot who reportedly had been diagnosed with narcolepsy; the diagnosis wasn't noted on FAA form eight-four-two-zero-dash-two, so we assume it was made by a person other than a designated examiner. Would you please check your records to see if Scott Oakley was a patient?"

Only five people asked if I was with the Federal Aviation Agency or the National Transportation Safety Board. When I admitted to being a private investigator working for the victim's mother, two cut me off, citing confidentiality of patient records, but the remainder made searches. All the searches came up negative.

Maybe Clark Morris, Scott's friend who tended bar at The Assay Office, could steer me toward the right doctor.

EVENING ON THE STRIP: THE sun was sinking over the Sierras and the light was golden, vying with the garish neon and coming up a winner. The sidewalks were crowded with people out for a Saturday-night good time—or looking for trouble. A drunken guy in cowboy garb bumped into a middle-aged couple and yelled an obscenity. They stared him down until he slunk off, muttering. I spotted three drug deals going down, two of them to minors. A trio of young Native Americans, probably fresh off one of the nearby reservations, paid an older, cynical-eyed man to buy them a six-pack. Hookers strolled, lonely men's gazes homing in on them like airplanes to radar transmitters. And on the curb a raggedly dressed girl of perhaps thirteen hunched, retching between her pulled-up knees.

I thought of Hy's ranch house, the stone fireplace, the shelves of western novels and Americana to either side of it. Of the easy chairs where we should now be seated, wineglasses to hand. Of quiet conversation, a good dinner, and bed. . . .

\*     \*     \*

"SCOTT'S DOCTOR?" CLARK MORRIS SAID. "I don't think he had one."

"He must've gone to somebody for his student pilot's medical exam."

"Excuse me a minute." The moustached bartender moved to a couple who had just pulled up stools, served them Bud Lights, and returned to me. "You were asking about the medical exam. I think he got it in Sparks—and only because he had to. Scott hated doctors; I remember him and Christy having a big blowup once because he wouldn't get a yearly physical."

The cocktail waitress signaled that she needed an order filled. Morris complied, poured me another glass of wine when he came back.

"Thanks. The reason I'm asking about the doctor is that Scott saw one the day before he died—"

"No way. He took Christy on a picnic that day, out at Pyramid Lake, one of their favorite places. They left real early."

"Well, maybe his mother got it wrong. It could've been the day before that."

"I don't think so. Scott was working construction in Sparks all that week."

"Oh? He wasn't dealing cards anymore?"

"That too—at Harrah's. He needed the money because he wanted to get married. He was going to talk to Christy about setting the date while they were on their picnic. He really loved that woman, said he had to marry her before it was too late."

"Too late for what?"

Morris frowned, then spread his hands. "Damned if I know."

LYNDA COLLINS, CHRISTY HERTZ'S FRIEND, wore one of the camp-follower costumes and looked exhausted. When the time came for her break from her duties in The Shaft, she sank into the chair opposite me and kicked off her high-heeled shoes, running her stockinged toes through the thick carpet.

"So who hired you?" she asked. "It couldn't've been that no-good bastard of a stepfather of Christy's, trying to find out where she's living now. I know—poor, wimpy Scott."

"You haven't heard about Scott?"

"Heard what?"

"He's dead." I explained the circumstances, watching the shock register in Collins's eyes.

"That's awful!" she said. "I wonder why Christy didn't let me know? I wonder if *she* knows?"

"I take it you didn't like Scott."

"Oh, he was all right, but he couldn't just let go and have a good time, and he was stifling Christy. The flying was the one real thing he ever did—and look how that turned out."

"I understand he and Christy went on a picnic at Pyramid Lake the day before he died."

"They did? Oh, right, now I remember. Funny that I haven't heard from her since then. I wonder how Scott took it?"

"Took what?"

"Christy was going to break it off with him when they were up there. She met somebody else while Scott was living down at his mom's place—a guy from Sacramento, with big bucks and political connections. Since Scott got back, she couldn't get up the nerve to tell him, but she had to pretty soon because she and this guy are getting married next month. God, I hope she let Scott down easy."

AGAIN THERE WAS NO ANSWER at Christy Hertz's mobile home, but lights shone next door. I went over, knocked, and asked the woman who responded if she'd seen Hertz recently.

"Oh no, honey, it's been at least two weeks. She's probably on vacation, planning her wedding. At least that's what she told me she planned to do."

"When was the last time you saw her?"

"It was . . . Yes, two weeks ago last Thursday. She was leaving with that good-looking blond-haired boy. I guess he's the lucky fellow."

"Did she take any luggage?"

"She must have, but all I saw was a picnic hamper."

THE PARK OFFICE WAS CLOSED. I stood on its steps, debating what could be a foolhardy move, then doubled back to Hertz's. The lights still shone next door, but to the other side all the trailers were dark. I went that way and checked Hertz's windows till I found one that was open a crack, then removed the screen, slid the glass aside, and entered.

Inside I stood listening. The mobile home had the feel of a place that is unoccupied and has been for some time. I took my flashlight from my purse and shone it around, shielding the beam with my hand. Neat stacks of magazines and paperbacks, dishes in a drainer by the sink, a well-scrubbed stovetop and counters. My impression of Hertz as a tidy housekeeper was contradicted, however, by a bowl of rotting fruit on the dining table and milk and vegetables spoiling in the fridge.

A tiny hallway led to a single bedroom and bath. The bed was made and clothing hung neatly in the closet. In the bathroom I found cosmetics and a toothbrush in the holder and a round compact containing birth control pills. The date above the last empty space was that of the day before the picnic at Pyramid Lake.

On my way out I spotted the glowing message light on the answering machine.

"Christy, this is Dale. Just checking to see how it went. I love you."

"Christy, are you there? If you are, pick up. Okay, call me when you get this message."

"Christy, where the hell are you? For God's sake, call me!"

"Okay, let me guess: You patched it up with Scott. The least you could do is tell me. But then you couldn't tell him about *me*, now could you?"

"I'm giving you one more chance to explain. If you don't return this call within twenty-four hours, that's it for us!"

Christy Hertz hadn't been too wise in her choice of either man.

I'D NEVER BEEN TO PYRAMID Lake before, but as I stood on a boat-launching ramp on its western shore, I felt as if I'd come home. Like Tufa Lake, it was ancient and surreal, the monolith from which it had taken its name looming darkly; on the far shore clustered domes and pinnacles very like the Tufa towers. A high, milky overcast turned the still water to silver; a few boats drifted silently in the distance; above, the migratory waterfowl wheeled, swooping low in their quest for food.

The lake was some thirty miles north of Reno, surrounded by a Paiute Indian reservation. Upon my arrival I'd driven along the shore to Sutcliffe, a village whose prefab homes and trailer parks and small commercial establishments seemed to have been scattered beside the water by some gigantic and indiscriminate hand. There I'd shown the picture Scott Oakley's mother had given me to clerks in grocery stores and boat rental and bait shops—anywhere a couple on a picnic might have stopped—but to no avail. At the offices of the Pyramid Lake Tribal Enterprises—whose function seemed to be to sell fishing licenses—I was advised to try Saltby's Bait and Tackle, some ten minutes north. But Saltby's was closed, and I was fresh out of options.

A sound made me turn away from the water. A rusted-out white pickup, coming this way. It pulled up next to the little store, and an old man got out; he unlocked the door, went inside, and turned the Closed sign over to Open. I hurried up the boat ramp.

The man had longish gray hair and a nut-brown complexion weathered by years of harsh elements, and the reception he gave me was as one of his own. My great-grandmother was a full-blooded Shoshone, and my looks reflect her part of the family gene pool; sometimes that's a hindrance, but it can also be a help.

I showed him Scott's picture. "Two weeks ago Thursday, did you see this man? He would've been with a redheaded woman—"

"Yes. They've come here many times. They always rent one of my motorboats and take a picnic to the east shore."

"And you're sure about the date?"

He nodded.

"What time did they get here?"

He reached under the counter and produced a rental log, ran a gnarled finger down the listings. "Ten in the morning. They brought the boat back at four—a long time for them."

"When they brought it back, who returned the keys and paid?"

"The young man."

"Did you see the woman?"

He considered. "No. No, I didn't."

The only other thing I needed to ask him was how to find the office of the tribal police.

THE TRIBAL POLICE LOCATED WHAT was left of Christy Hertz's body at a little after three that afternoon. It was concealed in a small cavern fashioned by the elements out of a dome on the east shore, and beside it lay a bloodstained rock. Her skull had been crushed.

I could imagine the scenario: Scott pressing her to set a wedding date; Christy telling him she already had, but with someone else. And Scott—the good kid who took life so seriously, who worked hard at doing the right thing and now couldn't understand what he'd done wrong—striking out at her. Striking out in blind anger, because everything he cared about was being taken from him.

After he hid the body, he went through the motions—returning the boat, driving down to Vernon as scheduled. When he was unable to conceal his distress from his mother, he'd come up with a lie that would make his suicide look to be an accident. And then he'd taken the Cessna trainer around the pattern at Tufa Tower—three times, perfectly, so Hy could get out of the plane. Perfectly, so he could end his own life.

THE NEXT AFTERNOON I WAS at the controls of the Citabria, and Hy rode in the backseat. I put it into a steep-banked turn, keeping the tip of the left wing on Plover Island, where Scott had crashed and burned.

Through our linked headsets, Hy said, "A decent kid is pushed too far, kills somebody he loves, and then kills himself. He was so intent on dying and such a good actor that I hadn't a clue."

"And now his mother will have to live with what happened."

"At least she's got the comfort of knowing he tried to spare her."

"Small comfort."

"Dammit, McCone, why don't suicides think of the people they'll be leaving behind?"

For a moment I didn't speak, concentrating on fighting the winds aloft, trying to keep the wingtip centered on the island. It's an exercise in directional control you learn during flight training, and normally I enjoy it. Not today, though, not in these winds.

I gave up on it and headed south, to check out the obsidian domes at the volcanic field. "Ripinsky," I said, "suicidal people are very self-involved, we all know that. And a lot of them, like Scott, just plain don't want to take responsibility for their own lives."

"So they crap up everybody else's life too."

I put on full throttle and pulled back on the stick; instead of flying over the domes, I'd take it way up, practice some aerobatic maneuvers. Nothing amused Hy more than being along for the ride when I managed to turn a simple loop into something that resembled a corkscrew. And he badly needed to be cheered up right now.

"You know," I said, "it occurs to me that a life lived well is a lot like a solo flight. You accept responsibility, do the best you can, and go on from there."

I glanced back at him; he nodded.

"And that's enough philosophizing for today," I added.

I leveled off, pulled back on the stick, and pushed the throttle in all the way. The plane shot upward on the vertical. In ten seconds, I had him laughing.

Melissa Mia Hall is a writer and editor who lives in Fort Worth, Texas. Her anthology *Wild Women* was published in 1997. Short fiction by her appears in *Marilyn: Shades of Blonde* and *Car Crimes III*. In "Psychofemmes," she examines not only what happens when people take the law into their own hands, but the aftermath of their choices.

# Psychofemmes
## MELISSA MIA HALL

### Karen

"Are you crazy?—don't do this—please, I'm begging you, sweetheart—don't do this . . ."

The man, already soaked in sweat, pees in his pants and the stink of urine and BO makes the already stale air in the storeroom thicker and more horrible to bear. His executioner twitches her nose like Samantha, a TV character on the old sitcom *Bewitched*, but nothing happens. TV magic is just that, TV magic caught in random airwaves after being played with by a bunch of show-biz folk, amateur illusionists. This is real. The stench gets worse. He no longer looks like a successful accountant. Her patience finally pops like a chewing gum bubble.

"I don't think I'm crazy, at least not the last time I looked," she says, calmly pulling the trigger. "Are you crazy?"

He doesn't say much, since he is dead.

Her aim has been magnificent, ending the nightmare with a perfect bullet hole to the heart. All those weeks practicing at the range have paid off. No longer will the bastard be conducting the criminal business he ran alongside his legit C.P.A. services, making kiddie porn.

The last seedy epic starred her now deceased daughter, Alison. The weight of the cassette bumps her hip where it nestles in the pocket of her Donna Karan jacket like a defanged rattlesnake.

She has not erased this last piece of evidence, although often she has longed

43

to destroy it. It could be just an example of self-punishment. Karen has no intention of ever viewing it again, not the way she does the home movies of happier times. The school concerts Alison soloed in as a talented singer and dancer. The family holidays. Alison's father, still alive, not a middle-aged victim of heart disease. Alison, still alive, not a suicide at fifteen. Her dream to be an actress coincided too neatly with Mom's new boyfriend's plan to put her to work in cheesy blue videos.

Her mom's boyfriend—the thought tickles down her throat like curdled milk she can't spit out. She let the animal, even encouraged the animal to enter their normal lives. At least he has now been returned to the cosmic zoo, hopefully the one in the hotter regions.

A tentative knock on the door signals the time to leave has arrived. "Hurry . . ." the whisper from her sister jolts her out of her despondent and futile reverie. Karen Perkins carefully subtracts any detail of her presence and takes the service elevator to the parking garage. She walks past the almost empty slots with the intent of a panther stalking its kill, but the kill has already been completed.

Her sister Jill meets her in the all-night coffee shop on the corner where several hospital workers just getting off the late shift congregate. Jill lifts her mug of double espresso. "To justice . . ."

Karen slides into the booth and glances at the cappuccino waiting for her. "Did you order me a BLT?"

"Sure did." She has to use the rest room. With a weary nod, she leaves Jill. The gun is still in her purse, wrapped in a scarf, alongside many other articles. Made of dark brown Italian leather, sturdy, but sleek, the bag also holds many other things. The heat of the gun seems to radiate through the bands of woven leather. At any minute she thinks a cop will burst through the rest room to arrest her. She has just killed a man; well, maybe "man" is the wrong term for that worm.

She washes her face and scrubs her hands furiously. Doesn't she smell? She squirts massive amounts of DIVA on her wrists and then combs her long, blond hair. She finds a barrette in the bottom of her suit pocket and clips her hair back neatly. She reapplies her lipstick and mascara.

The light in the rest room isn't so good. She leans closer to the mirror and notices one eyelid seems a little droopy. She is only thirty-two but she feels like sixty-two. She bugs her eyes wide and wonders how on earth she can live with what she has just done.

Veronica Esmeralda Luna, from the group, comes in. "You okay?"

"Are you checking up on me?"

"You completed the assignment. You're a psychofemme, no doubt about it." She hands her the plane ticket and the traveler's checks without a smile or a handshake, just a cool stare that gives Karen a shiver. Veronica never smiles.

"Okay."

"You got the job done—now get on with your life. We cannot tolerate injustice. It's not about power, it's about being whole, not a fragment, doing what's right for you and not because someone tells you it is."

The bathroom seems to shrink. Karen can hardly breathe.

"Good luck." Veronica takes Karen's bag, fishes out the gun and slips it into her attaché case. "Did the silencer work out—did you notice any possible problem spots during the assignment that we need to be aware of?"

"No."

"Fine." Veronica gives her a nod, unlocks the rest room door, and vanishes. Karen splashes some more cold water on her face and leaves.

The BLT waits for her. Her sister tries to smile but her lips keep slipping back into a worried wrinkle. "I had them do you another cappaccino because I drank yours."

Karen eats part of the sandwich and ingests the caffeine. She has to stay awake.

"I'll miss you."

"You can come and visit after I get settled."

"I will."

"With Sissy dead I just don't have much of a life here."

"I know." Her sister lowers her gaze and tears her napkin into tiny pieces. "So, was it bad?"

"Yeah."

"Were you scared?"

Karen can't answer her. A waitress watches them with a little too much attention. "Say, I've gotta run. Would love to stay and talk, but duty calls."

"Later . . ." Jill manages, knocking back tears Karen is sure will fall all the way back to her home in Arlington.


## Jill

Her husband thinks Jill is a member of a book review club that is an offshoot from the Junior League or a continuing ed. class at the local university. He has no idea what they do or what they are doing.

"What's on the agenda tonight—a Sandra Brown romance or a naughty Stephen King book?" Brad hollers on his way out to the ball game.

"Neither. Try Margaret Atwood—she's a Canadian feminist writer."

"Cool," he says as he loads their two boys into the Explorer.

Jill waves as they leave the cul-de-sac.

Her neighborhood seems like an oasis of peace. She blinks back tears as she thinks about Karen leaving town as if it is something she does every day.

The club will begin arriving soon. She goes inside to get the table ready. The dogs, Labs that are affectionate if somewhat slobbery and always underfoot, allow her to sweep the faded Oriental rug. They seem to know something is up. She's not crazy about dogs, prefers cats, but the children and Brad really love dogs. She tolerates them. At least they're not wild dogs, really tame, actually—Pete sits quietly in the corner by the patio door and Marsha snuggles beside him, working on a rawhide chew toy.

Jill keeps checking the clock. Everything looks lovely. She lights the candles, not for romantic effect but to mask the faint doggy smell she is always so sensitive about.

The cars begin arriving in the cul-de-sac around seven. Jill welcomes the group with a strained smile. She recognizes some regulars and a few strangers. A disparate crowd—a curious assortment of age, ethnicity, talents, economic worth, and temperament. Jill feels both fear and pride to be among them.

Everyone clusters around the table heavy with food and drink. One woman, who looks especially impoverished and malnourished, takes up a quiet post at the end of the table, eats several helpings without looking up. She sniffs at the eggplant casserole. "Needs more garlic," she says, then finally heads to the sofa, coffee, and éclair in hand.

Veronica sips merlot and nibbles on celery dipped in crab dip.

"Karen—" Jill's voice freezes in her throat as Veronica's eyebrows shoot up. You are never supposed to bring up the name of any graduate. Her exploits are never supposed to be discussed. It is over; Karen is over, done with. Through. Still, Jill can't let it go. The sisters had discussed it beforehand, over and over. With tears and pleading, she had resorted to their Christian upbringing. " 'Vengeance is mine,'" saith the Lord.' Karen, don't you think, when it all comes down to Judgment Day, he will get his just reward?"

Her sister's pain rang shrilly in her voice. "I can't wait for that. My child is dead. She killed herself over what he did to her—a man I even slept with. Now she's gone, my baby's gone, suicide at fifteen because I didn't believe her, my own daughter, and then, there it was on the TV, playing with blood all over the floor. My baby's blood? She'd timed it so I'd find her when I came in from work. Come on, Jill, you've said it yourself, you'd like to be the one to pull the trigger." Her sister had looked so strong, so full of righteous glory, like an angel with a sword. Jill had pushed away the little voice that said, "Let Jesus handle it." They had gone to church every Sunday, growing up. They had prayed. Jill finds herself praying now. God help me get out of all this.

Veronica's voice startles her back to reality. She has one of those musical throaty voices at once hypnotic and awakening. "Your sister is dead—I am so sorry to hear about it. It was on the news at five P.M."

"What?" Jill feels shock spread throughout her body, numbing it.

"Plane crashed."

"Excuse me?" Jill will not believe her ears. It has to be some sort of cover or hidden message.

"Yes, I imagine it will be hard for you to adjust to the loss. We're all so sorry."

Jill's legs can't support her. The group all stares at her, pairs upon pairs of dead eyes unblinking, dry.

"She was a queen."

"Queen."

"Master of the Game."

"Blessed Demoiselle of Psychofemmedom," Babette says. The almost-super model just in from the Paris collections lifts her wineglass in tribute, then drains the wine in one gulp.

"Was there anything else on the agenda tonight?"

"Leslie's assignment."

Leslie Trenton is in the corner, studying the sculpture of Mother and Child Brad gave Jill for their tenth anniversary. Her dark red hair obscures her expression. One perfectly manicured hand rests on the head of the mother.

"The newspaper publisher."

"Maybe," Veronica says. The impoverished woman, on her second éclair, licks a chocolate smear off her thumb and mutters under her breath. "Excuse me, Hazel. Did you have something to share with us?"

"Gotta happen right away. My source says she's leaving the country for a sabbatical in three days after her elective surgery."

"Good work."

Leslie sits down, watching Veronica with unabashed respect. "The arrangements are all in place?"

"I'll let you know when it's time and also the confirmation of the victim's identity. There could be a last-minute emergency."

Babette raises her hand and waves it like a child.

"What is it?" Veronica says a little impatiently.

"I want my assignment verified. The girls are watching me too closely. They think something is up. If I'm going to do it—I've got to do it soon."

"Something is up."

"I want to do it real bad but the girls don't think he is so bad."

"The girls—the girls—are you all under eighteen, or what?" Jill says, wishing they could get back to Karen.

"Almost—"

"And you are almost as old as Cindy Crawford, Babette—you are not a girl. You are a woman," Jill says suddenly, her head pounding. The impoverished woman suddenly pulls out a platinum diamond-studded cigarette case and proceeds to light up. "Not in my house," Jill snaps.

"What's her problem?" a strange woman with short white hair says with a gasp. She is about seventy, wearing Armani and Ralph Lauren in a haphazard mix. She digs in her Chanel handbag and produces a cigar. "See this, honey? I'll smoke anytime, anywhere I damn well please, and so can Hazel!"

"No, you won't," Jill says.

Veronica shakes her black hair back and groans. "Oh, for heaven's sake, to smoke or not to smoke is not even in the ballpark."

"Excuse me?" the smoker arches a perfectly plucked eyebrow but puts her stogie back in her purse.

"Let's get back to what's really important. Is my sister really dead?" Jill's teeth chatters. Her whole body trembles as if an unseasonable arctic blast had blown through the room.

Hazel puts her cigarette case back into the shabby pocket of her dirty trench coat and produces a small pocketknife. She begins cleaning her fingernails.

Babette fidgets with her short see-through plastic skirt. She reaches into her silver thong and scratches. "I need some sex." She turns to look at Veronica pointedly.

"Not now—you little slut," Veronica says.

"I know—and not ever—I just like to pull your string, like I pull on mine. So sue me. I like pussy."

Babette loves flaunting her lesbianism. Right now Jill just wants her to stop playing with herself and to leave. She wants all of them to leave. She flinches when she thinks she hears Brad's Jeep pull up outside.

"Did you sabotage the plane? Did you kill her and how many innocent people along with her?"

"She's breaking the rules," a quiet woman says softly from her position near the Monet reproduction of water lilies. To Jill she looks like the waitress.

"Karen broke the rules," Babette says. "I don't break rules. I make them and I say that I want my assignment. I want to kill that two-faced jerk who doesn't want lesbians on the cover of *Vogue* or *Elle* or any damn magazine that promotes Miss Perfect GIRLIE GIRL as MS HETERO."

"Shut up," Veronica says, staring at Jill.

"I don't have to."

"We will end our meeting today without following *Robert's Rules of Order*. Jill will soon be deluged with company."

"This is my house and I demand answers."

Veronica just looks at Jill and shakes her head.

"How did she break the rules?" Jill almost screams, one hand digging into Veronica's thin shoulders.

"Don't touch me!" Veronica pushes her away.

Babette laughs. "Yes, don't touch Veronica, don't ever touch Veronica."

The dark woman's brown eyes shine with hatred. "Babette, I am warning you—don't make me lose my temper. I have killed twelve people. Maybe it's time for a lucky thirteen."

The group hushes. For a few moments no one can speak, then one at a time, members get up to leave. As each passes Jill, they make the club's crooked peace sign and say "Good luck," then disappear out the front door.

Veronica is the last to leave.

"I want out," Jill tells her, searching for signs of intelligent life in the face of the club's president. Jill suspects "Veronica" isn't even her name. Intelligence has long ago been replaced by a mask that chills and repels Jill even as it impresses her.

"We don't do that," she says. "You knew that going in. Karen knew that going in. Accidents happen. You give us too much power, Jill. Do you really think the club would kill innocent women and children?"

Jill has to admit that doesn't make much sense.

"A tragic accident, that's all."

"I still want out," Jill says.

"I'm afraid that's just not possible," Veronica says. "Remember: *Mi casa* is my house."

This time it is Brad's Jeep. Jill doesn't want the club president to see him, but it is too late. He brushes by the curvaceous brunette with an appreciative smile. He starts to introduce himself, but Veronica's exit is too quick.

"What's wrong with her?"

"She's in a hurry," Jill says. "She's just always in a hurry."

"Hey—look—is that your mother coming?"

Her mother's Oldsmobile squeals as she parks it haphazardly and runs, crying up the drive. "OH, MY GOD, JILL—I've had some just horrible news . . ."

The dogs begin barking then. It will be an hour before the house has any semblance of calm. Calm, not joy. Jill feels it will be years before she can ever find that again.

Too many secrets corrupt. Revenge corrupts. Evil destroys. All means do not justify the cause. Her head keeps getting larger and thicker with confusion.

Karen can't be dead, she just can't be.

## Hazel and Leslie

"I used to be married to a guy who worked for a *Fortune* 500 company. He was a vice president. He gave me diamond bracelets and gold necklaces. One time he gave me a ruby. We were so rich we had platinum toothpicks and towel warmers in every bathroom, not to mention a housekeeper."

"That's right, Hazel. Would you like a Big Mac? I'm making a run."

"No, I ate real good tonight."

"Sure you don't want some French fries?"

"Well, maybe I'd share some." Hazel belches. "But I did eat me more than one chocolate éclair and you wouldn't want me to lose my girlish figure, Isaac."

"No, now that would be just terrible."

"Yes, it would," Hazel says with a laugh. The ER tech gave her back a slap and Hazel belched, as if on cue.

"How do you do that?" he says, escaping between the automatic doors.

Hazel watches him with a grin. Magic.

Everything is magic.

Dr. Leslie Trenton passes Hazel and winks. "What is it this time? An ingrown toenail?"

"Sarcasm gets you zippo, *nada*, nothing." Hazel slips an envelope in the doctor's white coat and whispers in her ear. "Your orders, ma'am." Then she turns and leaves. "I'm going home."

"Don't forget to take a bath," Dr. Trenton calls after her, fumbling in her pocket, a frown slitting her forehead like a badly done suture.

She joined the club by accident, although Veronica always says there are no accidents, after trying to save Lois, a new recruit of the group in the ER, who had finally gotten the courage to divorce her abusive husband. She had died of a cerebral hemorrhage when her ex had surprised her in the parking lot of their former home. Too many blows to the head from a golf club.

Another group member, Nancy, had brought Lois in on the night Leslie was on duty. She had also been her next-door neighbor. "I told her this was going to happen. She kept thinking he would change. Leopards don't change their spots. I told her, you know," the woman kept saying over and over. "This didn't have to happen."

"I know," Leslie said under her breath. "Maybe she was just too scared. Where's the guy?"

"Drunker than the lord. Police should've taken him downtown by now."

"Next of kin?"

"How about a boy, age eight? He's in the waiting room with my husband, Marlon, and my daughter, Sara."

"I wish this stuff wouldn't happen." A policeman approached her, flipping through papers. "Doc? Can I talk to you about—about—"

"Lois Benson," Nancy interrupted. "What—you get so many you can't keep the names straight?"

"Excuse me, are you related to the victim?"

"We all are," Nancy said.

Leslie had been so impressed. When she got the invitation to the first meeting, something had told her to go.

Now she wasn't so certain it had been a good idea. A doctor doesn't get into death. A doctor is supposed to save lives, not take them.

Of course, there's always a first time.


## Babette

The Glamour Café in New York City appears deserted. A goofy, rather brainless imitation of the Fashion Café and Planet Hollywood with a dash of McDonald's, it had been opened by a trio of television actresses formerly of a hit sitcom that once been the epitome of Trend. They had made a fortune, become stars almost overnight, authorities upon glamor and style to the twentysomething and whateversomething group who dined on tabloid TV-style with the hunger of cats who haven't eaten in days, then when fed, gobble so fast they have to throw up an hour later. Bulimic chic. Babette nurses her gin and tonic and stares at her empty shot glass that had held overpriced tequila.

The Man sits across from her.

"So my contract has been terminated."

"You can make this easy or you can make this hard. Face it, Babette, you had a good run."

The Other Man had done it to her.

"Who made him God? Stop it, don't answer that. I know, the billboards make him God. His fucking empire of designer shops, lines, commercials, perfumes, and farts makes him God. So I mean, what's the big deal? So I wouldn't fuck him? He fucks everyone. Why was my turn down so special?"

The Man looks away politely, ignoring her tirade. He stares at the giant face of the actress with the super hair and big mauve mouth. "She's so Not Important. . . ."

"Don't try to change the subject." Babette's hands shake as she tries to light a cigarette.

"You're not supposed to smoke in here," their chirpy waitress reminds her.

Babette curses and throws the unlit cigarette down. "And now I'm supposed to say I'm not important or it's not important that bastard has so much effing power, he can just do this to me?"

"You did it to yourself. You can't expect to be a role model to teenagers with your stupid attitude. You're selfish, Babette. Who cares who you sleep with? Moms care. Not the kids, certainly, but let's face it, you are not the *Seventeen* cover girl anymore. Hell, you couldn't even make *Sassy*, and *Vogue* thinks you're trashy; *Elle* thinks you are no longer thin enough; and *Playboy* only wants to do a spread because you're so good at showing everyone you don't have to wear panties or bras. Europe's the only place for you. Our agency is no longer representing you but I'm sure someone will like you over there, where they don't understand English so well. Face it, Babs, baby, you just talked too much."

"About him."

"You blew it."

All the money, too. "I was *Clairvoyant*. I made all that money for that stinking perfume."

"I know, go into acting." The man examines his manicure. His cell phone buzzes. "Sorry," he turns his attention to his call, moving away from Babette, speaking quietly.

Babette stares into the painted eyes of the actress reportedly now an alcoholic whore.

The man ends his call and smiles at Babette. "We can still be friends, at least. I can tell Hayley we're square."

Hayley is his boss, her real boss, not this thing. She has to work to recall his name. Clark something. Not Clark Kent. More like Clark Fart. He has pale green eyes and pale white skin with moles on his cheek and a hairless chest he has waxed regularly. She wonders if he has armpit hair and if this also gets removed weekly.

"Just admit it. He's put out the word, hasn't he?"

"God, Babette, you're so *noir*. Things like that just don't happen. Do you think he gives a damn about you? Simply put, your time in the spotlight has passed. Move on. Get a life." Clark strokes the plastic salt shaker in the shape of one of the actresses. "Take acting lessons. . . ."

Very funny. Babette looks down at her manicure, at her pale blue nails. It had seemed a good idea at the time. Now it just seems pathetic.

"Are you screwing him?"

Clark turns red. "Wha-at?"

"The Big Kahuna. I know he does boys and girls. See, that's the thing I don't understand. Why does he have to pick on me?"

"Look, I have a meeting." Clark stands and stares at her icily. "See ya— good luck." He leaves a paper she needs to sign and send back to the agency. She may or may not sign it. She could make things hard.

Or easy. It might be very easy. To do him. Not Clark. The other man. The Emperor of Star, the Showman of Style without Substance, He Who Will Be Obeyed.

The chirpy waitress returns. "Anything else?"

Some tourists have landed. All is right with the world.

"Yeah, some cyanide, if you have it."

"Oh, you models are so funny," she says with a laugh.

Right.

Babette grubs around in her bag for a mirror. She studies her mouth. The bluish-brownish-reddish stain upon her lips suddenly seems totally hideous. She is not going to wait for the club to give her approval for what must be done. There comes a time when you have to break from the pack.

He wanted to do her in the rear. He wanted to hear her say she preferred him to his wife. She just couldn't do it.

She starts to light the cigarette again. The chirpy waitress is busy and doesn't notice. But her hand's shaking too much.

She could do him, all right. A woman could do anything once she really focuses. The actresses beam down from the walls, smiling, always smiling or pouting with just the right finesse, sparkling with glamor. Look what they had done with minimal talent and looks, thanks to Nielsen numbers and smart TV writers and directors and producers and money. Money.

Money talks. Money listens. Advertising. Image.

Clairvoyance. This is the face of the future.

"I see a line that leads to you," she says. Suddenly a line of coke dances in her brain. Nope, she can't afford to do that again. She has to remain *clairvoyantly* clear. On what must be done.

## Jill and Hazel

"I just want it to stop," Jill says very softly.

The bag lady doesn't say anything at first, she just sighs and scrambles around in the plastic bag. "Hate these things—always prefer paper, brown paper, but they're too lazy to open them up and bag the groceries in 'em. Have to ask, and they act like it's a special gift. Bottles are too heavy for plastic. Waste paper. They always waste paper because they're lazy. Want to load up your arm with 'em." Hazel remembers how simple the beginning of the club had been. Years ago it had been just a sisterhood of women who wanted to take charge of their lives, to seize their own power, to avenge those who had none. How had it become more of a powerhood than a sisterhood? She sighs. It began with the first killing. A man who had gotten away with murder. Of his own mother. Hazel's mother. Hazel's brother a murderer. She sighs, wanting to forget. She will forget. Somehow.

"Can't we make it stop? I'm a Christian. Christians don't kill."

"Yes, sometimes they do." The bus stop was still pretty empty, but soon it would fill up. "Let's walk down to Sundance Square and look at the courthouse. I like looking at that thing. Downtown Fort Worth is just so much easier to walk around in than downtown Dallas. President Clinton stopped here, you know, rather than Dallas. Probably the Kennedy thing. Bad karma. But Dallas isn't a bad place, entirely. They have the State Fair. Ever been to the State Fair? I think Big Tex oughta be black once in a while. But then he'd need to be Hispanic, and then Vietnamese. Lots of Orientals here now. Texas is a melting pot. Melting pot. That can be good and that can be bad, I suppose."

"Hazel, killing people is a bad thing. I just don't think it's a good thing. You just shouldn't. 'Vengeance is mine,' saith the Lord.' Jesus didn't approve of it."

"It's a little late in the day to start having a conscience. I don't approve of it either, but sis, it happens, for a very good reason. An eye for an eye, and isn't it better to be organized? To this day my first kill remains 'accidental death' on the books, and he ain't going around burning churches and temples of good God-fearing, God-loving folk any longer, praise God. Jill, he was a very bad man. I can even say it was self-defense. He tried to rape me and . . ." Hazel is lying, of course.

That no-account fool church-burning fool did deserve to die. But the first real kill had been her own brother. Her boyfriend on the police force had found her crying over her mother's inert form, oblivious to dead Jay in the corner, where she whooped him on the side of the head with her mom's iron skillet, still dripping warm bacon grease. Hazel had looked up, crying, ignoring her own knife wounds. "Jay said he wouldn't take no back talk no more. He was going to take the rent money and Mama said no. . . ." Maybe it was justified, righteously so. Jill's whimpering brings her back to the present.

"Look, I want it to stop, for me, at least. Can't I please leave the group? I really think she sabotaged the whole plane Karen was on—I really do. Why would she kill Karen?"

"You know why," Hazel says unhappily.

"No, I don't."

"Maybe Veronica believed she was going to snitch on us. Maybe she even had proof that she had already begun talking to someone at the *Dallas Morning News*. But let me ask you this, little sister: If you leave us, how are we to be sure you wouldn't go to someone about your suspicions? At least Karen was a murderer. You're still a greenhorn. And seriously, now, Veronica wouldn't sabotage a whole plane. It was just a horrible accident."

"If she was going to do that, we'd all get into trouble—so I don't believe Karen was going to tell anyone about us. And why would I want to get myself in trouble? It doesn't make any sense. Besides, Karen would've told me—we never kept secrets from each other. And furthermore, she wouldn't have wanted me to pay for her crime. I just don't trust Veronica."

Hazel smiles her trademark crooked smile. "I wouldn't either, if I were you, child."

"What does that mean?"

"You know, sister, any woman doing my man would be sure enough suspect in my eyes."

Jill turns to look at Hazel slowly, her breath coming and going in ragged little gasps. It feels like someone is squeezing her chest. She could be having a heart attack. Her blood pressure could be going through the roof. She could be dying. "What are you saying?"

"Don't tell me you don't know." She had chosen Veronica to be her successor to the throne. Now it is time to dethrone Veronica, now a liability, a disgrace through bad judgment, ill will, and pure, unadulterated instability. If the center does not hold, chaos always erupts. Hazel sees that Jill might be the right one to take over. The simplicity of her rage appears both holy and organized. That's what the club needs, if it is to endure such tragedy.

Jill touches her bare neck. The short, sassy haircut she'd just gotten earlier that morning suddenly feels too bare and mannish. Her skin feels cold. What she needs is more hair and it is gone, all gone. A wind kicks up. She watches Hazel's plastic bag take to the air like a balloon that has been deflated by the prick of a malicious child. Karen did that once, just to be mean because Jill had gotten the red balloon Karen wanted, while she got stuck with a boring white one on Valentine's Day.

Hazel takes a bite out of a Ding Dong. She swallows happily and shakes her head. "Damn, you girls slay me. The wives are always the last to know even when it's right there, in front of their face.

"I think I'm ready to stop this routine. I want to go back to being rich. It will be good getting back home to Highland Park. Or maybe I'll go back to my Santa Fe condo or maybe open up the beach house in Malibu. Or the mountains. I could buy a place in Aspen. Or no, Montana, a ranch in Montana or Wyoming. No, it's too cold up there. Europe—haven't been there in a while. France. Rich black women always do well in France. . . ." She wipes her mouth daintily on the sleeve of her jeans jacket.

"Hazel!" Jill's whole body turns to Hazel's, trembling vaguely like a poodle held back by a strong leash. "Hazel, come on, tell me what you know!"

"Tell me what *you* know, sweetie."

"I don't know anything—what you're saying. He wouldn't be unfaithful to me. We have a good marriage. It was like a romance novel, how we met. And he brings me little surprises. Especially Godiva chocolates and sometimes flowers or jewelry. Charms for this sterling silver bracelet—hearts, lots of little hearts—"

"But I bet he never quotes Maya Angelou."

"He doesn't like poetry."

"Honey, he doesn't like you and I bet you get these little surprises after every time he's unfaithful."

"He loves me," Jill whispers.

Hazel coughs and studies her feet in the ugly old nurse's shoes Doc had given her for her masquerade. "Liking should come first. Then when the loving gets harder, the man's more liable to stick around to wait for the tide to come back in."

"What's that?"

"Loving goes in and out like the tides. But if you don't like the ocean you're swimming in, what can I say, baby, but watch what happens when the moon comes out and he's thinking, whoa—'I got to get to the Pacific' when he oughta stick to the Atlantic, if you know what I mean."

Jill doesn't exactly know what she means but she remembers the last charm Brad gave her. The little coyote. She hates coyotes. When she was a little girl, she tried to pet a wild dog that bit her. The emergency room doctor had to give her twelve stitches. Her father had told her, "That's what you get for petting a coyote." How had Brad forgot? After all this time, she still has the scars.


## Veronica

His body reminds her of a glove her mother used to keep in the bottom drawer of her antique bureau. It smelled of old moisture, almost a mildew smell but scented lightly with old rose petals and ancient ghost clothes no longer stored there. Nightshirts, long johns, silken underthings no longer in fashion, teddies and slips, hosiery that needs washing. Panties that are not quite clean. Memories of ancient couplings. White-people clothes. It should remind her of her father, the lost bullfighter from Madrid, the one in the storybook her mother gave her when she was six. "This is your father." It was a drawing. He had on fancy clothes, almost girl clothes. He even had a little cape and a funny hat only an old crazy woman would wear.

Carlos. Pedro. Juan. She does not know his name. Her mother was such a liar. She will never know his name.

Veronica once owned a petticoat that her mother said belonged to his mother. Later she found out it came from JCPenney. There are no traces of her heritage. She practically took apart the bureau once, looking for a secret drawer to see if she could find the love letters. Her mother said her father used to write the most beautiful, ardent letters any woman could wish for, in Spanish, never in English. Her mother met her father while she was on vacation in Spain, an innocent young student he deflowered and impregnated but never married. "He killed many bulls, my conquistador."

"Excuse me?"

Veronica's exquisite body turns on the creamy silken sheets. Her lovely head in profile, her dark, shiny hair fanned across the pillowcase fringed with lace shot through with golden thread urges him to touch her. She watches him fondle her right breast, the nipple coming awake. "My father killed bulls."

"My father was as stubborn as an old bull," he says with a laugh.

Veronica tenses. "You shouldn't make fun of your father."

The hand falls in supplication. She grabs it and places it between her legs. "What are we going to do about her?"

"Who?"

"Your wife. She is in the way."

"I'll divorce her."

"And the children?"

"Do you want to have children?"

"Your children?"

"Mine? 'Rica—my 'Rica, you are mine, mine. I love you; I love you . . ." His mouth litters her body with his sloppy kisses and he comes down on her like a devouring angel.

Veronica pretends to care. "We can keep the children but she's in the way, the mother is in the way. She won't give them up without a fight—and today we started a family, I think, I really believe it is so,"

He moans, unable to answer. He will do anything for her. She will make sure. Jill is a mess. Karen was a disaster. The whole thing's crashing down on her head. She still recalls the voice in the night on her answering machine. Karen had panicked. Karen had to come clean. No time to plan. She just had to do it. It was messy. Sometimes the voices scream in her head. The headlines dance in her brain, accompanied by that awful song, the one they said originated in Mexico. Sometimes Selena is singing it. Sometimes it is Garth Brooks. But the worst dream is when the passengers of the plane she doomed to death do it, dripping blood and tears. Blood and tears. It is driving her crazy. Psycho. For real. A woman who is crazy.

Jill must get out of the way. She knows. No one must know.

The man's body falls off of her and she thinks of the seed spilled upon her and how they may sprout something inside her. It's not enough that she gets rid of her. She must show her who has the power to create, take charge.

Her father's body created her. Then abandoned her. Veronica rises, stands naked over her lover. He looks up at her hungrily. "Come back to bed; turn around, let me kiss your ass."

"You promise to tell her."

He looks suddenly toward the bedroom door slowly opening. "I don't have to."

Veronica smiles, looking over her shoulder at the foolish girl he calls a wife.

Jill's pale white face has no blood in it. Just pain and the powdery blush she probably got in her Lancôme gift bag when she bought the exfoliant that was supposed to make her fake tan look better. Veronica wants to laugh out loud at the streaks on her silly white legs.

Veronica smells her fingers. It's repulsive but she wants to get her point across. "Baby, look, it's not what you think, not exactly. Brad, darling, we are not alone, we have a visitor, I'm afraid." His exhausted penis is exposed. "Cover yourself, Brad, your wife has just joined us. I think we need to have a talk, just the three of us, to set things straight. Don't you?"

He's not even embarrassed or even ashamed, just disgusted. Veronica puts on his white shirt stiff with extra starch. "Brad and I are getting married," she says, "I hope we can still be friends, though. It just happened—we didn't plan it, Jilly."

Jill makes the sign of the cross. She hates anyone to call her Jilly, and today she also hates Veronica. It is a sin to hate.

Veronica's eyes suddenly rest on the crucifix hanging over their bed. It is her turn to feel terrified and hideous. "You didn't say you were Catholic," she splutters, loosing composure for just a second, for just one brief second. Veronica thinks her father was Catholic. Certainly he has been crucified on the cross as long as Jesus.

Jill has left the room, unable to digest the grotesque display, the aftermath of illicit sex.

Veronica rummages through Jill's lingerie drawer, stealing some Dior hose and some fresh panties. She will not clean herself. She needs to be pregnant. She hopes to be pregnant. There's a gun there. The convenience of the gun unnerves her. It is too perfect.

He sits on the side of the bed, head in hand. "It is not what I thought it would be. I shouldn't have let it go this far. I have to make it up to her. What we did was cruel, unspeakable. Did you see her face? Oh, God, how can I live with myself?" The tone in his voice is both insincere and almost humorous.

How can anyone? Veronica finds gloves in Jill's drawer, under a tangle of silken scarves and discarded hair ornaments. They are old-fashioned, probably belonged to Jill's mother or grandmother. Blue as a sky, soft, delicate. She puts them on, smiling at the mother-of-pearl closing. The gun is loaded. She can shoot him. Instead of her. Or herself. She chooses to do neither. Instead she puts the gun into her purse. Then she goes to him, naked with blue gloves on her hands. "Don't worry, darling, I will not leave you," she says, kneeling before him.

It starts all over again. She is almost disappointed he is so weak.

## Leslie and Babette

"How did it really happen?"

"How does anything?"

"He just fell in front of the car and I ran over him. The traffic is terrible in New York City. Someone in the back squealed their tires and honked and someone was running down the street, screaming about a purse snatcher or a kid, I don't know. I just hit him. It was an accident. A fortunate one, but an accident nonetheless. He was drunker than the Lord. The autopsy proved that. Higher than a Good-year blimp on Super Bowl Sunday."

"You had been stalking him, Babette. We all knew you wanted him to be your kill, and now he's dead. Are you telling me it was an accident?"

"The police said it was. Didn't you hear the news report? It's in every magazine and every newspaper and every tabloid show in the nation. It was an accident, I tell you." Babette pulls at the hair on her forehead nervously. Her eyes seem wild, directionless. She will not look at Leslie directly.

Leslie doesn't like her assignment. It is not the one she expected, the publisher in bed with the drug cartel. And the drug in the syringe? She doesn't even know what it is. All she has is an educated suspicion, and this hotel room is not an operating room.

Killing a sister was never part of the agreement. Her stomach aches, and she longs to pop an antacid. She feels nauseous. A doctor doesn't kill people, at least not on purpose. Swallowing down bilge, she forges on bravely. "You need to play by the rules, Babette. If you can't play by the rules you shouldn't be allowed to be in the club."

"The club? Good heavens, Leslie, you sound like you belong to the NFL or something—no, I know—you sound like you're talking about my mother's country club. They had rules. Oh, didn't they. I got kicked out when I was fifteen for swimming naked in front of a bunch of little boys."

"Babette, you know what happens to psychofemmes who don't follow the rules agreed upon by their sisters."

"Psychos don't follow rules. And femmes—what's with that, anyway? I'm the one with the French genes and I don't go around speaking French. It's stupid. It sounds dumb. Psychofemmes? Excuse me, but what does that mean? Crazy women who like French food or what? And sisters? I don't think I have a family anymore. When I really needed help, you all deserted me, ignored me. I had to strike out on my own if anything was to get done. Sometimes you just have to make your own rules."

Leslie touches the filled syringe gently. It hides in her hand, underneath the Hermès scarf filled with the drug that will put Babette out of her misery. For surely she must be sorry for what she has done. She should be, sick little bitch. And foolish one, at that, for the club had not okayed the death. Leslie won't be the only fashion lover of the world who would miss the famous designer's fabulous creations.

Babette suddenly stares at the doc with amazing intensity. Leslie is shocked for a moment by the reality of her considerable charm. Luminescent, transcendent, Babette's hands lift, palms upward, gesturing happily like a child. "It was fate. Now my life has come together. Have you heard? I've gotten an acting part in a movie. My career is really hot again. I'm not just another over-the-hill muse. It's like when the accident happened, the curse lifted. Don't you see? It was an accident even if he needed to die. He just happened to be at the wrong place at the right time.

"Anyway, he was keeping the sisterhood down, you know. We were just tools for him to make money. I'd gotten rusty, see, but now I'm clean." Her eyes slide upward, inspecting the ceiling of the hotel room. "I'm so happy."

Horribly drawn to Babette's sudden irresistible madness, Leslie feels a wanton and despicable urge to kiss her. She is so tall but delicate, and her breasts are like two oranges that should be squeezed. As if reading her feelings, Babette impulsively grabs her, hitting Leslie's knee. Unnerved by her own desire, Leslie jumps and accidently pierces the soft flesh of her own thigh.

Babette stands, gaping at the syringe sticking in Leslie's skin. Leslie pulls it out quickly, although it might be too late. "Call 911—Babette—please hurry—I need . . ." Babette just looks at her, shocked, almost hurt.

"You were going to kill me?"

"Ba-ba—bet-t—pl-ease—mis—take—sor-ry . . ." Her tongue is going numb and the room is getting fuzzy. "Pi-ll—p-purse." Rhymes with hearse. Leslie has to have an antacid, anyway. She will at least burp before she dies.

Babette is wiping all signs of her presence from Leslie's room. The model was not registered here. She'd never stay in this part of New York City. Only on the good side of Central Park. Soon it won't matter. In fact, she's moving to L.A. She's going to be a star. She's just going to drop out of this club business. Maybe write her autobiography. Take music lessons. Maybe form a group called the Powerbabes. She grins.

Some things you just outgrow. She could find the damn pill and give it to the bitch or she could just let her die.

"I'm not crazy, you know, but you are."

Still—another dead body? "If I let you live, will you leave me alone?"

Leslie stares at her, almost unblinking, mouth agape, drool descending from the corners of her mouth.

"And you call yourself a doctor? What was in that syringe? What kind of poison? Will a pill save you? Would a pill have saved me?

"Is this what you want? A little pill like this? I don't know, it looks like a birth control pill to me. You want me to call 911?" She laughs as she shoves the pill down the doc's throat.

Leslie tries to nod but gags instead. Babette splashes water down the front of her silk shirt as she aims water in the vicinity of her throat. Leslie watches the water stain spread, and her hands don't seem to work right. Nothing is working right. There is no magic pill, only an antacid that could only, through some miracle, postpone the end of the world. She will soon go crazy with grief. Speechless, then soon, lifeless, too. And the slut/whore/bitch/queen/model/actress/whatever is going to get away with it.

Using a Kleenex, Babette uses the phone in a distress call, pretending to be a maid. Then she walks out, stepping over the dying body lightly, as if she were slipping down a catwalk amid lightbulbs popping, cameras whirling.

Mercifully, Leslie does manage a burp.


## Jill

"Everything's going to be all right."

The boys are digesting news of the separation, and eventually, a divorce. It was not an enjoyable discussion.

Kent and Keith focus on the dogs now, ignoring their mother, eager to get back to normal life, whatever that is.

"Go on, take the dogs for a walk. Your father will come see you on Saturday. Remember, I will never get in the way. I know how much you love your dad and he loves you. Maybe . . ." Jill hopes there might be a maybe if Brad ever comes to his senses. She doesn't believe Veronica loves him. She doesn't believe Veronica loves anyone.

The doorbell rings. She goes to meet her visitor. He's a TV reporter, of all things, a bit wilder than a newspaper reporter, more dangerous. He has a reputation for confidentiality and going out on a limb.

"Come in," she says softly, surprised how intense the man is in person. He reeks of power and a dangerous quality she cannot quite identify until she's close enough to smell him. He needs sex and he wants hers. Their eyes lock for a second, and she can sense he is drawn to her, which surprises her. She looks at his ringless hands with curious satisfaction. She had heard he was divorced. They share something. He glances around at her home. He can figure out she is not without resources. For some men it is an aphrodisiac.

"No cameras, like I promised. Everything is off the record. For now. Unless you're ready to go to the DA—I always protect my sources."

She shows him into the small room off the porch she sometimes uses for her office. For many years she has fancied herself a romance novelist, but it's been hard completing anything. Especially when your belief in romance begins faltering. "Please sit down." She feels more in control sitting at her little cluttered desk with the old computer Brad gave her when he got a new one.

"So this group you're talking about. They kill people?"

She smiles softly. "Sometimes."

"So tell me, Mrs. Compton, have you ever killed anyone?"

"No, sir."

"Just Marvin," he says.

Marvin Wilson is very attractive. Jill wants him, she realizes, with a disturbing shock. Carelessly, he pushes his dark brown hair out of his eyes and waits a little impatiently for her to speak. Something begins throbbing inside her. Excitement courses through her skin and radiates through her flushed cheeks. His body seems to be aimed at her like a bow with an arrow drawn across it.

"Marvin, that's a funny name." Jill tingles. She should write this down, she should write all of this down. Sometimes life is like a romance novel if you play your cards right.

He relaxes just a little, laughs. "I know. You've made some serious allegations. I think we should talk about it, don't you? I don't want to pressure you, though. Please take your time."

"First of all, I had no idea that they were actually going to kill anyone when my sister convinced me to join."

"Your sister, the one on the plane that crashed?"

"Yes. Do you recall the C.P.A. who turned out to be a child pornographer who was allegedly killed by a thief in the rest room of—"

Marvin stops her with a raised hand. "May I tape this?"

Jill finds herself drawing her chair closer to his. She gently touches his Armani-clad thigh. "What do you think?"

"I think I'm going to be hired by a major affiliate on the East Coast."

"Excuse me?" Jill laughs. Their eyes lock again. She is glad he has a sense of humor. Brad's sense of humor is somewhat lacking.

## Hazel

She looks at the favorite pieces of her wardrobe. She favors an African designer but chooses the snooty Escada suit and the Charles Jourdan pumps. She sighs as she puts on her pearls. Pearls always make her feel old, but today she has decided to leave Dallas. She has just gotten off the phone with her stockbroker, and her maid has just finished the packing. The house in Highland Park has already been sold. Her assets in America have been liquidated and she's flying to Switzerland in a matter of hours.

The club has fallen apart. There were no good-bye meetings this time, just meltdown, pure, utter disintegration due to that idiot Veronica she had trusted to lead the band to new heights. She had trusted her sincerity and had misjudged the tiger underneath her skin, had misunderstood how sick mentally Veronica had become, how deranged. Things happen that are out of your control. Hazel is learning that. Better now than never. She is mature enough to know when to let go. If she had only known about the strange circumstances surrounding the death of Veronica's first husband or known about the identity of her father, the bullfighter.

Jill has gone to the media as ordered, to deal with another failure that must be turned into a success. She has been sworn in as new club president should anything happen to Hazel while she is on "vacation," although she plans on playing it safe in the near future and helping the club to rise again when the scales of justice need to be balanced again. She has utter confidence in Jill. She has been coached thoroughly on what to say and do. Everything is going to be all right.

However, Hazel still aches over the misfires. The biggest failure and heartbreak has to be the plane crash and all of those lives lost. She had no idea Veronica would kill innocent women and children just to get rid of one possible loose cannon. Karen. That damn Karen. She had liked her so much. Her kill had been magnificent, the lioness protecting her dead cub so other cubs would go free, able to grow up the way the goddess had intended.

She sips champagne from Waterford and shakes her head, admiring the wig that makes her look like Tina Turner.

"To a new beginning—you lose some; you win some." She toasts her image.

## Veronica

Her father is coming up the walk. She looks through the blinds at the Mercedes-Benz. And at the other car, a Pontiac, she thinks, or maybe an Oldsmobile or a Honda. She has never been good at cars. She only knows the sign of the Mercedes because that is what her husband and her father drove. She doesn't know that for sure, about her father. It is something she has dreamed about. She dreamed about her father again last night. He had killed a bull and had hung it in her closet. She thought he was dead but her mother lied. He is coming up the walk.

She searches her apartment for Brad. He is sleeping in her bed. He won't wake up.

She dresses slowly. The short white dress pleases her. It clings to her body gently, not cheaply. Her father will approve. He would also like the blue gloves, but she has misplaced them.

"Brad, you have to leave now. Get up!" She tugs at him. He won't obey her. She covers him with the downy red comforter, hiding his inappropriate naked body and praying her father won't come upstairs. They'll have coffee in the dining room. "Stay there, then—don't you breathe a word. He won't understand if there's a man in here, in his own daughter's bedroom and we're not married. It is against the faith."

The pounding is loud, so masculine and brave. He doesn't use the doorbell. Her heart flutters like a cape in the wind. His cape! Her mother had shown her one she said he'd worn, but she had not believed her. It appeared so limp, and, well, dirty. Then, of course, her mother was so unclean. She only swept the floors once a month, if then. Veronica is so clean her baseboards shine. And you can eat off her kitchen floor anytime.

"Veronica E. Luna?"

"Papa?" He is not alone. Another man, with blond hair, stands beside him. He looks angry. Her father looks sad.

"Read her her rights, Sam."

"Papa?" She has been waiting all of her life for him to come home, and he won't even touch her. Her body waits for an embrace that will never come.

Another man, with gray hair, paunchy and small, appears. "Compton's car is in the parking lot. We've got a warrant to search the premises. . . ."

They keep babbling. Veronica covers her ears, trembling. Her father is not here. The Hispanic man is too young, like José Luna. He wanted babies, too; they all want babies. The old man is going upstairs. He is going to find Brad with the horn in his gut. She has killed him. She told him she was pregnant and he told her he was going back to his wife because she was crazy. It was not a big thing. Just a temper tantrum. She wore gloves, though. She learned about gloves from her mother. "Make sure and put it on before you put it in. He didn't put one on, and look what I got. You're a fine substitute for a bullfighter. . . ."

Her head aches with all the disappointments. "I want to go to Spain," she says. "I want to go find my father."

"You have the right to . . ." The dark man sighs. He seems very sad. He keeps spitting out words she does not understand.

He tried to make her wear a condom. She never understands. The man is the one who's supposed to do that, not the girl. He really hurt her feelings. He didn't understand. He would have told someone. The woman has the power, so Veronica has to be a woman, not a man. He had to shut up. Although she is sad, very sad. Brad's kisses had been so unlike her mother's.

## Karen

Karen stands on the Eiffel Tower, her hand resting lightly on a metal railing. She gathers the courage to go to the next *étage*. She is afraid of heights and wishes stupidly that she could jump off the Eiffel Tower. Too bad only there are so many tourists down there. She would hate to splatter them with her guts. It would not be a nice thing to do, and Marc would not understand.

Marc comes around the corner, his sulky French mouth waiting for just one word, one glance from her to let him know she is the least bit happy. He is so kind and patient. He can also cook. His fresh French bread is a marvel and he doesn't use a bread machine. *"Vite, vite—"*

"I don't want to hurry," she says.

She just saw a young girl who looked like her sweet lost baby, a student from the States. She laughs and points, her wild hair blowing in the strong western breeze. "Take my picture!" she tells a friend.

"Carrie—"

Karen Perkins is Carrie Olivier now. A plane overhead causes hot tears to spring to her eyes. She still remembers the headlines. She was right to follow her gut instincts, not to get on that plane and to take another, although now she worries about that woman she sold her identity to. She hopes she died quickly.

"Let's go to the top, okay? If you go with me I can do it."

*"Pourquoi, Carrie? C'est ton vie."*

*"D'accord. Tôt ou tard?"* She can tell he wants her to be first.

*"Je parle anglais, aussi.* First! *Et à premiere vue* I love you, Carrie, *toujours*—always. . . .* He pushes her forward, brandishing their tickets. "We pay all way. Go," he says with a laugh, cocking his head toward the stairs.

She puts one foot forward. "I am crazy," she says, taking a big breath and one step up. And then another. "I am a psychofemme." The label sounds funny, archaic, a term from the past from a language she has almost forgotten.

*"Si! Ma femme—mais je ne sais pas—*psycho? *Non, mon Dieu,"* he mutters behind her.

She tries to think how to explain what she is. "Wild" in French is *sauvage* or maybe *extravagant* or *étrange*. Maybe she is a wild girl—*une étourdie* or *une bête sauvage,* a wild beast. She keeps climbing. She does not look down. She hears her lover's labored breath behind her. There is so much to learn. She is not free, though. She killed a man, and his blood is on her hands. A wild woman should be free, but if she's crazy, she can't be. Not ever.

When they ascend the last step they can take up the tower, Marc holds her while she gets the courage to see what there is to be seen. He warns her not to look down at first, to look outward slowly.

The sun has begun to set in the west, and streaks of ruddy color freshen the melancholy blue sky. A cloud like her child's face appears to float toward her.

Then she looks down at her feet. This time she doesn't feel dizzy; this time she doesn't see blood. She must be brave.

"I thought I did the right thing. I did it for you!" she cries. Her child cannot answer her. Her child is still dead.

*"Je t'aime; je t'aime,"* he murmurs in her hair.

In her daydreams she can jump off the tower. In reality she cannot. Alison won't let her. Carrie watches the cloud face melt into a purple orange streak. It reminds her of a crayon drawing Alison made when she was six.

The saddest thing of all is how you can forget a face, how you sometimes have to work to remember your own child's face. She shuts her eyes and feels the fading warmth.

"Time we go?" Marc says.

First and last. Wild women keep moving. One step in front of the other, up or down.

From below a girl laughs and screams, "Thank you. *Merci, merci beaucoup!*" Someone has taken her photograph, with her permission.

Carrie pretends it is Alison.

Richard T. Chizmar is primarily known for his work in the horror field, most notably as the editor of the World Fantasy Award-winning magazine *Cemetery Dance*, a showcase of dark fantasy and horror fiction. The best of the magazine's run was recently collected in *The Best of Cemetery Dance*. His short fiction, which has appeared in *White House Horrors* and *Cat Crimes at the Holidays*, is both poignant and disturbing. The best of his short stories was collected in the anthology *Midnight Promises* in 1997. "Blood Brothers" takes a chilling look at the familial ties that bind so much so that the only recourse might be to sever them completely.

# Blood Brothers
## RICHARD T. CHIZMAR

I grabbed the phone on the second ring and cleared my throat, but before I could wake up my mouth enough to speak, there came a man's voice: *"Hank?"*

"Uh, huh."

*"It's me . . . Bill."*

The words hit me like a punch to the gut. I jerked upright in the bed, head dizzy, feet kicking at a tangle of blankets.

"Jesus, Billy, I didn't recog—"

*"I know, I know . . . it's been a long time."*

We both knew the harsh truth of that simple statement and we let the next thirty seconds pass in silence. Finally I took a deep breath and said, "So I guess you're out, huh? They let you out early."

I listened as he took a deep breath of his own. Then another. When he finally spoke, he sounded scared: *"Hank, listen . . . I'm in some trouble. I need you to—"*

"Jesus H. Christ, Billy! You busted out, didn't you? You fucking-a busted out!"

My voice was louder now, almost hysterical, and Sarah lifted her head from the pillow and mumbled, "What's wrong? Who is it, honey?"

I moved the phone away from my face and whispered, "It's no one, sweetheart. Go back to sleep. I'll tell you in the morning."

She sighed in the darkness and rested her head back on the pillow.

*"Hey, you still there? Dammit, Hank, don't hang up!"*

"Yeah, yeah, I'm here," I said.

*"I really need your help, big brother. You know I never woulda called if—"*

"Where are you?"

*"Close . . . real close."*

"Jesus."

*"Can you come?"*

"Jesus, Billy. What am I gonna tell Sarah?"

*"Tell her it's work. Tell her it's an old friend. Hell, I don't know, tell her whatever you have to."*

"Where?"

*"The old wooden bridge at Hanson Creek."*

"When?"

*"As soon as you can get there."*

I looked at the glowing red numbers on the alarm clock. 5:37.

"I can be there by six-fifteen."

The line went dead.


## Two

I slipped the phone back onto its cradle and just sat there for a couple of minutes, rubbing my temple with the palm of my hand. It was a habit I'd picked up from my father, and it was a good thing Sarah was still sleeping; she hated when I did it, said it made me look like a tired old man.

She was like that, always telling me to stay positive, to keep my chin up, not to let life beat me down so much. She was one in a million, that's for damn sure. A hundred smiles a day and not one of them halfway or phony.

Sitting there in the darkness, thinking of her in that way, I surprised myself and managed something that almost resembled a smile.

But the thought went away and I closed my eyes and it seemed like a very long time was passing, me just sitting there in the bed like a child afraid of the dark or the boogeyman hiding in the bottom of the closet. Suddenly— and after all this time—there I was thinking so many of the same old thoughts. Anger, frustration, guilt, fear—all of it rushing back at me in a tornado of red-hot emotion . . .

So I just sat there and hugged myself and felt miserable and lost and lonely and it seemed like a very long time, but when I opened my eyes and looked up at the clock, I saw that not even five minutes had passed.

I dressed quietly in the cold darkness. Back in the far corner of the bedroom. I didn't dare risk opening the dresser drawers and waking Sarah, so I slipped on a pair of wrinkled jeans and a long sleeve t-shirt from the dirty laundry hamper. The shirt smelled faintly of gasoline and sweat.

After checking on Sarah, I tiptoed down the hallway and poked my head into the girls' room for a quick peek, then went downstairs. I washed my face in the guest bathroom and did my business but didn't flush. For just a second, I thought about coffee—something to help clear my head—but decided against it. Too much trouble. Not enough time.

After several minutes of breathless searching, I found the car keys on the kitchen counter. I slipped on a jacket and headed for the garage.

Upstairs, in the bedroom, Sarah rolled over and began lightly snoring. The alarm clock read 5:49.


## Three

He saved my life once. A long time ago, back when we were kids.

It was a hot July afternoon—ninety-six in the shade and not a breeze in sight. It happened no more than thirty yards downstream from the old Hanson Bridge, just past the cluster of big weeping willow trees. One minute I was splashing and laughing and fooling around, and the next I was clawing at the muddy creek bottom six, seven feet below the surface. It was the mother of all stomach cramps; the kind your parents always warned you about but you never really believed existed. Hell, when you're a kid, the old "stomach cramp warning" falls into the same dubious category as "never fool around with a rusty nail" and "don't play outside in the rain." To adults, these matters make perfect sense, but to a kid . . . well, you know what I'm talking about.

Anyway, by the time Billy pulled me to the surface and dragged me ashore, my ears had started to ring something awful and the hell with seeing stars, I was seeing entire solar systems. So Billy put me over his shoulder and carried me a half-mile into town and Dad had to leave the plant three hours early on a Monday just to pick me up at the Emergency Room.

I survived the day, more embarrassed than anything, and Billy was a reluctant hero, not only in our family but all throughout the neighborhood. Old widow Fletcher across the street even baked a chocolate cake to celebrate the occasion with Billy's name written out in bright pink icing.

I was thirteen, Billy twelve, when all this happened.

Like I said, it was a long time ago, but the whole thing makes for a pretty good story, and I've told it at least a couple hundred times. In fact, it's the one thing I always tell people when the inevitable moment finally arrives and they say, "Jeez, Hank, I didn't know you had a brother."

I hear those words and I just smile and shrug my shoulders as if to say, "Oh, well, sorry I never mentioned it" and then I slip right into the story.

This usually happens at social gatherings—holiday work parties, neighborhood cook-outs, that sort of thing. Someone from the old neighborhood shows up and mentions Billy's name, asks what he's been up to, and another person overhears the conversation. And then the questions:

"What's your brother's name? Does he live around here? What's he do for a living? Why haven't you mentioned him before, Hank?"

Happens two, three times a year. And when it does I just grin my stupid grin and tell the drowning story one more time . . . and then I make my escape before they can ask any more questions. "Excuse me, folks, I have to use the restroom." Or "Hey, isn't that Fred Matthews over there by the pool? Fred, wait up. I've been meaning to ask you . . ."

It works every time.

BILLY WAS JUST A YEAR behind me, but you never would've guessed it growing up. He looked much younger; two, maybe even three years. He was short for his age and thin. Real thin. Dad always used to say—and at the time we could never figure out just *what the hell* he was talking about—that Billy looked like a boy made out of wire. Little guy is tough as wire, he'd always say, and give Billy a proud smile and a punch on the shoulder.

Despite his physical size, Billy was fast and strong and agile and much more athletic than me. His total lack of fear and dogged determination made him a star; my lack of coordination made me a second-stringer. But we both had fun, and we stuck together for the three years we shared in high school. We played all the same sports—football in the fall, basketball in the winter, baseball in the spring.

Baseball. Now, that's where Billy really shined. All-County second-base as a sophomore. All-County and All-State as a junior and again as a senior.

A true-blue hometown hero by the time he was old enough to drive a car.

After graduation, I stayed in town and took business classes over at the junior college. Summer before sophomore year, I found an apartment a few miles away from home. Got a part-time job at a local video store. Played a little softball on Thursday nights, some intramural flag football on the weekends. Stopped by and saw the folks two, three times a week. Ran around with a few girlfriends, but nothing serious or lasting. For me, not too much had changed.

Then Billy graduated and went upstate to college on a baseball scholarship and *everything* seemed to change.

First, there was the suspension. Billy and three other teammates got caught cheating on a mid-term English exam and were placed on academic probation and suspended from the team.

Then, a few months later, in the spring, he was arrested at a local rock concert for possession of marijuana. It shouldn't have been that big a deal, but at the time, he'd been carrying enough weed to warrant a charge for Intent to Distribute. Then, at the court trial, we discovered that this was his second offense and the university kindly asked him to clear out his dorm room and leave campus immediately. His scholarship was revoked.

He was lucky enough to receive a suspended sentence from the judge but instead of moving back home and finding a job—which is what Mom and Dad hoped he would do—Billy decided to stay close to campus and continue working at a local restaurant. He claimed he wanted to make amends with his baseball coach and try to re-enroll after the next semester if the university would allow him. So he moved in with some friends and for a time it appeared as though he'd cleaned up his act. He kept out of trouble—at least as far as we (and his probation officer) could tell—and he stopped by on a regular basis to see Mom and Dad, and he even came by my place once or twice a month (although usually only when he needed to borrow a couple of bucks).

So anyway things went well for awhile . . .

Until the rainy Sunday midnight the police called and told Mom and Dad they needed to come down to Fallston General right away. Billy had been driven to the Emergency Room by one of his roommates; just an hour earlier he'd been dumped in the street in front of his apartment—a bloody mess. Both hands broken. A couple of ribs. Nose mashed. Left ear shredded. He was lucky to be alive.

We found out the whole story then: it seemed that my baby brother had a problem with gambling. The main problem being that he wasn't very good at it. He owed some very dangerous people some very significant amounts of money. The beating had been a friendly reminder that his last payment had been twelve hours late.

Billy came home from the hospital ten days later. Moved into his old room at home. This time, Mom and Dad got their way without much of an argument. A month or so later, when Billy was feeling up to it, Dad got him a job counting boxes over at the plant. Soon after, he started dating Cindy Lester, a girl from the other side of town. A very sweet girl. And pretty, too. She was just a senior over at the high school—barely eighteen years old—but she seemed to be good for Billy. She wanted to be a lawyer one day, and she spent most of her weeknights studying at the library, her weekends at the movies or the shopping mall with Billy.

One evening, sometime late October, the leaves just beginning to change their colors, Billy stopped by my apartment with a pepperoni pizza and a six-pack of Coors. We popped in an old Clint Eastwood video and stayed up most of the night talking and laughing. There was no mention of gambling or drugs or Emergency Room visits. Instead, Billy talked about settling down, making a future with Cindy. He talked about finding a better job, maybe taking some classes over at the junior college. Accounting and business courses, just like his big brother. Jesus, it was like a dream come true. I could hardly wait until morning to call the folks and tell them all about it.

To this very day, I can remember saying my prayers that night, thanking God for giving my baby brother another chance.

That night was more than eight years ago.

I haven't seen him since.

## Four

I drove slowly across the narrow wooden bridge. Clicked on the high-beams.

There were no other cars in sight.

Just empty road. Dense forest. And a cold December wind.

My foot tapped the brake pedal and I thought to myself: *Hank Foster, you've lost your mind. This is crazy. Absolutely crazy.*

I reached the far side of the bridge and pulled over to the dirt shoulder. I sat there shivering for a long couple of minutes. Looking up at the rearview mirror. Staring out at the frozen darkness.

I turned the heater up a notch.

Turned off the headlights.

It was 6:17.

I LOOKED AT MY WATCH for the tenth time. 6:21.

Jesus, this really *was* crazy. Waiting in the middle of nowhere for God knows what to happen. Hell, it was more than crazy, it was dangerous. Billy had sounded scared on the phone, maybe even desperate, and he'd said he was in trouble. Those had been his exact words: *I'm in some trouble.* Even after all this time, I knew the kind of trouble my brother was capable of. So what in the hell was I doing out here? I had Sarah and the girls to think about now, a business to consider . . .

Or maybe, just maybe, he had changed. Maybe he had left the old Billy behind those iron bars and a better man had emerged. Maybe he had actually learned a thing or two—yeah and maybe Elvis was still alive and catching rays down on some Mexican beach and the Cubs were gonna win the god-damn World Series.

Nice to imagine, one and all, but not real likely, huh?

I was starting to sweat now. *Really* sweat. I felt it on my neck. My face. My hands. And I felt it snaking down from my armpits, dribbling across my ribcage. Sticky. Cold and hot at the same time.

I leaned down and turned off the heat. Cracked the window. Inhaled long and deep. The sharp sting of fresh air caught me by surprise, made me dizzy for a moment, and I realized right then and there what was going on: I was scared. Probably more scared than I had ever been in my entire life.

With the window open, I could hear the wind rattling the trees and the creek moving swiftly in the darkness behind me. In the dry months of summer, Hanson Creek was slow-moving and relatively shallow, maybe eight feet at its deepest point. But in the winter, with all the snow run-off, the creek turned fast and mean and unforgiving. Sometimes, after a storm, the water rose so quickly, the police were forced to close down the bridge and detour traffic up north to Route 24. One winter, years ago, it stayed closed for the entire month of January.

The old house where we grew up—where Mom and Dad still live today—was just a short distance north from here. No more than a five minute drive. Back when we were kids, Billy and I walked down here most every morning during the summer. All the neighborhood kids came here. We brought bag lunches and bottles of pop and hid them in the bushes so no one would steal them. Then we swam all day long and held diving contests down at the rope swing. When the weather was too cool to swim, we played war in the woods and built forts made out of rocks and mud and tree branches. Other times, we fished for catfish and carp and the occasional bass or yellow perch. On *real* lucky days, when it rained hard enough to wear away the soil, we searched for (and usually found) Indian arrowheads wedged in with the tree roots that grew along the creek's steep banks. We called those rainy days *treasure hunts,* and took turns acting as "expedition leader." The creek was a pretty wonderful place.

I thought about all this and wondered if that was the reason Billy had chosen the bridge as our meeting place. Was he feeling sentimental? A little nostalgic maybe? Probably not; as usual, I was probably giving the bastard too much credit . . .

LIKE I TOLD YOU, I haven't seen him in more than eight years. Not since that long ago autumn night we spent together talking at my apartment. One week later, Billy just up and disappeared. No note, no message, nothing. Just an empty closet, a missing suitcase, and eighty dollars gone from Mom's purse.

And to make matters worse, Mr. Lester called the house later that evening and told us that Cindy hadn't been to school that day, was she with Billy by any chance?

The next morning, Dad called Billy's probation officer. He wasn't much help. He told us to sit tight, that maybe Billy would come to his senses. Other than that, there was really nothing we could do but wait.

And so for two weeks, we waited and heard nothing.

Then, on a Sunday afternoon, Mom and Dad sitting out on the front porch reading the newspaper, still dressed in their church clothes, there was a phone call: *I know I know it was a stupid thing to do but you see Cindy's pregnant and scared to death of her father he's a mean sonofabitch real mean and California is the place to be these days heck we already have jobs and a place to stay and there's lots of great people out here we've got some really nice friends already c'mon please don't cry Mom please don't yell Dad we're doing just fine really we are we're so much in love and we're doing just fine . . .*

Six months later, Cindy Lester came home. Alone. While walking back from work one night, she had been raped and beaten in a Los Angeles alley. She'd spent three days in the hospital with severe cuts and bruises. She'd lost her baby during the first night. Cindy told us that she'd begged him over and over again, but Billy had refused to come home with her. So she'd left him.

Over the next three years, there were exactly seven more phone calls (two begging for money) and three short handwritten letters. The envelopes were postmarked from California, Arizona, and Oregon.

Then, early in the fourth year, the police called. Billy had been arrested in California for drug trafficking. This time, the heavy stuff: cocaine and heroin. Dad hired Billy a decent lawyer, and both he and Mom flew out to the trial and watched as the judge gave Billy seven years in the state penitentiary.

I never went to see him. Not even once. Not at the trial. Not when Mom and Dad went for their twice-a-year visits. And not when Billy sent the letter asking me to come. I just couldn't do it.

I didn't hate him the way Mom and Dad thought I did. Jesus, he was still my baby brother. But he was locked up back there where he belonged, and I was right here where I belonged. We each had our own lives to live.

So no I didn't hate him. But I couldn't forgive him, either. Not for what he had done to this family—the heartbreak of two wonderful, loving parents; the complete waste of their hard-earned retirement savings; the shame and embarrassment he brought to all of us—

—bare knuckles rapped against the windshield and I jumped so hard I hit my head. I also screamed.

I could hear laughing from outside the car, faint in the howling wind, but clear enough to instantly recognize.

It was him alright.

My baby brother.

Suddenly a face bent down into view. Smiled.

And I just couldn't help it. I smiled right back.


**Five**


We hugged for a long time. Car door open, engine still running. Both of us standing outside in the cold and the wind. Neither of us saying a word.

We hugged until I could no longer stand the smell of him.

Then we stopped and sort of stood back and looked at each other.

"Jesus, Billy, I can't believe it," I said.

"I know, I know." He shook his head and smiled. "Neither can I."

"Now, talk to me. What's this all about? What kind of trouble are—"

He held up his hand. "In a minute, okay? Lemme just look at you a while longer."

For the next couple of minutes, we stood there facing each other, shivering in the cold. The Foster boys, together once again.

He was heavier than the last time I'd seen him; maybe fifteen, twenty pounds. And he was shaved bald, a faint shadow of dark stubble showing through. Other than that, he was still the Billy I remembered. Bright blue eyes. Big stupid smile. That rosy-cheeked baby face of his.

"Hey, you like my hair," he asked, reading my thoughts.

"Yeah," I said, "who's your barber?"

"Big black sonofabitch from Texas. Doing life for first-degree murder. Helluva nice guy, though."

He waited for my response and when I didn't say anything, he laughed. This time, it sounded harsh and a little mean.

"How's the folks?" he asked.

I shrugged my shoulders. "You know, pretty much the same. They're doing okay."

"And Sarah and the girls?"

My heart skipped a beat. An invisible hand reached up from the ground and squeezed my balls.

"Mom and Dad told me all about 'em. Sent me pictures in the mail," he said.

I opened my mouth, but couldn't speak. Couldn't breathe.

"They're twins, right? Let's see . . . four years old . . . Kacy and Katie, if I remember right."

I sucked in a deep breath. Let it out.

"I bet you didn't know I carry their picture around in my wallet. The one where they're sitting on the swing set in those fancy little blue dresses—"

"Five," I said, finally finding my voice.

"Huh?"

"The girls," I said. "They just turned five. Back in October."

"Halloween babies, huh? That's kinda neat. Hey, remember how much fun we used to have trick-or-treatin'? 'Member that time we spent the night out back the old Myer's House? Camped out in Dad's old tent. Man, that was a blast."

I nodded my head. I remembered everything. The costumes we used to make. The scary movies we used to watch, huddled together on the sofa, sharing a glass of soda and a bowl of Mom's popcorn. All the creepy stories we used to tell each other before bedtime.

Suddenly I felt sorry for him—standing there in his tattered old clothes, that dumb smile refusing to leave his face, smelling for all the world like a dumpster full of food gone to spoil. I suddenly felt very sorry for him and very guilty for me.

"I didn't break out, you know," he said. "They released me two weeks ago. Early parole."

"Jesus, Billy. That's great news."

"I spent a week back in L.A. seeing some friends. Then I hitched a ride back here. Made it all the way to the state line. I walked in from there."

"I still can't goddamn believe it. Wait until Mom and Dad see you."

"That's one of the things I need to talk to you about, Hank. Why don't we take a walk and talk for awhile, okay?"

"Sure, Billy," I said. "Let's do that."

So that's exactly what we did.


## Six

I still miss him.

It's been four months now since that morning at the bridge. And not a word.

I read the newspaper every day. Watch the news every night.

And still there's been nothing.

I think about him all the time now. Much more often than I used to. Once or twice a week, I take a drive down to the old bridge. I stand outside the car and watch the creek rushing by, and I think back to the time when we were kids. Back to a time when things were simple and happy.

God, I miss him.

HE WANTED MONEY. PLAIN AND simple, as always.

First, he tried to lie to me. Said it was for his new "family." Said he got married two days after he got out of prison. Needed my help getting back on his feet.

But I didn't fall for it.

So then he told me the truth. Or something close to it, anyway. There was this guy, an old friend from up around San Francisco. And Billy owed him some big bucks for an old drug deal gone bad. Right around thirty grand. If he didn't come up with the cash, this old friend was gonna track him down and slit his throat.

So how about a little help, big brother?

Sorry, I told him. No can do. I'd like to help out, but I've got a family now. A mortgage. My own business barely keeping its head above water. Sorry. Can't help you.

So then he started crying. And begging me.

And when that didn't work, he got pissed off.

His eyes went cold and distant; his voice got louder.

He said: okay that's fine. I'll just hit up the old man and the old lady. They'll help me out. Damn right they will. And if they don't have enough cash, well, there are always other ways I can *persuade* you to help me, big brother. Yes, sir, I can be mighty *persuasive* when I put my mind to it . . .

Let's start by talking about that store of yours, Hank—you're paid up on all your insurance, aren't you? I mean, you got fire coverage and all that stuff,

don't you? Jeez, I'd hate to see something bad happen when you're just starting out . . . And how about Sarah? She still working over at that bank Mom
and Dad told me about? That's a pretty dangerous job, ain't it? Working with
all that money. Especially for a woman . . . And, oh yeah, by the way, what
school do the girls go to? Evansville? Or are you busing them over to that
private place, what's it called again?

I stabbed him then.

We were standing near the middle of the bridge. Leaning against the thick
wooden railing, looking down at the water.

And when he said those things, I took out the steak knife—which had been
sitting on the kitchen counter right next to where I'd found my car keys—I
took it out from my coat pocket and I held it in both of my hands and brought
it down hard in the back of his neck.

He cried out once—not very loud—and dropped to his knees.

And then there was only the flash of the blade as I stabbed him over and
over again . . .

LAST NIGHT, IT FINALLY HAPPENED. Sarah confronted me.

We were alone in the house. The girls were spending the night at their
grandparents'—they do this once a month and absolutely love it.

After dinner, she took me downstairs to the den and closed the door. Sat
me down on the sofa and stood right in front of me. She told me I looked a
mess. I wasn't sleeping, wasn't eating. Either I tell her right now what was
going on or she was leaving.

She was serious, too. I think she thought I was having an affair.

So I told her.

Everything . . . starting with the phone call and ending with me dumping
Billy's body into the creek.

When I was finished, she ran from the room crying. She made it upstairs
to the bathroom, where she dropped to her knees in front of the toilet and
got sick. When she was done, she asked me very calmly to go back downstairs
and leave her alone for awhile. I agreed.

An hour or so later, she came down and found me out in the backyard
looking up at the moon and the stars. She ran to me and hugged me so tight
I could barely breathe and then she started crying again. We hugged for a
long time, until the tears finally stopped, and then she held my face in her
hands and told me that she understood how difficult it had been for me, how
horrible it must have felt, but that it was all over now and that I had done
the right thing. No matter what, that was the important thing to remember,
she kept saying—I had done the right thing.

Then we were hugging again and both of us were crying.

When we finally went inside, we called the girls and took turns saying
goodnight. Then we went to bed and made love until we both fell asleep.

Later that night, the moon shining silver and bright through the bedroom window, Sarah woke from a nightmare, her skin glistening with sweat, her voice soft and frightened. She played with my hair and asked: "What if someone finds him, Hank? A fisherman? Some kids? What if someone finds him and recognizes him?"

I put a finger to her lips and *ssshed* her. Put my arms around her and held her close to me. I told her everything was going to be okay. No one would find him. And if they did, they would never be able to identify him.

"Are you sure they won't recognize him?" she asked. "Are you sure?"

"Absolutely positive," I said, stroking her neck. "Not after all this time. Not after he's been in the water for this long."

*And not after I cut up his face the way I did.*

*No one could recognize him after all that . . . not even his own brother.*

Simon Brett is one of several authors from the other side of the pond in this year's volume. Adept at both the traditional mystery as well as the historical, his latest novels include *Mrs. Pargeter's Plot* and *Sicken and So Die*. However, he's also quite accomplished in the short form, as well. Here, a famous author proves the truth of the title as she tries to remove the source of her success.

# Ways to Kill a Cat
## SIMON BRETT

*"There are more ways to kill a cat than choking it with cream."*
—old proverb

### 1. Putting the Cat Among the Pigeons

Seraphina Fellowes felt very pleased with herself. This was not an unusual state of affairs. Seraphina Fellowes usually felt very pleased with herself. This hadn't always been the case, but her literary success over the previous decade had raised her self-esteem to a level that was now almost unassailable.

Only twelve years before, she had been no more than a dissatisfied, mousy-haired housewife, married to a Catholic writer, George Fellowes, whose fondness for "trying ideas out" rather than writing for commercial markets, coupled with an increasingly close relationship with the bottle, was threatening both his career and their marriage.

Seraphina clearly remembered the evening that had changed everything. Changed everything for her, that is. It hadn't affected George's fortunes so much, even though the original life-changing idea had been his. This detail was one of many that Seraphina tended to gloss over in media interviews about her success. George may have given her a little help in the early days, but he had long since ceased to have any relevance, either in her career or her personal life.

When the idea first came up, Seraphina hadn't even been Seraphina. She had then just been Sally, but "Sally Fellowes" was no name for a successful author, so that was the first of many details that were changed as she created her new persona.

Like an increasing number of evenings at that stage of the Fellowes' marriage, the pivotal evening had begun with a row. Sally, as she then was, had crossed from the house to the garden shed in which her husband worked and found George sprawled across his desk, fast asleep. Cuddled up against his head had been Mr. Whiffles, their tabby cat. Well, the cat was technically "theirs," but really he was George's. George was responsible for all the relevant feeding and nurturing. Sally didn't like cats very much.

It was only half past six in the evening, but already in George's wastepaper basket lay the cause of his stupor, an empty half bottle of vodka. That had been sufficient incentive for Sally to shake him rudely awake and pull one of the common triggers of their rows, an attack on his drinking. George's subsequent picking up and stroking the disturbed Mr. Whiffles had moved Sally on to another of her regular criticisms: "You care more about that cat than you do about me."

George had come back, predictably enough, with: "Well, this cat shows me a lot more affection than you do," which had moved the altercation inevitably on to the subject of their sex life—George's desire for more sex and more enthusiastic sex, his conviction that having children would solve many of their problems, and Sally's recurrent assertion that he was disgusting and never thought about anything else.

Once that particular storm had blown itself out, Sally had moved the attack on to George's professional life. Why did he persist in writing "arty-farty literary novels" that nobody wanted to publish? Why didn't he go in for something like crime fiction, a genre that large numbers of the public might actually want to *read*?

"Oh, yes?" George had responded sarcastically. "What, should I write mimsy-pimsy little whodunits in which all the blood is neatly swept under the carpet and the investigation is in the hands of some heartwarmingly eccentric and totally unrealistic sleuth? Or," he had continued, warming to his theme and stroking Mr. Whiffles ever more vigorously, "why don't I make a cat the detective? Why don't I write a whole series of mysteries that are solved by lovable Mr. Whiffles?"

The instant he made the suggestion, Sally Fellowes's anger evaporated. She knew that something cataclysmic had happened. From that moment, she saw her way forward.

At the time, though the cat mystery was already a burgeoning sub-genre in American crime fiction, it had not taken much of a hold in England. Cat picture books, cat calendars, cat quotation selections, and cat greeting cards all sold well—particularly at Christmas—but there didn't exist a successful home grown series of cat mysteries.

Sally Fellowes—or rather Seraphina Fellowes, for the name came to her simultaneously with the idea—was determined to change all that.

George had helped her a lot initially—though that was another little detail she tended not to mention when talking to the media. She rationalized this on marketing grounds. The product she was selling was "a Mr. Whiffles mystery, written by Seraphina Fellowes." To mention the existence of a collaborating author would only have confused potential purchasers.

And George didn't seem to mind. He still regarded the Mr. Whiffles books as a kind of game, a diversion he took about as seriously as trying to complete the crossword. Seraphina would summon him by intercom buzzer from his shed when she got stuck, and he, with a couple of airy, nonchalant sentences, would redirect her into the next phase of the mystery. George was still, in theory, working on his "literary" novels, and regarded devising whodunit plots as a kind of mental chewing gum.

Seraphina proved to be a quick learner, and an assiduous researcher. She negotiated her way around library catalogues; she established good relations with her local police for help on procedure; she even bought a gun, which ever thereafter she kept in her desk drawer, so that she could make her descriptions of firearms authentic.

As the Mr. Whiffles mysteries began to roll off the production line, the summonings of George from his shed grew less and less frequent. While Seraphina was struggling with the first book, the intercom buzzer sounded every ten minutes, and her husband spent most of his life traversing the garden between shed and house. With the second, however, the calls were down to about one a day, and for the third—except to unravel a couple of vital plot points—Seraphina's husband was hardly disturbed at all.

The reason for this was that George had made the first book such an ingenious template that writing the rest was merely a matter of doing a bit of research and applying the same formula to some new setting. Seraphina, needless to say, would never have admitted this, and had indeed by the third book convinced herself that the entire creative process was hers alone.

As George became marginalized from his wife's professional life, so she moved him further away from her personal life. As soon as the international royalties for the Mr. Whiffles books started to roll in, Seraphina organized the demolition of George's working shed in the garden, and its replacement by a brand-new, self-contained bungalow. There her husband was at liberty to lead his own life. Whether that life involved further experimentation with the novel form or a quicker descent into alcoholic befuddlement, Seraphina Fellowes neither knew nor cared.

She didn't divorce George, though. His Catholicism put him against the idea, but Seraphina also needed him around to see that Mr. Whiffles got fed during her increasingly frequent absences on promotional tours or at foreign mystery conventions. Then again, there was always the distant possibility that she might get stuck again on one of the books and need George to sort out the plot for her.

Besides, having a shadowy husband figure in the background had other uses. When asked about him in interviews, she always implied that he was ill and that she unobtrusively devoted her life to his care. This did her image no harm at all. He was also very useful when oversexed crime writers or critics came on to her at mystery conventions. Her assertion, accompanied by a martyred expression of divided loyalties, that "it wouldn't be fair to George" was a much better excuse than the truth—that she didn't, in fact, like sex.

As the royalties mounted, Seraphina had both herself and her house made over. Her mousey hair became a jet-black helmet assiduously maintained by costly hairdressing; her face was an unchanging mask of expertly applied makeup; and she patronized ever more expensive couturiers for her clothes. The house was extended and interior designed; the garden elegantly land-scaped to include a fishpond with elaborate fountain and cascade features.

And Seraphina always had the latest computer technology on which to write her money-spinning books. After taking delivery of each new state-of-the-art machine, her first ritual action was to program the "M" key to print on the screen: "Mr. Whiffles."

So, twelve years on from the momentous evening that changed her life, Seraphina Fellowes had good cause to feel very pleased with herself. The previous day, she had achieved a lifetime ambition. She had rung through an order for the latest model Ferrari. There was a year-and-a-half waiting list for delivery, but it had given Seraphina enormous satisfaction to write a check for the full purchase price without batting an eyelid.

She looked complacently around the large study she had had built on to the house. It was decorated in pastel pinks and greens, flowery wallpapers, and hanging swaths of curtain. The walls were covered with framed Mr. Whiffles memorabilia: book jackets, publicity photographs of the author cuddling her hero's namesake, newspaper bestsellers listings, mystery organizations' citations and awards. On her mantelpiece, amongst lesser plaques and figurines, stood her proudest possession, the highest accolade so far accorded to the Mr. Whiffles industry: an Edgar statuette from the Mystery Writers of America. Yes, Seraphina Fellowes did feel very pleased with herself.

But even as she had this thought, a sliver of unease was driven into her mind. She heard once again the ominous sound that increasingly threatened her well-being and complacency. It was the clatter of a letterbox and the solid thud of her elastic-band-wrapped mail landing on the doormat. She went through into the hall with some trepidation to see what new threat the post-man had brought that day.

Seraphina divided the letters into two piles on her desk. The left-hand pile comprised those addressed to "Seraphina Fellowes, Author of the Mr. Whiffles Books"; the right-hand one was made up of letters addressed to Mr. Whiffles himself. A lot of those, she knew, would be whimsically written by their owners as if they came from other cats. In fact, that morning over half of Mr. Whiffles's letters had paw prints on the back of the envelopes.

But that wasn't what worried Seraphina Fellowes. What really disturbed her—no, more than disturbed—what really twisted the icy dagger of jealousy in her heart was the fact that the right-hand pile was much higher than the left-hand one. This was the worst incident yet, and it confirmed an appalling trend that had been building for the last couple of years.

Mr. Whiffles was getting more fan mail than she was!

The object of her jealousy, with the instinct for timing that had so far preserved intact all nine of his lives, chose that moment to enter Seraphina Fellowes' study. He wasn't, strictly speaking, welcome in her house—he spent most of his time over in George's bungalow—but Seraphina had had cat-flaps inserted in all her doors to demonstrate her house's cat-friendliness when journalists came to interview her, and Mr. Whiffles did put in the occasional appearance. To get to the study he'd had to negotiate four cat-flaps: from the garden into a passage, from the passage into the kitchen, kitchen to hall, and hall to study.

He looked up at his mistress with that insolence that cats don't just reserve for kings, and Seraphina Fellowes felt another twist of the dagger in her heart. She stared dispassionately down at the animal. He'd never been very beautiful, just a neutered tabby tom like a million others. Seraphina looked up at one of the publicity shots on the wall and compared the cat photographed five years previously with the current reality.

Time hadn't been kind. Mr. Whiffles really was looking in bad shape. He was fourteen, after all. He was thinner, his coat more scruffy, he was a bit scummy round the mouth, and he might even have a patch of mange at the base of his tail.

"You poor old boy," Seraphina Fellowes cooed. "You're no spring chicken any more, are you? I'm rather afraid it's time for you and me to pay a visit to the vet."

And she went off to fetch the cat basket.

AT THE SURGERY, EVERYONE MADE a great fuss over Mr. Whiffles. Though he'd enjoyed generally good health, there had been occasional visits to the vet for all the usual, minor feline ailments and, as the fame of the books grew, he was treated there increasingly like a minor royal.

Seraphina didn't take much notice of the attention he was getting. She was preoccupied with planning the press conference at which the sad news of Mr. Whiffles's demise would be communicated to the media. She would employ the pained expression she had perfected for speaking about her invalid husband. And yes, the line "It was a terrible wrench, but I felt the time had come to prevent him future suffering" must come in somewhere.

"How incontinent?" asked the vet once they were inside the surgery and Mr. Whiffles was standing on the bench to be examined.

"Oh, I'm afraid it's getting worse and worse," said Seraphina mournfully. "I mean, at first I didn't worry about it, thought it was only a phase, but there's no way we can ignore the situation any longer. It's causing poor Mr. Whiffles so much pain, apart from anything else."

"If it's causing him pain, then it's probably just some kind of urinary infection," said the vet unhelpfully.

"I'm afraid it's worse than that." Seraphina Fellowes choked back a little sob. "It's a terrible decision to make, but I'm afraid he'll have to be put down."

The vet's reaction to this was even worse. He burst out laughing. "Good heavens, we're not at that stage." He stroked Mr. Whiffles, who reached up appealingly and rubbed his whiskers against the vet's face. "No, this old boy's got another good five years in him, I'd say."

"Really?" Seraphina realized she'd let too much pique show in that one, and repeated a softer, more relieved, more tentative, "Really?"

"Oh, yes. I'll put him on antibiotics, and that'll sort out the urinary infection in no time." The vet looked at her with concern. "But you shouldn't be letting worries about him prey on your mind like this. You mustn't get things out of proportion, you know."

"I am *not* getting things out of proportion!" Seraphina Fellowes snapped with considerable asperity.

"Maybe you should go and see your doctor," the vet suggested, gently. "It might be something to do with your age."

Seraphina was still seething at that last remark as she drove back home. Her mood was not improved by the way Mr. Whiffles looked up at her through the grille of the cat basket. His expression seemed almost triumphant.

Seraphina Fellowes set her mouth in a hard line. The situation wasn't irreversible. There were more ways to kill a cat than enlisting the help of the vet.

## 2. Fighting Like Cats and Dogs

"Are you sure you don't mind my bringing Ghengis, Seraphina?"

"No, no."

"But I thought, what with you being a cat person, you wouldn't want a great big dog tramping all over your house."

A great big dog Ghengis certainly was. He must have weighed about the same as the average nightclub bouncer, and the similarities didn't stop there. His teeth appeared too big for his mouth, with the result that he was incapable of any expression other than slavering.

"It's no problem," Seraphina Fellowes reassured her guest.

"But he doesn't like cats." Seraphina knew this; it was the sole reason for her guest's invitation. "I'd hate to think of him doing any harm to the famous Mr. Whiffles," her guest continued.

"Don't worry. Mr. Whiffles is safely ensconced with George." The mastiff growled the low growl of a flesh addict whose fix is overdue. "Maybe Ghengis would like to have a run around the garden . . . to let off some steam?"

As she opened the back door and Ghengis rocketed out, Seraphina looked with complacency toward the tree under which a cat lay serenely asleep. "No, no!" her guest screamed. "There's Mr. Whiffles!"

"Oh dear," said Seraphina Fellowes with minimal sincerity. Then she closed the back door, and went through the passage into the kitchen to watch the unequal contest through a window.

The huge, slavering jaws were nearly around the cat before Mr. Whiffles suddenly became aware and jumped sideways. The chase thereafter was furious, but there was no doubt who was calling the shots. Mr. Whiffles didn't choose the easy option of flying up a tree out of Ghengis's reach. Instead, he played on his greater mobility, weaved and curvetted across the grass, driving the thundering mastiff to ever-more frenzied pitches of frustration.

Finally, Mr. Whiffles seemed to tire. He slowed, gave up evasive action, and started to move in a defeated straight line towards the house. Ghengis pounded greedily after him, slavering more than ever.

Mr. Whiffles put on a sudden burst of acceleration. Ghengis did likewise, and he had the more powerful engine. He ate up the ground that separated them.

At the second when it seemed nothing could stop the jaws from closing around his thin body, Mr. Whiffles took off through the air and threaded himself neatly through the outer cat-flap into the passage, and then the next one into the kitchen.

Seraphina Fellowes just had time to look down at the cat on the tiled floor before she heard the splintering crunch of Ghengis hitting the outside door at full speed.

Mr. Whiffles looked up at his mistress with an expression that seemed to say, "You'll have to do better than that, sweetie."

As Seraphina Fellowes was seeing her guest and bloody-faced dog off on their way to the vet's, the postman arrived with the day's second post. The usual thick rubber-banded wodge of letters.

That day two-thirds of the envelopes had paw prints on the back.

### 3. Letting the Cat Out of the Bag

It was sad that George's mother died. Sad for George, that is. Seraphina had never cared for the old woman.

And it did mean that George would have to go to Ireland for the funeral. What with seeing solicitors, tidying his mother's house prior to putting it on the market, and other family duties, he would be away a whole week.

How awkward that this coincided with Seraphina's recollection that she needed to go to New York for a meeting with her American agent. Awkward because it meant that for a whole week neither of them would be able to feed Mr. Whiffles.

Not to worry, Seraphina had reassured George, there's a local girl who'll come in and put food down for him morning and evening. Not a very bright local girl, thought Seraphina gleefully, though she didn't mention that detail to George.

"Now, Mr. Whiffles is a very fussy eater," she explained when she was briefing the local girl, "and sometimes he's just not interested in his food. But don't you worry about that. If he hasn't touched one plateful, just throw it away and put down a fresh one—okay?"

Seraphina waited until the cab taking George to the station was out of sight. Then she picked up a somewhat suspicious Mr. Whiffles with a cooing "Who's a lovely boy then?" and opened the trapdoor to the cellar.

She placed the confused cat on the second step, and while Mr. Whiffles was uneasily sniffing out his new environment, slammed the trap down and bolted it.

Then she got into her BMW—she couldn't wait till it was a Ferrari—and drove to the Executive Parking near Heathrow, which she *always* used when she Concorded to the States.

SERAPHINA MADE HERSELF CHARACTERISTICALLY DIFFICULT with her agent in New York. Lots of little niggling demands were put forward to irritate her publisher. She was just flexing her muscles. She knew the sales of the Mr. Whiffles books were too important to the publisher, and ten percent of the royalties on them too important to her agent, for either party to argue.

She also aired an idea that she had been nurturing for some time—that she might soon start another series of mysteries. Oh yes, still cat mysteries, but with a new, female protagonist.

Her agent and publisher were both wary of the suggestion. Their general view seemed to be "If it ain't broke, don't fix it." An insatiable demand was still out there for the existing Mr. Whiffles product. Why put that guaranteed success at risk by starting something new?

Seraphina characteristically made it clear that the opinions of her agent and publisher held no interest for her at all.

On the Concorde back to London, she practised and honed the phrases she would use at the press conference that announced Mr. Whiffles's sad death from starvation in her cellar. How she would excoriate the stupid local girl who had unwittingly locked him down there in the first place, and then not been bright enough to notice that he wasn't appearing to eat his food. Surely anyone with even the most basic intelligence could have put two and two together and realized that the cat had gone missing?

THERE WAS INDEED A PRESS conference when Seraphina got back. The story even made its way onto the main evening television news—as one of those heartwarming end pieces that allow the newsreader to practice his chuckle.

But the headlines weren't the ones Seraphina had had in mind. "PLUCKY SUPERCAT SUMMONS HELP FROM CELLAR PRISON," "MR. WHIFFLES CALLS FIRE BRIGADE TO SAVE HIM FROM LINGERING DEATH," "BRILLIANT MR. WHIFFLES USES ONE OF HIS NINE LIVES AND WILL LIVE ON TO SOLVE MANY MORE CASES."

To compound Seraphina's annoyance, she then had to submit to many interviews, in which she expressed her massive relief for the cat's survival, and to many photographic sessions in which she had to hug the mangy old tabby with apparent delight.

Prompted by all the publicity, the volume of mail arriving at Seraphina Fellowes's house rocketed. And now almost all the letters were addressed to Mr. Whiffles. Scraphina thought if she saw another paw print on the back of an envelope, she'd throw up.

## 4. Playing Cat and Mouse

In July 1985, in a speech to the American Bar Association in London, Margaret Thatcher said: "We must try to find ways to starve the terrorist and the hijacker of the oxygen of publicity on which they depend."

Seraphina Fellowes, a woman not dissimilar in character to Margaret Thatcher, determined to apply these tactics in her continuing campaign against Mr. Whiffles. His miraculous escape from the cellar had had saturation coverage. The public was, for the time being, slightly bored with the subject of Mr. Whiffles. Now was the moment to present them with a new publicity sensation.

She was called Gigi, and she was everything Mr. Whiffles wasn't. A white Persian with deep blue eyes, she had a pedigree that made the Apostolic Succession look like the invention of parvenus. Whereas Mr. Whiffles had the credentials of a street fighter, Gigi was the unchallenged queen of all she surveyed.

And, Seraphina Fellowes announced at the press conference she had called to share the news, Gigi's fictional counterpart was about to become the heroine of a new series of cat mysteries. Stroking her new cat, Seraphina informed the media that she had just started the first book, *Gigi and the Dead Fishmonger.* Now that "dear old Mr. Whiffles" was approaching retirement, it was time to think of the future. And the future belonged to a new, feisty, beautiful, young cat detective called Gigi.

The announcement didn't actually get much attention. It came too soon after the blanket media coverage accorded to Mr. Whiffles's escape and, though from Seraphina's point of view there couldn't have been more difference between the two, for the press it was "just another cat story."

The only effect the announcement did have was to increase yet further the volume of mail arriving at Seraphina Fellowes's house. At first she was encouraged to see that the majority of these letters were addressed to her rather than to her old cat. But when she found them all to be condemnations of her decision to sideline Mr. Whiffles, she was less pleased.

Seraphina, however, was philosophical. Just wait till the book comes out, she thought. That's when we'll get a really major publicity offensive. And by ceasing to write the Mr. Whiffles books she would condemn the cat who gave them their name to public apathy and ultimate oblivion. She was turning the stopcock on the cylinder that contained his oxygen of publicity.

So Seraphina Fellowes programmed the letter "G" as the shorthand for "Gigi" into her computer, and settled down to write the new book. It was hard, because she was canny enough to know that she couldn't reproduce the Mr. Whiffles formula verbatim. A white Persian aristocrat like Gigi demanded a different kind of plot from the streetwise tabby. And Seraphina certainly had no intention of enlisting George's help again.

So she struggled on. She knew she'd get there in time. And once the book was finished, even if the first of the series wasn't quite up to the standard of a Mr. Whiffles mystery, it would still sell in huge numbers on the strength of Seraphina Fellowes's name alone.

While she was writing, the presence—the existence—of Mr. Whiffles did not become any less irksome to her.

She made a halfhearted attempt to get rid of him by a plate of cat food laced with warfarin, but the tabby ignored the bait with all the contempt it deserved. And Seraphina was only just in time to snatch the plate away when she saw Gigi approaching it greedily.

Mr. Whiffles took to spending a lot of time in the middle of the study carpet, washing himself unhurriedly, and every now and then fixing his green eyes on the struggling author with an expression of derisive pity.

Seraphina Fellowes gritted her teeth and, as she wrote, allowed the back burner of her mind to devise ever more painful and satisfying revenges.

## 5. The Cat's Pajamas

"I've done it! I've finished it!" Seraphina Fellowes shouted to no one in particular, as she rushed into the kitchen, the passive Gigi clasped in her arms. The author was wearing a brand-new designer silk blouse. Mr. Whiffles, dozing on a pile of dirty washing in the utility room, opened one lazy eye to observe the proceedings. He watched Seraphina hurry to the fridge and extract a perfectly chilled bottle of Dom Perignon.

It was a ritual. In the euphoria of completing the first Mr. Whiffles mystery, Seraphina and George had cracked open a bottle of Spanish fizz and, even more surprisingly, ended the evening by making love. Since then the ritual had changed. The lovemaking had certainly never been repeated. The quality of the fizz had improved, but after the second celebration, when he got inappropriately drunk, George had no longer been included in the festivities. Now, when Seraphina Fellowes finished a book, she would dress herself in a new garment bought specially for the occasion, then sit down alone at the kitchen table and work her way steadily through a bottle of very good champagne. It was her ideal form of celebration—unalloyed pampering in the company she liked best in the world.

When her mistress sat down, Gigi, demonstrating her customary lack of character, had immediately curled up on the table and gone to sleep. So the new mystery star didn't hear the rambling monologue that the exhausted author embarked on as she drank.

Mr. Whiffles, cradled in his nest of dirty blouses, underwear, and silk pajamas, could hear it. Not being blessed with the kind of anthropomorphic sensibilities enjoyed by his fictional counterpart, he couldn't, of course, understand a word. But, from the tone of voice, he didn't have much problem in getting the gist. Continued vigilance on his part was clearly called for.

Seraphina Fellowes drained the dregs of the last glass and rose, a little unsteadily, to her feet. As she did so, she caught sight of Mr. Whiffles though the open utility room door. She stared dumbly at him for a moment; then an idea took hold.

Seraphina moved with surprising swiftness for one who'd just consumed a bottle of champagne, and was beside Mr. Whiffles before he'd had time to react. She swept up the arms of the silk pajama top beneath the cat and wrapped them tightly round him. Then she tucked the bundle firmly under her right arm. "You're getting to be a very dirty cat in your old age," she hissed. "Time you had a really good wash."

She was remarkably deft for someone who'd had a woman to come in and do all her washing for the previous ten years. Mr. Whiffles struggled to get free, but the tight silk tied in his legs like a straitjacket. Though he strained and meowed ferociously, it was to no avail. Seraphina's arm clinched him like a vise, and he couldn't get his claws to work through the cloth.

With her spare hand, she shoveled the rest of the dirty washing into the machine, finally pitching in the unruly bundle of pajamas. She pushed the door to with her knee, then turned to fill the plastic soap bubble.

Claws snagging on the sleek fabric, Mr. Whiffles struggled desperately to free himself. Somehow he knew that she had to open the machine's door once more, and somehow he knew that that would be his only chance.

The right amount of soap powder had been decanted. Seraphina bent down to open the door and throw the bubble in. With the sudden change of position, the champagne caught up with her. She swayed for a second, put a hand to her forehead, and shook her head to clear it.

"Quietened down a bit, have you?" she crowed to the tangled bundle of garments; then slammed the door shut. "Won't you be a nice clean boy now?" She punctuated the words with her actions, switching the dial round to the maximum number of rinses, then vindictively pulling out the knob to start the fatal cycle.

SERAPHINA FELLOWES WAS A BIT hung over when she woke the following morning. And the first thing that greeted her pained eyes when she opened them was a ghost.

Mr. Whiffles sat at the end of her bed, nonchalantly licking clean an upraised back leg.

Seraphina screamed, and he scampered lazily out of the bedroom.

She was far too muzzy and confused to piece together that Mr. Whiffles must have jumped out of the washing machine during the few seconds when the alcohol had caught up with her. She was too muzzy and confused for most things, really.

Her bleared gaze moved across to the chair, over which, in the fuddlement of the night before, she'd hung her new designer shirt.

The rich silk had been shredded into a maypole of tatters by avenging claws.

## 6. Cat on Hot Bricks

It was nine months later. A perfect summer day, drawing to its close.

On such occasions, a finely tuned heat-seeking instrument like a cat will always know where the last of the day's warmth lingers. Mr. Whiffles had many years before found out that the brick driveway in front of the house caught the final rays of sunlight and held that warmth long after the surrounding grass and flowerbeds had turned chilly. So, as daylight faded, he could always be found lying on the path, letting the stored heat of the bricks flow deliciously through his body.

\*    \*    \*

SERAPHINA FELLOWES FELT VERY PLEASED with herself. Her self-esteem had taken something of a buffeting through the last months, but now she was back on course. She was on the verge of greater success than she'd ever experienced. And, to make her feel even better, she had taken delivery that morning of her new Ferrari.

Seraphina was driving the wonderful red beast back from the launch of *Gigi and the Dead Fishmonger*, and she felt powerful. The party had been full of literati and reviewers; the speech by her publisher's managing director had left no doubt about how much they valued their top-selling author; and everyone seemed agreed that the new series of books was destined to outperform even the success of the Mr. Whiffles mysteries.

Oh, yes, it might take a while for the new series to build up momentum, but there was no doubt that Mr. Whiffles would quickly be eclipsed forever.

Seraphina looked fondly down at Gigi, beautiful as ever, deeply asleep on the passenger seat. The cat had been characteristically docile at the launch, and the pair of them had been exhaustively photographed. Gigi was much more of a fashion accessory than Mr. Whiffles could ever have been, and Seraphina had even begun to buy herself clothes with the cat's coloring in mind. One day, she reckoned, they could together make the cover of *Vogue*.

She leant across to give Gigi a stroke of gratitude, but her movement made the Ferrari swerve. She righted it with an easy flick of the steering wheel, and reminded herself to be careful. In the euphoria of the launch, she'd probably had more to drink than she should have done. Not the only occasion recently she'd overindulged. Must watch it. George was the one with the drink problem, not her.

The thought drove a little wedge of unease into her serenity. It was compounded by the recollection of a conversation she'd had at the launch with a major book reviewer. He'd expressed the heresy that he thought she'd never top the Mr. Whiffles books. Those were the ones for him; no other cat detective could begin to replace Mr. Whiffles in the public's affections.

The wedge of unease was now wide enough to split Seraphina's mind into segments of pure fury. That wretched mangy old cat was still getting more fan mail than she was! Bloody paw prints over bloody everything!

Her anger was at its height as she turned the Ferrari into her drive. And there, lying fast asleep on the warm bricks, lay as tempting a target as Seraphina Fellowes would ever see in her entire life.

There was no thought process involved. She just slammed her foot down on the accelerator and was jolted back as the huge power of the engine took command.

Needless to say, Mr. Whiffles, alerted by some sixth or seventh sense, shot out of the way of the huge tires just in time.

The Ferrari smashed into a brick pillar at the side of the garage. Seraphina

Fellowes needed five stitches in a head wound. Gigi, who'd been catapulted forward by the impact, hit her face against the dashboard and was left with an unsightly, permanent scar across her nose. For future publicity, the publishers would have to use the photographs taken at the launch; all subsequent ones would be disfigured.

And the Ferrari, needless to say, was a write-off.


## 7. Shooting the Cat

One morning a few weeks later, along with the rubber-banded brick of fan mail—almost all with bloody paw prints on the back—came an envelope from the publicity department of Seraphina Fellowes's publishers. She tore it open and, reading the impersonal note on the "With Compliments" slip ("These are all the reviews received to date"), decided she might need a quick swig of vodka to see her through the next few moments.

It wasn't actually that morning's *first* swig of vodka, but, Seraphina rationalized to herself, she had been under a lot of stress over the previous weeks. Once she got properly into the second Gigi book, she'd cut back.

Through the vodka bottle, as she raised it to drink, Seraphina caught sight of Mr. Whiffles, perched on her mantelpiece. The refraction of the glass distorted the features of his face, but the sneering curl to his lips was still there when she lowered the bottle.

Seraphina Fellowes firmly turned her swivel chair to face away from the fireplace, took a deep breath, and started to read the reviews of *Gigi and the Dead Fishmonger*.

She had had inklings from her publisher over the previous few weeks that the reaction hadn't been great, but still was not prepared for the blast of universal condemnation the cuttings contained. Setting aside the clever quips and snide aphorisms, the general message was: "This book is rubbish. Gigi is an entirely unbelievable and uninteresting feline sleuth. Get back to writing about Mr. Whiffles—he's great!"

As she put the bundle of clippings down on her desk, Seraphina Fellowes caught sight once again of the tabby on the mantelpiece. She would have sworn that the sneer on his face had now become a smirk of Cheshire cat proportions.

Seized by unreasoning fury, Seraphina snatched open her desk drawer and pulled out the gun she had bought all those years ago when researching the first book. Her wavering hand steadied to take aim at the cat on the mantelpiece. As she pulled the trigger, she felt as if she were lancing a boil.

Whether her aim was faulty, or whether another of Mr. Whiffles's extra senses preserved him, was hard to judge. What was undoubtedly true, though, was that the bullet missed, and before the echo of the shot died down, it had been joined by the panicked clattering of a cat-flap.

Mr. Whiffles had escaped once again.

Seraphina Fellowes's Edgar, however, the precious ceramic statuette awarded to her by the Mystery Writers of America, had been shattered into a thousand pieces.

## 8. All Cats are Gray in the Dark

What had started as a niggle and developed into a continuing irritation was by now a full-grown obsession. Seraphina couldn't settle down to anything—certainly not to getting on with the second Gigi mystery. The critical panning of the first had left her battered and embittered. It was a very long time since Seraphina Fellowes had felt even mildly pleased with herself.

She now spent her days lolling in the swivel chair in front of her state-of-the-art computer, gazing at the eternally renewed moving pattern of its screen saver, or drifting aimlessly around the house. She ceased to notice what clothes she put on in the mornings—or, as her sleep patterns got more erratic, afternoons. More and more white showed at the roots of her hair, but the effort of lifting the phone to make an appointment at her hairdresser's seemed insuperable. The vodka bottle was never far away.

And, with increasing certainty, Seraphina Fellowes knew that only one event could restore the self-esteem and success that were hers by right.

She could only be saved by the death of Mr. Whiffles.

ONE DAY SHE FINALLY DECIDED there would be no more pussyfooting. He was just a cat, after all. And if one believed in the proverbial nine lives, his stock of those was running very low. Seraphina decided that she really would kill him that day.

Bolstered by frequent swigs from the vodka bottle, she sat and planned.

George was away for the day, on one of his rare visits to hear his agent apologize about her inability to find a buyer for the latest George Fellowes "literary novel." So Seraphina went down to the bungalow, checked carefully that Mr. Whiffles wasn't inside, and locked the cat-flaps shut.

Then she looked in her house for Gigi. That didn't take long. The characterless, but now scar-faced, white Persian was, as ever, asleep on her mistress's bed. Seraphina firmly locked the bedroom door and the cat-flap that was set into it. The little fanlight window was still open, but Gigi would never overcome her lethargy sufficiently to leap up and climb through a fanlight.

Seraphina went down to the kitchen and prepared a toothsome plate of turkey breast, larded with a few peeled prawns. Then she sat down by the cat-flap, and waited.

In one hand she held the vodka bottle. In the other, the means that would finally bring about Mr. Whiffles's quietus.

After lengthy consideration of more exotic options, Seraphina had homed in on the traditional. From time immemorial, it had been the preferred way of removing unwanted kittens, and she saw no reason why it shouldn't also be suitable for an aging tabby like Mr. Whiffles.

She must've dozed off. It was dark in the kitchen when she heard the clatter of the outer cat-flap.

But Seraphina was instantly alert, and she knew exactly what she had to do.

It seemed an age while her quarry lingered in the little passage from the garden. But finally a tentative paw was poked through the cat-flap into the kitchen.

Seraphina Fellowes held her breath. She wasn't going to put her carefully devised plan at risk by a moment of impetuousness.

She waited as the metal flap slowly creaked open. And she waited until the entire cat outline, tail and all, was inside the room, before she pounced.

The furry body kicked and twisted, but the contest was brief. In seconds, the cat had joined the three bricks inside, and Seraphina had tied the string firmly round the sack's neck.

She didn't pause for a second. She allowed no space for the finest needle of conscience to insert itself. Seraphina Fellowes just rushed out into the garden and hurled the meowing sack right into the middle of the fishpond.

It made a very satisfying splash. A few bubbles, then silence.

THE NEXT MORNING, SERAPHINA WOKE with a glow of well-being. For the first time in weeks, her immediate instinct was not to reach for the vodka bottle. Instead, she snuggled luxuriously under her duvet, feeling the comforting weight of Gigi across her shins, and planned the day ahead.

She would go up to London, for the first time in months. The morning she would devote to having her hair done. Then she'd visit a few of her favorite stores and buy some morale-boostingly expensive clothes. She wouldn't have a drink all day, but come back late afternoon, and at five o'clock, which she'd often found to be one of her most creative times, she'd start writing the first chapter of *Gigi and the Murdered Milkman*. Yes, it'd be a good day.

Seraphina Fellowes stretched languidly, then sat up, and looked down at the end of the bed.

There, licking unhurriedly at his patchy fur, his insolent green eyes locked on hers, sat Mr. Whiffles.

## 9. Cat's Cradle

After that, Seraphina Fellowes really did go to pieces. She didn't change her clothes, falling asleep and waking in the same garments, in a vodka-hazed world where time became elastic and meaningless. Her hair hung, lank and unwashed, now more white than black.

And the thought that drove all others from her unhinged brain was the imperative destruction of Mr. Whiffles.

Now that Gigi wasn't around—a sad, white, bedraggled lump had indeed been pulled out of the sack in the fishpond—there was no longer any limitation on the means by which that destruction could be achieved. There was no longer any risk of catching the wrong victim by mistake.

Mr. Whiffles, apparently aware of the murderous campaign against him, went into hiding. Seraphina cut off his obvious escape route by telling George the cat had died, and organizing a carpenter to board over the cat-flaps into the bungalow. George was very upset by the news, but Seraphina, as ever, didn't give a damn about her husband's feelings.

All through her own house, meanwhile, she organized an elaborate network of booby traps. "Network" was the operative word. Seraphina set up a series of wire snares around every one of the many cat-flaps. She turned the floors into a minefield of wire nooses, which, when tightened, would release counterweights on pulleys to yank their catch up to the ceiling. Designer-decorated walls were gouged out to accommodate hooks and rings, gleaming woodwork peppered with screws and cleats. The increasingly demented woman lived in a cat's cradle of tangled and intersecting wires. She ceased to eat, and lived on vodka alone.

And she waited. One day, she knew, Mr. Whiffles would come back into the death trap that had been her house.

And one day—or rather one evening—he did.

The end was very quick. Mr. Whiffles managed to negotiate the snares on the two cat-flaps into the house. He skipped nimbly over the waiting booby traps on the kitchen floor. But, entering the hall, he landed right in the middle of a noose, which, as he jumped away, tightened inexorably around one of his rear legs. He tried to pull himself free, but the wire only cut more deeply into his flesh. He let out a yowl of dismay.

At that moment, Seraphina, who had been waiting on the landing, snapped the light on, and shouted an exultant "Gotcha!" Mr. Whiffles, frozen by the shock of the sudden apparition, looked up at her.

Had Seraphina Fellowes by then been capable of pity, she might have noticed how thin and neglected the cat looked. But her mind no longer had room in it for such thoughts—no room, in fact, for any thoughts other than felicidal ones. She reached across in triumph to free the jammed counterweight that would send her captive slamming fatally up against the ceiling.

But, as she moved, she stumbled, caught her foot in a stretched low-level wire, and tumbled headfirst down the staircase.

Seraphina Fellowes broke her neck and died instantly.

Mr. Whiffles, jumping out of the way of the descending body, had moved closer to the anchor of the noose around his leg. Its tension relaxed, the springy wire loosened, and he was able to step neatly out of the metal loop.

And he started on his next set of nine lives.


## 10.  The Cat Who Got the Cream

George Fellowes was initially very shocked by his wife's death. But when the shocked receded, he had to confess to himself that he didn't really mind that much. And that her absence did bring with it certain positive advantages.

For a start, he no longer had the feeling of permanent, brooding disapproval from the house at the other side of the garden. He also inherited her state-of-the-art computer. At first he was a bit sniffy about this, but as he started to play with it, he quickly became converted to its many conveniences.

Then there was the money. In the press coverage of Seraphina Fellowes's death, her recent doomed attempt to start a new series of cat mysteries had been quickly forgotten. But interest in Mr. Whiffles grew and grew. All the titles were reissued in paperback, and the idea of a Hollywood movie using computer animation, which had been around for ages, suddenly got hot again. The agents of various megastars contacted the production company, discreetly offering their client's services for the year's plum job—voicing Mr. Whiffles.

So, like a tidal wave, the money started to roll in. And, because his wife had never divorced him, George Fellowes got the lot.

More important than all of this, Seraphina's death freed her Catholic husband to remarry. And there was someone George had had in mind for years for just such an eventuality.

THE EVENING OF SERAPHINA'S FUNERAL, George was sprawled across his desk, asleep in front of the evermoving screen saver of his late wife's computer, so he didn't hear the rattle of the reopened cat-flap. He wasn't aware of Mr. Whiffles's entrance, even when the old cat landed quietly on his desk top, but a nuzzling furry nose in his ear soon woke him.

"How're you, old boy?" asked George, reaching up with his left hand to scratch Mr. Whiffles in a favorite place, just behind the ear. At the same time, George's right hand reached out instinctively to the nearly full litre of vodka that stood on the edge of his desk.

Mr. Whiffles, however, had other ideas. Speeding across the surface, he deliberately knocked the bottle over. It lay sideways at the edge of the desk, its contents glugging steadily away into the wastepaper basket.

George Fellowes looked at his cat in amazement, as Mr. Whiffles moved across to the computer. One front paw was placed firmly on the mouse. (That bit was easy; for centuries cats have been instinctively placing their front paws on mice.) But, as the screen saver gave way to a white screen ready for writing, Mr. Whiffles did something else, something much more remarkable.

He placed his other front paw on the keyboard. Not just anywhere on the keyboard, but on one specific key. The "M."

Obedient to the computer's programming, two words appeared on the screen. "Mr. Whiffles."

George Fellowes felt the challenge in the old green eyes that were turned to look at him. For a moment he was undecided. Then, out loud, he said, "What the hell? I'm certainly not getting anywhere with my so-called 'literary' novels."

And his fingers reached forward to the keyboard to complete the title: "Mr. Whiffles and the Murdered Mystery Writers."

Bill Pronzini can be considered one of the cornerstone authors of the modern mystery field. His detectives, whether they be in present day San Francisco like the Nameless Detective or the Old West like Quincannon, are always complex and engaging, solving crimes and tackling social issues of both then and now. His recent novels include *A Wasteland of Strangers* and *Boobytrap*. He is also a perennial in the best of year anthologies such as this series. The following story puts Quincannon right in the middle of a logging camp where trees aren't the only things that fall in the forest.

# The Horseshoe Nail
## BILL PRONZINI

The High Sierra sawmill camp was spread out on a flat along the Truckee River south of Verdi, just across the Nevada state line. It was larger than Quincannon had expected: several barns and corrals, storehouse, cookhouse, a pair of bunkhouses, blacksmith's shop, lumberyard, string of rough-log cabins for the foreman and crew bosses, and the huge steam-powered mill built back into the mouth of a canyon rimmed by high volcanic cliffs. A railroad spur cut through the camp, as did a pair of rutted wagon roads, one from Verdi, which followed the rail line, and the other connecting the sawmill with its logging camp higher up in the mountains.

The place was a swarm of activity: teamsters, swampers, and handlers working with horses and oxen; freighters shunting mule-drawn wagons laden with supplies; men working with long pike poles on the logs that clogged the pond alongside the mill; men stacking and cutting and loading rail cars with lumber and cordwood. The air rang and hummed with the steady metallic whine of the circular saws. The mill cut better than thirty thousand feet of lumber each day in peak season—and there was a rush on now, as autumn lengthened, to maintain a high production pace before the snows came and shut down operations for the winter.

There was no taste yet of snow in the air; the woods scent mixed with the sharp tang of fresh-cut logs was almost summery. The sun lay warm on Quincannon's face as the bullwhacker beside him drove the big Studebaker freight wagon down the Verdi road into camp. It was a fine day to be in the mountains, he thought. An early frost had colored the leaves of the cottonwoods fringing the river, and far up on the mountainside he could see patches of shimmering gold where quaking aspens grew among the pine. Fall days like this one reminded him of his youth. And of the season he had spent working in a sawmill camp in the Oregon woods. That season would make the job that had brought him here easier; once he took his bearings, he would neither look nor feel out of place.

He glanced down at the rough timber-cruiser's outfit he wore. With his thick freebooter's beard, he even *looked* like a lumber-man. A smile bent the corners of his mouth. Ah, if Sabina could see him now, a fine Bunyanesque figure of a man, steely-eyed, with the mountain wilderness all around him and the hot blood raging in his veins . . . would she finally weaken, find herself overcome with uncontrollable passion? She wouldn't succumb to wit, sophistication, or clever subtleties; perhaps raw earthiness was the secret route to her heart and her bed. He would have to find out when he returned to San Francisco, riding yet another triumph as the mighty Bunyan rode Babe the Blue Ox. . . .

The bullwhacker brought his mules to a stop at the rear of the cookshack. Two men waited there, a long-queued Chinese cook in a white apron and a shaggy-bearded beanpole of about fifty dressed in congress boots and a pair of high-topped pants. The cook's interest was in the wagonload of stores; the beanpole's was in Quincannon. He approached as Quincannon swung down, warbag in hand, and looked him over with a blearily critical eye.

"You the new cheater?" he demanded in a rusty-file voice.

"Cheater?" Quincannon's memory jogged. "Timekeeper and scaler—that's right. But only an assistant and only temporary."

"How temporary?"

"No more than a week. I won't be needed past then."

"Too bad for you. This here's a highball camp, best in the Sierras. I ought to know. What's your name?"

"John Quincannon."

"Scot, eh? I got nothing against Scots." He scratched at a scrawny neck as wrinkled as an old pair of logger's tin pants. His own trousers were stiff with dirt and held up by the most enormous galluses Quincannon had ever seen. Oddments such as twists of baling wire decorated the galluses; a miscellany of hand tools hung from a belt around his waist. "Mine's Ned Coombs. Nevada Ned, they call me. I'm the bullcook here—best damn bullcook in this or any other camp. What do you say to that?"

Quincannon shrugged. A bullcook was a camp chore boy, usually a superannuated logger and often and often enough a souse suffering from locomotor ataxia. Despite the name, a bullcook had nothing to do with the preparation of food; his workday consisted of sweeping out the bunkhouses, cutting and bringing in fuel, washing lamps, and the like. "If you say you're the best, I'll take your word for it."

"Damn well better," Nevada Ned said. "You got any drinkin' likker in your kick?"

"No."

"No? How come?"

"I don't use it."

"Hell you say. A cheater that don't use likker." He spat on the ground at Quincannon's feet and then produced a four-ounce bottle from a pants pocket, yanked out the cork, and took a long draught. After which he made a face and said, "Jakey. Can't afford better, and now I'm almost out. Sure you ain't got any good likker?"

"I'm sure. Where do I find Jack Phillips?"

"Camp office." Nevada Ned had lost interest in him. "Ask anybody," he said and turned his back and disappeared around the corner of the cookshack.

Quincannon found his way to the camp office, a cottonwood-shaded building near the lumberyard. Jack Phillips, High Sierra's foreman, turned out to be a burly gent in his late thirties, with a black beard almost as thick and piratical as Quincannon's. An unlit corncob pipe jutted at an authoritative angle from the midst of all the facial brush. When they were alone in the foreman's private cubicle, Quincannon presented him with the letter of introduction he'd been given in Sacramento. Phillips scowled as he read it, and when he was finished he slapped it down on his desk and transferred the scowl to his visitor.

"How is it a flycop has such pull with Cap Fuller?" he asked. Cap Fuller was the head of the High Sierra Logging Company and Phillips's boss.

"I don't know Mr. Fuller," Quincannon said. "It so happens he's a friend of Senator Johannsen, and the senator—"

"—is a friend of yours."

"Satisfied former client would be more accurate."

Phillips grunted. "Well! I'll cooperate because I've been ordered to. But I don't mind telling you, I don't like it."

"Why is that, Mr. Phillips?"

"Flycop sneaking around my camp, pretending to be somebody he's not, putting the arm on one of my men—it's bad for morale."

"If all goes according to plan, no one but you and me and Mr. Fuller need ever know about it."

Another grunt. "Besides, Guy DuBois is my best sawyer. I hate like hell to lose him this late in the season."

"He's also a thief."

"You sure about that? No doubt he's the one stole that woman's jewelry?"

"None," Quincannon said.

"Rich San Francisco widow taking up with a French Canadian logger—don't make much sense to me."

"DuBois's sister was one of Ida Bennett's maids. Mrs. Bennett was the one who sent the wire notifying him when the sister died unexpectedly two weeks ago. She met him at the funeral, felt sorry for him, and invited him to her home for dinner. Matters evidently progressed rapidly from that point."

"Talked her out of her drawers, eh?"

"Not that she admitted, but I suspect so. It wasn't until after DuBois left the city that she discovered the three valuable items of jewelry were missing."

"A brooch, a pendant, and a ring worth fifty thousand dollars?"

"Diamonds, rubies, and platinum gold, Mr. Phillips."

"Well, what makes you think he brought them back here with him?"

"A strong hunch backed by facts. I traced his movements from San Francisco; he went straight to Sacramento and straight from there to Verdi."

"Could've stashed the loot somewhere along the way, couldn't he?"

"He could, but where? He's a timber beast—no permanent home, no relatives now that his sister has passed on, no safe-deposit box that I've been able to locate. I like the odds that the booty is still in his possession."

"Why in hell would he do such a fool thing as to come back and resume his work as a sawyer if he has fifty thousand in jewelry in his kick? If it were me, I'd've kept right on traveling east."

Quincannon said, "My guess is that his motive is a fool's mix of cleverness and uncertainty. The widow Bennett knows he was working here; he might believe it's the last place anyone would look for him. And because he's not a professional thief, it's likely he hasn't a clear idea of how to dispose of the swag. By continuing at his job until the camp shuts down he can finance a winter search for a fenceman, one who'll give him top dollar."

"All well and good," Phillips said, "but I still don't see why you can't just arrest him now instead of skulking around on the sly first."

"The safe return of the jewelry is Mrs. Bennett's paramount concern," Quincannon explained. "Punishment for DuBois is secondary."

"So? If he has the goods with him, he'd tell you where they are or you'd find them on your own."

"Not necessarily. He may have found a clever hiding place in all this wilderness that will elude my searches. And thieves in his position, once caught, sometimes develop the sly notion of remaining silent so they can return for the swag when they get out of prison."

"Beat the hiding place out of him, then. That's what I'd do."

"A last resort, Mr. Phillips. I prefer to use my wiles rather than my fists." Particularly with a client as rich as Mrs. Ida Bennett, who was paying Carpenter and Quincannon, Professional Detective Services, a handsome daily retainer.

"No more than a week of you and your wiles?"

"No more than that, and with any luck, considerably less. If I haven't recovered the jewelry by this time next week, I'll arrest DuBois—quietly, of course—and adopt the persuasive approach."

"Well, I still don't like it, but since I don't have a vote in the matter . . ." Phillips lit his corncob with a sulphurous lucifer and puffed up a cloud of acrid smoke. "Where do you want to be quartered, bunkhouse or private cabin?"

"Where does DuBois hang his hat?"

"He has a cabin."

"I'd prefer one near his, then, if that can be arranged."

"It can. Anything else?"

"Names of his friends, and something about his habits."

"He has no friends. DuBois isn't well liked—he's a loner and owns a surly disposition, the more so when he's been drinking. We don't permit the public consumption of alcohol, and drunkenness is grounds for dismissal, but some of the men . . ." Phillips shrugged. "Sawmill camps are rough-and-tumble places. As I assume you know, since Cap Fuller's letter says you're familiar with the business."

Quincannon nodded. "Is drinking DuBois's only vice?"

"No. Stud poker's another."

"Ah. Does he play with a core group?"

"Ben Irons, his setter at the mill. Okay King, the blacksmith. Hank Ransome, one of the teamsters. No one else on a regular basis."

"How often?"

"Most nights for a few hours after supper."

"His cabin?"

"No. Usually Okay King's."

"Good," Quincannon said, smiling. "Very good."

"If you say so." The foreman squinted at him through tendrils of smoke. "One more thing I'd like to know, Quincannon. Do you intend to just prowl around camp all day, taking up space, or will you make yourself useful in your sham role?"

"Useful?"

"You're supposed to be an assistant timekeeper. There's plenty of work to be done by the man holding that position. I'd feel better about your presence if you'd do your share between skulks and searches. Assuming you'll be here more than one day, that is. And assuming you can handle the job."

"Oh, I can handle it," Quincannon told him. "For the standard assistant's wages, of course."

"Wages?" Phillips was indignant at first; then his mouth shaped into a crooked smile. "By God, you've got gall, I'll give you that. Wages! All right, then—wages paid for work done. Agreed?"

"Agreed, Mr. Phillips. And you'll not regret it. No man works harder for an honest dollar than John Quincannon."

\*     \*     \*

THE CABINS, SOME TEN IN ALL, were arranged in a staggered row, some shaded by tall pines, others afforded a measure of privacy by elderberry and choke-cherry bushes. All were small, single-room affairs, and the one Quincannon was given was as spare as a monk's cell: sheet-iron stove, puncheon table, wall bench, and a pole bunk mattressed with finely cut fir boughs and covered with wool blankets. That was all, save for a lantern hanging from a wall peg. A small glass-paned window admitted tree-filtered shafts of sunlight. The only means of protection against intruders was a pair of iron brackets mounted one on each side of the door, into which a heavy wooden crossbar could be fitted.

Quincannon stowed his warbag under the bunk and took himself to the cabin three away from his that Phillips had pointed out to him as Guy DuBois's. There was no one else in the vicinity; he slipped around to the side to have a look through the window. The interior was similar to his, except that it was considerably more cluttered. DuBois's duffel, jammed under the bunk, bulged invitingly.

Back at the front, he made sure he was still alone and unobserved and then quickly slipped inside and shut the door again behind him.

The cabin stank of unwashed clothing, woodsmoke, and alcohol. The ripe blend of odors set him to breathing through his mouth as he knelt beside the bunk.

The duffel was not the only item wedged underneath. Pushed back behind the bag was a small wooden case. He checked the case first. It contained half a dozen identical dark-brown bottles; the label on one he lifted out bore a steel-engraved photograph of a healthy-looking gent and the words Perry Davis's Pain Killer. Quincannon was familiar with the product—a patent medicine that claimed to have great thaumaturgic powers, good for man and beast, but whose main ingredient was pure alcohol. It was more potent, in fact, than most lawfully manufactured whiskies.

He turned his attention to the duffel and its contents. Wads of soiled shirts, socks, and union suits. A new, sealed deck of playing cards. A torn dime novel featuring the exploits of a character named Mexican Bill, the Cowboy Detective. And a leather drawstring pouch that clinked and rattled when he shook it. The pouch, however, turned out to be a disappointment. All it contained was a collar button, a woman's corset stay, two Indian head nickels, the nib of a pen, and half a dozen other odds and ends of value only to DuBois.

He replaced the pouch and the rest of the items, pushed the duffel and the case of Pain Killer back under the bunk. Then he searched the remainder of the room, beginning with the pair of calked boots, coil of rope, and other logger's paraphernalia littering the floor against the wall under the window. He even went so far as to feel in among the fir boughs lining the bunk and to check the stove's ash box and flue.

There was no sign anywhere of the stolen jewel-work.

Well, he thought philosophically, he hadn't really expected to find the swag so easily, had he? Time was on his side—time, and a handsome fee and day wages besides. He cracked the door open, peeked out. A foraging jay had the area to itself; it flew off squawking and scolding when Quincannon emerged and sauntered away along the river bank.

Before returning to the camp office to begin his assistant time-keeper's duties, he detoured to the sawmill for a gander at Guy DuBois in the flesh. The widow Bennett had described the French Canadian to a bitter tee, but Quincannon preferred to take the measure of an adversary himself well in advance, if possible, of any sort of face-to-face confrontation.

The huge circular saws were quiet when he stepped inside the cavernous enclosure. This was because a fresh log, just winched up from the pond below, was being rolled into place on the saw carriage and clamped down by means of iron "dogs." The setter—Ben Irons, he assumed, a keg of a man with drooping, tobacco-stained moustaches—used his levers to move the log into position for the first cut. The sawyer, DuBois, then stepped in close to the two blades, one set directly above the other, their sharp teeth almost touching. When he started the carriage, steadying its progress as the saws bit deep into the wood, streams of sawdust flew high and the screech of steel against wood was deafening.

Quincannon watched DuBois as he and Irons sliced off a slab of rough bark and wood that would be chopped up into firewood, then commenced reducing the log to thinner strips of board lumber. The French Canadian was a much less imposing figure than Ida Bennett had led him to believe; in fact, DuBois was anything but a "handsome little devil." Short, long-necked, knobby-armed, with a nose like a cant hook, a sullen mouth, and eyes sunk deep under wire-brush brows—altogether an unlovely specimen, in Quincannon's estimation. Mrs. Bennett must have been lonelier than he'd thought, and with poorer eyesight, to have taken DuBois into her home and bed.

He was smiling as he left the mill. He had six inches in height and fifty pounds in solid weight on the sawyer, not to mention years of experience in the niceties of handling felons; he would have no trouble with DuBois when the time came to make his arrest. This job was looking better all the time—a veritable lark compared to some he'd had in recent months. The only challenge was locating the whereabouts of the stolen jewelry, and for a detective with his talents, he didn't see how he could fail to meet it successfully, sooner or later.

SUPPER WAS SERVED IN THE cookshack, at a single table that ran the length of the room and was flanked by wooden benches. Quincannon contrived to find a seat across from DuBois, the better to observe him and to listen in on his conversations. A good plan, except that it produced no results. DuBois sat alongside Ben Irons and a barrel-chested gent with a lion's mane of blond hair—Okay King, the blacksmith—but spoke to neither of them nor to anyone else. He kept his eyes on his plates of boiled potatoes, corned beef, baked beans, and cornstarch pudding, ate hurriedly and wolfishly, and then left the table, alone, before any of the other men were finished.

When DuBois was gone, Quincannon tried to strike up conversations with both Irons and King. Neither man showed more than a cursory interest in him. Loggers and sawmill camp workers could be standoffish with newcomers until they got to know them, and Quincannon, despite his gregarious nature, was no exception. It would take some doing to cultivate Irons and King to the point where he could ask them probing questions about DuBois and expect straightforward answers. He could begin the cultivation, he thought, at the stud game tonight.

But he was wrong. The game, in Okay King's cabin, was already in progress when he arrived, and all six places were filled. And they stayed filled for the next hour, forcing him into a passive kibitzing role. Conversation among the players was desultory; DuBois, again, had almost nothing to say to anyone. The stakes were low—coins rather than greenbacks—but the French Canadian played as if he were in a cutthroat, high-stakes game, betting conservatively, keeping his hole cards close to his chest, and studying them, the cards faceup on the table, and the faces of his opponents with a brooding concentration.

His luck was poor tonight; he lost steadily, often with second-best hands. His expression darkened into a sullen glower and he began nipping at a bottle of Perry Davis's Pain Killer without offering it to any of the others. Not a good loser, DuBois. When his nine-high straight was beaten by Okay King's queens full, he slammed his fist down on the table and growled, *"Sacre Dieu! If I do not know better, mon ami, I think maybe you make your own luck."*

King glared back at him. "But you do know better, don't you, Frenchy?" he said in a deceptively mild voice.

"Perhaps. But the cards are yours."

"Same cards we always play with."

"I say we play with a new deck."

"And I say we don't. Anybody else think there's something wrong with this one?"

Headshakes. Irons said, "Whose deal is it? Mine?"

DuBois's eyes were still on the blacksmith. He said angrily, *"J'en ai plein le cul!"*

"You want to cuss me," King said, laying his massive hands flat on the table, "by God, do it in English."

"Bah! I am sick of this game, that's what I tell you."

"Then quit, why don't you?"

DuBois bounced to his feet, kicking over the box he'd been sitting on, and scraped up his few remaining coins. "So!" he said. "I quit!" And he stormed out of the cabin and banged the door behind him.

Quincannon moved over to right the upended box. "Mind if I sit in, lads?"

The men around the table looked him over. Okay King shrugged and said, "Sit. Your money's good as anybody's."

"New cheater, ain't you?" the teamster, Hank Ransome, asked.

"Assistant. And a more honest cheater you'll never meet."

The men liked that; all of them except Okay King laughed. The humorless blacksmith asked him, "What's the name again?"

"Quincannon. John Quincannon."

"Scot, eh? Well, I reckon a Scot's got a better chance than most of being honest."

"He has for a fact. And I'm not half so feisty as the former occupant of this seat. That French Canadian has a fine temper."

"You don't know the half of it," Irons said. "Ought to work with him on a saw carriage all day long."

"Difficult fellow?"

"Difficult? Grizzly bear's got a better disposition."

"What's the source of his bile?"

"Born with it, and it's eating his vitals."

"Along with that Perry Davis he's so fond of," Ransome said.

"Is that what makes him such a poor loser?"

"Among other things. Fact is, he don't like losing at nothing. Don't trust nobody either, that Frenchy. Anything goes wrong for him, he figures it's somebody else's fault—somebody out to do him dirt. Only one doing him dirt's his own self."

"To hell with DuBois," Okay King said. "We're here to play stud and time's growing short. Deal the cards, Ben, and let's get on with it."

They played until ten o'clock, with Quincannon winning more hands than he lost. He tried twice more to steer the sporadic table talk around to DuBois, but the others wanted no more of the French Canadian tonight. He counted the evening a success, nonetheless. He'd learned enough about his quarry and the men's feelings toward the man to discard the notion that any of them, or anyone else in the camp, was in cahoots with him; DuBois was too much of a loner and too suspicious of others to have let on to anyone about the stolen jewelry. Nor would he have hidden the swag anywhere it was likely to be found by accident. He would have it close at hand, where he could check on it regularly to make sure it was safe.

Quincannon whistled a jaunty tune as he walked back to his cabin. Not only was he one step closer to finding the loot, but he had won twelve dollars at stud—another little bonus to add to his accumulating pile. Today had been profitable in more ways than one. Tomorrow might be even more so.

DuBois's cabin, he noticed as he passed by, was dark, and not even a dribble of smoke came from its stovepipe chimney. No fire to ward off the night's chill? Well, loggers in general, and French Canadians in particular, were a hardy lot. Sleep well, *mon ami*, he thought cheerfully. Your time is about up.

He didn't know until morning how right he was.

DuBois's time was up, for a fact. Permanently.

IT WAS THE BULLCOOK, NEVADA Ned, who brought the news. When Quincannon trudged sleepily through the frosty five A.M. darkness to the cookshack, summoned by the cook's bell, there was no sign of the sawyer; and when DuBois still hadn't arrived by the middle of breakfast, an annoyed Jack Phillips sent Ned to find out what was keeping him. The bullcook came rushing back inside of ten minutes, as the men were finishing the last of their boiled coffee, waving his arms and shouting at the top of his voice.

"He's dead! By grab, he's deader than a boiled owl!"

Phillips, sitting near Quincannon, was on his feet first. He called over the general commotion, "What're you babbling about, Ned? Who's dead?"

"DuBois. Frenchy. Lyin' on the floor of his cabin, deader than a boiled owl."

"The devil you say! How? What happened to him?"

"Side of his head's busted in. Looks like he tripped on a coil of rope and cracked his skull wide open on the stove."

The cookshack emptied swiftly, Phillips leading the rush of men and Quincannon, muttering "Hell and damn!" under his breath, close behind. Pale dawnlight had begun to seep into the eastern sky, but the shadows were still long and thick in the surrounding woods and across ground so heavy with frost it looked snow-patched; Phillips carried a lantern he'd claimed from Nevada Ned, and several of the others had lighted their lamps as well. When they reached DuBois's cabin, the foreman reached out for the latch.

"Can't get in that way," Ned told him. "Barred inside—I tried it before I come running."

They hurried around to the side window. Phillips held the lantern up close to the dusty glass; Quincannon crowded in next to him. The lamplight threw wavery shadows over the dark interior, over the figure of DuBois sprawled facedown in front of the stove, his arms drawn back against his sides. Dried blood gleamed faintly on the raw wound above his left temple.

Phillips half turned to scan the faces behind him. "Ned," he said to the bullcook, "you're not much wider than a fence pole. Think you can squeeze through here?"

"Sure thing, once I shuck my mackinaw. Want me to bust out the glass?"

"I'll do it. Give me your hammer."

Ned slipped the hammer free of its belt loop, handed it over, and Phillips broke the window and cleaned shards from the frame. Then the bullcook wriggled his beanpole body through the opening and went to unbar the door.

Quincannon made sure he was the first man inside after Phillips, the first to kneel down for a close look at the dead man. Caught around DuBois's left ankle was a loop of hemp from the coil against the wall under the window. Blood was smeared on a lower corner of the stove, as well as on DuBois's hair and cracked skull. Quincannon touched an edge of it with his forefinger: dried to a crust. When he grasped one of the backflung arms he found it stiff and unyielding: the early stages of rigor mortis.

Dead since sometime last night, he thought. Eight or nine hours. Dead, by God, when I walked by at ten o'clock.

Behind him Okay King said, "Drunk, likely. Drunk on Perry Davis and staggering around in the dark."

"Damn fool," Phillips agreed disgustedly.

"Ain't much of a loss, you ask me."

"Poor excuse for a man, I'll grant you that, but good at his job. It's too late in the season to find another sawyer. That means extra shifts for everyone at the mill, same as when he was in Frisco."

During this exchange, and while the mill hands were grumbling at the foreman's words, Quincannon made a quick, deft search of DuBois's clothing. If the brooch, pendant, and diamond ring had been on the body, he'd have found them. And he didn't.

Veritable lark, eh? Minor challenge? Faugh!

As Quincannon straightened, Ben Irons said, "Blasted Frenchy, makin' trouble dead as well as alive. If he had to have a freak accident, why couldn't he wait until we shut down for the winter?"

Wrong, Mr. Irons, Quincannon thought darkly. Not a freak accident. Not on your tintype.

Murder.

Murder plain and simple.

ON PHILLIPS'S ORDERS, THREE OF the men removed DuBois's corpse and carried it to the loading dock, where it was to be held for shipment to Verdi on the morning train. The rest, except for Quincannon, dispersed to begin their day's work. He faded away to his own cabin, so as to avoid, for the time being, another private talk with Phillips in the camp office. The foreman would want to know his intentions now that DuBois was dead, and he wasn't ready yet for that discussion, or to reveal the truth about his quarry's demise.

He waited fifteen minutes, ruminating over a pipeful of shag tobacco. Then he transferred his Navy Colt from his warbag to his belt, buttoned his shirt over it, and returned to DuBois's cabin.

It was deserted now. He let himself inside. Sunrise was only a few minutes away, but little of the morning light penetrated the broken window; he lighted DuBois's lantern. In its glow he first examined the stove and the floor around it. Next he studied the door, the iron brackets mounted on either side of it, and the wooden crossbar. There was a tiny hole, almost a gouge, high up on the door. And near one end of the bar he found a fresh, five-inch vertical furrow.

He lowered the lantern and searched the floor here. Among the boot-crushed remains of window glass he spied a horseshoe nail, two inches long and slightly bent. It hadn't been there long; it was shiny new, free of dust. He nodded in satisfaction and dropped the nail into his shirt pocket.

Only one question remained now.

Had DuBois been killed for the stolen jewel work or for some other reason?

He continued his search, leaving no corner of the room and nothing in it uninspected. He felt along the underside of the table, probed the walls and floor for loose boards and the legs of the table and the bunk poles for hollows. He reexamined the stove and its flue, the logger's boots, and other items strewn under the window. He sifted once more through the four bottles of Perry Davis's Pain Killer, through the clothing and other contents of DuBois's duffel.

"Hell and damn!" he muttered aloud when he was done.

He had the answer to his question of motive. But what he still didn't have was Ida Bennett's expensive baubles.

THE BLACKSMITH SHOP STOOD ON the bank of a shallow creek that flowed into the Truckee, not far from the barn and corrals. Made of unbarked logs like the other camp buildings, it had a steep shed roof but neither doors nor windows. As Quincannon approached the wide entrance he saw Okay King and another man working at a heavy wooden crib set alongside the forge and bellows. Inside the crib, slung from a windlass-drawn harness fashioned of heavy bands of leather and rope, its four legs tied to the corner timbers, was a wild-eyed and bellowing ox.

The second man, a bullwhacker from the looks of him, was saying to the ox, "Quit your hollerin', Tex. This ain't hurtin' you none," as Quincannon entered.

King was hunched over by the animal's near hind foot, trimming off the rough edges of the hoof and cleaning it with a sharp knife. Finished with that, he laid one half of a new shoe against the hoof. The fit wasn't right; he took the shoe to the forge, thrust it under the coals with a pair of tongs, and pumped the bellows until the coals flared a smoky red. When he stepped back to wait for the heat to soften the iron, he spied Quincannon. His sweating face pinched into a scowl.

"What is it *you* want?"

"Two minutes of your time."

"You've got eyes, man, you can see I'm busy."

"It's important," Quincannon told him. "Did you know DuBois long enough and well enough to make a guess as to where he might have hidden something of value?"

"Hidden something? Hidden *what*? What the devil are you gabbling about?"

"There's no time to explain now. Can you make a guess?"

"No," King said. "All I know about Frenchy is that I didn't like him any more'n a horse's hind end. He went his way, I went mine. Stud poker's all we had in common, and damn little there. Talk to Ben Irons and Hank Ransome—they knew him better than I did."

Quincannon produced the horseshoe nail and held it up for King to see. "One of yours, I'll warrant."

The blacksmith squinted at it, wiping his hands on a fire-blackened leather apron. "Looks like. Why?"

"It was on the floor of DuBois's cabin. Would he have had any reason to keep horseshoe nails?"

"A sawyer? Not hardly. Somebody might've tracked it in on a boot sole this morning. Anyhow, what's a blasted nail got to do with anything?"

"A great deal," Quincannon said. "Oh, a great deal, Mr. King."

He asked two more questions, the answers to which were just as he'd expected. By this time the caged ox had begun to toss its head in a frenzy, hurling flecks of slobber all the way over to where Quincannon stood. Its bawling increased in volume.

King growled to the bullwhacker, "Hell's fire, Joe, can't you shut that critter up?"

"Tex ain't never took well to a shoein', you know that."

"He ain't the only one."

Joe prodded the animal with his goad, and when that had no effect, he commenced to swearing at it. If anything, this caused the ox's complaints to grow even more frantic.

The smith glared at Joe, at the ox, and then at Quincannon.

"No damn peace in this camp since you showed up," he said aggrievedly. He stalked back to the forge, yanked out the glowing shoe, laid it on his anvil, and began hammering it with a vengeance, as if trying to drown out both the ox's bellows and Joe's steady cussing.

HANK RANSOME WAS AWAY FROM the settlement, delivering a load of supplies to the logging camp higher up in the mountains. Quincannon went from the teamsters' barn to the mill, avoiding the camp office on the way. Inside the mill, he watched Ben Irons and DuBois's towheaded replacement saw a massive redwood log into board lumber. When they were done and a fresh log was being winched up, he approached Irons and drew him aside.

The setter frowned at his question about DuBois. "What would that Frenchy have that's valuable enough to hide?"

"Something he stole in San Francisco."

"Stole? Well, that don't surprise me none. Money, is it?"

"Expensive jewelry. Three small pieces."

"Don't say. How come you know so much about it?"

"It's a long story and time is short. I'll explain later. In or near his cabin, would you guess? Or somewhere else in camp?"

"No place else DuBois spent much time, except Okay's cabin and right here in the mill."

"Would he have chanced hiding it here?"

"No spot safe enough. My pick is his cabin."

"Mine, too, but I've searched it twice."

"Maybe he buried it somewhere outside. . . ." Irons paused and then shook his head. "No, not him. He'd be afraid somebody'd see him do it. Got to be *inside*. He'd play that hand like he played his cards—close to the vest, no risks. Hide valuables where he could keep a close eye on 'em, particularly if they was stolen goods."

Cards, Quincannon thought.

Cards!

Half to Irons and half to himself he said, "Last night DuBois all but accused Okay King of doctoring the deck. Not for the first time when he lost?"

"Hell; no. He was always tryin' to blame somebody."

"Did he ever bring his own cards to the game?"

"Time or two."

"Recently?"

"Not since he come back from his sister's funeral."

"Yet he called for a deck last night."

"Yeah, he did. What—?"

Quincannon said, "That's the answer, then," and spun on his heel and hurried out of the mill.

For the third time that morning he entered DuBois's cabin. He went straight to the bunk, hauled out the duffel, and rummaged around inside until he located the sealed box of playing cards. It had the feel of a brand-new deck, and at a casual glance it had the look of one. But on closer inspection he found that the original seal had been pried loose, probably with a knife blade, and then carefully reglued. He slit the seal with his thumbnail, opened the box.

It contained no more than two dozen cards, separated into two halves to help create the illusion of a full deck; and sandwiched tightly between the cards, in a wrapping of tissue paper, were the widow Bennett's brooch, pendant, and diamond ring.

Quincannon offered himself congratulations and at the same time cursed himself for a rattlepate, a difficult feat even for him. An ingenious hiding place, to be sure, but he should have inspected the card box more closely on his first search, or at least his second. After all, he was no stranger to the ploy of card mechanics bilking suckers with resealed decks—

Sounds outside. Someone was approaching the cabin.

Swiftly and silently he stood and moved to the wall behind the door. He had just enough time to pocket both the card box and the jewelry, and to unbutton his shirt above the handle of his Navy, before the door swung inward.

The man who entered kicked the door shut behind him without turning. As Quincannon had done minutes earlier, he made straight for DuBois's bunk and knelt beside it. But it wasn't the duffel that he was after. Eager fingers drew out the case containing the four remaining pint bottles of Perry Davis's Pain Killer. He put one of these into the pocket of his mackinaw, was lifting out a second when Quincannon made his presence known.

"Hello, Ned," he said. "Come after the rest of the spoils, have you?"

The bullcook twisted around on one bony knee. His expression in that instant was one of surprise and trapped fear; but in the next, as he recognized Quincannon, he managed to reclaim some of his usual arrogance and bluster. He gained his feet, still clutching the pint of Pain Killer.

"Oh, it's you. The cheater. What're you doin' here?"

"Same as you, Ned. Only it's altogether different spoils that interest me."

"I don't know what you're talkin' about. Foreman sent me down to gather up DuBois's gear. This here Perry Davis ain't gonna do him no good, so I figured I might as well help myself."

"Just as you helped yourself last night, eh?"

"Last night? Wasn't nowhere near here last night."

"Around nine or so," Quincannon said. "Helping yourself to a pint of Pain Killer while DuBois was away playing stud."

"That's a damn lie!"

"Fact. One of several. You told me yesterday you were almost out of jakey and you're a man who sorely needs Demon Rum in one form or another to keep his bones together. You knew DuBois brought a case of Pain Killer back with him from San Francisco; saw him unloading it, likely. And you thought he might not miss one bottle, or wouldn't know for certain who'd pilfered it if he did. But you picked the wrong night, Ned. DuBois left the stud game early and caught you at the job. A brief struggle, perhaps, and you sent him to his reward."

"I never did no such thing."

"Hit him with that hammer of yours, I'll wager, and down he went. If he wasn't dead then, you made sure he was by thumping his cranium against the stove."

Nevada Ned's seamed face had lost its color. The look of trapped fear was back in his eyes. "You're crazy as a one-winged jay. DuBois was drunk, he tripped on that coil of rope and fell against the stove and busted his own skull—"

"No, that's how you made it look. After which you took two pints of Pain Killer instead of one and went on your merry way. There were six bottles in the case when I was here yesterday, looking for my spoils, and only four when I searched again earlier."

"The door," Ned said desperately, "the door was barred on the *inside*. You was here when we busted in, you saw that same as everybody else. Wasn't nobody but DuBois could have barred it. Nobody!"

"Except you," Quincannon said. "You and your trusty hammer and one little horseshoe nail—"

Ned threw the pint of Pain Killer at him. Launched it in one sudden, fluid motion, with not even a flicker of his eyes as warning. Quincannon was caught off guard. The bottle fetched him a glancing blow on the cheekbone—if he hadn't twisted his head at the last second it would have struck him squarely between the eyes—and staggered him backwards into the wall. The impact was jarring enough to upset his balance; his right foot slid, then his left, and he toppled to one knee. By the time he lunged upright again, Ned was past him and out the door.

Quincannon wasted breath on a smoldering six-jointed oath, shook his head to clear out the cobwebs, drew his revolver, and gave chase. The bull-cook had a fifty-yard lead, running spraddle-legged along the riverbank to the north. Quincannon mowed down an elderberry shrub, but the shrub paid him back by scratching his hands and chin. It also slowed him enough for Ned to add ten more yards to his lead.

"Stop or I'll shoot, you damned blackguard!" Quincannon bellowed, wasting more breath. Nevada Ned threw a look over his shoulder but not even sight of the big revolver broke his stride. Whether he realized it or not, however, he had nowhere to go. The river ran too fast here for swimming, if in fact Ned could swim, and the terrain offered neither a hidey hole nor an escape route.

Younger and in better physical condition, Quincannon soon closed the gap between them to thirty yards. Ahead was the mill pond, pole-wielding men wearing steel-calked boots balanced on the floating logs; he couldn't risk a shot that might miss the bullcook and hit one of them. Catch up and tackle him, that was the best way to end the chase. But before he could gain any more ground, Ned veered away from the river at an angle toward the lumberyard and loading dock.

Men working there stopped to watch as Nevada Ned and Quincannon pounded toward them. One shouted something that was lost in the screaming whine of the mill saws, the chuffing of a yard engine on the spur track. The

bullcook stumbled around a huge cone of sawdust, and when he dodged between stacks of board and slab lumber, Quincannon lost sight of him. Hell
and damn! He put on a burst of speed, reached the stacks, cut through them—
and then skidded to a halt.

Ned had pulled up next to a jumble of cut firewood. And in his hands now,
drawn up menacingly, was a double-bitted axe.

Quincannon sleeved sweat from his eyes. Both he and Ned were panting
like dray horses in the thin mountain air. "Put the axe down," he managed,
"and give yourself up. Don't make me shoot you."

"Hell I will! Stay away from me, you heathen murderer!"

Half a dozen burly lumbermen were closing in around them. One called,
"What's this all about, Ned?"

"DuBois . . . he didn't die accidental. Cheater here killed him and now he's
tryin' to blame it on me."

"So that's your game, is it?" Quincannon said. "Well, it won't work." He
drew another ragged breath and said to the others, "I'm not a timekeeper,
lads, I'm a detective from San Francisco. Come here undercover to arrest
DuBois for theft."

A surprised muttering greeted this pronouncement. Two lumbermen who
had been edging closer to Quincannon stopped and held their ground.

"He's lying!" Nevada Ned shouted. *"He's* the thief. He killed DuBois for
his stash of Perry Davis's Pain Killer."

Quincannon shifted the Navy to his left hand, and with his right fished the
brooch and pendant from his pocket. When he held them high, sunlight
glinted off the diamonds and rubies and gold settings. Sharp exclamations
came from the gathering crowd this time.

"These are what DuBois stole. Ned's the one who murdered him—not for
these but for the Pain Killer. One of you fetch Jack Phillips. He'll vouch for
who I am."

"No need to fetch me, I'm already here." The foreman appeared at a trot
from behind a stack of redwood burls. "Quincannon is who he says he is, all
right, a flycop from—"

Phillips didn't finish the sentence because Nevada Ned, trapped and lost
and impelled by hate, chose that moment to attack the flycop with his axe.

Again without warning, he rushed forward and swung the weapon in a
vicious horizontal arc, as if he were about to fell a sapling. Quincannon
twisted aside just in time; the blade sliced air two inches from his jugular. He
didn't dare fire the Navy with the workers milling around. Instead, as the
bullcook pivoted back toward him, lifting the axe for another swipe, he drove
the toe of his boot into Ned's shin, staggering him; then he slammed the Colt's
barrel against his knobby wrist. The bone snapped with a dry, brittle sound,
like the crack of an old pine cone under a heavy tread. Ned screamed in pain.
And the axe dropped harmlessly at his feet.

Phillips shoved up next to Quincannon as some of the others dragged the moaning bullcook away. "By God, that was close. He nearly sliced that blade clean through your neck. Are you all right?"

"Never better," Quincannon lied. "Close, true, but history was on my side, Mr. Phillips."

"History?"

He smiled ruefully. "No member of the Quincannon clan has ever lost his head in a fight."

A SHORT WHILE LATER, IN Phillips's private cubicle, he was feeling his old self again. This was due in large part to the grudging mix of awe, admiration, and respect now being accorded him by the foreman—a mix that grew richer still as he made his explanations.

"When did I first suspect DuBois had been murdered?" he said, leaning back comfortably in his chair. "Why, from the first moment you held the lantern up to his cabin window. I knew it for certain as soon as we were inside."

"Even though the door was barred?"

"Even though."

"But how, man? How?"

Quincannon applied a fresh match to the tobacco in his pipe. When he had it drawing to his satisfaction he said, "From the position of the body. If DuBois had tripped and fallen against the stove, drunk or sober, he would not have been lying as he was."

"I don't see what—"

"His arms, Mr. Phillips. When a man trips and falls, his instinctive reaction is to throw his arms out in front of him to break the fall. DuBois's should have been outflung *toward* the stove, or at least caught under his body, but they weren't. They were drawn back *along his sides*. Therefore, he hadn't died where he lay—his body had been moved."

"Of course. Now why didn't I notice that myself?"

"You haven't the trained eye of a master detective."

"What else did your trained eye notice?"

"The location of the coil of rope," Quincannon told him. "It was against the wall under the window, a placement where it was unlikely to snare the foot of even a drunkard who was familiar with his surroundings. But much more telling is the fact that in the darkness this morning, even with the aid of your lantern, I couldn't see the coil from outside the window. Nor the loop of rope caught around DuBois's ankle. The angle was wrong and the shadows inside too thick."

"Ah."

"Ah, indeed. When Ned burst into the cookshack he told you it looked as though DuBois had 'tripped on a coil of rope and cracked his skull wide open on the stove'—his exact words. But he couldn't have seen the rope from outside the window any more than I could; he had to've been *inside* the cabin. And if he was inside, then he must be the one who killed DuBois and rearranged the position of the body."

"And the barred door? How did he manage that trick?"

"Oh, it wasn't difficult," Quincannon said. "The trick likely isn't original with him; he's not clever enough to devise spur-of-the-moment subterfuges. I'll wager that somewhere in his travels he saw it done or heard of it being done, and since it takes very little time to arrange and he had all the tools he needed on his person, he seized on it as a way to ensure that DuBois's death would be taken as accidental."

"What tools?" Phillips asked.

"The hammer in his toolbelt. And a horseshoe nail, which I later found, slightly bent, on the cabin floor. Okay King told me Ned sometimes helped him around the blacksmith's shop, and a bullcook by nature fills his pockets with all manner of miscellaneous items gathered on his rounds."

"True enough. But a hammer and a horseshoe nail . . . that's *all* he used?"

"That's all," Quincannon said. "He drove the nail into the door high up near its outer edge no more than a quarter-inch deep. Then he set one end of the crossbar into the bracket on the hinge side, and rested the bar's other end on the nail. The door could still be opened inward with the bar in that diagonal position. Not far, only a few inches, but far enough for a man as thin as Ned to squeeze through. I found a vertical gouge in the bar where the bracket had cut into it during the squeeze. Once Ned was outside, he had only to pull the door closed once or at the most twice with enough force to dislodge the nail. When the nail bent and fell, the upper end of the bar dropped into the second bracket and completed the seal. As simple as that."

Phillips was shaking his head. "You're a marvel, Quincannon, you really are. How many other detectives could've done what you've done here, and in such a short time?"

Quincannon smiled modestly around the stem of his briar. "None, Mr. Phillips," he said. "Not even Allan Pinkerton himself."

LATER THAT DAY, AFTER HE had returned to Verdi and handed Nevada Ned over to the sheriff there, Quincannon sent a wire to Sabina in San Francisco.

ARRIVING HOME SIX PM TRAIN TOMORROW STOP DUBOIS MURDERED BUT BAFFLING CRIME SWIFTLY SOLVED AND CULPRIT ARRESTED AFTER FIERCE STRUGGLE STOP ALL BENNETT

JEWELRY RECOVERED STOP MASTER DETECTIVE AND DOTING
PARTNER SURELY DESERVING OF CELEBRATION AND SPECIAL
REWARD COMMA DONT YOU AGREE QM

He had her reply in less than an hour. It said simply and eloquently:

NO

Of course, one of the qualifications to be a successful mystery writer is a knack for figuring out puzzles. Some writers have more than just a knack for puzzle-solving, they have a love for it. John Harvey deals in puzzles of human relationships, much like his series detective Charlie Resnick. Resnick recently appeared in the novels *Easy Meat* and *Cutting Edge*. Here he makes a welcome return to our pages as well, solving the case of a burglar who isn't what he seems.

# Bird of Paradise
## JOHN HARVEY

It was still surprisingly cold for the time of year, already well past Lent, and Sister Teresa kept her topcoat belted but unbuttoned, so that the lower part of it flared open as she strode through the stalled traffic at the corner of Radford Road and Gregory Boulevard, revealing a knee-length grey wool skirt and pale grey tights which Grabianski, watching from the window of the Asian confectioner's, thought were more than pleasingly filled.

He popped something pink and sugary into his mouth and smiled appreciatively. One of life's natural observers, he never failed to enjoy those incidental pleasures that chance and patience brought his way: a brown flycatcher spied on the edge of Yorkshire moorland, the narrow white ring around its eye blinking clear from its nest; a chink of light just discernible through the blinds of a bedroom window four storeys up, suggesting the window may have been left recklessly unfastened; the stride of a mature woman, purposeful and strong, as she makes her way through the city on an otherwise unremarkable April day.

Casually, Grabianski stepped out onto the street. He was a well-built man, broad-shouldered and tall, no more than five or six pounds overweight for his age, somewhere in the mid forties. His face was round rather than lean, and freshly shaved; the dark hair on his head had yet to thin. His eyes were narrowed and alert as he angled his head and saw, away to his right, the woman he had noticed earlier, passing now between two youths on roller blades before rounding the corner and disappearing from sight.

Dressed in civilian clothes as Sister Teresa was, Grabianski would have been surprised to learn that she was a nun.

THE SISTERS OF OUR LADY of Perpetual Help were dedicated to the deliverance of succour and salvation to the needy, those who were, for whatever reason, less fortunate than their neighbours. Or, as Sister Teresa's fellow worker, Sister Bonaventura, expressed it, the more, economically challenged members of the urban underclass. Sister Bonaventura was a *Guardian* reader through and through.

Originally, the sisters had continued to wear their traditional vestments while working in the community and could often be seen setting up their late-night soup stall in the market square or ascending the steps towards the old General Hospital, for all the world like sumptuous magpies denied the power of flight. But with the decline of the city into an awkwardly romanticised version of its former self, fake minstrels and archers on every street corner and working models of everything from flour mills to four-loom weaving, no one gave credence to the belief that nuns perambulating in their proper habit were real nuns at all. Resting actors employed by the city council to entertain the tourists, drama students supplementing their grants in ecclesiastical drag, that was what people assumed. So now Sister Teresa and the others wore their simple white shifts and coarse grey wool only when they knelt to prayer each morning at six in the small community house where they lived, changing into civilian clothing before stepping out into the jostling world.

Most of what they wore came to them as a result of charitable donations or after-hours visits to the nearest Oxfam shop, though rumour, of necessity unsubstantiated, had it that Sister Marguerite's underwear was silk and had been ordered on approval from one of the boxed advertisements at the back of the *Sunday Times*.

The three of them, Sister Teresa, Sister Bonaventura, and Sister Marguerite, had been working together now for almost two years and in the summer they were due to return to their convent outside Felixstowe for six months of silent contemplation and spiritual healing. As Sister Bonaventura put it, an enforced visit to the health farm without any of the benefits of whirlpools or colonic irrigation.

The house they lived in was attached to the community centre in Hyson Green, itself a former church which had fallen on agnostic times. Deconsecrated, it was home to a variety of worthy enterprises, from a twice-weekly mother-and-toddler club, through yoga and enabling sessions for recovering alcoholics, to the evening youth club and disco. Fridays, Saturdays, and alternate Thursdays, Sister Marguerite, whose room was closest to the dividing wall, was lulled to sleep by the insistently sampled bass lines of Jazzmatazz and the near-ecclesiastical pleading of black rappers whose every third injunction included the word "bitch" or worse.

This and other highly colourful expressions had been tagged on the walls and stairwells of the low block of flats Sister Teresa was now entering, no longer even bothering to try the lift, but walking instead up to the third-floor balcony where cat shit and used works shared space with several tubs of late daffodils and bright purple pansies and washing hung from lines diagonally stretched from wall to railing, railing to wall.

Teresa rang the bell of number thirty-seven and waited while Shana Palmer turned down the television, hushed the baby, pushed aside the three-year-old, and paused to light another Embassy Filter on her way to the door.

"Sister . . ."

"Shana, how are we today? The little one, she got over her cough, did she?" Teresa said nothing about the bruise that was thickening around the young woman's left eye. Eighteen, nineteen? For certain she had not reached twenty-one.

"Cup of tea, Sister?"

"That'd be lovely, thanks."

Teresa followed her through the narrow hallway, jammed with pushchair and tricycle, free newspapers, unopened junk mail, and broken toys, into the kitchen where the three-year-old pulled at the legs of her mother's jeans and whined for whatever she couldn't have. Waiting for the kettle to boil, Teresa looked out through the postage-stamp window at the block of flats opposite, almost identical save that more of them were boarded up.

"Biscuit, Sister?"

"No, thanks."

They went into the living room and sat at either end of the sofa that served as the three-year-old's bed, the baby cossetted in blankets and sucking on its dummy in half-sleep. In the corner, on TV, a modishly efficient woman in a floral-print dress and that morning's makeover explained how to choose the best cuts of lamb from your local organic butcher.

Teresa waited until she had finished her first mug of tea and declined a second before leaning towards Shana and touching her lightly on the forearm. "Don't you think it's time, Shana, we had another talk about finding you and the children a place in a refuge?"

GRABIANSKI HAD WAITED SEVERAL MINUTES more before heading east along the Boulevard, his meeting with Vernon Thackray timed for the quarter-hour and Thackray, like himself, was a stickler for punctuality. And sure enough, there was the car, a dark blue Volvo estate, pulled in at the upper corner of the space on the Forest Recreation Ground allotted to drivers wishing to Park & Ride.

Grabianski skirted the parking area, so as to approach the vehicle from the driver's side. Thackray was behind the wheel, head resting back against the padded extension to the seat, eyes closed, the music seeping out through the inch of lowered window something Grabianski recognised as baroque and nothing more. Albinoni, Pergolesi, one of those. Vivaldi, he was certain Thackray would have considered too common by half.

He was three strides away from the car when Thackray opened his eyes and smiled. "Jerzy. Good to see you again. Come on, get in, why don't you? We'll take a drive."

The interior smelt of leather polish and astringent, doubtlessly expensive cologne. Anyone else who knew Grabianski well enough to greet him by his first name would have used the Anglicised "Jerry."

As they pulled out onto the main road, Thackray made a vague circling gesture with his head. "Find things much changed?"

Grabianski's response was noncommittal, vague.

"Three years, is it?"

"Four."

"I'm surprised you haven't been back before."

Beneath his coat, Grabianski was aware of his shoulders tensing. "I'm surprised I'm here now."

Thackray laughed and swerved to the inside of a Jessop's van that was signalling right ahead of the Clarendon roundabout. "Clumber Park. I thought we'd take a trip out to feed the ducks."

WHEN HE HAD LAST BEEN in the city, those four years before, Grabianski had been partnered up with a skinny second-storey artist named Grice, an individual of notably limited imagination, save where gaining illegal access was concerned—there he was almost second to none.

Jewelery, that was their speciality, that and the few antiques Grabianski recognised as not only genuine but likely to fetch a good return; the baubles they sent by express to a silversmith with premises on Sauchiehall Street, Glasgow, the eventual proceeds making their discreet way into a pair of pseudonymously held accounts a safe interval later.

All had been going well until they had the misfortune to come across a sizable quantity of almost pure cocaine in someone's bedroom safe and Grabianski had allowed Grice to convince him it was a good plan to sell it back to the owner, a television director of decidedly moderate stature. Unfortunately, he turned out to be only holding the coke for one of the local suppliers, after which things not only got complicated but nasty. And that was without Grabianski falling in lust with the director's wife.

In the end, the only way Grabianski could avoid a lengthy prison term was to help the police with their enquiries, set up the aforementioned dealer, and turn Queen's evidence on his partner. The result, a suspended sentence and an invitation from the local constabulary to get out of town. And now he was back.

No wonder his neck muscles were uncomfortably tight.

\*     \*     \*

THERE WAS THE USUAL SELECTION of mallards and pintails, along with a small flock of shovellers, consisting entirely of flatheaded, blue-winged drakes. Lower down, at the far northern end of the main lake, a clamour of Canada geese stalked the two men incessantly, greedy for anything they might have in their pockets and be prepared to throw away. The water looked grey and cold, its surface turning in the wind.

"I've had it checked four weeks out of the last five," Thackray was saying. "Leaves the house between seven and seven-twenty and never back before eleven-fifteen."

"Theatre? Cinema?"

"Bridge club. Up on Mansfield Road. Duplicate. Quite good, seemingly. Plays a modified Acol."

"Hmm." Grabianski nodded, unimpressed. He was a straightforward never-mess-with-a-minor-suit, four-no-trumps-is-strong-and-asking-for-aces kind of player himself.

"Here." Thackray took a sheet of graph paper from his inside pocket and the nearest dozen geese started honking in earnest.

The plan of the house interior had been neatly drawn in violet ink, the position of the alarm in red, the paintings marked clearly in green, one angled above the other on the drawing room wall, their exact dimensions noted at the bottom right corner of the sheet. Neither so large that they could not be fitted into a large holdall.

"And the alarm, it's not connected directly through to the police?"

Thackray shook his head and they walked on, turning into a stiffening breeze. "Not anymore."

"Any idea how she got hold of them?" Grabianski asked. "Dalzeils. Hardly ten a penny."

"Handed down, apparently. In the family for a couple of generations. Gambling debt originally."

"Sentimental value, then. Seems a shame."

Thackray fingered a three-inch cigar from his breast pocket and let the cellophane wrapping waft out across the lake. "Look at it this way, Jerzy, what we're doing, it's a public service. Liberating art for the nation."

"At least there'll be the insurance."

"Not so, apparently. Let the policy lapse last day in March. Cost of the premiums, I suppose. Works of art like that in private hands, can't be cheap."

"So if she loses them she's left with nothing."

"Social work now, is it? Distressed gentlefolk?"

Grabianski growled and continued walking.

"At least," Thackray went on blithely, "they're going to a good home, so that's one thing you don't have to fret about. Japanese banker, anniversary present for his second wife." Thackray's face broke into a rare smile. "Just the kind of sentimental gesture, Jerzy, I should have thought you would have appreciated more than most."

RESNICK HAD BEEN WOKEN THAT morning soon after four, without being sure of the reason why. The smallest of the cats was nestling near the edge of his pillows; he had lain there aware of a vague sense of foreboding, listening to the birds outside the window and watching the steadily brightening light.

At half five, certain now he would not fall back to sleep, he had risen and padded to the bathroom and the shower. By the time he had pulled on some clothes and reached the kitchen, the other cats had joined him, all save Dizzy content to wait patient by their bowls while Resnick opened a fresh can of food and found milk in the fridge. The six o'clock news summary told of slaughtered cattle and bankrupt British beef farmers, bombs in the Lebanon, first reports of a police officer being shot dead in Liverpool, more details promised as they became known. The magnolia tree that leaned across the low wall from his neighbour's garden had started, at last, to unfold into bloom. When he stood for a moment at the back door, staring out, he felt the first fall of rain against his face, faint and indefinite as if it too would not last.

He arrived at the police station early, earlier than usual; Kevin Naylor, the young DC who had drawn first shift, still sorting through the duty officer's report of the night's activities, breaking it down into categories before setting the file on Resnick's desk. Burglaries Naylor would initially deal with himself, the rest would be for Resnick, as Detective Inspector, to prioritise and hand on to the other members of the squad.

"Quiet night?" Resnick asked, glancing at a fax that had come in from Manchester CID during the night, asking for information about a runaway girl of fourteen.

"Passable, sir. Usual bit of activity in the Park. Three houses broken into on Tennis Drive; last one, the owner got up for a pee round about two, looked out the window, and there were these blokes lifting his twenty-three-inch Sony into a van."

"Blokes?"

"Two of them; another in the driver's seat, he thinks. Not sure."

"And the van?"

"Green, apparently. Dark green. If you can trust colours under those antique gas lamps they're so proud of. Old post-office van, sounds like, sprayed over."

"He wrote down the number?"

"Two letters missing. Like I say, the lighting . . ."

"Yes. I know. You'll get around there sharpish."

"First call."

The Park was not a park at all: a private estate principally made up of large

Victorian houses sporting stained glass and ornate decoration and originally designed to show off the wealth and taste of the mine owners and lace merchants who had lorded it in the latter half of the last century. Now it was home to barristers and account executives and Porsche owners who never seemed to work at all. Smack in the centre of the city as it was, the place attracted burglars the way a mangy dog had fleas.

"Remember that couple who worked the Park a few years back," Naylor said, making conversation as he poured the tea. "One of them built a bit like you, big, the other a scrawny little bugger. Turning over this place when the bloke as lived there come back unexpected, took one look at 'em and had a heart attack. Big bloke called emergency services, hung around to give him mouth-to-mouth."

"Saved his life."

"What was his name now? Something foreign. Polish, wasn't it?"

"Grabianski," Resnick said, of Polish ancestry himself. "Jerzy Grabianski."

"Wonder what became of him then?"

Resnick shrugged broad shoulders. "Retrained, maybe. Paramedic, something of the sort." It was a nice idea and one he didn't believe for a minute.

Three hours later, when Resnick was in conference with his superintendent and Naylor was still out and about knocking on doors, Grabianski was watching with considerable pleasure as Sister Teresa crossed Gregory Boulevard. And a little more than an hour after that, Resnick selecting cheese and turkey breast for his sandwich at the nearby deli while Naylor checked through vehicle licences and registrations in the CID office, Grabianski was enjoying the fresh air and the ducks and contemplating the detailed drawing of the house in the Park which was home, just for the present, to a pair of watercolours by the British Impressionist Herbert Dalzeil.

SISTER TERESA HAD MADE THREE more home visits after calling on Shana Palmer, that particular issue no more resolved than it had been when she had arrived. At lunchtime, she had stopped off at the Help Line centre run in conjunction with the local BBC radio station and busied herself with everything from sorting through the previous week's backlog of mail to counselling a fifteen-year-old boy who feared he might be gay, feared what his father would do if he found out, feared he might already have contracted AIDS.

She then went into the studio for her regular weekly spot on the afternoon show, answering questions from callers about spiritual and other problems that were bothering them, mostly, she found, the latter. As usual, she ended by asking for donations or volunteers for the Help Line, thanked both presenter and producer, and exited through the rear car park, having promised Sister Marguerite she would pop into Tesco's and buy a Sara Lee pecan pie for her birthday.

A dozen paces into the car park a hand grabbed at her hair, an arm was thrown tight about her neck, and she was wrenched backwards and thrown heavily against the rear wall.

"Help?" Paul Palmer said, brandishing a fist in Sister Teresa's face. "I'll give you help. All the help you soddin' need."

And he began to punch her in the face and breasts, kick viciously against her legs, and drive his knee into her groin.

THACKRAY DROPPED GRABIANSKI AT THE York Street entrance to the Shopping Centre and carried on his way towards the London Road roundabout and the river; within the hour he would be safely ensconced behind closed doors in Stamford, hotting up his modem with faxes to the Far East and cryptic messages on the Internet.

Grabianski had one of the swing doors half open, mind set on a bottle of vodka and some designer potato chips, when he heard cries coming from somewhere behind him: cries of pain and shouts of anger from the other side of the narrow street, from somewhere amongst the vehicles that were tightly clustered beyond the low brick wall. Others, passing, heard them and hurried on. Grabianski vaulted the wall and saw the couple towards the rear door, the man lashing out wildly and the woman half spread-eagled on the ground.

"Come near my wife again, you interfering bitch, and—"

Palmer broke off, hearing the sound of someone at his back, half-turned, another warning on his lips, and met the heel of Grabianski's outthrust hand full force upon his nose. The snap of cartilage was dredged through snot and blood.

"Bastard!" Palmer tried to shout, but something blurred and muffled was all that emerged. Grabianski picked him off his feet and half-threw, half-pushed him across the front of a Ford Orion, Palmer screaming as he fell.

"Don't . . ." began the woman, easing herself up onto all fours. "Please, don't . . ." as she levered herself back against the wall, head sinking gingerly forward till it came to rest against her knees.

"Don't what?" asked Grabianski gently, bending down before her.

"Don't hurt him."

He recognised the dull sparkle of the ring upon her hand. Why was it they always defended them, no matter what? One of her eyes was already beginning to close.

"A beating," Grabianski said, "no more than he deserves."

"No, no. Please." She fumbled for, then found, his wrist and clutched it tight. "I pray you."

Something about the way she said it made Grabianski think twice; he recognised her then, the woman who had been striding out in shades of grey, and felt a quickening of his pulse. Somehow, instead of her holding his wrist, he was holding her hand. Behind them, he heard her attacker scurry slew-footed away.

The muscles in the backs of Grabianski's legs were aching and he changed position, sitting down against the wall. Sister Teresa, blood dribbling from a cut alongside her mouth, was alongside him now, shoulders touching, and he was still holding her hand.

She found it strangely, almost uniquely, reassuring.

She said, "Thank you."

He said it was fine.

She asked him his name and he hers.

"Teresa," she said.

"Teresa what?"

And she had to think. "Teresa Whimbrel," she said and he smiled.

"What's amusing?" she asked, though a pain jolted through her side each time she spoke.

"Whimbrel," Grabianski said. "It's a bird. A sort of curlew." He was smiling. "Notably long legs."

He looked, she thought, decidedly handsome when he smiled, and something else besides. She wondered if that something might be dangerous.

"But I expect you know that already," he said.

She was looking at the fingers of his hand, broad-knuckled and lightly freckled with hair and curved about her own smaller hand. And showing no intention of letting go. She nodded to signify yes, she knew. There was a bird book back at the community house and Sister Bonaventura had pointed out the illustration. "A black and white cap on its head," she had said. "Just the way we would have looked once upon a time. Those unenlightened times."

"I think you should let go," she said.

"Um?"

"Of my hand."

"Oh." He asked another question instead. "Was that your husband? The man."

"Not mine."

He could feel the ring, though he could no longer see it. "But you are married?"

"In a way."

Grabianski raised an eyebrow, continuing to smile. "Which way is that?"

"A way you might find difficult to understand."

SHE LAY ON A NARROW bed in Accident and Emergency, bandaged, strapped, and salved. They had examined her carefully, wheeled her down to X-ray and back on two separate occasions, confirmed that two of her ribs were broken, but that, aside from internal bruising, there were no further injuries invisible to the naked eye.

"Lucky your saviour, he happen along when he did," the nurse said.

"Hmm," Sister Bonaventura commented, eyeing Grabianski appraisingly, "so that's who he is. He looks a little different in the pictures I've seen."

She and Sister Marguerite had rushed to the hospital as soon as they had heard, filling the small cubicle with anger, advice, and concern. When the young police officer had arrived to take a statement, Grabianski had discreetly removed himself, returning an hour later with flowers, an artfully wrapped box of dark soft-centred chocolates from Thorntons, and a copy of the *Collins' Field Guide to the Birds of Britain and Europe*; with the section on curlews clearly marked.

"Are you sure you're going to be all right?" Sister Marguerite asked, declining a second chocolate.

"Perfectly," Teresa replied. "The doctor's assured me there's no need for me to stay in overnight. And they'll provide an ambulance to take me home."

"That wasn't what I meant," Sister Marguerite said.

"I know what you meant."

Grabianski's presence filled the cubicle to the point of overflowing.

Leaving, the sister pressed an extra crucifix into Teresa's hand for good measure. The curtain she left ostentatiously open, and after a few moments Grabianski reached across and pulled it closed. The bustle of Accident and Emergency went on around them, muffled but nonetheless real.

"There's one question . . ." Grabianski began.

Teresa laughed. "There always is. Prostitutes and nuns, it's always the same one: How did a nice girl like you . . . ?"

But Grabianski was shaking his head; that wasn't the question.

NAYLOR KNOCKED ON RESNICK'S DOOR and waited. Behind him, the CID room was the usual monkey house of movement and overlapping conversations; telephones rang and were curtly answered or left to flounder in their own impatience; officers scrolled down VDUs, pecked two-fingered reports from keyboards, doodled loved ones' names on the backs of envelopes, listened on leaking headphones to taped interviews. At his desk near the head of the room, Naylor's sergeant, Graham Millington, was sporting a new haircut and freshly trimmed moustache and an almost-new check sports jacket, in the inside pocket of which nestled reservations for seats on the London train and two tickets for that evening's performance of *Sunset Boulevard*. Andrew Lloyd Webber and Petula Clark in the one evening; it was almost more than ordinary flesh and blood could stand.

Naylor heard Resnick's call of "Come in" just above the sergeant's shrilly whistled version of "As If We Never Said Goodbye."

"Kevin?" Amongst the papers littered over Resnick's desk were the remains of a toasted tallegio and ham sandwich and several empty takeout cups still smelling of strong espresso.

"Licence plate on the van, sir. Likely belongs to a ninety-four Fiesta reported stolen out in Bulwell three weeks back."

"Dead end, then."

"Not exactly. Youth as reported it missing, Tommy Farrell, been walking the thin and narrow since he left school."

"Charges?"

"Fraudulently claiming benefit, passing stolen cheques, possession of illegal substances, handling stolen goods. Probation on one, the others all dismissed."

"Insurance scam, then, the car? Nicked by his mates, switch the plates, sit back and wait for General Life or whoever to pay over the cheque."

"It's possible."

"So if one of Farrell's friends happened to own an old post-office van . . ."

"Exactly."

Resnick leaned forward in his chair. "That piece of paper in your hand, Kevin—wouldn't be a list of Farrell's known associates, would it?"

Grinning self-consciously, Naylor placed the sheet upon the desk.

"Mickey Redthorpe," Resnick read, "Michael Chester, Sean McGuane—he's in Lincoln doing three to five. Victor Canning, Barry Fielding, Billy Murdoch, Paul Palmer . . ."

Resnick looked up, fingers drumming across the name. "Aggravated burglary, Palmer, eighteen months inside?"

"Yes, sir. Released March first. Good behaviour."

"I wonder," Resnick said, smiling a little, "what the chances might be of finding friend Palmer the owner of a resprayed van?"

"A warrant or . . . ?"

"Too early. Take Mark with you, have a little nose around. Palmer's got a wife and kids, hasn't he? Probably not going anywhere in a hurry."

Naylor nodded. "Unless it's back inside."

GRABIANSKI WAS NOT AS CAUTIOUS. And although he preferred making his way into other people's property under the cover of darkness, on this occasion he was happy enough with the sound of the *EastEnders* theme tune and the sight of the living room door to the Palmer's flat closing behind Shana as she carried through the three-year-old.

Paul himself had made his way from the betting shop to the pub.

Grabianski checked both ways along the balcony, inserted the strip of plastic between front door and frame, and slipped the lock.

As soon as he was standing inside, the adrenalin grabbed him, jolting his veins. Being inside: forbidden. It was like sex, only better, purer; more controlled. He stood for several minutes, listening to sounds, breathing the air. Then made his way silently from room to room.

There was a rusted bayonet at the back of the cupboard alongside the double bed and a shoe box containing half a dozen stolen credit cards underneath it; burglary tools were secure in a duffel bag behind the waste pipe of the kitchen sink. The baby was sleeping in the back bedroom in a cot surrounded by several thousand pounds' worth of electrical equipment, including a top-of-the-range wide-screen Sony TV.

Just as Grabianski stepped out into the hallway, the living room door opened and Shana stood facing him, the almost empty mug of tea slipping from her hand.

"It's all right," Grabianski said softly. "There's no need to be afraid."

Which was when Paul Palmer entered through the front door, a six-pack of Special Brew at his side.

"You!"

Grabianski had the advantage of surprise and some forty extra pounds in weight; he grabbed Palmer by the front of his leather jacket and jerked him forward, kicking the door closed.

"You . . ."

"You already said that."

Palmer's voice was distorted by the width of plaster taped across his nose. Grabianski spun him round and, firmly holding his shoulders, smacked him, face first, against the wall.

Shana screamed and Paul fainted, unused to having his nose broken twice in the same day. When he came to and saw Grabianski was leaning over him, he flinched.

"Listen," Grabianski said, "if you ever go near that person again, I will break every other bone in your body. You know who I mean?"

Palmer blinked and grunted yes.

"And you believe me?"

He did.

"Good," Grabianski said, leaning away. "A little belief, it's a wonderful thing." He turned back at the door. "It might be an idea if you stopped thumping your wife, too. I imagine there's a self-help group you could go to, men and violence, something like that. You should look into it." And he walked off along the balcony, taking his time, though time was something he had precious little of—the owner of two rare Impressionist paintings would soon be sitting down to her first hand of the evening, busily counting points.

SINCE RESNICK HAD STOPPED USING the Polish Club with any regularity, when he did appear committee and staff fussed round him like swans with their wayward young; which only served to curtail his visits all the more. But halfway through a bottle of Polish lager with only the cats and CDs for company, he made a sudden decision to call a cab and go, even though it meant exchanging *Miles Davis Live at the Plugged Nickel* for an accordionist with a ruffled shirt and his heart on his sleeve.

He hadn't been in the club more than twenty minutes when, reflected in the mirror above the bar, he saw, approaching, someone he had thought he was unlikely ever to see again. He waited until Grabianski had taken the stool alongside his before holding out his hand. "Jerzy."

"Inspector."

"Charlie would do. Not as if I'm on duty."

"Ah." Grabianski smiled and ordered a bison-grass vodka, Resnick declining with a shake of the head. "Maybe not."

"No coincidence, then? You being here like this?"

"I phoned ahead."

"Something that couldn't wait till morning."

Grabianski shrugged.

"You're here on business?" Resnick asked.

"An old friend to meet." A smile spread across his face. "Two, if we include you."

It was Resnick's turn to smile. "That's what we are? Friends?"

They sat there awhile longer, not speaking, two men who might easily have been mistaken for brothers: big men with broad, heavy features whose families had fled their mother country in the first months of the war. In that room, with so many framed photographs of generals and fighter pilots on the walls, it was unnecessary to ask which war.

"Paul Palmer," Grabianski said, paying for his second vodka. The slight shift of expression on Resnick's face told him the name was not unknown.

"What about him?"

"If he was caught with a quantity of stolen goods on his premises, a few choice artifacts of the burglar's trade, what are the chances he might see serious time?"

"Depends. Sometimes, as well you know, there are extenuating circumstances."

"Not for the likes of Palmer."

Resnick thought he would chance another lager after all; if they were going to pull Paul Palmer it would be before the milk, and Graham Millington could take charge. Just the thing to get an overdose of Andrew Lloyd Webber out of his system.

"This isn't professional rivalry, I take it?" Resnick asked. "I mean, he's hardly in your class."

"Let's just say there are reasons for shutting him away where his temper won't do more harm."

Resnick frowned. "There's some history of domestic violence, I know. Is that what this is about? The wife? Shana, isn't it?"

"Not only her."

Resnick laughed. "I should have known with you there'd be a woman involved."

"It's not like that, Charlie."

"No?"

"Not this time."

Resnick remembered the alacrity with which the television director's wife had taken Grabianski to bed, bosom, and bath. "Whatever happened to Maria Roy?" he asked.

Grabianski shook his head, grinning despite himself. "You don't want to know."

"And this time?"

"I told you. . . ." But Resnick was staring at him from close range, and for a confirmed criminal Grabianski could be a hopeless liar. "This is different."

"Yes," Resnick said, not meaning it.

"Platonic."

"Of course."

"Charlie, she's a nun, for Christ's sake!"

Resnick's laughter was abrupt enough to turn heads way back across the room.

"No laughing matter, Charlie."

"So I've heard."

"This kid Palmer, he went for her. Could have been serious. Angry because she's been talking to his wife, advising her, you know, getting into a refuge, taking the kids."

Resnick nodded. "How come you're so certain about these stolen goods? They wouldn't be planted, by any chance, to lend us a helping hand?"

Grabianski shook his head. "Not my way."

"Okay. This is the second time I've got you to thank. Always assuming it pans out."

"Oh, it will." Draining his glass, Grabianski swung round on the stool and rose to his feet.

"You'll likely not be around to see it go down?"

"Likely not."

"Well," Resnick stood and again the two men shook hands, "it was good to see you again."

Grabianski nodded and began to turn away.

"I suppose I'd be wasting my breath telling you to keep your hands to what's rightfully yours?"

Grabianski kept on walking, through the door, along the broad corridor, and out onto the forecourt, where he climbed into the taxi he had instructed to wait. Before it had pulled away, Resnick was speaking to Lynn Kellogg on the telephone, informing her of the cab company and registration. "Get onto their controller, find out their position; if you can get the destination without arousing suspicion, so much the better. Then call in Mark and Kevin, sort out the surveillance between you, let me know how it's going. Send a driver to pick up my car and collect me here."

\*     \*     \*

GRABIANSKI STOOD IN THE FIRST-FLOOR drawing room, heavy velvet curtains drawn against the night. He was wearing the same dark blue suit as earlier, smartly polished shoes, new white cotton gloves. He was holding a torch in one hand, a Polaroid camera in the other. The canvas holdall was on the floor near his feet.

He positioned himself carefully before taking the pictures, capturing the paintings separately and together. They were, he thought, a wonderful pair. The first, earlier by some fifteen years, showed a farm boy close by the half-open gate to a field, some half-dozen sheep in the middle distance, an avenue of poplars making a diagonal right to left behind. It was a perfectly respectable, cleanly executed rural painting of its time; the kind the Royal Academy in the 1880s would have cherished. Possibly still did.

But it was the second which Grabianski cherished, an earlier study for what most critics considered Dalzeil's masterpiece, "Departing Day." It showed a stubbly, tilled landscape through the blur of fading light, the sun a yellow disc, faint through mottled sky. Patched along the low horizon were sparse purplish shadows, whether outbuildings or carts, or even cattle, it was neither possible nor desirable to know.

What had happened to Dalzeil between the two paintings, Grabianski was uncertain. Had he been smitten by the influence of Seurat, sudden as Saul on the road to Damascus, or had he fallen under the spell of Monet, who had exhibited in London only a few years before this work would have begun? More prosaically, had Dalzeil's failing health and badly deteriorating sight meant that this hazy vision of the world was the only one he had left?

It didn't matter. For Grabianski, most of what gave him pleasure in painting was here: the interplay of light and colour, the shifting texture of the paint, the mystery.

It was exquisite.

He felt a thread of envy for the woman who had lived with the joy of this painting for so long and considered what he was about to do. He checked his watch and unzipped the canvas bag.

DIVINE TURNED HIS BACK IN the direction of Resnick's car before uncapping his flask and tipping an inch or more of whisky into Kevin Naylor's coffee and then his own. Lynn Kellogg and Carl Vincent were somewhere off in the shrubbery, keeping guard over the rear of the house, while Divine and Naylor had positioned themselves to watch both the main entrance and the fire escape angling rustily down the side of the building. Resnick's driver had parked in shadow fifty yards along the street.

"Tell me why we're hanging about here like this, Kev?" Divine asked, "when there are nice warm pubs in spitting distance."

"Overtime?"

"Oh, yeah. Knew there was a reason."

"Hush up!" Naylor hissed. "Here he comes now."

They watched as Grabianski, somewhat larger than life, nonchalantly let himself out of the front door and headed for the low wrought-iron gate, swinging the holdall a little as he walked. Beneath the even crunch of his feet on the gravel came the firm click of a car door and then the sound of Resnick's feet approaching.

Fifteen yards along, Grabianski stopped. "Coincidence, Charlie?"

"Hardly that."

Grabianski scarcely turned as Divine and Naylor moved up on him from behind.

"You wouldn't care to show us, Jerzy, what you've got in the bag?"

Grabianski hesitated but not for long. "Why not?"

Naylor shone his torch as the zip was eased back; save some gloves, a torch, and a camera, the bag was empty.

"Not much of a haul," Divine observed.

"I've a receipt for the camera," Grabianski said, "if you think that's really necessary."

Resnick looked at him thoughtfully. "Why don't you come and sit in the car? Mark, Kevin, give the place the once-over just in case. Tell the others to call it a night."

RESNICK TOLD HIS DRIVER TO take a walk. He pushed a cassette into the car stereo and kept the volume low: Monk playing "April in Paris," "I Surrender, Dear.""Why the change of mind?" he asked. "Or was it a change of heart?"

"How about a conversion?" Grabianski's smile was an angular as the music.

"How about you realised the risk you took in coming to me was too great? You must have known there was a chance I'd have you followed."

Grabianski leaned back against the inside of the door. "The truth?"

"What passes for it, maybe."

"You do know about the paintings? You know they're rare."

Resnick nodded. "A little. The owner was in touch awhile back about security."

"Always been a special favourite of mine, Dalzeil. Soon as I heard they were here, I had to see them. And what chance would I have otherwise?"

"Written and asked permission? Knocked on the door?"

"Not my way, Charlie. Besides, half an hour with one of the unsung masters, worth any amount of risk. Like standing up to your armpits in cold water for hours just to catch a glimpse of an Ivory Gull that's got lost on its way from the Arctic."

"Any amount of risk?" Resnick said.

"Come on, Charlie," Grabianski laughed. "You'll not bother charging me with this, scarce worth the paperwork. Besides, your lads, they'll not find as much as a speck of dust disturbed. And then there's always that small favour to repay."

Resnick reached over and clicked open the door. "London nowadays, isn't it? Notting Hill? Camden? Work enough down there, I should have thought. Art galleries, too."

Grabianski held out his hand but this time Resnick didn't take it; instead he watched in his rearview mirror as the tall figure merged into the dull glow of street lamps until he was no more than a purple shadow without shape or contour.

A WEEK LATER A PACKAGE arrived at the community house addressed to Sister Teresa. It contained two Polaroid pictures of a landscape painting, which Sister Bonaventura assured her was firmly in the Impressionist tradition, and a single feather, mottled brown and white, close to five inches long. Sister Marguerite thought it might have come from a curlew, but Teresa assured her it was a whimbrel and produced her book as evidence. There was neither letter nor note.

Only later, looking at the photographs alone, did she see, faintly to the side of one of them, the reflection of a man seemingly holding a camera. Her saviour. At least, that's what she believed.

Jan Grape made her mark as an editor in the mystery field with the publication of *Deadly Women*, co-edited by Dean James and Ellen Nehr, a critical study of the female mystery writer. Her short fiction has appeared in the anthologies *Malice Domestic II* and *Midnight Louie's Pet Detectives*. "Front Row Seat" makes the case that sometimes revenge is best viewed from a distance.

# A Front-Row Seat
## JAN GRAPE

I awoke on that cold wet March morning with a fierce sinus headache over my right eye. Things went downhill from there. I broke a fingernail and tore a run in my panty hose. I had to dress twice because I snagged my sweater and had to change. When I walked out the front door I banged my little toe against the potted plant I'd brought inside for protection from the cold. "Damn Sam." I limped out to my car and sank into the seat gratefully.

Some mornings should be outlawed, I thought, but I managed to get to the office which I own and operate with my partner, Cinnamon Jemima Gunn, at eight-thirty A.M. on the dot. C. J., as she's known to all except a few close friends, would have killed me if I'd opened up late. With the way things were going, death didn't sound half bad.

At nine a man pushed open the door with its distinct sign, G & G investigations. He stopped cold in the middle of the reception area and looked around as if searching for someone.

He wasn't handsome. His nose was too long and it hooked at the end, ruining his overall attractiveness. Dark, blue-black hair waved across his head and curled down over the tips of his ears. His eyes were blue-gray and crinkle lines radiated outward from the corners. He was probably no taller than five feet ten with a rounded abdomen and torso, like he'd rather sit in front of the tube and veg out than work out. I'd guess his age around fifty.

"May I help you?" I asked.

His navy suit looked expensive, but off-the-rack, and he added a floral print tie to spiff up his white shirt. He wore a black London Fog-style raincoat, open and unbelted, and a perplexed look.

"Do you need an investigator?" I asked when he didn't answer my first question.

"Is Mr. Gunn here?" His voice was husky, like he had a cold.

"There is no Mr. Gunn. Only C. J., but she's in court . . ."

"She? I don't understand. I want to talk to Mr. C. J. Gunn." His annoyance was obvious in his derisive tone.

"C. J. isn't a mister. C. J.'s a woman."

"I'll speak to your boss, then."

"I'm it." I smiled. "I mean, I own this agency. Well, C. J. and I are co-owners actually. I'm Jenny Gordon."

"You mean this detective agency is run by a bunch of damn women?"

"That's about it, sir."

"Well, shit." He turned, walked out, and slammed the door.

"Up yours, fella," I said to his retreating footsteps.

I didn't waste time wondering about him. It happened occasionally—some macho pea brain unable to hire a female private eye because of his own ego. I shrugged and turned back to the computer terminal.

Electronic technology baffles me. I think I'm a little intimidated to think a machine is smarter than I am. But C. J., who's a computer whiz, had set up a program for our business invoices and all I had to do was fill in the blanks, save, and print. I could handle that much.

G & G's bank account was dangerously low and unless we collected on some delinquent accounts or came up with a rich client or two, we were in deep doo-doo.

We'd worked too hard for that, but it meant sending out timely statements and following up with telephone calls. Our biggest headaches were large insurance companies that always seemed to run sixty to ninety days past due.

I got all the blank spaces filled on the next account and saved the file, but before I could push the button to print, the telephone rang.

"Ms. Gordon, this is Dr. Anthony Randazzo." The husky voice was familiar. "I want to apologize for the way I acted a few minutes ago."

So, the piggy chauvinist was a doctor. His name rang a bell in my head, but I couldn't connect it. My first impulse was to hang up in his ear, but he kept talking fast—as if he could read my mind.

"Ms. Gordon, I've been under a lot of stress . . ." He laughed, sounding nervous not jovial. "Boy, does that sound trite or what?"

I waited, unsure if he expected an answer.

"I honestly am sorry for storming out of your office. I acted like some idiot with a caveman mentality. I need an investigator and your firm was highly recommended."

I'm not a die-hard feminist, but the emotional side of my brain was yelling hang up on this bastard while the practical left brain was reminding me we needed a paying client and the doctor could be one. I wondered who was wicked enough to send this clown in our direction. "May I ask who recommended you?"

"My niece works as a receptionist for Will Martin's law firm."

Oh, hell. Will and Carolyn Martin were counted among my closest friends. Good friends aren't supposed to send the jerks of the world to you.

"I've never met Mr. Martin," he continued, "but my niece thinks highly of him."

Whew! That explained it. When asked, Will automatically would have said, "G & G." Knowing this guy wasn't a client of Will's made me feel better. "Dr. Randazzo, perhaps I should refer . . ."

"Please, Ms. Gordon, don't judge me too quickly. My wife and I desperately need help. It's a matter of life or death."

Now that he was contrite he was much easier to take, but I still wasn't sure I wanted to work with him. "I'm not . . ."

"Please don't say no yet, let me explain briefly. Two months ago, I was involved in a malpractice suit. You probably heard about it."

The bell in the back of the old brain pinged. Anyone old enough to read or watch television had heard. Because of the high costs of health care nowadays, which the medical profession tried to blame on things like malpractice suits, the media had talked of nothing else. Randazzo was a plastic surgeon. A woman had sued him for ruining her face. She hadn't looked too bad on TV, but the jury awarded her a huge amount. Mostly for pain and anguish, as I recalled. The doctor had lost and lost big.

"Yes, I recall," I said, wondering why he needed a PI now. "But the lawsuit's over, isn't it?"

"Yes. Except for working out the payment schedule." He cleared his throat. "But I think our problem has a definite connection. I'm really worried and will be happy to pay a consulting fee for your time."

"I, uhmmm . . ."

"Would five hundred be appropriate?"

He got my attention. Five big ones would certainly help our bank account. I could probably work for Attila the Hun for five hundred dollars. Okay, so I can be bought. "Would you like to make an appointment?"

"If you're free this evening, my wife and I are having a few friends over for drinks and hors d'oeuvres. If you and Ms. Gunn could join us—whatever you decide to do afterward is entirely up to you, but the five hundred is yours either way."

"What time?"

"Seven, and thanks for not hanging up on me."

Dr. Randazzo gave me directions to his house and we hung up.

I had the invoices ready to mail by the time C. J. returned.

She remembered the Randazzo lawsuit. "Five hundred dollars just to talk?"

"That's what the man said."

"Are you sure he's not kinky?" A knowing look was on her cola nut-colored face and her dark eyes gleamed wickedly.

"Maybe. But he said his wife and other people would be there. It didn't sound too kinky."

"Hummm. Guess the lawsuit didn't bankrupt him if he's got five C notes to throw around." C. J. worked her fingers across the computer keyboard.

"He probably has hefty malpractice insurance," I said.

I watched as she punched keys and letters appeared on the monitor in front of her eyes. C. J. can find out the most illuminating information about people in only a matter of minutes. With my technology phobia I don't understand modems, networks, and E-mail and have no idea what it is that she does. I've also decided I really don't want to know any details.

"Let's just check on his finances. I'm sure he has investments, stocks and bonds, real estate and what have you. Never knew a doctor who didn't." A few minutes later she muttered an "Ah-ha. Looks like Randazzo was shrewd enough to put a nice nest egg into his wife's name, but his medical practice *is* close to bankruptcy." She printed up some figures, stuck the papers in a folder, and we closed the office and left.

Since my apartment is only a few blocks from our office and her place is halfway across town, C. J. keeps a few clothes and essentials there for convenience. We took turns showering and dressing.

C. J. wanted to drive. Since she liked to change cars about every six months she'd recently leased a Dodge Dakota SE pickup truck. As roomy and as comfortable as a car. But what she was proudest of was a fancy sound system, tape deck, and CD player. She popped a CD in and turned up the volume.

A woman sang, "I wanna be around to pick up the pieces, when somebody breaks your heart."

"All right." I laughed and she raised an eyebrow. I picked up the box and read about the songs and the artists. These were golden oldies by Peggy Lee, Nancy Wilson, Sarah Vaughn, Judy Garland, and others. It wasn't her usual type of music.

"That's Dinah Washington," she said. "I knew you were gonna get a kick out of this one."

I'd been hooked on country music forever but a couple of years ago I discovered Linda Ronstadt singing ballads from the '30s and '40s. And the funny thing is, I remember my parents playing records and dancing to music like this. It's an early memory and a rare one with my parents having fun. Somehow my mother's long unsuccessful battle with cancer had wiped out too many good memories.

I listened to Dinah singing about her old love getting his comeuppance, and how sweet revenge is as she's sitting and applauding from a front-row seat.

"Cripes," I said. "That really knocks me out. I've gotta have a copy."

"I'll give you this one, girl, after I've listened to it."

The Randazzos' house was located in the hills above Lake Travis, west of Austin. After a couple of wrong turns we found the brick pillars that flanked the entrance of the long drive. The blacktop curved into the front of the house and ended in a concrete parking area. C. J. pulled up between a dark green Jaguar and a tan Volvo.

The Spanish-modern house was large and rambling, made of tan brick with a burnt-sienna tile roof and built onto the side of a hill. The arched windows were outlined in the same color tile as the roof and black wrought-iron bars covered the bottom halves. The Saint Augustine grass was a dun-muckle brown with little shoots of green poking out—normal for this time of year.

We got out, walked up to the ornately carved double doors, and I pushed the oval-lighted button beside the facing.

"Some joint," C. J. said, as we waited.

A young man dressed in a cable-knit sweater with a Nordic design and charcoal gray slacks opened the door. Late twenties, blond and blue eyed with a Kevin Costner smile. He was so handsome my breath caught in my throat to look at him.

When I said Dr. Randazzo expected us he frowned, but stepped back and said, "Come in."

We were in an entry hall that ran across most of the width of the front and was open-ended on both sides. I couldn't recall ever seeing a house where you entered into a width-wise hallway.

We were directly in front of and looking into a large square atrium. Behind the glass wall was a jungle of green plants, shrubs, and trees, with a spray of water misting one side. The darkening sky was visible through the roof and I saw a couple of small green birds flitting back and forth between some trees.

The scene was exquisite and several moments passed before I could find my voice. "I—I'm Jenny Gordon and this is C. J. Gunn. We were to see Dr. Randazzo at seven."

"I'm Christopher Lansen and I work with Tony Randazzo." His voice was nasal and high-pitched and it sure didn't go with his looks. "And I'm sorry, Tony isn't here at the moment."

"Oh?" I asked, "A medical emergency?"

"I don't think so. I mean, I don't know exactly."

"I'm sure Tony will be back shortly, please come in," said a woman coming into the hall from the right side. Her voice was soft and there was no trace of a Texas accent. She sounded as if she'd had elocution lessons and had graduated at the top of the class.

She was dressed in a soft blue silk shirtwaist dress, belted with a gold chain, and wore gold hoop gypsy earrings. She was tall and willowy with dark hair pulled severely back into a bun. She would have looked elegant except she hunched her shoulders instead of standing straight.

She had high cheekbones and almond-shaped dark eyes. There was a hint of Spanish or American Indian in her tight, unlined and unblemished face. Her age could have been anywhere from thirty to sixty. Probably has had a face-lift, I thought.

"I'm Marta Randazzo. Are you the investigators my husband hired?"

"Uh . . . yes," I said. "And please call me Jenny. My partner is C. J."

The young man put his hand on her arm. "Marta, why don't you go back inside and I'll talk . . ."

"No, Chris. I, I want to speak to them now." Her voice sounded tentative, as if she hated to contradict him. She turned abruptly and walked down the hallway toward the left, leaving us no choice except to follow.

"Mrs. Randazzo," said C. J., who was walking directly behind the woman. "I should clarify something. Your husband asked us over for a consultation only. He hasn't actually hired us."

Marta Randazzo entered a huge den/family room. At least half of my apartment could fit into this one room, but maybe it seemed bigger because of the glass wall of the atrium. Another wall was taken up by a fireplace large enough to roast a side of beef. The room's decor was in Southwestern Indian colors. Navajo rugs and wall hangings, Kachina dolls, framed arrowhead and spear points, Zuni pottery, turquoise and silver jewelry knick-knacks were everywhere. In a small alcove to one side of the fireplace was a wet bar. A sofa, love seat, and three chairs were covered in Indian-design fabrics.

It felt like déjà vu until I remembered I'd once been in a living room decorated with Indian things. Inexplicably, I couldn't remember when or where. "It's a lovely room," I told her. "I like it."

"Thank you." She motioned for us to sit, indicating the sofa, and she sat on a chair to our right. Christopher Lansen took a spot standing near the fireplace.

"I believe Chris told you Tony isn't here at the moment," Marta said. "He should be back soon."

But she didn't sound too certain. "I'm sure . . . I, uh, know he didn't forget you were coming. . . ."

Chris Lansen said, "Marta, I don't think . . ."

"Chris?" Marta Randazzo stiffened. "Let me finish, please."

Lansen turned away and walked to the window staring out into the darkness. His body language indicated he didn't like something she'd said or was about to say.

"Tony mentioned you were coming." Marta got up, walked to the mantel, ignoring Lansen, and took a piece of paper out from under a Zuni bowl. "He had me write out a check for you." She walked over and held it out to me.

I automatically reached for the paper and looked at her. I glimpsed a flicker of something in her eyes just before she turned and sat down, but then it was gone. Fear maybe? Or despair. I couldn't be sure.

The check was made out to G & G investigations for five hundred dollars and signed by Marta Randazzo.

"Mrs. Randazzo," said C. J. "Perhaps we should wait until your husband returns and we can talk to him."

"I agree," said Chris. He looked at Marta with a stern expression. Some battle of wills was going on between the two of them. "He'll be back soon." Lansen's tone was emphatic. "He and I planned to talk about the surgery I'm doing on Mrs. Franklin tomorrow. He wouldn't forget about that."

"Oh, you're a doctor, too?" I asked, hoping to ease the tension. He and Marta were definitely uptight.

"Yes. I'm an associate of Tony's. A junior partner."

"We could wait a little while for him if it won't inconvenience you, Mrs. Randazzo." I tried to hand the check back to her. She ignored it, so I placed it on the end table next to me.

"Please, call me Marta," she said. She jutted her chin slightly. "That check means you are working for *me*, doesn't it?"

"We're here on consult. That was my agreement with Dr. Randazzo."

"Then, in that case I'm consulting you. It must be obvious to you both . . . I should explain."

Chris Lansen cleared his throat and Marta Randazzo looked at him, her face creased with a frown. Her chin jutted out again briefly before she relaxed. "Jenny, C. J.? Would you like something to drink? Coffee or something stronger?"

"Coffee would be fine," said C. J. and I agreed.

"Chris? Would you go make coffee for my guests?" Her tone sounded like an order, but she didn't raise her voice.

He gave her a look as if she'd just asked him to wash the windows or something equally distasteful, but he left the room without speaking.

"Jenny, my husband has disappeared," she said when Lansen was gone. "I was taking a shower. After I dressed and came out here, Tony was gone. I assumed he'd gone for a walk, but that was at five o'clock and he still isn't back yet."

"Have you looked for him?" I asked. She reminded me of someone, but I didn't know who.

"Yes. Chris came over about six and when I mentioned I was getting worried about Tony, Chris got into his car and drove around looking. He didn't find Tony."

"Your husband walks regularly?" C. J. asked.

"Yes, if something is bothering him. It's his way of relieving stress. But he's usually back after about twenty to thirty minutes."

"Could his disappearance have something to do with why he wanted to hire us?" I noticed out of the corner of my eye that C. J. was poised on the edge of her seat.

C. J. got up, muttering something about going to help with the coffee and went in the same direction Chris had gone. I knew she was using the old divide-and-question-separately technique.

"Maybe," said Marta.

"Do you know why he . . ."

"Yes," said Marta. "Someone's trying to kill me."

"What makes you think someone is trying to kill you?"

"Someone followed me all last week. The same man I think, I'm sure it was the same car." She began twisting the hem of her skirt as she talked and I noticed bruises on her inner thigh near her left knee.

"After I became aware of this man," she continued, "I realized he'd probably followed me even before that. Then night before last that same car tried to run my car off the road. You drove up here and saw those treacherous curves. And the cliffs are pretty steep. I almost went over the edge. It scared me silly."

"Why would anyone want you dead?"

"I don't know, uh . . . maybe it's someone from the Davis family—wanting to get back at Tony."

"The Davis family?"

"The people who sued my husband."

"But why? They won their case."

C. J. and Chris came back into the room. He was carrying a silver serving tray with four china cups sitting in saucers.

Chris said, "My thoughts exactly. Why would anyone from the Davis family . . ."

"Money might not be enough," said C. J.

"What?" asked Marta.

"Revenge can be sweeter than money." C. J. sat on the sofa where she'd been before while Chris placed the tray on the coffee table. "Mrs. Davis feels she has suffered," she said. "And now it's Mrs. Randazzo who must suffer."

Chris carefully handed a saucered cup of coffee to each of us and then took his and returned to the fireplace. "That's what Tony thought," he said, placing his coffee on the mantel. "But I think it's all hogwash."

"I know what you think, Chris. You've been vocal enough about it." Marta's voice got lower and that made her words sound more ominous. "You think I'm imagining all this, but you don't know. You just don't know." Marta began stirring her coffee, banging the spoon against the cup. "Tony believed me. And now something has happened to him."

"Oh, Marta," said Chris with a there, there, little lady tone. "Tony's only been gone a couple of hours. He's gotten sidetracked, that's all."

"Maybe he twisted his ankle and fell into one of the canyons," I said. "He could even be unconscious."

"I looked in all the likely places," said Chris.

"Maybe you should call the search and rescue squad," I said.

"Law enforcement won't be inclined to do anything until he's been missing for twenty-four hours or so," said C. J.

"I want to hire you to find my husband and find out who . . ."

The doorbell rang and Chris, without asking Marta, left to answer it. He acted as if this were his house not hers.

"Will you try to find Tony?" Marta asked, ignoring the interruption.

C. J. and I glanced at each other and I saw her imperceptible nod of agreement.

"Okay, Mrs. Randazzo," I said. "You've just hired us." I picked up the check. "Consider this a retainer for two days."

My partner, who believes in being prepared, said, "I have a contract with me." She pulled papers out of her shoulder bag, handed a page to Marta Randazzo who scanned it quickly, and took the pen C. J. offered, and signed it.

"Marta?" I asked. "Does one of the cars out front belong to your husband?"

"The Jag is his. My Caddy is in the garage."

"And the Volvo belongs to Chris?"

Marta nodded.

Chris walked in with a man and woman trailing behind. The man was stocky, about fifty with heavy dark eyebrows and a hairline that receded back past his ears. The strands left on top were plastered to his reddish scalp. He was dressed in a three-piece suit and looked as if he'd rather be anyplace else except here. He walked straight to the bar without speaking and poured a drink.

The woman came over to where Marta now stood. "Chris told us Tony is missing."

She was short with a voluptuous figure and blond Farah Fawcett hair. "Oh, Marta, you poor dear." The woman put her arms around Marta and kissed the air near Marta's cheek.

"I'm fine, Sonja." Marta recoiled from the woman's touch, but forced a smile. "I'm sorry, the party is canceled. Chris was supposed to call you."

"Oh, he came by about six-thirty. Said he was looking for Tony," said the woman. "He called back later and left a cancellation message on the infernal machine. I just thought we'd drop by on our way out to eat."

The woman noticed C. J. and I for the first time. She looked at Marta and said in a stage whisper as if we weren't there, "Are they from the police?"

"No, uh, Sonja Bernard." She nodded, and we stood. "This is Jenny Gordon and C. J. Gunn. They're private investigators."

The man who'd come in swayed over a double shot of amber liquid in a glass. I assumed he was Sonja Bernard's husband.

"Private dicks, huh?" he said and laughed uproariously. From his slurred words it was obvious this drink was not his first. "Don't think I've ever met a female dick before, black or white. How do?"

He took a big swallow and said, "Tough gals, huh? Do you carry guns? Which one is the dyke? I'll bet it's the black one."

"Bernie, don't be crude," said Sonja. "Their sexual preference is none of your damn business."

Marta's face turned red. "I apologize . . ."

I hated it, too, because I knew C. J.'s sharp tongue would slash and trash Bernie before he could stagger another step. And that was if she decided to only chew him up instead of knocking him on his can. My partner's an ex-police woman, six feet tall, and trained in Tukong Martial Arts. She could put him down and out.

I felt her body tense and spoke quickly, "C. J.? We probably should go." But I wasn't quite fast enough.

"He doesn't bother me, Mrs. Randazzo," said C. J. She smiled sweetly at the man, and then back at Marta. "His whiskey-soaked miniscule brain is ruled by his own penile inadequacy." Her next words were directed to me and spoken through clenched teeth. "You're right, Jenny. We must be on our way, but perhaps Marta will show us out. I have a couple more questions."

"What did she say?" asked Bernie. "Did she just insult me?"

"Of course, Bernie," said Chris, who walked over and took the man's arm. "But turnabout's fair play, wouldn't you say? Let's refresh your drink." Chris took the man's arm and turned him toward the bar.

The man needed another drink like a cowboy needed a burr under his saddle, but the maneuver had moved him out of C. J.'s reach.

The man followed, muttering something about how he'd bet a hundred dollars Tony was shacked up with a blonde someplace.

"I'm terribly embarrassed . . ." said Sonja.

"And I'm terribly sorry for you," I said to her.

Marta Randazzo looked as if she'd like to climb into a hole someplace, but she walked out of the room instead.

C. J. and I followed. Marta veered off into a small sitting room where we stood and asked our questions.

C. J. made notes as Marta gave us descriptions of the car and the man who had followed her. She hadn't seen the license number. She said the people who sued her husband were Ellen and Herbert Davis.

"First," said C. J. "We'll check the local hospitals and emergency clinics, in case Dr. Randazzo has been brought in unconscious. And we'll try to check up on who's been following you. It won't be easy without that plate number."

"Will you call? No matter how late?" Marta asked. "I mean even if the news is . . ."

"Yes," I said. "We'll call if we hear anything." She gave us a recent photo of her husband.

"This could turn into an all-night job," I said as we got into the truck and headed to town.

"Did you catch that last remark from old Bernie?" I asked.

"No, I was having too much trouble trying to keep from decking the guy."

"I figured. Bernie mumbled something about Tony being shacked up someplace."

"Which is why the police are reluctant to get involved in domestic squabbles," said C. J. "The missing usually turn up the next day looking sheepish."

"Did you learn anything from Chris?"

"Only that he knew his way around the kitchen."

"You think the Randazzos quarreled?"

"Didn't you see the bruises on Marta's neck?"

"No, I missed those, but I saw bruises on her leg. That muddies up the waters a bit, doesn't it?"

THE NEXT MORNING WE DROVE to work separately in our respective vehicles. My partner is a morning person and her energy and excitement greeting a new day bugs the hell out of me. I needed time for my body to wake up slowly and the short drive without her helped.

Last night we'd checked all the emergency rooms without turning up the doctor. I'd called a friend, Jana Hefflin, who worked in Austin Police Department communications to see if her department had taken a call regarding a John Doe of anyone fitting Dr. Randazzo's description. She checked with the 911 operators, the EMS operators, and police dispatcher, all at APD headquarters. It was a negative on our man.

Finally, I called Marta Randazzo to report that there was nothing to report. It was almost two A.M. when we made up the bed in the guest room for C. J. and called it a night.

The new day was filled with sunshine and blue skies—reminding me of why I love central Texas.

Austin's built over the Balcones Fault, an ancient geological plate that eons ago rumbled and formed the hills, canyons, and steep cliffs around west Austin. The land west of Austin is known as the Texas Hill Country. The city's east side slopes into gentle rolling hills and fertile farm land. Our office is in the LaGrange building which sits on a small knoll in far west Austin near the MoPac Freeway and from our fourth-floor office there's a fantastic view of limestone cliffs and small canyons to the west.

At the office, C. J. ran computer checks on the Davises. Ellen Davis had never sued anyone before and neither she nor her husband had a police record. She also ran three other names: Sonja and Hirum "Bernie" Bernard and Christopher Lansen.

Mr. Bernard had a DUI and a resisting arrest charge pending. He also had a couple of business lawsuits resulting in settlements. Sonja Bernard had called the police recently in regard to a domestic dispute. Dr. Lansen had one bad debt on his credit record and a couple of unpaid parking tickets. A bunch of ordinary people, nothing to set off any alarm bells.

C. J. learned from a friend on the computer network that Ellen and Herbert Davis had left three weeks ago on an extended vacation to Hawaii. "That lets them out as revenge seekers," she said.

"You got that right," I said, using one of her favorite sayings. I called Mrs. Randazzo to see if she'd heard anything. She hadn't, and afterward I made follow-up calls to the hospitals.

I told C. J. a trip to Dr. Randazzo's office might be helpful. "Maybe the doctor has a girlfriend and someone from his office knows about it."

"Maybe he even plays with someone from work."

Having spent a few years around doctors myself, I knew the long hours of togetherness sometimes bred familiarity. "This whole thing just doesn't make good sense to me. If Randazzo and his wife had an argument and he stormed out, why didn't he go off in his Jag, not just head out on foot someplace?"

"Unless," said C. J., "he wanted to stage a disappearance. That malpractice suit left him in bad shape financially except for those assets in his wife's name."

I liked it. "What if he has other assets, hidden ones, and worked out a scheme? What better way than just walk off? Leave everything. And if another woman is involved she could meet up with him later. Intriguing, huh?"

"Yeah, but what about someone trying to kill Marta? If the Davises are out spending their newfound money, then who?"

"So," I said, "Randazzo hired someone to scare Marta in order to throw suspicion off of his own plans."

We couldn't come up with any more ideas, so I left to talk to the doctor's employees.

Randazzo's office was in the Medical Professional high-rise building next door to Seton Hospital on Thirty-eighth Street, a few miles north of downtown and only a fifteen-minute drive from my office.

Years ago, I had worked at an X-ray clinic in this building. My husband, Tommy, used to pick me up for lunch and we'd go around the corner to eat chicken-fried steak. The restaurant went bust a while back and of course, Tommy was killed a couple of years ago. Nothing stays the same, I thought, as I pulled into an empty parking spot and got out.

Randazzo's suite of offices were on the second floor. A typical doctor's suite. Comfortable chairs in the waiting room, popular magazines scattered on tables, and modernistic art prints hanging on the wall. A curly-top redheaded young woman, about eighteen, sat in the glassed-in cubicle.

Were receptionists getting younger or was I only getting older? After I explained who I was and what I wanted, I was asked to wait. Ms. Williams, the head nurse, would be with me in just a few minutes, I was told.

It was a good half hour before Ms. Williams called me. Her office was small, more like a closet under the stairs, but there was a desk and secretary-type chair. A telephone and a computer sat on the desk and file folders covered all the remaining space. She was about my age of thirty-five and every year showed on her face today. I'd guess a missing boss could upset routines.

"Ms. Williams, I'm sorry to bother you but if you'll answer a few questions, I'll get out of your way."

"Please call me Tiffany. Ms. Williams reminds me of my mother and I'd just as soon not think of her."

"I hear that," I said. "And I'm Jenny." Even though she didn't ask me to, I sat down.

"I don't know if you've talked to Mrs. Randazzo today, but she's hired my partner and me to try to find her husband."

"Wow, I've never talked to a private detective before. It must be exciting." Tiffany Williams ran her hand through her brown hair which was cut extremely short and was two shades lighter than my own chestnut color.

"It's not exactly like it is on TV. Most of my work involves checking backgrounds on people. Nothing too exciting there."

She looked disappointed. "Dr. Lansen told us Mrs. Randazzo had hired someone to try to locate Dr. Tony. How do you go about finding a missing person?"

"Pretty much like I'm doing now with you. You talk to friends, family, and coworkers. See if they have any knowledge or ideas."

"I don't know where he's gone. I just work here."

"I understand. But sometimes coworkers overhear things and that chance remark might give a clue." She nodded and I continued, "Tell me about Dr. Randazzo."

"Tell you what?"

"What kind of boss is he? It helps if I can get some feel for the person. Did he seem unusually upset or worried about anything lately?"

"He's always upset about something. He's a very intense person. A control freak. He got upset whenever people wouldn't do as he said."

"You mean his patients?"

"Everyone. His wife, his employees, the hospital staff." Tiffany Williams began chewing her fingernails. They looked red and ragged as if she'd already spent a lot of time gnawing. "Everyone is afraid of him and no one would knowingly cross him—about anything."

"When I worked in X-ray I ran across doctors like that and I always called it the prima-donna syndrome. Some doctors let a little power go to their heads." Tiffany was nodding in agreement after her initial surprise that I'd once worked in medicine.

"Yes. And when a second doctor comes in and is so nice, you see how things *could* be."

"You mean Dr. Lansen?"

"Yeah, he's so easygoing, but a great doctor, too. The patients all love him and the employees, too." She thought a moment. "I think everyone responds to his kindness but that didn't go over with Dr. Tony."

"I can imagine. Do you know how Marta Randazzo got along with Dr. Lansen?"

"I don't know if I should say. It's not professional."

"I understand and I don't blame you. Let me tell you what I've observed and see if you agree."

She nodded and I said, "There's an undercurrent of something between them. It goes deeper than an . . ."

"Very definitely," she interrupted. "I think Chris hopes to get ahead by being attentive to Marta."

"That doesn't sound too smart or ethical."

"I never said Chris is an angel. He has his faults. He wants a partnership with Dr. Tony and he wants to reach the top as quickly as possible."

Okay, I thought, the young Dr. Lansen is ambitious. But was that enough to have caused Randazzo's disappearance? "How did Tony feel about Chris's ambitions?"

"Pleased as long as Chris kept Marta occupied."

"Oh?"

"Our patients are mostly female and women find Dr. Tony's bedside manner quite charming. If Marta's attention was elsewhere then . . ." Realizing she was saying too much, she stood. "I've got to get back to work. It's gonna be one of those days."

I stood also. "Okay, but one more question. Was there one lady Dr. Tony was especially close to lately?"

She walked to the door, looking as if she were a little girl who'd just tick-a-locked her mouth shut. She then sighed. "I probably shouldn't, but you'll find out anyway if you keep digging. Dr. Tony is having a relationship with a patient—or was. We all knew about it."

"Who?"

"Sonja Bernard, a neighbor of theirs. He did surgery on her and they got involved a few months ago. They were going hot and heavy and it was beginning to get sticky."

"Did Marta know?"

She nodded. "Chris let it slip but I'm sure it wasn't by accident. Chris always does things for a reason." Tiffany went out into the hallway. "I really do have to get busy."

"Okay and thanks." I turned to leave, but remembered something she'd just said. "You said Dr. Tony and Sonja *were* going hot and heavy?"

"Yes, but they broke up last week. And remember you didn't hear any of this from me."

"My lips are sealed."

On my way back to the office I wondered why Lansen had wanted Marta to know about Tony and Sonja. Somehow, that didn't fit with my image of the young doctor on his way up. You can get fired for getting the boss's wife upset.

I pulled onto the street behind the LaGrange and Jana Hefflin from APD communications rang my car phone.

"Jenny, I've been listening in on a call one of my 911 operators is working. Dr. Randazzo was located about an hour ago—he's dead."

"Damn. What happened?"

"He was shot. Body was in a deep ravine about a half mile from his house. The police aren't calling it homicide yet, they're still investigating."

"You're sure it's Randazzo?"

"Yep. He had identification. Sorry, Jenny."

"Thanks, I appreciate it. I owe you one," I said. I knew Jana had an abiding affection for chocolate-covered strawberries made by a local candy company— Lamme's. I'd make sure she received a box the next time they were offered for sale.

When I got inside, I plopped in a customer chair in front of C. J.'s desk and told her our missing person had been found dead.

She was pulling apart sheets of computer paper as they came out of the printer. "Should we call Marta Randazzo?"

"We'll wait. The police have to make their notifications."

We discussed my conversation with Tiffany and when the printer's clatter abruptly stopped, C. J. held up the pages. "I came up with more info about Mrs. Randazzo. She comes from an old West Texas ranching family. She inherited more money than you or I could ever imagine.

"I think," she added, "Dr. Lansen changed horses in mid-stream. When he realized Randazzo was losing the lawsuit and the medical practice would go down the tubes, he figured Marta was his best bet. She's got enough money to set up two or three practices.

"And personally, I think young Lansen is involved right up to his pretty blue eyes," said C. J.

I thought about how Marta and Chris Lansen had acted when we were there. C. J. could be right. If Chris wanted to get ahead and if he felt Marta could help. But I didn't think Marta was involved. She had seemed genuinely worried about Tony's disappearance and, besides, I liked her. "No, I can't buy it."

"Why not?" C. J. prided herself on her judgment of people and she got a little huffy because I didn't agree. "Look, he's hot after the missus and he probably saw a quick and dirty way to take out the husband."

She was working up her theory hoping to convince me. "He probably began stalking Marta to use as a cover for his real target . . ."

When I said I couldn't buy it, I meant I couldn't buy Marta's involvement. I did have many doubts about Chris Lansen. "Possibly. He says he went out looking for Randazzo. Maybe he found him and killed him."

"The stalking tale could have been just that, a tale."

"What about your 'Good Buddy,' Bernard?" I asked. "His wife's infidelity could have sent him into a jealous rage. Or what about the woman scorned, Sonja Bernard?"

C. J. said, "Bernard might strike out in the heat of passion if he caught his wife with Tony. But he's a drunk and I doubt he'd have the balls to plan anything sophisticated.

"And Mrs. Bernard is out from the same mold as Randazzo. She's played around for years, but she always goes back to her husband. He needs her."

"Surely you didn't find that out from your computer," I said.

"No, I called Carolyn Martin, she filled me in on the Bernards."

My friend, Carolyn, who's hip-deep in society happenings, knew all about the skeletons in the jet-setters' closets. If Carolyn said Sonja had the morals of a rock-star groupie, then it was true. "Okay, so where does that leave us?"

C. J. stared at me. "Back to Marta Randazzo. She's one cool bitch."

"No, I think she's putting on a front. Acting cool when she really isn't." The more I thought about it the more I felt I was right. "Marta couldn't kill . . ."

"Listen to you, Jenny, listen to that nonsense coming from your mouth. The husband abused her regularly, he played around—even had an affair with a friend." C. J.'s tone was curt.

"Chris Lansen and Marta Randazzo together," she said. "They have the best motive and Chris sure had the opportunity . . ."

I thought about the vulnerability I had seen in Marta's eyes and was determined to give her every benefit of the doubt. "If Chris did it he was acting alone."

"No way. Marta is involved, believe me. She was fed up with her husband." C. J. shook her finger at me and raised her voice. "Randazzo acted like a horse's ass routinely. Now he's lost his medical practice—suddenly, Marta and Chris both see a solution to all their problems."

"Dammit, we don't even know yet that it was murder. Maybe Randazzo killed himself. What do the police say?"

C. J. shrugged.

"Take it from me—if Randazzo was murdered Marta didn't do it." I stood and walked out of the reception area and into my inner office, slamming the door behind me.

Once inside I started cooling off immediately. I've always been that way. I can get angry enough to chew nails, spout off, then quickly my anger subsides. When C. J. began to get angry with me, I should've backed off. It was stupid and I knew it.

My partner can stay mad for hours—days even. The only way to head it off was to try and make her laugh. If I could get her to laugh things would smooth out quickly.

I stayed in my office for about five minutes, rehearsing what I would say to C. J., but when I went back out to her desk in reception—she was gone.

She'd left a note saying she'd gone to APD to see what she could find out from Larry Hays. Hoo-boy, I thought. When she's too angry to tell me when she's leaving, she's really mad.

Lieutenant Hays worked in homicide and he'd been my late husband's partner and best friend. After Tommy died Larry took on the role of my brother/protector. For a private investigator, having a friend on the force was a huge bonus. If Larry hadn't worked on the Randazzo case, he'd know who had and would be able to give C. J. all the inside dope.

Talking to Larry was another good way for C. J. to get over her anger. If she could talk shop with him—she'd chill out fast.

I tidied up my desk, set the answering machine, and left.

But instead of going home, I found myself heading to the Randazzos'. Something about Marta pushed my buttons and I had to see if I could find out why.

MARTA RANDAZZO WASN'T PARTICULARLY GLAD to see me, but she didn't slam the door in my face. She just said, "Come in, if you like." I followed her down the hall to the den.

Once again I had the feeling I'd been in this room before, the Indian colors and Kachina dolls and arrowheads were so familiar it was spooky. I refused the drink she offered and sat down.

Marta certainly didn't look like a woman who only a few hours ago had learned of her husband's death. Her makeup was impeccable. No red eyes or tears. Her whole demeanor was changed, she acted poised and self-assured. She picked up her glass and drank, standing regally by the fireplace, and then stared at me over the rim. "You expected tears?" Her tone was defiant.

"Everyone handles grief differently."

"I can't pretend grief when there's nothing there. I can't pretend when deep down I'm glad Tony's dead."

Suddenly, I was ten years old again and memories came flooding back. My mother and I were at my aunt's house, in her living room decorated with Indian artifacts. Decorated much like this room was.

I could even hear my mother's voice. It sounded tearful and sad. *"Everyone handles grief differently."*

I recalled Aunt Patsy saying, "I can't pretend grief when deep down I'm glad Stoney is dead."

My mother said, "But, Patsy, I don't understand. What did you do?"

Both of my aunt's eyes were blackened and she had a plaster cast on her arm. I'd never seen anyone look so defiant. Aunt Patsy said, "I killed him. I got his pistol and I shot him. I just couldn't take the beatings anymore. Not with this baby coming."

"Shhh," said my mother turning to me. "Jenny, why don't you go play outside. Aunt Patsy and I need to talk grown-up stuff."

I could now remember everything I'd blocked out. My aunt being arrested, and there was a trial or something. Later, she was sent away, probably to a women's prison. She didn't even come to my mother's funeral three years later. Maybe she couldn't if she was in prison, but as a child I didn't know that. I only knew how hurt I was because she wasn't there. I'd been crazy about Aunt Patsy and I guess I couldn't deal with all the emotional trauma and had buried it.

Until I met Marta Randazzo.

I looked at Marta. "You killed him, didn't you? You killed him because he beat you and cheated on you and you'd finally had enough. His affair with Sonja Bernard was the last straw."

Marta began shaking her head no, but I continued. "You wanted a way out."

"No," she said. And for the first time since I'd met her, she stood straight with her shoulders back. "He scarred Ellen Davis's face, but he wasn't sorry. He even laughed about it. Just like he laughed over what he did to me." Marta pulled her sweater up and off her head in one fluid motion. She was braless and I winced at the misshapen breasts and the hideous red-surgical-scar tissue.

"See! See what he did to me?" She was crying now and could barely speak. "I—I killed him . . . be-because I didn't want him to get away with ruining another woman."

"But he didn't . . ."

"Y-you think giving Ellen Davis thousands of dollars could ever be enough? And it didn't even faze him. He was going to disappear. Move to another state and start all over. Start butchering women again. I couldn't let him. I—I had to stop him."

"So, THAT'S WHY YOU HAD a blind spot about her. What did you do when she just up and confessed?" asked C. J.

"I told Marta I knew one of the best defense lawyers in Texas. I called Bulldog Porter. He came over and together they drove downtown to police headquarters." I looked at C. J. "Thanks for not reminding me how right you were."

She shrugged. "What about Marta being stalked?"

"Randazzo probably set that up for his disappearing act."

"And Chris Lansen wasn't involved?"

"Bulldog wouldn't let Marta talk to me. I believe Chris dumped the body for her, but killing Tony was her own solitary act." I thought about that Dinah Washington song, then. "Marta sure had a front-row seat for her revenge."

Deloris Stanton Forbes is an author who should be familiar to readers of the monthly mystery magazines, particularly *Alfred Hitchcock's Mystery Magazine*. In the following story, she deftly illustrates the perils of modern hospital care when one of the staff is only trying to make sure a patient lives "A Long and Happy Life."

# A Long and Happy Life
## DELORIS STANTON FORBES

Somebody said (dogs' years ago) the best reaction to falling off a horse is getting back on the horse and riding the heck out of him. That's what I did in essence when I went back to the very same hospital where my husband had died (they'd said, sorry, Mrs. Glenn, we've done all we can) and took a volunteer job as a Pink Lady. I didn't say anything about Victor's death (it happened in room 213; you can put me down as a firm believer in triskaidekaphobia, I avoid entering that room even to this day), and I couldn't see that they connected me with the hospital in any way, which was not surprising because Fairland General is a good-sized hospital and sometimes their left hand doesn't know what their right hand is doing, so do be careful when you check in via the emergency entrance. I mean, sure, doctors are only human and so are nurses and they can make mistakes, so don't take anything for granted, especially something simple-seeming like replacing a weakening pacemaker with a new improved model . . .

I'm rambling on, excuse me, please, I have to go. I'm delivering flowers to the third floor this afternoon, but first it's the book cart for the second floor; the men don't read as much as the ladies do, but what they do read is more interesting I believe. I'll take thrillers and Westerns over the quote romance unquote novels that go so well with the gals any day. This is my usual routine, I cover a lot of ground in one afternoon. People say I'm the fastest Pink Lady in the west wing.

In room 201 we have Mr. Eberhardt and Mr. Burt. Mr. Eberhardt is postoperative. They've put his knee back together, and he's due to go home this weekend, even though he's certain that he can't manage with crutches and a brace, and believes he should stay a little longer in order to have more physical therapy, but his insurance company says, "I don't think so." Mr. Burt (colon problems; I have a hunch he's a tippler, his nose has that look, if you know what I mean) has just come in and is feeling edgy as he waits for his surgery. "Good afternoon, Mr. Eberhardt, I've rounded up a Louis L'Amour for you. Have you seen this one?—it should be a quick read. Good afternoon, Mr. Burt, how about a Mickey Spillane? It's an oldie but goodie, so says Mr. Cooper in 207."

Mr. Cooper in 207 is a real character. Angie on the afternoon nursing shift says his trouble is prostate, but you wouldn't know it the way he carries on. He even flirts with me, calls me an old cutie and an old sweetie, grabs my hand and pulls me down for a cheek kiss. I must confess that I don't find it offensive even though Mr. Foss, his recent roommate, told him to watch it or I'd file suit for sexual harassment, to which I replied, "Such foolishness, the way you two do carry on," at which they laughed and seemed pleased with themselves and that's all right with me. That's what I'm here for, to make patients feel better. That and to keep an eye on things. Just in case.

The man I felt sorriest for was poor Mr. Fallon in 220. His debilitating diabetes having reached a serious stage, they put him in here to try to get his sugar reregulated. Among his many troubles was a persistent problem with his feet. They were afraid of gangrene and I think that really frightened him, but the main reason I felt sympathy was because of his wife. Arlene Fallon is blind, she showed up daily, suddenly materializing at the visitor's desk. I never saw her come, she was just there, and one of us Pink Ladies took her up to visit her husband. She is one of those little women, petite in stature, in voice, in mannerisms, everything about her is small. I figure her for a size four shoe and a size two dress. I get the idea that Mr. Fallon, she called him Ronnie, saw to her every need, even picked out her clothes, and she did look well turned out from tiny black patent pumps to the single strand of pearls (real, I believe) around her birdlike neck. She looked like Barbie the doll's grandmother if Barbie the doll had a grandmother, but since her mother (Barbie the doll's mother) was a plastic mold, even I can't envision a family tree. I say even I because my husband Victor used to comment that no Christian need perish in torment for me, and when I said what does that mean, for heaven's sake, he said, "Shaw said it in the Epilogue to *St. Joan*. He said, 'Must then a Christian perish in torment in every age to save those who have no imagination?'" Victor was very literary.

When Mrs. Fallon speaks, she sounds like a little radio girl (remember Fanny Brice?), and the thought crossed my mind that thirty or forty years (they're of the generation that married once and forever) of listening to that voice could have resulted in self-inflicted psychological deafness, but he always listened attentively and answered in soft, fatigued tones (at least when I was in the room), so it would seem his hearing and his patience were up to par. Anyway, she arrived promptly at ten A.M. each day and sat by his bedside until five, when a man in a chauffeur's uniform showed up and took her away. I watched one day from the window at the end of the hall that looks out on the hospital entranceway and saw her departure. In a limousine, yet. So I guessed they were well off, the Fallons. Financially, that is. I wonder how much money they'd have given if she could see and he hadn't come down with diabetes?

If I sound as though my gentlemen patients interest me more than my female charges, I must confess that they do. Except for Sara Dobbs. Women patients require less of my tender loving care, they are, by and large, more self-reliant, and since I enjoy being needed, I cater to the men. No matter how strong, how virile they are, in the hospital they so often revert to the status of little boys, and it pleases me to mother.

I mention Sara Dobbs not because she is any less self-reliant but because she has the magic ingredient—imagination. She's a writer, she tells me. She is writing a screenplay. "It's a natural, honey. I can't understand why they haven't already done it. It's all about the *MASH* people twenty years later. You know, what happened to Hawkeye and B. J. and Colonel Potter and Margaret Houlihan and Radar. Especially Radar. I was very taken with Radar, weren't you honey? I mean, everybody was. *MASH* was the most popular TV show for the longest time ever, more beloved than *Gunsmoke* or *All in the Family* or Lucille Ball, sure they were all good, but *MASH* . . . it had laughter and tears, it had suspense, and everybody in it was so human, I mean there weren't any solid, one hundred percent heroes, you know, honey, except maybe Radar . . . and I just hated that Frank Burns, but by the end of his stay I'd begun to feel sorry for him and Klinger, Klinger was a real hoot, wasn't he, honey . . . ?"

She'd go on like that, she had every character memorized, she could tell me episode by episode what happened next. I found it rather amazing because of her ailment. Sara was in the hospital because her daughter claimed Sara was coming down with Alzheimer's or something along those lines. Sara's doctor, that was Dr. Edgars, he was a doll, not a Barbie doll but a real doll, wasn't sold on that idea at all, so Sara was in for tests.

If there was anything wrong with Sara's brain, I certainly couldn't put a name to it. We used to have long girl-to-girl chats. She didn't say much about her life outside the hospital, mostly she just went on about *MASH*. I told her all about Victor and me, what a happy marriage we'd had, it was great to talk to someone about it, I guess I don't have many close friends. Not that I mind. It's better, I find, to sort of keep people at a short distance. Be friendly but be private, my best friend in my whole life was my husband. Sara was a perfect girl chum. I could see her when I wanted to, I could stay just as long as I wished. As long as we had something of interest to say to one another. I think she felt the same. I kept urging her to get on with her TV screenplay. It did indeed sound like a natural to me.

When I volunteered as a Pink Lady, I knew I'd be running into Dr. Faubus. After all, the hospital was big but it wasn't that big, and he was a prominent physician, in line for chief of cardiology, I'd heard, but I'd schooled myself—no, schooled isn't the right word—I'd talked things over with myself and decided that encountering Dr. Faubus wouldn't disturb me in the least. After all, it wasn't as though he committed malpractice. He couldn't help it if the atria and the ventricles of Victor's heart fell totally out of coordination and brought on a Stokes-Adams heart block which led to loss of consciousness accompanied by convulsions just before Victor's scheduled pacemaker insertion. Dr. Faubus couldn't help it if he was out on the golf course when I called, frantically called I might add, for his help. He couldn't help it if I had failed to take a course in cardiopulmonary resuscitation, and he couldn't help it if the paramedics got involved in an accident on the way to Victor, and he couldn't help it if Victor died when he was only sixty-two years old in this day and age when more and more people are living to be a hundred—just listen to Willard Scott on the *Today* show!—Dr. Faubus couldn't help it . . . I keep telling myself that. Dr. Faubus couldn't help it.

For the first few months I saw him seldom, passed him in the hall occasionally, a tall authority figure in his white coat (on nonoperating days) or green suit (postsurgery). He didn't recognize me, or if he did, he didn't acknowledge the recognition. Which was fine with me.

But then he turned out to be Mr. Fallon's doctor. It seemed that, in addition to his diabetes, Mr. Fallon had developed heart palpitations due to his vascular problems—that's what I gathered from the conversational bits and pieces I'd managed to string together. I'd overheard Dr. Faubus using his placate-the-patient voice tell Mrs. Fallon, "It's nothing to worry about just now. I'm keeping a close watch on his condition, and I've instructed the nurses to call me immediately in any emergency." To which she'd replied in her I'm-ever-so-helpless tones, "I am so grateful, doctor. I have complete trust in you, I just know you'll be able to fix it so Ronnie can come home again. It's so hard without him. I just don't know what I'd do if I didn't have someone to depend on."

One day early this week I saved a book for Mr. Fallon, a new John Grisham thriller that I knew would interest him because I'd learned that Mr. Fallon was Ronald G. Fallon, Esquire, successful attorney-at-law, make that very successful attorney-at-law, which explained the limousine and the real pearls. "That's very sweet of you—" Mrs. Fallon never bothered to look in my direction when she spoke to me, I guess that was because since she didn't see she needn't bother "—but Dr. Faubus says he should use his eyes sparingly. The diabetes affects eyesight, says Dr. Faubus. He says Ronnie should ration his television viewing and . . ."

"My eyes are fine," Mr. Fallon interrupted. He spoke abruptly, surprising me because he was always so gentle when he spoke to her. I could understand his irritation. Confined to a hospital bed, one had to have some diversion. If she had her way, her husband would do nothing but lie there and listen to her. Maybe that was her purpose.

She was, I concluded, completely spoiled. His fault, of course, but still . . . I could understand his reasons. How long had she been blind, I wondered. Was she blind when he married her? If so . . .

"Thank you for the book," said Mr. Fallon taking it from my hesitating hand. "I should imagine it's much in demand. I'm most grateful."

"I saved it for you because you're a lawyer," I told him and seized the opening. "I know it's pesky, and I apologize, but may I ask you a legal question?" Bad manners, Bea, I thought. Like describing your symptoms to a doctor at a cocktail party.

"Of course." Any annoyance he felt, he hid. Mrs. Fallon bridled slightly and opened her mouth to speak, but I hurried on. "In the course of your practice, do you ever do any malpractice suits?"

His eyebrows rose. He was still a rather a nice looking man even though he was so very pale and had lost much of his hair. My husband had never lost his hair. He might have, I suppose, had he lived long enough, but I doubted it. He had such thick, wavy, brown, still brown at sixty-two, hair. I loved to touch it, to feel it, to run my fingers through . . .

"No, I don't. I specialize in corporate law." He warmed his tone, "Have you some problem requiring a trial lawyer?"

I smiled reassuringly. "No. No, I was merely asking. For a friend. I told her I didn't think you were that sort of lawyer. I couldn't imagine you appearing in one of those ads on TV . . ." I smiled to show the foolishness of the mere possibility.

"Really, miss . . ." Mrs. Fallon was obviously irritated, she even bothered to glance in my direction. "My husband is ill, and you are imposing."

"Yes. I'm sorry. Do excuse me. Have a good day, Mr. Fallon. Mrs. Fallon. I'm on my way." I'd been out of line, I knew. Why I'd even bothered to bring up the subject I had no idea, Dr. Faubus couldn't be sued for playing golf, could he? Of course not. My question was a result of my controlled—I thought—animosity toward Dr. Faubus. You'll have to do better than that, Bea, I told myself. So I faced facts and came up with a new idea.

As I wheeled my cart out of the room in what I hoped was a dignified exit, I collided with none other than Dr. Faubus. "Watch it!" he barked and almost pushed me aside. He should have said, "Sorry," because he was the one who'd run into me, but no, of course not. Dr. Faubus could do no wrong.

I had a fact to face, so I faced the fact. I hated Dr. Faubus. I faced the fact that I firmly believed Dr. Faubus was the cause of Victor's death. I faced the fact that until I did something to avenge Victor's death I would sour my disposition and even undermine my mental health. I faced the fact that I would have to come up with a plan, a successful plan, for my inner satisfaction. That's when the idea came to me.

If I could see to it that Mr. Fallon passed away . . . he was going to die anyway, wasn't he? Sooner or later? He looked so sad, so tired, he looked as though he would welcome death. I thought I saw a look in his eyes that said, "I'm ready. Come and get me." If Mr. Fallon died in such a way that Dr. Faubus would be blamed for it, then Mrs. Fallon (if I knew her) would find a malpractice lawyer all right. Mrs. Fallon would be a wonderful witness in a court of law, the tiny little widow, the little handicapped widow—my God, they'd take all the doctor's money, they'd take away his license, maybe they'd even put him in jail. One way or another, Dr. Faubus would be done for, Dr. Faubus would pay.

The only problem now was how. I caught my reflection in the hospital comfort station mirror. My eyes were sparking, my face was pink like my smock, I didn't look like myself at all. I sighed, shook my head at myself. This was all theoretical, of course. An exercise in plotting. To exorcise my demons. One demon. In a white coat. A scheme not to be taken seriously, not at all.

I went to my friend Sara for theoretical help. "How's the play coming, Sara?" I asked. "I'd love to see what you've written."

Sara looked blank, and I thought, maybe she does have Alzheimer's after all. "I'm blocked," she said. "I got this pad of paper and a six-pack of Bic pens, and I'm blocked. I can't seem to get started. All I think about is the way they were on *MASH*, but when I try to think about them now, I'm blocked."

"Oh. Well, maybe all you need is an idea. Let's see, you said you disliked that Dr. Burns . . ."

"Yeah. But he's such a wimp; to tell the truth, he's not a very interesting character. I'd rather do one of the others. Like Radar. I was really crazy about Radar."

"Well, maybe Radar became a doctor . . ."

She shook her head of lank gray hair. "Radar wasn't that well educated. It isn't that he wasn't smart, he just didn't have the background. 'Course, he could have become a male nurse."

"That's it. A male nurse. And he works in this hospital . . ."

"Yeah. That could be. Maybe with Hawkeye. The same hospital with Hawkeye."

"And this Hawkeye, he was a doctor, wasn't he? Right. He could have caused the death of a patient through malpractice and Radar knows it . . ."

She shook her head again, this time with vehemence. "Hawkeye wouldn't do that. He just wouldn't. It won't sell. Never."

"Well, how about another doctor? Somebody with an attitude, you know, like Dr. Faubus, for instance. Have you run into Dr. Faubus? I use him as an example because he's so full of himself he strikes me as the kind of doctor who would make a mistake and never own up to it. Isn't there a doctor that it could happen to—because of arrogance? In *MASH* wasn't there some full-of-himself doctor from Harvard . . . ?"

"Dr. Winchester! Yes. That could be. Arrogant is the word for Dr. Winchester. Hawkeye and Radar and Dr. Winchester could all be at the same hospital, so Radar tells Hawkeye about Dr. Winchester . . ."

"But how would Dr. Winchester kill his patient? And how could Radar find out? That's what we've got to figure. How did he do it? So Radar could prove it?"

Sara cocked a grackle eye at me. "Doctor kills patient, that's your idea? You figuring the viewers will eat up the malpractice bit? Seeing as how they're already mad at the medics on account of high health costs? But that calls for lawyers, and the public's down on doctors and lawyers. I don't know . . ."

"I think you're wrong there. On both counts. The public loves doctors, look at the hospital shows on TV. But they especially like it when a doctor gets into a jam, it pays back for all the times they've had to wait for an appointment and the high price of health care and all the pain . . ."

"You don't go for the image of the doctor as God? You've had a problem with the AMA? Or with one M.D.? That Dr. Faubus?" She swung her legs over the side of her bed, tugged at her hospital gown for decency's sake. "Tell me more, lady. Maybe we can work it in . . ."

"I'm going to have to kick you out, Mrs. Glenn," said Ms. Freeble, R.N. and boss lady on Sara's floor. "Sara's got to go down to X-ray for another scan."

"See you tomorrow, Sara." I waved goodbye. "You think about it. You'll have that white pad filled in no time."

"White pad?" I heard Ms. Freeble ask as I went out into the hall.

"I'm writing my will," I heard Sara tell her. "I'm cutting my daughter off without a cent . . ."

Leaving for the day, I borrowed a volume from the hospital library. Diabetes was the subject of a section. I decided a little knowledge might indeed be a dangerous thing—for Dr. Faubus. (Theoretically, of course.) I looked up diabetes mellitus, which "becomes increasingly common with age." The cause, it seems, is when the pancreas' output of insulin is insufficient for the body's needs. The article said that the effectiveness of modern treatment has changed this often fatal disease into one from which deaths are extremely rare. "However," it went on, "there are still risks." I paid close attention. Insulin-dependent diabetics (Mr. Fallon) risk falling into diabetic coma when the body uses fat as a substitute for glucose to provide energy, which causes poisonous substances called ketones to form as a byproduct. Complications include diabetic retinopathy (an eye disorder—aha!), peripheral neuropathy (a nerve disease), chronic kidney failure, and atherosclerosis with its attendant risks of stroke and heart attack—oh yes. Diabetics cannot eat sugar, candy, cake, jam, etc. Yeah, yeah, everybody knows that. And they should avoid sugar-sweetened drinks . . . another given. But "even if you keep strictly to your diet, you may find that your tests show your condition to be worsening, in which case your physician may prescribe hypoglycemic tablets, which lower blood sugar, but some tablets may have unpleasant side effects; in that case another type of hypoglycemic tablet may be prescribed. . . . Hypoglycemia" (low level of glucose in the blood and the opposite of diabetes mellitus) "may come from overdoses of insulin, not keeping to one's diet, or unusually strenuous or prolonged exercise, and may result in convulsions and coma; hence the treating physician will give you an injection of glucose in a vein in your arm." An injection of glucose in a vein in your arm. Hmmm. I'd read through all that and maybe found my answer at the tag end. A shot of glucose in the arm. Interesting. And Mrs. Fallon couldn't see.

I was reading at the desk in my living room. There is a mirror hanging on the wall over the desk, and I looked up and saw myself in that mirror then, saw my new self, Bea Glenn as Dr. Jekyll turning into Hyde. I slammed the book shut. I was overly warm, my forehead was damp, my eyes were shining, no, not shining, gleaming. An unholy gleam. I shut the gleam off, I told the mirror to "Stop this! Stop this right away." I threatened the mirror, "If you can't behave yourself, you'll have to quit the Pink Ladies. And you know you enjoy being a Pink Lady, you know you do. So straighten up and fly right . . . slow down, baby, don't you blow your top!" Words to an old song, Victor used to sing that old song . . . Victor would be so ashamed . . . I groaned and went to bed, where I dreamed ugly dreams at first but by morning sweet dreams. Victor and I were floating down a river in a canoe, it was sunset, and the sky was filled with such divine colors, gold and pale gold, almost silver, and orange becoming coral turning to peach. Then blue-gold, fade to black.

Mr. Burt greeted me with a message. "A woman's been looking for you. She's a patient. Old dame with gray hair. Looks like a witch."

And from Mr. Cooper, "Hello there, sweetie pie. Old gal named Sara's been asking for you. Give me a kiss, girl, I'm all alone now." He gestured to the adjacent empty bed. "Fossy's gone."

"Mr. Foss—oh yes, your roommate—he's passed on?"

He made a face. "Nah. Gone home. Come on, sugar. Just a little kiss. You know the song, just a spoonful of sugar makes the medicine go down . . ."

But Sara wasn't in her room, her room was empty. Ms. Freeble, sought out, had the answer. "Dr. Edgars sent her to Pinevale," she told me. "She'd started fantasizing. Something about murder in a hospital. She had you involved in it for some reason. Some wild tale about somebody named Radar and a diabetic patient. You shouldn't get so chummy with the patients, Mrs. Glenn. Sometimes you give out the wrong message, you know. Leave the nursing to the professionals, please. We know what we're doing."

"Sorry," I said and almost trotted away. Maybe *I* needed a stay at Pinevale. Whatever had I been thinking? Out of my mind, that was it. Just plain out of my mind.

The corridor in front of Mr. Fallon's room was blocked. A gurney stood outside, there were people in the doorway, nurses and orderlies, over their heads I got a glimpse of a green operating cap. Someone was weeping, *waa, waa, waa* like a child. To me, standing outside, it was like a tableau, everyone frozen until my arrival, and then, as though I'd thrown the switch, everyone moved. Two orderlies came for the gurney, wheeled it inside. At the end of its path I saw Dr. Faubus, and Dr. Faubus saw me. For the first time, it seemed, he recognized me. He knew who I was, I could tell by the look in his eye, and I thought, oh dear God, he knows everything. He knows of my plan, my abandoned plan, he knows my feelings.

I backed away from the door. A cluster of hospital people moved out, at their core Mrs. Fallon. She was the weeper, and I knew that Mr. Fallon was dead. It was Mr. Fallon they were loading on the gurney, it was his body they were bringing out on the gurney escorted by Dr. Faubus, an angry Dr. Faubus, I could almost smell his fury. I let them all go by, then caught the arm of a nurse who trailed the procession. "What happened?"

She looked blank for a moment, then shrugged. "Embolism," she said. "Dr. Faubus said it was an embolism." She looked ahead to make sure everyone was out of earshot. "He's wild, claims somebody gave the patient an overdose of glucose. Heads are gonna roll." She rolled her eyes to show how. "Thank God I never went near the man today. Dr. Faubus can be a holy terror."

I took a deep breath, swallowed, and thus controlled my stomach acid. "What about his wife?" I asked. "She's blind, isn't she? What will happen to her?"

The nurse, her nametag said Connors, shrugged again. "Family Services will take over. Me, I've got patients to attend to. Calm them down. Some of them are sure to know what's happening . . ."

Mr. Fallon's room was empty now. His blood pressure cuff dangled from its tubing; on the table beside the bed was the Grisham book I'd left him. My knees felt weak, I sank into Mrs. Fallon's chair. Guilty as sin, said my head. The old Chinese curse, be careful what you wish for, you might get it. Guilty as sin.

Staff was returning, I could hear them coming down the hall. As I picked up the Grisham book, two nurses in conference with Nurse Connors passed. I could hear one of the nurses saying, "I hate it when we lose one, but I try to think of it this way: he lived a long and happy life . . ."

"That's dumb, Shirley," said Nurse Connors. "How do you know his life was . . ." I added the Grisham book to my collection and went back down to Mr. Burt and Mr. Cooper, who were not, so far as I knew, on the verge of dying.

But when I told him, Mr. Burt said, "Ah well, he lived a long and happ
life."

I could have slapped him.

I THINK I KNEW THEY were police before anybody else. They came, two of them, in semi-uniforms of blue blazers and tan pants, Florida's idea of plain-clothes, the day after Mr. Fallon died. (Guilty as sin, guilty as sin, said the litany in my head.) They talked to the nurses. They prowled around the corridors. They even chatted with patients. I heard through the grapevine that they had a long conference with Dr. Faubus. (He's getting his, he's getting his! Shut up, shut up, guilty as sin.)

They even cornered me. They introduced themselves, Detectives Beaumont and Laird, they said. Beaumont was tall, Laird was shorter. Other than that they looked a good deal alike. Maybe it was the blue blazers? They had a few questions, they said. They'd heard I spent a lot of time on this floor. They'd heard that I spent a lot of time in Mr. Fallon's room.

"But I didn't," I protested. "No more than in anyone else's. Who told you that?"

It seemed Mrs. Fallon thought I spent a lot of time in Mr. Fallon's room.

Oh dear. Could the little bird lady be jealous?

"I don't think I spent more time there than anywhere else. I just took him a book now and then. And a cheery word. He was a very sick man. You say you have questions, I have a question. Why are you here? I mean, the poor man passed away. A heart attack. A natural way of dying, he had a heart problem. Why are the police interested in that? Unless you think the doctor . . ."

"It's because of the doctor that we're here," said Beaumont. "Doc Faubus says somebody caused the heart attack. We're trying to find out if he's right."

"Somebody caused . . . what does he mean? How could anybody cause . . . ?"

"Doc Faubus says the deceased got an overdose of glucose."

My heart threw in an extra beat for good measure. "An overdose. Oh dear. Some nurse . . . ?"

"None of the regular nurses gave him a shot of any kind. They all swear to it. We're trying to locate another nurse, maybe she's private, maybe she's from another floor, although there's no record of any Nurse Houlihan on the hospital's roster. Mrs. Fallon says some nurse named Houlihan came into her husband's room that afternoon . . ."

"Houlihan?" Nurse Houlihan.

"Doc Faubus and the hospital are walking on eggs with the lady. Seems she plans to instigate a suit against the doc and the hospital, she's talking about F. Lee Bailey."

"Nah," said Laird. "Not Bailey. Dershowitz."

d Beaumont. "She's a tough one, that little old gal. Looks
reeches like a . . ."

l. "Screeches like a parrot. Ever hear one of those parrots
one out to the zoo that'll break your eardrums. My kids
every other week, I swear I'll take to wearin' ear plugs.
You know, those birds live to be like a hundred years old, you know that?
Long lives, those parrots. As long as somebody takes care of them. Long and
happy lives."

Nurse Houlihan. They were walking away from me, they were almost out
of earshot. I took a deep breath. "I think," I said softly, "you'd better check
out Pinevale. The sanitarium. To see if a patient named Sara Dobbs is still
there."

They didn't hear me, they were almost at the end of the hall.

What could they do to her anyway? Put her in an institution?

But suppose they believed she knew what she was doing? Knew right from
wrong (wasn't that the insanity rule)? Then they could try Sara Dobbs and
find her guilty of murder and even send her to the electric chair. Old Sparky.
That's what they call it. Old Sparky.

And she could implicate me. Couldn't she? Wasn't there some sort of crime
called aiding and abetting?

Then, too, what if Mr. Fallon *wanted* to die? Facing possibly years of in-
capacitation and all the while having to listen to Mrs. Fallon's high-pitched
piping monotone . . .

I needed to think, I needed to think about the right thing to do, I needed
to go home and think . . .

Just then, as I reached that sensible conclusion, Dr. Faubus came into the
hall, appeared at the same far end where the police had gone, came toward
me. And before I could stop myself, I called out, "Dr. Faubus!"

He walked right by. He brushed right past me as though I weren't there at
all. I watched him stride off down the hall, he was a big man, something
about the way he moved made me think of bulldozers. He passed through the
double swinging doors at the far end, they went *slaaaap, slaaap, slaap,
slap* . . .

I stood there a few minutes before turning my cart around and heading for
the elevators. I had work to do up on the third floor (books for Mrs. Egbert
and Miss Donatelli, flowers for Mr. Ponsonby, who'd come out of surgery
that very morning), and time was a-wasting. But I had lots of time to think
about Mr. Fallon and Sara Dobbs and Dr. Faubus . . . all the rest of my (probably) long and happy . . . happy? . . . all the rest of my probably long (considering what medical science can do today) life.

John Lutz is one of the most skilled mystery writers working today with his most recent novels being *The Ex* and *Final Seconds*, co-authored with David August. His settings and descriptions always have the ring of authenticity, whether he's writing about the blues scene in New Orleans or the relationships between men and women. His series characters are also in a class by themselves, whether it be the hapless Alo Nudger, or Fred Carver, who appears in the following tale of corruption and death in the Florida swamps.

# Night Crawlers
## JOHN LUTZ

There's plant life in parts of the Everglades that's to be found nowhere else in the country, spores carried by hurricane winds from the West Indies that take root and flourish in the steamy tropical climate and are exotic and primitive and sometimes dangerous. Some say that in Mangrove City there's animal life to be found nowhere else.

Mangrove City isn't really a city unless you use the term generously. It's a stretch of ramshackle, moss-marred clapboard buildings where the road runs through the swamp along relatively dry land. The "city" is a few small shops, a restaurant, a service station with a sign warning you to fill your gas tank because the swamp's full of alligators, a barber shop with a red and white barber pole that's also green with mold. There's a police station in the same rundown frame building as the city hall, and a blackened ruin that was Muggy's Lounge until it burned down five years ago. Next to the ruin is the new and improved Muggy's, constructed of cinder block and with a corrugated steel roof. Not a city, really. Barely a town. More like something unfortunate that happened on the side of the road.

A mile before you get to Mangrove City, that is *before* if you're driving west the way Carver had, is the Glades Inn, a sixteen-unit motel. It's a low brick structure, built in a *U* to embrace a swimming pool. Carver couldn't imagine anyone ever actually swimming in the thing. The algae on its surface was green and thick. A diving board sagged toward the water and was draped with Spanish moss. From the far corner of the pool came a dull *plop* and a stirring of sluggish water as a bullfrog, tired of Carver's scrutiny, hopped for

165

green cover. Carver set the tip of his cane on the hot gravel surface of the parking lot and limped toward the office.

As he pushed open the door, a bell tinkled. That didn't seem to mean much. The knotty-pine-paneled office was deserted. Behind the long counter, whose front was paneled to match the walls, was a half-eaten sandwich on a desk, next to an old black IBM Selectric typewriter. The only furniture on Carver's side of the desk was a red vinyl chair with a rip in its seat that revealed white cotton batting struggling to get out. On the wall near the chair was a framed color photograph of a buxom woman in a bikini and cowboy boots, riding on the back of a large alligator. She was grinning with her mouth open wide and had an arm raised as if she were waving the ten-gallon hat in her hand. Carver leaned close and studied the photograph. The woman was stuffed into the bikini. The alligator was just stuffed.

"Some sexy 'gator, don'tcha think?" a voice said.

Carver turned and saw a stooped old man with a grizzled gray beard that refused to grow over a long, curved scar on his right cheek. The right eye, near the scar, was a slightly different shade of blue from that of the left and might have been glass. The man had a wiry build beneath a ragged plaid shirt and dirty jeans. He was behind the desk, and Carver couldn't see much of the lower half of his body, but what he could see, and the way the man moved, gave the impression he was bowlegged. His complexion was like raw meat, almost as if he'd been badly burned long ago.

"I didn't see you there," Carver said, noticing now a paneled door that matched the wall paneling behind the desk.

"I was in back, heard the bell, knowed there was somebody out heah." He had an oddly clipped southern accent yet drew out the last words of his sentences: *heeah.* He leaned scrawny elbows on the desk and grinned with incredibly bad teeth, shooting a look at Carver's cane. "What can I do ya, friend?"

Carver saw now that he had a plastic nametag pinned to his shirt, but it was blank. He immediately named the man "Crusty" in his mind. It fit better than the baggy shirt and pants the man wore. And it certainly went with his faint but acrid odor of stale urine. "You can give me a room."

Crusty looked surprised. Even shocked. "You sure 'bout that?"

"Sure am. This is a motel, right?"

"Well, 'course it is. 'S'cuse my bein' put back on my heels, but this heah's the off-season."

Carver wondered when the "on" season was. And why.

Crusty got a registration card out of a desk drawer and laid it on the counter along with a plastic ballpoint pen that was lettered *Irv's Baits.* "You want smokin' or nonsmokin'?"

Carver thought he had to be kidding, but said, "Smoking. Every once in a while I enjoy a cigar."

"Be eighty-five dollars a night with tax," Crusty said.

"That's steep," Carver commented as he signed the register.

Crusty shrugged. "We're a val'able commodity, bein' the only motel for miles."

"You might be the only anything for miles that doesn't swim or fly."

"Then how come you're heah"—Crusty looked at the registration card—"Mr. Carver from Del Moray?"

"The fishing," Carver said.

Crusty's genuine-looking eye widened. "Not many folks come here for the fishin'."

"No doubt they just come to frolic in the pool," Carver said. "You take Visa?"

"Nope. Gotta be good ol' U.S. cash money."

Carver got his wallet from his pocket, held it low so Crusty couldn't see its contents, and counted out 850 dollars. The cost of doing business, he thought, and laid the bills on the desk.

Now both of Crusty's eyes bulged. The glass one—if it was glass—threatened to pop out.

"Ten nights in advance," Carver explained. "I always give myself enough time to fish until I catch something."

Crusty took the money and handed him a key with a large red plastic tag with the numeral 10 on it. "End unit, south side," he said.

Carver thanked him and moved toward the door.

"You got one of the rooms with a TV, no extra charge," Crusty said. "Ice machine's down t'other end of the buildin'. Just keep pressin' the button till the ice quits comin' out brown."

"I'll make myself at home," Carver told him and limped out into the sultry afternoon, astounded to realize it was cooler outside than in the office.

Number 10 was a small room with a dresser, a tiny corner desk, and a wall-mounted TV facing a sagging bed. The carpet was threadbare red. The drapes were sun-faded red. The bedspread matched the drapes. An old air conditioner was set in the wall beneath the single window that looked out on the unhealthy hole that was the pool, then across the road to the shadowed and menacing swamp.

Carver tossed his single scuffed-leather suitcase onto the bed, then went over and opened a door, flipped a wall switch that turned on a light, and examined the bathroom. The swimming pool should have prepared him. There was no bathtub, only a shower stall with a pebbled-glass door. The commode and sink were chipped, yellowed porcelain and so similar in design that they looked interchangeable. A fat palmetto bug, unable to bear the light, or maybe its surroundings, scurried along the base of the shower stall and disappeared in a crack in the wall behind the toilet.

I guess I've stayed in worse places, Carver thought, but in truth he couldn't remember when.

As he was unpacking and hanging his clothes in the alcove that passed for a closet, he laid his spare moccasins up on the wooden shelf and felt them hit something, scraping it over the roughwood. He reached back on the shelf and felt something hard that at first he thought was a coin, but it was a brass Aztec calendar, about two inches in diameter and with a hole drilled in it off-center, as if to make it wearable on a chain.

Carver stood for a moment wondering what to do with the brass trinket, then tossed it back up on the shelf. People might have been doing that with it for years.

He sat down on the bed and picked up the old black rotary-dial phone. Then he thought better of talking on a line that would undoubtedly be shared by Crusty the innkeeper and replaced the receiver. He decided to drive into town and make his call.

Outside Muggy's Lounge was a public phone, the kind you can park next to and use in your car, if you can park close enough and your arm is long enough. There was a dusty white van parked next to the phone, with no one in it. So Carver parked his ancient Olds convertible on the edge of the graveled lot, climbed out, and limped through the heat to the phone. If the humidity climbed another few degrees, he might be able to swim.

He used his credit card to call Ollie Frist in Del Moray. Frist was a disabled railroad worker who'd retired to Florida ten years ago with his wife and teenage son. The wife had died. The son, Terry, had grown up and become a cop in the Del Moray police department. Terry had come to Mangrove City six months ago, telling anyone who'd asked that he was going on a fishing trip. Ollie Frist had gotten the impression his son was working on something on his own and wanted to learn more before he brought the matter to the attention of his superiors. Two days later Ollie Frist was notified that Terry had been found dead in the swamp outside Mangrove City. At first they'd thought the death was due to natural causes and an alligator had mauled and consumed part of the body afterward. Then the autopsy revealed that the alligator had been the natural cause.

The Del Moray authorities had gotten in touch with the Mangrove City authorities. Accidental death, they decided. The grieving father, Ollie Frist, didn't buy it. What he *had* bought were Carver's services.

"Mr. Frist?" Carver asked when the phone on the other end of the line was picked up.

"It is. That you, Carver?" Frist was hard of hearing and roared rather than spoke.

"Me," Carver said. He knew he could keep his voice at a normal volume; Frist had shown him the special amplifier on the phone in his tiny Del Moray cottage. "I'm checked into the motel where Terry stayed."

"It's a dump, right? Terry said when he phoned to let me know where he was staying that the place wasn't four-star."

"Astronomically speaking, it's more of a black hole. Did Terry actually tell you he was coming to this place to fish?"

"That's what he said. I didn't believe it then. Should I believe it now?"

"No. There's some fishing here, I'm sure. But there's probably more poaching. It's the kind of backwater place where most of the population gets by doing this or that, this side of the law or the other."

"You think that's what Terry was onto, some kinda alligator poaching operation?"

"I doubt it. He wouldn't see it as that big a deal, or that unusual. He probably would have just phoned the Mangrove City law if that were the case." A bulky, bearded man wearing jeans and a sleeveless black T-shirt had walked around the dusty white van and was standing and staring at Carver. Maybe waiting to use the phone. "I'll hang around town for a while," Carver said, "see if I can pick up on anything revealing. There's something creepy and very wrong about this place. As of now it's just a sensation I have on the back of my neck, but I've had it before and it's seldom been wrong." The big man next to the van crossed his beefy arms and glared at Carver.

"Keep me posted," Frist shouted into the phone. "Let me know if you need anything at this end."

Carver said he'd do both those things, then hung up the phone.

He set the tip of his cane in the loose gravel and walked past the big man, who didn't move. His muscular arms were covered with the kind of crude, faded blue tattoos a lot of ex-cons sport from their time in prison, and on his right cheek was tattooed a large black spider that appeared to be crawling toward the corner of his eye. He puffed up his chest as Carver limped past him. He probably thought he was tough. Carver knew the type. He probably was tough.

The striking thing about Mangrove City's main street, which was called Cypress Avenue as it ran between the rows of struggling business establishments, was how near the swamp was. Walls of lush green seemed to loom close behind the buildings on each side of the road. Towering cypress and mangrove trees leaned toward each other over the road as if they yearned someday to embrace high above the cracked pavement. The relentless and ratchety hum of insects was background music, and the fetid, rotting, life-and-death stench of the swamp was thick in the air and lay on the tongue like a primal taste.

The humid air felt like warm velvet on his exposed skin as Carver crossed the parking lot and entered Muggy's Lounge.

Ah! In Muggy's, it was cool.

There were early customers scattered among the booths and tables, and a few slumped at the long bar. Carver sat on a stool near the end of the bar and asked the bartender for a Budweiser.

The bartender brought him a can and let Carver open it. He didn't offer a glass. He was a tall, skinny man with a pockmarked face, intent dark eyes set too close together, and a handlebar moustache that was red despite the fact that his hair was brown.

"So whaddya think of our little town?" he asked.

It's conducive to insanity, Carver thought, but he said, "How do you know I'm not from around here?"

The bartender laughed. "There ain't that many folks from around here, and we tend to know each other even if we ain't sleeping together." Someone at the other end of the bar motioned to him and he moved away, wiping his hands on a gray towel tucked in the belt of his cut-off jeans.

Carver sipped his beer and looked around. Muggy's was a surprisingly long building with booths lining the walls beyond where the bar ended. On a shelf high above the bar was a stuffed alligator about five feet long, watching whatever went on with glass eyes that nonetheless seemed bright with evil cunning. There were box speakers mounted every ten feet or so around the edges of the ceiling, tilted downward and aimed at the customers as if they might fire bullets or dispense noxious gas. Right now they were silent. The only sound was the ticking of one of the half-dozen slowly revolving ceiling fans, stirring the air-conditioned atmosphere and moving tobacco smoke around. It occurred to Carver that the clientele in Muggy's might have stopped talking to each other when he walked inside.

The bulky man who'd been watching Carver outside entered the lounge and swaggered toward him. He was about average height but very wide, with muscle rippling under his fat like energy trapped beneath his skin and trying to escape. He smiled thinly at Carver, then sat down on the stool next to him as if using the phone in succession had formed some sort of bond between them. When he smiled, the spider tattoo near his eye crinkled. Carver had seen real spiders do that after being sprayed with insecticide.

"You Mr. Fred Carver?" the man asked in a drawl that moved about as fast as the alligator above the bar.

"How did you guess?" Carver asked, continuing to stare straight ahead at the rows of bottles near the beer taps.

"Didn't guess. I was told you checked in at the Glades Inn. I went and talked to the desk clerk, found out who you was."

"Why?"

"Curious. Stranger here's always news. Ain't much happens to amuse us 'round these parts. We take our pleasure when we can."

"You think I'm going to amuse you?"

"You got possibilities fer sure."

Carver decided to meet this cretin head-on. "Ever hear of a man named Terry Frist?"

"Sure. Got his fool self killed and damn near et up by a 'gator a while back. Terrible thing."

"Alligators usually kill their prey, then drag it back to their den at water's edge where they hide it and let it rot until they can tear it apart easier with their teeth. The way I understand it, Terry Frist's body was found on land."

"Yeah. What was left of it. He was a cop, we found out later. From over in Del Moray. Say now, ain't that where you're from?"

Maybe not such a cretin. "It is," Carver said, "but Frist and I didn't know each other. I read in the newspaper about what happened to him here."

"What is it you do for a livin' there in Del Moray?"

"I'm in research. Decided to come here for the fishing."

"Really? We ain't known for the fishin'."

"Didn't I see a bait shop when I drove into town?"

"Oh yeah. Irv's. Well, there's *some* fishin'. More likely you'll catch yourself a 'gator like that Frist fella did. Fishin' suddenly becomes huntin' when that happens, and you ain't the hunter."

The pockmarked bartender came over and asked what the big man was drinking.

"Nothin'." He slid off his stool and looked hard at Carver. "Fishin's no good this time of year at all. Not much reason for you to stay around town."

"I like a challenge."

"You're more'n likely to get one if you go fishin' in them swamp waters."

"Can I rent an airboat anywhere around here?"

"Nope. Nowheres close, neither. Fella name of Ray Orb rents 'em some miles east, but the swamp's too thick around these parts for airboats to get around in it. I think you best try someplace in an easterly direction." He winked, then turned to leave.

"You didn't mention your name," Carver said.

"I. C. is what I'm called. Last name's Unit. The I. C. stands for Intensive Care." The spider crinkled again as if dying, and I. C. threw back his head and roared out a laugh. Carver watched him swagger out through the door, noticing that all the other customers averted their gazes.

"That his real name?" Carver asked the bartender when I. C. had left.

"He says it is. Nobody much wants to differ with him."

"He as tough as he acts?"

"Oh yeah. Him and his buddies from over at Raiford."

"Raiford? The state penitentiary?"

"That's right. The three of 'em, I. C., Jake Magruder, and Luther Peevy, was in there together after they come down from Georgia and committed some heinous type crime. Some say it was murder. Luther Peevy, his folks died and left him a place nearby, so I guess that's why they all settled in here 'bout a year ago."

"I'll bet the town was happy about that," Carver said.

"This town was never happy," the bartender said and moved away and began wiping down the bar with his gray towel.

Carver finished his beer, then walked around the town for a while before going into its only restaurant, Vanilla's, for lunch, even though it was just eleven o'clock. He was hungry and he was here, and he didn't know if the Glades Inn had a restaurant and didn't want to find out. Crusty was probably the cook.

Though Vanilla's was a weathered clapboard building that leaned on its foundation, it was surprisingly neat and clean inside. Small but heavy wooden tables were grouped evenly beneath a battery of ceiling fans rotating only slightly faster than the ones in Muggy's. There was a small counter and double doors into the kitchen. Carver saw an old green Hamilton-Beach blender behind the counter and wondered if Vanilla's sold milk shakes.

There were two men in white T-shirts and bib overalls at the counter, drinking coffee and eating pie. One of them, a red-headed man wearing a ponytail, turned on his stool, glanced at Carver, then went back to work on his apple pie. They seemed to be the only other warm bodies in Vanilla's.

" 'Nilla!" the redheaded man yelled. "You got yourself a customer."

The double doors opened and a heavyset, perspiring woman in her fifties emerged from the kitchen. She had a florid complexion, weary blue eyes, and wispy gray hair that stuck out above one ear as if she'd slept too long on that side. She was wearing maroon slacks and a white blouse and apron and had a faint moustache. "Sit anywhere you want," she told Carver in a hoarse voice as deep as a man's.

He was aware of her looking at his cane as he limped to a table near the wall, well away from the counter. Fly-specked menus were propped between the salt and pepper shakers. He opened one and saw that the selection was limited.

Vanilla came over with an order pad and Carver asked for a club sandwich. Then he asked her if she served milk shakes and she said she did. He said chocolate.

"Why do people call you Vanilla?" he asked when she returned with his food and a thick milk shake, half in a glass, half remaining in the cold metal container that had fit onto the mixer.

"I used to be a blonde," she said simply, then put his lunch on the table and went back into the kitchen.

Carver had eaten a few bites of the sandwich when he heard the door open and close. He looked in that direction and saw that a uniformed cop had come in, a short, obese, sixtyish man in a neatly pressed blue uniform with a gold badge on his chest.

He waddled directly to Carver's table. "I'm Mangrove City Police Chief Jerry Gordon," the cop said. He was one of those very fat men who breathe hard all the time, even when they speak.

Carver shook hands with Gordon and invited him to sit down.

"You're Fred Carver from Del Moray," Gordon said, settling his soft and wheezing bulk into the chair across the table from Carver.

"Your job to know," Carver said, unsurprised. Everyone in town apparently knew his name and where he lived.

"It is that." Gordon smiled. "You're the only guest out at the Glades Inn. Only outsider in town, matter of fact. So you're bound to be noticed. We ain't exactly Miami here, Mr. Carver."

"I guess you were told I'm here for the fishing," Carver said.

"Oh, sure. I got a yuk out of that. Most folks'd rather drop a line in water where there's more likely to be fish than something that's gonna eat their bait then have them for dessert."

"There must be some *good* fishing. Terry Frist came here a while back. He usually knew where they were biting." A different lie for Gordon. He'd told I. C. Unit he hadn't known Frist in Del Moray. Which had been the truth. Or part of the truth. The useful thing about lies was that they were so adaptable.

Chief Gordon gave Carver a dead-eyed, level look, the kind cops were so good at. "Way I recall it, Terry Frist didn't catch nothin' but a big ol' 'gator. I'd be careful walkin' in his footsteps."

"Are you warning me to be careful in and out of the swamp, Chief?"

"Cautionin' you, is the way I think of it." He put his elbows on the table and leaned toward Carver. "I gotta tell you, there's some angry people out there, in and around the swamp, all through these parts."

"Angry at what?"

"Ever'thin' from violence on TV an' in the movies to supermarket bar codes. You don't wanna do no verbal joustin' with 'em. We got folks around here, Mr. Carver, would shoot you dead over violence on TV."

"You think that's what happened to Terry Frist? An argument over politics or the price of something in produce?"

"I think somebody shoulda warned Terry Frist. I read he was a cop. Maybe he was workin' undercover, an' this was no place for him to be."

"Maybe he found out about something. Say, a drug-smuggling operation."

Chief Gordon grinned. "Why, you're fishin' already, Mr. Carver."

"Maybe. But Mangrove City's near enough to the coast that drug shipments from the sea could be brought here by airboat through the swamp, and the law would never be able to figure out the routes or the timing. A cop—as you say, maybe working undercover—was killed here recently. And I met I. C. Unit this morning in Muggy's and was told he's part of a set and recently of the Union Correctional Institution over in Raiford. And now here you are . . ."

"The local cop on the take?" Gordon didn't seem angry at the suggestion, which made Carver curious. "That's so preposterous I ain't even gonna respond to it, Mr. Carver, except to say we got creatures in the swamp more deadly than any 'gator. Maybe one of 'em killed Terry Frist."

"And you don't want to be next, is that it?"

"Nor do I want you to be, Mr. Carver. I. C. and that Peevy and Magruder, those are bad men. A 'gator grab one of 'em an' it'd spit him right out. I did feel compelled to warn you, an' now I have." Chief Gordon shoved back his chair and stood up, tucking in his blue shirt around his bulging stomach.

Carver felt sorry for him. He was past his prime and dealing with local toughs who had him and the rest of Mangrove City under their collective greasy thumb.

"Do you think Terry Frist was murdered?" Carver asked.

Again Chief Gordon was impassive. "What all I think publicly, it's all in my report, Mr. Carver. If you're really serious about doin' any fishin' while you're here, you oughta see Irv down at his bait shop. He'll tell you where they're bitin' an' you might not get bit back." He raised a pudgy forefinger and wagged it at Carver. "You remember I said might." He turned and waddled out, swinging his elbows wide to clear his holstered revolver and the clutter of gear attached to his belt.

Carver poked his straw into the thick milk shake and took a long sip. It was the best thing he'd encountered since arriving in Mangrove City.

THAT AFTERNOON, CARVER SET OUT from the Glades Inn wearing loose-fitting green rubber boots, old jeans, a black pullover shirt, and half a tube of mosquito repellent. He carried a casting rod and wore a slouch cap with an array of colorful feathered lures hooked into it. He hadn't been fishing for years and didn't really know much about it, but he figured if his cover story was fishing, he'd better fish. Maybe he'd even catch something.

Irv of Irv's Baits seemed to know a lot about fishing and had recommended his night crawlers, explaining to Carver that it took the fattest, juiciest worms to catch the biggest fish. Carver thought that made an elemental kind of sense and bought two dozen of the wriggling monsters squirming around in an old takeout fried chicken bucket half full of rich black loam.

He loaded all of this into the cavernous trunk of the Olds, then drove along the road toward town until he came to a turnoff he'd noticed on his previous trip.

The narrow gravel road soon became even narrower, and the gravel became mud that threatened to bog down the big car's rear wheels. Carver braked the Olds to a stop and turned off the engine. Silence somehow made deeper by the ceaseless drone of insects closed in. Off to his right, through dense foliage shadowed by overhead tree limbs and draped Spanish moss, he saw the dull green sheen of water.

He climbed out of the Olds, got his rod and reel and bucket of worms from the trunk, then muddied the tip of his cane as he limped from what was left of the road and trudged in his boots toward the water. His motion made sensory waves in the swamp. The humming insect tone varied slightly at his passing. He heard soft and abrupt watery sounds and the quick and startled beat of wings.

When he reached a likely spot, he stopped, placed the bucket on a tree stump, and stood in the shade. He disengaged the barbed hook from the cork handle of his casting rod, used it to impale one of Irv's ill-fated night crawlers, and moved slightly to the side. Careful not to snag his line on nearby branches, he used the weight of the bait, a small lead sinker, and a red and white plastic float to cast toward a clear circle of water in the shade of an ancient cypress tree. Line whirred out, there was a faint *plop!* and Carver was ready to reel in a fish.

Irv's worm must have loafed underwater. Nothing happened for about fifteen minutes. Then the red and white float bobbed, went completely underwater, and Carver reeled in an empty hook.

So what did it matter? He was really here to establish himself as a genuine fisherman, in case anyone might be watching him. He reached into the bucket for another worm.

The fishing got better at the spot Carver had chosen. It took him only about an hour to feed the fish the rest of Irv's worms. He removed the fishing cork, cut the leader line above the hook and sinker, then selected the feathered and multiple-barbed Oh Buggie! lure and unhooked it from his cap. He attached it to the line, cast it to where he'd lost all his worms, and almost immediately a fish took it.

Carver reeled in a tiny carp. Since he didn't like to clean fish, and this one was too small to keep anyway, he worked the hook from its mouth and tossed it back. Catch and release, he thought, hoping that wouldn't happen with whoever killed Terry Frist.

He caught nothing the rest of the afternoon. That evening he drove into town and had the family meatloaf special at Vanilla's, then stopped in at Muggy's for a beer before driving back to the motel. He saw no sign of I. C. Unit or his two confederates and was pretty much ignored by the townspeople. They saw him yet they didn't, as if someone had planted in them the post-hypnotic suggestion that he didn't exist, and there was a short-circuit between their eyes and their brains that made him invisible to them.

That night Carver awoke in his bed in the Glades Inn to an odd, snarling sound outside in the dark. He lay on his back in total blackness, his fingers laced behind his head, and realized he was listening to the sound of an airboat deep in the swamp. Maybe one of Ray Orb's boats. But according to I. C. Unit, Orb didn't operate in this part of the swamp because it was too dense and dangerous. And how could you not believe I. C.?

Carver fell back asleep listening to the faraway sound of the airboat and dreamed that it was a gigantic insect droning in the swamp. In the dawn and the halfway country between waking and sleep, he thought maybe his dream was possible.

It was more possible, he decided when fully awake, that the late-night droning from the swamp was indeed an airboat's engine, and the cargo was illegal narcotics.

CARVER ESTABLISHED A ROUTINE OVER the next five days, not doing much other than fishing with rod and reel and Oh Buggie!, going to secluded fishing spots in the evenings and staying late, tossing his infrequent catches back into the water. Carrying his fishing gear, he explored the swamp around Mangrove City. Though he came across tracks in the mud once, he never saw an alligator. And he didn't again hear the snarl of an airboat engine in the night.

Until the sixth night, when he was standing ankle-deep in water near the gnarled roots of a mangrove and heard the sudden roar of an engine, as if a boat that had been drifting nearby had abruptly started up. A light flashed, the swinging beam of a searchlight illuminating the swamp, and for an instant through the trees he saw the shimmering whir of an airboat's rear-mounted propeller spinning in its protective cage as it powered the flat-bottomed boat over the water. Judging by the size of the prop and cage, it was a large boat. Carver heard voices, then a single shouted word: *"Cuidado!"* A man yelling in Spanish to whoever was steering the boat to be careful, probably of some looming obstacle the light had revealed.

Carver stood motionless until the snarling engine had faded to silence. He could still hear water lapping in the boat's wake, even see ripples that had found their way to the moonlit patch of algae and floating debris where he was pretending to fish.

He reeled in Oh Buggie! and a tangle of weed, then returned to where the Olds was parked and drove back to the motel.

Maybe tonight he'd finally caught something.

After showering away mosquito repellent and swamp mud, he put on a fresh pair of boxer shorts, made sure the room's air conditioner was on high, then went to the alcove closet. He reached up on the shelf and found the half-dollar-size bronze Aztec calendar again and stood staring at it. No one knew for sure that the ancient circular Aztec design actually was a calendar. It was only a theory.

Carver stared at the trinket, then placed it back on the shelf. Now he had a theory, and one he believed in. Tomorrow he'd do something about it.

He sat on the edge of the sagging mattress, flicked the wall switch off with his cane, and dropped back on the bed in the warm darkness. With so much resolved, and with a clear course of action before him, he dozed off immediately and slept deeply.

\*      \*      \*

HE SENSED IT WAS TOWARD morning when he dreamed again of the giant insect droning in the swamp. Only this time he was surprised to hear it buzz his name.

Abruptly he realized someone was in the room speaking to him. Without moving any other part of his body, he opened his eyes.

I. C. Unit was standing at the foot of the bed. He was holding a shotgun casually so that it was pointed at Carver.

"Carver. Carver. You best wake up. You're gonna go fishin' early this mornin'. Gonna get yourself an early start well afore sunrise. Ain't no need for you to worry about bringin' any bait."

Carver knew why. He was going to *be* bait. And not for fish.

At I. C.'s direction, he climbed out of bed and dressed in jeans and a pull-over shirt, then put on his green rubber boots. His fishing outfit.

"Don't forget your rod and reel," I. C. said. "Gotta make this look realistic. Hell, maybe we'll even let you catch a fish."

When they went outside, Carver met Peevy and Magruder. There were no introductions and none were necessary. Peevy was a short man with a beer gut and a pug face. He was tattooed, like I. C., with the crude blue ink imagery of the amateur prison artist without adequate equipment. Magruder was tall and thin, with a droopy moustache and tragic dark eyes. Each man was armed with a semiautomatic twelve-gauge shotgun like I. C.'s. Their shells were probably loaded with heavy lead slugs rather than pellets, the rounds used by poachers to kill large and dangerous alligators. Awesome weapons at close range.

"He don't look like much," Magruder said in a southern drawl that sounded more like Tennessee than Georgia.

"Gonna look like less soon," Peevy said in the same flat drawl. He dug the barrel of his shotgun into the small of Carver's back, prodding him toward the parked Olds.

I. C. laughed. "Shucks, that's 'cause there's gonna *be* less of him."

Peevy drove the Olds, and I. C. sat in back with his shotgun aimed at Carver, who sat in front and wondered if he could incapacitate Peevy with a jab of his cane, then deal with I. C. and the shotgun. But he knew the answer to that one and didn't like it. Magruder followed, driving a dented black pickup truck with a camper shell mounted on its bed. As they pulled out of the Glades Inn parking lot, Carver was sure he saw a light in the office go out.

"You weren't smuggling drugs," Carver said, as they bumped over the rutted road. "You were bringing in illegal aliens from Mexico."

"From there and all over Central America," I. C. said. Now that Carver knew, he was bragging. Nothing to lose. "Boat from Mexico transfers 'em to airboats on the coast, and we know the swamp well enough to boat 'em in here. The Glades Inn is the next stop, where they pay the rest of what they owe and then are moved by car and truck on north.''

"And if they can't pay?''

I. C. laughed hard and Carver felt spittle and warm breath on the back of his neck. "That's the same question that poor Terry Frist asked. Answer is, if they can't pay, they don't go no farther north.''

"Nor any other direction," Peevy added, wrestling with the steering wheel as they negotiated a series of ruts.

"And Terry Frist?'' Carver asked.

" 'Gator got him, all right," was all I. C. said.

Peevy smiled as he drove.

They wound through the night along roads so narrow that foliage brushed the Olds's sides. Finally they reached the most desolate of Carver's fishing spots, a pool of still water glistening black in the moonlight, its edges overgrown with tall reeds and sawgrass.

As soon as they'd stopped, I. C. prodded the back of Carver's neck as an instruction, to get out of the car. Carver climbed out slowly, feeling the hot, humid night envelop him, listening to the desperate screams of nocturnal insects. Magruder parked the pickup behind the Olds, then climbed out and walked forward to join them. The only illumination was from the parking lights on the Olds.

While I. C. held his shotgun to Carver's head, Magruder looped a steel chain around the ankle of Carver's right boot and fastened it in place with a padlock. Then he shoved him toward the center of the shallow pool of water. Carver noticed a thick cedar post protruding from the water.

When they reached the knee-deep center of the pool, Magruder strung the chain through a hole in the post, wrapped it tight around the thick wood, then used another padlock to secure it. He clipped his key ring back onto one of his belt loops, then stepped back. Peevy was standing nearby, his shotgun aimed at Carver.

I. C. handed Carver the casting rod. "You hold onto your prop here," he said, then snatched Carver's cane away and effortlessly snapped the hard walnut over his knee. He let both ends of the splintered cane drop into the water.

"The desk clerk at the Glades Inn knows you left with me," Carver said. "He's probably already called Chief Gordon.''

"He knows ever'thin'," I. C. said. "So's Chief Gordon know, though he don't like to let on, even to his own self.''

Both men backed away from Carver, leaving him standing alone and unable to move more than a foot or so in any direction.

"You wanna pass the time fishin'," I. C. said, "you go right ahead. Now us, we gotta drive back into town and do some minor mischief, establish an alibi. Magruder'll stay here an' keep you company till you don't need no company. He ain't afraid of the dark, and he likes to watch."

"Watch what?"

"This here's a special part of the swamp, Carver. It ain't at all far from where that Terry Frist fella got hisself tore all to hell by a 'gator. This here area is crawlin' with 'gators. They figured out some way in their mean little brains that there's plenty to eat here from time to time."

I. C. and Peevy sloshed through the dark water and onto damp but solid ground. "We gonna be back to pick up Magruder later," I. C. said without bothering to look at Carver. He and Peevy climbed into the cab of the battered black pickup and the engine kicked over.

When the old truck had rattled its way out of sight, Magruder sat himself down on a stump about fifty feet away from Carver and settled his shotgun across his knees.

"Now then," he said, "you go ahead and fish if you want. You an' me's jus' gonna wait a while an' see who catches who."

Carver stood leaning against the post driven into the earth beneath the water. He knew it was firm, driven deep or maybe even set in concrete, and the locks and chain were unbreakable. He stared into the dark swamp around him, listening to the drone of insects, the gentle deadly sounds of things stirring in the night. Though he told himself to be calm, his heart was hammering. He glanced over at Magruder, who had a lighted cigarette stuck in his mouth now and smiled at him.

When Magruder was on his third cigarette, there was a low, guttural grunt from the dark, and off to the side water sloshed as something ponderous moved. Carver looked down and saw the water around his knees rippling. He tried swallowing his terror, tried desperately to think, but fear was like sand in the machinery of his mind.

The tall black grass stirred, and something low and long emerged. Carver knew immediately what it was.

The huge 'gator slithered out into plain view in the moonlight, sloshed around until it was at a slight angle to him, and regarded him with a bright, primitive eye.

"Sure is a big 'un!" Magruder said, obviously amused.

The 'gator switched its tail, churning the water. Carver's heart went cold. He wielded the casting rod like a weapon, as if that might help him.

And it might.

He made himself stop trembling, turned his body, and leaned hard against the post, setting his good leg tight to it.

The 'gator gave its fearsome, guttural grunt again.

"Hungry!" Magruder commented, looking from Carver to the 'gator with a sadist's keen anticipation.

Carver raised the casting rod, whipping it backward then forward. The line whirred out and fell across Magruder's shoulder. Carver reeled fast as Magruder reached for the thin but strong line. It simply played through his fingers, cutting them. He yanked his hand away and Carver gave the rod a sharp backward tug, feeling the Oh Buggie! with its many barbed hooks set deep in the side of Magruder's neck.

Magruder yelped and jumped up in surprise, the shotgun dropping to the ground. He reached down for the shotgun but Carver yanked hard on the rod, pulling him off balance and making him yelp again in pain. He'd stumbled a few steps toward Carver, and now he couldn't get back to the gun.

Carver began reeling him in.

Magruder didn't want to come. He tried to work the lure loose from where it clung like a large insect to the side of his neck, but each time Carver would yank the rod and pain would jolt through him. The alligator was still and watching with what seemed mild interest.

Carver had Magruder stumbling steadily toward him now, led by excruciating pain. Magruder raised his right hand and tried frantically to loosen the barbed hooks, but found he couldn't withdraw the hand. It was hooked now too, held fast to the side of his neck. Blood ran in a black trickle down his wrist. With his free hand he removed the cigarette stuck to his lower lip and tried to hold the ember to the fishing line to burn through it. Carver yanked harder on the rod, and the cigarette dropped to the water. Magruder was splashing around now, falling, struggling to his feet, fighting to pull away.

And something else was splashing.

Carver looked over and saw the massive low form of the alligator gliding toward him.

Magruder was still fifty feet away.

The alligator was about the same distance away but closing fast, cutting a wake with its ugly blunt snout, its impassive gaze trained on Carver.

Carver began screaming as he worked frantically with the reel. In the back of his mind was the idea that noise might discourage the alligator. And Magruder was screaming now, thrashing panic-stricken in the shallow water.

The alligator hissed and slapped the water with its tail, sending spray high enough to drum down for a few seconds like rain.

Carver and Magruder screamed louder.

THE DENTED BLACK PICKUP TRUCK approached slowly and parked in the moonlight beside the still water.

I. C. and Peevy climbed down from the cab and slammed the doors shut behind them almost in unison. They stood carrying their shotguns slung beneath their right arms.

"Been paid a visit here," Peevy said, motioning with his head toward the two lower legs and boots jutting up from the bloody water. It was obvious from the shallow depth of the water and the angle of the legs that they were attached to nothing. Other than the right leg, with the padlock and chain around its booted ankle.

"Magruder!" Peevy called.

"Will you look at that!" I. C. said. He pointed with his shotgun toward the huge alligator near the water's edge, its jaws gaping.

Neither man said anything for at least a minute, standing and staring at the alligator, their shotguns trained on it.

"Ain't movin'," Peevy said after a while.

I. C. dragged the back of his forearm across his mouth. "C'mon."

"Don't like it," Peevy said, advancing a few steps behind I. C. toward the motionless alligator.

"Nothin' here to like," I. C. said.

When they were ten feet away from the alligator they saw the black glistening holes in the side of its head, from the lead slugs Magruder used in his shotgun rounds.

Then they saw something else. The alligator's jaws were gaping because they were propped open with something—a stick or branch?

No, a cane! A broken half of a cane!

I. C. whirled and looked again at the booted legs jutting from the bloody surface of the barely stirred water.

"Them boots got laces!" he said. "Crippled man didn't have no laces in his boots! He musta somehow got Magruder's keys off'n him, then his gun!"

He and Peevy turned in the direction of a slight metallic click in the blackness near the edge of the pond, a sound not natural to the swamp. Together they raised their shotguns toward their shoulders to aim them at the source of the sound.

But Carver already had them in his sights. He squeezed the trigger over and over until the shotgun's magazine was empty.

In the vibrating silence after the explosion of gunshots, he heard only the beating of wings as startled, nested birds took flight into the black sky. They might have been the departing souls of I. C. and Peevy, only they were going in the wrong direction.

Using the empty shotgun for a cane, Carver limped out of the swamp.

Carolyn G. Hart was already collecting both accolades and awards for her cozy mystery series featuring bookstore owners Annie Laurence and Max Darling, when she decided to strike out with a new series protagonist, Henrietta O'Dwyer Collins, a 70-something reporter with one of the sharpest detecting minds since Miss Marple herself. Judging by the recognition, with one Agatha award and one Agatha nomination, the series is off to a grand start. Henry O appears in *Death in Lover's Lane*, and in the following story, pursuing crime among the wealthy in South Carolina.

# Remembrance
## CAROLYN G. HART

Dislike was instantaneous. And mutual.

Natalie Wherry Pearson's high-bridged nose and chiseled lips were elegant and haughty, her face as serenely arrogant as those pictured in the family portraits that lined her study. Directly behind her desk was a portrait of Colonel Amos Wherry, who died on Omaha Beach. Natalie's father.

I had now lived in Derry Hills long enough to become familiar with the local icons. Amos Wherry was a brave man, by all accounts. The glass-encased medals beneath the portrait attested to that. But it didn't mean Amos Wherry was a likable man, not if the artist's brush was true. I saw the supercilious curl to Wherry's mouth, the posture of command born not of rank but of lineage.

I was underwhelmed. I've never excelled in deference, and obeisance to wealth and position ignites in me a contrariness that borders on the pugnacious.

This visceral response isn't unique to me, of course. All reporters have a stripe of irreverence in their mental makeup. It usually keeps them from turning into toadies, a danger for those who associate, even in an adversarial way, with the rich and powerful.

Natalie Pearson knew I was disdainful. That accounted for the tightening of those thin coral lips, the firming of her chin. She glanced down at my card, lying face up on her black-lacquered antique Chinese desk with its lovely inlays of copper. On the card, beneath my name, Henrietta O'Dwyer

Collins, I had written, "I wish to speak with you concerning Judith Montgomery."

She picked up the card. "I'm rather rushed this morning, Mrs. Collins. Since Miss Montgomery is no longer in my employ, I don't believe there is any point in our conversing." Her sharply planed face was all bones and unguent-smoothed skin. Her silvered hair fit her head in sleek waves designed by a stylist at an expensive salon. Glacial gray eyes surveyed me.

I smiled, even though I knew my eyes were as icy as hers. "But you've agreed to see me, Mrs. Pearson. That's quite interesting, you know."

Sudden red patches of anger flamed in her gaunt cheeks.

First score to me.

But now was the time to be wily. It wouldn't help Judith's cause for me to be summarily dismissed.

Before she could speak, I continued briskly. "I'm sure, of course, that your willingness to see me reflects your status as a community leader, your family tradition of noblesse oblige."

I kept my expression bland, a look perfected through years of interviewing.

As I had expected, after a flicker of surprise, she fished as nicely as a striped bass on a lazy summer afternoon.

Those thin red lips curved into a tight bow of satisfaction. "Yes. Yes, of course. Although I don't quite see that much can be done for poor Judith." Her voice was as cool as shaved ice.

"If you could just give me the circumstances . . ."

Old fish can be cautious. She was close to taking the lure, but not quite. "What is your interest in this unfortunate matter, Mrs. Collins?"

"Judith Montgomery is one of my students." And, I didn't add, a rather prickly one, charming one moment, confrontational the next. But, nonetheless, a student who had caught my attention and who now had asked for my help.

It still seems odd to think of myself as a teacher. I spent almost a half century as a reporter, and, after my retirement, found myself in a new career at a small liberal arts college in Missouri as a member of the journalism faculty made up, with glorious élan, of old professionals. This semester I was teaching basic reporting. I still see myself as a writer who teaches, not a teacher who writes.

The fact that the *Clarion*, the Derry Hills daily newspaper, was a product of the journalism school kept me firmly rooted in news reality. It bridged town and gown in a way unusual for a college community.

"At the college." Her tone warmed a degree.

I could see a cloak of respectability settling around me.

Useful things, occupations. But deceptive, too. Doctor. Lawyer. Indian chief. Reporter. Professor. The mind responds with a stylized image. That's why con artists dress so well, smile so often.

"I am a trustee, you know." A be-ringed hand reached up to smooth an almost invisible strand that had dared to straggle loose from her spray-stiff coiffure.

"Of course."

Actually, I'd learned it only that morning after skimming through the *Clarion* file on Natalie Pearson. Then I'd dropped by the desk of Vicky Marsh, who writes the kind of personal column found only in small-town newspapers.

I wasn't especially interested in what had appeared in Vicky's column. I wanted the information that never surfaced, the behind-the-hand whispers that rustle across a small town like discarded newspapers on a windy day.

I got a lot.

Natalie Pearson would be shocked at what I knew.

But that could come later. Right now I wanted entrée.

"I understand you hired Judith to serve as your social secretary on a part-time basis."

"Yes. It is my custom to employ a student in that role. This is the first time I've ever had a bad experience. I do appreciate the college being concerned about this matter."

I could have corrected her, made it clear I did not represent the college.

I could have, but I didn't. I had in no way suggested that I represented the school. It wasn't my job to correct her misperceptions.

"It is always a matter for concern when a student is suspected of theft. You understand that she will be suspended if charges are filed?"

Once again high red flagged her sharp cheeks.

"I am sorry to say," the words came quick and sharp, "that the police have declined to file charges. They say there is insufficient evidence." That high-bridged nose wrinkled in disdain. "However," her tone was grudging, "they've assured me they have ways of finding out when stolen goods change hands. Chief Holzer feels confident the thief will ultimately be caught."

I wished I had heard the exchange between Mrs. Pearson and Derry Hills Police Chief Everett Holzer.

Holzer and I are not simpatico. In his view, it's a (white) man's world. Everyone else (women, blacks, gays, the elderly, et al) simply get in the way and cause no end of trouble because of their uppity ways. Holzer believes the fifties marked the height of civilization.

So yes, Holzer is a chauvinist pig.

But he's smart and he's honest.

If Mrs. Pearson accurately recalled his words, if Holzer spoke of "the thief," it indicated the police were not convinced of Judith Montgomery's guilt.

"Perhaps we can help the chief."

Her eyes widened in surprise. "How would that be possible?"

"We can work together to find out the truth."

"But what can we do?"

"Talk to people. Someone else in the house may have noticed something."

"It's Judith," she said harshly.

"Then I know you'll be glad when that is proven."

"I want it over. Over." There was a flash of sheer unhappiness in her cool gray eyes.

Why should she be distressed? Judith Montgomery was the one in trouble.

"Tell me what happened."

She took a deep breath. Her voice was clipped. "It was the night of the Hospital Ball, October fifteenth."

One week ago.

"We have it here, of course. The board counts on it." She gestured toward French windows to her left. "We have so much room. The terraces are quite perfect. And the weather is usually pleasant in October. We have a seated dinner. Three hundred this year, I believe. And an orchestra. And dancing. And, of course, I wore the diamond and ruby necklace. I always wear it at this kind of event. Everyone expects it." She said it perfunctorily, without pleasure. As if it were a burden.

"So everyone who attended the ball could have seen the necklace, known it was there in the house."

"Oh yes. But the ball ended. As balls always do." There was the faintest undertone of sadness and regret. Her thin mouth drooped.

Did she wish for life to be filled with light and music, beautiful clothes and handsome people? Was it only then that her dreams were met?

She put the letter opener on a tray, also black and lacquered. She laced together her thin, heavily ringed fingers. Sunlight glanced off those diamonds. "I was very tired. So tired. And there was the usual commotion, the caterers striking the tables, the staff cleaning. But finally, the house was quiet. So you see, it doesn't matter that everyone saw it at the ball. The ball was over." Again, that breath of regret. "I'd asked Judith to stay the night. There are always so many little things a secretary can see to. I was in my room and I just felt too weary to come down and put the necklace away. I rang for Judith. She knew the combination, of course. She took the necklace—and that's the last time anyone has seen it." She said it matter-of-factly, as if it didn't matter a whit to her.

Perhaps it only mattered to Judith.

Judith, of course, had told me what happened next: She'd come downstairs, placed the necklace in the safe, and gone straight up to the room assigned to her. ". . . a tiny hot little hole up on the third floor."

Natalie Pearson's eyes dared me to disagree.

"When did you discover the necklace to be missing?"

"The next morning. The door to the safe was ajar." She pushed back her chair, walked to the fireplace. Her silk dress, a striking pattern of cream and black, glistened in the sunlight spilling through the terrace windows.

I joined her at the fireplace.

She tugged and a square of paneling swung open, revealing the dull gray metal of the safe.

Instead of a dial, an electronic pad was inset to the left.

Her fingers punched the numbers, 5-3-9-1-0.

The *Clarion* files included her birth date, May 10, 1939.

The door opened and a light came on, revealing three shelves.

She pointed at the top shelf. "There's where I keep my jewelry. I found the safe door open and the case on the floor."

"What else was taken?"

She swung the door shut. "Oh, I checked at once. But only the necklace was gone."

I looked at her curiously. "Don't you find that surprising?"

She shrugged and the silk rustled. "I suppose she was afraid to take more. Perhaps something disturbed her. Or perhaps only the necklace was wanted. It's very famous, you know. It's called Remembrance. My grandfather had it made for my grandmother when he came home safely from World War One. There have been many stories written about it. Perhaps Judith was commissioned to steal it."

I didn't argue. But, with a quick memory of Judith's defiant face, her dark blue eyes blazing, her lips tight in a defiant frown, I had difficulty casting her as anyone's accomplice. Judith was a loner as, of course, are many aspiring journalists, aloof enough to welcome a life of observation. But I had difficulty also in being sure of my judgment of Judith. I thought she was innocent because I didn't pick up either the cockiness of a clever criminal or the too-cautious fear of the guilty. What I sensed was anger, pulsing as steadily as a heartbeat.

Moreover, early in the fall Judith had found my purse in the parking lot—I still wasn't clear how it had been taken from my locked office while I was in class—and nothing was missing. Not that I would have expected anything to be, but once a thief, always a thief, and she need not have returned the purse at all, had she wished to strip it of cash and credit cards.

But there was something about Judith I couldn't gauge.

However, I simply said mildly, "Leaving the safe door open immediately exposed Judith to suspicion. If the door had been shut, when might you have discovered the necklace to be missing?"

Her eyes swung toward me, widening in surprise. Clearly, this had not occurred to her. "Why . . . I suppose . . . not until the Hall of Fame dinner. Next week."

I let her think about it.

She spoke quickly. "But no one else knows the combination, only I and my secretary."

I made no comment. Her family and staff would know her birthday and I felt sure if those dates were the basis for this combination, she'd used them elsewhere. "Do you have voice mail?"

"Yes."

"What is your pass code? One, nine, three, nine?"

Her silence answered me.

I didn't bother to ask about her credit card PIN. If it wasn't the same, I'd be very surprised.

Anyone with access to the safe could have tried various combinations: her birthday, the home address, hell, the telephone number. Savvy burglars do a little homework before breaking in.

But if I'd harbored any doubts about Judith's innocence, the open safe door answered them. All Judith had to do was swing the safe shut and she would be no more suspect than anyone who'd been in the house until the next time the safe was opened. To be sure, Judith would have been the last person to have handled the jewels, but that proved nothing.

In my interview with Judith, she'd sworn she'd closed the safe. ("Mrs Collins, I pulled on the handle to be sure.")

"It's an interesting point." I paused, then said, as if the thought had just come to me, "I suppose a necklace that famous has always been a security concern?"

She stood as stiffly as a dog scenting a snake-infested log. I pressed on. "When did you install a safe here in the library?"

"Some years ago." Her tone was wooden.

"Since the earlier theft of the necklace? From your mother's bedroom?"

Her face drained of color, leaving her cheeks as pasty as puddled candle wax.

It was so quiet I could hear her thin, quick breaths.

"The necklace *was* stolen some years ago, wasn't it? The police were called in, then suddenly the matter was dropped. Is that right?"

"No. No. There was a mistake, that's all. The necklace was simply mislaid."

"But wasn't there some question of someone on the staff being involved?"

I could hear Vicky Marsh's low breathless voice, "Henrie O, it was a four-alarm scandal. Some people thought Natalie's mother sold it for gambling debts. Another camp was sure Natalie's older brother got drunk and gave it to a current girlfriend. All anyone can be sure of is that Calvin Wherry, her grandfather, called the cops, then it was dropped like a rock. But the maid and chauffeur were gone the next week. Everybody clammed up. And six months later, Natalie married Tolman Pearson, the most boring old bachelor in town but a golfing buddy of Natalie's grandfather. They say she cried all night before the wedding. He must be twenty-five years older than she is." Vicky pushed tortoiseshell glasses higher on her nose. "No children. But her brother still lives with them. Old Mrs. Wherry's in a rest home, gaga, so I hear."

Mrs. Pearson turned away, walked stiffly back to her desk. "It was a long time ago. No one knows exactly what happened. But the necklace turned up. So it doesn't matter." She faced me. Her arms pressed tightly against her body.

If it didn't matter . . .

I smiled. "Funny, the stories that get around. But this time there has definitely been a theft?"

"As I said," her tone was venomous, "the necklace was simply mislaid some years ago. Now it has been stolen."

"But you want to find out what happened?"

"Of course."

"All right, I'll be glad to help, if I can." I spoke as if I'd been invited. "I'll talk to the others who were in the house." I kept my voice easy. "They may have seen something which will give us information."

"It's Judith. Of course it is." She rubbed one temple. "All right, talk to them. I want it settled."

THE PIERCING WHISTLE EASED AS the woman picked up the tea kettle. "Only way to make tea. Good hot water."

Steam plumed in the air as she splashed the boiling water into two pots. "No tea bags in this kitchen, thank you, ma'am." She brought the tray to the sunny breakfast table where I waited.

Ruth Fitch settled into the chair opposite me, her pudgy face pink with exertion. "Well, we've had us a week, that's for sure. I had to make the tea double strong the morning the necklace went missing. I thought Mrs. Pearson was going to faint. She was white as a ghost. Whiter! And that girl was just downright rude."

"Judith?" I poured the tea through the silver strainer.

The housekeeper nodded vigorously, her gray curls bouncing. "Yes, ma'am. When Mrs. Pearson asked if she knew where the necklace was, that girl flung up her head and snapped back that she'd put it away and if it was gone, someone else had taken it, and she didn't like the suggestion she'd had anything to do with it and she wasn't going to stay someplace where her honesty was doubted and she quit. And then she whirled around and ran out of the house. Set off all the alarms, too. And that was upsetting. She didn't even take her overnight bag. We had to send it the next day. And poor Mrs. Pearson, she didn't know what to do. Mr. Pearson came wandering in and he said I'd better call the police. Then the police came . . ."

Ruth Fitch had a runaway tongue, but it didn't take long to learn what she knew:

The burglar alarm didn't go off that night.

Mr. Pearson was interested in the missing jewelry, but Mrs. Pearson didn't want to talk about it, and she shut herself up in her room and said she had a sick headache.

Mrs. Pearson's brother, Harley Wherry, was, as usual, under the weather. (I took this as a euphemism for drunk.)

The catering staff was gone before the house was locked for the night.

Five people slept in the Wherry house the night of the theft: Judith Montgomery, Natalie Pearson, Tolman Pearson, Harley Wherry, and Mrs. Fitch.

The Pearsons occupy separate suites.

No, so far as she knew, Judith didn't know the code for the alarm system.

It wasn't like the good old days with a big staff, including a fulltime maid and a chauffeur. No indeed. Now a cleaning service came in every week, a girl came in twice a week to dust, Mrs. Fitch handled the housekeeping, except for large parties, and Mr. and Mrs. Pearson drove themselves.

I sipped at the Earl Grey. "Were you working here when the necklace disappeared some years ago?"

She glanced over her shoulder, then spoke softly, "I'm surprised Mrs. Pearson told you about that. Did you know she's always hated that necklace? Ever since that time? It was the strangest thing. To this day nobody knows what really happened. Later everybody guessed that Terry Parker—he was the chauffeur—took it. No one ever saw him here again after it was gone." She pulled her chair closer to mine, with another swift glance at the closed kitchen door. "But Leola, his wife, was as honest as anybody ever could be, and she left, too. She was the maid. I heard she took their little girl and moved to Springfield, but nobody knows for sure. Years later, somebody told me Leola lived in Springfield, and she'd remarried, so I don't know what happened to Terry. He was too good-looking to ever last for any woman. You know the kind, eyes that tell you you're the most gorgeous woman in the world and a wicked smile, the kind that makes women forget they've got any sense at all. Oh, he could charm everybody. And laugh! He'd get you laughing till you almost cried. He always had a kind word for everybody. Leola adored him and so did their little girl. I remember he always called her Baby. I thought to myself, a schoolgirl should have a name, but that was Terry, making everybody feel special. He called Leola Dream Girl." She ducked her head. "Why, he called me Petunia." Her cheeks dimpled. "Anyway, the necklace was kept in Mrs. Wherry's jewel box. It disappeared and then everybody was so shocked when it turned up the next week, hidden in the toe of one of Mrs. Wherry's dancing slippers." Suddenly her pink mouth formed a sudden perfect O of surprise. "Why, it was after the Hospital Ball that time, too! Why, isn't that the strangest coincidence!"

Coincidences do happen.

But I always give them a second look.

TOLMAN PEARSON SIGHTED ALONG THE imaginary line from his golf ball to the hole. He had beautiful form, firm wrists, his arms and shoulders moving together, just like a pendulum. Easy to describe, difficult to do. The ball rolled obediently eight feet and curled into the cup.

"Change the holes every week. Still, you get to know the turf. But it's nice to have my own putting green."

Only the top of the three-story stone house was visible from the putting green, which was over a hill from the terraces.

"You're a good golfer." I didn't make it a question.

"Yes. Best sport in the world. Nothing else can compare."

He was seventy-nine and looked sixty-five. Indolence agreed with him.

"I'm interested in the disappearance of your wife's necklace."

He bent down, picked up the ball, walked a few paces, dropped the ball over his shoulder. "Don't mind if I putt, do you?"

I didn't suppose it mattered to him if I did. "Of course not."

Once again, he eyed the imaginary line. "Quite a magnificent necklace, you know." He studied the grass. "Funny thing is, it disappeared for a while the year Natalie and I got married. She told me Harley pinched it, but her grandfather made him put it back. I tried to talk to Calvin about it, but he wouldn't ante. Suppose it was true about Harley. But, there it is, it was a long time ago." Once again, that sure, confident stroke, and the ball rolled to the cup, dropped in. "Don't suppose it matters. Natalie doesn't like to talk about it." He walked to the hole, picked up the ball. "Actually, I don't even think she would have called the police this time if I hadn't insisted. I came downstairs for breakfast and found everyone in a panic. But you can't lose a fortune and not do something. The insurance fellows wouldn't like it."

"So you've made a claim for the necklace."

Pale blue eyes swung toward me. For an instant, they lost their good-natured gleam. "Of course."

HARLEY WHERRY WAS AMIABLY DRUNK, but it was such an habitual state there was only the slightest thickening to his voice. ". . . so that's why old Tolman's never wanted to make any investments with me. Trust my dear little sister to queer my pitch. But," he moved languidly in the massive red leather chair in a dim corner of a downstairs clubroom, "that's all right. Poor old Nat. She's never had much fun. I've always had fun. My number one rule in life is to do whatever the hell I want to. Makes sense, right? So, I'll let Tolman keep on thinking I'm the light-fingered Harry. Thing about it is, I think Sis stole the jewels the first time around. And, somehow, the Old Man—that's my grandfather, and he was the closest thing to a Prussian general you ever met—caught her at it. Why else did she marry Tolman? She sure as hell didn't want to." A chuckle ended in a hiccup. He reached out a thin, languid hand, so like his sister's but ringless, and picked up a full tumbler. He lifted it and drank. "But this time, it has to be the secretary. Too bad. Cute little thing." His mouth curved in a salacious smile. His face was almost a replica of his sister's except his cheeks sagged with dissipation, and his eyes were rheumy. "Can't see why Sis would do it. Of course, I never knew why she did it the first time."

DON BROWN LOOKS LIKE AN average thirtyish guy, almost nondescript, not too tall, slender, with a narrow, often weary face. But a perceptive viewer will note the quick intelligence in his eyes, the deliberate lack of expression, the wiry athletic build of a long-distance runner.

He's a cop, a good one.

And he's my friend, one of the best. A good enough friend that he now calls me Henrie O, the nickname given to me by my late husband Richard. Richard said, "Sweetheart, you pack more surprises into a single day than O. Henry ever put in a short story."

Don Brown and I met when I'd first moved to Derry Hills and a young blond woman was strangled in the apartment next to the one where I was staying temporarily.

We've come a long way since that day. I'd thought him too young to be a detective. He'd thought me too old to be of any assistance. We were both wrong.

On Sunday afternoon, he lounged comfortably in a rattan chair on my screened porch, a mug of coffee cradled in his slender hands. "I copied the file." He nodded at the manila folder on the rattan coffee table. "Sue Rodriguez has the case. She thinks it's clearly an inside job, but it's a puzzler because the primary suspect, Judith Montgomery, doesn't strike Sue as stupid. So, why didn't Montgomery shut the safe, delay the discovery? Moreover, there are no fingerprints on the safe door and the buttons on the electronic panel were smudged. The last person to punch the numbers wore gloves. Why would Montgomery wear gloves? She was supposed to put the necklace away. Her prints should be there. Moreover, she slammed out of the house the next morning—apparently they made her mad—and she was wearing, according to the housekeeper and Mrs. Pearson, a thin chambray blouse and jeans tight enough to fit an eel and carrying a tiny purse. The necklace is big. No way she could have taken it out in a pocket or in that purse. Judith Montgomery didn't know the house alarm system and it hadn't been turned off when she left. When she yanked open the front door, the alarm sounded and Mrs. Fitch had to turn it off. So Montgomery didn't snitch the necklace and pass it to a confederate. Any opened window or door would have sounded the alarm."

"We can't be certain she hadn't somehow learned the alarm code." I sipped at my coffee and pushed the plate with sugar cookies closer to Don.

He took one. A crumb straggled down his chin as he continued. "True. But if Montgomery took the necklace, she's made no move to unload it. Sue's had her under around-the-clock surveillance." He finished the cookie. "So now, Henrie O, tell me how you got involved."

"Judith's one of my students."

"Investigating a jewel theft isn't in your job description. I guess your reputation as a sleuth is getting around."

I shrugged it away, but I suppose it was flattering to think students saw me as something other than a teacher or a retired reporter. "I'm afraid I haven't come up with much this time."

I told him what I'd learned. Not enough to clear Judith. Not even enough to implicate anyone else, and the list of others had to be confined to Natalie Pearson, Tolman Pearson, Harley Wherry, or Mrs. Fitch, and a less likely crew of jewel thieves I'd never seen.

I shook my head. "Nothing makes sense, Don. Why? Why would any one of them do it? Money? The family has money. As for Judith and Mrs. Fitch, how could they make the right kind of connection to fence a necklace like that?"

I refilled our mugs. "Don, there's something odd about the whole setup. I keep thinking there's some connection to the disappearance of the necklace some years ago. I found a story in the *Clarion*, October seventeenth, nineteen eighty-three. There was only one story, then the investigation was dropped. There was no hint it was thought to be an inside job."

Don drank his coffee, his eyes squinted in thought. But, finally, he shook his head. "Got me, Henrie O. It has a funny feel to it. But you'll get there. You always do."

I didn't share his confidence.

MONDAY MORNING AFTER MY NINE-O'CLOCK class, I returned to my office to find two messages.

I called Don first.

"Henrie O, talk about twists and turns! In Sue's mail this morning, there was a typed note with this message: *The necklace is hidden in Natalie Pearson's closet. Ask her why.* Sue's already had the note to the lab. It's written on Tolman Pearson's stationery and it has his fingerprints on it. Sue's huddling with the chief right now."

"The insurance company will find this quite interesting."

"Won't they?" Don agreed. "And, of course, it's a misdemeanor to report a false crime. I'd say Natalie Pearson's got some problems."

I've been around investigations of all kinds for a good many more years than Don. "Actually, Don, I doubt it. I'll bet you a ticket to the Cards' opening day next spring that it will be déjà vu all over again: The lost shall be miraculously found and no more will be said."

There was an instant of silence. "It would simplify life for the chief, wouldn't it? I'll let you know, Henrie O."

The second call was to the registrar's office in Greene County. I wrote down the information I'd asked for—the issuance of a marriage license sometime after 1983 to Leola Parker.

I wanted to talk to Leola Parker, find out more about handsome Terry, who was seen no more after the first disappearance of the necklace. And if Leola had moved to Springfield, been rumored to have married again, there was a good chance that second marriage took place in Springfield.

It had.

Sometimes basic reporting, going after facts to flesh out a story, can turn up surprising leads. I stared down at the names I'd written:

Leola Baker Parker to John Milton Montgomery.

Oh, oh, and oh.

I tapped my pen against the paper.

I ran through some facts in my mind:

1. The open safe door.
2. Smudged fingerprints.
3. Leola Parker was an honest woman.
4. Natalie Wherry wept the night before she wed.

I now had an idea why.

But I still needed certain facts.

Mrs. Fitch had her own telephone line at the Wherry house. When she answered, I had one question.

What time did Natalie Pearson eat breakfast the morning the jewels were discovered missing?

As she concluded, I said, "Thank you, Mrs. Fitch. I'll—"

"Mrs. Collins, have you heard? Mrs. Pearson found the necklace in her closet. Why, it's just the strangest thing! In the toe of a pump, just like last time! Mrs. Collins, have you ever heard of such a thing?"

"I imagine it will turn out to be some kind of a joke, Mrs. Fitch."

"Well, Mrs. Pearson doesn't think it's funny!"

"I'm sure she doesn't. Nor," I said a trifle grimly, "do I. Thank you, Mrs. Fitch."

I hung up the phone.

I had one more person to talk to—if she would see me.

\* \* \*

OUR SHOES GRATED AGAINST THE pebbled walk. The Italian terraces rose behind us. There was no one near.

Natalie Pearson walked with her head down, her hands clasped tightly behind her back. "Mrs. Collins, I have to know *why*. Not because it matters legally. The matter is officially closed, both by the police and the insurance company. Actually," Natalie Pearson's voice was bitter, "everyone seems to think I took the necklace and hid it, even though that makes no sense at all." Her eyes glittered with anger. "But I have to know why. Why would this young woman whom I don't know involve me in this—this grotesque charade? Why, Mrs. Collins?"

"I believe I know."

She stopped, faced me, her gaze demanding.

But this time I didn't see pride or arrogance. This time I saw pain and despair.

"I will explain what happened, Mrs. Pearson, if you will tell me the truth about the first disappearance."

A pulse throbbed in her throat.

I spoke quietly. "Terry Parker took the necklace from your mother's room. Is that right?"

A breeze rustled the cedars behind us. In the sunlight, her quite perfect, lifeless hair was touched with gold.

I could see that she'd had a fragile beauty when she was younger, before her eyes lost hope.

Natalie Pearson met my gaze squarely. "No, Mrs. Collins. I took the necklace. I gave it to Terry."

We gazed at each other.

Her mouth quirked in a wry, sad smile. "You don't look surprised."

"No. I understand he was handsome. And charming."

"Oh yes. He made love to me. We were going to run away together. I gave him the necklace and the next night I was to meet him at the train station." She stared down at the shadows splashed along the sidewalk. "He didn't come."

Three little words, and the sorrow and loss they conveyed could never be summed up or judged or understood.

"And the necklace?"

"The next week Leola Parker came to see my grandfather. I don't know how she knew about the necklace. She must have found it in Terry's things and demanded to know what it was all about. She gave the necklace to my grandfather and told him it was all my fault, that I'd persuaded Terry to take it and that Terry had now deserted her. My grandfather said I had a choice." Her voice was toneless, all the passion and pain leached away by the passage of time. "Be publicly revealed as a woman involved with the family chauffeur—or marry Tolman."

"You married Tolman, and all of this was behind you—until now."

"Yes. Now, Mrs. Collins, tell me why this has happened."

"Terry Parker—what did he look like?"

"He was very handsome. Black hair. Dark blue eyes. High cheekbones. A magical smile and a funny way his mouth crooked when he thought everything was wonderful . . ." Her voice trailed away.

She could have been describing Judith Montgomery.

"Oh, my God. It's Baby," she whispered.

I FOUND JUDITH IN THE *Clarion* newsroom, at one of the desks used for general reporting.

She looked up from her computer as I stopped beside her.

"If you have a moment, Judith?"

"Oh yes, Mrs. Collins. What's happened?"

"Quite a bit." I led the way to my office and closed the door. I settled behind my desk.

She sat demurely in a chair, facing me.

But she was electric with excitement, her eyes bright, a becoming flush in her cheeks.

"Have you heard that the necklace has been found?"

Pleasure glistened now in her eyes. Pleasure and an almighty cockiness. "Oh, really? Then they owe me an apology, don't they? I'll demand it. And if they don't—if *she* doesn't apologize—I'll write a story for the *Clarion*."

"No."

Suddenly, her face was still, smooth, stiff. "No? Why not? I've been accused of theft. And they had no right. It's just like—" She stopped short.

"Yes, Judith? Like what?"

She stared at me, knowing something was wrong.

"Why don't you tell me about it—Baby."

Her face twisted with fury. "*She* took the necklace. Years ago. *She* took it. But she blamed my father—and so he ran away. That's what happens when people are rich and powerful, they can put the blame on someone else. Mother told me all about it, how *she* went after my dad, turned his head, persuaded him to run away with her. It's all *her* fault."

"Fault." I sighed. "That's what you've done, isn't it? You've blamed Natalie for your dad's running away. But think a little further, Judith; he didn't have to run away. Your mother returned the necklace. Your father left because he wanted to. Maybe he changed his mind about Natalie, maybe your mother faced him down. It doesn't matter. Yes, Natalie took the necklace, but she took it for him, to have him."

"No." It was a child's cry. "No. If it weren't for her, I would have had my dad, he wouldn't have gone away."

"Oh yes. Someday he would have. Because that's who and what he was.

Your mother blamed Natalie because she didn't want to blame him. Everyone always made excuses for Terry Parker. Wherever he is now, you can bet he's left behind people who loved him. And he's left behind a legacy of bitterness. You spent years thinking about it, and thinking how you could pay back the woman you blame for losing your father. That's why you came to school here. That's why you applied for the job as Natalie Pearson's secretary. Tell me, how many jobs did you turn down, for one reason or another, until you got what you wanted? You became her secretary and you waited for the right opportunity. The night you put the necklace away, you added sleeping pills to Mrs. Pearson's drink."

Her eyes widened, her mouth opened.

"How did I know? Because she overslept the next morning, by more than an hour. When she came down to breakfast, she mentioned feeling headachy to Mrs. Fitch. That could have been dangerous, Judith. You don't know what medicines she takes. But you were focused on your plan.

"That night, as she slept heavily, you crept into her room and hid the necklace in her closet, in the toe of a shoe, just as you'd heard that the necklace was found so long ago. From Mrs. Fitch, I imagine. I imagine you polished it so it would have no fingerprints. You made yourself a suspect, but you were careful to make it look wrong, the safe door open, no fingerprints on the door, the fingerprints smudged on the electronic panel. And the next morning, leaving in tight clothes with a small purse, not taking your overnight bag, setting off the alarm. You thought of everything."

She eyed me carefully. "You can't prove anything."

"I don't need to. I know. And you know."

She shoved back her chair, her face defiant. "What are you going to do?" She was poised to run.

"It is a crime to lie to a police officer during the course of an investigation."

"So?"

"It could be grounds for suspension from school."

She waited, her body tense. "What are you going to do?"

"That depends upon you, Judith. You see, I'd like for you to let go of the past, focus that thought and energy and passion on the future. Your future. You're smart, quick, clever. For example, you wanted someone to take up your cause. That's where I came in. You took my class and very quickly you figured out that I have a passion for the underdog and I thumb my nose at the powerful. You figured out a way to use me. First, you set it up so that I would be sure of your honesty. What did you do? This is an old building, did you try a bunch of keys until you found one that opened my office, then wait for a good time to snatch my purse?"

Her eyes flickered.

"I thought so. And then you called on me to help an underdog in need. And I couldn't wait to put on my Superman cape and get into the fray."

Something in my tone surprised her.

I managed a wry grin. "Yes. I'm at fault here, too. How rebellious do I come across in class? I need to give some thought to that. You see, Judith, as hard as it ever is to know someone else, it is harder to know ourselves. So let's make a deal: You put the necklace—Remembrance—behind you for good, for always, and look to yourself for the direction of your life, not your father or your mother or Natalie Pearson. And I promise that I won't—next time—assume that the underdog is always right."

As I told Don later, one is never too young to change—or too old to learn.

M. D. Lake's fiction has appeared in anthologies such as *The Mysterious West* and *Malice Domestic II*. His most recent novel is *Midsummer Malice*. A writer with a gift for dialogue and a natural talent for description, here he is at his best in this rather one-sided conversation over a nice cup of tea where several not so nice discoveries are made.

# Tea for Two
## M. D. LAKE

The door opens and a tall, elegantly clad woman with sleek black hair strides into the restaurant. She glances around, spots Jane already seated at a table against the front window, and marches over to her. Other guests, mostly middle-aged women having late-afternoon tea, glance up at her as she passes and comment in undertones that she looks familiar.

"It's remarkable," she exclaims as she slides into the chair opposite Jane. "I recognized you the moment I came in. You haven't changed at all." She shrugs out of her mink stole, letting it fall over the back of her chair. "You should exercise more, though, Jane—as much for health reasons as for appearance. I exercise an hour every day—even have my own personal masseuse now, an absolutely adorable man!"

She peers into Jane's cup, sniffs. "What're you drinking? Herbal tea!" She shakes her head in mock disbelief. "Same old Jane! You were the first person I ever knew who drank the stuff—you grew the herbs yourself, didn't you? Not for me, thanks. Oh, well, since you've poured it anyway, I suppose I can drink a cup of it for old times' sake. But when the waiter gets here, I want coffee. What are these? Tea cakes? I shouldn't, but I'll take a few. It's my special day, after all."

She puts some on her plate and one in her mouth. "Um, delicious! Did you make them yourself? Of course you did! It's just amazing what a clever cook can do with butter and sugar and—cardamom? A hint of anise? What else?" She laughs gaily. "You're not going to tell me, are you? Oh, you gourmet cooks and your secret recipes! Well, it would be safe with me, since I don't even know how to turn on the stove in either of my homes."

She eats another cookie, washes it down with a swallow of tea, and then makes a face. "Needs sugar. Oh, look! I haven't seen sugar bowls like this on a restaurant table in years. Nowadays all you see are those hideous little sugar packets that are so wasteful of our natural resources." She spoons sugar into her cup, tastes the result. "That's better," she says.

She looks at her jeweled watch. "Unfortunately, Jane, I don't have a lot of time. I told the escort to be back to pick me up in an hour—one of those damned receptions before the awards banquet tonight, you know. I don't know why I bother going to those things anymore. Vanity, I suppose, but this one is special, after all."

She glances around the room, an amused smile on her lips.

"So this is your little restaurant! Such a cozy place, just like you—and I mean that in the kindest possible way! You started out as a waitress here, didn't you? Then you became the cook, and finally, when you inherited some money and the owner died, you bought the place. See, I didn't cut *all* ties with you when you suddenly dropped out of my life, Jane. I've kept myself informed through our mutual friends."

She smiles. "It's ironic, isn't it? The author of cozy little mysteries featuring the owner of a cozy little restaurant quits writing and becomes the owner of a cozy little restaurant of her own! You've turned fiction into reality, Jane, haven't you? It's usually the other way around."

Becoming more serious, she goes on: "Oh, Jane, I've wanted so much to see you again, to try to clear the air and restore the trust that was lost twenty years ago through misunderstandings—but I wasn't sure you would want to, or that you were ready for it. I was afraid that your wounds, real and imagined, might never heal. But they have, haven't they?

"I can't tell you how happy I was when my secretary told me you'd called and wanted to get together while I'm in New York. 'My cup runneth over,' I thought—isn't that what they say? To get a lifetime achievement award from my peers and, on top of that, to see you again—all on the same day!"

She swallows a cookie, chokes on it, and tries to wash it down with tea.

"It came as such a shock," she continues when she's recovered, "when you threw your writing career away and went to work as a waitress! I mean, over just one little rejection!"

She laughs. "If I'd known it was going to do that to you, I might have accepted the manuscript. I mean, you should have talked to me about it before doing anything so drastic—we could have worked something out. Our relationship, after all, was more than just editor-slash-author. Much more—we were *friends*!

"Your manuscript *was* bad, of course, but your track record was good enough that you could have survived one weak effort like that. Not that I don't think I was right to reject it! As an editor, I had an obligation to my company, and I couldn't let friendship cloud my professional judgment. I did what I thought was right, without considering the consequences. And damn, Jane, there wouldn't have been any consequences if you'd been strong! You could have taken the rejection as a challenge to rise to another plateau. And I thought you were strong—everybody did. 'Strong Jane,' we all called you. Quiet, unassuming—maybe even a little dull and drab—but strong. How wrong we were!"

She wags a long, slim finger playfully in Jane's face. "And I don't feel a single twinge of guilt. Don't think for a moment I do, Jane! I'm sure that the rejection couldn't have been the sole reason you gave up writing! Admit it! Doing something that drastic is a lot like suicide. Something had been building up in you for a long time, and my rejection of the manuscript was just the last, but not the only, straw that broke the camel's back. Am I right? Of course I am! You were burned out, or burning out, weren't you? I could sense it in the manuscript. No—no more tea for me or I'll be spending most of the evening in the Ladies, instead of at the head table as guest of honor! Besides, it's a little too bitter, even with the sugar. Well, half a cup, then, since my throat's so dry—probably because I've been doing most of the talking, haven't I? Well, you always were the quiet type, weren't you?"

She spoons sugar into the cup and stirs it, sips tea and scrutinizes Jane across the table, a look of concern on her face. "Are you happy, Jane?"

She rolls her eyes and shakes her head in resignation. "Why do I ask! I don't think you were ever happy, were you? You always went around with a frown on your face, you were always concerned that you weren't writing enough, you were afraid you'd run out of ideas. You once told me you died a little every time you sent in a manuscript, wondering if I'd like it enough to buy it. Well, you look happy now—not happy, exactly, but content—even pleased with yourself, it seems to me. God, I'd give anything to be content! Well, not anything—I don't know any successful author who's content, do you? But you know what I mean. Here I am, about to receive a lifetime achievement award—a *lifetime* achievement award, Jane, after only twenty years, isn't that funny!—and I'm still not content. I don't think I'm writing enough, or good enough, and except for that first book, none of my books has been successfully translated into film. And I'm afraid I'm going to run out of ideas! I've pretty well taken up where you left off in the worry department, haven't I?"

Suddenly she leans across the table, rests one hand lightly on one of Jane's. "Look, Jane, I accepted your invitation this afternoon because on this, what should be the happiest day of my life, I don't like the thought that you might blame me for your career going into the toilet the way it did. I don't want that shadow over my happiness. I'm here because I want us to be friends again—you do see that, don't you?

"Don't frown at me like that! I know what you're thinking, but you're wrong! When I rejected the manuscript, I didn't have any intention of—of appropriating your plot! I rejected it on its own merits—its own *lack* of merits, I should say."

She lowers her voice. "But then the plot began to haunt me, you see. It was so original, so clever—and you hadn't known what to do with it! You'd played it out with such small people—your heroine, that drab little owner of a cozy little restaurant, for Chris-sakes! Her friends, the kitchen help, and her dreary little husband—not to speak of her poodle and her parakeet!"

She laughs harshly. "And all those suspects, the sort of people who patronize restaurants like that—cozy people with cozy middle-class lives and cares and secrets! Who's going to pay good money to read books about characters like that?

"I saw immediately that your plot could be applied to talented and successful characters—characters who were larger than life, the kind that most people want to read about. Characters who own horses and big, expensive cars—not poodles and parakeets! And I took it from there, and it was successful beyond my wildest dreams—and beyond anything you could ever have achieved, Jane!"

She laughs a little wildly. "My God—even I'll admit I've been living off that book ever since. One critic actually went so far as to say that I haven't written seventeen books, I've written the same book seventeen times! That hurt, but there's some truth in it. Even I'll admit it—as I laugh all the way to the bank!

"Oh, I know, I can see that you've caught me in a little contradiction. First I said I didn't have any intention of appropriating your plot and then I said I saw immediately that it could be put to so much better use than you'd put it to. But there's really no contradiction, Jane. Once I'd read your manuscript, I couldn't get the plot out of my head! It haunted me day and night. I couldn't sleep, couldn't think of anything else. I'd been trying to write a mystery for years—God knows, as an editor, I'd read enough of them to know how to do it—but after reading your manuscript my own seemed to turn to ash."

She arranges her mink stole around her shoulders, shivers. "It's cold in here. And where's the damned waiter? I'd like coffee. You'd think he'd be dancing attendance on us, Jane, considering he works for you."

She lowers her voice. "Was what I did so wrong? Your plot was like a succubus, eating away at my creativity. And since your creativity destroyed mine, didn't I have a right to steal from you? But I didn't think it would end your career! I assumed you'd go on writing those miserable little mysteries featuring Maggie O'Hare—or whatever her name was—forever, earning tidy little advances, a steady dribble of royalties, and tepid reviews. Damn it, Jane, I wasn't stealing *everything* from you—just that one brilliant little plot!"

A sheen of perspiration glistens on her forehead and upper lip, and she glances quickly around the room. "Sorry! I didn't mean to raise my voice like that. But you can see how aggravated it still makes me when I think of how you were going to waste it. I thought of you as a bad parent, Jane, and I felt it was my moral obligation to take your child from you to save it. You should have thanked me for that, not quit writing and disappeared without so much as a by-your-leave."

She picks up the teapot and starts to pour tea into Jane's cup, but, when she sees it's full, refills her own instead.

"And when your apartment burned down," she goes on after a moment, "and with it your computer and all the diskettes, it seemed to me that that was a sign from God—or whoever it is who watches over the really creative people in this world—that I should seize the moment! I mean, after the fire your plot was in the air, so to speak, wasn't it—just ashes floating in the air for anybody to grab who had the moral courage to grab it. And I did. I grabbed it, since I was left with the only copy of your manuscript still in existence!"

She dabs at her forehead with the napkin bunched in her hand. "Don't you think it's too hot in here?" she asks, shrugging out of her mink stole again.

"Even then," she continues after a moment, "I'm not sure I would have done it—taken your plot, I mean, changing the names and occupations of the characters—if it hadn't been for your husband. In fact, I'm not sure it wasn't Brad's idea in the first place! You see, he'd grown tired of being the husband of a plump, rather drab, lower mid-list mystery author, and one afternoon when we were lying in bed idly chatting about this and that, I happened to mention how possessed I was by the plot of your latest manuscript and how I thought it was bigger, much bigger, than your abilities to do anything with it. It needed larger characters and a larger milieu, I told him—perhaps a strikingly beautiful gourmet cook who has studied with some of the best chefs in France or Italy and is married to a remarkably handsome stockbroker—strong, self-possessed characters who move with casual grace in a world of money, power, and elegance!"

She smiles at a memory. "And you know how it goes when you're lying in bed after sex with your lover. Brad remarked—in all innocence, I'm sure—that unfortunately you weren't equipped to write about such a world. You didn't know it. You only knew the world of the middle class.

"And then I said that, well, *I* knew the world of the beautiful people very well! After all, as an editor I'd had to attend the kind of literary soirees that now, as one of the world's best-selling authors of romantic suspense, I'm forced to attend all the time.

"And that's how it happened, you see, Jane. I rejected your book because it wasn't up to your usual standards, Brad and I discussed what I could do with its marvelous plot—and the next thing I knew, your apartment burned down with all your records! You were lucky to get out with your life, if I remember correctly—although you did lose the poodle and the parakeet you'd loved so much. I remember that because Brad hated them both and was glad they were gone, although he did feel badly about everything else you lost."

She nibbles a cookie. "And your miscarriage, of course," she adds. "Brad was very, *very* sad about that, as was I. Brad had ceased to love you by that time, of course, but he still *cared* about you. *Deeply.*"

She smiles compassionately across the table at Jane. "If you need money, Jane—for expansion or to get more help—and God knows you could use another waiter!—I'd be glad to give you some. I've got more than I know what to do with now. I'll even give you a little monthly stipend if you want it, even though I don't have to and I certainly don't feel any moral qualms about what I did."

She picks up her cup and brings it to her lips, pauses suddenly, and then puts it down and stares at it thoughtfully for a long moment. Then she laughs uneasily, shrugs, and picks it up again and takes a big swallow.

"Funny," she says, "in your manuscript it's in a pot of tea that Nora Smith puts the poison that kills first her husband and then her husband's lover in Maggie—Margie?—O'Hare's restaurant. Do you remember, or has it been too long ago for you? I'd probably have forgotten about it myself except I had a big quarrel with my editor, who wanted me to make the poison a faster-acting one, cyanide or strychnine. I pointed out that if it acted that fast, the police would have no trouble tracing where the victims ingested it, but by making it take several days, nobody would know—until Maggie or Margie figures it out in the end, that is. Of course, by the time I rewrote it my way, it wasn't Maggie's—Megan's?—drab little restaurant anymore, it was the elegant bistro belonging to my heroine, Titania Oakes, a culinary artist, which attracted only the beautiful people—the trendsetters, the movers and the shakers. And the victims weren't a dowdy schoolteacher and an insurance salesman either—they were famous Broadway stars! That's how I made your wretched little story into a blockbuster, Jane! But I kept the poison the same as yours, except in my book it wasn't in tea, it was in a lovely risotto, for which Titania's restaurant was famous."

She frowns in thought, her eyes moving involuntarily to the teapot. "What was the name of that poison, anyway—do you remember? Something odorless and tasteless that leaves no trace, unless the medical examiner knows what to look for. I remember asking you where you got the idea for it and you said you'd had mushrooms like that growing in your backyard when you were a kid. Your mother had warned you against eating them. Once they got into your system, she said, you were done for—nothing could save you."

She shudders, picks up her teacup, and starts to take another swallow, then changes her mind and puts the cup down with a clatter.

"God, how you must hate me!" she whispers. "First I steal your husband and then your novel. Then you lose your poodle, your parakeet, and your baby—and finally your career. It sounds awful now, in the cold light of a gray autumn day in this cozy god-awful place—but it seemed so right at the time! And I didn't mean to hurt you, Jane! I expected you to bounce back stronger than ever. And probably meaner, too."

She tries to laugh but coughs instead. "I even imagined you'd write a novel in which you murdered me in the most horrible possible way! Isn't that ridiculous? Instead, you just dried up and blew away, didn't you?

"But you did get Brad back! When it didn't work out between us and I was forced to show him the door, right around the time my novel hit the *New York Times* best-seller list, he crawled back to you, didn't he? I seem to recall hearing that somewhere. As I said, I've kept track of you all these years, Jane. I don't know why. I guess I just don't know how to let go of a friend, even one who's turned her back on me the way you did. Call me a fool, but at least I'm a *loyal* fool!"

She frowns at a sudden memory. "But then Brad died, didn't he? I recall hearing that, too. First, you got remarried, and then, a year or so later, he came into some money. And then he died—suddenly, although he wasn't very old."

She's pale and breathing hard now, but she manages a ghastly smile. "Did you have him cremated, Jane?" she asks with forced humor. "So they'd never be able to find out if you'd put something in his food?"

Her voice rising, she asks, "What was it called again—the poison? There's no known antidote for it, is there? And a little goes a long way. Isn't that what your Megan or Maggie or Margie told the homicide inspector? 'No known antidote, inspector—and a little goes a long way.' " She laughs. "How much better that line sounded in my Titania's mouth than in—in your dreary little protagonist's!

"But once you've got it in your system," she goes on slowly, ominously, "it doesn't do any good to pump your stomach, does it? It doesn't do any good at all! Isn't that right, Jane?"

She jumps up and stares down at Jane in horror. "How long before you begin to feel the effects?" she shouts. "Do you remember? Of course you do—how could you forget? And the symptoms—chills and fever that mimic the flu, aren't they?" She wipes her forehead with her soggy napkin, stares at her shaking hand.

"And then, shortly after Brad died, the owner of this place died too, didn't he, Jane? Suddenly. And you bought the restaurant form his heirs with the money you'd inherited from Brad!"

She looks around the room wildly. "Why hasn't the waiter come over to our table? It's because you told him to leave us alone, didn't you? The tea and cookies were already here, waiting for me. It was in the tea, wasn't it? You never touched a drop of it. Or was it the cookies, or the sugar? Damn you, Jane, tell me!"

Without waiting for an answer, she turns to the others in the room and shouts, "She's killed me! As sure as if she'd pointed a pistol at me and pulled the trigger, she's killed me because I stole her plot, her story, her husband— everything—and she's never forgiven me! And I won't die quickly, either. No—it'll be tomorrow or the next day and I have to live with that knowledge and with the knowledge that it's going to be a slow and painful death. And I'll be conscious every moment of the hideous ordeal!"

She rushes around the table and throws herself on Jane. "Monster!" she screams. "Mass murderer! First your husband, then the owner of the restaurant, now me!"

The waiter runs over and pulls her off Jane. She struggles violently for a moment, then collapses onto the floor.

"Oh, God!" she whispers. "This was supposed to be the happiest day of my life, and now look what you've done! How cleverly you've plotted your revenge, Jane!"

Her face lights up briefly when something occurs to her. "But you won't get away with it this time. They'll do an autopsy! After my long, slow, agonizing death, they'll open me up and find what you murdered me with—and then you'll spend the rest of your life in prison—or worse!"

She chuckles madly and closes her eyes. "Will somebody please cover me with my mink stole?" she says plaintively. "But try not to let it touch the floor. Oh, how like you, Jane, to add insult to injury—poisoning me in such a grubby little place, among such drab people!"

She pulls the stole up over her face, after which her muffled voice can still be heard complaining that the pains have already begun, the poison is acting faster than Ms. Know-It-All thought it would.

As Jane waits for the ambulance and the police to arrive, she stirs sugar into her cold tea (she likes cold tea), helps herself to a couple of the remaining cookies, and begins planning tomorrow's menu. She remembers to turn off the tape recorder in her purse, too. That goes without saying.

Reginald Hill is another British author who excels at every form of fiction he tries. His recent novels *On Beulah Height* and *Asking for the Moon* have only extended this string of successes. The following story, a tale of a patient who divulges more than his doctor really wants to know, was the winner of the Crime Writer's Association's Golden Dagger Award. After reading it, you'll know why.

# On The Psychiatrist's Couch
## REGINALD HILL

I hate these things.

You come in with angst, you go out with back-ache. Aversion therapy. That'll be fifty guineas.

What's it stuffed with anyway? Rocks? Or electronic equipment? Perhaps it's really the couch that's listening to me, you're just a cut-out. Could be I'd get more sense out of it. Sorry, I don't really mean that.

Funny if it could talk, though. What tales it could tell! There must be more dirt spilled here than in a prozzie's pit.

Did I see you twitch there? One minute into the session and the patient makes first aggressive sexual reference to women. Worth a note, I'd say.

Please yourself.

I just want you to know that I've been here before. I know what's going on as much as you do. More. Think about it. You lot are all dying to find out what made me a serial killer.

Well, I know already.

So who's in control, eh?

OK, where shall I start? That's your cue for saying, where do you want to start, Jamie? So let's take that as read, and I'll say, the very beginning.

My father, God rest his soul, had a heart attack while he was on the job. Fatal. But his last shot was a bull's eye. Me.

Must have been a bit of shock for my dear mother, realising that she'd screwed the poor sod to death. Probably a lot bigger shock when she found she was pregnant. Still, no problem those days. Back in the swinging sixties, you travelled fast and you travelled light and the next stop could always be the terminus.

But it wasn't. She had me. Don't ask me why. Clearly she didn't want me. How do I know that? Well, she gave a pretty strong hint by buggering off soon as she could stagger and leaving me high and dry. Or, knowing the way babies are, probably high and wet.

I didn't know this at the time, of course. I must have been three or so when I first asked why I didn't have a mum. Your mother died giving birth to you, I was told. Bit baffling for a three year old! What did I know about birth or death?

But at least the motive for this lie was probably kindness, you say.

No way!

More chance of a hand job from the Venus de Milo, coming as it did from my paternal grandmother.

No, I suspect it was just wishful thinking. When it came to penal policy, she and her husband were Old Testament throwbacks. The way they saw it, my mother dying having me might just have evened things up for their son dying having her.

It was them that raised me till I was five. Not a labour of love, believe me. Love was pretty short in that household, but it fairly creaked with Victorian values, prime among which was, spare the rod and spoil the child. He wasn't too bad, more of a tokenist than the real thing. The disgrace of a beating was the true punishment, he reckoned. Not *her* though. *Whatsoever thy hand findeth to do* was her favourite text, and she did it with all her might. Across the knuckles just to keep you honest; back of the legs for minor offences; bare bum for the big ones.

This hurts me more than it hurts you, she once said. Oh, how I hoped it did, but I didn't really believe it.

You must have read all this stuff already. I'm not exactly the best advert for patient confidentiality you wankers have ever had!

Never mind. I don't mind going over it all again.

So how did I feel about her?

I hated her, of course. How else was I supposed to feel?

Even a guileless child soon gets the message when he's told everyday he ought to consider himself a very lucky little boy and this wasn't how she'd envisaged spending the years of her prime and if I knew what was good for me I'd sit there very quiet and not draw attention to myself as I was only there on sufferance and there were plenty of places where bad little boys were taken care of as they truly deserved.

Firm but fair, that was how she described her pediatric philosophy.

Strict and stark staring bonkers was nearer the mark.

That bit of my life ended that last Christmas, not long before my fifth birthday. I'm a Capricorn, by the way. That any help? No, I didn't think so. Not scientific. You and your science. Lot of good it's done me.

My grandparents had always gone to hotels for Christmas. Their Old Testament attitudes didn't extend to depriving themselves of any of life's little luxuries. Also hotels saved them the bother of mucking up their own house with pine needles and tinsel and mince pie crumbs, though I can't imagine a lot of people beating a path to their door in search of seasonal cheer. Perhaps that was another reason for hotels. Company without commitment, the desideratum of the self-righteous egotist since time began. No, not my phrase. Another of you lot. I've picked up quite a lot of the jargon as I've bounced from couch to couch.

Far from changing their festive arrangements, my arrival probably simply confirmed their wisdom. Hotels offering traditional Christmas breaks really cater for kids. Creches, child minders, special entertainment—they could dump me on arrival and hardly see me again till it was time to go.

Funny that. Despite what's happened to me, which I think you'll agree has hardly been calculated to inspire religious fervour, I still get a warm glow whenever Christmas comes around. The few good memories I've got of my earliest years all centre on those three days spent in the care and company of strangers.

That last Christmas had a real bonus in that it was white. Snow everywhere. We had snowball fights and went sledging and built huge snowmen with coal eyes and carrot noses. I loved it so much I didn't want to leave, and when it got to the day after Boxing Day, I went into hiding. By the time they tracked me down it was late morning. My grandparents were surprisingly laid back about it, on the surface anyway. Thing was, there were other people around who'd helped in the search and they'd all made a jolly game out of it, so what else could they do but join in the merriment at the comical antics of a lovable little scamp? But I saw the long teeth behind my grandmother's wide smile and I knew what to expect once we were alone.

We set off at midday. Before we got out of the hotel grounds, the tongue lashing had begun. Things weren't helped by the fact that it was starting to snow again. We should have been home by now, my grandmother told me. It was all my fault, I was a wicked ungrateful child who thought about nothing but my own pleasure, just like my slut of a mother who had clearly known what she was doing when she ran off and abandoned me at birth. This was the first time I got the revised, and as it turned out authorised, version of the story. My grandmother was the kind of woman who could use truth like a whip to draw blood.

The only good thing about the situation was that she was driving (she always drove; she wouldn't trust my grandfather to drive sheep, she would say) and keeping two hands on the wheel meant she had to stick to verbal punishment. But she made plenty of promises, and she was a woman of her word.

The main roads which had been cleared were beginning to whiten over again and traffic was heavy and slow. My fault, of course. She decided to turn off and go across country, despite my grandfather's weak protests. Perfectly safe, she said. The only danger in these conditions was from all those incompetent idiots who insisted on hogging the main road back there. Give her an empty highway and she could guarantee to negotiate any obstacle unscathed.

I enjoyed these few minutes of relief while she directed her venom at her husband, but it was a short respite. Soon I was the target again. The weather was worsening and as the snow came down harder and harder, so her abuse of me increased till suddenly I could bear it no longer. I had to get out. We'd slowed down a lot because of the conditions and I suppose the all enveloping whiteness blurred my impression of movement, so I probably thought we were almost at a standstill. It was a two door car and I was in the back so normally there was no way I could get out till one of the front seats was empty. But I couldn't wait for that.

Suddenly I clambered over my grandfather, heading for the passenger door. He shouted, my grandmother swung her left hand at me, either to grab or more likely, to hit me, I kicked out and caught her in the face, and next thing the car was spinning round like a duck landing on a frozen pond.

At first it was quite a pleasant sensation. Then we went through a fence and down a steep embankment, and it stopped being pleasant.

We rolled over two or three times, hit something hard, and came to a halt upside down.

That was it. The situation as I discovered later was that we were upside down against a stone wall under a snowdrift with the doors so badly buckled they couldn't be opened. My grandfather was already dead. Heart failure. The same weakness that killed my father, I suppose, which could mean my grandmother's revulsion from the idea of sex for pleasure gave him a couple of decades of extra life. Some prezzies aren't worth the pain, are they?

As for my grandmother, she was badly injured. Nothing wrong with her tongue, though. It took her a day and a half to die, during which time she never ceased to heap accusations on me and catalogue my failings. The one thing which did change was her language. Normally so precise, measured and magisterial, now she demonstrated a command of obscene abuse terminology which might have amazed me, if I'd been in any condition to be amazed.

The funny thing was that I didn't really become afraid till she finally fell silent. I wasn't too badly injured, in fact just scratches and bruises it turned out, but I was firmly trapped between my grandfather's body underneath me, and my grandmother's above. In a way, I suppose that saved my life. Kept the cold off. Gave me something to . . . hang on to.

Anyway, it was another two days before they finally found us. The snow had covered the car and it wasn't till a beginning thaw revealed the gap in the fence that someone thought of looking down the embankment.

I was taken to hospital where I recovered. Physically anyway. And then, in the absence of any other known relatives, I was put into care.

Care!

There's a four letter word for you to lecture on, doc.

The shelter I got from the decomposing bodies of my grandfather and grandmother was the last protection I was to receive from any adult human for many a long year.

Am I boring you?

God, how many times have I seen that same steady, blank, compassionate, nonjudgmental gaze! What it says is, I know all this. I'm way ahead of you. I understand why you did what you did, and I can help you confront it, understand it, and finally come to terms with it. Trust me.

Well, it's crap, you hear me? Crap!

You people want to trace everything back to those early years. Adolescence, childhood, in my case birth even! Like there's some burden I was born with and it's got bigger and bigger over the years as other stuff's got loaded onto it, till finally my mind and personality cracked under the weight.

Well, you're wrong. Not altogether wrong. You lot are clever buggers, I've never denied that. You understand things about the human mind I could never grasp. Where you fail is in being too self important. In not acknowledging that some people can shed their burden without your help. And shed it completely. Not a trace left. A completely new start. A rebirth, if you like. *Tabula rasa*, a born again personality. Like I say, I know the jargon.

There's another way you go wrong too. Not arrogance this time. Almost the opposite. But I'll get to that later.

The point I'm trying to make here is that whatever it was I was suffering from, I was cured before any of you couch-artists got within sniffing distance of me. I remember my first meeting with Mr Barnfather. You'll know his work, of course. Really high powered, with enough letters after his name to write a paper on me, which in fact he did.

Later we came to be good mates, at least that's how I saw it. That first time, he naturally wanted to hear everything, so I told him everything. But even with him that first time, when I got to this point, I caught on his face the same expression I think I've just detected on yours—a little flicker of impatience, like he'd made his mind up already that everything I'd done had to stem from those very early experiences and the rest of my sad story was just mere confirmation, so let's get a wiggle on and get to the killings.

He was probably right. You are probably right. Like I say, I know what clever buggers you lot are. But bear with me, I feel I've got to make sure you have the full story. But I will keep it as short as possible, knowing you can fill in the gaps yourself.

OK, where was I?

Oh yes, Care. I went into care.

Was I unlucky or was what I experienced just the norm? You'll probably have access to more statistics than are ever likely to come my way, so I'll let you be the judge. All I know is that I experienced three different children's Homes over the next ten years and all they had in common was that there was someone in there waiting to fuck you up. Mentally, physically, emotionally, every which way.

I was fostered too. Three times. Generally speaking that was worse. At least in the Homes it was sometimes someone else's turn.

Worst of all was the last time. *He* was away most of the time. *She* used to treat me as a servant. Then her mood would swing and I'd be "her baby". She used to give me baths. I was eleven. Then she started getting in with me. 'I've lost the soap, Jamie. See if you can find the soap, there's a love.'

I wanted to push her big fat smiling face under the water and hold it there till the bubbles stopped coming up.

But I didn't. In fact I never harmed anyone I was closely connected with. I mean, that would have been like leaving an arrow pointing right at myself, wouldn't it?

That was sensible, you must agree. That was rational. That alone surely points to my underlying sanity.

You don't look convinced. You're thinking, but he killed four women! Point taken, I can see your problem. Let me make no bones about it, if you'll excuse the expression. I murdered four women. Only four, mind you. If you believed some of the tabloids, I must have been responsible for every unsolved prostitute death from Jack the Ripper on!

But even four is too many. Even tarts have a right to live. I acknowledge it freely. I was right out of order. I was wrong.

I should only have killed one.

The one who started it all.

The one who should have died when I was born.

Odd, isn't it? I finally came round to my grandmother's way of thinking. Justice would have been served if my uncaring, unloving, hard-hearted, self-centred, runaway mother had died having me.

So you see, if only I'd known before I started what I found out within a very short time of being caught, none of this would have happened.

Say what you will about the tabloids, when it comes to digging up the past, they leave Egyptian tomb robbers eating their dust.

Me, I'd often thought of looking for her, but I didn't know where to start.

Nobody knew nothing, nothing they were going to tell me anyway. But within a few days of the fuzz releasing details of my arrest to the media, those Wapping weevils had burrowed into my past and come up with the truth about my mother's vanishing trick.

Simple really. She'd died.

When she walked out of the hospital leaving me to to field all the crap that life was about to throw at me, she headed back up north to the little Lancashire town she'd been born in. Up there she'd kept them as ignorant of her life down south as she'd kept those down south of her origins up there.

So when she got killed in a drunken car crash, enough was known about her locally to get her buried without need of any wider enquiry.

All those years of festering ignorance. Of wild imaginings. Of cancerous resentment.

If only I'd known . . .

But I knew now, and the knowledge had set me free.

There's the irony of it, you see. Before any of you lot had got down attempting a diagnosis of the causes of my disfunction, I was already cured.

I tried to explain this to Mr. Barnfather, of course, and he smiled and he nodded and made notes, but I could see I wasn't getting through. It didn't bother me, however. Please yourself, I thought. Makes no odds. That's how I saw things then.

You see, and this is further evidence of my return to sanity, I *knew* I'd done wrong. Even though the deaths of those woman had been in the strict sense of the word *accidental*, this didn't absolve me from responsibility. I knew I had to face up to this and I was ready to pay my debt to society, eat my porridge, whatever phrase you like to use.

I worked out that with remission for good behaviour, I could be out in seven years, perhaps less. Even with the worst-case scenario in which they threw the book at me, I couldn't possibly do more than ten.

I was so taken up with this long term planning for the rest of my post-prison *normal* life that I didn't pay enough attention at the trial. I was eager to cooperate, and determined to let them all see just how much I *was* cooperating. I was a little taken aback to hear myself being sentenced to a secure mental institution rather than jail, but my solicitor assured me I'd be much better off there than in some draughty old nick with four to a cell and slopping out every morning.

I was a model inmate. Whatever they told me to do, I did. Read the records, it's all there. No black marks against my name. I was on the best of terms with all the officers and nurses. And when it turned out that Mr. Barnfather was the head trick cyclist there, all I thought was, here's a chap who's got all the background. We'd established a good relationship, even though I knew I hadn't been able in our few pre-trial sessions to overcome his natural caution.

But now with so much time on our hands, he must eventually come round to admitting the truth of my mental condition.

We had weekly sessions. Nice and relaxed, me on the couch talking about my dreams, my hopes, my fears; him taking notes, asking the odd question, always very kind and sympathetic. I never mentioned getting out unless he brought up the outside world.

Like I say, I admitted my guilt, and was very willing to serve my time and wipe the slate clean.

But after seven years, I did feel entitled to bring the question of my release up.

He was very optimistic. Not just him, all the staff. They talked about necessary procedures, and safeguards, and reassuring the public, and all that stuff. But always it was made clear to me that it was just a matter of form, of getting the bookkeeping right.

And time went on.

At the start of my tenth year, I began to be a little more assertive. Not aggressive, you understand. Assertive.

Mr. Barnfather was very open with me. Yes, my release was under consideration. Decisions were taken by the Board Of Managers, some such body, consisting of representatives of all professionally concerned parties plus some outside lay members. In a case like mine, there were two major aspects to consider. First, was it in my interests to be released? Second was it in the public's interest?

As to the first, I assured him, the answer was obviously yes. I had plans. I wanted to get down to catching up with all the normal life I had lost thorugh my own foolishness. As for the second, there was probably no one in the free world less likely to harm any of his fellow humans than me! I had known this from the moment I heard that my mother was dead. Mr Barnfather must surely have reached the same conclusion after our years of consultation. And with his great reputation, how could the Board fail to be convinced if he offered them a copper-bottomed assurance about my condition?

The day of meeting arrived. I didn't expect to be summoned personally, not for examination anyway. But I held myself in readiness just in case they decided to give me the good news direct.

I waited.

And waited.

And waited.

Nothing.

I wasn't even told officially that I'd been turned down.

Naturally it was the first thing I brought up in my next session with Mr. Barnfather.

He looked uncomfortable and said he couldn't talk about what had been said at the meeting, it was more than his job was worth. But I mustn't give up hope.

It was a short session, which was probably just as well. I was ready to explode but I knew that any outburst would just confirm the Board in its wisdom. I sat on my bed and worked out what had probably happened.

I had no doubt Mr. Barnfather was on my side, and I knew how much of a favorite I was with both the nursing and the prison staff. So clearly it was the lay members of the Board who had decided in their ignorant fear, doubtless underpinned by a political agenda, to keep me locked up. I knew how such things worked. They'd be on the government's Quango list, picking up all kinds of undemanding but lucrative little jobs. All they had to do was make sure they toed the official party line and above all never got involved with anything which could be potentially embarrassing.

Like releasing a prisoner who immediately reoffended.

There was only one way to prove to the world what a bunch of short sighted idiots they were.

I escaped.

It was easy. Like I say, I was a model prisoner. I could have walked out of there via any one of a dozen routes any time over the last several years. There again, the fact that I didn't just goes to show how sane and belanced I am.

I had money in a Building Society account. It was mainly what had come to me from my grandparents who, happily for me, had died intestate. No one knew about the account except myself and my solicitor who had set it up for me during the pre-trial period. Even then, knowing I was going to plead guilty and face a long sentence, I was preparing for my release. Knowing from their work on my mother just how good the press hounds were, and not wanting them to have an easy scent to follow on my release, I had taken considerable precautions—a slight change of name, a branch in a town with which I had no connection—so I was able to get at my money without arousing any particular interest.

After that, it was easy. None of the old photos they had was in the least like the well fed, healthy looking chap I'd become, and a moustache soon removed even the last glimmer of resemblance. I took a room. I got casual work. I moved around a bit, each time taking with me another small piece of official evidence of my existence, till finally for the last six months, I settled down in one community, became a regular both in my local pub and my local church, played in the darts team, sang in the choir, and all in all established myself as a perfectly acceptable, indeed desirable, member of any community.

At the end of a year and a day, I went back to the Institution.

While I knew the period had no official legal function, I felt that its historical standing gave it some weight. It took some time to persuade them I really was who I said I was, and when it finally got through, I really enjoyed seeing their jaws drop.

'Here I am,' I said. 'I've been free for a year and a day, and even under the difficulties of having no official existence, I have not only survived without breaking the law. I have become a useful and well-liked member of the community. Now let me hear how you justify my continued incarceration.'

How naive I was! All you do when you demonstrate to closed minds that they are wrong is to drive them to even greater extremes in their search for self-justification.

Instead of being received like the conquering hero I felt I was, I found myself kept from all contact with fellow inmates and pumped full of drugs till I didn't know what time of day it was, let alone what I'd been up to for the past year!

I begged to see Mr. Barnfather and was further devastated when they told me he had retired from the public service and was now back in private practice in London.

The new man was most unsympathetic, obviously in the pockets of the self seeking Quangoites. There was another meeting of the Board, this one (so the grapevine told me) in the full glare of media publicity.

And the decision?

They were unanimous that my irrational behaviour in first effecting my escape and then returning with my grandiose claims to being a pillar of the community merely confirmed my basic unsoundness of mind. What outlet my violent impulses might have found had not yet become apparent, but I'd had plenty of time, and the kind of woman I attacked was often not readily or quickly missed in society.

My reaction to this decision and also to their drugs kept me in bed for several weeks. As I slowly returned to health I began to see very clearly where I'd gone wrong. I should have used my time outside to gain the confidence and support of the government's political enemies, those who knew as well as I did the hidden agendas which warped so many decisions in public institutions. And I should have worked through the media also, and returned in a spotlight of publicity which would have prevented them dealing with me as they had done. Also it would have got the papers concentrating on my struggle to prove my sanity rather than rehashing with gory details all those old killings that had put me here in the first place.

Above all, once out, I should have offered myself for examination by an independent psychiatrist, far removed from all the pressures of a job within the system.

Gradually hope began to revive in me. What I had done once I could do again. Only this time I would set the rules of the game myself.

It wasn't so easy getting out this time. Once bitten, twice shy, and they were very much on the alert. But I'd learned a thing or two. I faked being in a much more depressed state than I really was. Injections I resisted with all my strength. Of course, they just used more and more force to start with, but eventually I wore them down, and besides, they realised the bruising necessarily involved didn't look so good, and in the end I was taking all medication by mouth. They watched very carefully to make sure I took this, but I was way ahead of them here. What they concentrated on was my mouth, watching me put the pills in and drink the water, then checking to make sure I'd swallowed. But from one of my fellow patients who was diabetic I'd stolen a bottle of sweeteners which in size, colour and shape resembled my tablets, and I'd made myself expert at palming the real pills and substituting these. Also I developed an allergy to light and took to lying in my bed during the day with the sheet pulled over my head.

So it was easy to slip out one afternoon at the change of shifts, leaving a bolster taken from an unoccupied bed under the sheets, help myself to some clothing from the nurses' locker room, and make my way out of the building by a door most of those who worked there didn't know the existence of. Ten years of exploration and observation had made me probably the world's leading expert on the topography of that institution.

My idea was to lay low for a while. Even under the delusion of the certain success of my first plan, I had still (superstitiously rather than in belief I'd ever need it) hidden away a fair sum of cash before I gave myself up.

This I now collected and headed into London where I reckon anyone can drop out of sight into the huge underground world of runaways and derelicts.

Next day I bought a paper and read all about myself. God, it sounded like Rasputin and Attila the Hun had broken loose together! This was no more than I'd expected, but what did shock and surprise me was an alleged interview with Mr. Barnfather, now in private practice in Knightbridge, and thus, I would have hoped, able to speak frankly. Instead, according to the tabloid, he declared that during all our acquaintance he had never detected what he would call any real remorse, and he doubted whether a man with my powers of self-delusion would ever have been safe to release into the community!

This was so obviously the old party line that I was certain some hack had merely gone through his years old notes and had a quick chat with Mr. Barnfather on the phone in which he tricked him into saying something which could be interpreted as support for this garbage.

I didn't doubt that he would come forward with an indignant denial that he'd ever said these things, but by the time the Press Complaints people dealt with it, nobody would remember what it was all about. If on the other hand I could get to him while he was still angry, perhaps his indignation plus his natural sense of justice would persuade him to accompany me to a press conference and declare his belief in my sanity to the world.

What a coup this would be!

And so I set off to Knightsbridge with my hopes once more soaring high.

Alas, what another huge disappointment awaited me.

I bluffed my way into his consulting room quite easily. His reaction when he realised who I was I put down to natural surprise and I made sure I kept between him and his alarm button until he'd had time to adjust.

It was a wiser move than I realised. At first as I explained the purpose of my visit, he nodded and smiled and said, yes, of course, he'd be only too happy to go along with me and do all he could to persuade the world that I presented no danger to the public at large. But something about his eyes told me a different tale. I put on a vulnerable face and pressed him for reassurance that I was doing the right thing, giving the impression that I would let myself be advised by him. Slowly his manner changed as he felt himself back in control. He talked with the easy sympathy he had shown in the old days, but the message that came across was that the best thing for me was to return to the Institution in his company and once there we could settle down with everyone concerned and sort things out.

Oh, he was smooth, and soothing and convincing, but as I listened I realised the truth I'd been denying for these many years.

It wasn't just the self-interest of the lay members of the Board which had been preventing my release. This man whom I had trusted with sight of my naked soul had been speaking against me at their meetings! I had never had a cat in hell's chance of getting out!

What his agenda had been I didn't stay to ask. All I knew was that here where I had looked for my closest ally I had found my worst enemy.

But not for that did I give up hope. I had been stupid to seek an ally against an unjust system from within the system itself. But just because one of their number was self-seekingly unprofessional didn't mean that all practicioners in the independent sector were tarred with the same brush.

So I set out to find an honest, independent psychiatrist who would assess my case without fear or favour, and that's why I've come knocking on your door.

So what do you say? You've heard my story from start to finish. Do I come across as a maniac, a potential menace to civilised society, and totally unfit to be released into the community? Or have you penetrated to the man within, more sinned against than sinning, who has paid his debt and now deserves, not special treatment, but simple natural justice?

To put it bluntly, as it might be put to you by journalists and lawyers, Is this man you see before you sane? Answer yes or no.

You nod your head. Vigorously. I am encouraged.

But it is not *at* your head I wish to look, but *into* it.

I mean, through your eyes, the portals of the soul.

Oh, there I read another story.

You can stop nodding, doctor. I quite understand. Any man in your position, lying on his own consulting couch, with his arms strapped and his mouth taped, would probably nod his head as vigorously as you.

But your eyes give a quite different answer.

Or rather they ask a quite different question.

To wit, how many psychiatrists have I killed since Mr. Barnfather?

You'll be the seventh.

Bill Crider is another writer who is at home in several time periods and just about any facet of the mystery. His Sheriff Dan Rhodes series is running strong, with the most recent installment being *Death by Accident*. Recently he also teamed up with well-known ex-television weatherman Willard Scott to create a series of bed-and-breakfast cozies, the first entitled *Murder Under Blue Skies*. Of course, he's just as proficient at the short story as well, particularly when dealing with Hollywood in the 1940s.

# The Easter Cat
## BILL CRIDER

Let me give you a little piece of advice: Never stop to help the Easter Bunny change a flat tire. I would never have done it myself except that it was obvious that he was totally incompetent and no one else was even giving him a second glance. Besides, I thought I recognized him.

So I drove on by and coasted to a stop by the curb about half a block in front of the Bunny's pre-war Chevy. It was the same model as mine, in fact, a 1940 model, but mine was in better shape. The Bunny obviously wasn't a very good driver.

I got out of my car, stretched, and took a deep breath. It was a beautiful California day, all blue skies and sunshine, low humidity, and the smell of oranges drifting in from one of the groves that still remained nearby. If I'd had any sense at all, I would have kept right on driving. But then no one ever accused me of having any sense at all.

I walked back to the Bunny's Chevy. The passing cars ignored both of us. We were out near the studios, and you don't have to live in Hollywood for very long to get used to some pretty strange sights out there. Or anywhere else, for that matter.

The Bunny was trying to loosen a lug nut. He was down on his knees, straining so hard that his long pink ears were quivering. As I watched him strain, his hands slipped off the lug wrench. He looked over on his side and hit the pavement.

"Goddammit," he said, which I thought was pretty strong language for the Easter Bunny, and I told him so.

"Yeah? And who the hell asked you?" He didn't bother to get up. He just lay there on his side with his puffy white tail sticking out toward the traffic.

"Nobody asked me. Nobody asked me to stop and help a bunny in distress, either."

He sat up then, and turned to look at me through eyes narrowed against the sunlight. He was who I'd thought he was, all right, Ernie Wiggins, dressed out in a bunny suit. Rabbits' noses were supposed to be pink, I think, but his was a bright shiny red.

"Ferrel?" he said. He put a hand up to shade his eyes. His eyes were a little red, too. "Bill Ferrel, private dick?"

"It's me, all right," I said. "And better a dick than a bunny rabbit. You got a part in something?"

It was a natural question. *Ernie* Wiggins was a has-been comic who'd started out with a couple of bits in Leon Errol shorts and then done one with the Three Stooges. Someone at Gober Studios spotted him in that one and gave him a try as the comic sidekick in a Rick Torrance jungle epic, *Johnson of Java*, I think, but it might have been *Benson of Borneo*. I can never remember which one came first.

Torrance and Wiggins hit it off, and Ernie had been funny enough to get a couple of good mentions in the trades. Not only that, but the box-office take was a little better than Torrance's last picture. So naturally they put Ernie in another movie with Torrance, *Johnson* or *Benson*, whichever, and it looked like Ernie was on his way.

He was on his way, all right—on his way out. As it happened he was a lush. Now that's no big thing in Hollywood, of course. If they fired all the lushes tomorrow, every studio in town would close down. But Ernie was the wrong kind of lush. He started showing up drunk on the set, forgetting his lines, and missing his marks. Even that might not have been so bad on some pictures, but Rick Torrance's directors weren't exactly top of the line. They preferred the methods of William. "One Shot" Beaudine. So after one more picture, *Andrews of the Amazon*, Ernie was out on the streets.

And not only that. Now he was dressed like the *Easter Bunny*.

Ernie stood up, none too steadily, and brushed haphazardly at the knees of his bunny suit. He didn't say anything about having a part. What he said was, "Cun y' gimme a hand wi' th' tire?"

Even the exhaust fumes from the passing cars couldn't disguise the fact that he'd been sipping on the Old Overholt, or whatever he favored. Did I say sipping? He'd probably slugged down a filth of the stuff by now, and it was only a little after noon. He'd never get the tire changed by himself.

So fool that I was, I said, "Sure."

I took off my hat and jacket and laid them on the hood of Wiggins's Chevy. Then I picked up the lug wrench and got to work. Ernie stared vacantly off into space and leaned his back against the car as if he needed a brace to help him stand up. While I worked at getting the wheel off, he slid slowly down the side of the car, an inch at a time.

I got the wheel off, put on the spare that Ernie had left lying in the street behind his car, and tossed the hat into the trunk. By that time Ernie had slid all the way down the side of the car. He was sitting in the street, his back to the Chevy, snoring heavily.

I jacked down the car, tightened the lug nuts, and threw the wrench and jack into the trunk with the flat tire. I slammed down the trunk lid as hard as I could, hoping the noise would wake Ernie up. It didn't.

I wiped my hands off on my handkerchief, then put on my hat and jacket and looked down at Ernie, who was still snoring. He'd drawn a bunch of little black lines straight out from the sides of his nose. Whiskers, I guess.

I kicked one of his feet. Gently. I'm not some tough peeper like Bogart in *The Maltese Falcon*. "Wake up, Ernie," I said.

He opened one eye. "Ri'. Wakey, shakey, Gotta job."

If he had a job, it wasn't at Gober Studios. I'm on retainer to Gober, the big cheese himself, and I know the casts of every picture on the lot, which is how I got to know Ernie in the first place. Wayward starlets, oversexed leading men, pregnant ingenues—I'm the one who tries to keep them out of trouble and, when that fails, to keep their names out of the papers.

In fact, I was on my way to do a little job for the studio at the moment, or I was supposed to be. I didn't think Mr. Gober would appreciate my helping out the Easter Bunny.

"Where are you working?" I asked Ernie.

"Rick's place. Kid's party. All I can ge' 'ese days."

He shut his eye and began snoring again. I hunkered down beside him and slapped him on both cheeks, gently. That didn't work, so I shook him. Gently, of course.

"Stop," he said. "Stopstopstopstop."

"Not until you wake up."

"Can't wa' up."

He slumped forward into my arms, and I shoved him back against the car. He opened one eye again. "Gotta ge' to Rick's. Gotta be bunny a' party."

I couldn't just leave him there, so I dragged him around to the passenger side of the car and held his head up by the ears to keep it off the street while I opened the door. Then I tried to get him inside. It was like working with a very heavy dummy filled with flour dough, but I finally managed it. Of course his feet were in the seat and his upper body was on the floor, but at least he was in the car. His head was practically up under the dash.

I shut the door and looked down the street at my own car. It would be all right where it was for a while. I could drive Ernie to Rick's house. Maybe he would sober up on the way.

Sure he would.

And maybe MGM would call me to replace Robert Taylor in some big-budget foreign intrigue film because I was so much better-looking than he was. My nose has been broken twice, I'm going bald on top, I'm a little overweight, and my eyes are too close together. You figure the odds.

I sighed, walked around to the driver's side of the Chevy, and slid in. As it happened, the little job I was supposed to do was at Rick Torrance's house. It seemed that there was some kind of dispute going on, and Mr. Gober wanted me to settle it. He hadn't said what it was, which is why I wasn't in much of a hurry. It apparently wasn't an emergency, and I didn't like settling arguments. That wasn't my idea of what my job was all about.

But I was going to do it. That's what I got paid for.

RICK TORRANCE LIVED NOT FAR off Sunset in Beverly Hills. I'd been to his place once before, when some starlet had nearly drowned in his pool, where she'd fallen after being goosed by a chimpanzee that had wandered in from Rick's private jungle.

The house was a big, three-story stucco job, painted pink and set back from the street behind a pink stucco wall on a couple of acres of ground, only a little of which was given over to a well-manicured lawn and a drive lined with bougainvillea bushes. The rest was covered with the jungle: three or four kinds of palm trees, banana trees, creeping vines, climbing vines, and a few varieties of exotic flowers.

God knows what the water bill was, but it didn't matter to Rick. The studio paid it. The jungle was good publicity, giving the place the semblance of the kind of terrain Rick Torrance was supposed to prefer.

Anyone familiar with the Rick knew that he actually preferred the terrain of a nice shady bar to a jungle anytime, but most of the ticket-buying public didn't know Rick at all. Instead they read about his private jungle in the fan magazines and had fantasies about his running around among the palm trees with his shirt off. Most of his pictures didn't require a big wardrobe. He never wore a shirt if he didn't have to, and I didn't blame him. If I had pecs like his, I'd go shirtless, too.

I stopped Ernie's Chevy at the gate in the pink wall. The gatekeeper, an old geezer with bifocals and white hair growing out of his ears, recognized me from the last time I'd been there. He was willing to let me inside, but he wanted to know who was on the floor.

"The Easter Bunny," I said.

The *geezer* wasn't surprised. "Oh, yeah, him. He's late. Mr. Torrance and Mr. Gober are having a fit."

"He's a little under the weather," I said. "You say that Mr. Gober's here?" I hadn't realized that Gober was calling from Rick's place.

"In the flesh," the gatekeeper said. "He's the kid's godfather or something.

He's fit to be tied because the bunny hasn't showed up. If I was you, I'd do something about your buddy there and get him ready. Mr. Torrance and Mr. Gober, they don't want the kid to be disappointed."

I didn't want the kid to be disappointed either, and I didn't want Ernie to get into any trouble. But I didn't know what to do about it.

The gatekeeper had a suggestion, however, which is how I wound up in the bunny suit, walking up the drive with a basket of colored eggs in each hand. The eggs and baskets had been in the Chevy's back seat, and now and then I stopped along the drive to hide an egg or two in a bougainvillea bush.

I was careful not to wander off into the jungle. There was no telling what was in there. I thought I could hear spider monkeys calling to one another, and then there was that chimp. So I stuck to the drive.

The gatekeeper and I'd had a hell of a time getting Ernie out of the bunny suit, and I was having a hell of a time wearing it. It was hot, it was too tight, and it smelled a lot like Ernie. I wasn't a happy bunny when I hammered the brass knocker against the front door of Torrance's house. Ernie, lying asleep in the gatehouse in his underwear, was considerably happier than I was.

No one answered my knock on the door, so I tried the knob. It was open, and it swung back into the house.

I looked inside just in time to see a familiar-looking man hurtling down the hallway toward me. He had a cat in his arms, a huge tabby that was dark and light gray on top, with a lot of orangy gold mixed in, and a solid white stomach. It was colored almost like an egg—sort of an Easter cat.

I thought maybe it had something to do with the party, and I was trying to get a better look when there was a thunderous explosion and the door frame shattered above my head.

Maybe the little dispute Mr. Gober had called me about was more serious than I'd thought.

I looked around for a place to run, but before I could move, the man from the hallway crashed into me. I'm pretty sturdy, but I don't think I slowed him down much. It was hard to tell. I couldn't see very well because I was lying flat on the tiles in front of the door. There were colorful hardboiled eggs all around me.

There was another explosion and I raised my head cautiously. I could see Rick Torrance back in the hallway. He had an elephant gun to his shoulder. At least it looked like an elephant gun. Maybe it was only a .30—.30. Pistols I know a little bit about; rifles are something I don't generally have to deal with.

I squirmed out of the way before he could run over me too. He ran past me and headed down the drive. Then Mr. Gober, who must have been behind him, came outside. He stopped and looked at me.

"You're not Wiggins," he said. Studio heads have to be perceptive.

"No, sir. I'm not."

He recognized me then. "Goddammit, Ferrel, what are you doing in that outfit?"

He always says that *Goddammit, Ferrel*, I mean. I'm thinking of having my first name changed, since he can't seem to call me anything else.

"I'm taking Ernie's place," I said, standing up.

I started gathering up the eggs. Most of them were cracked, but I put them in the baskets anyway.

"Goddammit, Ferrel!" Gober said. "You're not supposed to be playing with Easter eggs. You've got to stop Rick. He's going to kill somebody if you don't."

"What about the party?" I asked. I didn't want to disappoint the kids, not after I'd gone to the trouble of getting dressed like a bunny.

Gober, however, didn't care about the kids. He was more interested in his star. "Forget the party. The kids have waited this long, they can wait a little longer."

"Where are they?"

"They're in the back yard. Peggy's with them. They're fine. Now get going!"

"I need to know what's going on here first," I said.

Mr. Gober took a deep breath and tried to control himself. Patience wasn't his strong suit. "The guy that ran you over is Lawrence Berry. Rick's going to kill him."

I didn't think so. It was widely known that Rick was a terrible shot. But I was curious. "Why?"

"He got Felicia pregnant, that's why. Now—"

I interrupted him. "Felicia? I thought Rick's wife was Penny Turnage."

Gober's face was turning a truly amazing shade of red. It was almost the same color as Ernie's nose. I wondered if Gober had been drinking. He took another deep breath.

"Felicia's the cat," he said. "Rick's cat."

"And Larry Berry got her pregnant? Illicit pregnancy is one thing, but bestiality? And cross-species breeding? Wow! Wait till the fan mags get hold of this one! Not to mention *Scientific American!*"

Berry was a well-known womanizer who generally played the villain's role in films. He'd been in a couple of Rick's pictures, playing an evil white hunter in *Kent of Kilimanjaro* and a murderous guide in *Clive of the Congo*. Or maybe he was a guide in *Kent* and a hunter in *Clive*. As I said, it's easy to get confused. The pictures are a lot alike. Plenty of shots of Rick with his muscles showing, and lots of stock footage of crocodiles sliding off sandbanks into rivers . . . things like that.

"Not Henry, you idiot!" Gober yelled. "He didn't get Felicia pregnant! His cat got her pregnant! Berry lives next door, and the cat comes sneaking over the wall to assault Felicia."

"Was that his cat Larry was holding?" I asked.

A rifle boomed.

"Yea! Now are you going to do something to earn your retainer, or do I have to turn things over to the Continental Agency?"

I handed him the Easter baskets. "Hold these," I said.

AS AN EASTER BUNNY, I was more of an urban type of animal. I didn't really belong in the jungle.

For one thing, my ears kept getting caught on the vines that dangled from the palm trees. It wasn't so bad once I realized what was happening in time to extricate myself, but once or twice I'd nearly jerked my own head off.

For another thing, the ground was squishy and wet underfoot. Rick had some kind of irrigation system for all the plants, even an overhead mister, and it was doing a very efficient job. Water dripped down out of the palms and soaked into my fur.

And for still another thing, I didn't like the noises, especially since I didn't really know what kind of wildlife Rick Torrance had stocked the place with. There were rumors in the fan magazines that monkeys weren't the only things in there. Pythons had been mentioned more than once. And boa constrictors.

Of course snakes don't make noises. That's one of the things I don't like about them. They're very sneaky, snakes are. But lions make noise, and one article had hinted that Rick had a lion on the property. I wondered if lions liked to eat rabbits.

Even though I wasn't exactly an old jungle hand, it was easy to follow along behind Rick and Larry. They were crashing along like a couple of rhinos in rut, and now and then Rick would let off another volley with his cannon.

When he did, a screeching like nothing I'd ever heard in real life would arise, and the trees above me would come alive with terrified monkeys. They weren't any more terrified than I was. I was afraid that if Rick saw me, he'd shoot me. He probably didn't have any rabbit heads mounted on his trophy wall.

Larry was probably even more frightened than I was. Rick was actually trying to kill him, which he'd done often enough in the movies but never before in real life. It was pretty stupid considering the circumstances, but then Rick probably hadn't taken the time to think about that. Maybe it wouldn't have made any difference even if he had.

There was a sudden frenzied fluttering off to my right, and I jumped about five feet straight up. I was a credit to the bunny clan. It wasn't a lion, however; it was only a bunch of colorful birds that were no doubt as scared as I was. They were cockatoos, which reminded me of my last case for Gober. That one had involved a cat, too. I was beginning to think that everyone at Gober's studio was nuts, though even that wouldn't be big news in Hollywood.

I looked down at my shoes, which I'd managed to force onto my feet over the bunny costume. They were ruined, naturally. I'd put them on the expense account, but I was still upset.

What with the noise and my shoes, I momentarily lost track of Rick and Larry, but then I heard something that sounded the way *Tarzan* might yell if he'd pulled a hernia. When I looked up, Larry was swinging toward me on a thick vine that he had gripped in his right hand. He had his multi-colored cat cradled in his left arm.

This time I was able to get out of his way, but I didn't really have to. From somewhere in the jungle a rifle roared, the vine parted, and Larry splatted on the wet ground, flat on his back.

He didn't fall far, but he was stunned. He lay there in the dappled shade with his eyes rolled back into his head. His cat, demonstrating the loyalty for which cats are renowned, took off for the tall timber.

Rick Torrance came crashing through the undergrowth, his rifle at the ready.

"All right, you son of a bitch," he said when he spotted Larry, "say your prayers."

"That's more like a Monogram Western than a jungle epic," I said.

Maybe Torrance had seen me on his stoop or maybe not. At any rate, he seemed pretty surprised to see a six-foot bunny in his jungle.

"Jesus Christ," he said, and I didn't bother to reprimand him for it. It seemed appropriate enough, considering the season.

What didn't seem appropriate was the barrel of the rifle that he had leveled at me. It might not have been an elephant gun, but the bore looked big enough to stuff a python into.

"Who the hell are you?" Rick asked.

"Bill Ferrel, private bunny."

He didn't laugh. "What're you doing in that outfit? I thought Ernie was supposed to be here."

"It's a long story. Why don't you give me that rifle and we'll talk about it."

"Forget it." He aimed the rifle at Larry's head. "I'm going to plug this varmint."

"Monogram again," I said. "Or maybe Republic. Have you ever starred in a Western?"

"No, but I like to watch 'em. Now why don't you just get out of here and let me do what I have to do."

Larry's eyes were no longer rolled up in his head. They were wide and bulging as he stared into the rifle barrel. I think he was holding his breath. He'd looked into plenty of rifle barrels in his movies, being a villain most of the time, but he wasn't used to them when he wasn't acting.

"Killing Larry would be bad publicity for the studio," I said. There was no need to bring morality into it; stars don't understand morality. So I was appealing to his practical side. "And had publicity for you, too. What about that picture you're working on now?"

"*Manfred of Madagascar*? What about it?" He moved the rifle pointing it at the wet ground, and Larry let out a slow hiss of air.

"Think how it would look to the fans if you murdered your co-star," I said. "Larry's in the picture, isn't he?"

"Yeah, he's in it, but I wouldn't call him a co-star. He's just the bad guy. I don't have co-stars."

"Right. But it still wouldn't be a good idea to kill him, not over something as silly as a pregnant cat."

The rifle barrel came up. Now it was pointing at me again. Right at my pink bunny stomach.

"There's nothing silly about a pregnant cat," Rick said. "Especially not about Felicia. She's a pedigreed Siamese, really expensive. Very classy. I've got all the papers on her. And now she's been polluted by alley trash."

"You should've kept her up. That's what people usually do."

"She was in the back yard. She likes to get out a little *in* the daytime. Get some exercise. There's a fence, so she should have been safe. Besides, Berry's the one who should have taken precautions."

Torrance turned the rifle barrel back toward Larry. I have to admit to feeling a guilty twinge of relief. But I can never resist asking questions when I shouldn't.

So I said, "What precautions?"

"He could have had his alley cat fixed."

"I thought about that," Larry said.

His voice, always firm in his movie roles, quavered just a little. Not that I blamed him.

"But I just couldn't do it," he continued. "If I had a wife, she could prob-ably have had it done, but I just couldn't."

It was clear that Larry had certain psychological problems that we weren't going to be able to resolve for him. Or it was clear to me. Rick seemed to think he could resolve them easily enough.

He pointed the rifle in the general direction of Larry's reproductive organs and said, "I could fix *you* right here and take care of the cat later."

While Rick was focused on Larry, I made my move. I'm not generally a very quick guy, but maybe the bunny suit inspired me. I jumped to Rick's side and grabbed the rifle, trying to twist it out of his grasp.

He didn't want to give it up, and he twisted back, which caused both of us to fall to the squishy ground. Luckily, I landed on top.

We thrashed around for a while, but neither of us could get the advantage. Rick's muscular chest wasn't just a movie illusion, though. He managed a powerful roll that turned the two of us over and put him on top. Then he began slowly wresting the rifle from my grip.

I thought that if I could hold out long enough. Larry would get up and help me out, but I was wrong about that. You can never trust a villain. I heard the frantic rustling of palm fronds, and I know that Larry was leaving the area. Possibly he was extremely worried about his cat and wanted to find him as soon as possible. More than likely, however, he didn't really care what happened to me, just as long as it didn't happen to him.

I could tell it was going to be up to me to rescue myself, so I resorted to low bunny cunning.

"Rick," I gasped.

He didn't stop trying to get the rifle, but he said. "What?"

"Are there any tarantulas in this jungle?"

"No." He sounded a little nervous, which was good. "Why?"

"Well, there's a couple of big hairy black spiders on your back. I thought maybe—"

"Spiders? Spiders?"

Rick let go of the rifle and jumped to his feet, brushing wildly at his back with both arms.

"Did I get them? Where are they? Step on them! Step on them!"

I stood up, holding the rifle. My formerly fluffy white tail was soaking wet, and it dragged down the rest of my suit. I was willing to bet it wasn't white anymore, either.

"The spiders are gone," I said. "They probably weren't tarantulas, anyway."

He seemed happy to hear that, but he kept looking around anxiously until he noticed who was holding the rifle.

"You son of a bitch," he said. "You're going to let Larry get away."

"He probably won't leave without his cat," I said. "Let's see if we can find them."

It didn't take long. We found Larry at the base of a tall palm tree, trying to coax the cat down with a toy mouse. I didn't bother to ask where the mouse had come from. Larry probably carried it around in his pocket.

Rick and I stood quietly behind a banana tree until Larry had the cat safely in hand. Then I took over.

WE MARCHED BACK TO THE house with Rick in front, Larry and his cat behind him, and me bringing up the rear. A guy wearing a bedraggled bunny costume and carrying a rifle. I felt like an escapee from an Abbott and Costello set.

To add to the fun, Rick and Larry yapped at each other all the way to the house.

"You'll regret this, Berry," Rick said. "I'm going to get you and that cat if it's the last thing I do."

"Fat chance. As soon as I leave here, I'm calling my lawyer. I'm going to sue you for every cent you've got. You'll be living in a jungle, all right—a hobo jungle!"

Stuff like that, I didn't try to keep them quiet. I knew someone who could do that for me when we got to the house.

And he did. Four or five words from Gober, and they were sitting in a pair of leather-covered chairs, as quiet as a couple of rocks. Larry's cat was spread out all over his owner's lap, sleeping calmly.

"That's better," Gober said. Then he looked at me. "Goddammit, Ferrel, you've got to settle this. I can't have two of my stars running around trying to kill each other."

"I didn't try to kill anyone," Larry said. "It was Rick. He—"

"Shut up!" Gober roared.

Larry shut up.

"Larry's no star!" Rick said. "*I'm* the star. I—"

"You too!" Gober thundered, and Rick was quiet.

Gober turned to me. "What about it, Ferrel? You're a fixer. Fix it."

One of my ears kept flopping over my eye. Probably got broken by one of those stupid vines. I pushed it out of my face and said, "Well, Mr. Gober, I think we can take care of things. The way I see it, there's been no crime committed here. Rick got a little excited, but that can happen. He didn't hurt anyone, after all. And I'm pretty sure Larry's cat isn't guilty of anything."

Rick jumped to his feet. "The hell he's not! He . . . he raped Felicia! He—"

"Shut up and siddown!" Gober shouted.

Rick shut up and sat.

"I can't swear that Larry's cat—by the way, what's his name?"

"Slim," Larry said with a straight face.

I didn't smile, either. "I can't swear that Slim didn't have his way with Felicia. But I'd be willing to bet my month's retainer from Gober Studios that he didn't get her pregnant."

Rick jumped up again. "That's a lie! He—"

This time Mr. Gober didn't say a word. He just looked at Rick, who sat back down. I wished I could look at people like that.

I went on as if I hadn't been interrupted. "I'd be willing to bet that Slim didn't get anyone pregnant because I don't think he's capable of it."

Larry was incredulous. "Not capable? Are you kidding? Look at the size of his ba—"

Gober glared. Larry shut up.

"It's not the size that matters," I said. "The truth is that cats with as many colors as Slim are usually females. And when they're male, they usually can't reproduce. They're sterile."

"Is that really true?" Larry asked. I guess he had a suspicious nature.

"Of course it's true," Gober said. "Ferrel knows his cats. Isn't that right, Ferrel?"

I didn't really know all that much about cats, but I nodded. I'd heard something like that once, and it might even have been true.

Rick looked as if he believed me. Or if not, he believed Gober.

"So who knocked up Felicia, then?" he asked.

"I don't have any idea. But if you think a fence is going to keep male cats away when a female's in heat, you're crazy. You may have caught Slim with her, but you missed the others. And I'd bet there were plenty of them."

"I did hear some *howling* out in the back yard earlier," Rick admitted.

"So there you are," I said. "If you want pedigreed kittens, you'll have to make the proper arrangements. And if you want no kittens at all, you'll have to keep Felicia up or get her spayed."

It took a little more persuasion, but Rick eventually admitted that everything was mostly his fault, not that he ever came right out and said so. He even apologized to Larry, sort of, for trying to kill him. And then he asked him if his cat could stay for the party. With Felicia safely put away in the house, of course.

THE PARTY WAS A SUCCESS. I looked pretty crummy, even for a fake Easter Bunny, but the kids didn't care. I'd hidden the eggs, and that was all they really wanted. They ran down the drive looking for eggs in the bougainvilles bushes, yelling happily every time they found one.

But the real hit of the party was Slim, who was billed by Rick as the Easter Cat, the Easter Bunny's special guest and helper. Slim had the coloring for it, all right, and he wasn't the nervous type. Even after all the excitement he'd had, he let the lads rub him and scratch behind his ears and under his chin. I could hear him purring from ten feet away.

When the party was over, I went back to the gatehouse. I took a couple of hardboiled eggs with me, a blue one and a pink one. I figured on having them for dinner. I might as well get something out of my day's work.

Ernie was awake but still in his underwear. He was drinking coffee with the gatekeeper and looking right at home.

"Damn," Ernie said when he saw me. "What did you do to the bunny suit? It's rented, you know. You're going to have to pay for having it cleaned."

I gave him a look. It wasn't as good as one of Gober's, but it was a pretty good one.

"Ernie," I said, "I've never killed a man before. But I've never worn a bunny suit before, either. There's a first time for everything."

Ernie smiled weakly. "Oh. Yeah. Right. I see what you mean. I'll take care of the suit. Did you get my check?"

I reached inside the suit, pulled it out, and handed it to him.

He gave it the once over, started to stick it in his boxer shorts, then thought better of it and just held it in his hand.

"Great," he said. "Thanks, Ferrel. I mean it."

"Sure," I said, and I started peeling myself out of the bunny suit. "You're welcome."

"You know," he said, giving the gatekeeper the elbow, "you look pretty cute in that outfit, Ferrel. You ever think of getting into the movies yourself?"

They had a good laugh at that one, and while they were guffawing, I reached down and got the pink egg from the basket. It would have made a nice dinner with a little salt and pepper, but I had a better use for it now.

Holding the egg behind my back, I walked over to Ernie and said, "Open up and say Ah."

For some reason, he did it, and I shoved the egg into his mouth, slapping away his hands when he reached for it.

"M-m-m-m-m-m," he mumbled.

"Happy Easter, Ernie," I said.

Jerry Sykes is one of a new generation of British crime writers who are rapidly gaining acclaim for their gritty look at England's middle and lower classes. "Call Me Walt" illustrates this perfectly in a slice-of-life story where two generations of criminals, a father and son, come into conflict over two of the basic human needs, a woman and money.

# Call Me Walt
## JERRY SYKES

My father was already waiting outside the prison gates when I arrived a little before eight. It was a bright, February morning and frost lay in shadows that seemed to have been carved out of the grey pavement. I pulled into the forecourt of a small electrical store across the street and killed the engine. The clear blue sky stretched above the dark Victorian building hurt my eyes and I decided to stay in the car. I lit a cigarette and looked through the passenger's side window.

He was wearing the same navy blue suit he had been wearing twelve years ago when he had been escorted from the dock and into the bowels of the courthouse, a tuft of hair sticking up at the back of his head lending him a childlike innocence. It was the last time I had seen him.

Back then, his shoulders bunched to the world, the suit had fitted him like a blanket fits a derelict out in the cold; now his shoulders filled the cheap, thin material so that it shone in the winter sunlight as if spun through with quicksilver.

I had arrived early hoping to get a look at his face as he came through the heavy wooden gates, catch his eyes as they blinked at freedom. But the guards had obviously had other ideas and bundled him out before the shift change at eight.

I looked at him now as he watched the traffic go by, the sun bleaching one side of his face. He kept glancing in my direction, an arm raised to shield his eyes from the sun, but he didn't appear to recognise me.

I opened the window to flick the cigarette butt out. It wheeled through the air and landed in a bundle of sparks by a stone lion with graffiti-red genitals. In the silence between traffic I could hear the claustrophobic sounds of metal doors clanging.

My father shuffled his feet in the brogues that he had bought for the trial and that still looked brand new, kept glancing back at the dark prison walls, uncertain of his future.

I hit the horn.

His head jerked up and for an instant I saw a mask of fear appear on his face before quickly melting away. He punched a wave in the air and with one last look over his shoulder started walking across the street with long, deliberate strides.

He opened the passenger's side door and leaned in. I tried to catch his eyes, gauge his mood, but he was focused on something way beyond the windscreen. His lips moved silently as he scrambled for the right words. "Good to see you, boy," he said finally. "How're you keeping?" His voice was softer than I remembered it, and there was a slight lisp as if several of his teeth were broken.

I smiled, but the man whose quick temper and skinny legs I had inherited was a stranger to me.

MY FATHER MOVED AROUND THE house as if it were a private museum and every object in it a totem of his past. I had long since thrown out many of my parents' belongings, but the way in which he would hold my things, run his fingers over them, he would make them his own and as he replaced each object he would shake his head as if at the memories it evoked.

I watched him from the door. He had removed his jacket and I could see dark patches under his arms and along the ridge of his spine. After a circuit of the living room he lowered himself into the armchair facing the fire. I noticed that his knuckles were ingrained with dirt and it surprised me that he had had to work in prison.

"You want a coffee or something?" I said.

He didn't appear to have heard me. His eyes were locked and I followed his stare to an old stack of albums against the wall by the TV, one of the few things of his that I had held on to.

"Sorry," he said, blinking up at me. "Coffee's fine." There was a warmth to his voice for the first time that day; he was beginning to relax.

It was contagious: the words were out before I could stop them. "That cop was around here last week," I said.

My father eased himself out of the chair and crossed the room, knelt in front of the records. Slowly, he began to flip through them with stiff fingers.

"Stark. That was his name, wasn't it?"

Once more, my words fell on deaf ears.

He pulled out an album, looked at the back cover.

I took a deep breath and pressed on. "He still thinks you're sitting on a pile of cash."

He turned towards me, a dark sadness in his eyes. "What're you now, son? Twenty-one?"

I felt my shoulders push back. "Twenty-two," I said.

"Twenty-two," he echoed. "Guess you're all grown up now, huh? Too old to call me Daddy." He smiled, showing teeth blackened by jailhouse roll-ups. "Call me Walt."

WHEN I TOOK THE COFFEE through he was standing with his arms in the air and his back arched, stretching. I heard joints pop. He brought his arms back down again. He waved the record he held towards me. "It must be fifteen years since I heard this," he said. He slid the record out of the sleeve and carefully placed it on the turntable, lifted the stylus into the groove. There was a gentle rumbling sound, then a deep sorrowful voice began to sing: "Pack up all your dishes . . ."

He listened in silence, his lips mouthing half-remembered phrases. As the song returned to the rumble of the turntable an invisible hand shook him by the spine. "Still gets me," he said.

The unexpected lip made him sound faintly comical and the beginnings of a smile twitched at the corners of my mouth.

He turned to face me, a rush of nerves animating his arms. He splayed his hands out in front of him, twisted his palms together. "Do you . . ." A shake of the head. "Look, I don't suppose you could lend me some decent clothes, could you?" He pinched at the legs of his trousers. "I've only got this suit and it smells like it's spent the last twelve years underground." The words tumbled over each other in his nervousness.

"Yeah, sure. Whatever you want. Room at the front," I said, pointing my chin at the ceiling. I stepped aside to let him pass.

I heard him moving about upstairs. Then suddenly I felt cold fingers tugging on my heart. The photos.

I ran for the stairs, scrambling over the worn carpet. I stuck my head in the bedroom, white knuckles gripping the doorframe. I scanned the room— bedside cabinet, walls, ceiling. Everything was as it should be.

"You OK?" said Walt. He was standing by the bed with a bundle of clothes draped over his arm. Pale flesh rippled his torso.

I tried to control my breathing; deep breaths seared my throat.

"I just thought . . . I just thought I'd show you where everything is," I managed, my heart thumping in my throat.

He looked at me with flat eyes. "I think I can manage," he said.

I turned and went downstairs.

\*       \*       \*

THE NURSE WAS FAMILIAR: LOP-SIDED smile, long eyelashes that would hold tears long after they were born. I was trying to figure out where I might know her from when I heard my father coming down the stairs. I found myself sinking in the armchair. He stopped in the doorway and looked down at me, a Happy-Families mask on his face.

He was wearing a denim shirt with a button-down collar, maroon tie, black jeans and his old brogues. The shower had flushed his face a vital red and his hair was slicked back from his forehead.

"This OK?" he said. He lifted his arms away from his torso.

"Fine." I shrugged and turned back to the nurse; her laugh had brought her closer to recognition.

He stood in silence for a moment, doing the old soft shoe, and then in a voice that was a broken whisper said, "I don't suppose you could lend me a few quid, could you?"

I must have hesitated a beat too long because he took a step closer and followed through with, "It's hidden in a tree in Sherwood Forest. I need the train fare."

I shifted uncomfortably in my chair. It was the first time he had acknowledged the existence of any booty: the pickings of his short-lived life of crime, the change from his one-way ticket to Strangeways.

Such riches had become a part of family folklore, my mother spinning tales of fat rolls of cash, hidden from her slippery fingers, into the fabric of my childhood as she fought the DSS for the control of my welfare.

The day I turned sixteen she gave up the fight. I came home from school to find a gift tag on the front door handle that read, "Happy Birthday. Have a good life." The word 'good' had been crossed out.

But as the first-born son I had always seen the legendary booty as my birthright; the only problem was in persuading the present guardian to give it up.

"How much do you need?" I said. I pulled my wallet from my back pocket.

As he looked down at me, the bags under his eyes puffed out and his eyes receded into darkness. "I don't know. You tell me. I'm meeting someone for lunch." He licked his upper lip.

I sat up. "Sorry?"

"Lunch. You know—"

I twisted round to face him. "Who? You just got out of prison."

"This woman, she's . . . She's been writing to me."

"A nun? You're meeting a nun for lunch?"

"She's not a nun," he said, but the word broke apart on his lips. "No. The letters—"

"Who else would write to a prisoner? Nuns and fuckin' do-gooders. Nuns out of uniform."

"No," he said slowly, drawing out the word, as if he might bite it back at any moment.

"You got a picture? Let me see a picture."

He went over to the table and pulled a bundle of envelopes from his bag. He flicked through them before withdrawing a small passport-size photo. As he handed it to me I felt my pulse quicken and my hand start to twitch; I snatched the photo from his fingers.

The face was more familiar to me than that of the nurse on TV. Dark eyes that spoke of hidden demons; deep lines that bracketed full lips.

"You know who this is?" I said.

My father's mouth slackened and I could see his blackened teeth, turrets in the darkness.

"You know her?" he said, astonishment in his voice.

"No, but I'll bet this is not the woman who's been writing to you." I waved the photo at him. "This'll be her good-looking friend."

His hands balled into fists, knuckles bled white. The tension spread through his body; a muscle in his temple pulsed. He snatched the photo back. "You gonna lend me the money or not?"

I LAY IN BED LISTENING for his key in the lock. I blew smoke towards the ceiling and watched as the moon chased ghosts through the room. Around twelve-thirty I heard a scratching at the front door, a scratching that continued long enough to let me know that he was drunk.

He headed for the kitchen, his footsteps heavy and irregular. He bounced off the walls before flipping the kitchen door open, the handle cracking the wall behind it. A light went on that echoed under my door; shadows scooted from behind the furniture.

Rolling words, as if he was singing. The fridge door slamming, footsteps.

The flat went quiet. All I could hear was the rattle of heels on the street outside. A moment later I heard him heading back down the hall. The living room door creaked open. A muffled thud told me he had collapsed on the sofa.

THE FOLLOWING MORNING I CREPT downstairs and into the kitchen as soon as I awoke. I made myself a cup of coffee and stood at the window, lit a cigarette. I could see a kid of about eight chasing a dog around the playground of the school opposite. Grubby, disembodied faces bubbled at the windows and gawped at the impromptu circus. The kid was chasing the dog with a stick and hitting it every few strides; the dog was turning dizzy circles and making increasingly desperate swings at the stick with its teeth.

I went back down the hall.

I put my ear to the door, one beat, two beats, carefully eased it open. Cold air enveloped me; a window was open.

The smell of stale alcohol lingered in the air, otherwise there was no sign of my father. Maybe he had made it up to bed after all. I went up to his room. His bag was still in the centre of the bed where he had left it the night before.

I could only assume he had gone for a walk to clear his head.

IT WAS THREE DAYS BEFORE I heard anything.

I was chasing a mouthful of dry pizza with cold beer when the phone rang. I licked my fingers and picked up on the second ring.

Ragged breathing; familiar background noise. "Dana? That you?"

"I'm scared, Mike."

"I told you not to call." I found myself whispering through gritted teeth.

"He was here."

"Who?" It popped out automatically.

"The fuck d'you think?" Her words sounded like they were being shot from a pistol at the back of her throat.

"Okay. A'right." I breathed out through my nose. Tried to slow things down a little. "You say he was there?"

"Uh-huh."

"You know he hasn't been back here since the day after he got out."

"Right across the street."

"He didn't call, ring the bell?"

"He just stands there. It's givin' me the fuckin' creeps."

"Is he there now?"

I heard the phone being put down on the table, the rhythmic squeak of floorboards, the phone being picked up again. "I don't think so. I can't see him."

I thought back to the night I had last seen him. "Did you say anything to him?"

She was immediately on her guard. "Like what?"

A wave of anger swelled in my chest. "Dana, no, tell me you didn't . . ."

Her silence screamed at me.

THE FOLLOWING MORNING I DECIDED to go look for him. I was too jumpy to just sit tight and, besides, who knew what buttons Dana had pushed.

The Metro started first time, but as I sat there waiting to pull out, I realised that I hadn't the slightest idea of where to start looking. I turned off the engine and slumped back in the seat.

I had been nine-years-old when he was arrested, ten at the trial. What did I know of his old haunts, old friends, hidden women?

I reached for the ignition; he was out there somewhere.

It must have been a couple of hours later when I found myself passing the building society where my father had attempted to steal himself a new lifestyle.

I pulled into a side street and walked back to the red brick building. I knew the street well, but today the building looked darker than usual.

There was only one customer, an elderly man in a tweed jacket and baggy grey flannels. His hands were shaking as he lifted his passbook from the counter, a tuft of notes stuck out from between the covers.

I glanced up at the ceiling. There was a single camera, in the corner to the right of the counter. Had it been there when my father had drawn his gun?

I walked back outside and stood at the top of the steps. I lit a cigarette and watched the traffic pass by, tyres crackling on the wet tarmac.

HIS BAG WAS STILL ON the bed. I pulled out clean underwear that felt like parchment in my fingers, a white shirt still in its wrapper, black socks. I stuffed my hand in the bag, pulled out the bundle of letters.

I recognised the first letter immediately, but even though it was only a few months since it had been written, the words escaped me. But what magical words they must have been: a cheap prison envelope had landed on her mat less than two weeks later.

We had celebrated by getting noisily drunk on cheap red wine and tugging at each others' pants on the way home.

I had then stepped aside and allowed Dana's naturally flirty manner to continue the correspondence, my only contribution being a whispered, "I only want what's mine." Judging by the bundle of letters in my hand she had written at least twice a week since then. I pulled one at random from the pile and tossed the rest on to the bed. I held it to my nose, sniffed—sweat and something I didn't care to think about.

The letter had been written about three weeks ago. It started with Dana thanking him for his letter and then rambling on about what she had been doing since she had last written; I skipped pages. Towards the end, though, I felt my face flush, my stomach curdle. She had begun to describe in vivid detail what they would get up to on his release. There were even simple drawings of people having sex, limbs woven into positions that looked like letters of the alphabet, in the margins. I tossed the letter aside, grabbed another from the bed. Ditto: more of the alphabet.

I felt my hands prickle with perspiration and blood swirl around in my head. My heart kept punching me in the chest and I had forgotten how to breathe. I flipped through a couple more letters. But confirmation was the last thing I needed: I didn't have to see the rest of the A-to-Z of Fucking to know where my father was.

I bundled the letters together and hurried down the stairs. I unlocked the back door and walked over to the paved area in the far corner of the garden. There were a few bricks around and I formed them into a small circle. I stuffed the letters between the bricks, stood up, and pulled my lighter from my jeans.

The wind was gusting between the houses and I couldn't get the paper to burn. I kicked the bricks over and went back into the house.

IT WAS JUST STARTING TO get dark when I pulled up across from Dana's building, a three-storey Victorian terrace; she had a bedsit on the top floor. I looked up at her window and saw pale light bleeding through cheap curtains.

I crossed the street. Hit the buzzer and pushed on through the door; the lock had been broken for as long as I could remember. I was halfway to the stairs when her voice crackled over the intercom. I stepped back.

"It's me," I said.

"Where have you been. Tell me what's going on." Her voice sounded weak and flat, turning the question into a statement.

"I'm coming up," I said.

The door was ajar when I reached the landing and I pushed it open with the back of my hand. I stepped into the room and saw her sitting on the bed, her legs tucked under her. She was wearing a baggy white T-shirt and grey cords. Her brown hair looked greasy and her face was pale; eyes once quick to laugh were now dull and rimmed red. The cigarette in her hand had been burning for ever if the stain on her fingers was anything to go by.

In my mind I saw little stick fingers crawling over her breasts.

Dana uncoiled herself from the bed and walked towards me. I thought she was going to hug me but she threw a punch at my head and began pummelling my chest. She made ugly grunting noises as I let her punch herself out. Her last punch displaced air and I pushed her back on the bed.

"Where is he?"

Dana scrambled to sit up.

"Where is he?" I said again, my voice a dark whisper.

Dana shook her head, gestured to the window. "Outside," she said. "He was outside."

"He's been staying here, hasn't he?"

Her eyes flickered back into life, as if an electric current had passed through them. "What're you talking about?"

"He hasn't been home in three days."

"So? He has no friends?" A scowl pinched her face.

"You're fucking him."

"Wha—"

"I saw the drawings, the letters." I took a step closer.

She raised her palms to me as a look of terrible realisation appeared in her eyes. "Look, he's gotta trust me. How else is he gonna give up—"

I saw my hand come out of my jacket, the knife a glint in the darkness. Dana's face became a blur, her words white noise. My hand flicked out and a crimson ribbon appeared at her throat, splashed down her chest. She threw back her head and fingers disappeared at her neck.

I watched as she thrashed around on the bed, as her words became gurgles and then became nothing. I watched as her life became nothing.

I HEARD FROM HER AGAIN today.

My father found the letters, blowing around in the garden, and stuck them back together. Every week he photocopies one and sends it to me, drawing over her signature in red ink.

I put them under my pillow.

Carole Nelson Douglas is best known for her two mystery series, one featuring Irene Adler, the only woman to outsmart Sherlock Holmes, and the other current, series which stars a large black tomcat named Midnight Louie, and his Las Vegas publicist Temple Barr. Louie last appeared on the scene in *Cat in a Flamingo Fedora*. But Victorian historical novels and cat cozies aren't all she can do. For example, "Cold Turkey" shows a perhaps not-so-surprising darker side of her fiction.

# Cold Turkey
## CAROLE NELSON DOUGLAS

"Hey, Big Blind Bertha, betcha can't get me!"

The boy jammed his hand in her chest, pushed, and ran.

Bertha hardly noticed the jibe. She was one of those people born under the unlucky star stuck on the wand of a bad fairy, and she had figured it out at an early age.

Maybe the dead paternal aunt had been a lovely person, which was why her parents had perpetuated her name in their only daughter, but the aunt would have needed to be a lovely person with a name like that even seventy years ago.

Surely thirty-eight years ago the name was clearly on the comical list, but her parents had been losers like herself and ever ready to make what was bad worse.

Bertha.

She had fulfilled the prophecy of herself and became a chubby, pale child with poor eyesight who had to get spectacles at an early age so she could see for herself how hopeless she was.

She stuttered in school because the other kids laughed when she was called on. On the playground, they called her Big Bertha.

Only the boys, though. The girls didn't call her anything and they didn't ask her to play jump rope because her name was so ugly no one wanted to sing it out in one of the venerable rhymes. Not like Lin-da and Kar-en and Bam-bi. Besides, Bertha knew that she was clumsy and that her clothes were as ugly and laughable as she was (and always would be) and that her fat (and

241

especially the fat where the boy had jammed his hand) would jiggle if she jumped.

She worked on the power of positive thinking as she rode the bus home after school, alone in the pandemonium of others at play. She repeated endlessly and silently, *invisible/disappear*. But she never was and she never did. Not enough.

She wasn't brilliant, but stubborn. All through school, she took home solid B's. Her parents seemed oblivious to her social flaws, but then they were fat, simple people too stolid to know how unworthy they were. Her brother was no better than herself, only older and a boy, and therefore mean in his frustration.

If the city streets and schoolyards were purgatory, the family's annual summer weeks on her uncle's farm were hell. All her cousins were older and boys, or seemed so, because the girls avoided her. The girls wanted to walk into town to slow-sip chocolate malts at the drug store soda fountain and then stroll the dusty, shaded streets in their new outfits so the older boys could watch them, and sometimes even say something nasty but nice.

Bertha was never asked to go with them, but she desperately wanted to, not because she had delusions of strolling around like a southern belle. She just wanted to get away from the nasty boys on the farm, who liked to dismember insects because it made her face pucker up and hot tears run into the creases and turn them raw.

The boy cousins had endlessly inventive fun on the farm. Usually it involved tormenting something. She tried to forget most of it as she grew older and didn't have to go there anymore.

"But *why* don't you want to go?" her parents would harp at her when she was old enough to stay home in the city alone. "Such good country air and so much fun, and all your cousins are there. Silly girl."

Her brother was off in the military by then, the only way he'd get educated beyond high school.

Bertha had held firm about the farm. She couldn't tell her parents why, but surely they knew. She remembered, when she didn't want to, pranks involving the animals, especially chickens and firecrackers. Her mind winced at the details. She could conjure only scenes of laughter and of frantic birds running and clucking and bursting apart in panic and pain.

That's how they saw her, she thought, a stupid, clucking, running thing worth only laughing at.

Over the years, she had smothered the things too terrible to remember with food and then fat and then more food. She wasn't quite morbidly obese, but fat enough to sometimes almost disappear inside it. And sometimes too fat to disappear. She had been granted a quiet tenacity that got her through leaving home to go on her own, but she lost an early job or two with a craven phone call not to come back because her coworkers complained that she smelled.

She was meticulous about grooming and cleanliness, and she didn't smell, but she looked like she could. And her hair was the curly kind that seemed to have been subjected to a bad permanent, and everything she chose, from eyeglass frames to clothes, was somehow instantly out of date once it became hers.

So she plodded and still said *invisible/disappear* to herself on the bus, and sometimes lately she had even caught her lips moving, but maybe they would think she was praying. She put herself through nursing school because she thought it would be rewarding to take care of sick people and they might actually say thank you sometimes.

She hadn't counted on the laboratory dissections. That was awful, the frogs screaming as the needle pithed their brains, frog after frog, and the live specimens that sometimes mercifully didn't survive to lay before her dissecting team on the table. At least with all the formaldehyde no one could say for sure that she smelled.

She hated scalpel work, but her dissection partners were so clumsy that she took over. At least this way the animals would not be butchered. She had always been neat with her hands. After a while, she learned what the lab sessions were designed to teach her, to disassociate from the gore and fluids and smells, to do what she had to do professionally, and without fuss. To be a nurse.

She got so good at disassociation that when the hospital put her in the emergency room, she handled it with her usual slightly flustered competence. Haste and blood and moans had become white noise to her by then. *Invisible/ disappear*. And the patients moved on so fast—either quick or dead, and that was that.

Disassociation worked off the job, too. On the rare times that scattering feathers and hysterical clucks fluttered into her mind, they vanished faster now. Even the wincing glimpse of a shadowed barn and the boys' voices low and laughing and mean and herself screaming the silent scream . . . fun on the farm.

She never ate chicken, or any fowl, or meat. She never ate eggs or milk or cheese. She liked what they called that. She was a vegan, she would tell people, and they looked at her like she had come from Mars, or even Venus.

I am a vegan. *Invisible/disappear*. Some day she just might.

But for now she was just Bertha the nurse, and she worked the night shift because all the most undesirable tasks always came to her. She volunteered to work holidays; she thought they might like her, then, and, besides, she lived alone in a semirural place crowded with the vagrant animals she had taken in. No one ever thought to invite her to a family holiday dinner, though she was always free or she wouldn't have been able to work those days. No one ever thought about Bertha. *Invisible/disappear* had finally worked.

And it was just as well. She hated holiday dinners and the roasted birds brought in headless, eviscerated, their vital organs extracted and chopped up and reinserted, then gobbled down by all the laughing, talking mouths. Assholes. She rarely even thought bad words, but that was one expression too deserved to pass by.

Bertha was working night shift the day before Thanksgiving. Funny that only Christmas and New Year's and Halloween had an "Eve" the day before, she often thought. She often thought of odd, insignificant facts other people never noticed. Just as they never noticed her.

Thanksgiving was hardly a busy holiday: a few accidental choking victims maybe, or the bloody but minor cuts from a carving knife. No one ever really lost a finger. Then the usual appendicitis and asthma cases. And once in a blue moon, a very blue moon, one of the truly freaky cases that descends on every emergency room eventually, that gets talked about forever after, and laughed about at cocktail parties in hushed corners where nasty boys still gather, only they call themselves doctors now, and they always know best and there are still certain crude things they let women hear only tiny, titillating, terrifying parts of, as if they were still in some barn plotting deviltry.

Dr. Cavanaugh the intern heard it first, by radio from the ambulance crew, and came out grinning in his greens. He was tall and thin and wore little round glasses like he'd been to an eastern med school, when he was really from Indiana.

"Got a live one coming in. Grease the latex gloves."

Everyone knows from *ER* on TV that a hospital emergency room is always busy, except during the rare dead time, and this was one of those down times.

"You aren't gonna believe this," Dr. Cavanaugh added. "A little early Thanksgiving turkey for one and all."

By then the ambulance was cruising silently into the parking zone by the intake entrance and Dr. Cavanaugh was first to greet it.

They could hear the guy squawking all the way in, calling on Jesus Christ like it was already Christmas.

They wheeled him in, accompanied by a similarly scruffy pal, one step up from wino, the blanket over his torso heaving with a life of its own.

"Jesus Christ! You gotta help me. Get me outta this!" His shouts hit the high notes of hysteria like a trumpet solo.

Bertha watched him pass, a man in his late twenties with long, dirty-blond hair, his unshaven lower face masked in wheatfield stubble, and blood on his grimy hands. His friend was no more appetizing, but who was a fat nurse to judge?

"Bertha," Dr. Cavanaugh called. "We need some big-time left to hold this guy down."

The blanket reared up over the injured man's crotch; people with an obscene cast of mind might try to imagine what was going on under it.

Bertha thought she heard hoarse cries and saw pale, soft feathers swirling like snow in the summertime, amid a shower of fine, bloody raindrops.

She rushed alongside the gurney into an examining room. When the door hushed shut she could hear the ambulance attendants already answering questions from the jabbering staff. Then they all were laughing so hard no one could speak.

And she was inside, doing important things. Trying to calm the impatient patient and assisting Dr. Cavanaugh.

"Jesus Christ."

This time Dr. Cavanaugh echoed the words as he lifted the blanket off the writhing man.

A bird appeared, like a pretty little dove from under a magician's handkerchief, except a blanket was much bigger and so was the bird.

It flapped its clumsy wings and gargled piteously in the sudden light, bound to the patient's lower torso with torn, dirty sheeting, its beaked face a nightmare framed by obscene flaps of lumpy crimson skin. Turkeys were unattractive birds, like vultures, and considered stupid. But you never know, Bertha thought, still too surprised to grasp the situation.

The blood flowed from the man's pantless thighs and stomach, where the turkey's formidable, flailing talons had dug in. Horrible, deep rakes seven inches long. Urine and bowel smells mingled under the warm examining lights, man and turkey's.

"What a mess." Dr. Cavanaugh sounded disgusted. "How'd you get yourself into this, man?"

Bertha frowned, finally beginning to grasp what had happened. Mercifully, she felt the room miniaturize and pull away, like the barn shadows had done so long ago.

The turkey's wings sawed in hopeless racial memory of flight.

"My buddy and me, we got a chance to get this live turkey for Thanksgiving cheap, a couple of days ago. So, we thought, let's get some double duty from the bird, right? Hey, we were drinking Dos Equis all day and didn't have nothin' better to do.

"Now I'm fuckin' stuck and gettin' clawed to hell and I'm stuck. Nobody can get this damn bird off me. Do it, Doc."

Dr. Cavanaugh rubbed his chin with a gloved hand. "Never had a case like this. Nurse!"

Bertha rushed to his side, her soft-soled shoes quiet as falling feathers on the vinyl tile floor.

"This guy needs a little tranquilizer. Phenergan should do it, whichever way it's easier to administer. You got someone can drive you home? Been drinking in the past couple hours?"

The guy nodded and shook his greasy head in turn. Dr. Cavanaugh withdrew to the door, Bertha accompanying him, and lowered his voice.

"We need him tranqed when we unwrap that winding sheet and do in the bird. Have to break its neck, I suppose. Or cut its throat with a scalpel. You didn't happen to do that on a farm, did you? I'll ask the others. Wonder what this thing weighs. What do you think? You're a woman. You cook these things."

She didn't, but she prided herself on knowing any information needed. "Ah . . . twenty-five pounds, maybe. It's a big one, bigger than a chicken."

"Not quite big enough," Dr. Cavanaugh added under his breath, his mouth quirking into a sneer. "Jeez. Maybe that guy will learn to be more choosy about where he stuffs it."

They could overhear staff titters outside in the hall. A rare moment of humor and idleness. Then all talk stopped as they heard a sudden flutter.

"Stat!" a man's voice ordered. "Stats" started echoing off the hard hospital walls like machine-gun fire. Stat-a-stat-a-stat.

"Sounds like all hands are needed." Dr. Cavanaugh opened the door. "Get him started on the tranq."

As the door whooshed open and closed, Bertha heard the words "apartment" and "fire." Seconds later the wails of arriving ambulances began.

"God, that bastard can't leave!" The man on the Gurney shouted. "I've got a situation here. Get this damn bird off me."

"This medication will help. It's actually for nausea, but has a calming side effect. Just a moment, sir."

She had to call him "sir."

"It better not be no needle! I don't need nothin'. The turkey's the problem. Whatcha gonna do about that, huh?"

"I believe the doctor intends to . . . kill it." Bertha hesitated over the supplies, then picked the Phenergan in suppository form. "Just relax."

"God! What're you doing down there? Hey!"

"Just a small suppository, sir. Like a toothpick compared to what's in the turkey. This won't get stuck. It'll melt away."

And still the bird flapped and emitted its pathetic squawks.

Bertha suddenly saw the bird plucked and headless, protruding from the man's groin, its own life blood minging the red runes its claws had drawn on his flesh.

She saw the bird as white, plump, stupid and defenseless, like the babies they brought in, sometimes blue already, the pale flesh marked with the signs of nasty things done in shadowy corners, of mutilated orifices. Dead sometimes. And more often, unfortunately living to remember.

Or to disassociate.

She had disassociated from the bizarre scene before her. She was a nurse. She would do her duty. But the victim always paid, always suffered more, was always punished somehow, just for being there.

"Get this thing off me!" the man was screaming, barely audible above the rhythmic rise and fall of the sirens' warning chorus.

These whould be burned people. Pained people. Helpless people. Victims of circumstance. Not victims of deliberate abuse. Why did the perpetrators prove so hard to convict, and to punish? Why did they go on and on, to victimize again?

"Get this fucking bird off me, you stupid bitch!" the man screamed.

She really was in no position to object to his language, so she did exactly what he said.

"It was really simple," Bertha told the rape counselor from down the hall an hour later, a middle-aged lady with a plain face who looked as if she knew about invisible/disappear.

They had given her hot coffee and saltine crackers, but Bertha was a nurse and knew she wasn't really in shock.

"These boys like to think they're so mean, that it's so hard, like a bone. But that's a delusion of the circulatory system. It's all just blood and bluster. That's all. Not hard to cut, and once the blood leaked out, it shriveled and came out of the turkey like nothing. Like a narrow little thermometer. Poor bird. Don't let them kill her, please. She shouldn't be abused like that and then just die. I've a place in the country, I could take her home and I would never, ever eat her. Boys can be so mean, you know?"

The rape counselor's face looked odd, like she was disassociating, too. *Invisible/disappear.*

"I did the only thing I could," Bertha said. "I saved the victim. And they saved the leftover. They can sew it on again. And next time, he might think twice. Wouldn't you have done the same thing? Is it right to kill the victim? I'm not sorry. Wouldn't you have done the same thing?"

The woman never answered her, but Bertha was used to that.

A master of psychological fiction in both novel length and short form, Joyce Carol Oates is arguably among the top authors in the nation. She examines the usually fragile bonds that hold people together, whether it be by marriage or blood, then introduces the catalyst that more often than not tears that relationship apart, all the while imbuing her characters with a fully-realized life of their own that practically makes them walk off the page. Her most recent novel is *My Heart Laid Bare*, and she recently edited the anthology *Telling Stories: An Anthology for Writers*. In "Death Cup" she is at her sly best, telling the story of two very different brothers and how their lives are fatally intertwined.

# Death Cup
## JOYCE CAROL OATES

*Amanita phalloides* he began to hear in no voice he could recognize.

Murmurous, only just audible—*Amanita phalloides*.

More distinctly that morning, a rain-chilled Saturday morning in June, at his uncle's funeral. In the austere old Congregationalist church he only entered, as an adult, for such ceremonies as weddings and funerals. As, seated beside his brother Alastor of whom he disapproved strongly, he leaned far forward in the cramped hardwood pew, framing his face with his fingers so that he was spared seeing his brother's profile in the corner of his eye. Feeling an almost physical repugnance for the man who was his brother. He tried to concentrate on the white-haired minister's solemn words yet was nervously distracted by *Amanita phalloides*. As if, beneath the man's familiar words of Christian forbearance and uplift another voice, a contrary voice, strange, incantatory, was struggling to emerge. And during the interlude of organ music. The Bach Toccata and Fugue in D Minor which his uncle, an amateur musician and philanthropist, had requested be played at his funeral. Lyle was one who, though he claimed to love music, was often distracted during it; his mind drifting; his thoughts like flotsam, or froth; now hearing the whispered words, only just audible in his ears *Amanita phalloides, Amanita phalloides*. He realized he'd first heard these mysterious words the night before, in a dream. A sort of fever-dream. Brought on by his brother's sudden, unexpected return.

He did not hate his brother Alastor. Not here, in this sacred place.

*Amanita phalloides. Amanita phalloides . . .*

How beautiful, the Bach organ music! Filling the spartan plain, dazzling white interior of the church with fierce cascades of sound pure and flashing as a waterfall. Such music argued for the essential dignity of the human spirit. The transcendence of physical pain, suffering, loss. All that's petty, ignoble. *The world is a beautiful place if you have the eyes to see it and the ears to hear it*, Lyle's uncle had often said, and had seemed to believe through his long life, apparently never dissuaded from the early idealism of his youth; yet how was such idealism possible, Lyle couldn't help but wonder, Lyle who wished to believe well of others yet had no wish to be a fool, how was such idealism possible after the evidence of catastrophic world wars, the unspeakable evil of the Holocaust, equally mad, barbaric mass slaughters in Stalin's Russia, Mao's China? Somehow, his uncle Gardner King had remained a vigorous, good-natured, and generous man despite such facts of history; there'd been in him, well into his seventies, a childlike simplicity which Lyle, his nephew, younger than he by decades, seemed never to have had. Lyle had loved his uncle, who'd been his father's eldest brother. Fatherless himself since the age of eleven, he'd been saddened by his uncle's gradual descent into death from cancer of the larynx, and had not wanted to think that he would probably be remembered, to some degree, in his uncle's will. The bulk of the King estate, many millions of dollars, would go into the King Foundation, which was nominally directed by his wife, now widow, Alida King; the rest of it would be divided among numerous relatives. Lyle was troubled by the anticipation of any bequest, however modest. The mere thought filled him with anxiety, almost a kind of dread. *I would not wish to benefit in any way from Uncle Gardner's death, I could not bear it.*

To which his brother Alastor would have replied in his glib, jocular way, as, when they were boys, he'd laughed at Lyle's over-scrupulous conscience: *What good's that attitude? Our uncle is dead and he isn't coming back, is he?*

Unfortunate that Alastor had returned home to Contracoeur on the very eve of their uncle's death, after an absence of six years.

Still, it could only have been coincidence. So Alastor claimed. He'd been in communication with none of the relatives, including his twin brother Lyle.

How murmurous, teasing in Lyle's ears—*Amanita phalloides.*

Intimate as a lover's caressing whisper, and mysterious—*Amanita phalloides.*

Lyle was baffled at the meaning of these words. Why, at such a time, his thoughts distracted by grief, they should assail him.

In the hardwood pew, unpleasantly crowded by Alastor on his left, not wanting to crowd himself against an elderly aunt on his right, Lyle felt his lean, angular body quiver with tension. His neck was beginning to ache from the strain of leaning forward. It annoyed him to realize that, in his unstylish matte-black gabardine suit that fitted him too tightly across the shoulders and too loosely elsewhere, with his ash-colored hair straggling past his collar, his face furrowed as if with pain, and the peculiar way he held his outstretched fingers against his face, he was making himself conspicuous among the rows of mourners in the King family pews. Staring at the gleaming ebony casket so prominently placed in the center aisle in front of the communion rail, that looked so forbidding; so gigantic; far larger than his uncle Gardner's earthly remains, diminutive at the end, would seem to require. *But of course death is larger than life. Death envelops life: the emptiness that precedes our brief span of time, the emptiness that follows.*

A shudder ran through him. Tears stung his cheeks like acid. How shaky, how emotional he'd become!

A nudge in his side—his brother Alastor pressed a handkerchief, white, cotton, freshly laundered, into his hand, which Lyle blindly took.

Managing, even then, not to glance at his brother. Not to upset himself seeing yet again his brother's mock-pious mock-grieving face. His watery eyes, in mimicry of Lyle's.

Now the organ interlude was over. The funeral service was ending so soon! Lyle felt a childish stab of dismay, that his uncle would be hurried out of the sanctuary of the church, out of the circle of the community, into the impersonal, final earth. Yet the white-haired minister was leading the congregation in a familiar litany of words beginning, "Our heavenly father . . ." Lyle wiped tears from his eyelashes, shut his eyes tightly in prayer. He hadn't been a practicing Christian since adolescence, he was impatient with unquestioned piety and superstition, yet there was solace in such a ritual, seemingly shared by an entire community. Beside him, his aunt Agnes prayed with timid urgency, as if God were in this church and needed only to be beseeched by the right formula of words, and in the right tone of voice. On his other side, his brother Alastor intoned the prayer, not ostentatiously but distinctly enough to be heard for several pews; Alastor's voice was a deep, rich baritone, the voice of a trained singer you might think, or an actor. A roaring in Lyle's ears like a waterfall—*Amanita phalloides! Amanita phalloides!* and suddenly he remembered what *Amanita phalloides* was: the death-cup mushroom. He'd been reading a pictorial article on edible and inedible fungi in one of his science magazines and the death-cup mushroom, more accurately a"toadstool," had been imprinted on his memory.

His mouth had gone dry, his heart was hammering against his ribs. With the congregation, he murmured, "Amen." All volition seemed to have drained from him. Calmly he thought, *I will kill my brother Alastor after all. After all these years.*

OF COURSE, THIS WOULD NEVER happen. Alastor King was a hateful person who surely deserved to die, but Lyle, his twin brother, was not one to commit any act of violence; not even one to fantasize any act of violence. *Not me! not me! Never.*

\* \* \*

IN THE CEMETERY BEHIND THE First Congregationalist Church of Contracoeur the remainder of the melancholy funeral rite was enacted. There stood Lyle King, the dead man's nephew, in a daze in wet grass beneath a glaring opalescent sky, awakened by strong fingers gripping his elbow. "All right if I ride with you to Aunt Alida's, Lyle?" Alastor asked. There was an edge of impatience to his lowered voice, as if he'd had to repeat his question. And Lyle's twin brother had not been one, since the age of eighteen months, to wish to repeat questions. He was leaning close to Lyle as if hoping to read his thoughts; his eyes were steely blue, narrowed. His breath smelled of something sweetly chemical, mouthwash probably, to disguise the alcohol on his breath; Lyle knew he was carrying a pocket flask in an inside pocket. His handsome ruddy face showed near-invisible broken capillaries like exposed nerves. Lyle murmured, "Of course, Alastor. Come with me." His thoughts flew ahead swiftly—there was Cemetery Hill that was treacherously steep, and the High Street Bridge—opportunities for accidents? Somehow Lyle's car might swerve out of control, skid on the wet pavement, Alastor, who scorned to wear a seat belt, might be thrown against the windshield, might be injured, might die, while he, Lyle, buckled in safely, might escape with but minor injuries. And blameless. Was that possible? Would God watch over him?

Not possible. For Lyle would have to drive other relatives in his car, too. He couldn't risk their lives. And there was no vigilant God.

A SIMPLE SELF-EVIDENT FACT, THOUGH a secret to most of the credulous world: Alastor King, attractive, intelligent, and deathly "charming" as he surely was, was as purely hateful, vicious, and worthless an individual as ever lived. His brother Lyle had grown to contemplate him with horror the way a martyr of ancient times might have contemplated the engine of pain and destruction rushing at him. *How can so evil a person deserve to live?* Lyle had wondered, sick with loathing of him. (This was years ago when the brothers were twenty. Alastor had secretly seduced their seventeen-year-old cousin Susan, and within a week or two lost interest in her, causing the girl to attempt suicide and to suffer a break-down from which she would never fully recover.) Yet, maddening, Alastor had continued to live, and live. Nothing in the normal course of events would stop him.

Except Lyle. His twin. Who alone of the earth's billions of inhabitants understood Alastor's heart.

And so how shocked Lyle had been, how sickened, having hurried to the hospital when word came that his uncle Gardner was dying, only to discover, like the materialization of one of his nightmares, his brother Alastor already there! Strikingly dressed as usual, with an expression of care, concern, solicitude, clasping their aunt Alida's frail hand and speaking softly and reassuringly to her, and to the others, most of them female relatives, in the visitors'

waiting room outside the intensive care unit. As if Alastor had been mysteriously absent from Contracoeur for six years, not having returned even for
their mother's funeral; as if he hadn't disappeared abruptly when he'd left,
having been involved in a dubious business venture and owing certain of the
relatives money, including Uncle Gardner (an undisclosed sum—Lyle didn't
doubt it was many thousands of dollars) and Lyle himself (three thousand
five hundred dollars).

Lyle had stood in the doorway, staring in disbelief. He had not seen his
twin brother in so long, he'd come to imagine that Alastor no longer existed
in any way hurtful to him.

Alastor cried, "Lyle, Brother, hello! Good to see you!—except this is such
a tragic occasion."

Swiftly Alastor came to Lyle, seizing his forearm, shaking his hand vigorously as if to disarm him. He was smiling broadly, with his old bad-boyish
air, staring Lyle boldly in the face and daring him to wrench away. Lyle
stammered a greeting, feeling his face burn. *He has come back like a bird of
prey, now Uncle Gardner is dying.* Alastor nudged Lyle in the ribs, saying in
a chiding voice that he'd returned to Contracoeur just by chance, to learn the
sad news about their uncle—"I'd have thought, Lyle, that you might have
kept your own brother better informed. As when Mother died, too, so suddenly, and I didn't learn about it for months."

Lyle protested, "But you were traveling—in Europe, you said—out of communication with everyone. You—"

But Alastor was performing for Aunt Alida and the others, and so interrupted Lyle to cry, with a pretense of great affection, "How unchanged you
are, Lyle! How happy I am to see you." It wasn't enough for Alastor to have
gripped Lyle's hand so hard he'd nearly broken the fingers, now he had to
embrace him; a rough bearlike hug that nearly cracked Lyle's ribs, calculated
to suggest to those who looked on *See how natural I am, how spontaneous
and loving, and how stiff and unnatural my brother is, and has always been,
though we're supposed to be twins.* Lyle had endured this performance in the
past and had no stomach for it now, pushing Alastor away and saying in an
angry undertone, "You! What are you doing here! I'd think you'd be damned
ashamed, coming back like this." Not missing a beat, Alastor laughed and
said, winking, one actor to another in a play performed for a credulous, foolish audience, "But why, brother? When you can be ashamed for both of us?"
And he squeezed Lyle's arm with deliberate force, making him wince; as he'd
done repeatedly when they were boys, daring Lyle to protest to their parents.
*Daring me to respond with equal violence.* Then slinging a heavy arm around
Lyle's shoulders, and walking him back to the women, as if Lyle were the
reluctant visitor, and he, Alastor, the self-appointed host. Lyle quickly
grasped, to his disgust, that Alastor had already overcome their aunt Alida's
distrust of him and had made an excellent impression on everyone, brilliantly

playing the role of the misunderstood prodigal son, tender-hearted, grieved by his uncle's imminent death, and eager—so eager!—to give comfort to his well-to-do aunt.

How desperately Lyle wanted to take Aunt Alida aside, for she was an intelligent woman, and warn her *Take care! My brother is after Uncle Gardner's fortune!* But of course he didn't dare; it wasn't in Lyle King's nature to be manipulative.

IN THIS WAY, ALASTOR KING returned to Contracoeur.

And within a few days, to Lyle's disgust, he'd reestablished himself with most of the relatives and certain of his old friends and acquaintances; probably, Lyle didn't doubt, with former women friends. He'd overcome Alida King's distrust and this had set the tone for the others. Though invited to stay with relatives, he'd graciously declined and had taken up residence at the Black River Inn; Lyle knew that his brother wanted privacy, no one spying on him, but others interpreted this gesture as a wish not to intrude, or impinge upon family generosity. How thoughtful Alastor had become, how kind, how *mature*. So Lyle was hearing on all sides. It was put to him repeatedly, maddeningly: "You must be so happy, Lyle, that your brother has returned. You must have missed him terribly."

And Lyle would smile wanly, politely, and say, "Yes. Terribly."

The worst of it was, apart from the threat Alastor posed to Alida King, that Lyle, who'd succeeded in pushing his brother out of his thoughts for years, was forced to think of him again; to think obsessively of him again; to recall the myriad hurts, insults, outrages he'd suffered from Alastor; and the numerous cruel and even criminal acts Alastor had perpetrated, with seeming impunity. And of course he was always being thrown into Alastor's company: always the fraudulent, happy cry, "Lyle! Brother"—always the exuberant, rib-crushing embrace, a mockery of brotherly affection. On one occasion, when he'd gone to pick up Alastor at the hotel, Lyle had staved Alastor off with an elbow, grimacing. "Damn you, Alastor, stop. We're not on stage, no one's watching." Alastor said, laughing, with a contemptuous glance around, "What do you mean, Brother? Someone is always watching."

It was true. Even on neutral ground, in the foyer of the Black River Inn, for instance, people often glanced at Alastor King. In particular, women were drawn to his energetic, boyish good looks and bearing.

*As if they saw not the man himself but the incandescent, seductive image of the man's desire: his wish to deceive.*

While, seeing Lyle, they saw merely—Lyle.

What particularly disgusted Lyle was that his brother's hypocrisy was so transparent. Yet so convincing. And he, the less demonstrative brother, was made to appear hesitant, shy, anemic by comparison. Lacking, somehow, manliness itself. Alastor was such a dazzling sight: his hair that should have been Lyle's identical shade of faded ashy-brown was a brassy russet-brown, lifting from his forehead in waves that appeared crimped, while Lyle's thinning hair was limp, straight. Alastor's sharply blue eyes were alert and watchful and flirtatious while Lyle's duller blue eyes were gently myopic and vague behind glasses that were invariably finger-smudged. Apart from a genial flush to his skin, from an excess of food and drink, Alastor radiated an exuberant sort of masculine health; if you didn't look closely, his face appeared youthful, animated, while Lyle's was beginning to show the inroads of time, small worried dents and creases, particularly at the corners of his eyes. Alastor was at least twenty pounds heavier than Lyle, thick in the torso, as if he'd been building up muscles, while Lyle, lean, rangy, with an unconscious tendency to slouch, looked by comparison wan and uncoordinated. (In fact, Lyle was a capable swimmer and an enthusiastic tennis player.) Since early adolescence Alastor had dressed with verve: At the hospital, he'd worn what appeared to be a suit of suede, honey-colored, with an elegantly cut jacket and a black silk shirt worn without a tie; after their uncle's death, he'd switched to theatrical mourning, in muted-gray fashionable clothes, a linen coat with exaggerated padded shoulders, trousers with prominent creases, shirts so pale a blue they appeared a grieving white, and a midnight blue neckie of some beautiful glossy fabric. And he wore expensive black leather shoes with soles that gave him an extra inch of height—so that Lyle, who had always been Alastor's height exactly, was vexed by being forced *to look up at him.* Lyle, who had no vanity, and some might say not enough pride, wore the identical matte-black gabardine suit in an outdated style he'd worn for years on special occasions; often he shaved without really looking at himself in the mirror, his mind turned inward; sometimes he rushed out of the house without combing his hair. He was a sweet-natured, vague-minded young-old man with the look of a perennial bachelor, held in affectionate if bemused regard by those who knew him well, largely ignored by others. After graduating summa cum laude from Williams College—while Alastor had dropped out, under suspicious circumstances, from Amherst—Lyle had returned to Contracoeur to lead a quiet, civilized life: He lived in an attractively converted carriage house on what had been his parents' property, gave private music lessons, and designed books for a small New England press specializing in limited editions distinguished within the trade, but little known elsewhere. He'd had several moderately serious romances that had come to nothing yet he harbored, still, a vague hope of marriage; friends were always trying to match him with eligible young women, as in a stubborn parlor game no one wished to give up. (In fact, Lyle had secretly adored his cousin Susan, whom Alastor had seduced; after that sorry episode, and Susan's subsequent marriage and move to Boston, Lyle seemed to himself to have lost heart for the game.) It amused Lyle to think that Alastor was considered a "world traveler"—an "explorer"—for he was certain that his brother had spent time in prison, in the United States; in Europe, in his late twenties, he'd traveled with a rich older woman who'd conveniently died and left him some money.

It wasn't possible to ask Alastor a direct question, and Lyle had long since given up trying. He'd given up, in fact, making much effort to communicate with Alastor at all. For Alastor only lied to him, with a maddening habit of smiling and winking and sometimes nudging him in the ribs as if to say *I know you despise me, Brother. And so what? You're too cowardly to do anything about it.*

AT THE FUNERAL LUNCHEON, LYLE noted glumly that Alastor was seated beside their aunt Alida and that the poor woman, her mind clearly weakened from the strain of her husband's death, was gazing up at Alastor as once she'd gazed at her husband Gardner: with infinite trust. Aunt Alida was one of those women who'd taken a special interest in Lyle from time to time, hoping to match him with a potential bride, and now, it seemed, she'd forgotten Lyle entirely. But then she was paying little attention to anyone except Alastor. Through the buzz and murmur of voices—Lyle winced to hear how frequently Alastor was spoken of, in the most laudatory way—he could make out fragments of their conversation; primarily Alastor's grave, unctuous voice. "And were Uncle Gardner's last days peaceful?—did he look back upon his life with joy?—that's all that matters." Seeing Lyle's glare of indignation, Alastor raised his glass of wine in a subtly mocking toast, smiling, just perceptibly winking, so that no one among the relatives could guess the message he was sending to his twin, as frequently he'd done when they were boys, in the company of their parents. *See? How clever I am? And what gullible fools these others are, to take me seriously?*

Lyle flushed angrily, so distracted he nearly overturned his water goblet.

Afterward, questioned about his travels, Alastor was intriguingly vague. Yet all his tales revolved around himself; always, Alastor King was the hero. Saving a young girl from drowning when a Greek steamer struck another boat, in the Mediterranean; establishing a medical trust fund for beggars, in Cairo; giving aid to a young black heroin addict adrift in Amsterdam . . . Lyle listened with mounting disgust as the relatives plied Alastor with more questions, believing everything he said no matter how absurd; having forgotten, or wishing to forget, how he'd disappeared from Contracoeur owing some of them money. Alastor was, it seemed, now involved in the importing into the United States of "master-works of European culture"; elliptically he suggested that his business would flourish, and pay off investors handsomely, if only it might be infused with a little more capital. He was in partnership with a distinguished Italian artist of an "impoverished noble family". . . . As Alastor sipped wine, it seemed to Lyle that his features grew more vivid, as if he were an actor in a film, magnified many times. His artfully dyed brassy-brown hair framed his thuggish fox-face in crimped waves so that he looked like an animated doll. Lyle would have asked him sceptically who the distinguished artist was, what was the name of their business, but he knew that Alastor would give glib, convincing answers. Except for Lyle, everyone at the table was gazing at Alastor with interest, admiration, and, among the older women, yearning; you could imagine these aging women, shaken by the death of one of their contemporaries, looking upon Alastor as if he were a fairy prince, promising them their youth again, their lost innocence. They had only to believe in him unstintingly, to "invest" in his latest business scheme. "Life is a ceaseless pilgrimage up a mountain," Alastor was saying. "As long as you're in motion, your perspective is obscured. Only when you reach the summit and turn to look back, can you be at peace."

There was a hushed moment at the table, as if Alastor had uttered holy words. Aunt Alida had begun to weep, quietly. Yet there was a strange sort of elation in her weeping. Lyle, who rarely drank, and never during the day, found himself draining his second glass of white wine. *Amanita phalloides. Amanita* . . . He recalled how, years ago, when they were young children, Alastor had so tormented him that he'd lost control suddenly and screamed, flailing at his brother with his fists, knocking Alastor backward, astonished. Their mother had quickly intervened. But Lyle remembered vividly. *I wasn't a coward, once.*

LYLE DROVE ALASTOR BACK TO the Black River Inn in silence. And Alastor himself was subdued, as if his performance had exhausted him. He said, musing aloud, "Aunt Alida has aged so, I was shocked. They all have. I don't see why you hadn't kept in closer touch with me, Lyle; you could have reached me care of American Express anytime you'd wanted in Rome, in Paris, in Amsterdam . . . Who will be overseeing the King Foundation now? Aunt Alida will need help. And that enormous English Tudor house. And all that property: thirty acres. Uncle Gardner refused even to consider selling to a developer, but it's futile to hold out much longer. All of the north section of Contracoeur is being developed; if Aunt Alida doesn't sell, she'll be surrounded by tract homes in a few years. It's the way of the future, obviously." Alastor paused, sighing with satisfaction. It seemed clear that the future was a warm beneficent breeze blowing in his direction. He gave Lyle, who was hunched behind the steering wheel of his nondescript automobile, a sly sidelong glance. "And that magnificent Rolls Royce. I suppose, Brother, you have your eye on *that?*" Alastor laughed, as if nothing was more amusing than the association of Lyle with a Rolls Royce. He was dabbing at his flushed face, overheated from numerous glasses of wine.

Quietly Lyle said, "I think you should leave the family alone, Alastor. You've already done enough damage to innocent people in your life."

"But—by what measure is 'enough'?" Alastor said, with mock seriousness. "By your measure, Brother, or mine?"

"There is only one measure—that of common decency."

"Oh well, then, if you're going to lapse into 'common' decency," Alastor said genially, "it's hopeless to try to talk to you."

At the Black River Inn, Alastor invited Lyle inside so that they could discuss "family matters" in more detail. Lyle, trembling with indignation, coolly declined. He had work to do, he said; he was in the midst of designing a book, a new limited edition with handsewn pages and letterpress printing, of Edgar Allan Poe's short story "William Wilson." Alastor shrugged, as if he thought little of this; not once had he shown the slightest interest in his brother's beautifully designed books, any more than he'd shown interest in his brother's life. "You'd be better off meeting a woman," he said. "I could introduce you to one."

Lyle said, startled, "But you've only just arrived back in Contracoeur."

Alastor laughed, laying a heavy hand on Lyle's arm, and squeezing him with what seemed like affection. "God, Lyle! Are you serious? Women are everywhere. And any time."

Lyle said disdainfully, "A certain kind of woman, you mean."

Alastor said, with equal disdain, "No. There is only one kind of woman."

Lyle turned his car into the drive of the Black River Inn, his heart pounding with loathing of his brother. He knew that Alastor spoke carelessly, meaning only to provoke; it was pointless to try to speak seriously with him, let alone reason with him. He had no conscience in small matters as in large. *What of our cousin Susan? Do you ever think of her, do you feel remorse for what you did to her?*—Lyle didn't dare ask. He would only be answered by a crude, flippant remark which would only upset him further.

The Black River Inn was a handsome "historic" hotel recently renovated, at considerable cost, now rather more a resort motel than an inn, with landscaped grounds, a luxurious swimming pool, tennis courts. It seemed appropriate that Alastor would be staying in such a place; though surely deep in debt, he was accustomed to first-rate accommodations. Lyle sat in his car watching his brother stride purposefully away without a backward glance. Already he'd forgotten his chauffeur.

Two attractive young women were emerging from the front entrance of the inn as Alastor approached. Their expressions when they saw him—alert, enlivened—the swift exchange of smiles, as if in a secret code—cut Lyle to the quick. *Don't you know that man is evil? How can you be so easily deceived by looks?* Lyle opened his car door, jumped from the car, stood breathless and staring at the young women as they continued on the walk in his direction; they were laughing together, one of them glanced over her shoulder after Alastor (who was glancing over his shoulder at her, as he pushed into the hotel's revolving door) but their smiles faded when they saw Lyle. He wanted to stammer—what? Words of warning, or apology? Apology for his own odd behavior? But without slowing their stride the women were past, their glances sliding over Lyle; taking him in, assessing him, and sliding over him. They seemed not to register that Alastor, who'd so caught their eye, and Lyle were twins; they seemed not to have seen Lyle at all.

RECALLING HOW YEARS AGO IN circumstances long since forgotten he'd had the opportunity to observe his brother flirting with a cocktail waitress, a heavily made-up woman in her late thirties, still a glamorous woman yet no longer young, and Alastor had drawn her out, asking her name, teasing her, shamelessly flattering her, making her blush with pleasure; then drawing back with a look of offended surprise when the waitress asked him his name, saying, "Excuse me? I don't believe that's any of your business, miss." The hurt, baffled look on the woman's face! Lyle saw how, for a beat, she continued to smile, if only with her mouth; wanting to believe that this was part of Alastor's sophisticated banter. Alastor said, witheringly, "You don't seem to take your job seriously. I think I must have a conversation with the manager." Alastor was on his feet, incensed; the waitress immediately apologized, "Oh no, sir, please—I'm so sorry—I misunderstood—" Like an actor secure in his role since he has played it numberless times, Alastor walked away without a backward glance. It was left to Lyle (afterward, Lyle would realize how deliberately it had been left to him) to pay for his brother's drinks, and to apologize to the stunned waitress, who was still staring after Alastor. "My brother is only joking, he has a cruel sense of humor. Don't be upset, please!" But the woman seemed scarcely to hear Lyle, her eyes swimming with tears; nor did she do more than glance at him. There she stood, clutching her hands at her breasts as if she'd been stabbed, staring after Alastor, waiting for him to return.

IT WOULD BE CREAM OF *Amanita phalloides* soup that Lyle served to his brother Alastor when, at last, Alastor found time to come to lunch.

An unpracticed cook, Lyle spent much of the morning preparing the elaborate meal. The soft, rather slimy, strangely cool pale-gray-pulpy fungi chopped with onions and moderately ground in a blender. Cooked slowly in a double boiler in chicken stock, seasoned with salt and pepper and grated nutmeg; just before Alastor was scheduled to arrive, laced with heavy cream and two egg yolks slightly beaten, and the heat on the stove turned down. How delicious the soup smelled! Lyle's mouth watered, even as a vein pounded dangerously in his forehead. When Alastor arrived in a taxi, a half-hour late, swaggering into Lyle's house without knocking, he drew a deep startled breath, savoring the rich cooking aroma, and rubbed his hands together in anticipation. "Lyle, wonderful! I didn't know you were a serious cook. I'm famished."

Nervously Lyle said, "But you'll have a drink first, Alastor? And—relax?"

Of course Alastor would have a drink. Or two. Already he'd discovered, chilling in Lyle's refrigerator, the two bottles of good Italian chardonnay Lyle had purchased for this occasion. "May I help myself? You're busy."

Lyle had found the recipe for cream of mushroom soup in a battered Fanny Farmer cookbook in a secondhand bookshop in town. In the same shop he'd found an amateur's guide to fungi, edible and inedible, with pages of illustrations. Shabby mane, chanterelles, beefsteak mushrooms—these were famously edible. But there amid the inedible, the sinister look-alike toadstools, was *Amanita phalloides*. The death cup. A white-spored fungi, as the caption explained, with the volva separate from the cap. Highly poisonous. And strangely beautiful, like a vision from the deepest recesses of one's dreams brought suddenly into the light.

The "phallic" nature of the fungi was painfully self-evident. How ironic, Lyle thought, and appropriate. For a man like Alastor who sexually misused women.

It had taken Lyle several days of frantic searching in the woods back beyond his house before he located what appeared to be *Amanita phalloides*. He'd drawn in his breath at the sight—a malevolent little crop of toadstools luminous in the mist, amid the snaky gnarled roots of a gigantic beech tree. Almost, as Lyle quickly gathered them with his gloved hands, dropping them into a bag, the fungi exuded an air of sentient life. Lyle imagined he could hear faint cries of anguish as he plucked at them, in haste; he had an unreasonable fear of someone discovering him. *But those aren't edible mushrooms, those are death cups, why are you gathering those?*

Alastor was seated at the plain wooden table in Lyle's spartan dining room. Lyle brought his soup bowl in from the kitchen and set it, steaming, before him. At once Alastor picked up his soup spoon and began noisily to eat. He said he hadn't eaten yet that day; he'd had an arduous night—"well into the morning." He laughed, mysteriously. He sighed. "Brother, this *is* good. I think I can discern—chanterelles? My favorites."

Lyle served crusty French bread, butter, a chunk of goat's cheese, and set a second bottle of chardonnay close by Alastor's place. He watched, mesmerized, as Alastor lifted spoonfuls of soup to his mouth and sipped and swallowed hungrily, making sounds of satisfaction. How flattered Lyle felt, who could not recall ever having been praised by his twin brother before in his life. Lyle sat tentatively at his place, fumbling with icy fingers to pick up his soup spoon. He'd prepared for himself soup that closely resembled Alastor's but was in fact Campbell's cream of mushroom slightly altered. This had never been a favorite of Lyle's and he ate it now slowly, his eyes on his brother; he would have wished to match Alastor spoon for spoon, but Alastor as always ate too swiftly. The tiny, near-invisible capillaries in his cheeks glowed like incandescent wires; his steely blue eyes shone with pleasure. *A man who enjoys life, where's the harm in that?*

Within minutes Alastor finished his large deep bowl of steaming hot creamy soup, licking his lips. Lyle promptly served him another. "You have more talent, Brother, than you know," Alastor said with a wink. "We might open a restaurant together: I, the keeper of the books; you, the master of the kitchen." Lyle almost spilled a spoonful of soup as he lifted it tremendously to his lips. He was waiting for *Amanita phalloides* to take effect. He'd had the idea that the poison was nearly instantaneous, like cyanide. Evidently not. Or had—the possibility filled him with horror—boiling the chopped-up toadstool diluted its toxin? He was eating sloppily, continually wiping at his chin with a napkin. Fortunately Alastor didn't notice. Alastor was absorbed in recounting, as he sipped soup, swallowed large mouthfuls of bread, butter, and cheese, and the tart white wine, a lengthy lewd tale of the woman, or women, with whom he'd spent his arduous night at the Black River Inn. He'd considered calling Lyle to insist that Lyle come join him—"As you'd done that other time, eh? To celebrate our twenty-first birthday?" Lyle blinked at him as if not comprehending his words, let alone his meaning. Alastor went on to speak of women generally. "They'll devour you alive if you allow it. They're vampires." Lyle said, fumblingly, "Yes, Alastor, I suppose so. If you say so." "Like Mother, who sucked life out of poor Father. To give birth to *us*—imagine!" Alastor shook his head, laughing. Lyle nodded gravely, numbly; yes, he would try to imagine. Alastor said, with an air almost of bitterness, though he was eating and drinking with as much appetite as before, "Yes, Brother, a man has to be vigilant. Has to make the first strike." He brooded, as if recalling more than one sorry episode. Lyle had a sudden unexpected sense of his brother with a history of true feeling, regret. Remorse? It was mildly astonishing, like seeing a figure on a playing card stir into life.

Lyle said, "But what of—Susan?"

"Susan?—who?" The steely blue eyes, lightly threaded with red, were fixed innocently upon Lyle.

"Our cousin Susan."

"Her? But I thought—" Alastor broke off in mid sentence. His words simply ended. He was busying himself swiping at the inside of his soup bowl with a piece of crusty bread. A tinge of apparent pain made his jowls quiver and he pressed the heel of a hand against his midriff. A gas pain, perhaps.

Lyle said ironically, "Did you think Susan was dead, Alastor? Is that how you remember her?"

"I don't in fact remember her at all." Alastor spoke blithely, indifferently. A mottled flush had risen from his throat into his cheeks. "The girl was your friend, Brother. Not mine."

"No. Susan was never my friend again," Lyle said bitterly. "She never spoke to me, or answered any call or letter of mine, again. After . . . what happened."

Alastor snorted in derision. "Typical!"

" 'Typical'—?"

"Female fickleness. It's congenital."

"Our cousin Susan was not a fickle woman. You must know that, Alastor, damn you!"

"Why damn *me*? What have I to do with it? I was a boy then, hardly more than a boy, and you—so were *you*." Alastor spoke with his usual rapid ease, smiling, gesturing, as if what he said made perfect sense; he was accustomed to the company of uncritical admirers. Yet he'd begun to breathe audibly; perspiration had broken out on his unlined forehead in an oily glisten. His artfully dyed and crimped hair that looked so striking in other settings looked here, to Lyle's eye, like a wig set upon a mannequin's head. And there was an undertone of impatience, even anger, in Alastor's speech. "Look, she did get married and move away—didn't she? She did—I mean didn't—have a baby?"

Lyle stared at Alastor for a long somber moment.

"So far as I know, she did not. Have a baby."

"Well, then!" Alastor made an airy gesture of dismissal, and dabbed at his forehead with a napkin.

Seeing that Alastor's soup bowl was again empty, Lyle rose silently and carried it back into the kitchen and a third time ladled soup into it, nearly to the brim: This was the end of the cream of *Amanita phalloides* soup. Surely, now, within the next few minutes, the powerful poison would begin to act! When Lyle returned to the dining room with the bowl, he saw Alastor draining his second or third glass of the tart white wine and replenishing it without waiting for his host's invitation. His expression had turned mean, grim; as soon as Lyle reappeared, however, Alastor smiled up at him, and winked. "Thanks, Brother!" Yet there was an air of absolute complacency in Alastor as in one accustomed to being served by others.

Incredibly, considering all he'd already eaten, Alastor again picked up his spoon and enthusiastically ate.

So the luncheon, planned so obsessively by Lyle, passed in a blur, a confused dream. Lyle stared at his handsome ruddy-faced twin, who spoke with patronizing affection of their aunt Alida—"A befuddled old woman who clearly needs guidance"; and of the King Foundation—"An anachronism that needs total restructuring, top to bottom"; and the thirty acres of prime real estate—"The strategy must be to pit developers against one another, I've tried to explain"; and of the vagaries of the international art market—"All that's required for one thousand percent profits is a strong capital base to withstand dips in the economy." Lyle could scarcely hear for the roaring in his ears. What had gone wrong? He had mistaken an ordinary, harmless, edible mushroom for *Amanita phalloides*, the death cup? He'd been so eager and agitated out there in the woods, he hadn't been absolutely certain of the identification.

Numbed, in a trance, Lyle drove Alastor back to the Black River Inn. It was a brilliant summer day. A sky of blank blue, the scales of the dark river glittering. Alastor invited Lyle to visit him at the inn sometime soon, they could go swimming in the pool—"You meet extremely interesting people, sometimes, in such places." Lyle asked Alastor how long he intended to stay there and Alastor smiled enigmatically and said, "As long as required, Brother. You know me!"

At the inn, Alastor shook Lyle's hand vigorously, and, on an impulse, or with the pretense of acting on impulse, leaned over to kiss his cheek! Lyle was as startled as if he'd been slapped.

Driving away he felt mortified, yet in a way relieved. *It hasn't happened yet. I am not a fratricide, yet.*

GARDNER KING'S WILL WAS READ. It was a massive document enumerating over one hundred beneficiaries, individuals and organizations. Lyle, who hadn't wished to be present at the reading, heard of the bequest made to him from his brother Alastor, who had apparently escorted Aunt Alida to the attorney's office. Lyle was to receive several thousand dollars, plus a number of his uncle's rare first-edition books. With forced ebullience Alastor said, "Congratulations, Brother! You must have played your cards right, for once." Lyle wiped at his eyes; he'd genuinely loved their uncle Gardner, and was touched to be remembered by him in his will; even as he'd expected to be remembered, to about that degree. *Yes and there's greater pleasure in the news, if Alastor has received nothing.* At the other end of the line Alastor waited, breathing into the receiver. Waiting for—what? For Lyle to ask him how he'd fared? For Lyle to offer to share the bequest with him? Alastor was saying drily, "Uncle Gardner left me just a legal form, 'forgiving' me my debts." He went on to complain that he hadn't even remembered he owed their uncle money; you would think, wouldn't you, with his staff of financial advisors, Gardner King could have reminded him; it should have been his responsibility, to remind him; Alastor swore he'd never been reminded—not once in six years. Vividly Lyle could imagine his brother's blue glaring eyes, his coarse, flushed face, and the clenched self-righteous set of his jaws. Alastor said, hurt, "I suppose I should be grateful for being 'forgiven,' Lyle, eh? It's so wonderfully Christian."

Lyle said coolly, "Yes. It is Christian. I would be grateful, in your place."

"In my place, Brother, how would you know what you would be? You're 'Lyle' not 'Alastor.' Don't give yourself airs."

Rudely, Alastor hung up. Lyle winced as if his brother had poked him in the chest as so frequently he'd done when they were growing up together, as a kind of exclamation mark to a belligerent statement of his.

Only afterward did Lyle realize, with a sick stab of resentment, that, in erasing Alastor's debt to him, which was surely beyond $10,000, their uncle had in fact given Alastor the money; and it was roughly the equivalent of the amount he'd left Lyle in his will. *As if, in his uncle's mind, Alastor and he were of equal merit after all.*

SHE CAME TO HIM WHEN he summoned her. Knocking stealthily at his door in the still, private hour beyond midnight. And hearing him murmur *Come in!* and inside in the shadows he stood watching. How she trembled, how excited and flattered she was. Her girlish face, her rather too large hands and feet, a braid of golden-red hair wrapped around her head. In her uniform that fitted her young shapely body so becomingly. In a patch of caressing moonlight. Noiselessly he came behind her to secure the door, lock and double-lock it. He made her shiver kissing her hand, and the soft flesh at the inside of her elbow. So she laughed, startled. He was European, she'd been led to believe. A European gentleman. Accepting the first drink from him, a toast to mutual happiness. Accepting the second drink, her head giddy. How flattered by his praise *Beautiful girl! Lovely girl!* And: *Remove your clothes please.* Fumbling with the tiny buttons of the violet rayon uniform. Wide lace collar, lace cuffs. He kissed her throat, a vein in her throat. Kissed the warm cleft between her breasts. *Lee Ann is it? Lynette?* In their loveplay on the king-sized bed he twisted her wrist just slightly. Just enough for her to laugh, startled; to register discomfort; yet not so emphatically she would realize he meant anything by it. *Here, Lynette. Give me a real kiss.* Boldly pressing her fleshy mouth against his and her heavy breasts against his chest and he bit her lips, hard; she recoiled from him, and still his teeth were clamped over her lips that were livid now with pain. When at last he released her she was sobbing and her lips were bleeding and he, the European gentleman, with genuine regret crying *Oh what did I do!—forgive me, I was carried away by passion, my darling.* She cringed before him on her hands and knees, her breasts swinging. Her enormous eyes. Shining like a beast's. And wanting still to believe, how desperate to believe, so within a few minutes she allowed herself to be persuaded it had been an accident, an accident of passion, an accident for which she was herself to blame, being so lovely, so desirable she'd made him crazed. Kissing her hands pleading for forgiveness and at last forgiven and tenderly he arranged her arms and legs, her head at the edge of the bed, her long wavy somewhat coarse golden-red hair undone from its braid hanging over onto the carpet. She would have screamed except he provided a rag to shove into her mouth, one in fact used for previous visitors in Suite 181 of the Black River Inn.

"HOW CAN YOU BE SO cruel, Alastor!"

Laughing, Alastor had recounted this lurid story for his brother Lyle as the two sat beside the hotel pool in the balmy dusk of an evening in late June. Lyle had listened with mounting dismay and disgust and at last cried out.

Alastor said carelessly, " 'Cruel'?—why am I 'cruel'? The women love it, Brother. Believe me."

Lyle felt ill. Not knowing whether to believe Alastor or not—wondering if perhaps the entire story had been fabricated, to shock.

Yet there was something matter-of-fact in Alastor's tone that made Lyle think, yes, it's true. He wished he'd never dropped by the Black River Inn to visit with Alastor, as Alastor had insisted. And he would not have wished to acknowledge even to himself that Alastor's crude story had stirred him sexually.

*I am falling into pieces, shreds. Like something brittle that has been cracked.*

The day after the luncheon, Lyle had returned to the woods behind his house to look for the mysterious fungi; but he had no luck retracing his steps, and failed even to locate the gigantic beech tree with the snaky exposed roots. In a rage he'd thrown away *The Amateur's Guide to Fungi Edible & Inedible.* He'd thrown away *The Fanny Farmer Cookbook.*

Since the failure of the *Amanita phalloides* soup, Lyle found himself thinking obsessively of his brother. As soon as he woke in the morning he began to think of Alastor, and through the long day he thought of Alastor; at night his dreams were mocking, jeering, turbulent with emotion that left him enervated and depressed. It was no longer possible for him to work even on projects, like the book design for Poe's "William Wilson," that challenged his imagination. Though he loved his hometown, and his life here, he wondered despairingly if perhaps he should move away from Contracoeur for hadn't Contracoeur been poisoned for him by Alastor's presence? Living here, with Alastor less than ten minutes away by car, Lyle had no freedom from thinking of his evil brother. For rumors circulated that Alastor was meeting with local real estate developers though Gardner King's widow was still insisting that her property would remain intact as her husband had wished; that Alastor was to be the next director of the King Foundation, though the present director was a highly capable man who'd had his position for years and was universally respected; that Alastor and his aunt Alida were to travel to Europe in the fall on an art-purchasing expedition, though Alida King had always expressed a nervous dislike, even a terror, of travel, and had grown frail since her husband's death. It had been recounted to Lyle by a cousin that poor Alida had said, wringing her hands, "Oh, I do hope I won't be traveling to Europe this fall, I know I won't survive away from Contracoeur!" and when the cousin asked why on earth she might be traveling to Europe if she didn't wish to, Alida had said, starting to cry, "But I may decide that I do wish to travel, that's what frightens me. I know I will never return alive."

Cocktail service at poolside had ended at 9 P.M.; the pool was officially closed, though its glimmering synthetic-aqua water was still illuminated from below; only boastful Alastor and his somber brother Lyle remained in deck chairs, as an eroded-looking but glaring bright moon rose in the night sky. Alastor, in swim trunks and a terry cloth shirt, trotted off barefoot for another drink, and Lyle, looking after him, felt a childish impulse to flee while his brother was in the cocktail lounge. He was sickened by the story he'd been told; knowing himself sullied as if he'd been present in Alastor's suite the previous night. As if, merely hearing such obscenities, he was an accomplice of Alastor's. *And perhaps somehow in fact he'd been there, helping to hold the struggling girl down, helping to thrust the gag into her mouth.*

Alastor returned with a fresh drink. He was eyeing Lyle with a look of bemusement as he'd done so often when they were boys, gauging to what extent he'd shocked Lyle or embarrassed him. After their father's death, for instance, when the brothers were eight years old, Lyle had wept for days; Alastor had ridiculed his grief, saying that if you believed in God (and weren't they all supposed to believe in God?) you believed that everything was ordained; if you were a good Christian, you believed that their father was safe and happy in heaven—"So why bawl like a baby?"

Why, indeed?

Alastor was drunker than Lyle had known. He said commandingly, his voice slurred, "Midnight swim. Brother, c'mon!"

Lyle merely laughed uneasily. He was fully dressed; hadn't brought swim trunks; couldn't imagine swimming companionably with his brother, even as adults; he who'd been so tormented by Alastor when they were children, tugged and pummeled in the water, his head held under until he gasped and sputtered in panic. *Your brother's only playing, Lyle. Don't cry. Alastor, be good!*

Enlivened by drink, Alastor threw off his shirt and announced that he was going swimming, and no one could stop him. Lyle said, "But the pool is closed, Alastor"—as if that would make any difference. Alastor laughed, swaggering to the edge of the pool to dive. Lyle saw with reluctant admiration and a tinge of jealousy that his brother's body, unlike his own, was solid, hard-packed; though there was a loose bunch of flesh at his waist, and his stomach had begun to protrude, his shoulders and thighs were taut with muscle. A pelt of fine glistening hairs covered much of his body and curled across his chest; the nipples of his breasts were purply-dark, distinct as small staring eyes. Alastor's head, held high with exaggerated bravado as he flexed his knees, positioning himself to dive, was an undeniably handsome head; Alastor looked like a film star of another era, a man accustomed to the uncritical adoration of women and the envy of men. The thought flashed through Lyle like a knifeblade *It's my moral obligation to destroy this man, because he is evil; and because there is no one else to destroy him but me.*

With the showy ebullience of a twelve-year-old boy, Alastor dived into the pool at the deep end; a less-than-perfect dive that must have embarrassed him, with Lyle as a witness; Lyle who winced feeling the harsh slap of the water, like a retributive hand, against his own chest and stomach. Like a deranged seal, Alastor surfaced noisily, blowing water out of his nose, snorting; as he began to swim in short, choppy, angry-looking strokes, not nearly so coordinated as Lyle would have expected, Lyle felt his own arm and leg muscles strain in involuntary sympathy. How alone they were, Lyle and his twin brother Alastor! Overhead the marred moon glared like a light in an examination room.

Lyle thought *I could strike him on the head with—what?* One of the deck chairs, a small wrought-iron table caught his eye. And even as this thought struck Lyle, Alastor in the pool began to flail about; began coughing, choking; he must have inhaled water and swallowed it; drunker than he knew, in no condition to be swimming in water over his head. As Lyle stood at the edge of the pool staring he saw his brother begin to sink. And there was no one near! No witness save Lyle himself! Inside the inn, at a distance of perhaps one hundred feet, there was a murmur and buzz of voices, laughter, music; every hotel window facing the open courtyard and the pool area was veiled by a drape or a blind; most of the windows were probably shut tight, and the room air conditioners on. No one would hear Alastor cry for help even if Alastor could cry for help. Excited, clenching his fists, Lyle ran to the other side of the pool to more closely observe his brother, now a helpless, thrashing body sunk beneath the surface of the water like a weighted sack. A trail of bubbles lifted from his distorted mouth; his dyed hair too lifted, like seaweed. How silent was Alastor's deathly struggle, and how lurid the bright aqua water with its theatrical lights from beneath. Lyle was panting like a dog, crouched at the edge of the pool, muttering, "Die! Drown! Damn your soul to hell! You don't deserve to live!"

The next moment, Lyle had kicked off his shoes, torn his shirt off over his head, and dived into the water to save Alastor. With no time to think, he grabbed at the struggling man, overpowered him, hauled him to the surface; he managed to get Alastor's head in a hammerlock and swim with him into the shallow end of the pool; managed to lift him, a near-dead weight, a dense body streaming water, onto the tile. Alastor thrashed about like a beached seal, gasping for breath; he vomited, coughed, and choked, spitting up water and clots of food. Lyle crouched over him, panting, as Alastor rolled onto his back, his hair in absurd strings about his face and his face now bloated and puffy, no longer a handsome face, as if in fact he'd drowned. His breath was erratic, heaving. His eyes rolled in his head. Yet he saw Lyle, and must have recognized him. "Oh God, Lyle, w-what happened?" he managed to say.

"You were drunk, drowning. I pulled you out."

Lyle spoke bitterly. He too was streaming water; his clothes were soaked; he felt like a fool, a dupe. Never, never would he comprehend what he'd done. Alastor, deathly pale, weak and stricken still with the terror of death, not hearing the tone of Lyle's voice or seeing the expression of impotent fury on Lyle's face, reached out with childlike pleading to clutch at Lyle's hand.

"Brother, thank you!"

THE WORLD IS A BEAUTIFUL *place if you have the eyes to see it and the ears to hear it.*

Was this so? Could it be so? Lyle would have to live as if it were, for his brother Alastor could not be killed. Evidently. Or in any case, Lyle was not the man to kill him.

A WEEK AFTER HE'D SAVED Alastor from drowning, on a radiantly sunny July morning when Lyle was seated disconsolately at his workbench, a dozen rejected drawings for "William Wilson" scattered and crumpled before him, the telephone rang and it was Alastor announcing that he'd decided to move after all to Aunt Alida's house—"She insists. Poor woman, she's frightened of 'ghosts'—needs a man's presence in that enormous house, Brother, will you help me move? I have only a few things." Alastor's voice was buoyant and easy; the voice of a man perfectly at peace with himself. Lyle seemed to understand that his brother had forgotten about the near-drowning. His pride would not allow him to recall it, nor would Lyle ever bring up the subject. Lyle drew breath to say sharply, "No! Move yourself, damn you," but instead he said, "Oh, I suppose so. When?" Alastor said, "Within the hour, if possible. And, by the way, I have a surprise for you—it's for both of us, actually. A memento from our late beloved Uncle Gardner." Lyle was too demoralized to ask what the memento was.

When he arrived at the Black River Inn, there was Alastor proudly awaiting him at the front entrance, drawing a good deal of admiring attention. A tanned, good-looking, youthful man with a beaming smile, in a pale pink-striped seersucker suit, collarless white shirt, and straw hat, a dozen or more suitcases and valises on the sidewalk; and, in the drive beneath the canopy, a gleaming-black chrome-glittering Rolls Royce. Alastor laughed heartily at the look on Lyle's face. "Some memento, eh, Brother? Aunt Alida was so sweet, she told me, 'Your uncle would want both you boys to have it. He loved you so—his favorite nephews.' "

Lyle stared at the Rolls Royce. The elegant car, vintage 1971, was as much a work of art, and culture, as a motor vehicle. Lyle had ridden in it numerous times, in his uncle's company, but he'd never driven it. Nor even fantasized driving it. "How—did it get here? How is this possible?" Lyle stammered. Alastor explained that their aunt's driver had brought the car over that morning and that Lyle should simply leave his car (so ordinary, dull, and plebian a car—a compact American model Alastor merely glanced at, with a disdainful look) in the parking lot, for the time being. "Unfortunately, I lack a valid driving license in the United States at the present time," Alastor said, "or I would drive myself. But you know how scrupulous I am about obeying the law—technically." He laughed, rubbing his hands briskly together. Still Lyle was staring at the Rolls Royce. How like the hearse that had borne his uncle's body from the funeral home to the church it was; how magnificently black, and the flawless chrome and windows so glittering, polished to perfection. Alastor poked Lyle in the ribs to wake him from his trance and passed to him, with a wink, a silver pocket flask. Pure scotch whiskey at 11 A.M. of a weekday morning? Lyle raised his hand to shove the flask aside but instead took it from his brother's fingers, lifted it to his lips, and drank.

And a second time, drank. Flames darted in his throat and mouth, his eyes stung with tears.

"Oh! God."

"Good, eh? Just the cure for your ridiculous anemia, Brother," Alastor said teasingly.

While Alastor settled accounts in the Black River Inn, using their aunt's credit, Lyle and an awed, smiling doorman loaded the trunk and plush rear seat of the Rolls with Alastor's belongings. The sun was vertiginously warm and the scotch whiskey had gone to Lyle's head and he was perspiring inside his clothes, murmuring to himself and laughing. *The world is a beautiful place. Is a beautiful place. A beautiful place.* Among Alastor's belongings were several handsome new garment bags crammed, apparently, with clothing. There were suitcases of unusual heaviness that might have been crammed with— what? Statuary? There were several small canvases (oil paintings?) wrapped hastily in canvas and secured with adhesive tape; there was a heavy sports valise with a broken lock, inside which Lyle discovered, carelessly wrapped in what appeared to be women's silk underwear, loose jewelry of all kinds— gold chains, strings of pearls jumbled together, a silver pendant with a sparkling red ruby, bracelets and earrings and a single brass candlestick holder and even a woman's high-heeled slipper, stained (bloodstained?) white satin with a carved mother-of-pearl ornament. Lyle stared, breathless. What a treasure trove! Once, he would have been morbidly suspicious of his brother, suspecting him of theft—and worse. Now he merely smiled, and shrugged.

By the time Lyle and the doorman had loaded the Rolls, Alastor emerged from the inn, slipping on a pair of dark glasses. By chance—it must have been chance—a striking blond woman was walking with him, smiling, chatting, clearly quite impressed by him—a beautiful woman of about forty with a lynx face, a bold red mouth, and diamond earrings, who paused to scribble something (telephone number? address?) on a card and slip it into a pocket of Alastor's seersucker coat.

Exuberantly Alastor cried, "Brother, let's go! Across the river and to Aunt Alida's—to our destiny."

Like a man in a dream Lyle took his place behind the wheel of the Rolls;

Alastor climbed in beside him. Lyle's heart was beating painfully, with an almost erotic excitement. Neither brother troubled to fasten his seat belt; Lyle, who'd perhaps never once driven any vehicle without fastening his seat belt first, seemed not to think of doing so now as if, simply by sliding into this magnificent car, he'd entered a dimension in which old, tedious rules no longer applied. Lyle was grateful for Alastor passing him the silver flask, for he needed a spurt of strength and courage. He drank thirstily, in small choking swallows: how the whiskey burned, warmly glowed, going down! Lyle switched on the ignition, startled at how readily, how quietly, the engine turned over. Yes, this was magic. He was driving his uncle Gardner King's Rolls Royce as if it were his own; as he turned out of the hotel drive, he saw the driver of an incoming vehicle staring at the car, and at him, with frank envy.

And now on the road. In brilliant sunshine, and not much traffic. The Rolls resembled a small, perfect yacht; a yacht moving without evident exertion along a smooth, swiftly running stream. What a thrill, to be entrusted with this remarkable car; what sensuous delight in the sight, touch, smell of the Rolls! Why had he, Lyle King, been a puritan all of his life? What a blind, smug fool to be living in a world of luxury items and taking no interest in them; as if there were virtue in asceticism; in mere ignorance. Driving the Rolls on the highway in the direction of the High Street Bridge, where they would cross the Black River into the northern, affluent area of Contracoeur in which their aunt lived, Lyle felt intoxicated as one singled out for a special destiny. He wanted to shout out the car window *Look! Look at me! This is the first morning of the first day of my new life.*

Not once since Alastor's call that morning had Lyle thought of—what? What had it been? The death-cup mushroom, what was its Latin name? At last, to Lyle's relief, he'd forgotten.

Alastor sipped from the pocket flask as he reminisced, tenderly, of the old Contracoeur world of their childhood. That world, that had seemed so stable, so permanent, was rapidly passing now, vanishing into a newer America. Soon, all of the older generation of Kings would be deceased. "Remember when we were boys, Lyle? What happy times we had? I admit, I was a bit of a bastard, sometimes—I apologize. Truly. It's just that I resented you, you know. My twin brother." His voice was caressing yet lightly ironic.

"Resented me? Why?" Lyle laughed, the possibility seemed so far-fetched.

"Because you were born on my birthday, of course. Obviously, I was cheated of presents."

Driving the daunting, unfamiliar car, that seemed to him higher built than he'd recalled, Lyle was sitting stiffly forward, gripping the elegant mahogany steering wheel and squinting through the windshield as if he was having difficulty seeing. The car's powerful engine vibrated almost imperceptibly, like the coursing of his own heated blood. Laughing, though slightly anxious, he said, "But, Alastor, you wouldn't have wished me not to have been born, would you? For the sake of some presents?"

An awkward silence ensued. Alastor was contemplating how to reply when the accident occurred.

Approaching the steep ramp of the High Street Bridge, Lyle seemed for a moment to lose the focus of his vision, and jammed down hard on the brake pedal; except it wasn't the brake pedal but the accelerator. A diesel truck crossing the bridge, belching smoke, seemed then to emerge out of nowhere as out of a tunnel. Lyle hadn't seen the truck until, with terrifying speed, the Rolls careened up the ramp and into the truck's oncoming grille. There was a sound of brakes, shouts, a scream, and as truck and car collided, a sickening wrenching of metal and a shattering of glass. Together the vehicles tumbled from the ramp, through a low guardrail, and onto an embankment; there was an explosion, flames; the last thing Lyle knew, he and his shrieking brother were being flung forward into a fiery-black oblivion.

THOUGH BADLY INJURED, THE DRIVER of the diesel truck managed to crawl free of the flaming wreckage; the occupants of the Rolls Royce were trapped inside their smashed vehicle, and may have been killed on impact. After the fire was extinguished, emergency medical workers would discover in the wreckage the charred remains of two Caucasian males of approximately the same height and age; so badly mangled, crushed, burned, they were never to be precisely identified. As if the bodies had been flung together from a great height, or at a great speed, they seemed to be but a single body, hideously conjoined. It was known that the remains were those of the King brothers, Alastor and Lyle, fraternal twins who would have been thirty-eight years old on the following Sunday. But which body was which, whose charred organs, bones, blood had belonged to which brother, no forensic specialist would ever determine.

Like many lawyers these days, Carolyn Wheat has put her legal skills, honed by the Brooklyn chapter of the Legal Aid Society, to good use in her novels, which feature Cass Jameson. Recent novels include *Mean Streak* and *Troubled Waters*. However, her story chosen for this year's volume has nothing to do with law, and everything to do with a crime. "Love Me for My Yellow hair Alone" illustrates the prices people are willing to pay for their beliefs, especially in Hollywood.

# Love Me for My Yellow Hair Alone (32 Short Films About Marilyn Monroe)
## CAROLYN WHEAT

*Only god, my dear*
*could love you for yourself alone*
*and not your yellow hair*
> —W. B. Yeats

### 1. the watcher

The Hotel Del Coronado squats on the silver strand of beach like a fat, aging duchess. Huge, sprawling, its rust-red roof like a giant mushroom cap, it dominates the Coronado oceanfront.

The woman sits on a beach chair, her face upturned to catch the rays of the sun she professes to hate. She is blonde and pale; sun will dry and wrinkle her skin, she says often. Yet she inhales the sun's heat, she revels in the languorous feeling it spreads through her body. She undulates in her beach chair, shifting her perfect anatomy to expose more skin to the blinding light. She disdains the hat her companion proffers, waving it away with an impatient hand whose fingernails are meticulously manicured but unpainted. Not Hollywood hands, but the hands of a secretary or a bookkeeper.

The companion is a middle-aged woman with a soft, lived-in look. She wears a shapeless black dress; her feet are encased in support hose and orthopedic sandals. A Jewish housewife, thinks the man with the binoculars. He knows her husband is the high priest of Method acting, but he does not know that the Jewish housewife is herself an accomplished actress, a woman who is not permitted to work because of the blacklist. He thinks the high priest has sent his wife to baby-sit the temperamental star.

## 2. the extra

And, boy, was she ever temperamental! She never, but absolutely never, got to the set on time. Once she showed up at noon for a nine o'clock call, and the minute she got there, Mr. Wilder picked up his megaphone and called "Lunch."

I was an extra on that movie, one of twenty Coronado kids who got to sit around on the beach and get our pitchers took, as my Okie grandfather said with a cackle when I told him about my summer job.

We were military brats, my pals and me. We grew up surfing before anybody in the rest of the country knew what a surfboard was. We bummed around on the beach and took jobs at the Del for pocket money, clearing tables or carrying suitcases and waiting for the day when we'd take the ferry to San Diego and start college and never come back to boring old Coronado where there was nothing to do.

Johnny Benson told me about the movie coming. You remember Johnny—his dad was Navy all the way and Johnny was supposed to go to Annapolis, only he didn't want to. His idea of heaven was MIT; kid was great at math and science. Only his dad thought scientists were pointy-headed weirdos who were either Jewish or faggots or both, and he was god-damned if any son of his was going to—

Well, you get the picture. So that was Johnny, and you wouldn't think a kid like that would care much about the movies or even about Marilyn Monroe, but you would be wrong because Johnny was seriously in love with Marilyn and the minute he heard that movie was coming, he decided he had to meet Marilyn. Really meet her, not just sit on the same beach as her, watching her through binoculars like all the other goofballs on Coronado.

## 3. the private eye

I was a Rita Hayworth man myself. That long, red hair, those full lips. Plus, she could dance. I'm not much of a dancer myself, but I love a woman who can dance. Marilyn, you could see she'd had to take a lot of lessons before she danced on screen, but Rita was a natural.

But a job is a job is a job, to quote that dyke writer in Paris. And besides, I always had a soft spot for Joltin' Joe. So he was divorced from her, that doesn't mean he can't take an interest? He can't hire a guy or two to keep an eye on her, he knows she's in some kind of trouble?

I wouldn't of taken the job if I hadn't believed I was working for DiMaggio. Honest. I would have turned that money down cold, even though making a living as a P.I. in San Diego was no picnic in those days. America's Finest City was fine, all right—too fine to need a lot of guys wearing gumshoes.

But I wouldn't have taken the money if I'd of known.

Honest.


## 4. the director's assistant

Mr. Wilder was so patient with her. Like a father with a fractious child, he told her over and over again just what he wanted. He'd say the same thing twenty different ways, trying for the one phrase that would connect and bring out a performance. The other actors, Curtis and Lemmon and Raft, all they needed were one or two takes and they'd have it right. But Marilyn would shake her head and her lip would tremble and a tear would fall down the perfect face and then Makeup would have to come over and do her up again.

I'd stand there in the hot sun, holding an umbrella over Mr. Wilder's head so he wouldn't get heatstroke, and I'd watch her stumble over a line and stop, demanding another take.

Even when she got the lines right, she wasn't satisfied. "I need to do it again," she'd say in that baby voice. "It wasn't right."

Mr. Wilder would lean forward and whisper in her ear. I'd have to lean forward too, so the umbrella would shield him. She'd shake her head and wave him away. "I need to think," she'd say. "Don't talk to me, please. I'll forget how I want to play it."

As if she could know how to play the scene any better than Mr. Wilder did! As if she were some kind of genius and Mr. Wilder was nothing more than a ham-handed amateur who might screw her up.

The nerve of that little bitch, I thought, gripping the umbrella with white-knuckled hands.

Until I saw the rushes. Until I saw the tiny, subtle differences between the scene as Billy had instructed her to do it and the scene the way she felt it from within.

She was magic on the screen. Even Mr. Wilder said so. Later.

Much later.

## 5. the hotel maid

He was always in the room. Whenever I came to clean, there he'd be, sitting on one of the wicker chairs on the balcony or writing at the desk by the window. He'd nod politely and tell me to go ahead even though I always told him I could come back when it was more convenient. That was what the management wanted us girls to say, so I said it. Some rooms the maids didn't get to clean until 5:00 in the P.M. on account of the movie people kept pretty strange hours.

"My wife's on the set," he'd say. I'd nod as if to say, where else would the star of the movie be?

But she wasn't on the set. Everybody knew Mr. Wilder and the other actors were going nuts because Marilyn didn't show until afternoon. Everybody knew except Mr. Miller. Except the husband.

The husband is always the last to know.

## 6. on the beach

"She's just a *pretend* lady," the chubby little boy with the potbelly confided.

"I know," the little girl replied. She was an inch shorter than the boy and her hair was the exact same baby blonde as the real lady's hair.

"She's a man dressed up like a lady," the boy went on. "For the movie."

"I know," the little girl said again. She walked toward the approaching waves; she stood on the hard sand and waited for the cool water to lick her toes. When the wave washed over her feet, she jumped and squealed, then ran back to the soft sand.

The lady who wasn't a lady walked funny. She wobbled and her heels buckled under her and the people crowding around laughed.

The little girl wasn't sure why the people laughed when the pretend lady walked. The real lady wobbled when she walked, too, only the people didn't laugh.

Once she wobbled so much she fell down on the stairs. If the pretend lady had done that, everyone would have laughed. But nobody laughed when the real lady did it.

## 7. the New York journalist

"Hollywood," quips Bob Hope, "where every Tom, Dick, and Harry is Tab, Rock, and Rory." And where a white-trash California girl named Norma Jeane Baker transformed herself into the most glamorous sex symbol of her time.

California is the edge of America. It's where you go to reinvent yourself, where you can leave behind the person you were and become someone new, shedding the past like a worn-out snakeskin. You expect the freeways to be littered with crackling, near-transparent carapaces of dead selves.

I gotta cut that last bit. Too goddamn literary for this rag. Maybe I can pull it out and reshape it for a piece in the *Times*. Yeah, the *Times*'ll eat that crap with a spoon. But for the *Mirror*, I need a little dirt.

She's late on the set. She's always late, they tell me, but this time it's different. This time she's not in Hollyweird; she's at this godforsaken hole near San Diego. So what the hell's she doing every morning instead of showing up for work?

She's not doing the horizontal mambo with her hubby, that's for sure. She leaves the room, but she doesn't go down to the set.

Miller thinks she's with Wilder; Wilder thinks she's with Miller—and the whole thing smells to me like a nice big fishy story. A story I can clean up a little for the *Mirror* and spice up a little for *Hollywood Confidential*. In this business, there's nothing better than getting paid for the same story twice.

Three times, if I can toss in enough bullshit for the *Times*.

## 8. the watcher

He trains his binoculars on the silver strand of beach. The prop men from the movie have strategically placed several wicker beach chairs that wrap around the sitter like a cocoon. In the movie, Tony Curtis, dressed like a twenties playboy, will sit in one of the chairs and Marilyn will mince past him and strike up an acquaintance.

He thinks it would be interesting if someone walked past the wicker cocoon and discovered that the person sitting inside, facing the ocean, had been dead for some time.

## 9. the private eye

This thing is a security nightmare. I can't believe Wilder lets everyone and his twin brother watch the shooting on the beach. They put up ropes to hold back the crowds, but any nut could pull out a gun and shoot Marilyn where she stands. Hell, someone with a good aim could pot her from a passing boat—and a lot of boats go by, people training binocs on the shore to get a glimpse of the stars.

Wilder's there in his white cloth cap, a cigarette dangling from yellowed fingers. He looks like a cabbie, not a famous director.

Lemmon's wearing a girl's bathing suit from the twenties. He's standing next to Marilyn, and they're both laughing. I can't hear what they're saying, but I have a good idea why Lemmon, at least, is enjoying himself.

He doesn't have to wear high heels on the beach.


## 10. the drama student

I saw him on Orange Avenue this afternoon. I don't know why, but I thought he was taller. And I definitely visualized him wearing a suit and tie. But he had on a pair of slacks and a striped T-shirt and a baseball cap. He looked like a father on his way to his son's Little League game.

The most famous American playwright of our time, and he was walking along Orange Avenue just like anybody else.

He walked faster than everyone else; he kept moving around other people. I guess they walk a lot in New York City.

He's here because of Her, of course. I don't imagine a man like him would even step foot in California if it weren't for being married to Her.

How can he write with all the distractions She brings into his life? How can a man of his genius be content to play second fiddle to a silly movie star? Why doesn't he realize that she can bring him nothing but pain, that he needs a woman of high intellectual attainment, a woman who will devote herself to nurturing his art, not pursue her own meaningless career?


## 11. the actor

You do the work. Forget this self-indulgent bullshit about being ready or not ready. Forget this Method crap about getting in touch with your inner feelings. You show up, you hit the marks, you say the lines—hell, first you *know* the lines; you don't show up three hours late and ask for cue cards.

She was just off a movie with Larry Olivier. Can you feature that? I've been in the business since I was younger than Marilyn and nobody ever let me get close to a movie with Olivier, and that no-talent blonde gets a movie with him and screws it up.

I'm a character actor; you could see this movie nine times and still not really notice my performance. Which is another way of saying it's a good performance, since I'm not supposed to be noticed.

Her husband, now, he understood what professional was. He was a writer, he knew how to produce. He knew that you have to put your keister in the chair and pound away on the typewriter every day whether or not you feel like it. He wanted Marilyn to act like a pro, to give a damn about the other people on the set. Every time she threw one of her tantrums or burst into tears, he died a little.

You could see it; he'd grimace like a father whose kid is acting bratty at the officers' club.

## 12. the acting coach

I know what they call me on the set: the wicked witch of the East. They hate Easterners out here, which is amusing, really, because so many of them are from the East themselves. But they've gone Holly-wood and I haven't.

The sun gives me terrible headaches, which is why I dress like a Bedouin, and yet I sit with Marilyn on the Ocean Terrace, going over lines and working on the scenes. I pass on bits of wisdom from my own acting days, spiced with little sayings from Lee, from the Studio.

"A scene is like a bottle," I tell her. "If you can't open it one way, try another."

She mumbles something I have to ask her to repeat.

"Maybe I should just throw the bottle away," she says in her wispy voice, which almost but not quite gets swept out to sea by the strong breeze.

## 13. the cameraman

You know how they say in Hollywood that the camera loves somebody. It sounds kind of stupid when you say it; I mean, how can a camera love anyone? But it's true. You take Marilyn, now. All I do is point the camera at her and she lights up. Her face plays to the camera, tilting ever so slightly to catch an angle of light. Or she widens her eyes and the camera zooms right in on her baby blues. She tosses her head and the camera records the swirl and fall of fine, golden hair.

We're shooting black-and-white, remember. And yet the camera catches, somehow, the precise shade of her blonde hair, the wide blue eyes. She is going to look wonderful on screen, lit from within like a Japanese lantern.

We're shooting black-and-white because of the boys. Wilder says if we were doing the movie in color, the drag bits wouldn't work; the makeup would be too garish.

He's right. The studio bitched at first, said nobody would ever pay good money to see a black-and-white picture again, color was here to stay. But for this movie, they'll pay. Curtis is great, Lemmon is greater, and then there's Marilyn.

The camera loves her, and I think I do too.

### 14. the local reporter

I can't believe this quote! Little old me from sleepy little San Diego with a quote that's going to make headlines around the world.

TONY CURTIS ON MARILYN: "KISSING HER LIKE KISSING HITLER."

Can you believe my luck in being actually in the room when Tony Curtis tells the world his glamorous costar is really more like the hated dictator?

Of course, I go on to explain in the article that what he really means is that in her relentless drive for perfection in every little thing she does, Marilyn sometimes drives her costars to distraction. But rest assured, I intend to tell the movie-going public, the results on screen will be worth it! They always are with La Monroe, aren't they?


### 15. the studio doc

You don't get rich in Hollywood by saying no to big stars. And Marilyn was one of the biggest. When she was in a picture, everyone on the set lived on Marilyn time. The stars, the extras, the director all sat around waiting for Her Highness to show up. On a good day, she made it before the lunch break. On a bad day, she didn't make it at all.

She lived on champagne, caviar, and Nembutal. Once, I tried to tell her she needed to taper off, not use the pills every night, especially if she was serious about wanting a baby. She looked at me with her beautiful, bleary eyes and said, "What night? My life is one long, goddamned horrible day that never ends."

I shut up and wrote another prescription.


### 16. the continuity girl

That last picture she made with Wilder, she didn't even have a name. Her character was called The Girl. That's all, just The Girl, as if any bubble-headed blonde in the world could have walked in and played the part.

That's what Wilder really wants from her. That she play The Girl, not a real person.

I'm forty-two years old. I've been in the picture business since I was nineteen. When I started, I *was* a girl, I guess. But now, it sounds pretty silly when people introduce me as "the continuity girl." Not bothering to find out my name, just calling me "the girl."

Just like Marilyn in *Seven Year Itch*.

I know where she goes in the mornings. I've seen her. I know I should tell Mr. Wilder. And I will—the first time he calls me by my name.

## 17. the drama student

He's writing a movie for Her. The greatest playwright of the twentieth century, and he's wasting his time writing a stupid movie.

I can't believe it. I can't believe he's that besotted.

If only I could talk to him. If only I could make him understand that he has a duty to his art. He needs to know there are people like me, who love him for what he's done. He needs to know he doesn't have to prostitute himself.

I have to talk to him.

## 18. the psychiatrist

It was a classic case of Electra complex. Marrying an older man, a father figure. And of course, there was already a father figure in Lee Strasberg, not to mention her way of playing bad little daughter with her directors. She craved their approval, and she refused to earn it by behaving properly.

Classic.

Classic, and tragic. By the time she was making that movie, any competent therapist could have told her the marriage was coming apart at the seams. Anyone could have told her nothing would save it; certainly not a baby.

## 19. the hairdresser

Sweetie, this movie is going to be a *hoot*. You haven't *lived* until you've seen macho Tony Curtis mincing around in high heels! The poor boy looks *so* uncomfortable. I'd just *die* if one of his butch friends like Kirk or Burt came on the set and saw his Cupid's bow lips. Honey, he's the *spitting image* of Clara Bow!

Oh, all right, I'll lay off the camp. Just for you, sweetcheeks.

Oh, don't be such a closet queen. I won't tell your Navy buddies who you like to kiss on weekends, so just relax, will you?

What's she like?

The truth? She's like a poisoned bonbon, beautiful to look at, but, oh, Mary, don't—

All *right*.

She's like a child. A mean little child who'll do anything to get her own way.

God, what hets go through for a little taste of sex on the silver screen!

## 20. on the beach

"Here comes the lady," the boy said. He squatted on the sand next to the sand castle he'd made with his pail and shovel. It was a simple castle; all he'd done was turn over a pailful of hard, wet sand and dug a little moat around it for the water to run in.

The little girl kicked at the shell and drew her foot back with a cry. "It hurts," she said. "It's too sharp." She picked up the offending object and threw it as hard as she could into the water. It landed with a plop about three feet away.

The lady came every morning. She walked along the beach in her bare feet, but she wore pants instead of a bathing suit. And she wore a scarf over her blonde curls. It was a funny way to dress for the beach, the little girl thought. Her mother wore a bathing suit and a white cap with a rubber flower on the side.

Maria turned the pages of her book. It was a book with pictures, and it was written in Spanish. She watched the approaching woman with an expression of indifference. She knew the blonde lady was in the movie they were making at the big hotel, but it would never have occurred to her that the pasty gringa with the capri pants and the head scarf was *La Magnifica* herself.

The blonde scuffed her feet in the water, sending salt spray up in little fountains.

"Hi," she said as she got closer. "Catch any fish today?"

"How could we?" the boy replied with a crowing laugh. "We don't have any fishing poles."

"Oh, you don't need poles," the lady said with a shake of her head. "All you have to do is want the fish, and they'll swim right over and ask you to catch them."

"That's silly," the boy retorted.

"Would the fish die if we caught them?" the little girl wanted to know. "I wouldn't like it if they died."

"Oh, no," the lady answered. "That wouldn't be nice at all. The fish wouldn't die. They'd swim into your little moat here and you could scoop them up and take them home and put them in a glass bowl and watch them swim around."

"You still need poles," the little boy pronounced. He walked over to his sand castle and began to kick it with his tanned bare feet. "I saw the men fishing on the pier, and they all had poles."

"The fish I'm talking about are called grunions," the blonde lady explained. Her forehead creased as she talked, like someone who really wanted them to understand. "They swim very close to shore, and you can really catch them in a bowl if you want to."

"Do you have any little girls?"

The lady stood very still. She looked toward the place where the sun would be if the fog weren't so thick. One hand touched her tummy very lightly and she said, "I hope I'm going to. Very soon."

She smiled, and the smile was like the sun breaking through the Southern California morning fog. "Very, very soon," she repeated.

## 21. the extra

If Johnny had just kept his mouth shut, he might have gotten away with it. But then, if he had, nobody would have believed him, so what would have been the point?

The whole point was that he had to kiss Marilyn and all the guys on Coronado had to know he kissed her. That way, his father couldn't get away with calling him a faggot on account of he wanted to go to MIT instead of Annapolis.

He started out just wanting to meet her, but all the guys razzed him when he talked about it, so he bet Carl Rasmussen that he wouldn't just meet Marilyn, he'd kiss her.

He'd kiss her right in front of the Del.

And Carl could watch, and then Carl could pay up, 'cause he, Johnny, was going to do it, and when he said he was going to do a thing, that thing was as good as done.

Which I could have told Carl was the truth because I was there that time in seventh grade, which Carl wasn't, being as his father was stationed in Hawaii that year. And I knew that if Johnny Benson said he was going to kiss Marilyn Monroe, then she was going to get kissed, come hell or high water.

What I didn't know was exactly how much hell there was going to be.

## 22. the director's assistant

"When Marilyn Monroe walks into a room, nobody's going to be watching Tony Curtis playing Joan Crawford."

That's an exact quote, I can assure you. I was in the room when she said it, right to Mr. Wilder's face. She made him reshoot the opening, said she wouldn't finish the picture unless he—

Yes, she said Joan Crawford—and isn't Miss Crawford just going to die when she sees that in print? I mean, I can't look at Tony in his costume any more without thinking of Joan.

Did I hear what Mr. Wilder said about doing another movie with Marilyn?

Well, yes, but I don't think I really ought to—

Well, since you already know, I guess it won't hurt to—

He said, "I've discussed the matter with my doctor and my accountant, and they tell me I am too old and too rich to go through this again."

Yes, that's what he said. But please don't quote me.

## 23. the studio doc

You've had two tube pregnancies, I reminded her. And then I had to explain for probably the fifteenth time exactly what that meant. You have two Fallopian tubes, Miss Monroe, I said. And what they're supposed to do is carry your eggs down to your womb so that if you get pregnant, the baby can grow in your womb like it's supposed to.

Understand?

I was using words I'd use to explain menstruation to a slow thirteen-year-old, and the look I'd get from her was as if I was trying to explain Einstein's theory. No comprehension.

Your trouble is that your eggs don't travel all the way to the womb. They stay in the tubes, so that when the sperm fertilizes the egg, it starts growing in the tube. This is called an ectopic pregnancy, and it won't work. The baby can't grow that way.

Your chances of having a normal pregnancy, Miss Monroe?

Slim to none, I'd answer. With your history, slim to none.

## 24. the private eye

This job is pointless. I've got a film of Unguentine on my face so thick it traps gnats, that's how long I've been out in the sun watching Monroe. And so far, nobody's come close to her except a couple of toddlers, only it was her got close to them instead of the other way around.

If something doesn't happen by the end of the day, I'm off this job. Money or no money, DiMaggio or no DiMaggio.

## 25. the drama student

He wouldn't listen. He wrote me an autograph and said I should keep studying. He said he'd write me a recommendation to the Yale Drama School if I wanted him to, but he wouldn't listen.

I looked up into his face, all white and drawn with suffering, and I knew what I had to do.

I was wrong trying to talk to him. He's too noble and good to betray the woman he loves. The woman he thinks he loves.

Next time I'll talk to Her.

Only I won't just talk.

## 26. the extra

Johnny had it all planned. He needed a diversion, he said. Just like in the war. He needed somebody to help distract the people around Marilyn so he could step in and make his move.

He didn't mean any harm.

Honest.

He was just a kid who wanted to impress his buddies.

So we started by tossing a flying saucer back and forth on the beach. You know, those round disks you throw and somebody catches them? Anyway, Tug Murphy had one and we tossed it around, getting pretty close to where the grips were setting up the next shot. One of the grips yelled at us to move away, but we hollered and pretended not to hear. So the grip steps over to Tug and says something and Tug said something back, and pretty soon a lot of grips were walking over to straighten things out.

Marilyn was just standing there, in this funny bathing suit that didn't show nearly enough of her attributes, if you know what I mean. She was shivering on account of it was breezy out there by the shore. Nobody from the movie was standing near her. It was weird, like none of them wanted to be close to her. The funny old lady with the big black hat was sitting in one of the canvas chairs, watching like a hawk, but she was too far away to do anything.

Which was why Johnny made his move. He ran out of the crowd and made straight for Marilyn.

## 27. the drama student

I was watching in the crowd, waiting for my opportunity. I'd been there the day before, and the day before that, and there hadn't been an opportunity, but I was certain that today was the day my luck would change. And it did.

It was a boy, a stupid boy. He ran out of the crowd toward Her as if he was going to catch her in a flying tackle.

She screamed and her hand flew to her mouth and she jumped back. She jumped back toward me. Toward where I stood in the crowd with my knife at my side, waiting for my opportunity.

Waiting to liberate the greatest playwright in the English language from his stupid mistake.

### 28. the private eye

Like everybody else, I saw the kid. Like everybody else, I reacted—only, being a professional, I reacted a little faster. The trouble was, I was reacting to the wrong threat. I didn't see the girl until it was too late.

Until the little bitch raised the knife and screamed like a banshee in heat and lunged at Marilyn.

I had the kid in a wrestling hold I learned in high school, but I let him go and went after the girl.

But the kid was young and strong and I was getting beerbellied and slow. He got there first—and so did the knife.

By the time the cops came, I had her under control and the knife in my hand.

But the kid had been cut. Cut bad, too, judging from the amount of blood seeping into the white sand.

### 28. the extra

Johnny saved her life. At least that was what she said.

All around her, people were yelling and screaming. Some of the women ran backwards, screeching as if they'd seen a hundred mice. The big guy grabbed the girl around her waist and took the knife away from her, but she wouldn't stop crying that she was going to kill Marilyn and nobody was going to stop her. Johnny and the big guy already had stopped her, but she didn't recognize that.

With all the yelling and running, you'd have thought Marilyn would take off for safety, run over to the old lady in the black hat or something. But she didn't. She just stood there while everyone else went crazy and then she knelt down in the sand and picked up Johnny's head and put it in her lap.

And when the guys with the stretcher came pushing through the crowd, she bent down and kissed him on the lips.

Which is when I turned to Carl Rasmussen and told him he'd better pay up or else. I didn't spell out what the "or else" was going to be because my voice was shaking so bad I thought I was going to cry.

Which was pretty weird on account of all that happened was that Johnny did what he said he was going to do.

### 29. the cop

Sure, the movie people hushed it up. Can you blame them? The kid was okay—well, okay if you think thirty-eight stitches in the shoulder is okay, but you get my point. Nobody died or anything. They took the girl over to the state hospital, but this kind of publicity the movie didn't need, so they asked us all to keep it as quiet as possible.

And no, this isn't Hollywood, it's Coronado, but have you ever been anyplace where money doesn't talk?

Well, I haven't. So when the Chief said the whole thing never happened, I saluted smartly and said, What never happened, sir?

You'll go far, boy, the old man replied. And he was right.


## 30. the actor

Three words of dialogue; sixty-five takes. Sixty-fucking-five. That's the story of this picture in a nutshell. Wilder's going nuts, the actors are going nuts, the crew's loving the overtime, and this picture may sink into the ocean like a chunk of cliff in an earthquake.


## 31. the letter

She sits at the little round table in her room. There's a piece of Hotel Del stationery in front of her, and a powder-blue typewriter in a plastic case.

She smiles at the paper, picks up a pencil, and draws on the hotel's logo at the top of the page. It shows the sprawling building, with its distinctive mushroom rooftop, beside the beach. She makes a quick stick-figure drawing of herself in the billowing waves and writes the word "help" next to it, as if the figure were drowning.

Then she slips the paper into the carriage return, smartly maneuvers it to a space below the logo, and types in the date: September 11, 1958.


*Dear Norman,*

*Don't give up the ship while we're sinking. I have the feeling this boat is never going to dock. We are going through the Straits of Dire. It's rough and choppy but why should I worry I have no phallic symbol to lose.*


She smiles wryly, then hits the carriage bar several times to leave room for the oversized signature she intends to write. Another thought strikes her, and she adds:


*PS "Love me for my yellow hair alone"*

## 32. the local doctor

"I asked for a doctor, not a nurse," the tall man with the dark-rimmed glasses said when he answered my knock.

I've heard this before; female doctors are not usual, even in the field of gynecology. "I am a doctor," I said, keeping my tone even. "May I see your wife, please?"

He stepped aside and let me in.

"She's in the bathroom," he said. There was an edge of disgust in his tone; he turned abruptly and made for the door. "Tell my wife I'm going down to the set to tell the director that she's too sick to film today." He was speaking loudly enough for the woman in the bathroom to hear, and he pronounced the word "sick" with quotation marks around it. I had the distinct feeling I had been summoned as a witness to the fact that Miss Monroe was feigning her illness.

I'd heard the rumors; I'd even read a movie magazine or two. I knew Marilyn's reputation as a difficult actress, and as a woman who ingested pills the way other people chewed gum.

So I stepped into the bathroom with a brisk, businesslike air, expecting to see a spoiled star with a barbiturate hangover.

She squatted on the toilet seat, her head between her knees. She groaned weakly and sobbed as I approached. Her arms hugged her stomach; on the floor next to the commode lay a silk slip soaked in blood.

Postscript

*Marilyn Monroe, who had all but completed shooting the new Billy Wilder comedy Some Like It Hot, was hospitalized today in Southern California. Doctors announced she had suffered a miscarriage; Miss Monroe is married to Pulitzer prize-winning playwright Arthur Miller. Mr. Miller, emerging from his wife's bedside at an undisclosed hospital, declined to be interviewed.*

—New York Mirror

Edward Bryant began writing professionally in 1968, and has since published more than a dozen books. His work has appeared in such anthologies as *Orbit, Night Visions,* and *Blood Is Not Enough,* as well as such magazines as *Omni, Writer's Digest,* and *Locus.* He's won the Nebula Award (twice) and is currently living in North Denver finishing his next novel. "The Clock That Counts the Dead" combines mystery and horror with his usual trademark style.

# The Clock That Counts the Dead
## EDWARD BRYANT

"I finally looked up the clock last night. Brian's right. It says when I'm gonna die. Right down to the second." Benjamin does not look delighted by the prospect.

The four of them sit in the lovingly recreated Naugahyde booth, two facing two, and consider the variety of healthful breakfasts. It's a nostalgic wonderland of chrome and neon. Mel's Drive-in is a Southern California chain, but it's not bad in terms of either price or selection, Del thinks, surveying the menu. He's from out of town; *a prince from a distant land,* his agent laughingly describes him as she lines Del up with studio meetings.

Del's no different than any other writer with moderate credits in the winding-down bargain years—1998, 1999—leading into the new millennium. He's had books published and he's won a few mid-level awards. Not a big deal for the literary world, but the young execs in Hollywood are always impressed by this kind of thing. Awards. Books. Something in Hollywood reeks of a dubious lack of professional self-esteem. These days, Del hails from elsewhere. Therefore he's exotic. Fresh meat.

There's never a guarantee of a sale or a script assignment; but he always gets the meetings. He's always believed he'll Make It. It just hasn't happened yet.

Del senses he has never quite grown into his capabilities.

Later in the afternoon, before he shows up for the appointment at Universal, he'll don his writer's outfit: sharp, new, washed-once, razor-creased denim jeans. The 501s are okay because he's from Out West—actually east from

California. It's a reverse snobbery. Designer jeans would be required for a Southern California citizen. Then there will be the subdued, solid-print, expensive (or at least as expensive as upscale-but-cheap Structure puts on sale) open-collar shirt. And the comfortable, tailored-look, all-natural-fibers, British import jacket. No suede elbow patches. That's antiquated. And no pipe. This is no-public-smoking California.

Benjamin, directly opposite Del, says, "I don't want to know when my life's going into turnaround."

Beside him, Brian says, "Man, it was all a goof. I called up 'deadsite.end' as a joke. You're not going to die." He smiles. "I mean, well, you are going to die. We all will. But not when the program specified. *Capiche?*"

Raju looks mildly bewildered. "Deadsite.end? I have never heard of such a URL suffix."

"Well, there is now," Brian says.

Del makes his decision to order the turkey hash and add a side of fresh citrus. And coffee. Lots of coffee. With caffeine. "What are you guys talking about? More of that dead pool crap?"

Benjamin jerks his napkin off the table and flatware clatters perilously close to the edge.

"Well, it started with the dead pool," Brian says. He's a tanned expatriate Brit, 40-something, moderately successful with low budget horror flicks, starting to bald and slide into fat. "Did I tell you? Someone put Benjamin on his entry list—and then told him."

Benjamin mumbles something that sounds less than pleased. His eyes and slicked-back hair are dark. The beard gives him that Steve Cannell sort of distinguished look. If facial expressions can darken, Benjamin's albedo is so slight he doesn't seem to be reflecting light at all.

"Ben was not amused," Brian continues.

"Well, Christ," Benjamin interjects. "It's one thing for us all to pore over lists with everyone from Betty Bacall to Marilyn Manson pulling down odds in terms of whether they'll cash in this year, just so one of us ghouls can rake in a few hundred bucks. I'll cop to putting in my ten along with a list that included Macaulay Culkin and that Dano guy from *Hawaii Five-O*—what's his name? James MacArthur."

"You should have picked Mr. Jack Lord," says Raju, showing some interest for the first time in minutes. Raju was once a hot Calcutta film director. Now he basks in the Southern California sun and endlessly exhausts the battery of his cell phone setting up cheap action flicks in weirdly configured Indian exhibitor packages.

"Don't I know it," Benjamin says. "But nobody should have picked me for their list."

"Take it as a compliment," Brian suggests. "You're a somebody. None of the rest of us made it into the pool."

Del has been vaguely aware back in Boise that both on and off the Internet, dead pools have become the rage. Pick a list of VIPs and celebs you think are going to meet their maker in the coming year. Place a wager. Then wait for entropy to make your fortune.

Not being entirely sure what he thinks of the whole concept of betting on death—Del does know he's generally against sad endings on principle—he hasn't pursued the subject. But now, in a Ventura Boulevard Mel's Drive-in on a sunny January morning in the San Fernando Valley, the whole issue's caught up with *him*.

He thinks about the ratty paperback of John O'Hara's *Appointment in Samarra* he's been rereading back in his room at the Sportsman's Lodge. Del's been doing his homework, both because he remembers loving the novel back in college, and because he figures he may derive some inspiration for the pitch he's going to make this afternoon. He's always been fascinated by the inevitability implicit in performing superhuman efforts to avoid death, and by doing so, to escape right into the waiting arms of the Reaper himself.

"It wasn't just being in the pool as a target," Benjamin says testily. "The dismal thing was when my *friends* exploited an already grim situation to generate a few laughs."

"Cheap laughs, at that," Brian says with a flash of ready grin. "I'd just found out about deadsite.end. I wanted to try it out."

"So why didn't you look *yourself* up?" says Benjamin. He mumbles something else into a mug half full of cold coffee.

"The dead pool spread sheet had just come in," Brian says. "Your name was right in front of me." He shrugs. "You think I'm going to check out my own mortality? It's true I do know people in the pool such as Jerry Weinstein and Woody Allen. But not well. Ben, you I know. I know your birthdate and your age, I can guess accurately at your weight, and I know if you smoke. I know certain other realities about your personal habits. You made a good test subject."

Benjamin shakes his head. "But nobody said you had to share."

"Bad news needs an audience. And I did not want to talk about you behind your back."

"Hold on," Del says. There's something about this all that is beginning to intrigue him. "What's the Internet thing?"

"Deadsite.end," Brian says. "It's an interactive program that asks you a number of questions, then gives you a predicted time and date of death, right down to the hour and minute. Hardly takes any time at all."

"Quite fascinating," Raju says.

The waiter comes by to refill coffee mugs, bring Del his own mug, and take their orders. Del notices that Benjamin is ordering food as if there is no tomorrow. "Hungry?" he says.

"Comfort food. It's all stuff my parents wouldn't let me eat when I was a kid. Right now, I think I need it."

"But . . . grits?" says Brian doubtfully.

"They were snobs."

"I am not sure I see the root of the dispute," Raju says, his soft accent bearing the weight of apparent serious thought.

"About grits or snobs?"

"About your evident discomfort with this computer prediction. We all of us must die. If we were to know the precise time, would it not enable us to make our transitions more carefully considered?"

"You mean like wrapping things up, getting the bills paid, saying good-bye, all that?" Benjamin says. "I'd just sit around worrying. I mean, if I was *sure* I knew when I was going to die."

"So you do not believe in the literal truth of the information Brian obtained?" Raju's gaze does not waver from Benjamin's face.

Benjamin shakes his head vehemently.

"Then there's the voodoo effect," says Brian.

Raju raises one eyebrow quizzically. "You are referring to the power of suggestion?"

"Absolutely. Voodoo works. I shot on location in Haiti two years ago. On the second day of principal photography, I heard one of the local production assistants was cursed by some kind of priest. The guy started getting sick. Finally I thought I was going to have to lay him off." He pauses.

"You didn't?" Del finally breaks the silence.

"Didn't have to. He died the day before we wrapped. Some of the crew lobbied to put his name into the end credits as a memorial. Studio nixed that. Thought it would just confuse the teenagers."

"I remember that," Benjamin says. "The PR people used it like crazy, though. 'The voodoo curse that threatens the stars.' You got a lot of mileage out of it in the trades."

"Didn't get us any Oscar nods."

Benjamin smiles for the first time that hour. "For chrissake, it was a cheap-jack zombie epic. Any Oscar nods, it'd mean Oscar was nodding *off.*"

Brian looks momentarily defensive. "The controlling metaphor was that tropical zombies beautifully embody the whole concept of a regimented modern American lifestyle."

Raju shakes his head. "What a reach."

Likewise Benjamin. "What a crock."

"It made nearly sixty million worldwide," Brian says.

"No accounting for taste." Benjamin looks grim. "Maybe it's creative accounting for taste."

"Benjamin's death thing," Del says persistently.

"You would bring that back up." Benjamin looks pensive. "I guess what really startled me was not the specificity of the prediction. It was the proximity."

"Meaning?"

Benjamin releases what sounds suspiciously like a sigh. "I'm going to die early tomorrow morning. Three fifty-three, to be precise."

"You are not *going* to die," says Brian. "It's only a software prediction."

"And this query was made, when, yesterday?" Raju looks serious. "That seems a bit precipitous for an input I assume only included such general risk factors as age, weight, gender, and so forth."

Brian nods. "I thought it was perhaps an overstatement. But I fear young Ben is taking it all too seriously."

"Yes," says Benjamin. "I am. Taking it too seriously, I mean. I am trying not to let the power of suggestion get to me. Tomorrow at three fifty-three I'll be home. I'll make sure of that. The doors will be locked. I just had my studio physical last month. Heart was fine. Everything else checked out. I should do great, other than not getting much sleep."

"Perhaps you *should* sleep through this experience," says Raju. "Then enjoy the feeling of release when you wake."

"I'd dream," Benjamin says. "I don't want to dream. At least not tonight. I don't think there's any way I could avoid thinking about this. I'm not going to get any rest anyway, I might as well just stay up and watch videos."

"I'll lend you the director's cut of *Spree 2000: Zombie Uprising*," Brian says.

Benjamin doesn't dignify the offer with a response.

The food arrives. Conversation ceases temporarily while flatware clinks and jaws exercise silently.

Del chews and swallows his turkey hash, and thinks about Benjamin's situation. "It's gotta be a software glitch," he finally says. "Something's fouled up in the program. No one would dare tell dial-up people they were going to die within 48 hours."

Raju speaks slowly. Thoughtfully. "Unless, perhaps, the source of the program actually does have an accurate line on mortality."

"Thanks a lot," says Benjamin. He fumbles for his check. "I think I've got to get back to my office. I think I hear the fax."

"Just to check up," Brian says, "I'll call you tomorrow morning." He smiles gently. "Or I'll use my wife's Ouija board."

Benjamin offers a small, highly rude gesture; gets up, tosses some money down by the register; leaves.

"Poor man," says Raju. "He has not been the same since his wife died."

The other two say nothing. Del feels a cold blade transfix his heart.

The good-byes are awkward. As Raju walks past Del toward his own car, he says, "Later, my friend. Good luck. I've always thought you are destined for major things."

Del smiles. "A movie of the week?"

"Major things," Raju repeats seriously. He does not smile. "I have understood all too little about you, Del. I suspect you are a person of great, unrealized potential." He shakes his head.

A silence grows. Del picks his way through a suddenly unsure vocabulary. "Thank you for the vote of confidence."

Raju shrugs, smiles now but slightly. "Call it more an expression of fatalism."

Del wonders about that final remark all the way to his car.

DEL DRIVES THE RENTAL CAMRY back to his room in Studio City. For a January day, it's getting uncomfortably warm. When he turns on the Toyota's air conditioner, it puffs, whirs, and then expires.

Del wonders if there's an Internet web site that predicts the demise of one's automobile. There would be a market. But he knows the invention would be suppressed by the Southern California Association of Automobile Dealers.

He wishes Raju had not brought up the matter of Monica's death; brought the issue into the foreground of reality simply through the articulating of it.

Del glances to the right, fully expecting to see Monica's completely realized shade sitting in the passenger seat. He tries to prepare himself to see the sapphire eyes and dark, tousled hair, the slightly crooked mouth grinning back at him. He can hear her voice, words charged with energy and promise. She is, of course, not really there.

There exists death. He knows that. He also knows that nothing comes after. It has always been an article of faith.

Monica's death. He wonders, would she have died the same miserable way had she not married the unpredictable and moody Benjamin? Would she be dead at all on this January morning? What if she had married Del?

Could he have protected her, advised her not to drive the rainslick 101 at *that* hour on *that* day? Would he have done what Benjamin could not?

He squelches that last treacherous thought by doing what any good California driver does—he swerves into the faster left-hand lane without signaling; indeed, without even taking more than a cursory glance at the possibility of disaster. Del grins. It's an accomplished tourist who can be so easily taken for a native.

But then, he thinks, I lived here for eleven years before I moved back home. Time enough to pick up many of the native customs and folkways.

*Was it only eleven years? It seems far, far longer.*

His room at the Sportsman's Lodge is small, but clean and serviceable. Del wonders what sort of tradeout Universal has for these rooms. The last time he flew out to talk with them, the studio had quite reasonably put him up at the Universal Hilton. Easy walking distance to the meeting. This time he's rather more isolated. Possibility one—this is a deliberate slight. Possibility two—the studio doesn't want him noticed by industry rivals out vultching. Not until the deal's inked.

Del laughs aloud. He never talks like the text style of *Daily Variety* except when he crosses the California border.

He's got just over ninety minutes until the meeting. Maybe he should settle his nerves. He fills the coffee maker on the bathroom sink counter and brews a full carafe of caffeinated. It's not like the good old days when he'd line a windrow of prime Bolivian blow on the slick bathroom tile, a line as long as the width of his palm. The '90s are a healthier time, indeed. Also more austere. Writing for Hollywood from Idaho is not the most lucrative pursuit. Most of Del's recent income has been cashing minuscule residuals from series like *X-Monsters*, just syndicated in Australia, and teaching an adult extension course in screenwriting at Two Forks Community College.

When the coffee's done, all acrid and sludgy, but at least hot, he sits at the small table and pulls up his notes on the laptop. In three minutes he's coached and bored. The laptop's actually for subsequent drafts only. First drafts generate from the yellow lined tablet and the hard lead pencil sitting beside the keyboard. He's a lungfish still struggling to find its land-legs after an easy, comfortable youth in the saline amniotic sea.

Del picks up the sharpened pencil, taps it haft first on the table. The eraser's long since been chewed away. He glances back toward the computer. He checked out the modem hookup the night before, so he knows it works. On a whim he calls up the Internet with a flourish of bleeps and electronic static-whirs.

Del types in the URL that ends with deadsite.end.

His hand hesitates over the trackball. To click or not to click.

Later.

Maybe.

There's one other thing he thinks he really ought to check. Del unlatches the top of the suitcase he brought as checked luggage on the plane. He unzips one of the many smaller compartments and takes out the carefully wrapped little bundle.

What's inside the suede cloth is a compact dark metal device. It's .32 caliber and cheap. Perfectly disposable. Del bought it in Hayden Lake for chump change. He unwraps the clip and slips it into the butt, pushes it into place and it locks with a nice, positive, metallic *snap*.

He looks at the clock by the bedside and knows it's time.

THAT NIGHT, DEL BUYS HIS supper from a Wolfgang Puck fast-foodaria and carries it back to the Sportsman's Lodge in a bright take-out bag. He has to admit the roasted veggie pizza is good, but he wasn't about to spend three times the meal cost on souvenir tee shirts or a baseball cap.

He pulls the curtain back, somehow comforted to remind himself that the room overlooks a grove of California oak.

Taped to the inside of the glass door are a dozen faded photographs of Monica.

The TV's been playing its subtle background score as he eats, though he really hasn't been paying attention to the content. He understands from the tone, though, that some kind of silly season phenomenon is spooking the public. But when his attention perks up, the format shifts to business news and then sports. What the hell, he'll catch the headlines come the half-hour.

Speaking of time checks, he looks at the clock.

He had planned his most important California errand for four in the morning. He has reassessed his plans after Benjamin's tirade this morning. Should he alter his careful timetable? No, he thinks, probably not.

It's hard to concentrate on his primary mission. His memory still slips back to the meeting at Universal. It had not gone as well as he'd hoped. He had the feeling he'd managed to snow most of the staff—but that was the problem. It was the producer who had wanted to add his own valuable input. And that represented 51% of the vote.

The producer loved the idea of updating O'Hara. No problem there. He *loved* the classics. After all, look at the grosses for Jane Austen and Charles Dickens, not to mention *some* of Henry James. Never discount what romance and/or nudity could do to crank up an old text.

*But,* the producer wanted to see a bit more conflict when the protagonist met up with Mr. Death. Del's epiphany when parsing out his notes for the treatment had been that in the final confrontation, the protagonist had to realize that *he himself* was Death. He was his own foremost opponent. The producer thought that was way too confusing for the demographics he was reaching for.

What the guy really wanted was some kind of Hong Kong kick-ass martial arts competition between the terrified guy fleeing his fate, and the Grim Reaper himself. Nun-chuks against the scythe, maybe. The stunt coordinator would figure it out.

Now that's plot resolution, the producer had said. *That's* how to end a character arc.

Del respectfully disagreed.

Thanks for coming in, had been the reply.

And so now Del is eating Wolfgang Puck pizza in his motel room and wondering how the rest of his trip will go.

What the hell. He switches on the laptop and joins the Internet. Once again he keys in deadsite.end and this time does not hesitate. He presses return and waits for the clicks and whirs.

He knows it cannot be a valid destination, but it beats thinking about the producer's heralded but unwelcome input. The screen flickers, the image downloading and resolving. After all the conversation earlier, he's expected something a little spiffier. But no, the design is austere, almost monochrome.

The deadsite letters draw from a simple serif font. The background is dark, almost black. The letters are a dark crimson that nearly fades into the sable.

The first thing he sees is the visitor total box. According to today's date, he reads, the site has been visited by 6.8 billion people. He blinks. Isn't that something like the total global population? The counter clicks up as he watches. The right-hand digits whirl faster than he can register.

He clicks the next-screen command.

The new screen beckons him to enter his name and age, and then to fill in the rest of the necessary information.

Why not? he thinks.

Then he hears the TV behind him, the volume seemingly increasing. It's time for the semi-hourly headlines. The news reader seems genuinely bewildered by what she's reporting. Apparently the Internet site for the death predictor is doing land office business. All over the earth, phone lines are tied up, networks are starting to crash. One thing about the Internet. This is a genuinely global phenomenon.

The oddest revelation is that everyone's predictor is set at 3:53 the following morning, or at the equivalent time for their location on the planet. Political figures and religious leaders are denying there is any reason for concern.

It's probably all an enormously elaborate hoax. Are 6.8 billion human beings going to die simultaneously at fifty-three minutes past the hour?

Maybe.

Del turns back to the computer and, as is his habitual approach, writes the answers down on the yellow pad. Then, if he wishes, he can enter them into the laptop and hit return.

But he's not yet sure. He's not certain he wants to learn if his predicted death will be at 3:53 in the morning this coming day. Del registers the electronic clock at the top of the screen. This coming day has already arrived. Time is passing faster than he had expected.

He senses he no longer has much time. He has already checked the throwaway pistol. He really ought to make sure the lock-pick set is with the weapon. He has to put on the dark clothing and make sure the black knit balaclava is balled up in the fanny pack. He needs to check the map again, to make sure he knows the route to Benjamin's home.

Obsessive revenge is a bitch, he thinks. He never fought hard for Monica in life. So why is he going out to kill Benjamin now that she's dead?

Del suspects the answer to that would also explain why he's never been able to plot out a satisfactory story for a relationship-based movie of the week. It's a puzzlement. The dramatic tension between fiction and real life has always baffled him.

He has always wished to create a genuine epic, and has been forever frustrated.

*Until now.* He blinks. Where did that thought come from?

The commentator on the television screen is talking about mass hysteria, the power of suggestion, and millennial apprehension. The word voodoo does not pass his lips.

Or maybe, Del thinks, it really is all a silly little software glitch that will weigh heavily on the conscience of some overworked, underpaid programmer.

But now he's not so sure. He's starting to think about what kind of man would fly to L.A. under cover of show business to kill another guy who did nothing more heinous than to steal the love of the first man's life.

Hey, what could better encapsulate life?

It is all getting too confusing. Del wishes he had a better line on what death means, what it portends, what will come after.

It appears as though there is one simple way to get a clue. He checks the answers on the yellow lined pad again, makes up his mind, starts to type them into the electronic form onscreen.

He wonders, will he die at 3:53 in the morning, too?

It's a surprising world of possibilities.

The sharp hard lead pencil

*could* fly up, transfix the eye, pierce the brain

*or* draw its own map across the chest, furrowing blood and tissue until it discovers its private channel to the inner heart

*or* it slips from the fingers and describes the long, slow, lazy parabola to the soft carpet.

All the possibilities are linked by precisely that—*possibility.* Benjamin might be right, or Brian or Raju. Or no one. Answers may surpass human understanding.

The pencil moves. Death comes to life in his hand, he senses. He opens his fingers.

*The possibilities.*

All he regrets is that he can never know. That is sufficient sadness.

Or can he? Del's always suspected he truly possessed hidden depths.

With the index finger of his other hand, he punches "return."

And then the surprise. The clock reads: 3:52. Time, or at least some variety of time—*someone's time*—is almost up.

His eyes return to the screen as the pencil reaches the floor.

The pixels flicker and the new image resolves. He instantly forgets about the waiting pistol, and Benjamin and Monica recede to a distant, small part of his attention. He thinks of sharp objects.

The letters arrange themselves: YOU WILL NOT DIE

Del is afraid he understands why. Maybe he always has.

It's 3:53.

Life was such a warm chrysalis.
The walls collapse around him. His body is no longer a hindrance.
He knows he has a job to do.
And appointments to keep.

Donald Westlake's series characters couldn't be more different than night and day. Parker is a hard-boiled professional thief who's made a well-deserved return after almost twenty years in the novel *Comeback*. Dortmunder is a bumbling burglar whose capers inevitably fall apart, the only question being how spectacularly it happens. The short story "Too Many Crooks" garnered Dortmunder's author an Edgar award, proving that it's not always the hard-boiled or serious mystery stories that deserve recognition. He also writes excellent stand-alone fiction, most recently the chilling downsizing-leads-to-murder story "The Ax." In "Take it Away" he combines one world-weary cop with a criminal who has an unusual sense of humor, for a tale only he could write.

# Take It Away
## DONALD E. WESTLAKE

"Nice night for a stakeout."

Well, *that* startled me, let me tell you. I looked around and saw I was no longer the last person on line; behind me now was a goofy-looking grinning guy, more or less my age (34) and height (6'1½"), but maybe just a bit thinner than my weight (190 lbs). He wore eyeglasses with thick black frames and a dark blue baseball cap turned around backward, with bunches of carroty red hair sticking out under it on the sides and back. He was bucktoothed and grinning, and he wore a gold and purple high school athletic jacket with the letter X hugely on it in Day-Glo white edged in purple and gold. It was open a bit at the top, to show a bright lime green polo shirt beneath. His trousers were plain black chinos, which made for a change, and on his feet were a pair of those high-tech sneakers complete with inserts and gores and extra straps and triangles of black leather here and there, that look as though they were constructed to specifications for NASA. In his left hand he held an *X-Men* comic book folded open to the middle of a story. He was not, in other words, anybody on the crew, or even *like* anybody on the crew. So what was this about a stakeout? Who *was* this guy?

Time to employ my interrogation techniques, which meant I should come at him indirectly, not asking *who are you* but saying, "What was that again?"

He blinked happily behind his big glasses and pointed with his free hand. "A stakeout," he said, cheerful as could be.

I looked where he pointed, at the side wall of this Burger Whopper where it was my turn tonight to get food for the crew, and I saw the poster there advertising this month's special in all twenty-seven hundred Burger Whoppers all across the United States and Canada, which was for their Special Thick Steak Whopper Sandwich, made with U.S. government–inspected steak guaranteed to be a full quarter-inch thick. I blinked at this poster, with its glossy color photo of the Special Thick Steak Whopper Sandwich, and beside me the goofy guy said, "A steak out, right? A great night to come out and get one of those steak sandwiches and bring it home and not worry about cooking or anything like that, because, who knows, the electricity could go off at any second."

Well, that was true. The weather had been miserable the last few days, hovering just around the freezing point, with rain at times and sleet at times and at the moment, nine-twenty P.M. on a Wednesday, outside the picture windows of the Burger Whopper, there crowded a thick misty fog, wet to the touch, kind of streaked and dirty, that looked mostly like an airport hotel's laundry on the rinse cycle.

*Not* a good night for a stakeout, not my kind of stakeout. All of the guys on the crew had been complaining and griping on our walkie-talkies, sitting in our cars on this endless surveillance, getting nowhere, expecting nothing, except maybe we'd all have the flu when this was finally over.

"See what I mean?" the goofy guy said, and grinned his bucktoothed grin at me again, and gestured at that poster like the magician's girl assistant gesturing at the elephant. See the elephant?

"Right," I said, and I felt a sudden quick surge of relief. If our operation had been compromised, after all this time and energy and effort, particularly given my own spotty record, I don't know what I would have done. But at least it wouldn't have been my fault.

Well, it hadn't happened, and I wouldn't have to worry about it. My smile was probably as broad and goofy as the other guy's when I said, "I see it, I see it. A steak out on a night like this, I get you."

"I'm living alone since my wife left me," he explained, probably feeling we were buddies since my smile was as moronic as his, "so mostly I just open a can of soup or something. But weather like this, living alone, the fog out there, everything so cold, you just kinda feel like you owe yourself a treat, you know what I mean?"

Mostly, I was just astonished that this guy had ever *had* a wife, though not surprised she'd left him. I've never been married myself, never been that fortunate, my life being pretty much tied up with the Bureau, but I could imagine what it must be like to have *been* married, and then she walks out, and now you're not married anymore. And what now? It would be like, if I screwed up *real* bad, much worse than usual, and the Bureau dropped me, and I wouldn't have the Bureau to go to anymore. I'd probably come out on foggy nights for a steak sandwich myself, and talk to strangers on the line at the Burger Whopper.

Not that I'm a total screwup, don't get me wrong. If I were a total screwup, the Bureau would have terminated me (not with prejudice, just the old pink slip) a long time ago; the Bureau doesn't suffer fools, gladly or otherwise. But it's true I have made a few errors along the way and had luck turn against me, and so on, which in fact was why I was on this stakeout detail in the first place.

All of us. The whole crew, the whole night shift, seven guys in seven cars blanketing three square blocks in the Meridian Hills section of Indianapolis. Or was it Ravenswood? How do I know, I don't know anything about Indianapolis. The Burger Whopper was a long drive away, that's all I know.

And we seven guys, we'd gotten this assignment, with no possibility of glory or advancement, with nothing but boredom and dyspepsia (the Burger Whopper is not my first choice of food) and chills and aches and no doubt the flu before it's over, because all seven of us had a few little dings and dents in our curricula vitae. Second-raters together, that's what we had to think about, losing self-esteem by the minute as we each sat alone there in our cars in the darkness, waiting in vain for Figuer to make his move.

Art smuggling; has there ever been a greater potential for boredom? Madonna and Child; Madonna and Child; Madonna and Child. Who cares what wall they hang on, as long as it isn't mine, those cow-faced Madonnas and fat-kneed Childs? Still, as it turns out, there's a lively illegal trade in stolen art from Europe, particularly from defenseless churches over there, and that means a whole lot of Madonnae und Kinder entering America rolled up in umbrellas or disguised as Genoa salami.

And at the center of this vast illegal conspiracy to bore Americans out of their pants was one Francois Figuer, a Parisian, now resident in the good old U.S. of A. And he was who we were out to get.

We knew a fresh shipment of stolen art was on its way, this time from the defenseless churches of Italy and consisting mostly of the second favorite subject after M & C, being St. Sebastian, the bird condo. You know, the saint with all the arrows sticking out of him for the birds to perch on. Anyway, the Bureau had tracked the St. Sebastian shipment into the U.S., through the entry port at Norfolk, Virginia, but then had lost it. (Not us seven, some other bunch of screwups.) It was on its way to Figuer and whoever his customer might be, which is why we were here, blanketing his neighborhood, waiting for him to make his move. In the meantime, it was, as my new goofy friend had suggested, a good night for a steak out.

Seven men, in seven cars, trying to outwait and outwit one wily art smuggler. In each car, we had a police radio (in case we needed local backup), we had our walkie-talkie, and we had a manila folder on the passenger seat beside us, containing a map of the immediate area around Figuer's house and a blown-up surveillance photo of Figuer himself, with a verbal description on the back.

We sat in our cars, and we waited, and for five days nothing had happened. We knew Figuer was in the house, alone. We knew he and the courier must eventually make contact. We watched the arrivals of deliverymen from the supermarket and the liquor store and the Chinese restaurant, and when we checked, all three of them were the normal deliverymen from those establishments. Then we replaced them with our own deliverymen and learned only that Figuer was a lousy tipper.

Did he know he was being watched? No idea, but probably not. In any event, we were here, and there was no alternative. If the courier arrived, with a package that looked like a Genoa salami, we would pounce. If, instead, Figuer were to leave his house and go for a stroll or a drive, we would follow.

In the meantime, we waited, with nothing to do. Not allowed to read, even if we were permitted to turn on a light. We spoke together briefly on our walkie-talkies, that's all. And every night around nine, one of us would come here to the Burger Whopper to buy everyone's dinner. Tonight was my turn.

Apparently, everybody in the world felt thick fog created a good night to eat out, to counteract a foggy night's enforced slowness with some fast food. The line had been longer than usual at the Burger Whopper when I arrived, and now it stretched another dozen people or so behind my new friend and me. A family of four (small, sticky-looking children, dazed father, furious mother), a young couple giggling and rubbing each other's bodies, another family, a hunched solitary fellow with his hands moving in his raincoat pockets, and now more beyond him.

Ahead, the end was in sight. Either the Whopper management hadn't expected such a crowd on such a night, or the fog had kept one or more employees from getting to work; whatever the cause, there was only one cash register in use, run by an irritable heavyset girl in the clownish garnet-and-gray Burger Whopper costume. Each customer, upon reaching this girl, would sing out his or her order, and she would punch it into the register as though stabbing an enemy in his thousand eyes.

My new friend said, "It can get really boring sitting around in the car, can't it?"

I'd been miles away, in my own thoughts, brooding about this miserable assignment and the miserable weather, and without thinking I answered, "Yeah, it sure can," but then immediately caught myself and stared at the goof again and said, *"What?"*

"Boring sitting around in the car," he repeated. "And you get all stiff after a while."

This was true, but how did *he* know? Thinking, What is going *on* here? I said, "What do you mean, sitting around in the car? What do you mean?" And at the same time now thinking, Can I take him into protective custody?

But the goof spread his hands, gesturing at the Burger Whopper all around us, and said, "That's why we're here, right? Instead of over at Radio Special."

Well, yes. Yes, that was true. Radio Special, another fast-food chain with a franchise joint not far from here, was set up like the drive-in deposit window at the bank. You drove up to the window, called your order into a microphone, and a staticky voice told you how much it would cost. You put the money into a bin that slid out and back in, and a little later the bin would slide out a second time, with your food and your change. A lot of people prefer that sort of thing, because they feel more secure being inside their own automobiles, but us guys on stakeout find it too much of the same old same old. What we want, when there's any kind of excuse for it, is to be *out* of the car.

So I had to agree with my carrot-topped friend. "That's why I'm here, all right. I don't like sitting around in a car any more than I have to."

"I'd hate a *job* like that, I can tell you," he said.

There was no way to respond to that without blowing my cover, so I just smiled at him and faced front.

The person next ahead of me on line was being no trouble at all, for which I was thankful. Slender and attractive, with long, straight, ash blond hair, she was apparently a college student, and had brought along a skinny green loose-leaf binder full of her notes from some sort of math class. Trying to read over her shoulder, I saw nothing I recognized at all. But then she became aware of me and gave a disgusted little growl, and hunched further over her binder, as though to hide her notes from the eavesdropper. Except that I realized she must have thought I was trying to look down the front of her sweater—it would have been worth the effort, but in fact I hadn't been—and I got suddenly so embarrassed I automatically took a quick step backward and tromped down on the goof's right foot.

"Ouch!" he said, and gave me a little push, and I got my feet back where they belonged. "Sorry," I said. "I just—I don't know what happened."

"You violated my civil rights there," he told me, "that's what happened." But he said it with his usual toothy grin.

What *was* this? For once, I decided to confront the weirdness head-on. "Guess it's a good thing I'm not a cop, then," I told him, "so I *can't* violate your civil rights."

"To tell you the truth," he said, "I've been wondering what you do for a living. I know it's nosy of me, but I can't ever help trying to figure people out. I'm Jim Henderson, by the way, I'm a high school math teacher."

He didn't offer to shake hands, and neither did I, because I was mostly trying to find an alternate occupation for myself. I decided to borrow my sister's husband. "Fred Barnes," I lied. "I'm a bus driver, I just got off my tour."

"Ah," he said. "I've been scoring math tests, wanted to get away from it for a while."

Mathematicians in front of me and behind me; another coincidence. It's all coincidence, nothing to worry about.

"I teach," Jim Henderson went on, "up at St. Sebastian's."

I stared at him. "St. Sebastian's?"

"Sure. You know it, don't you? Up on Rome Road."

"Oh, sure," I said.

The furious mother behind us said, "Move the line up, will ya?"

"Oh," I said, and looked around, and my girl math student had moved forward and was now second in line behind the person giving an order. So I was third, and the goof was fourth, and I didn't have much time to think about this.

Was something up, or not? If I made a move, and Jim Henderson was merely Jim Henderson just like he'd said, I could be in big trouble, and the whole stakeout operation would definitely be compromised. But if I *didn't* make a move, and Jim Henderson actually turned out to be the courier, or somebody else connected with Francois Figuer, and I let him slip through my fingers, I could be in big trouble all over again.

I realized now that it had never occurred to any of us that anybody else might listen in on our walkie-talkie conversations, even though we all knew they weren't secure. From time to time, on the walkie-talkies, we'd heard construction crews, a street-paving crew, even a movie crew on location, as they passed through our territory, talking to one another, but the idea that Francois Figuer, inside his house, might have his own walkie-talkie, or even a scanner, and might listen to us, had never crossed our minds. Not that we talked much, on duty, back and forth, except to complain about the assignment or arrange our evening meal—

Our evening meal.

Who was Jim Henderson, what was he? I wished now I'd studied the picture of Francois Figuer more closely, but it had always been nighttime in that damn car. I'd never even read the material on the back of the picture. Who was Francois Figuer? Was he the kind of guy who would do . . . whatever this was?

Was all this—please God—after all, just coincidence?

The customer at the counter got his sack of stuff and left. The math girl stood before the irritable Whopper girl and murmured her order, her voice too soft for me to hear; on purpose, I think. She didn't want to share *anything*, that girl.

I didn't have much more time to think, to plan, to decide. Soon it would be my turn at the counter. What did I have to base a suspicion on? Coincidence, that's all. Odd phrases, nothing more. If coincidences didn't happen, we wouldn't need a word for them.

All right. I'm ahead of Jim Henderson, I'll place my order, I'll get my food, I'll go outside, I'll wait in the car. When he comes out, I'll follow him. We'll see for sure who he is and where he goes.

Relieved, I was smiling when the math girl turned with her sack. She saw me, saw my smile, and gave me a contemptuous glare. But her good opinion was not as important as my knowing I now had a plan, I could now become easier in my mind.

I stepped up to the counter, fishing the list out of my pants pocket. Seven guys, and every one of us wanted something different. I announced it all, while the irritable girl spiked the register as though wishing it were *my* eyes, and throughout the process I kept thinking.

Where did Jim Henderson live? Could I find out by subtle interrogation techniques? Well, I would say, we're almost done here. Got far to go?

I turned. "Well," I said, and watched the mother whack one of her children across the top of the head, possibly in an effort to make him as stupid as she was. I saw this action very clearly because there was no one else in the way.

Henderson! Whoever! Where *was* he? All this time on line, and just when he's about to reach the counter he *leaves?*

"The man!" I spluttered at the furious mother and pointed this way and that way, more or less at random. "He—Where—He—"

The whole family gave me a look of utter unalterable treelike incomprehension. They were going to be no help at all.

Oh, hell, oh, damn, oh, gol*darn* it! Henderson, my eye! He's, he's, he's either Figuer himself or somebody connected to him, and I let the damn man escape!

"Wenny sen fory three."

I started around the family, toward the distant door. The line of waiting people extended almost all the way down to the exit. Henderson was nowhere in sight.

"Hey!"

"Hey!"

The first hey was from the irritable Whopper girl, who'd also been the one who'd said wenny sen fory three, and the second hey was from the furious mother. Neither of them wanted me to complicate the routine.

"You gah *pay* futhis!"

Oh, God, oh, God. Time is fleeting. Where's he gotten to? I grabbed at my hip pocket for my wallet, and it wasn't there.

He picked my pocket. Probably when I stepped on his foot. Son of a *bitch!* Money. ID.

"Cancel the order!" I cried, and ran for the door.

Many people behind me shouted that I couldn't do what I was already doing. I ignored them, pelted out of the Whopper, ran through the thick gray swirling fog toward my car, my face and hands already clammy when I got there, and unlocked my way in.

Local police backup, that's what I needed. I slid behind the wheel, reached for the police radio microphone, and it wasn't there. I scraped knuckles on the housing, expecting the microphone to be there, and it wasn't there.

I switched on the interior light. The curly black cord from the mike to the radio was cut and dangling. He'd been in the car. *Damn* him. I slapped open the manila folder on the passenger seat and wasn't at all surprised that the photo of Francois Figuer was gone.

Would my walkie-talkie reach from here to the neighborhood of the stake-out? I had no idea, but it was my last means of communication, so I grabbed it up from its leather holster dangling from the dashboard—at least he hadn't taken *that*—thumbed the side down, and said, "Tome here. Do you read me? Calling anybody. Tome here."

And then I noticed, when I thumbed the side down to broadcast, the little red light didn't come on.

Oh, that bastard. Oh, that French . . .

I slid open the panel on the back of the walkie-talkie, and of course the battery pack that was supposed to be in there was gone. But the space wasn't empty, oh, no. A piece of paper was crumpled up inside there, where the battery used to be.

I took the paper out of the walkie-talkie and smoothed it on the passenger seat beside me, and it was the Figuer photo. I gazed at it. Without the thick black eyeglasses, without the buck teeth, without the carroty hair sticking out all around from under the turned-around baseball cap, this was him. It was *him*.

I turned the paper over, and now I read the back, and the words popped out at me like neon: "reckless" "daring" "fluent unaccented American English" "strange sense of humor."

And across the bottom, in block letters in blue ink, had very recently been written: "They forgot to mention master of disguise. Enjoy your steak out. FF"

Stuart Kaminsky is another writer whose two mystery series are nothing like each other. Inspector Porfiry Rostnikov is an intelligent Moscow policeman forever distrusted by his superiors and always being assigned "impossible" cases, which he solves with aplomb. Private detective Toby Peters lives and works in and around Hollywood of the 1940s, taking on cases for stars like Judy Garland and the Marx Brothers. Kaminsky's short fiction has appeared in anthologies such as *Guilty as Charged* and *The Mysterious West*. "The Man Who Beat the System" shows his lighter touch with crime, a humorous look at the wheelings and dealings of a Florida city council.

# The Man Who Beat the System
## STUART M. KAMINSKY

"You Fonesca?" the voice behind me said as I scooped at my regular-size chocolate-cherry Breeze at the Dairy Queen across the parking lot from my office-home. I have to stick with frozen yogurt because I have a lactose intolerance.

I felt like answering the voice that had interrupted my late breakfast with, "No, I can't Fonesca, but I can do a pretty mean tango when my life depends on it."

I didn't say anything. I was in a good mood. It was a typical summer morning in Sarasota. The sun was hot. The air was humid. The ultraviolet index, which I could never understand, was over ten, which meant that if you stepped out into it you'd probably die of skin cancer faster than you would of exposure in the middle of winter at the North Pole. I sat at one of those round white painted aluminum tables with a DQ umbrella. I had the *Sarasota Herald-Tribune* laid out in front of me.

The tourists were gone until winter, and I didn't regret having left Chicago two years earlier so that I could exchange winters for constant heat and humidity, afternoon thundershowers, and possible hurricanes.

I was content. I even had a bicycle, almost two hundred dollars in cash, and my combination office-living quarters—two rooms not much larger than the dressing rooms at Burdine's or Saks.

I didn't give the voice my smart-ass answer. Instead I paused, adjusted the blue Albany State College baseball cap that shaded my eyes and helped cover my rapidly balding head, and turned around.

306

I recognized him.

"I'm Fonesca," I said.

"Went to your office," he said, nodding toward the open seat across from me. "Note on the door said I could find you here."

I invited him to sit. After all he was a distinguished local gadfly, a member of the city council, and the only African American in the city or county government.

The Reverend Fernando Wilkens was in the newspaper and on the two local television news stations almost every day. Now that I had cable in my room—for which I was two months behind in payments—I was not only up on the international news, the national news and whether Scully and Mulder would catch the giant worm before it turned the town of Feeney, North Dakota, into a larder of zombies. I now also had the privilege of knowing almost nothing about local politics.

The Reverend Wilkens was a big man, running toward the chunky side, in tan slacks and a white pullover short-sleeve shirt with a little green alligator on the pocket. I was wearing my faded jeans and a Chicago Bulls T-shirt. He was about my age, forty-four. He had good teeth, smooth skin, an even smoother bass voice, and a winning smile, which he was not sporting at the moment.

"Breeze?" I asked.

"No, thank you," he said. "I have eaten, and my doctor says I should stay away from snacks. You recognize me?"

"I read the paper," I said, tapping at the Local section in front of me, which featured an article on the mysterious death of more manatees. Now a scientist was blaming red tide. Red tide seemed to roll in once a month and linger in the warm water and hot sun over the Gulf of Mexico, stinking up the beaches and killing fish. It gave the Local section reporters surefire stories and once in a while made the front page.

The doings of both the city council and the county board, on the other hand, made the front page only when there was a controversy so major that at least twenty citizens protested with marches and placards and complaints before the open hearings of the council or the board. Few people went to meetings on the lingering issue of the new city library location and branch location with any real hope of convincing the council or board that the new library would cut off parking downtown, cost seventeen million dollars, and have fewer books than the library that was about to be torn down and that the proposed branch would be too far from human life to make it usable. Few people, in the midst of their passion, when addressing the council for their allotted three or four minutes, even expected their elected officials to listen to them. Often members of the council in the middle of an impassioned speech by an ancient resident would pass notes on the latest College World Series scores.

All of this was on television for those who chose to watch, who were few.

"There's a council meeting tonight," the Reverend Wilkens said soft and deep as I dug deep into my breakfast while a couple of shirtless boys, with lean bodies and a desire to sacrifice themselves to the sun, ordered large Oreo-cookie Blizzards.

"I know," I said.

Reverend Wilkens nodded, taken aback only slightly that a citizen actually knew when there was to be a council meeting.

"There's going to be an open hearing about six items," he said. "The last one is where to put a new branch library."

I nodded, thinking I could see where this was going but not what I had to do with it.

"I want the new branch in or near Newtown," he said. "I want it to serve the African American community. It will be the last item on the agenda and probably won't come up till after midnight. I've got the feeling that a few of my fellow board members who have a much different site in mind will have lots to say on the earlier items, such as tearing up Clark Road again or re-planting blighted trees on Palm Avenue. We'll listen to the public and then vote. The vote won't be subject to review unless there's a violation of the state or federal constitution."

I used to work for the state attorney's office in Cook County as a process server and investigator. One day I packed the little I owned in my car, called my landlord, called the office and quit over the phone, saying I'd let them know where to send my last check. I was still waiting for that check. My battered Toyota had barely got me from Chicago to Sarasota and away from the winter and an ex-wife whom I kept running into when she was with other men.

Newtown is the African American ghetto in Sarasota, running about four blocks or more in either direction north and south of Martin Luther King Jr. Street. The far south end of what could be called Newtown was within walking distance of downtown, where the new library with fewer books was going to go up. Members of the council, downtown business leaders, and community money people said the blacks could walk to the new library. The branch containing books would be out on the east side of town close to I-75, too far for any Newtown kid to walk and even six miles from my office behind the DQ. A pedal to the closest proposed branch would leave me looking like John Wayne in *Three Godfathers* when Ward Bond shoots his water bag and leaves him and his fellow robbers to wander in the desert.

I was about to say, "What's this got to do with me?" when Fernando Wilkens told me.

He leaned over and whispered,

"I've got the votes."

"The votes?"

"To get the library branch on Martin Luther King right on three-oh-one," he said. "Easy walk for my constituents. Easy drive for others."

There were five members of the city council. They took turns serving as mayor for two years, depending on seniority, the last time they served, when they were elected, and some computer math system beyond the comprehension of the Unabomber. Votes, sometimes involving contracts for millions of dollars, were decided by simple majority.

Maybe it was the way I slowly poked at the bottom of my Breeze searching for bits of chocolate clinging to the sides of the cup. Maybe my face is not as inscrutable as I like to think.

"This a privileged conversation?" he asked softly, though no one was listening. He looked around to see if we were being watched by anyone. Cars drove by, but on a day like this only out-of-work teens and the homeless wandered the streets of Sarasota.

"One question first," I said. "How did you find me?"

I'm not listed in the phone book either in the white pages or in the Yellow Pages. I don't know what I'd call myself anyway—asker of questions? researcher in obscure publications and mud that sometimes contained both animal and human snakes and gators?

"My lawyer, Fred Tyrell," he said.

I nodded. Tyrell was the token black in the downtown law firm of Cameron, Wyznicki, Forbes, and Littlefield. Tyrell's job was to take minority clients and even drum them up. Sometimes it worked. Sometimes even the most committed African American activists wanted a smart white lawyer, preferably a Jewish one. Cameron, Wyznicki, etc., had one of those too—Adam Katz. I had done work for both Katz and Tyrell. The partners had their own short list of investigators and process servers.

I nodded again, looked at my empty cup.

"You want another?" asked Wilkens.

I'm what is usually called medium height and probably seen as being on the thin side, but I pedal to the downtown Y every day, work out for at least an hour, and have grown hard in a town of white sand beaches and lazy hot days. I grew hard in my effort to stay away from my own tendency to turn into a vegetable.

"Patormi will vote with me," said Wilkens.

I nodded a third time. This was no surprise. Patormi was the closest thing we had to a liberal radical on the council. He was old and crusty, had moved down from Jersey thirty years ago, and would have gladly voted for Eugene Debs for governor if Debs had been alive and eligible. Sometimes the other council members kept certain issues to be addressed late in each session in the hope that Patormi would be too tired to protest or might even doze off. Patormi was too crafty an old Socialist to let that work. He sat with his thermos of black coffee, did crossword puzzles while he pretended to take notes, and waited for the big vote.

"Three votes," I reminded Wilkens.

The other three council members always voted in a block on money issues. They would debate furiously for hours whether they should approve an unbroken or broken yellow line down the middle of the recently widened Tuttle Avenue, and you'd never know how that one would go, but on expenditures they were closer together than the Statler Brothers.

"Zink," the Reverend Wilkens whispered, leaning even closer to me.

I thought delusions had set in on Wilkens and considered advising him to wear a hat and stay indoors.

I even considered inviting him across the parking lot to my barely air-conditioned office and living closet, but decided that whatever confidence he might have in me would evaporate with his first view of my professional headquarters.

"Zink is one of the solid three," I said.

Wilkens smiled. Nice teeth. Definitely capped.

"August Zink is dying," he said.

I was glad the prospect made him happy. He explained.

"Zink came to my office day before yesterday, told me. Said there was nothing they could do to him now and that he'd enjoy surprising the board by voting with me and Patormi. It would be a done deal."

"Still two questions," I said, pitching the empty cup toward the white-plastic-lined metal-mesh trash basket and sinking it for a solid two points. "First, what did Zink mean by saying there was nothing they could do to him now? Second, what do you need me for?"

"Zink wouldn't say much," said Wilkens, "but we were either talking past payoffs or things someone had on him for deals he might have made for his contracting business. Since Zink is up to his kneecaps in money, I'd say it was the contracting deals. We've got buildings in this town that crumble after a decade. Zink's company put up a lot of them, some of them public buildings. It doesn't cost him anything to meet his maker on the side of righteousness. Get him some good headlines and maybe a ticket to Heaven, though I think the Good Lord will look hard and long at the scales of this man's life before making a decision."

"And me?" I reminded him.

"Vote is tonight," he said tersely. "Zink is missing. I want you to find him, get him to that meeting so he can vote. If he doesn't show up, we deadlock. If Zink dies, we have an election fast and I have no doubt that, given the constituency and the inclination of both parties, the new member will not vote with me and Patormi, who stands a good chance of being defeated in the next open election if he lives long enough to run."

"You don't risk losing?"

"I'll be the token everything with Patormi gone," said the Reverend Wilkens. "The token black, the token liberal, the token clergyman. I am the exception that supposedly proves fairness. Every hypocrite on the council and in the business community will support me."

"How do you know Zink is missing?"

"I called his office," said Wilkens. "He hasn't come in for four days. I called his home. His wife didn't want to talk, but she said Zink was out of town on a family emergency and she had no idea when he would be coming back. I called the police and they asked me what the crime was."

"You think he's in town?" I asked.

"I pray he's in town," said Wilkens, clasping his hands. "He led me to believe that he didn't have very much time and that even coming to the meeting tonight was against his doctor's recommendation."

"Let's say one hundred and twenty-five dollars plus the cost of a car rental," I said. "I'll take care of my own meals, since I live here. If I have to slip someone cash, I'll try to keep it below fifty and I'll bill you."

"That will be satisfactory," he said, holding out a large right hand.

We shook, and he immediately reached into his pocket and counted out six twenties and a five. He also handed me his card. On the back in dark ink was his home number.

"Receipt?" I asked.

"Under the circumstances, I would prefer a strictly cash business arrangement," he said, rising. "For a change, Patormi and I will stall on other issues on the agenda. Members of my congregation will also be present to speak out at the open forum. I would guess that we can keep the meeting going till at least midnight. I would also guess, if they truly don't know yet, that the solid two will want to wait for Zink, assuming he will vote with them."

"Unless they know about his illness and the fact that he is missing," I said.

"Precisely," said the Reverend Wilkens, shading his eyes and looking toward the sun almost overhead and then at his watch.

"You'd best begin," he said.

"I'd best," I agreed.

"Find him, Lewis," he said. "I'll pray for you to find him."

He got into a clean, dark green five- or six-year-old Geo Metro about a dozen yards away in the small parking lot and pulled away, waving at me.

This wasn't going to be easy, but it was a day's work and I had just pocketed one hundred and twenty-five dollars.

I went back to my office. For about five minutes, I sat at my desk thinking and watching the air conditioner in the window drip into the bucket. I listened to the ancient machine shudder and clank and do its best to keep almost reasonably cool air coming in. In the adjoining room, where I slept on a cot and had my small-screen Sony and cable, I usually turned on a fan I'd purchased at Walgreen's last winter when the prices were down.

Then I got up and changed into my usual work clothes, an old, only slightly frayed pair of navy blue slacks well ironed, a light blue short-sleeved shirt, and my black patent leather shoes with dark socks.

It took Eb Farrell less than ten minutes to get there after I called him. I was back in the chair behind my desk when, even over the clatter of the air conditioner, I heard his motor scooter come into the DQ lot and park below. I didn't hear him climb the metal stairs to the second floor or hear his footsteps approach my door. Eb Farrell was polite, seventy-three years ago born a child of polite, God-fearing Methodists in Texas, near the Oklahoma Panhandle. Eb knocked. I told him to come in.

Eb had once been close to rich and lost it all. He trailed the partner who had cheated him to Sarasota, where the partner had changed his name and grown even richer, a steel pillar of philanthropy and high society. I found Eb's partner, and the two of them, in spite of my attempts to reason or threaten them out of it, had an old-fashioned shoot-out on the beach in the park at the far south end of Lido Key. Eb was the better shot. The former partner took a bullet in the heart. Eb served eight months for having an unregistered weapon and engaging in a duel, a law that still existed in Florida. Eb's age and the evidence of what his former partner had done kept the sentence reasonably short.

Now Eb lived in Sarasota. He had a room with a bed and old record player in the back of Edwardo's Bar and TexMex Restaurant on Second Street. Eb's job was to keep the place from being broken into at night. He got the room and food but no salary. It didn't cost Eb much to live, but even though he shopped at Goodwill, the motor scooter needed gas, and once in a while a man needs a new toothbrush.

Eb came in standing tall and lean in jeans and a long-sleeved shirt. The jeans were worn white in patches but clean, and the shirt was a solid khaki that looked more than a little warm. On his head was the battered cowboy hat he had putt-putted into town with more than a year ago. Once Eb must have been close to six-six. I figured age had brought him down a few inches. Age seemed to be the only thing that could bring Eb Farrell down.

"Have a seat," I said.

Eb sat.

"How've you been?" I asked.

Eb's face was the color and texture of high-quality tan leather. His hair was clear, pure white and recently cut almost military short either by himself or one of the four-dollar old-time places still trying to compete with First Choice and the other new chains.

"Fine," said Eb.

"Got a job for you," I said.

"You said on the phone," he reminded me.

"I'm looking for August Zink, the councilman. Heard of him?"

"Heard," said Eb, taking off his hat and putting it on his lap the way his mother had taught him back when Hoover was president.

"I need to find him soon," I said. "Today. Can you ask some of your friends and see what you can come up with?"

Eb nodded.

I was sending him among the homeless, the afternoon barflies, and the other Sarasotans that tourists were usually kept away from.

Eb got up.

Eb had once been an electrical engineer. University of Texas graduate. That was a long time ago. I pulled out the cash I'd received from the Reverend Wilkens and handed Eb twenty-five dollars. He gave five back. I gave the five back to him again.

"This is a rush job," I said in explanation.

He nodded, accepted the five, and left.

A short bike ride from my place, I rented a sub-subcompact car, double-cheap, more than slightly used, from a place on Tamiami Trail where I got my usual deal. I left the bike in the closet inside the rental office, as usual.

Then I was on my way. First stop, Zink's contracting office. Downtown, high up in a fifteen-year-old, sixteen-story building that Zink had no hand in building. The receptionist was well groomed and in her forties, with a nice smile. She seemed like more than receptionist material when she deftly parried my lunging questions about Zink. I figured her for a mom who was just rejoining the workforce and starting at the bottom.

She finally agreed to talk to Mr. Zink's secretary, which she did while I listened. She handled it perfectly, saying a Mr. Fonesca wished to speak to her on a matter of some urgency regarding Mr. Zink and that Mr. Fonesca would provide no further information. There was a pause, during which I assumed Zink's secretary asked if I looked like a badly dressed 'toon or acted like a lunatic. The receptionist said, "No."

Two minutes later I was sitting in a chair next to the desk of Mrs. Carla Free. Her desk in the gray-carpeted complex was directly outside of an office with a steel plate on the door marked AUGUST ZINK.

Mrs. Free was tall, probably a little younger than me, well groomed and blue-suited with a white blouse with a fluffy collar. She was pretty, wore glasses, and was black. Actually, she was a very light brown.

"I have to find Mr. Zink," I said.

"We haven't seen him in several days," she said, sounding like Bennington or Radcliffe, her hands folded on the desk in front of her, giving me her full attention. "Perhaps I could help you, or someone else in the office could?"

"Does he often disappear for days?" I asked.

Mrs. Free did not answer the question but said, "Can I help you, Mr. Fonesca?"

There was no one within hearing distance. Her voice sounded like all business and early dismissal for me. I decided to take a chance.

"Where do you live?" I asked.

She took off her glasses and looked at me, at first in surprise and then in anger.

"Is this love at first sight, Mr. Fonesca?" she asked.

"You don't live in Newtown," I said.

"No, I live in Idora Estates. My husband is a doctor, a pediatrician. We have a daughter in Pine View and a son who just graduated from Pine View and is going to go to Grinnell. Now, I think you should leave."

"I have reason to believe that if Mr. Zink goes to the city council meeting tonight, he will vote for a branch library in Newtown," I said.

I waited.

"Who are you working for?" she asked quietly.

"Someone who wants that branch library in Newtown," I said.

"I was born here," she said so softly that I could hardly hear her. "In Newtown. So was my husband. My mother still lives there. She won't move. I had a long bike ride to the Selby Library."

"Where is Zink?" I asked.

"Off the record, Mr. Fonesca," she said, "Mr. Zink is not well."

"Off the record, Mrs. Free," I said, "Mr. Zink is dying and you know it." She nodded. She knew.

"You really think he'll vote for the Newtown location?" she asked.

"Good authority," I said. "A black man of the cloth."

She looked away. She understood. The sigh was long and said a lot—that she was risking her job, that she was about to give away things a secretary shouldn't give away.

"You've heard of Nils Anderson," she said.

"I've heard," I said.

"He has a large estate on Casey Key," she said. "High walls, a high iron gate. I believe strongly that Mr. Zink is there. Being 'tended to' in his illness by a close friend who happens to also own two large pieces of land near I-75, large pieces of land where the branch library site is proposed."

"He owns both possible sites?" I said.

"You can check it out in the tax office right down the street," she said. "Which would be more than the local media have done."

"Thanks," I said, getting up.

"No need," she said, doing the same and accompanying me down the hall. "I've told you nothing."

"Nothing," I agreed.

When we stood in front of the receptionist's desk, she shook my hand and she said, "I'm sorry I couldn't help you, Mr. Fonesca, but I will give Mr. Zink your name and number as soon as he returns."

This was hard and easy at the same time. I probably knew where Zink was, but getting him out might be a bit tough. I was not a wall climber, a particularly fast talker, or a good threatener. My skill was in getting people to talk and listening to them.

I drove to Zink's house. It was big, new, not on a Key, and facing the bay. I rang the doorbell and waited. In about a minute, the door opened and I found myself facing the elusive Mrs. Zink. Mr. Zink had done his best to make excuses for the absence of his wife at social and public functions over the years. She was ill or she was touring Europe or visiting one of her brothers or sisters in Alaska, Montana, California, or Vermont. The Zinks had no children.

Mrs. Zink was hefty, in her sixties, dressed in a black silver-studded skirt and vest over a blue denim shirt. She wore boots and looked as if she were on her way to do some line dancing. She was a barrel of a woman, with too much makeup, large earrings, and the distinctly vacant look of the heavy drinker. Even through the heavy perfume, there was a smell of scotch, probably good scotch. I understood that she was known to hold her alcohol well, but once in a while there was a scotch overdose and the well-rounded Mrs. Zink turned honest and foul-mouthed.

"Who're you?" she asked.

"Lew Fonesca," I said. "I need to find your husband."

"I don't know where Gus is," she said.

"I do," I answered.

She looked me up and down.

"I know where he is and I know a lot more," I said. "I'd like to keep it all quiet."

"Blackmail, Fonesca?" she said.

"No," I answered. "I've got a client. I'm poor but honest."

"No crap," she said. "No self-respectin' blackmailer's be caught parboiled in that sorry-ass pair of pants and cracked leather shoes that should have been retired three seasons back. Come on in and have a drink."

I stepped in and she shut the door. The floors were smooth, expensive tile. The place was furnished ersatz Western.

"How you like it, Fonesca?" she asked, leading me to a living room with a view of the back and furniture that looked as if it belonged on the set of a Clint Eastwood Western. Wood, old brown leather, a rough-hewn table made from a thick slice of redwood, and animal skins for rugs. Two paintings on the wall looked like (and probably were) authentic Remingtons—galloping cowboys, Indians riding bareback.

"Western," I said.

"I mean your drink," said Mrs. Zink.

"Beer would be fine, Mrs. Zink," I said.

"That's not a drink," she said. "You can call me Flo. If you're stayin', you're drinkin'."

"I'm drinking," I said.

"That's better," she said. "I'm a flush lush and I don't like being cooped up and I don't like drinkin' alone."

She mixed drinks. I don't know what was in them. When she handed me mine, I sipped at it. It burned going down and tasted like molten plastic. She downed hers in two quick gulps and a satisfied smile.

She poured herself another, and I showed her that mine was barely touched. She shrugged and pointed to a leather chair with arms made from the antlers of something from the far north. She sat opposite me and went slowly on the second drink.

"Flo," I began, "I've got to find your husband."

"Out of town, business. Urgent," she said, working at her drink and glancing at mine.

"He told you he had to go out of town?" I said. "In person?"

"No," she said. "The usual way. On the answering machine from wherever he was."

"Didn't give you a number or address?" I asked.

"Hell, I don't even know what country he's in," she said. "Hey, didn't you say you know where he is and a lot more?"

"Do you know Nils Anderson?" I asked.

She paused in mid-sip, lowered her glass, and looked at me with her head bird-tilted.

"What's this got to do with that crooked pisshead?" she asked.

"I've got good reason to believe that your husband is at Anderson's house."

"What the hell for? He and Anderson are . . . Why would Gus go to Anderson's when . . ."

"When he's sick?" I asked.

Her eyes were moist now. She blinked them, blew out air, and took another drink.

"You know?" she asked.

"Your husband is very sick," I said.

"Shit, he's a dead rider on a dead horse," she said. "We've been up and down and had some good rides and made lots of money till we moved here and he wanted respectability. Wanted to be king of the city, meet movie stars who have houses on the Keys, and have his picture in the papers. I wouldn't change. Zink's wife's a lush and a little loony, with a foul mouth to go with it. Bunch of assholes and hypocrites. But you know what hurts, Fonsca?"

"Fonesca," I corrected.

"He never cheated on me that I know," she went on, talking to a spot somewhere a dozen yards from me where an overstuffed chair sat high and heavy with the indentation of a human behind. "He gave me what he thought I wanted and left me out as much because I wanted to be left out as he wanted me to be. I love Gus and, I'll be goddamned, the old fart loves me, always has."

"And so?" I prompted when she went silent.

"Gus is too sick to take business trips, and I'm for damn sure he'd want to spend his last days with me," she said. "He told me."

"Flo," I said, "I think we can help each other. I want your husband to be at the city council meeting tonight. There's an important vote and . . ."

"You're one of them," she said with a sigh.

"One of . . . No, your husband promised someone very reliable that he was going to vote to put the branch library in Newtown."

"Gus?" she said.

"Yes," I said.

"Gonna buy his way into heaven with a last good deed," she said. "He thinks God is one of those numnutz he's been conning for half a century. What you want me to do?"

"Call Anderson. Ask to speak to your husband. Tell him you want to come with a friend and get him."

She nodded, pursed her lips, and reached for the portable phone on the table. She opened a black phone and address book and dialed.

"Mitzi," she said amiably, "how are you? . . . That's good. Nils? . . . Pleased to hear it. Now let's cut the crap and put Gus on the phone . . . Bullshit. He's there."

Long pause and then, "Anderson, you son of a bitch, I want to talk to Gus, now."

Flo looked at me, burning red and ready to explode, while she listened to what Anderson was saying.

"We'll see what the police say," she said and hung up.

She looked at me and said, "If I smoked, I'd be smoking now."

Instead, she got up, topped off her drink, and said, "He's there. That gas-station-toilet-bowl Anderson says Gus doesn't want to talk to me or see me, that he wants to convalesce away from my vulgarity and drinking. Lew, Gus likes me vulgar. He respects me and he knows I love him. He's not convalescing. He's dying."

"The police won't help," I said. "Anderson's probably got a doctor with a big check who'll confirm that your husband can't be seen today and if they let you see him, they'll be sure he's asleep and will promise to have him call you tomorrow. Tomorrow is too late."

I reached for the phone and dialed one of the few numbers I knew in Sarasota. I called Edwardo's.

"Eddie? Lew Fonesca. You seen Eb? He is? Thanks. Eb?"

"He's at the house of a fella named Anderson," Eb said.

"I know. What I need is someone who knows how to get into a house, a big house with walls and maybe dogs and a guard or two."

"Wait," said Eb and put the phone down.

Flo stood looking down at me, her hands clasped tight. Eb came back in about two minutes.

"Got a fella right here—Snickers. Got one of them sweet teeth. Says he broke into the Anderson place two years back, doesn't want to talk about it. Says he'll get you in and out if the price is right."

I put my hand over the speaker and asked Flo Zink what she'd pay to have Gus back.

"Name a price," she said.

"Five thousand," I said.

"Hell, I've got that and a hell of a lot more in our safe," she said.

"Five hundred," I told Eb.

Eb left again and a nervous voice came on the phone.

"A cash thousand," Snickers said.

"Deal," I said. "Meet me across the street from Anderson's gate at eleven tonight. Don't be late. Cash comes half when you get there, half when we get out."

"Fair," Snickers said and hung up.

"What about the five thousand?" Flo asked.

"I've been dealing with the world of Snickers for a long time," I said. "He'd smell a big deal if we offered him five. He'd ask for ten. We give him ten and he feels he has to brag to his friends over whatever they put into their bodies. One of his friends tells . . ."

"I get it," she said.

She looked around and went for another drink.

I called the Reverend Fernando Wilkens and spoke to three people before he came on.

"Yes?" he said hopefully.

"If things go right," I said, "I'll have August Zink at that meeting by midnight. Stall."

"Won't be that hard unless the others know the way Zink plans to vote. They want him there too."

"I'll have someone call and say Zink is being held up by a flat tire," I said.

"Bring him, Fonesca."

"I'm pumping as fast as I can," I said.

I had Flo call the mayor, one third of the solid three. The mayor was a woman. She was all business and thought that Democrats were a little lower than University of Florida graduates. The mayor was a proud grad of Florida State University. Only the people in Florida and those who followed college football knew that there was a difference.

"Beatrice?" Flo said, sounding remarkably sober. "This is Flo Zink. Just got a call from Gus. He told me to call you and say he's on his way, but he'll be very late for the meeting. He said to tell you he knows the vote is important and he'll be there if he has to hijack an eighteen-wheeler."

Flo hung up before the mayor could ask any questions.

"Gus did hijack an eighteen-wheeler when he was about twenty-two and we were first married," she said with a smile. "Gus and a friend. That load of camera equipment gave Gus his start toward respectability. 'Course if you ever tell anyone, I'll say you're lyin'."

I crossed my heart.

"You can have the four thousand you saved me," she said.

"If we get your husband out and he makes it to the council meeting to vote, I'll take it," I said.

I stood and we shook hands.

We drove back to my office to wait until eleven. Eb or Wilkens might call and I wanted to be there to get the message. When I had told her I had no liquor where I lived and worked, she nodded and brought her own bottle and glasses. She also got the five thousand out of a safe somewhere deep in the house where I didn't follow and brought it.

Flo didn't seem to notice the stale smell of my office, the clatter of my air conditioner, or the cursing of the kids in the DQ parking lot. She drank and talked. I learned the life history of Gus, Flo, Flo's mother, father, and sister, and what she thought of every president of the United States, starting with Woodrow Wilson with leaps back to Jefferson, Grant, and Teddy Roosevelt.

I watched the clock, and we left a little earlier than we had to. We were across from Nils Anderson's impressive iron gate and high brick wall a little before eleven. I didn't stop. I drove around the neighborhood and came back on the dot, at least according to my watch. There were no other cars on the street of big houses, all of which had driveways and large garages.

Then I heard Eb's motor scooter coming. It was like a call to the curious. When he stopped behind me and turned the bike off, I was sure we had only minutes before we would be surrounded by police.

Eb and a very thin, very small, very nervous black man wearing a pair of dark pants, a black T-shirt, and a battered fedora that would have been the envy of Indiana Jones stopped me before Flo and I could get out of the car.

"Snickers," said Eb.

I shook hands through the window, and Snickers waved to Flo, who reached over and handed him five hundred-dollar bills. He kissed each one, pocketed the quintet, and motioned for us to get out of the car.

"The trunk," he said.

We moved behind the car and I opened the trunk. Since the car was a rental, the trunk was empty.

Snickers pointed at Eb's scooter.

"Inside," he said, standing back and looking both ways down the street, constantly adjusting his battered fedora.

Eb, Flo, and I managed to get the scooter in the trunk. Half of it hung out. Eb had a bungee cord and expertly tied the scooter down.

"Back in the car," Snickers whispered.

We all got back in. From the back seat, leaning over my shoulder, Snickers, who could have used a healthy dose of Scope, guided me slowly to a driveway two estates over from the Anderson place.

"They ain't home," said Snickers. "Go right over the lawn. Lights out. Park near the pool. Don't drive in. Cops won't look. Someone stays with the car. Back in front of Anderson's in fifteen minutes. Eb comes to back me up. Lady comes to tell me which guy we're pulling out."

"I think I . . ." I tried.

"Do it his way, Lew," said Eb.

I nodded, and the bizarre trio got out of the car and disappeared through a clump of bushes behind me. I sat watching the moonlight in the pool and checking my watch. Fifteen minutes took about three days. When the second hand made the call, I was around the house, Eb's scooter bouncing in the trunk, and then back across from Anderson's.

They weren't there. Suddenly the back door of my car opened and I turned around.

"What took you?" asked Snickers, as he and Flo helped August Zink into the car.

"I'm on time," I said.

Zink needed a shave. He also needed some clothes. He was barefoot and wearing pajamas.

Zink sat between Eb and Flo in the back seat. Snickers got in, patted me on the shoulder, and pointed down the street. In my rearview mirror I could see Zink, who muttered, "That bastard."

Flo smiled.

"Bastard kidnapped me," Zink went on. "Couple of Cuban giants stood outside the bedroom door. Wouldn't let me out."

Snickers did three things to reward himself. First, he tipped his fedora back. Second, he held his hand out to Flo, who filled it with five more hundred-dollar bills. Third, he took out a giant-size Snickers bar, peeled back the paper, and began to eat it.

"Mr. Snickers is a genius," said Flo. "Got a ladder from somewhere. Boom, we're inside and no dogs, no guards. Lights on, but Mr. Snickers takes us in back and up some stairs to the roof. Attic door opens slow and quiet."

"What about the Cubans?" I asked.

A very large old six-shooter jutted in front of my face. It was in the hand of Flo Zink.

"They're either considerin' a new career or makin' love in the very small closet where we locked 'em in after Eb tied them up. Best time I've had since we kicked crap out of those kids who tried to hold us up in Manhattan back in '63."

" '62," Zink corrected. "I think I'm gonna have Anderson killed. Hell, I'll kill him myself. What've I got to lose?"

"Hey, I know a guy . . ." Snickers began.

"Forget it," Flo said. "No hits. No runs. No errors. Do what you got to do, Gus, and let's tear ass out of this town. How you feel about dyin' in Texas?"

"I think I prefer Vermont," said Zink. "You can move to Texas when I'm gone."

There was silence as we drove, except for Snickers' happy munching. About a block from the town hall, I stopped. We got the scooter out. It looked all right and started without trouble.

"I can walk to Edwardo's from here," said Snickers, waving and wandering down the street.

"Call me tomorrow, Eb," I said. "Better yet, stop by."

Eb nodded and putted off into the night.

When I got into the hearing room, where almost all the faces in the audience were black, it was nearly midnight. Reverend Wilkens saw me and came to meet me at the back of the hall while a well-dressed young black man addressed the bored council members on the need for a library in Newtown.

"You found him?" whispered Wilkens.

Heads were turned toward us.

"Yes," I said, "but he needs a suit of clothes and a pair of shoes and socks."

Wilkens looked around the audience and waved at a man and woman near the front of the room. The couple came to join us. Now everyone was looking our way.

The discussion was fast. Five minutes later, still in need of a shave but wearing the white shirt and slacks of the man we had just spoken to, August Zink entered the hall with his wife.

The black man in the suit was still seated facing the council, which watched as Zink pulled himself together and marched down the aisle and took his seat at the table.

"Time," said Mayor Beatrice McElveny, looking at her watch.

The speaker rose and returned to his seat. I stood at the rear of the room with Flo Zink. A uniformed officer with arms folded stood next to us.

"It's late," said the mayor with a smile. "We've heard you. We've heard others. We have considered the advice of our planning committee and their consultants, and we think it is time to move into the future on this issue. I call for a vote on the branch library location. Objections?"

Patormi, the old radical, looked for a second as if he were going to speak, but something about the nearly bearded Zink changed his mind.

"In favor of the Newtown site?" the mayor asked.

Patormi and Wilkens' hands went up.

"Opp . . ." she began and stopped in horror as Zink's hand went up.

"Councilman Zink," she said. "Please wait till I finish asking for those opposed."

"I'm voting in favor of the Newtown site," said Zink. "Are you going blind in your old age, Bea?"

The crowd went wild.

The mayor found her gavel and pounded for quiet.

"Quiet, please," Reverend Wilkens said.

Patormi was grinning and shaking his head.

The audience went silent.

"Madame Mayor," said Patormi, "I believe we just passed a motion."

The mayor looked confused.

"The way it works now, you hit the gavel," said the old man gleefully. "And then you say, 'The motion carries.' You've been doing that for almost a year. It shouldn't be that hard."

The mayor tapped the gavel and, her voice breaking, said, "The motion carries."

THERE WAS A CELEBRATION PARTY late into the night at Edwardo's, but the Zinks didn't stay and I did little more than put in an appearance.

When I got back home, I found an envelope in my pocket. It contained four thousand dollars in hundred-dollar bills. I offered Eb half the next day, but he said he hadn't done two thousand dollars work for it. He did, however, accept three hundred.

The Zinks were packed and gone the next day. There was a hotly contested special election to fill Gus's place on the council. One of the biggest voter turnouts in Sarasota history. A Hispanic named Gomez who owned a big auto repair business was elected, and life went on.

Shortly after the election, I got a postcard in the mail. On the front was a photograph of the Alamo. On the back in neat letters was: "We had two good months together in Vermont, and now I'm doing what Gus and I both wanted me to do. Watch your ass."

It had no signature.

Lawrence Block creates characters that stand out no matter how hard they try to blend in. His long-running series detective Matthew Scudder made his latest appearance in *Everybody Dies* while light-fingered thief Bernie Rhodenbarr turned up in *The Burglar in the Library*. Even his short story characters got in on the game, with his philosophical hit man Keller's greatest exploits assembled in the collection *Hit Man*. Of course, no Keller collection would have been complete without a brand new appearance by the pensive assassin. Once again Keller takes on what appears to be a simple assignment, which swiftly grows more complicated by the minute.

# Keller on the Spot
## LAWRENCE BLOCK

Keller, drink in hand, agreed with the woman in the pink dress that it was a lovely evening. He threaded his way through a crowd of young marrieds on what he supposed you would call the patio. A waitress passed carrying a tray of drinks in stemmed glasses and he traded in his own for a fresh one. He sipped as he walked along, wondering what he was drinking. Some sort of vodka sour, he decided, and decided as well that he didn't need to narrow it down any further than that. He figured he'd have this one and one more, but he could have ten more if he wanted, because he wasn't working tonight. He could relax and cut back and have a good time.

Well, almost. He couldn't relax completely, couldn't cut back altogether. Because, while this might not be work, neither was it entirely recreational. The garden party this evening was a heaven-sent opportunity for reconnaissance, and he would use it to get a close look at his quarry. He had been handed a picture in the old man's study back in White Plains, and he had brought that picture with him to Dallas, but even the best photo wasn't the same as a glimpse of the fellow in the flesh, and in his native habitat.

And a lush habitat it was. Keller hadn't been inside the house yet, but it was clearly immense, a sprawling multilevel affair of innumerable large rooms. The grounds sprawled as well, covering an acre or two, with enough plants and shrubbery to stock an arboretum. Keller didn't know anything about flowers, but five minutes in a garden like this one had him thinking he ought to know more about the subject. Maybe they had evening classes at Hunter or NYU, maybe they'd take you on field trips to the Brooklyn Botanical Gardens. Maybe his life would be richer if he knew the names of the flowers, and whether they were annuals or perennials, and whatever else there was to know about them. Their soil requirements, say, and what bug killer to spray on their leaves, or what fertilizer to spread at their roots.

He walked along a brick path, smiling at this stranger, nodding at that one, and wound up standing alongside the swimming pool. Some twelve or fifteen people sat at poolside tables, talking and drinking, the volume of their conversation rising as they drank. In the enormous pool, a young boy swam back and forth, back and forth.

Keller felt a curious kinship with the kid. He was standing instead of swimming, but he felt as distant as the kid from everybody else around. There were two parties going on, he decided. There was the hearty social whirl of everybody else, and there was the solitude he felt in the midst of it all, identical to the solitude of the swimming boy.

Huge pool. The boy was swimming its width, but that dimension was still greater than the length of your typical backyard pool. Keller didn't know whether this was an Olympic pool, he wasn't quite sure how big that would have to be, but he figured you could just call it enormous and let it go at that.

Ages ago he'd heard about some college-boy stunt, filling a swimming pool with Jell-O, and he'd wondered how many little boxes of the gelatin dessert it would have required, and how the college boys could have afforded it. It would cost a fortune, he decided, to fill *this* pool with Jell-O—but if you could afford the pool in the first place, he supposed the Jell-O would be the least of your worries.

There were cut flowers on all the tables, and the blooms looked like ones Keller had seen in the garden. It stood to reason. If you grew all these flowers, you wouldn't have to order from the florist. You could cut your own.

What good would it do, he wondered, to know the names of all the shrubs and flowers? Wouldn't it just leave you wanting to dig in the soil and grow your own? And he didn't want to get into all that, for God's sake. His apartment was all he needed or wanted, and it was no place for a garden. He hadn't even tried growing an avocado pit there, and he didn't intend to. He was the only living thing in the apartment, and that was the way he wanted to keep it. The day that changed was the day he'd call the exterminator.

So maybe he'd just forget about evening classes at Hunter, and field trips to Brooklyn. If he wanted to get close to nature he could walk in Central Park, and if he didn't know the names of the flowers he would just hold off on introducing himself to them. And if—

Where was the kid?

The boy, the swimmer. Keller's companion in solitude. Where the hell did he go?

The pool was empty, its surface still. Keller saw a ripple toward the far end, saw a brace of bubbles break the surface.

He didn't react without thinking. That was how he'd always heard that sort of thing described, but that wasn't what happened, because the thoughts were there, loud and clear. *He's down there. He's in trouble. He's drowning.* And, echoing in his head in a voice that might have been Dot's, sour with exasperation: *Keller, for Christ's sake, do something!*

He set his glass on a table, shucked his coat, kicked off his shoes, dropped his pants and stepped out of them. Ages ago he'd earned a Red Cross lifesaving certificate, and the first thing they taught you was to strip before you hit the water. The six or seven seconds you spent peeling off your clothes would be repaid many times over in quickness and mobility.

But the strip show did not go unnoticed. Everybody at poolside had a comment, one more hilarious than the next. He barely heard them. In no time at all he was down to his underwear, and then he was out of range of their cleverness, hitting the water's surface in a flat racing dive, churning the water till he reached the spot where he'd seen the bubbles, then diving, eyes wide, barely noticing the burn of the chlorine.

Searching for the boy. Groping, searching, then finding him, reaching to grab hold of him. And pushing off against the bottom, lungs bursting, racing to reach the surface.

PEOPLE WERE SAYING THINGS TO Keller, thanking him, congratulating him, but it wasn't really registering. A man clapped him on the back, a woman handed him a glass of brandy. He heard the word "hero" and realized that people were saying it all over the place, and applying it to him.

Hell of a note.

Keller sipped the brandy. It gave him heartburn, which assured him of its quality; good cognac always gave him heartburn. He turned to look at the boy. He was just a little fellow, twelve or thirteen years old, his hair lightened and his skin lightly bronzed by the summer sun. He was sitting up now, Keller saw, and looking none the worse for his near-death experience.

"Timothy," a woman said, "this is the man who saved your life. Do you have something to say to him?"

"Thanks," Timothy said, predictably.

"Is that all you have to say, young man?"

"It's enough," Keller said, and smiled. To the boy he said, "There's something I've always wondered. Did your whole life actually flash before your eyes?"

Timothy shook his head. "I got this cramp," he said, "and it was like my whole body turned into one big knot, and there wasn't anything I could do to untie it. And I didn't even think about drowning. I was just fighting the cramp, 'cause it hurt, and just about the next thing I knew I was up here coughing and puking up water." He made a face. "I must have swallowed half the pool. All I have to do is think about it and I can taste vomit and chlorine."

"Timothy," the woman said, and rolled her eyes.

"Something to be said for plain speech," an older man said. He had a mane of white hair and a pair of prominent white eyebrows, and his eyes were a vivid blue. He was holding a glass of brandy in one hand and a bottle in the other, and he reached with the bottle to fill Keller's glass to the brim. " 'Claret for boys, port for men,' " he said, " 'but he who would be a hero must drink brandy.' That's Samuel Johnson, although I may have gotten a word wrong."

The young woman patted his hand. "If you did, Daddy, I'm sure you just improved Mr. Johnson's wording."

"Dr. Johnson," he said, "and one could hardly do that. Improve the man's wording, that is. 'Being in a ship is being in a jail, with the chance of being drowned.' He said that as well, and I defy anyone to comment more trenchantly on the experience, or to say it better." He beamed at Keller. "I owe you more than a glass of brandy and a well-turned Johnsonian phrase. This little rascal whose life you've saved is my grandson, and the apple—nay, sir, the very nectarine—of my eye. And we'd have all stood around drinking and laughing while he drowned. You observed, and you acted, and God bless you for it."

What did you say to that? Keller wondered. *It was nothing? Well, shucks?* There had to be an apt phrase, and maybe Samuel Johnson could have found it, but he couldn't. So he said nothing, and just tried not to look po-faced.

"I don't even know your name," the white-haired man went on. "That's not remarkable in and of itself. I don't know half the people here, and I'm content to remain in my ignorance. But I ought to know your name, wouldn't you agree?"

Keller might have picked a name out of the air, but the one that leaped to mind was Boswell, and he couldn't say that to a man who quoted Samuel Johnson. So he supplied the name he'd traveled under, the one he'd signed when he checked into the hotel, the one on the driver's license and credit cards in his wallet.

"It's Michael Soderholm," he said, "and I can't even tell you the name of the fellow who brought me here. We met over drinks in the hotel bar and he said he was going to a party and it would be perfectly all right if I came along. I felt a little funny about it, but—"

"Please," the man said. "You can't possibly propose to apologize for your presence here. It's kept my grandson from a watery if chlorinated grave. And I've just told you I don't know half my guests, but that doesn't make them any the less welcome." He took a deep drink of his brandy and topped up both glasses. "Michael Soderholm," he said. "Swedish?"

"A mixture of everything," Keller said, improvising. "My great-grandfather Soderholm came over from Sweden, but my other ancestors came from all over Europe, plus I'm something like a sixteenth American Indian."

"Oh? Which tribe?"

"Cherokee," Keller said, thinking of the jazz tune.

"I'm an eighth Comanche," the man said. "So I'm afraid we're not tribal bloodbrothers. The rest's British Isles, a mix of Scots and Irish and English. Old Texas stock. But you're not Texan yourself."

"No."

"Well, it can't be helped, as the saying goes. Unless you decide to move here, and who's to say that you won't? It's a fine place for a man to live."

"Daddy thinks everybody should love Texas the way he does," the woman said.

"Everybody should," her father said. "The only thing wrong with Texans is we're a long-winded lot. Look at the time it's taking me to introduce myself! Mr. Soderholm, Mr. Michael Soderholm, my name's Garrity. Wallace Penrose Garrity, and I'm your grateful host this evening."

No kidding, thought Keller.

THE PARTY, LIFESAVING AND ALL, took place on Saturday night. The next day Keller sat in his hotel room and watched the Cowboys beat the Vikings with a field goal in the last three minutes of double overtime. The game had see-sawed back and forth, with interceptions and runbacks, and the announcers kept telling each other what a great game it was.

Keller supposed they were right. It had all the ingredients, and it wasn't the players' fault that he himself was entirely unmoved by their performance. He could watch sports, and often did, but he almost never got caught up in it. He had occasionally wondered if his work might have something to do with it. On one level, when your job involved dealing regularly with life and death, how could you care if some overpaid steroid abuser had a touchdown run called back? And, on another level, you saw unorthodox solutions to a team's problems on the field. When Emmitt Smith kept crashing through the Minnesota line, Keller found himself wondering why they didn't deputize someone to shoot the son of a bitch in the back of the neck, right below his star-covered helmet.

Still, it was better than watching golf, say, which in turn had to be better than playing golf. And he couldn't get out and work, because there was nothing for him to do. Last night's reconnaissance mission had been both better and worse than he could have hoped, and what was he supposed to do now, park his rented Ford across the street from the Garrity mansion and clock the comings and goings?

No need for that. He could bide his time, just so he got there in time for Sunday dinner.

\*     \*     \*

"SOME MORE POTATOES, MR. SODERHOLM?"

"They're delicious," Keller said. "But I'm full. Really."

"And we can't keep calling you Mr. Soderholm," Garrity said. "I've only held off this long for not knowing whether you prefer Mike or Michael."

"Mike's fine," Keller said.

"Then Mike it is. And I'm Wally, Mike, or W. P., though there are those who call me 'The Walrus.' "

Timmy laughed, and clapped both hands over his mouth.

"Though never to his face," said the woman who'd offered Keller more potatoes. She was Ellen Garrity, Timmy's aunt and Garrity's daughter-in-law, and Keller was now instructed to call her Ellie. Her husband, a big-shouldered fellow who seemed to be smiling bravely through the heartbreak of male-pattern baldness, was Garrity's son Hank.

Keller remembered Timothy's mother from the night before, but hadn't got her name at the time, or her relationship to Garrity. She was Rhonda Sue Butler, as it turned out, and everybody called her Rhonda Sue, except for her husband, who called her Ronnie. His name was Doak Butler, and he looked like a college jock who'd been too light for pro ball, although he now seemed to be closing the gap.

Hank and Ellie, Doak and Rhonda Sue. And, at the far end of the table, Vanessa, who was married to Wally but who was clearly not the mother of Hank or Rhonda Sue, or anyone else. Keller supposed you could describe her as Wally's trophy wife, a sign of his success. She was young, no older than Wally's kids, and she looked to be well bred and elegant, and she even had the good grace to hide the boredom Keller was sure she felt.

And that was the lot of them. Wally and Vanessa, Hank and Ellen, Doak and Rhonda Sue. And Timothy, who he was assured had been swimming that very afternoon, the aquatic equivalent of getting right back on the horse. He'd had no cramps this time, but he'd had an attentive eye kept on him through-out.

Seven of them, then. And Keller . . . also known as Mike.

"SO YOU'RE HERE ON BUSINESS," Wally said. "And stuck here over the week-end, which is the worst part of a business trip, as far as I'm concerned. More trouble than it's worth to fly back to Chicago?"

The two of them were in Wally's den, a fine room paneled in knotty pecan and trimmed out in red leather, with western doodads on the walls—here a branding iron, there a longhorn skull. Keller had accepted a brandy and de-clined a cigar, and the aroma of Wally's Havana was giving him second thoughts. Keller didn't smoke, but from the smell of it the cigar wasn't a mere matter of smoking. It was more along the lines of a religious experience.

"Seemed that way," Keller said. He'd supplied Chicago as Michael Soder-holm's home base, though Soderholm's license placed him in Southern California. "By the time I fly there and back . . ."

"You've spent your weekend on airplanes. Well, it's our good fortune you decided to stay. Now what I'd like to do is find a way to make it your good fortune as well."

"You've already done that," Keller told him. "I crashed a great party last night and actually got to feel like a hero for a few minutes. And tonight I sit down to a fine dinner with nice people and get to top it off with a glass of outstanding brandy."

The heartburn told him how outstanding it was.

"What I had in mind," Wally said smoothly, "was to get you to work for me."

Whom did he want him to kill? Keller almost blurted out the question until he remembered that Garrity didn't know what he did for a living.

"You won't say who you work for," Garrity went on.

"I can't."

"Because the job's hush-hush for now. Well, I can respect that, and from the hints you've dropped I gather you're here scouting out something in the way of mergers and acquisitions."

"That's close."

"And I'm sure it's well paid, and you must like the work or I don't think you'd stay with it. So what do I have to do to get you to switch horses and come work for me? I'll tell you one thing—Chicago's a real nice place, but nobody who ever moved from there to Big D went around with a sour face about it. I don't know you well yet, but I can tell you're our kind of people and Dallas'll be your kind of town. And I don't know what they're paying you, but I suspect I can top it, and offer you a stake in a growing company with all sorts of attractive possibilities."

Keller listened, nodded judiciously, sipped a little brandy. It was amazing, he thought, the way things came along when you weren't looking for them. It was straight out of Horatio Alger, for God's sake—Ragged Dick stops the runaway horse and saves the daughter of the captain of industry, and the next thing you know he's president of IBM with rising expectations.

"Maybe I'll have that cigar after all," he said.


"Now, come on, Keller," Dot said. "You know the rules. I can't tell you that."

"It's sort of important," he said.

"One of the things the client buys," she said, "is confidentiality. That's what he wants and it's what we provide. Even if the agent in place—"

"The agent in place?"

"That's you," she said. "You're the agent, and Dallas is the place. Even if you get caught red-handed, the confidentiality of the client remains uncompromised. And do you know why?"

"Because the agent in place knows how to keep mum."

"Mum's the word," she agreed, "and there's no question you're the strong silent type, but even if your lip loosens you can't sink a ship if you don't know when it's sailing."

Keller thought that over. "You lost me," he said.

"Yeah, it came out a little abstruse, didn't it? Point is you can't tell what you don't know, Keller, which is why the agent doesn't get to know the client's name."

"Dot," he said, trying to sound injured. "Dot, how long have you known me?"

"Ages, Keller. Many lifetimes."

"Many lifetimes?"

"We were in Atlantis together. Look, I know nobody's going to catch you red-handed, and I know you wouldn't blab if they did. But *I* can't tell what *I* don't know."

"Oh."

"Right. I think the spies call it a double cutout. The client made arrangements with somebody we know, and that person called us. But he didn't give us the client's name, and why should he? And, come to think of it, Keller, why do you have to know, anyway?"

He had his answer ready. "It might not be a single," he said.

"Oh?"

"The target's always got people around him," he said, "and the best way to do it might be a sort of group plan, if you follow me."

"Two for the price of one."

"Or three or four," he said. "But if one of those innocent bystanders turned out to be the client, it might make things a little awkward."

"Well, I can see where we might have trouble collecting the final payment."

"If we knew for a fact that the client was fishing for trout in Montana," he said, "it's no problem. But if he's here in Dallas—"

"It would help to know his name." She sighed. "Give me an hour or two, huh? Then call me back."

IF HE KNEW WHO THE client was, the client could have an accident.

It would have to be an artful accident too. It would have to look good not only to the police but to whoever was aware of the client's own intentions. The local go-between, the helpful fellow who'd hooked up the client to the old man in White Plains, and thus to Keller, could be expected to cast a cold eye on any suspicious death. So it would have to be a damn good accident, but Keller had managed a few of those in his day. It took a little planning, but it wasn't brain surgery. You just figured out a method and took your best shot.

It might take some doing. If, as he rather hoped, the client was some business rival in Houston or Denver or San Diego, he'd have to slip off to that city without anyone noting his absence. Then, having induced a quick attack of accidental death, he'd fly back to Dallas and hang around until someone called him off the case. He'd need different ID for Houston or Denver or San Diego—it wouldn't do to overexpose Michael Soderholm—and he'd need to mask his actions from all concerned—Garrity, his homicidal rival, and, perhaps most important, Dot and the old man.

All told, it was a great deal more complicated (if easier to stomach) than the alternative.

Which was to carry out the assignment professionally and kill Wallace Penrose Garrity the first good chance he got.

And he really didn't want to do that. He'd eaten at the man's table, he'd drunk the man's brandy, he'd smoked the man's cigars. He'd been offered not merely a job but a well-paid executive position with a future, and, later that night, light-headed from alcohol and nicotine, he'd had fantasies of taking Wally up on it.

Hell, why not? He could live out his days as Michael Soderholm, doing whatever unspecified tasks Garrity was hiring him to perform. He probably lacked the requisite experience, but how hard could it be to pick up the skills he needed as he went along? Whatever he had to do, it would be easier than flying from town to town killing people. He could learn on the job. He could pull it off.

The fantasy had about as much substance as a dream, and, like a dream, it was gone when he awoke the next morning. No one would put him on the payroll without some sort of background check, and the most cursory scan would knock him out of the box. Michael Soderholm had no more substance than the fake ID in his wallet.

Even if he somehow finessed a background check, even if the old man in White Plains let him walk out of one life and into another, he knew he couldn't really make it work. He already had a life. Misshapen though it was, it fit him like a glove.

Other lives made tempting fantasies. Running a print shop in Roseburg, Oregon, living in a cute little house with a mansard roof—it was something to tease yourself with while you went on being the person you had no choice but to be. This latest fantasy was just more of the same.

He went out for a sandwich and a cup of coffee. He got back in his car and drove around for a while. Then he found a pay phone and called White Plains.

"Do a single," Dot said.

"How's that?"

"No added extras, no free dividends. Just do what they signed on for."

"Because the client's here in town," he said. "Well, I could work around that if I knew his name. I could make sure he was out of it."

"Forget it," Dot said. "The client wants a long and happy life for everybody but the designated vic. Maybe the DV's close associates are near and dear to the client. That's just a guess, but all that really matters is that nobody else gets hurt. Capeesh?"

" 'Capeesh?' "

"It's Italian, it means—"

"I know what it means. It just sounded odd from your lips, that's all. But yes, I understand." He took a breath. "Whole thing may take a little time," he said.

"Then here comes the good news," she said. "Time's not of the essence. They don't care how long it takes, just so you get it right."

"I UNDERSTAND W. P. OFFERED YOU a job," Vanessa said. "I know he hopes you'll take him up on it."

"I think he was just being generous," Keller told her. "I was in the right place at the right time, and he'd like to do me a favor, but I don't think he really expects me to come to work for him."

"He'd like it if you did," she said, "or he never would have made the offer. He'd have just given you money, or a car, or something like that. And as far as what he expects, well, W. P. generally expects to get whatever he wants. Because that's the way things usually work out."

And had she been saving up her pennies to get things to work out a little differently? You had to wonder. Was she truly under Garrity's spell, in awe of his power, as she seemed to be? Or was she only in it for the money, and was there a sharp edge of irony under her worshipful remarks?

Hard to say. Hard to tell about any of them. Was Hank the loyal son he appeared to be, content to live in the old man's shadow and take what got tossed his way? Or was he secretly resentful and ambitious?

What about the son-in-law, Doak? On the surface, he looked to be delighted with the aftermath of his college football career—his work for his father-in-law consisted largely of playing golf with business associates and drinking with them afterward. But did he seethe inside, sure he was fit for greater things?

How about Hank's wife, Ellie? She struck Keller as an unlikely Lady Macbeth. Keller could fabricate scenarios in which she or Rhonda Sue had a reason for wanting Wally dead, but they were the sort of thing you dreamed up while watching reruns of *Dallas* and trying to guess who shot J. R. Maybe one of their marriages was in trouble. Maybe Garrity had put the moves on his daughter-in-law, or maybe a little too much brandy had led him into his daughter's bedroom now and then. Maybe Doak or Hank was playing footsie with Vanessa. Maybe . . .

Pointless to speculate, he decided. You could go around and around like that and it didn't get you anywhere. Even if he managed to dope out which of them was the client, then what? Having saved young Timothy, and thus feeling obligated to spare his doting grandfather, what was he going to do? Kill the boy's father? Or mother or aunt or uncle?

Of course he could just go home. He could even explain the situation to the old man. Nobody loved it when you took yourself off a contract for personal reasons, but it wasn't something they could talk you out of, either. If you made a habit of that sort of thing, well, that was different, but that wasn't the case with Keller. He was a solid pro. Quirky perhaps, even whimsical, but a pro all the way. You told him what to do and he did it.

So, if he had a personal reason to bow out, you honored it. You let him come home and sit on the porch and drink iced tea with Dot.

And you picked up the phone and sent somebody else to Dallas.

Because either way the job was going to be done. If a hit man had a change of heart, it would be followed in short order by a change of hit man. If Keller didn't pull the trigger, somebody else would.

His mistake, Keller thought savagely, was to jump in the goddam pool in the first place. All he'd had to do was look the other way and let the little bastard drown. A few days later he could have taken Garrity out, possibly making it look like suicide, a natural consequence of despondency over the boy's tragic accident.

But no, he thought, glaring at himself in the mirror. No, you had to go and get involved. You had to be a hero, for God's sake. Had to strip down to your skivvies and prove you deserved that junior lifesaving certificate the Red Cross gave you all those years ago.

He wondered whatever happened to that certificate.

It was gone, of course, like everything he'd ever owned in his childhood and youth. Gone like his high school diploma, like his Boy Scout merit badge sash, like his stamp collection and his sack of marbles and his stack of baseball cards. He didn't mind that these things were gone, didn't waste time wishing he had them any more than he wanted those years back.

But he wondered what physically became of them. The lifesaving certificate, for instance. Someone might have thrown out his baseball cards, or sold his stamp collection to a dealer. A certificate, though, wasn't something you threw out, nor was it something anyone else would want.

Maybe it was buried in a landfill, or in a stack of paper ephemera in the back of some thrift shop. Maybe some pack rat had rescued it, and maybe it was now part of an extensive collection of junior lifesaving certificates, housed in an album and cherished as living history, the pride and joy of a collector ten times as quirky and whimsical as Keller could ever dream of being.

He wondered how he felt about that. His certificate, his small achievement, living on in some eccentric's collection. On the one hand, it was a kind of immortality, wasn't it? On the other hand, well, whose certificate was it, anyway? He'd been the one to earn it, breaking the instructor's choke hold, spinning him and grabbing him in a cross-chest carry, towing the big lug to the side of the pool. It was his accomplishment and it had his name on it, so didn't it belong on his own wall or nowhere?

All in all, he couldn't say he felt strongly either way. The certificate, when all was said and done, was only a piece of paper. What was important was the skill itself, and what was truly remarkable was that he'd retained it.

Because of it, Timothy Butler was alive and well. Which was all well and good for the boy, and a great big headache for Keller.

LATER, SITTING WITH A CUP of coffee, Keller thought some more about Wallace Penrose Garrity, a man who increasingly seemed to have not an enemy in the world.

Suppose Keller had let the kid drown. Suppose he just plain hadn't noticed the boy's disappearance beneath the water, just as everyone else had failed to notice it. Garrity would have been despondent. It was his party, his pool, his failure to provide supervision. He'd probably have blamed himself for the boy's death.

When Keller took him out, it would have been the kindest thing he could have done for him.

He caught the waiter's eye and signaled for more coffee. He'd just given himself something to think about.

"MIKE," GARRITY SAID, COMING TOWARD him with a hand outstretched. "Sorry to keep you waiting. Had a phone call from a fellow with a hankering to buy a little five-acre lot of mine on the south edge of town. Thing is, I don't want to sell it to him."

"I see."

"But there's ten acres on the other side of town I'd be perfectly happy to sell to him, but he'll only want it if he thinks of it himself. So that left me on the phone longer than I would have liked. Now what would you say to a glass of brandy?"

"Maybe a small one."

Garrity led the way to the den, poured drinks for both of them. "You should have come earlier," he said. "In time for dinner. I hope you know you don't need an invitation. There'll always be a place for you at our table."

"Well," Keller said.

"I know you can't talk about it," Garrity said, "but I hope your project here in town is shaping up nicely."

"Slow but sure," Keller said.

"Some things can't be hurried," Garrity allowed, and sipped brandy, and winced. If Keller hadn't been looking for it, he might have missed the shadow that crossed his host's face.

Gently he said, "Is the pain bad, Wally?"

"How's that, Mike?"

Keller put his glass on the table. "I spoke to Dr. Jacklin," he said. "I know what you're going through."

"That son of a bitch," Garrity said, "was supposed to keep his mouth shut."

"Well, he thought it was all right to talk to me," Keller said. "He thought I was Dr. Edward Fishman from the Mayo Clinic."

"Calling for a consultation."

"Something like that."

"I did go to Mayo," Garrity said, "but they didn't need to call Harold Jacklin to double-check their results. They just confirmed his diagnosis and told me not to buy any long-playing records." He looked to one side. "They said they couldn't say for sure how much time I had left, but that the pain would be manageable for a while. And then it wouldn't."

"I see."

"And I'd have all my faculties for a while," he said. "And then I wouldn't."

Keller didn't say anything.

"Well, hell," Garrity said. "A man wants to take the bull by the horns, doesn't he? I decided I'd go out for a walk with a shotgun and have a little hunting accident. Or I'd be cleaning a handgun here at my desk and have it go off. But it turned out I just couldn't tolerate the idea of killing myself. Don't know why, can't explain it, but that seems to be the way I'm made."

He picked up his glass and looked at the brandy. "Funny how we hang on to life," he said. "Something else Sam Johnson said, said there wasn't a week of his life he'd voluntarily live through again. I've had more good times than bad, Mike, and even the bad times haven't been that godawful, but I think I know what he was getting at. I wouldn't want to repeat any of it, but that doesn't mean there's a minute of it I'd have been willing to miss. I don't want to miss whatever's coming next, either, and I don't guess Dr. Johnson did either. That's what keeps us going, isn't it? Wanting to find out what's around the next bend in the river."

"I guess so."

"I thought that would make the end easier to face," he said. "Not knowing when it was coming, or how or where. And I recalled that years ago a fellow told me to let him know if I ever needed to have somebody killed. 'You just let me know,' he said, and I laughed, and that was the last said on the subject. A month or so ago I looked up his number and called him, and he gave me another number to call."

"And you put out a contract."

"Is that the expression? Then that's what I did."

"Suicide by proxy," Keller said.

"And I guess you're holding my proxy," Garrity said, and drank some brandy. "You know, the thought flashed across my mind that first night, talking with you after you pulled my grandson out of the pool. I got this little glimmer, but I told myself I was being ridiculous. A hired killer doesn't turn up and save somebody's life."

"It's out of character," Keller agreed.

"Besides, what would you be doing at the party in the first place? Wouldn't you stay out of sight and wait until you could get me alone?"

"If I'd been thinking straight," Keller said. "I told myself it wouldn't hurt to have a look around. And this joker from the hotel bar assured me I had nothing to worry about. 'Half the town'll be at Wally's tonight,' he said."

"Half the town was. You wouldn't have tried anything that night, would you?"

"God, no."

"I remember thinking, I hope he's not here. I hope it's not tonight. Because I was enjoying the party and I didn't want to miss anything. But you *were* there, and a good thing, wasn't it?"

"Yes."

"Saved the boy from drowning. According to the Chinese, you save somebody's life, you're responsible for him for the rest of *your* life. Because you've interfered with the natural order of things. That make sense to you?"

"Not really."

"Or me either. You can't beat them for whipping up a meal or laundering a shirt, but they've got some queer ideas on other subjects. Of course they'd probably say the same for some of my notions."

"Probably."

Garrity looked at his glass. "You called my doctor," he said. "Must have been to confirm a suspicion you already had. What tipped you off? Is it starting to show in my face, or the way I move around?"

Keller shook his head. "I couldn't find anybody else with a motive," he said, "or a grudge against you. You were the only one left. And then I remembered seeing you wince once or twice, and try to hide it. I barely noticed it at the time, but then I started to think about it."

"I thought it would be easier than doing it myself," Garrity said. "I thought I'd just let a professional take me by surprise. I'd be like an old bull elk on a hillside, never expecting the bullet that takes him out in his prime."

"It makes sense."

"No, it doesn't. Because the elk didn't arrange for the hunter to be there. Far as the elk knows, he's all alone there. He's not wondering every damn day if today's the day. He's not bracing himself, trying to sense the crosshairs centering on his shoulder."

"I never thought of that."

"Neither did I," said Garrity. "Or I never would have called that fellow in the first place. Mike, what the hell are you doing here tonight? Don't tell me you came over to kill me."

"I came to tell you I can't."

"Because we've come to know each other."

Keller nodded.

"I grew up on a farm," Garrity said. "One of those vanishing family farms you hear about, and of course it's vanished, and I say good riddance. But we raised our own beef and pork, you know, and we kept a milk cow and a flock of laying hens. And we never named the animals we were going to wind up eating. The milk cow had a name, but not the bull calf she dropped. The breeder sow's name was Elsie, but we never named her piglets."

"Makes sense," Keller said.

"I guess it doesn't take a Chinaman to see how you can't kill me once you've hauled Timmy out of the drink. Let alone after you've sat at my table and smoked my cigars. Reminds me, you care for a cigar?"

"No, thank you."

"Well, where do we go from here, Mike? I have to say I'm relieved. I feel like I've been bracing myself for a bullet for weeks now. All of a sudden I've got a new lease on life. I'd say this calls for a drink except we're already having one, and you've scarcely touched yours."

"There is one thing," Keller said.

HE LEFT THE DEN WHILE Garrity made his phone call. Timothy was in the living room, puzzling over a chessboard. Keller played a game with him and lost badly. "Can't win 'em all," he said, and tipped over his king.

"I was going to checkmate you," the boy said. "In a few more moves."

"I could see it coming," Keller told him.

He went back to the den. Garrity was selecting a cigar from his humidor. "Sit down," he said. "I'm fixing to smoke one of these things. If you won't kill me, maybe it will."

"You never know."

"I made the call, Mike, and it's all taken care of. Be a while before the word filters up and down the chain of command, but sooner or later they'll call you up and tell you the client changed his mind. He paid in full and called off the job."

They talked some, then sat a while in silence. At length Keller said he ought to get going. "I should be at my hotel," he said, "in case they call."

"Be a couple of days, won't it?"

"Probably," he said, "but you never know. If everyone involved makes a phone call right away, the word could get to me in a couple of hours."

"Calling you off, telling you to come home. Be glad to get home, I bet."

"It's nice here," he said, "but yes, I'll be glad to get home."

"Wherever it is, they say there's no place like it." Garrity leaned back, then allowed himself to wince at the pain that came over him. "If it never hurts worse than this," he said, "then I can stand it. But of course it will get worse. And I'll decide I can stand *that*, and then it'll get worse again."

There was nothing to say to that.

"I guess I'll know when it's time to do something," Garrity said. "And who knows? Maybe my heart'll cut out on me out of the blue. Or I'll get hit by a bus, or I don't know what. Struck by lightning?"

"It could happen."

"Anything can happen," Garrity agreed. He got to his feet. "Mike," he said, "I guess we won't be seeing any more of each other, and I have to say I'm a little bit sorry about that. I've truly enjoyed our time together."

"So have I, Wally."

"I wondered, you know, what he'd be like. The man they'd send to do this kind of work. I don't know what I expected, but you're not it."

He stuck out his hand, and Keller gripped it. "Take care," Garrity said. "Be well, Mike."

BACK AT HIS HOTEL, KELLER took a hot bath and got a good night's sleep. In the morning he went out for breakfast, and when he got back there was a message at the desk for him: *Mr. Soderholm—please call your office.*

He called from a pay phone, even though it didn't matter, and he was careful not to overreact when Dot told him to come home, the mission was aborted.

"You told me I had all the time in the world," he said. "If I'd known the guy was in such a rush—"

"Keller," she said, "it's a good thing you waited. What he did, he changed his mind."

"He changed his mind?"

"It used to be a woman's prerogative," Dot said, "but now we've got equality between the sexes, so that means anyone can do it. It works out fine because we're getting paid in full. So kick the dust of Texas off your feet and come on home."

"I'll do that," he said, "but I may hang out here for a few more days."

"Oh?"

"Or even a week," he said. "It's a pretty nice town."

"Don't tell me you're itching to move there, Keller. We've been through this before."

"Nothing like that," he said, "but there's this girl I met."

"Oh, Keller."

"Well, she's nice," he said. "And if I'm off the job there's no reason not to have a date or two with her, is there?"

"As long as you don't decide to move in."

"She's not that nice," he said, and Dot laughed and told him not to change.

He hung up and drove around and found a movie he'd been meaning to see. The next morning he packed and checked out of his hotel.

He drove across town and got a room on the motel strip, paying cash for four nights in advance and registering as J. D. Smith from Los Angeles.

There was no girl he'd met, no girl he wanted to meet. But it wasn't time to go home yet.

He had unfinished business, and four days should give him time to do it. Time for Wallace Garrity to get used to the idea of not feeling those imaginary crosshairs on his shoulder blades.

But not so much time that the pain would be too much to bear.

And, sometime in those four days, Keller would give him a gift. If he could, he'd make it look natural—a heart attack, say, or an accident. In any event it would be swift and without warning, and as close as he could make it to painless.

And it would be unexpected. Garrity would never see it coming.

Keller frowned, trying to figure out how he would manage it. It would be a lot trickier than the task that had drawn him to town originally, but he'd brought it on himself. Getting involved, fishing the boy out of the pool. He'd interfered with the natural order of things. He was under an obligation.

It was the least he could do.

D. A. McGuire is a regular contributor to leading mystery magazines such as *Alfred Hitchcock's Mystery Magazine*. With her usual attention to detail and setting, she takes us to "The House on the Edge," which leads two boys into the middle of a fifty-year-old mystery.

# The House on the Edge
## D. A. MCGUIRE

I didn't discover the bodies, which is something I'd like to point out. Everyone wants to leap to conclusions and assume that I, Herbie Sawyer, thirteen-year-old kid from Manamesset, Cape Cod, found them. Truth is, I was working on a school newspaper assignment with my friend when *he* found the bodies. But that didn't change a thing in most people's minds; all they knew was that "Herbie Sawyer's done it again."

Which continues to make me look like I have this strange affliction—that no matter where I go or what I do I practically stumble over dead people. That's not true at all. I've figured it out: I'm just the unlucky victim of circumstances. I mean, I wasn't even *there* when Remmy realized what they were. Of course that didn't make a bit of difference to his parents; they still blamed *me*, as if I'd buried them myself, for crying out loud.

In fact, Remmy's parents were giving me a bad name just two days before the bodies were discovered. . . .

"Bad influence?" I shouted at him. "What do you mean your parents say I'm a bad influence?"

We were out on Quinicut Point, a slim finger of land that juts into East Manamesset Bay at its northernmost edge. Quinicut once tried to incorporate itself as a town back in the late 1600's, but for some reason—probably political—it got "absorbed" into the larger town of Manamesset instead. Today it's known as the "Quinicut section" of town, a little point of land dotted with wetlands, cranberry bogs, and grown-over farmland. There are just a few paved roads in Quinicut, and the one going out to the end of the point

340

is a dusty dirt road. Tourist guidebooks and those pamphlets that the bed and breakfast industry puts out describe Quinicut as "one of the few truly unspoiled areas of Cape Cod left today." But personally I don't think it's very pretty at all. The only trees to speak of are junipers, scrub oaks, and pitch pines; the beaches are either rocky or covered by great stretches of mud flats; and the only reason the population is less than five hundred (in summer it swells to five fifty) is that nobody really wants to vacation in Quinicut, let alone live there.

So why were we riding out that way, Remmy with a backpack, me with a beatup Konica on a strap around my neck? Because we were on assignment for our school newspaper, going out near the tip of Quinicut to interview an old woman for our first feature article in the Manamesset *Mariner*.

Not an entirely original name, *Mariner*, but I missed the first meeting of the Newspaper Club and didn't get to vote. I heard later some kids had wanted to go with the Manamesset *Mohawk*, but our advisor got real nervous, imagining all us newspaper nerds running around with weird punk haircuts, so she nixed the name.

"It's a lame name," I'd been bold enough to say at our next meeting. "Every club or school on the Cape has a newspaper called the *Mariner*."

That's when the advisor (who was also my science teacher, Mrs. Thalassa Filiades) fixed me in her icy stare and said, "Herbert Sawyer, Jr., I can't believe you said that."

That was Mrs. Filiades' reaction to most things I said that she didn't like. It had been her idea that we interview Mrs. Louisa Valentina, an elderly woman who lived in a strange old house perched on the edge of a bluff out on Quinicut Point. According to Mrs. Filiades, Mrs. Valentina was a nice old woman, an antiques collector and a local history buff who just happened to live in a house that was in danger of pitching right over into the sea from the top of a forty-foot bluff. Despite repeated warnings from community officials that her property was a hazard and ought to be condemned, Mrs. Valentina steadfastly refused to move. I guess she was what people politely call an eccentric.

So Mrs. Filiades arranged for us to interview Mrs. Valentina. She felt it would make a good "human interest" story, plus she probably wanted to get Remmy and me off her back. I don't think Mrs. Filiades liked either one of us very much. 'Course it didn't help that Remmy immediately stuck up his nose at the assignment:

"Interview some old lady?" he snorted. "What are we going to ask her? What kind of walker she uses? How many naps she takes a day? If she uses wetness protection?"

Now I might have said the name Manamesset *Mariner* was lame, which it was, but I'm generally not a rude or disrespectful kid. It's just the way I've been raised; besides that, I have a few close friends who are up there in age, so when Remmy made those remarks, I backed off, stared at the ceiling, and waited for Mrs. Filiades to lay into him.

"Remington Rogers III!" she shouted. "I can't believe you said that! Don't you have a grandmother living with you? What would your parents say if they heard you make such disrespectful comments? If you have no interest in serving on this newspaper and completing the assignments that you and the staff have agreed on, you can tell me so right now."

"Sorry," Remmy muttered, his face turning bright red.

Apparently he looked contrite enough for her because she gave a kind of huffy sound, calmed herself down somewhat, and accepted his apology. Then she told Remmy and me what little she knew about Mrs. Valentina, the whole time giving Remmy dirty looks.

"You've got no common sense," I told Remmy later as we got our bikes, slung our gear around our necks, and started out of the parking lot. "You've got to *humor* Mrs. Filiades, go along with her. Don't you know *anything* yet? That's what you've got to do with *all* adults. God, Remmy, when are you going to learn?"

"Heck, I shouldn't even be going out to Quinicut with you," he whined as he tore open a juice pack and drank it down, one-handing his beatup mountain bike.

"What do you mean?" I asked. "You're not thinking of quitting the paper? This can lead to *big* things for both of us." I was starting to get mad.

"That's not what I mean, Herbie," he said. "What I mean is my parents aren't crazy about me hanging with you, that's all." And that's when he said, "They think you're a bad influence on me."

I nearly fell off my bike. I couldn't imagine anyone's parents not wanting their kid to hang around with me! Me! I've got to be the straightest, most normal, most average kid at Manamesset Junior High. I get good grades; I don't talk back; I don't do drugs; I don't smoke; I don't swear. In fact, I'm pretty boring, overall.

"Bad influence?" I shouted at him. "What do you mean your parents think I'm a bad influence?"

"They say you've got this bad habit of finding dead bodies."

"That's unfair," I shot back as I avoided a dead squirrel in the road. I kept pedaling right along so Remmy wouldn't want to stop and poke it with a stick. "Okay, once, twice . . . a few times that's happened. But it's not like I've ever *killed* anyone, for crying out loud."

I admit he kind of surprised me. Then I figured Remmy was just mad because we didn't get to interview the girls' field hockey team, which was playing a home game that afternoon. A couple of the other reporters had gotten that assignment: "Girl Sports Stars of Manamesset Junior High." It was the plum assignment we all wanted, and who wouldn't—interviewing a lot of sweaty girls in short skirts.

Remmy wiped his nose the length of his sleeve and slowed down to spit at the side of the road. The kid had no manners, no common sense, and he swore like a drunken sailor—one of my mother's expressions. Sometimes I wondered why *I* hung with *him*. I have a girlfriend, sort of, and she absolutely detests Remmy. She's asked me what I see in him, and I really have no answer. Still, for his parents to accuse *me* of being a bad influence was crazy.

Though I do admit, like I said before, that there have been a few times— just a few—where I've had the misfortune of being in the wrong place at the wrong time. An older friend of mine, a retired signpainter named Mr. Hornton, told me once that I was simply the "unfortunate victim of a string of strange coincidences."

So, in a funny kind of way, I was glad that if anyone had to discover those bodies, it wasn't me.

But I'll get to that soon enough. . . .

WE ARRIVED AT THE HOME of Mrs. Louisa Valentina about thirty minutes later. She was a short, plump, whitehaired, pleasant-faced woman who greeted us at the front door with a plate of cookies. When I said she was short, I mean it: she was shorter than either Remmy or me, probably four ten if she was lucky. She was standing in the doorway of this ancient two-story, gray-shingled saltbox with a smile on her face and a plate of oatmeal chocolate-chip cookies in her hand. It was as if that's how she greeted everyone who came to her door, with a smile and a plate of food.

But from the moment we stepped inside it was nearly impossible to get a word in edgewise. She started right off by asking us our names, our ages, and what grade we were in, then exclaimed over how tall we were. From there she went into what a lovely person Mrs. Filiades was and how they'd met at the funeral of a junior high school principal. After that she went on to tell us about her favorite subjects when *she* was in the eighth grade and how much schools had changed—mostly for the worse—in the last fifty, sixty years.

To which Remmy muttered under his breath, "Didn't know they had schools back in the Stone Age."

I stepped on his foot as Mrs. Valentina asked if we'd like to "look around a little bit, then sit and have some refreshments while we chat. How would that be, boys?"

"Yes, ma'am, that'd be fine," I answered.

This time Remmy made a face and mimicked, "Yes, ma'am," with a snicker. I stepped on his other foot as we followed Mrs. Valentina through the rooms of her house.

Now, I've been in some pretty wonderful and strange houses. I've been in a house that has towers on either end and at least twenty bedrooms and sits on Little Icy Bay like a castle. I've been in shacks and shanties and big houses and little ones, and despite being only thirteen, I've managed to get around a bit, but this house was different in a special way; it was unique.

It was packed. Crammed. With antiques. With furniture that even a jerk like Remmy had to guess was valuable. There were cabinets and dressers and things Mrs. Valentina called highboys and chests she said were coffers, and chairs—so many chairs that some were stacked one on top of the other. There were Chippendales and Hepplewhites and Victorian overstuffeds. As we followed her through her "front room," she pointed out one after another, telling us their names, the eras they came from, who made each and for what purpose. Then we entered what she called the sunroom, off the kitchen.

"Where we can sit and have that chat." She gave us a pleasant smile. "Imagine that, you boys are going to write about me in a lovely school newspaper. Have you been working on the newspaper very long?"

"Yes, and *we*—especially Remmy—have a lot of questions for you," I said, urging Remmy to say something. He was too busy stuffing cookies into his cheeks. "*He* wants to ask you about the history of your house, the house on the water's edge." I gave him a quick dirty look from the corner of my eye.

"Now, that's a misnomer, Henry," she said, waving me to a seat at a huge tilt-top table she paused to tell us was solid oak, circa 1870. We settled down, Remmy with his cookies and notepad, me with my camera.

I'd like to make this perfectly clear: it was Remmy's job to do the interview; I was there as the cameraman. But there he sat, notepad and pen under his arm, munching on cookies, saying nothing. The guy was a number one, first class, grade-A jerk.

"This house was originally built on the edge of a marsh. But as you can see, most of that has been destroyed by storms and the sea, and even by us. All have left their mark." She turned to stare pensively out a pair of great bay windows that overlooked a narrow strip of lawn. I hadn't realized until that moment how close we were to the edge. Probably less than fifteen yards to the bluff that dropped straight down about forty feet to the beach below.

She turned back to us. "One storm after another. Each hurricane and nor'easter, they all eat away at the bluff."

I decided to venture a bolder question. "Aren't you afraid . . . living so close to the edge like this? Mrs. Filiades wanted us to ask you about that." I nudged Remmy under the table; he just slid his chair farther away from me so I couldn't reach him.

"Afraid of what, Homer?" she asked, and before I could repeat my question, she looked at Remmy and said, "How about some iced tea, young man? Oh now, youngsters like you don't drink tea, do you? Well, let me see, I might have some nice juice. That lovely orange powder you mix with water. I bought it for my nephew's birthday party, oh, a little while back. I don't think we drank it all. I can look."

"Please don't go to any trouble," I insisted. "We have just a few questions and then—"

"Juice would be great," Remmy told her.

I glared at him.

"Let's see, it was the summer little Eddie turned fifteen, 1983. Or was it '84? No matter, there has to be some left. . . ."

"Tea would be better," I managed to say as she took a breath. There was no way I was going to drink any powdered juice that was probably a decade old.

"Then tea it is. I'll be right back. You two boys make yourselves at home. Feel free to look around. Oh, and I'm sure you'll want some pictures of the house." She glanced at the banged-up Konica hanging around my neck. "I'll take you out front to the beach path when we're done. You can get some lovely pictures for your newspaper. Will that be all right?"

"Fine," I mumbled, turning to Remmy the moment she was gone. "Hey, aren't you going to ask her any questions?"

"She talks too much," he said; we could hear rustling sounds from the kitchen, water taps turning on and off.

"I guess that's your problem, isn't it?" I said. "Look, Mrs. Filiades said the real story is why she's refused to move this house. The local historical society offered to help, but she said no. They were going to pay for everything. This is supposed to be one of the oldest houses in Manamesset. Anyhow, *you* have to find out why she won't let it be moved. Don't you see, stupid? That's the real story here."

"You do it," he blurted out.

"I do what?"

"You talk to her. I can't get a word in—she won't shut up. You ask why she won't move the house. Come on, Herbie, trade with me. Let me take the pictures."

"Damn it, Remmy, we agreed," I said sharply, snapping the cookie in half on what Mrs. Valentina had told us was "Fiestaware, circa 1930."

"Herbie, just this once," Remmy whined. "I don't know how to talk to old ladies. You're good at stuff like this."

"You live with your *grand*mother, for crying out loud," I reminded him.

"Yeah, but we don't talk. She can't even talk much, just mumbles a lot because she won't wear her dentures. Come on, this is the last time I'll do this to you, I swear."

"All right," I muttered as Mrs. Valentina came back, this time with something she called ladyfingers. They were a kind of soft white cake filled with cream. I ate two or three before I started the interview.

If interview is what you want to call it. Before I could ask anything, we had to listen to Mrs. Valentina tell us about every glass, every plate, every fork and knife and spoon, every picture on the wall, and everything else in the room right down to the rugs on the floor. That was what *she* wanted to talk about—her collection of antiques—not the house and why she refused to have it moved. Every time I tried to bring it up—doing Remmy's job for him—she skillfully turned the talk to something else.

Her past. Her childhood. What things were like when she was a girl.

Stories about her father, about the history of the town. About what she was doing and where she was when she bought a certain piece of furniture, or inherited it, or got it at auction or a yard sale, or even from a dealer who hadn't "recognized its worth, but of course my father would have," she'd tell us. "My father was one of the shrewdest antiques men on the Cape. Now, this little end table, he got that for a song in 1948, and this one—" a small chest of drawers that looked pretty nicked and banged up "—he picked up for a pittance in 1952."

There was no doubt that this was one knowledgeable but garrulous little lady, and that her expertise in antique furniture, porcelain, fabrics, and dinnerware was extensive, but there was also no doubt in my mind that she was going to tell us about her house only when she was darn good and ready.

It was a good forty minutes later, as we were taking a tour through the back rooms of the house, gazing at lowboys and highboys, tripod tables, gaming tables, and urn tables, sideboards and cupboards, that I saw I needed to take a different approach. Apparently Mrs. Valentina thought we were from an antiques magazine—either that or she was an extremely attention-starved little old lady who'd found herself a captive audience.

"So, how about this one?" I said, putting my hand down on a dresser-type table. It was about three feet tall, kind of fancy looking with funny overlapping butterfly shapes running in pairs down the front. It was varnished a bright gold color, and its drawer pulls were in the shape of metal tassels. "What is this one?"

"That, young man," she addressed me sternly, lifting my fingers off its top, "is a William and Mary walnut chest with inlays in boxwood combined with an oyster veneer, *and* with its original bun feet. It is a very rare and costly piece."

"Oh yeah?" Remmy couldn't see the look on her face; he was a bit to her side. "How costly?"

She gave him an equally stern look straight down the bridge of her pointed nose. "Ninety thousand dollars—at least."

"Damn." I pulled away from it, then paused as Remmy's eyes met mine. If this one piece of furniture were worth that much . . .

And we were standing in a room crammed with such furniture. In fact, this room, which she called the side parlor, was so crowded with tables and chairs, dressers and "coffers," that we had to move sideways to get around them.

"Then everything in this house must be worth close to a million bucks!" Remmy cried excitedly.

Quickly I seized on an opening: "But aren't you afraid if a big storm washes the house out to sea all this will be lost? I'd hate to think of this—" I touched the chest lightly, with new respect "—floating out in the ocean. Wouldn't the salt water ruin it?"

"Are you certain you're working for a *school* newspaper?" she asked, eyeing me shrewdly. "You sound like neighbors of mine, Senator Suddard and his brother Joseph. They have much the same sentiment. They worry more about my precious antiques falling into the sea than they do me."

"You've got to admit, Mrs. Valentina," I said, returning her shrewd look, "there's a story here."

"Which I tend to avoid, yes," she said. "Let's sit out on the back porch and I'll tell you about my house . . . the house on the ledge."

"As I said, the house was originally built on the edge of Great Mercy Marsh. But as you can see, most of the marsh is gone, just a few patches left here and there. It's been eaten up by the relentless power of Mother Nature." She paused, sighed, and stared out at the open water beyond. We were sitting on a small verandah made of weathered barnboard and native fieldstone. The sun was starting to drop to the west; terns flitted across the long, low, mud flats, and the crooked necks of a pair of cormorants were visible, bobbing in the swell. The tide was moving out, probably the best time to take some photographs from below. I had to speed this up.

But before I could speak, she went on. "Most of the sand is gone, too, carried off by longshore currents farther out. Of course, we humans did our share. A hundred years ago farmers grazed their cows on the marsh and filled it in in places. Others removed natural barriers out in the bay in order to widen and deepen it. In the process we destroyed the small islands that protected Quinicut. It's sad to say, but eventually all the point will be gone . . . but I plan to be gone myself before that day comes."

She gave me a curious look, then a quick glance at Remmy, who had lost interest and wandered off. He had walked to the edge of the bluff, possibly to see just how close he could get without falling over; now he was examining the statue of a large dog set about ten feet from the edge. It looked like a retriever, full size, with its head lifted and turned slightly toward the house.

Mrs. Valentina nodded toward it, said, "Now that piece there, the bronze dog, is relatively rare and probably worth quite a bit to a collector. When the house was built in 1840, the water's edge was over five hundred feet away. Ninety years later there was still a wide lawn here. It ran right to the edge of the bluff. My mother had a lovely row of cultivated roses there, the gentlest shade of lavender you can imagine, almost a mauve." Her eyes looked wistfully across the remaining lawn, then fell on Remmy again. He was fiddling with the bronze dog's head. "The dog was originally positioned at the edge of the cliff, so we've had to move it back several times. Fortunately the senator and his brother are always willing to help out. They've moved it a few times. There was a brass telescope that fitted atop the dog's head, but it's gone now, broken, discarded." She shrugged easily. "I think I will miss it, too . . . when it goes."

"Why can't you move it again?" I asked. "Why don't you just move the whole house?"

"It's too late now, dear child," she said to me, adjusting her position in the chair slightly. "Heavy moving equipment would further weaken the ground we're sitting on. No, I made an arrangement that when the house goes I shall go as well."

"And all your antiques? Your . . . William and whatever chest? You're going to let that go over the edge, too?"

"My goodness, Homer, don't look at me with such horror in your eyes!" she exclaimed with a small laugh. "Of course not! I'm not over the edge— not yet, that is. I intend to give away my things, some to charity, some to friends, and the rest will go to my nephew Edward, who up until now has shown very little interest in my lovely antiques. Still, I expect he'll sell them off, too."

"Wait. You've got this all timed? You're going to give all your stuff away, and then what? Wait out some storm or something and let the house fall into the sea with you in it?"

"How melodramatically you put it," she said, a strange little smile inching across her pleasant, plump face. Then she turned to face the sea; the water was deep blue, almost violet, and dappled with overlapping triangles of gold as the sun descended slowly in the west. "The house has done well; it has served its purpose. My father would have been satisfied. Oh my—" She glanced at me almost apologetically. "How silly of me, old woman talk. Now what about some photographs? You will be wanting some for your lovely magazine."

She had been speaking nonsense, as though I weren't there. Suddenly I had the unnerving feeling that she did this often. It was habit. What was not habit was to have a thirteen-year-old boy sitting beside her listening to it.

"I suppose so," I murmured, thinking to myself that now I'd heard everything, but also realizing we hadn't gotten what we came for . . . not at all.

I WILL NEVER FORGET MY trek down the side of that cliff—searching for a path that must have washed out years ago—despite Mrs. Valentina's insistence from up above: "Now, I know it's there somewhere. Oh, there used to be some lovely beach plums along the path. You be careful, Henry."

And me, stumbling, fumbling, and finding my footing on a small ledge of boulders that moved several inches deeper into the sandy slope with each step I took. There were some little tufts of grass along the rough outline of what might have been a path that led to another nearly vertical path held together by some brambles that managed to cling to the side. Finally I found the remnants of a real path, though even here the sand and gravel slid underfoot when I paused and tried to photograph the house.

The problem was I really had to go to the bottom to get a good shot, even though I managed a few pictures as I tumbled and stumbled downward.

Of course Remmy was supposed to be doing this, wasn't he? Hadn't I traded jobs with him? So what was I doing blundering down the bluff, aware that at any moment one misstep could toss me onto the muddy, rockstrewn flats at the bottom?

No, he stayed at the top where only moments ago he had informed Mrs. Valentina—and me—that "I'm afraid of heights; they make me throw up."

'Course, this was news to me. I could have strangled him with the cord to the Konica. Instead I gave him a look that promised his life wasn't worth an anthill in the snow, then gamely went ahead, Mrs. Valentina insisting: "Now, there's a lovely path, just a bit steep, that runs down the side, Hermie. Over to the left, just below where my mother's roses used to grow. Oh how I clambered up and down that path all summer long, picking lovely flowers, digging clams in the tidal flats . . ."

And so on, and so on. She watched from above, entertaining a suddenly engrossed Remmy while I half fell down the bluff, snapping pictures as I did.

Though I do admit this, once I made it to the bottom—with only one scraped knee and sand all over the seat of my pants—I think I got some pretty good shots. The tide was dead low, so I walked out across the mud into the shallow water, put the camera on zoom-focus, and fired away.

Then I had only to climb back up, thank Mrs. Valentina, and throttle Remmy, my so-called best friend. We didn't have the story we'd come for, but I'd had enough. Once I got to the top I wanted just one thing—to go home.

"THIS HAD BETTER BE PRETTY good," I warned Remmy as we went into the small room.

He made a hand signal to indicate I should drop my voice, so I did, repeating, "Did you hear me? This better be pretty damn good." I followed him to an old black-topped table, an ancient and discarded lab table. Spread over it were black-and-white five by sevens of Mrs. Valentina's house.

But they didn't matter as much as this. "You see this?" I told Remmy, waving the hall pass in his face. "This is a bathroom pass. I told Mrs. Filiades that's where I was going, so if anyone comes in here and checks, I'm in big trouble—and if I'm in big trouble, then *you're* in big trouble, too."

"Will you be quiet?" he snapped, nodding at an interior door.

We were in a small workroom where the photography club held their meetings. It was in this oversized cloakroom, situated between the darkroom and the faculty room, where I suddenly heard voices, including the raucous laughter of my new English teacher.

It seemed teachers were always in a better mood when they weren't teaching class.

Remmy had grabbed me in the hall between periods three and four, telling me I *absolutely* had to meet him in the photography room in ten minutes. "I lied to Mrs. Filiades," I said. "I told her I had to go! During the first test of the year! She didn't want to let me leave, but—"

"Will you shut up?" Remmy finally said, punching me in the arm, "Just take a look at these, will you?"

I was still nervous, my eyes on the connecting door to the faculty room. Remmy was here on a legitimate pass from study hall, but if I were caught—

"What's so important it couldn't wait?" I demanded, looking at the pictures.

They were black and whites, of course, and lay strewn across the table in no apparent order. I had to admit that I took a pretty decent picture: good contrast, good detail. Even the ones I'd waded out into the water to shoot looked good. The house looked like an aerie on the cliff and, from the angle I'd chosen, appeared even closer and more precariously perched near the edge than it really was.

"Nice, huh?" Remmy asked, and before I could say, yeah, thanks, he went on: "Steam did a good job, didn't he?"

"Steam" was Steamroller Rollins, actually Stephen Rollins, a senior who had but two talents. The first was the ability to move his tremendous bulk down a football field at a pretty good clip, mowing down anyone who dared threaten our star quarterback.

His second talent was developing crisp, clean, perfect photographs.

"Yeah, well, don't thank the photographer, whatever you do," I snapped.

"Just shut up and look at these." That's when I realized he was behaving very strangely—seriously, no wisecracks—and he was holding a magnifying glass, probably stolen from science class. "Look at this one, and this one especially." He shoved two pictures toward me, two which I didn't think— on first glance—were as good as the rest. They were more what we'd call "close-ups"; shots taken as I stumbled my way down the nonexistent footpath to the base of the cliff.

"These are no good, Remmy," I told him. "The distance shots are the best. These can be chucked . . ."

"Look at this!" he shouted; I gave an anxious glance at the faculty room door. "Look!" He put his finger down on a shot of the cliff, the rocks, and the rubble which loosely held the side of the bluff together. "I'm serious, Herbie, you look at this white thing and you tell me what it is!"

"Roots, Remmy." I studied the object he had his finger on: the long, white, knobby root of some tree which had once grown at the edge of the cliff. The last hurricane surge that had washed in and taken a bite from the cliff had probably swallowed the tree as well. "Roots from some tree."

"Damn it, Herbie, what shape are roots? Do they have these rounded edges?"

"I don't know, what the hell are you . . ."

"Look more closely!" He was nearly screaming at me. Of course *he* didn't care if a teacher from next door came in and found us—he had a pass to be here.

"What are you trying to say?" I asked, looking up at him, magnifying glass in hand.

"Roots? That is a bone, Herbie. *A bone.*" He was looking at me very levelly, both of us leaning over the table, our foreheads almost touching, our eyes meeting.

"Hell it is," I snorted.

"And there's more. Look!" He slid out another picture, a close-up showing where a rain of rocks, boulders, and . . . something suspiciously round and white lay among the litter at the base of the cliff. It looked like a large, pale, ostrich egg among the gray boulders. "Now look back at that thing again—look!"

I found myself swallowing. "Nah, you're nuts."

"Bones. I know bones when I see them. And I think they're probably human bones. Look at this one—the one sticking out of the dirt. Look at the rounded end of it—it's a . . . a . . . something that fits into the hip . . . you know!"

"You've got too much imagination, kid," I warned him.

"Yeah? Well, my parents told me I shouldn't hang around you so much," he said in disgust.

"These aren't bones . . . and even if they are . . ." I started muttering my way through a half-reasonable explanation, afraid to admit he was right. The longer I looked at them—the ostrich egg-sized white boulder, the one, or maybe two, that were sticking out of the side of the bluff about five feet below the surface—the more they did look like bones. I started thinking I could see another one or two lying on the bluff like thin, white twigs. Ribs?

"If they are, heck, they're probably just animal or dinosaur bones . . . or . . . hey, what about an Indian?"

But I was starting to work up a sweat. The long bone with the rounded end sticking out of the side of the bluff was slowly looking less and less rootlike and more and more . . . bonelike.

"There ain't any dinosaur bones on Cape Cod, and you know it," Remmy sneered. "This whole place is just one giant sand pile left by the glaciers ten thousand years ago."

"Look, how come you know so much about glaciers and stuff? Didn't you get a D in Earth Science last year?"

"Just because I got a D doesn't mean I'm stupid."

"Indian bones, then. Maybe Mrs. Valentina's house is sitting on an Indian graveyard, like in the movie *Poltergeist* or something."

"I don't think they're Indian bones, Herbie. Wouldn't she know if she were sitting on a graveyard? We've got to go back there and check. If we go down the bluff and find this one, we'll know for sure." He indicated with the handle of the magnifying glass the round one, the one that resembled—somewhat—the top of a skull.

I have to admit I was slowly starting to get interested: "Maybe, if it is an Indian graveyard, that explains why she wouldn't let them move her house?" I looked at him hopefully. "Desecration of Indian remains and all that. Maybe she's part Indian."

"You know something, Herbie, you talk nuttier than me sometimes. We going back?"

I heard a footstep near the interior door, the heavy, deep tones of a gym teacher I preferred not to run into.

"Yeah, sure," I said as I opened the door leading into the hall. "You won't be afraid to go down the bluff this time?"

"Sure, Herbie," he insisted, his face flushed and excited. "I really wasn't afraid, I just had a stomachache from all those cookies."

I MUTTERED A WORD I don't want to repeat here, then said, "Put it back down." I glanced up at the side of the bluff, incredulous that I could have missed this, that I'd taken pictures of bones sticking out of the side of a cliff and not even known it. Wasn't I a man of detail? Didn't I take care to notice everything? Both my friend Mr. Hornton, as well as Jake Valari, another friend who's just incidentally a cop, would be real disappointed in me.

Remmy squatted down and replaced the yellowish, discolored skull he had just lifted off the stones. He put it back, upper side down, gently. The bottom jaw was missing. Then we both looked up. There was no mistaking it now, there *was* more skeleton up there; that was a femur, or thighbone, sticking out of the bluff. And if we looked carefully enough in the sand and rocks on the slope, we would probably find . . .

Ribs? The pelvis maybe? A humerus, radius, ulna—or two? The vertebral column? Maybe, or pieces of it.

Fortunately we knew enough to leave everything right where it was.

"I have to call Jake," I told Remmy. "Let's go ask Mrs. Valentina if we can use the phone."

And this is where I made a big mistake, something I should have known better than to do but something that proves I'm not perfect. Because as soon as Mrs. Valentina answered her back door, surprised to see us back, I dashed past her like a bullet, shouting, "This is an emergency, Mrs. Valentina, I need to use your phone!"

Which meant I left *Remmy* to explain what was going on. I mean, this discovery was so extraordinary! I was upset and excited and confused. If I'd only exercised a little . . . well, maybe restraint is the word, and taken the time to tell her myself, I might have learned something.

You see, it should have been *me* who spoke to her and told her what we'd found outside in the bluff because if she had anything to do with it, or had any knowledge of it whatsoever, I might have been able to tell from the look on her face. Was she horrified? Or surprised? Relieved or revolted? Or was she frightened? I wouldn't know, and neither would anyone else who questioned her later. She would reveal that first startled expression only once, and she would reveal it to Remmy Rogers, of all people.

But I didn't realize what a mistake that was until some time later.

PEOPLE SAY THAT JAKE VALARI, Manamesset's only detective sergeant, is about the best thing that ever happened to Emily Sawyer, my mother. They met each other through me, and from my own observations, I think it's correct to say that the petite, dark-haired Emily Sawyer, widowed now ten years, and the burly, chainsmoking ex-Boston cop, divorced almost as long, were made for each other.

But it hasn't always been easy for my mother and me. We've had some tough times. For a while we had to get by on her salaries as a waitress and hotel chambermaid. We've lived in "winterized cottages," or cheap motel rooms in winter; in summer we've been lucky to afford what the locals charitably call "bungalows," roach-infested houses that most Cape Codders won't even touch.

There was even a brief period when we lived off state assistance. Then a little over a year ago my mother started dating Jake and things started to improve. Not only did she land a job with the local school department, but with Jake's help she got a "federally assisted" mortgage on a small, two-bedroom house in North Manamesset.

At any rate, Jake and I were friends, as much, at least, as you can be friends with the man who's dating your mother. And though I like to think there's a lot of mutual respect and admiration between us, Jake and I have had our ups and downs—the downs usually stemming from the fact that I tend to get mixed up in situations that involve sudden or unusual death.

But I don't go looking for trouble. As I said before, I just seem to fall into things. I'd avoid them if I could, which maybe I was trying to do that day, if only subconsciously. I didn't want to believe that a skeleton sticking out of the bluff below Mrs. Valentina's house meant a crime had been committed. Like I told Remmy, it could be an old graveyard out there in her back yard—one that erosion had slowly uncovered.

But when the police found that second skull in a small pile of barnacle-encrusted rocks, the skull with the bullet hole between its eye sockets, well, that kind of killed the graveyard idea. This was a crime all right, and a serious one, and whether I liked it or not, once again I was partly responsible for its grim discovery.

I WASN'T SURPRISED TO SEE yellow police tape strung up behind Mrs. Valentina's house when I pulled up on my bike, or the long line of cars, vans, and trucks beside the dirt road. There were at least a dozen vehicles parked against the wild brambles, grapevines, greenbrier, and other scruffy plants growing there. One car I knew right away: Jake Valari's red Mercury Firebird. Because Jake was a detective he usually used his own car.

It was early Saturday morning, and I had just snuck out of the house.

Last night Mrs. Rogers had my mother on the phone for the better part of an hour. On our end I'd heard my mother repeating, "Yes, I know. I'm sorry. Oh, is he really that upset? Nightmares? I'm so sorry."

It made me want to throw up. My mother was concerned enough without the Rogerses berating her—and me—for getting "poor Remmy involved in this situation." Though the truth is, I think the Rogerses kind of enjoyed all the attention; it had been Remmy the local news media contacted first. After all, he was one of two kids who, as the local cable news show put it, "guessed that some suspicious-looking white objects sticking out of the bluffs on Quinicut Point might actually be human remains." Initially I was overlooked, which was kind of a novelty for me, but later I wondered about that. Maybe Mr.—or Mrs.—Rogers had contacted the press themselves, though to hear them wailing and complaining you never would have known it.

When my mother got off the phone, I tried to avoid her, but she kept looking at me strangely. Then she called her sister. I heard part of that conversation, too: "Yes, Clemmie, can you believe it? Again!"

Thankfully my Aunt Clem was a pretty reasonable person, and she convinced my mother that it simply wasn't my fault; that anyone could have stumbled over those old bones. It was a wonder no one had found them before. And as it turned out, the bones were old, at least forty or fifty years old, if not more.

Or so Jake had told us when he stopped by late last night. I hadn't asked him any questions, and he didn't have any for me. I'd forced myself to be silent, speaking up only to agree with him and Mom about how "weird" the situation was. Jake just had too little information to give—even if he could have—for me to start pumping him for it. After a while I'd wandered off and pretended interest in some inane television show.

Later I got hold of the phone long enough to call my girlfriend. I'd wanted her opinion; I'd also wanted her to sneak out to Quinicut with me the next day. She would have gone, too; she's the most outrageous girl I've ever met. But she was gone, her mother had said, to spend the weekend with her father.

So I awoke this morning in the middle of a real dilemma. I didn't want to upset my mother, but what choice did I have? This had been my assignment, and I had to follow through. I mean how would it look if every newspaper reporter walked away from a story just because their mother disapproved? I really had no choice. I grabbed a granola bar, then left a note saying, "Gone out. Be back for lunch. Herbie."

Now here I was, making a mental tally of the vehicles along Quinicut Point Road. In addition to the Firebird, there was a black Geo, a pale ivory Range Rover, and a cobalt blue Mercedes with official state legislative plates. That startled me until I remembered Mrs. Valentina had said Senator Suddard lived farther on down the point. Must be him.

I recognized the medical examiner's blue Dodge pickup, and there was a green van with the state seal on the door and the words STATE HISTORICAL OFFICES. There was also a police van, two police cruisers, two state cruisers, and three news media vans, two of which had satellite dishes on top. One had the call letters of a Boston station, one was out of Providence, and the third—more beatup than the other two—was from the local cable station.

With all the cars and trucks parked outside it was bound to be total confusion inside—and out on the edge of the cliff. This would probably be the best time for doing a little investigating, that is, for sneaking around. There was no yellow tape stretched around the front of the house, so I went up to the door, tapped on it lightly, then let myself in when no one answered. From the kitchen and other rooms at the back of the house, I could hear voices rising and falling, some talking rapidly, others slowly; there was even a little bit of laughter mixed in. This was followed by the quick, pointed voices of reporters, firing off questions all at once.

I don't think Jake would have allowed that; he must have been outside with the Scene of the Crime Team.

Then one voice seemed to override the rest, asking—or demanding—that one question be asked at a time. I guessed it was the senator's. I knew for a fact the police captain wasn't here; he never was around, and I hadn't seen his car outside. After being informed of the situation's status, he'd probably told Jake to "take charge, do what needs to be done," then gone fishing off Nantucket.

I shut the door behind me quietly. I was in the front room, standing amidst sofas and sideboards, cabinets and cupboards, high chests, low chests . . .

"Anyone here?" I asked softly. What I wanted to do was get close enough so I could overhear what was going on. It was a cinch Jake would throw me out soon as he spotted me. I wanted to pick up all I could—for the newspaper of course—before that happened.

I stepped forward quietly, trying to hear, and then the voices from the kitchen stopped. Someone was talking in a fairly rapid and authoritative tone—some kind of lawyer talk about Mrs. Valentina's legal rights and a lot of other stuff I couldn't follow. That's when I was distracted by something— or someone—shuffling across the floor of the side parlor. I slipped through the front room and slowly eased into the doorway of the parlor . . .

To see a man on his hands and knees trying to move the William and Mary chest, the one with its original bun feet.

At first I thought he was a cop, crawling around on the floor in search of evidence. But what kind of evidence? Was it possible Mrs. Valentina was the front for some criminal gang? Was she hoarding antique furniture that had been stolen by the gang—a gang responsible for the shooting deaths of the bodies sticking out of the side of the cliff?

Yes, maybe she was even the gang's leader, and she'd had two men killed, then stuffed down a hole in her back yard years ago, and it was only now that her vicious crime was being uncovered.

Then I realized how stupid that was; besides, the guy was muttering, "Damn it, this is the real thing," as he tried to move the heavy chest.

I guess it was the sound of my breathing that made him jerk his head up and demand, "Who the hell are you?"

He was wearing jeans and a worn brown sport jacket over a plain white T-shirt. His hair was short, reddish-brown; he needed a shave; and he had that look real criminals do on television: pinched-in cheeks, pouches under the eyes, and thin, dark, mean-looking lips. He didn't look healthy is what I'm trying to say, and as he got to his feet, I saw that he was a small, runty kind of guy. He looked like he was in his late twenties, maybe older.

"Just a kid," I said, shrugging. I hadn't wanted to draw attention to myself, hoping to remain undiscovered at least long enough to see Mrs. Valentina and gauge her reaction to what was going on. Having screwed up already by losing the opportunity to see her first reaction, I hoped to see if now she looked or sounded nervous or frightened, upset, or merely fascinated by all this attention and commotion.

Because, you see, I wasn't a cop. And I was just barely a newspaper reporter. I had little access to any information in this case, if indeed it turned out to be a murder case.

"Just a kid, hey?" he snapped back, slapping his hand down on the walnut chest. "Do you realize what she's doing? Do you realize that she's giving everything away? Look at this, and this—" He spun around, pointing out another chest, one of darker wood, then a mirror stand, then the top of a large, rare, Tucker porcelain floor vase that stood about three and a half feet off the floor. "Every piece has a *name* on it. Do you know what *that* means?"

"No, sir, I'm sure I don't," I replied politely.

"Well, just take a look," he shouted belligerently, tipping the large vase to one side and indicating the bottom. "Well, go on, kid, take a look."

"Whatever you say . . ." I muttered, not wishing to draw the attention of anyone else. I bent over; there was a piece of sticky notepad paper attached to the bottom.

"Well, damn it, kid, read it!"

"It says . . ." It took me a moment to realize there was a name there. "Sud . . ." I stood back up. "Suddard."

"William Suddard! Joseph Suddard! Don't you see what this means? I can't believe it! I can't believe she's doing this to me! Every single item here has a name tag on it! She's giving it all away to them! And what I'd like to know is *why*—" he leaned in closer to me "—she's doing it."

I didn't know who he was or what any of this meant, but suddenly I wanted to keep him talking. He hadn't sent me away; in fact he didn't seem to care who I was or why I was there. Apparently these labels had upset him too much. So he wasn't a policeman, detective, or investigator, neither could he be from the state. He had to be a relative or friend, and he was taking the opportunity to do some snooping around.

"I mean, I can't believe this. Do you know what just this one piece is worth?" He seemed to be on the verge of tears as he put his hand down again on the William and Mary chest. "Hell no, why would you know anything about it? You're just a kid."

"Around ninety thousand dollars?" I offered.

"No," he said with a moan, "Closer to a hundred grand. "Just look at it, with the original feet." He ran his hand over the top, the way you'd caress a dog you really liked. "But the label says . . ."

"Suddard. She's giving her stuff away to the Suddards?"

"Damn it, yes, but what kind of person goes around giving away chests worth a hundred grand? Oh, I should have seen it was happening. But I was blind!" He moved away from me, eyes darting from chair to chair, finally settling on a rather nondescript Windsor chair with a broken spindle. He fell into it, then head in his hands said, "She told me I didn't care. She said I had no appreciation for the finer things. But what did I know about old furniture? I was just a kid then myself. But now that I do understand, she doesn't care, says it's all been arranged, that I'll get my share. But what does that mean? That she's got my name taped to some old teapot or set of dishes she keeps out in the kitchen? My name's not on any of *these!*" He flung his arms out wildly.

"You're Eddie Valentina, aren't you?" I slipped in. "You're Mrs. Valentina's nephew?"

"I'm Eddie *MacDonald*, but yes—" he stuck his hand out to me, and I took it "—I am Louisa's nephew and her only living relative. My grandfather was old Jim MacDonald, her father and the man who—" His face was filled with agony as he shook my hand. He had a surprisingly powerful grip for such a runty guy. "—did all this, who found these treasures and bartered and bought his way to . . . accumulating so much . . . beauty. But me, I'm just the no-account nephew who's lost his inheritance because he was such an idiot. I learned too late to appreciate, to understand . . ." He let go of my hand and, looking straight at me, asked again, "But who the hell are you? I don't suppose you're the local paperboy collecting this week's money?"

"No, me and a friend . . ." I paused, studying his face, trying to figure him out, then I corrected myself and told him, "I mean, it was me who found the bones sticking out of the cliff."

"You?" He frowned; he was puzzled. "Are you the one whose parents want to make a deal with the media?" He nodded toward the back of the house where the questioning voices had become a low din. "One of them said your parents acted like they'd found the bodies, not you."

So, a further insight into Remmy's home life? But I wasn't interested.

"I'm the *other* one," I emphasized carefully. "The one who really found them. That was my friend."

"Really." He nodded with false interest. "Well, listen, I guess this is all fascinating for you, but for me, it's a tragedy." He was up again, looking at the furniture, wandering through it, touching this piece and that, but always with his eyes turning sadly to the William and Mary chest. "I should have noticed long ago that they're always here. I don't think I've been to this house once in the last twenty years when they *haven't* been here. Oh, I know they bought my aunt out years ago, but they didn't buy these things. Just the shop and its inventory. So why does she keep giving things to them? Every time I see her, she's having something packed up, or there's a van outside waiting to take something away, a dresser, a chest, a mirror." He turned, stared at me almost defiantly; we were nearly the same height. "It's even occurred to me that maybe they know something about her, that they've . . . been blackmailing her all these years. Is that so farfetched? Or am I crazy? Now with these . . . these *bodies* out there and the police and . . ." Slowly, an eerie, almost malicious grin passed over the thin mouth, bringing color to the gray cheeks. "Hey, maybe I've stumbled onto something. Maybe *you* stumbled onto something, what do you think? Have Attorney Joseph R. Suddard and his brother, the politically ambitious William K. Suddard—have they knowledge about those bodies you found? What do you say? Is that why they were the first ones here, after the police, that is? What do you think?" He moved closer to me. "You should have seen her when I got here. She was nervous, and if that's the case . . ."

Suddenly he threw up his hands, gave a groan, and turned away. "What am I talking about! I must be mad to even think it! Aunt Louisa a murderer? It's nonsense. If anyone, it was old Grandpa Jim who killed and buried them, but then I heard that medical examiner say that they could have been in the ground as long as a hundred years. So it may turn out to be nothing. A curiosity, a freak thing. They could be Civil War veterans for all they know."

"You heard them say that?" I asked softly. "Civil War veterans? Was this house in your family at the time?"

"How should *I* know?" he blasted back at me. "She said *I* never showed any interest!" But then he sighed, slunk back into the chair, and looked at me almost apologetically. "Sorry, kid, didn't mean that. It's my own damn fault. I could have played the doting nephew and made it worth my while. I'm all she has, but it doesn't matter any more. She hates me, and she'll leave me a token in her will so I can't contest it. Like they say, you sow what you shall reap, right?"

"I don't think that's quite right," I said, "but I also think you're wrong. I think she does like you."

"Oh, come on, kid. How would you know that?"

"I interviewed her for my school newspaper. That's how we found the bodies, from some photographs I took." I settled on the edge of a Hepplewhite chair with a shield-shaped back and a stain on its seat. "She seemed to speak of you . . . fondly." It was a funny word, but it seemed to fit.

I wanted him to talk some more, even though I wasn't sure if all this was important or not. Unfortunately we could hear people coming our way. The reporters were leaving.

"Not a bad story," one said as he went by. "The bullet in the skull is a good angle." He barely glanced at us.

"Yeah," said another. "Hey, you think the old lady keeps a gun somewhere in all this junk?"

Then they were gone, Eddie MacDonald and I staring at their parting backs. I think he wanted to speak, but someone else was there, a man in a silver-blue suit and red silk tie, very expensive. He had a sharp look to his face and eyes. I put him in his mid- to late sixties, a slender, composed, but strangely self-important individual. There was another man behind him, dressed similarly but in dark gray; they could have been twins.

The second man hung back a bit, evidently talking to Mrs. Valentina: "Now you remember, Louisa, no answering any questions unless I'm with you."

But the silver-blue man was standing there staring at us . . . no, at Eddie MacDonald.

"Well, well," he said, his chisel-sharp gray eyes raking Eddie over. He never even saw me, I might as well have been a piece of furniture. "Look what the cat dragged in. The prodigal nephew, back again."

I'm just a kid, but I know arrogance, scorn, and sarcasm when I hear it; in this man's voice I heard all three.

"What's the problem, Eddie?" he went on, cruel laughter in his voice. "Out of cash again? Here—will this do?" He pulled a fat snakeskin wallet from his pocket and withdrew two twenties. "Will this keep you out of Louisa's hair for a day or two?" He waved the money toward Eddie.

"You're cheating her, aren't you? You're cheating her and robbing her blind," Eddie MacDonald said.

"Now, Eddie, that's not true." This was from the second man as he eased his way between the other two. "We're very fond of your aunt. We'd never hurt her." This man had a less severe look to him and a gentler tone to his voice, but the resemblance between the two was unmistakable. Brothers. The Suddard brothers, the state senator in silver-blue, the lawyer in dark gray.

"He knows that," Senator Suddard said snidely. He still hadn't taken his eyes off Eddie. "He knows we care more about his aunt than he does. But he learned too late, didn't you, Eddie, that eventually we all have to pay the piper." He laughed coldly, then left, dropping the money on the floor as he did so.

"Eddie." Joseph Suddard raised his hands, seeing that Eddie wanted to lunge at the senator. "Not a good idea. Take the money and go, and leave your aunt alone."

Eddie backed off, but I heard him say, "Bastards," as the two men left the house.

ONCE AGAIN I BLEW MY chance to see Mrs. Valentina, to read her reaction, to see if she were frightened, puzzled, or just plain scared at the prospect of having two bodies found in her back yard. I suppose she'd have called them "lovely skeletons," or maybe I'm being cruel, too. Because the fact is the moment I stepped into her kitchen I knew the opportunity was gone. She'd left, was walking across the lawn toward the edge of the bluff with a tray in her hands. Cookies and ten-year-old powdered drink maybe, for the small group assembled there: local and state police, people from the medical examiner's office, and the rest, which included two men leaning on shovels and another with a rope and ladder. It seemed they were stymied, uncertain how to proceed with the extrication of remains that were buried in such an unstable location. Jake was there, too, his huge, burly frame overshadowing those of the smaller medical examiner, Dr. Watson, and a third person, a young woman who was pointing and shaking her head a lot.

I still could have walked out there, said, hey, what's up, do you have anything you'd like to tell a junior reporter? But in front of his peers and colleagues Jake would have had no choice but to send me home.

Still, I didn't even get to consider it because there was a knock at the front door, and Eddie—whom I'd left in his anger and misery in the side parlor—was answering it.

It was Emily Sawyer, come to take her son home.

\*        \*        \*

FUNNY THING WAS, SHE WASN'T mad at me. Neither was Jake, who arrived a few hours later and stayed for supper. We talked a lot about trivial stuff, how I was doing in school, if I was going out for sports, that kind of thing. Jake complimented my mother on the meal, which really wasn't anything special, just hot dogs and baked beans.

The phone rang three times while we were eating. Mom answered each time, saying, "Sorry, you have the wrong number." The fourth time it rang, Jake insisted on getting it. His response was a bit more abrupt.

"News media, Herbie, trying to get ahold of you." He dived into his fifth plate of beans, his fourth hot dog. "Channel 8 that time. How many others?" He looked at my mother slyly.

She was up again, rinsing out the glass coffeepot. "I don't let Herbie take calls during meals. Case closed." She had her back to us.

"I can't tell them anything, Jake," I said, pushing my plate aside. I'd managed just one plate; beans were not my favorite. "I don't know anything."

Jake gave me a strange look, not the hard-eyed glare he usually used when confronted with a situation—or person—he found difficult to comprehend. No, this was a thoughtful, pensive, even a little bit curious kind of look. Maybe it was because I'd been doing a pretty decent job of sitting on all my questions, waiting him out.

"It's driving you crazy, isn't it?" he finally said.

"Damn it, Jake Valari!" My mother cried, turning from the sink, coffeepot in one hand, foil bag of vanilla roast in the other, "You know damn well you can tell him! I went to get him this afternoon because I didn't think he belonged out there interfering with the police, but the whole story will be in tomorrow's paper." She plunked herself down at the table, pot and bag of coffee still in hand, confronting a somewhat startled Jake across the table. "I saw on the news this morning—before I got Herbie—that the police, meaning you, are going to ask for the public's assistance. Apparently no one has even a rat's ass of an idea who those two men are. They don't even know how long they've been buried out there. So I really think Herbie deserves more than this from you."

"A rat's ass, Emily?" He was smiling at her.

"You know what I'm talking about." She went back to making coffee.

"I did talk to Mrs. Valentina's nephew today," I offered, watching Jake's reaction carefully. "He said a few things that . . . maybe you should know."

"Eddie MacDonald was born in 1968. I think that makes him at least twenty years too young to be a suspect."

"I wasn't suggesting he was a suspect, Jake. I just thought . . ." This wasn't working.

"Emily, would you mind bringing the coffee outside?" Jake asked suddenly. "Herbie and I are going to take in some fresh air . . . and have a little chat."

\*    \*    \*

AND A LITTLE CIGARETTE, WHICH my mother detested. But out here with a cool breeze coming off the water, the smoke drifted lazily away from us. It was a "jeans and sweatshirt evening," as my mother put it, cool and pleasant, early fall on upper Cape Cod. Jake was quiet and waited until she joined us, bringing the pot of coffee with her along with packets of sugar and a pitcher of cream that she set on our worn picnic table.

"So what have we got?" Jake asked, then went ahead, answering his own question. "Parts of two bodies. Both male. Both probably mid- to late twenties. The one you found first looks like a big guy; the other, with the bullet hole between the eyes, maybe a hair smaller. Both were close to, but probably not over, six feet." He looked at me out of the corner of his eye. I remained quiet.

"They were laid on top of each other, Herbie, buried together, so the odds are this is a double homicide. Doc Watson contacted an expert he met at some conference. You might have seen her out on the cliff with us? Dr. Abernathy, a forensic anthropologist who works for the state. She needs to do a lot more work; she wasn't crazy about the way some of the bones were found, tumbling down the side of the cliff. I convinced her that things hadn't been tampered with much, that was just the way they were found. We think most of the second skeleton, Mr. Bullet Hole, is still in the cliff. The other fellow—parts of him may never be found. Anyhow, she has a special procedure for digging up remains like this, uses the same techniques they do at archaeological sites. The problem right now is the stability of the cliff. It could give way any time."

He frowned, studied the tip of his cigarette, then looked over at me. The sun was starting to set behind his shoulders. I had to squint to see his face. "What was I saying? Oh yeah, this Abernathy woman thinks they've been buried about fifty years. I don't see how she came up with that figure. We've got a couple of ribs, two skulls, some vertebrae, and part of one pelvis." Jake shrugged, apparently conceding there were some things he just didn't understand. "Oh, and one large humerus with extensive muscle scarring. You know what a humerus is?"

"Upper arm." I clamped my hand on my left humerus.

"Right. Anyhow, she's guessing two white males, Nordic or Germanic ancestry." He looked at me as though this needed explaining and I never read anything. "Big faces. High cheekbones. Cause of death of the first man, unknown. The other, probably shot at close range with a high caliber pistol, maybe a shotgun or rifle. Oh, she also found a few scraps of cloth but no buttons, no metal hardware of any kind. It's slow going; the edge of the cliff is very unstable. She's requested help from a geologist and a stratigrapher. Know what that is?"

"Soil expert," I said confidently. "Anything from the cloth scraps?"

"No, but if we find anything . . ." He smiled. "It'll be in all the papers.

Your mom's right. We will need the public's help on this one. Abernathy says around fifty years, but Doc Watson puts a ten- to twenty-year leeway on either side until more testing can be done."

Doc Watson was a nice man, a physician who had served as county medical examiner for the last forty years. It wasn't that I didn't respect him, but if a forensic specialist said fifty years, then I was inclined to go with that.

"And you've started a missing persons check?" I asked.

"Sure have. Checking up on anyone in the area missing from 1920 on up through the sixties. Anything else you'd like to know, boss?" He was being astonishingly open with me; usually I had to pry everything out of him.

"And Mrs. Valentina? Is she a suspect? They were found on her property. And what about her father? Or her husband? She must have had a husband—"

Jake cut me off in mid-sentence. "Husband never came back from the war, but that doesn't necessarily rule him out. Her father, Jim MacDonald, was a lobster and shellfisherman, also a hunting guide. Ducks. They used to hunt ducks out there on Quinicut back in the thirties and forties. He was also a spotter during the war, you know, watching for enemy planes? I guess he made a bundle on a couple of estate deals and went into the antiques business in 1943. Did very well, had a real shrewd eye. Died in '62; the Suddards bought Louisa out in '82." He paused to take a drag on the cigarette, then looked over at my mother, sitting quietly, taking this all in. She wasn't happy about his smoking, but she was politely—just barely—tolerating it.

For a moment we were silent, Mom sipping vanilla roast, Jake enjoying a smoke in almost serene contemplation, and me watching the sun sink behind his back.

"The Suddard brothers," I heard myself whisper. I looked up, wondering if either of them had heard me.

"What about them?" Jake asked.

"I . . ." I studied him; there was a bright ring of sun just to his left. It was casting an eerie red glow against the white sport shirt he was wearing. But what to tell him? That Eddie MacDonald had some wild, cockeyed idea that the Suddards had been blackmailing his aunt? When Eddie himself thought it was a wild, cockeyed idea?

Or did I mention my theory about Louisa Valentina's being some crime syndicate boss-lady? And what if she pasted labels on the bottoms of her things? If the Suddards had bought her antiques business—and she had a house full of antiques—didn't it make sense that she would give stuff to them? They were her neighbors and evidently friends of long standing. Who was I to suspect them—of anything?

I shrugged. "I don't know. I met them briefly and—"

Jake suddenly leaned forward, cigarette in one hand, coffee mug in the other. "And what?"

"I didn't like him much, the senator. He was . . . mean to Eddie MacDonald."

"A lot of people don't care for William Suddard." That was my mother, sitting back in her molded plastic chair. "He's been described as arrogant, egotistical, and self-serving. But the truth is, he's done a lot of good for the people in this community. He supports numerous good causes, like homes for abused women and children, animal shelters. He's donated land for a new park here in Manamesset, and he's built more ballparks and playgrounds—for public use—than any elected official I know of."

Jake was still studying me, saying nothing. I turned to my mother.

"You know what he reminded me of?" I said. "A bluefish. A bluefish as it swims in close to shore at high tide, scooping up smaller fish in its mouth. I've seen them, Mom. They're absolutely voracious. Anything smaller and slower than them gets snapped right up. That's what Senator Suddard reminded me of."

Jake was still quiet, but when I turned to look at him, he was staring at my mother, nodding.

"Look, I know you're mad at me because I voted for him in the last election." Suddenly she was talking to him, not me. "His opponent tried to find something to slander him with and came up with nothing—nothing, Jake! Even the Boston papers admitted they'd never seen a cleaner record on any candidate." She turned back to me. "And you know very well, young man, you can't form an opinion about a person on just one meeting."

"It's instinct, Mom," I insisted. "He's not a nice man."

"He is a very *good* man," she said, her shoulders bristling. "I read about him years ago. Some people tried to ruin him then, too, said Bill Suddard avoided service during the war. What fools they looked when it came out that the senator received a deferral because he was his family's sole support. His father was a cartographer who died in a boating accident when Bill was seventeen. He took care of his invalid mother until she died and made sure his brother Joseph finished high school. Then he turned his own life around, went to college. It took him years to build a reputation in local and state politics. But when he did, he never forgot the Cape, or Manamesset. I've seen pictures of what their home looked like when they were children—a tiny little place out on Quinicut Point. But they've built it into a lovely place with a large house and boathouse, and even a swimming pool to which they invite handicapped children in the summer!" And with that she stopped to take an indignant breath.

I looked over at Jake. He was staring at Mom, the distant, dreamy look still in his eyes. He took a sip of coffee. It didn't seem the time to bring up what Eddie MacDonald had said about the Suddard brothers.

But it also didn't seem that Jake was as enamored of Senator William Suddard as was my mother.

Suddenly my mother rose, murmuring, "We need more sugar," and went up to the house. But I felt the coldness spill out of her as surely as I would have felt a frigid winter's blast.

I seized my opportunity. "She said *he* turned his own life around."

"Bill Suddard was on the highway to nowhere," he said, his voice distant, his attention on the house. "As my father used to put it, heading fast for jail or an early grave. No one was more surprised than my dad when he changed."

"He was wild," I said, a statement of fact. I understood.

"Talk of the town, 'course that's a little before my time. What I do remember are his first couple of runs for state office. I was about your age, and I remember folks being amazed at the change in him. Someone said, I forget who, that Bill Suddard had gone from being a mean son of a gun to an angel in less than a year." He smiled at me uneasily. "But it just goes to show you a person *can* change. Go from drinking too much and driving too fast, from stealing and lying and vandalizing and being just plain mean, to become an upright and outstanding citizen."

"What happened?" I was truly amazed, but knew I had detected in Senator Suddard some of what Jake was talking about; the meanness was still there in the cut of Bill Suddard's mouth, the way he had talked to Eddie MacDonald. "And how come his political opponents didn't bring any of that up?"

"People will forgive a wild youth, Herbie, as long as it stops there." He tapped cigarette ash into his coffee mug. "Heck, lots of people, judges, teachers, even cops, were wild and crazy when young." He grinned meaningfully at me.

We could pursue that some other time. "But most of them aren't mean, they're just being kids," I said. "They straighten themselves out."

"Well then, didn't Bill Suddard do just that?" he said, but there was still that look in his face, a look I now read as slight suspicion. The redness of the sun behind him merely emphasized it.

"You and Mom, you've argued about this before."

"According to your mom there's no finer man than Senator Bill Suddard. The day he announces his candidacy for governor she's going to be right there holding a banner."

"Eddie MacDonald says the Suddards are always at his aunt's house, that they're cheating her, taking her antiques, I mean. He feels he's being swindled out of his inheritance. He even suggested . . ." I watched Jake's face carefully; the light behind him was dying; it was nearly twilight. ". . . that maybe they're blackmailing her, that maybe they know something about those bodies and she's been buying their silence with the antiques she has left."

I took a breath, waited for his response.

"Eddie MacDonald is no prize himself, Herbie. It's probably just sour grapes."

"Yeah, maybe . . ." I glanced in the direction of our storage shed, an idea coming to me quickly. "Jake, I just remembered. I left my bike out at Mrs. Valentina's house. Could we . . . could you and I . . ."

"Well, how convenient," he said. This time I could see the glint in his eyes. "What the hell, I should take a drive out there anyhow, make sure everything's okay. I was thinking of putting an officer there in case some reporter gets the lamebrained idea of sneaking around in the dark; then I figured if someone's stupid enough to do that, they deserve to fall off a cliff. Go get your mother. We'll all take a drive."

IT SHOULD HAVE BEEN A pleasant evening, an enjoyable visit back to the house on the edge and a chance for Mom to meet Mrs. Valentina, but the moment Jake turned onto Quinicut Point Road, a dark shape—a car with no headlights—came barreling straight at us. Jake veered sharply to the right, nearly running off the dirt road and into the brush alongside it.

"Damn it!" Jake snapped. "Did you get a look at him? Did you get its plates?"

"No, Jake, I'm sorry . . ." I was excited but caught by surprise just as he had been. For a moment I thought he was going to whip out his portable light, stick it on top of the Firebird, and take off after the guy.

But not with us in the car. Grumbling and muttering, he pulled onto the road and headed out toward the point.

I COULD TELL MOM WAS shaken by the incident; she was giving me quick, nervous looks over her shoulder. But that was nothing compared to what we found at Mrs. Valentina's house.

"Now what—" Jake started as he drove up, slowing the car down.

The front door was open wide with a figure standing in it, a man; he was waving his arms at us. I knew him right away as Jake jammed on the brakes, jerking the car to a stop.

"Joseph Suddard," I said, recognizing the man's slight build as Jake jumped from the car. Mom and I were behind him.

"Thank God you're here!" he cried out. "Something's happened to Louisa!"

We found Mrs. Valentina lying across the doorway of the side parlor. She was dressed in an old housecoat and slippers, lying on her left side. There was a small pool of blood under her head, and she was breathing in a slow, agonized way. Next to her on the floor, in front of the William and Mary chest, was a gun, an old-fashioned twelve-gauge shotgun by the looks of it.

Both Jake and Mom fell to their knees beside her, Jake crying out, "Herbie, call the station! Now!"

"I've already done that, sergeant," Joseph Suddard said, but I rushed off to the phone anyway.

\* \* \*

"IT CAN'T BE A COINCIDENCE," I said to my mother. "I mean, two days after we find the bodies someone tries to kill Mrs. Valentina?" It was cool out at the edge of the bluff. The first-quarter moon was halfway up the sky, casting an eerie, silvery glow upon the water. Mom had her arms crossed atop the bronze dog as she stared out at the sea. It was low tide, and the smell of decay rising off the marsh was strong and ripe.

But to those accustomed to it, the odor was barely noticeable. Our minds were on other things, like the ambulance and firetruck that had responded to our call, and the two cruisers, their blue lights still flashing in front of the house, as well as the state police van, parked so its headlights glared toward the edge of the bluff. There was plastic sheeting over the gravesite now, held down by some wooden planks.

We had watched the EMTs take Mrs. Valentina out. Bundled up on a backboard she had looked like a small child, frightened and disoriented. There'd been attendants with her, and Joseph Suddard had been there, too, talking gently to her as they carried her out.

But for all we knew, he'd been the one who'd done it. That was the funny thing about all this. None of us knew what was going on. And none of it made any sense.

"All I know, Herbie—" my mother finally spoke in a low and solemn tone. She continued to stare across the silver-speckled water. "—is I wish you hadn't gotten involved in this."

"Mom, I didn't . . ." I stopped; she knew the rest.

"Besides—" She turned to me, one arm resting nonchalantly on the dog's head. It was tipped forward in the direction of the hole as though it were a pointer, not a retriever. "No one knows that someone tried to kill her. She wasn't shot, so she might have tripped and hit her head in the dark. Although it looks like that awful gun was hers; at least that's what Mr. Suddard said. Maybe she heard a noise, Herbie, came downstairs, and tripped."

"Or got pushed. Or got hit on the head," I said, wishing to exclude no possibility.

She was quiet as we watched a pair of state troopers examine the gun. One of them had laid it across the hood of a cruiser. Both men were wearing surgical gloves and were handling the gun gingerly.

She sighed and leaned back against the bronze dog. "I suppose they'll do their ballistics tests," she said kind of sourly. "Determine if that gun was used to kill . . ." Her head inclined in the direction the dog was pointing. "It's so sad, Herbie. If she did it . . . or her father . . . it was fifty years ago. She must have been . . . thirty? Younger than I am now, and who knows why it happened? Maybe it was self-defense." Her eyes turned to look at me; it was very strange there in the dark with the dog behind her and the silvery moonlight framing her face.

"And maybe they were murdered. We don't know, Mom," I reminded her. "We're just guessing."

"And isn't that what Jake does? Or part of what he does?" she said. "Makes guesses and checks up on them? And maybe she has nothing to do with those bodies, but that seems very unlikely right now, doesn't it?"

"Hey, you two." That was Jake, approaching us swiftly. It was dark in the yard, but the pale moonlight revealed the concerned look on his face. "Officer Cairns can drive you home. I'm going to be out here a while." He was looking at her. "Sorry about this."

"As if you knew it was going to happen?" Mom said with a slight laugh.

"No mention of the gun to anyone." Now his eyes shunted over to me. "But I need to ask you something; in fact I have two questions for you. Where were you when you had that conversation with Eddie MacDonald?"

I could hear the absolute seriousness in his voice.

"Right where we found her. She calls it the side parlor."

"The window in there was open, and this was on the floor near a big walnut chest. Does it mean anything to you?" He took from his jacket pocket a plastic bag containing what looked like a large white moth. Opening it very carefully, he removed a small pad of notepaper. The top sheet was curled over like a dry leaf, and written on it in large black letters was the name E. MacDONALD. I could feel Jake's eyes on me, waiting.

"She . . . puts labels like that on all her furniture and stuff. For the person who's going to get it, I guess . . . if she dies or . . . I don't know, Jake."

"You said Eddie MacDonald was upset that he hadn't found his name on any of her things?"

"Look, Jake, this is crazy. Are you saying maybe he was in there tonight? Putting his name on . . . stuff?" I looked at my mother, as though she'd be more practical about this, "But if he did that, she could just put new labels on it, right? She'd notice and . . ."

"Not if she had said in her will that her possessions were to be allocated according to the names on the labels," Mom said. "And then died before she noticed someone had changed them." She looked at Jake with a grim smile. "I had a cousin I always suspected did that, changed labels, that is. My aunt said she'd leave me her Hummel figurines. Problem was, my Cousin Tillie's name was taped to the bottom of every one of them."

"Are you saying he changed the labels," I asked, "and then tried to kill her so he'd get all her stuff?"

"He drives a black Geo, Herbie. What kind of car just nearly ran us off the road?"

"No, I don't think he'd hurt her. I mean, she likes him . . ."

Jake was ready to move on; my feelings about Eddie MacDonald were totally irrelevant: "Second question, how did Mrs. Valentina react when you told her you found some bones out on the bluff?"

I said that word, the one my mother dislikes, then quickly: "I didn't tell Mrs. Valentina. I'm sorry, Jake. Remmy did. I . . . was in such a hurry to reach you."

"Remmy." He said the name with a quick shake of his head, then: "Forget about it. Probably not important. Just remember, say nothing about this. I'll handle the press later."

"Are you going to pick up Eddie MacDonald?" I called after him, but he was already halfway across the lawn. He was done with me, but I shouted out, "And what about Mr. Suddard? He was here, too, Jake! Don't forget that. *He* was out here, too!"

IT DROVE ME CRAZY. EVERYTHING was going around and around in my head. Nothing connected, or if it did, it connected damned poorly. Could it be the Suddards were blackmailing Mrs. Valentina? At the same time that Eddie MacDonald was planning to murder his aunt—after changing the labels on all her valuable antiques?

What were the odds of two such separate scenarios occurring together? Or was Eddie MacDonald just a disgruntled, unprincipled creep who was taking advantage of the situation to play his own hand? I knew kids like that. If there were a sudden commotion—a fight in the hall maybe, or a bomb scare— they'd stuff their hand in some girl's handbag and grab what they could, using the confusion around them for cover.

Is that what Eddie MacDonald had been doing?

No, I refused to believe it. There had to be more to it. And though there was very little I could do to help Jake, this I *could* do: find out what, if anything, Mrs. Valentina had said to Remmy.

Fortunately Remmy's parents went to mass every Sunday—without Remmy. So the next morning I waited down the street and out of sight until I saw their big ugly Oldsmobile drive by, then went up to their door.

He didn't want to let me in. "Hey, I can't talk to you right now," he said while chewing on a bagel. I pushed the door in on him, smashing him against the side of the refrigerator.

"You jerk!" I shouted. He pretended to be gagging.

"My parents won't be happy about this," he warned.

"Your parents won't be happy until they get paid for you to talk." I'd finally had it with him. "Who do you think you are?"

"They want me to find some new friends, too." He was holding onto his throat. What an actor.

"So what. Find some. But before you do, I have something to ask you. What did Mrs. Valentina say to you when you told her we found those bones?"

He waved a bagel in the air. "I'm not supposed to talk unless my lawyer's with me. My parents told the police that and they left, but they'll be back, they'll be—"

"Hell they will. They don't care about you! They don't care what you might know, either." I moved closer to him, and he stepped backward into his cat's water dish.

"No." He was shaking his foot. "My dad says they'll be back. We're going to do an interview with this guy from Channel 8."

"Listen, you jerk!" I grabbed hold of his collar and dragged him right up to my face. "If the police thought you knew anything important, they'd have dragged you down to the station house by now and beat it out of you with a rubber hose. They do not care what you know, Remmy. They do not care."

"Yeah?" His bottom lip was trembling, and the bagel dropped out of his hand. "Then why are you here?"

I kind of pushed him back, like tough guys do on television.

"Because I'm not the police, that's why. So you have no choice but to answer my questions, Remmy, or I'll beat the crap out of you."

"Jeez, Herbie, you don't have to get so mad." He plunked himself down in a kitchen chair.

"What did she say? How did she react? When I was calling Jake, you talked to her. Tell me!"

"She said . . . she said she didn't know there were any bodies there."

I waited, hanging over him like the blade suspended on a guillotine. "And?"

"And that's it. That's all!" Suddenly he looked genuinely afraid. I decided to ease up on him.

"Okay, so *how* did she say it? Give me her exact . . . emphasis." I was thinking fast; maybe it didn't matter. Maybe Jake was right. "Repeat it to me slowly, word for word, exactly as she said it."

"You're crazy, you know that?"

"Do it." I leaned closer to him.

"*I didn't know*—" he eyed me carefully, exaggerating the emphasis on every word "—*there were . . . any bodies . . . there.*"

"I'm sure she didn't say it like that. Do it again."

"Damn it, Herbie!" He sat back, shut his eyes, then said, "Okay, okay, here's how she said it. 'I didn't know . . . there were any . . . bodies *there.*'"

"You sure?"

"Oh, come on, that's how she said it. I swear!"

"And how did she look?"

"Look? Well, kind of scared, I guess. Wouldn't you be?"

"Yeah, I guess I would be." I turned to go. "Thanks."

"Hey, Herbie."

I figured he was going to try to scare me, say he was telling his parents about this the minute they got back. Instead, he said, "Hey, we're still friends, aren't we?"

\*       \*       \*

FOR THE FOURTH TIME IN four days I was back out on Quinicut, leaving my
bike next to the front door. No hiding this time. And I ignored the looks of
the state troopers, the two local cops, the other guys in work uniforms who
were standing around not doing very much of anything. But no one stopped
me or spoke to me as I crossed the back lawn and walked toward the hole.

"Jake?"

He turned, surprised—and not surprised—to see me. It was an act, including the speech he was about to give. I cut him off, dealing with him as quickly
and as coolly as I had Remmy only minutes earlier. "I don't know what you've
learned since I saw you last, Jake, but I do know this: Mrs. Valentina knew
there were bodies buried in this yard, but she didn't know *where* they were
buried. Which means she knows who they are and probably who killed them.
If the Suddards are blackmailing her, that's a whole other story, but I think
murder takes precedence over blackmail every time. Am I right?"

"Sergeant?" That was the forensic anthropologist, motioning to him from
the hole.

He ignored her and looked at me.

"How do you—" he started, then stared sharply at me. He knew I wasn't
lying; everything about me told him so, my face, my eyes, right down to the
way I held my body. In fact I was so right and so serious I would have
willingly turned away and left, content to give him this piece of information
and nothing else.

"Sergeant." This was another voice; someone approaching from behind me.
"Got some answers for you."

I recognized Officer Cairns without turning around. He was the nice but
guarded fellow who had driven Mom and me home last night.

But now I would have to leave. I felt a sigh rise up inside my chest . . .

Then evaporate just as swiftly as Jake looked at Officer Cairns, nodding
his head ever so slightly. It was the signal for him to continue.

"No fingerprints on the windowsill, sarge. No footprints outside it either.
The window was probably opened from the inside. We spoke to Mr. Suddard.
He doesn't think anything's been taken, but he's not sure. I got a list of
persons who've been in there the last week or so. Kind of long. It includes
both Suddards, the nephew, a couple of workmen who moved some pieces of
furniture, and even . . ." I felt the man's eyes drop on me.

At Jake's nod, the man went on. "Ballistics tests on the shotgun are still
incomplete, but the size and caliber are compatible with the hole in Skull
Number 2. Or so say the experts. An old Remington shotgun, apparently
belonged to Mrs. Valentina's father. Only one set of prints on that, probably
hers, but state forensics also found traces of blood and hair on the rifle butt.
You were right about that."

Jake nodded again. I moved aside and watched Officer Cairns look up from his notepad. His expression grew grim. "I guess she's in pretty bad shape. Might not make it. They're airlifting her to Providence this morning."

Jake didn't react, just looked at the man until he composed himself and continued.

"As for Edward MacDonald, we've got him at the station. Says he went to bed early last night with a headache. Woke up this morning to find his car stolen." There was just a hint of irony in the man's carefully controlled voice. "Lives in a converted hotel over on Seaside Avenue, bog country. We're checking his story out, talking to his landlady, neighbors. He says he knows nothing about switching labels on any furniture but did seem concerned about his aunt. Could be an act. Oh, something else . . ." Just a bit of a sigh. "Senator Suddard's been calling the station, demanding to know when we plan to arrest MacDonald. Been a nuisance, sergeant, but we can't put him off forever."

"Sergeant Valari?" The woman who'd called out to him was walking our way.

"Find MacDonald's car," Jake said. "Then get both Joseph and William Suddard on the line." He turned to me as the woman stopped behind him; she had something in a glassine bag and was tapping her foot impatiently. Jake ignored her and said to me, "I want you to go home." His stare was steady, indicating he would tolerate no interruption, no complaint, no protest. "Come back tonight, six sharp. Do you understand?" He started to turn away, then looked back at me, adding as though it were an afterthought, "And bring your mother with you."

THIS TIME WE WERE USHERED into Mrs. Valentina's house by two state troopers, their faces wooden and unsmiling under their wide-brimmed hats. From the front room we were conducted toward the back by Manamesset officers Cairns and Andersen, the expressions on their faces equally taciturn.

We had spent a nerve-wracking afternoon, Mom off and on the telephone with Aunt Clem, me off and on the homework assignments I had spread wildly across my bed. Neither of us had been able to concentrate on anything for very long. When we finally left our house at five forty-five, it was with a sense of relief . . .

Soon to be replaced by nervous apprehension once we saw the police barricade at the end of Quinicut Point Road. A trooper there started to wave us away, then paused and let us through after checking his clipboard. This started an angry clamor from a group of reporters held back by the roadblock.

"Is it true they found two Nazis buried out on the cliff?" one of them shouted at us.

Or at least I think that's what he said.

Now we were being escorted into Mrs. Valentina's sunroom. The windows were open, a breeze coming off the water through them. A handful of people were sitting around the tilt-top table:

Eddie MacDonald, his legs crossed, his expression annoyed as he tapped his shoe with a pencil. Beside him, Doc Watson in his Red Sox baseball cap, leafing through a notebook. Across from them, Joseph Suddard staring out the dark windows, and Dr. Abernathy, with a bored expression on her face.

She was the only one who noticed us come in, her sharp eyes lifting to give us a quick once-over.

Mom went to sit at the other end of the table and, mimicking Dr. Abernathy, leaned back and folded her arms across her chest. No one said a word.

Officer Andersen was also there, stationed at the doorway. He gave me a nod of recognition. Officer Cairns was just outside the room with a small paper bag in his hand.

"Does anyone know what the hell is going on?" Eddie MacDonald suddenly said.

"Yes, I'd like to know that myself," said Senator Suddard as he came in, quickly glancing around but barely seeing us. His gaze even skidded past his own brother. He turned to address Officer Andersen rather sharply. "I demand to know what's going on here, officer. Some of us do have an agenda. Myself—" He turned his wrist to look at his watch, probably a Rolex. His entire attitude was one of impatient indifference. "I have an important fund-raiser to attend in Chatham. Even if I leave now, I'm going to be late."

As Officer Andersen was about to answer him, someone else spoke:

"Sorry to keep all you fine people waiting."

It was Jake, coming up behind me, his hands on my shoulders as he whispered, "I've always wanted to say this, Herbie. Have a seat and watch."

For a moment he stood, waiting for me to take a seat, and waiting, as it were, for the atmosphere to settle in on us. The wind was dying down, and the sea beyond the windows was drenched with sunset: red and orange, yellow and violet. But I knew what Jake was going to say; I could feel it, anticipate it . . .

"I suppose you're all wondering—" he paused; everyone held their breath "—why I asked you here tonight." His eyes scanned each of us quickly.

And for a moment it was like a scene out of an old English mystery movie: the suspects gathered in the drawing room waiting in suspense and apprehension; the capable and clever inspector with his assistants standing ready with their carefully collected evidence; and then the careful and artful explanations, followed by the denouement, the truth revealed, the mystery solved.

"Oh, damn," the senator drawled. "And pardon my English, ladies, but spare us the theatrics, sergeant. Evidently you've asked us all here and we've been good enough to comply, but is this really necessary?"

"Senator." Jake wheeled around on him, smiling strangely as he did. "Do you know Drs. Watson and Abernathy? Of course you do. And Mrs. Sawyer." A nod to my mother, then me. "And her son, Herbert. Oh, and of course, how could I forget. Officer Andersen?"

And before the senator could react, Officer Andersen was escorting an elderly woman with a small, soft face and a head full of white hair into the room.

"Mrs. Derry, everyone," Jake finished, guiding her to a chair.

"Mrs. Derry?" That was Eddie MacDonald, leaning forward, then explaining to us quickly, "My landlady?"

"Eddie." She nodded at him pleasantly as she sat down.

"All right, sergeant, I've had enough of this," Senator Suddard barked, still standing. "If this is some kind of foolish game, I'm really not in the mood for it—"

"No games, senator," Jake said to him, his expression and mood darkening just as the sun dipped below the horizon beyond. As if on cue, Officer Andersen turned on the Tiffany lamp hanging over the table. "Just a little story, a tale of murder, attempted murder, and blackmail. I don't think any of those are games, do you?"

The senator wasn't about to back down so easily: "Look, it's obvious to everyone that he—" he turned, pointed at Eddie MacDonald "—came back here last night, changed the tags Louisa had on her most valuable items, and then tried to kill her. That he didn't fully succeed is a testament to his continuing inadequacies. I told your aunt—" he was addressing Eddie directly now, his gray eyes blazing "—you weren't to be trusted. And I was right."

Eddie leaped to his feet, the senator stepped forward, and immediately Jake was between them.

"Sit down," Jake said, first to Eddie, then to the senator. "Sit down now."

Grudgingly the two men obeyed.

"Let's begin with what in a court of law might be known as Exhibit 1," Jake said, "which you may have noticed parked outside in the road." His gaze fell on Eddie. "A 1994 black Geo sedan, slightly dented in front, which my men pulled from the ditch of a cranberry bog about an hour ago."

"It was stolen—" Eddie began.

Jake put up a hand; Eddie was quiet. Jake went on. "A cranberry bog located off Seaside Avenue, not far from an apartment complex owned by Mrs. Patricia Derry." He looked at the elderly woman. She was smiling, apparently enthralled to be there. "Is that so, Mrs. Derry? The property at 323 Seaside? And your tenant at 323B is a Mr. Edward MacDonald?"

"Yes, oh yes," she said, hanging on his every word.

"Thank you, Mrs. Derry. We'll get back to you," Jake said. He turned to Joseph Suddard, who'd been quiet thus far. "Exhibit 2, the key to this house." He opened his palm to show a plain gray key. "However, this is not the key I am looking for. This one is Louisa Valentina's, taken from the key rack in the kitchen. No, the one I want is the one you used, Mr. Suddard, to enter this house last night. You do have one?"

"Yes, I do, sergeant," Joseph Suddard said with a heavy sigh, "but I didn't use it last night. I seldom do." He paused. "I often come up here in the evening, that is, I live just down the road, and it's quite reasonable for me to visit." He was looking around at the rest of us now. "Louisa's a neighbor. We often have tea and talk about antiques. She gave us a key so we could let ourselves in if there were a problem."

"You and your brother have known Louisa for a long time, haven't you?" Jake asked.

"Over fifty years, sergeant, since we were children."

"So how did you enter the house last night without a key?" Jake asked him. "Did she let you in?"

"No, no. The door was open, and I let myself in and . . . found her." He dropped his head.

"So the door was already open," Jake said. "Did she unlock it?"

"I don't know." Joseph Suddard was lifting his head slowly.

"Oh, damn it, sergeant," Senator Suddard snapped. "Evidently the thug—" he glared at Eddie "—who broke in through the windows ran out the front door when he heard my brother coming. What is so hard to figure out?"

Jake just looked at him. "Exhibit 3." He reached behind him. Officer Cairns took something from the paper bag and handed it to him. It was the plastic bag holding the sticky notepaper. He turned to Eddie. "Do you recognize this?" He held the bag out, and Eddie took it, realizing instantly what it was. "Is it yours?"

"Of course not. I mean, it's not even my handwriting."

"Exhibit 4," Jake moved on, turning to Officer Andersen, who handed him a police-issue shotgun: "The Remington 12-gauge, belonging to James Mac-Donald."

"I knew Jim MacDonald," Mrs. Derry said dreamily.

"I'm sure you did," Jake said. "At any rate, this will have to substitute for the shotgun found beside Louisa Valentina, with her blood and hair on it here . . ." He indicated the butt. "Now if we put together a possible scenario, it could have happened something like this: Louisa is upstairs and startled by a sound. She comes downstairs with her father's gun. However, when she realizes who has made the sound, she puts the gun aside, perhaps on a table or chest. It is then that this person, whom Louisa has every reason to trust, distracts her, grabs the gun, and then strikes her—" he demonstrated, lifting the gun and slashing the barrel downward "—in the back of the head. As she lies helplessly on the floor in her own blood, this person leaves this . . . either accidentally . . ." Jake's eyes were on Eddie as he retrieved the pad of paper ". . . or deliberately, in order to cast suspicion on the unfortunate Eddie. After which the window in the side parlor is opened, obviously to make it appear that entrance was gained that way, which we know it was not. At any rate, the intent was obviously murder. Would anyone disagree?"

"The only thing I disagree with are your methods," Senator Suddard grumbled.

"And you, young man, had a motive." Jake was addressing Eddie MacDonald again. "And, from what we can discern, ample opportunity."

"I went to bed early. I told you. I had a headache. I don't have a key. And someone stole my car," Eddie insisted.

"Yes, I know. We're running a hair and fiber analysis on your car," Jake told him, "despite the fact that it will prove nothing if you were the one who tried to kill Louisa. We'd expect to find your hair in your own car, wouldn't we? But would we expect to find someone else's? Maybe not. It all depends on *whose* hair we find, doesn't it? Say, someone who . . ." He turned to the woman. "Mrs. Derry, tell me again what color the car was you saw? The expensive car, you said it was, parked off the maintenance road that runs through the cranberry bog? You were walking your dog, you said."

"Blue," she said with a magnificent smile. "Deep blue, like the sea in winter."

"Ah, blue, an expensive blue car. Say . . . like a Mercedes?" Jake said, his voice dropping to a near whisper.

But I don't think Mrs. Derry would have known a Mercedes if one had run her over.

It barely made a difference because Senator Suddard was on his feet. "Damn you, you small town cops are all alike! I won't sit here and let you lead the witness this way! And I won't be accused of something I didn't do!"

"Witness?" That was Joseph Suddard, turning to his brother in surprise. "William, this is not a court of law, not even an inquest. We were *asked* to come here tonight."

"Asked?" the senator answered, his voice trembling, "Forced to come, more like it!"

"You needn't have obliged the sergeant, if you didn't want to," Joseph Suddard said. "You could have refused."

"And have it look as though I were guilty of something?" the senator roared.

"Didn't see one little old lady and her dog, did you? You tend to overlook quite a lot of things," Jake was saying, his voice surprisingly calm. "But she saw you."

"The hell she did!" Senator Suddard barked, but then he looked at Mrs. Derry's face, her nodding head. "This is crazy! This is preposterous!" He was confronting Jake. "If you want to charge me with something, then do so! But read me my rights! Because, damn you . . ." He spun around to confront his brother. "Joseph, tell them I don't have to answer one question unless I am formally charged and my rights are read."

"Tell them yourself, William," Joseph Suddard said, rising. "I resign as your lawyer."

"Resign! What the hell are you saying?" William Suddard cried. "You can't resign! You're my brother!"

"With the bodies discovered, your reasons for blackmailing Louisa were gone, weren't they? You could no longer force her to give you her most expensive antiques in order to buy your silence." Jake's voice was speeding up; he could see Eddie from the corner of his eye—a livid Eddie MacDonald, ready to lunge at William Suddard. Swiftly Jake motioned Officer Cairns to step in front of him.

The senator, confused, indignant, enraged, turned to look at Jake. "What the hell are you talking about?"

"This." Jake took a second plastic bag from Officer Cairns's hand, and as he did so, both Drs. Watson and Abernathy leaned forward expectantly. "Tell the good senator what is in this bag, doctor."

Dr. Abernathy, young, exuberant, and very excited, stepped forward to take the bag from Jake's hand. "It's a piece of ribbon." Opening the bag, she shook a tiny, soiled, and faded red, white, and dark-bordered ribbon onto the table. "We found it this morning on a piece of fabric taken from the gravesite. It was pushed through a buttonhole." She paused as Eddie, Jake, both Suddard brothers, and even my mother leaned in to get a closer look. "It was used to hold a medal given during World War II. The medal itself wasn't worn every day, but the ribbon was, to indicate the owner was a recipient of the Iron Cross, a decoration given to German soldiers and sailors."

Jake started in right after her, never missing a beat. "Jim MacDonald was a spotter during World War II; he watched for submarines, or U-boats, using the telescope stuck in that dog's head—" Jake pointed dramatically at the dog silhouetted on the bluff. "Fifty years ago he saw two men come ashore from a U-boat, two men he later killed and buried in this yard. And you knew about it." He was looking at the senator. "You witnessed it, or you learned about it somehow. Louisa knew about it, too. Her father must have told her he buried them in the yard, but he never told her *where* they were, possibly for her own protection. But you knew, didn't you?"

"You are crazy, absolutely crazy," William Suddard blurted out like a madman as he stepped back from us, the small group that had been huddled forward to look at Dr. Abernathy's grim find. "Me? Me blackmailing Louisa? Don't you know anything, man? *She's* been blackmailing *us!* For fifty years! Tell them, Joseph!" He was almost crying, or was it laughter?

I couldn't tell, just knew I felt my mother's arms around my neck suddenly, clutching me so tightly I could barely breathe . . . And then the senator was crying and falling back into his chair, tears running down his cheeks as he said over and over, "Tell them, Joseph. Tell them. Tell them how sweet little Louisa has been blackmailing us for fifty years . . ."

\*     \*     \*

"I UNDERSTAND WHY YOU DID it this way. There was so much you didn't know." Joseph Suddard was seated at the table, his hands clenched in a hard knot atop it.

"I know your brother saw an opportunity and seized it. Can you deny that?" Jake said.

Everyone was gone now. Drs. Watson and Abernathy, Eddie, the police officers. The senator had left in the custody of the state police. Only we were left, Joseph Suddard and Jake, Mom, and me. "Tell me first if Louisa is going to make it," Joseph Suddard replied.

"Tell me this before I do—when you found the door open, you knew your brother had been here, didn't you?"

"Sergeant, my brother was stealing cars before he was twelve. A thief, yes he was, but I truly did not think he was a murderer."

"Or a blackmailer?" Jake asked. "Can you explain that to me?"

"Ah, because of the two dead Nazis." Joseph Suddard smiled strangely. "You thought my brother was blackmailing Louisa because he had knowledge of those bodies."

Jake nodded. "And with the bodies uncovered, there would be no more blackmail. She would finally have to tell the police what she knew, about what her father did fifty years ago."

"Tell the police what? That her father shot and killed two German intelligence officers who trespassed on American soil? Despite your cleverness, you've got it backwards. William was right. Louisa has been blackmailing us.

"Our father was a cartographer," Joseph Suddard said, "as you know. He mapped every inch of this shoreline as far south as New York Bay. When he died, he left a house full of nautical maps, or charts as they're called. I don't know how William was contacted, supposedly through a Canadian fisherman he met. A collector he knew was interested in buying those charts. The only problem was that they were charts of the eastern coastline, and we were at war. In other words, such a transaction was illegal, and William knew it. So the plan was to meet this 'collector' at our dock, on May 9, 1943, a date your quite capable forensic scientist would love to hear."

Suddenly I spoke up. "And Mr. MacDonald, with his telescope, saw them come off a sub."

"You are a bright boy, aren't you?" Joseph Suddard said to me. He turned to look at Jake. "Jim MacDonald knew something was wrong, so he got out his gun and got in his old truck and drove down the road to see what it was. What he found were two boys, one eighteen and very sure of himself, the other fourteen and not so sure, arguing with two Germans, or Nazis if you will. They refused to deal with us. Oh, they had a big suitcase of money, sixty thousand American dollars in old, unmarked bills, but I have no doubt in my mind that when they saw we were just kids they planned to take our maps, keep the money, and kill us."

"Mr. MacDonald had to kill them." That was my mother, sitting with a blank look in her eyes.

"Yes. One had taken hold of me and put his pistol to my head. He told William to put the maps in the boat. They had a little inflatable craft. But old Jim . . . well, Jim was a crack shot. He took one between the eyes. The other . . ." He paused, sighed. "Look for damage in the midsection. Anyhow, Joe had us put the bodies in his truck; then he took the maps and the money. He told us to stay put and that he'd return. We were so scared, even William, that we didn't move all night."

"But I still don't understand," Jake said. "You're saying that Jim MacDonald . . . and Louisa? Blackmailed you?"

"My God," Mom cried, sitting back, putting both hands to her mouth. When we turned to look at her, her face was covered with tears. "She . . . he . . . Louisa and her father . . . they forced you and your brother . . . they . . . my God? To do . . . to do . . . good?"

"Yes, my good lady." Joseph Suddard was close enough to put his hand on her arm. "Yes, so they did. Jim told us we would never find the bodies, or the maps, that they would be buried somewhere on his property."

Mom was still crying. "So Louisa, she couldn't let anyone touch . . . or move . . . her house."

Joseph Suddard nodded.

"She's going to be all right," Jake murmured. "Though I still don't understand. Maybe I'm a fool, but these were German sailors, they—"

"They were Nazis, sergeant, German Intelligence, I believe, and old Jim did report the submarine. He reported many submarines, most of which turned out to be cormorants." A vague smile. "Jim told us that we had to do exactly as he said or he'd turn us in. He didn't want to, you see. What would become of a wild and reckless eighteen-year-old found guilty of treason? Maybe I would have gotten juvenile hall, but William? No, Jim had a heart, a firm and stubborn heart. He used that money to pay our bills so we could finish high school, and then he sent us to college. Some he used himself, yes, to start his antiques business, but he never lived lavishly. We were to do good, he said, to take this money that was meant for evil and do good with it."

"And the antiques? Marked with your names?"

"Well, I've no doubt that was William's doing, and that young Eddie Mac-Donald found him out. But Louisa did give us things, with orders to donate the proceeds to charity. As she herself did frequently, and as I hope she will do again."

At my mother's soft voice, we all turned to her. "You can force a man to do good . . ." She was drying her eyes. "But you cannot force a man to *be* good."

Joseph Suddard nodded again. "The location of the bodies and the maps were Jim's little safeguard in case William ever tired of 'doing good.' It hasn't been easy for William, fighting his own nature every day." He smiled grimly. "Now let me show you where old Jim hid the buttons he cut off the men's clothing; they had swastikas on them. And their guns, their belts. You see that?" He turned to point in the dark toward the edge of the bluff. "The dog? I guessed long ago and checked one night when Louisa and Jim were out of town. The head comes off; it turns so the telescope could be turned. Inside the dog is hollow." He rose and touched my mother's hand. "Come, let me show you."

And so he did.

While many authors write historical mystery fiction, only a handful regularly write twentieth-century ethnic historical mystery fiction. Walter Mosley is one of the few, and his Easy Rawlins series, set in Los Angeles in the 1940s and '50s, has won him acclaim from both critics and the President of the United States. His latest novel is *RL's Dream*. He pulls no punches, and his characters make no excuses for themselves. The protagonist in the following story, Socrates Fortlow, is a perfect example. In this selection from the short story collection *Always Outnumbered, Always Outgunned*, he creates a modern-day tale of two generations clashing at first, then finally coming to an uneasy cease-fire.

# Crimson Shadow
## WALTER MOSLEY

### One

"What you doin' there, boy?"

It was six a.m. Socrates Fortlow had come out to the alley to see what was wrong with Billy. He hadn't heard him crow that morning and was worried about his old friend.

The sun was just coming up. The alley was almost pretty with the trash and broken asphalt covered in half-light. Discarded wine bottles shone like murky emeralds in the sludge. In the dawn shadows Socrates didn't even notice the boy until he moved. He was standing in front of a small cardboard box, across the alley—next to Billy's wire fence.

"What bidness is it to you, old man?" the boy answered. He couldn't have been more than twelve but he had that hard convict stare.

Socrates knew convicts, knew them inside and out.

"I asked you a question, boy. Ain't yo' momma told you t'be civil?"

"Shit!" The boy turned away, ready to leave. He wore baggy jeans with a blooming blue T-shirt over his bony arms and chest. His hair was cut close to the scalp.

The boy bent down to pick up the box.

"What they call you?" Socrates asked the skinny butt stuck up in the air.

"What's it to you?"

Socrates pushed open the wooden fence and leapt. If the boy hadn't had his back turned he would have been able to dodge the stiff lunge. As it was he heard something and moved quickly to the side.

Quickly. But not quickly enough.

Socrates grabbed the skinny arms with his big hands—the rock breakers, as Joe Benz used to call them.

"Ow! Shit!"

Socrates shook the boy until the serrated steak knife, which had appeared from nowhere, fell from his hand.

The old brown rooster was dead in the box. His head slashed so badly that half of the beak was gone.

"Let me loose, man." The boy kicked, but Socrates held him at arm's length.

"Don't make me hurt you, boy," he warned. He let go of one arm and said, "Pick up that box. Pick it up!" When the boy obeyed, Socrates pulled him by the arm—dragged him through the gate, past the tomato plants and string bean vines, into the two rooms where he'd stayed since they'd let him out of prison.

THE KITCHEN WAS ONLY BIG enough for a man and a half. The floor was pitted linoleum; maroon where it had kept its color, gray where it had worn through. There was a card table for dining and a fold-up plastic chair for a seat. There was a sink with a hot plate on the drainboard and shelves that were once cabinets—before the doors were torn off.

The light fixture above the sink had a sixty-watt bulb burning in it. The room smelled of coffee. A newspaper was spread across the table.

Socrates shoved the boy into the chair, not gently.

"Sit'own!"

There was a mass of webbing next to the weak lightbulb. A red spider picked its way slowly through the strands.

"What's your name, boy?" Socrates asked again.

"Darryl."

There was a photograph of a painting tacked underneath the light. It was the image of a black woman in the doorway of a house. She wore a red dress and a red hat to protect her eyes from the sun. She had her arms crossed under her breasts and looked angry. Darryl stared at the painting while the spider danced above.

"Why you kill my friend, asshole?"

"What?" Darryl asked. There was fear in his voice.

"You heard me."

"I-I-I din't kill nobody." Darryl gulped and opened his eyes wider than seemed possible. "Who told you that?"

When Socrates didn't say anything, Darryl jumped up to run, but the man socked him in the chest, knocking the wind out of him, pushing him back down in the chair.

Socrates squatted down and scooped the rooster up out of the box. He held the limp old bird up in front of Darryl's face.

"Why you kill Billy, boy?"

"That's a bird." Darryl pointed. There was relief mixed with panic in his eyes.

"That's my friend."

"You crazy, old man. That's a bird. Bird cain't be nobody's friend." Darryl's words were still wild. Socrates knew the guilty look on his face.

He wondered at the boy and at the rooster that had gotten him out of his bed every day for the past eight years. A rage went through him and he crushed the rooster's neck in his fist.

"You crazy," Darryl said.

A large truck made its way down the alley just then. The heavy vibrations went through the small kitchen, making plates and tinware rattle loudly.

Socrates shoved the corpse into the boy's lap. "Get ovah there to the sink an' pluck it."

"Shit!"

"You don't have to do it . . ."

"You better believe I ain't gonna . . ."

". . . but I *will* kick holy shit outta you if you don't."

"Pluck what? What you mean, pluck it?"

"I mean go ovah t'that sink an' pull out the feathers. What you kill it for if you ain't gonna pluck it?"

"I'as gonna sell it."

"Sell it?"

"Yeah," Darryl said. "Sell it to some old lady wanna make some chicken."


## Two

Darryl plucked the chicken bare. He wanted to stop halfway but Socrates kept pointing out where he had missed and pushed him back toward the sink. Darryl used a razor-sharp knife that Socrates gave him to cut off the feet and battered head. He slit open the old rooster's belly and set aside the liver, heart, and gizzard.

"Rinse out all the blood. All of it," Socrates told his captive. "Man could get sick on blood."

While Darryl worked, under the older man's supervision, Socrates made Minute rice and then green beans seasoned with lard and black pepper. He prepared them in succession, one after the other on the single hot plate. Then he sautéed the giblets, with green onions from the garden, in bacon fat that he kept in a can over the sink. He mixed the giblets in with the rice.

When the chicken was ready he took tomatoes, basil, and garlic from the garden and put them all in a big pot on the hot plate.

"Billy was a tough old bird," Socrates said. "He gonna have to cook for a while."

"When you gonna let me go, man?"

"Where you got to go?"

"Home."

"Okay. Okay, fine. Billy could cook for a hour more. Let's go over your house. Where's that at?"

"What you mean, man? You ain't goin' t'my house."

"I sure am too," Socrates said, but he wasn't angry anymore. "You come over here an' murder my friend an' I got to tell somebody responsible."

Darryl didn't have any answer to that. He'd spent over an hour working in the kitchen, afraid even to speak to his captor. He was afraid mostly of those big hands. He had never felt anything as strong as those hands. Even with the chicken knife he was afraid.

"I'm hungry. When we gonna eat?" Darryl asked. "I mean I hope you plan t'eat this here after all this cookin'."

"Naw, man," Socrates said. "I thought we could go out an' sell it t'some ole lady like t'eat chicken."

"Huh?" Darryl said.

The kitchen was filling up with the aroma of chicken and sauce. Darryl's stomach growled loudly.

"You hungry?" Socrates asked him.

"Yeah."

"That's good. That's good."

"Shit. Ain't good 'less I get sumpin' t'eat."

"Boy should be hungry. Yeah. Boys is always hungry. That's how they get to be men."

"What the fuck you mean, man? You just crazy. That's all."

"If you know you hungry then you know you need sumpin'. Sumpin' missin' an' hungry tell you what it is."

"That's some kinda friend to you too?" Darryl sneered. "Hungry yo' friend?"

Socrates smiled then. His broad black face shone with delight. He wasn't a very old man, somewhere in his fifties. His teeth were all his own and healthy, though darkly stained. The top of his head was completely bald; tufts of wiry white hovered behind his ears.

"Hungry, horny, hello, and how come. They all my friends, my best friends."

Darryl sniffed the air and his stomach growled again.

"Uh-huh," Socrates hummed. "That's right. They all my friends. All of 'em. You got to have good friends you wanna make it through the penitentiary."

"You up in jail?" Darryl asked.

"Yup."

"My old man's up in jail," Darryl said. "Least he was. He died though."

"Oh. Sorry t'hear it, li'l brother. I'm sorry."

"What you in jail for?"

Socrates didn't seem to hear the question. He was looking at the picture of the painting above the sink. The right side of the scene was an open field of yellow grasses under a light blue sky. The windows of the house were shuttered and dark but the sun shone hard on the woman in red.

"You still hungry?" Socrates asked.

Darryl's stomach growled again and Socrates laughed.


## Three

Socrates made Darryl sit in the chair while he turned over the trash can for his seat. He read the paper for half an hour or more while the rooster simmered on the hot plate. Darryl knew to keep quiet. When it was done, Socrates served the meal on three plates—one for each dish. The man and boy shoveled down dirty rice, green beans, and tough rooster like they were starving men; eating off the same plates, neither one uttered a word. The only drink they had was water—their glasses were mayonnaise jars. Their breathing was loud and slobbery. Hands moved in syncopation; tearing and scooping.

Anyone witnessing the orgy would have said that they hailed from the same land; prayed to the same gods.

When the plates were clean they sat back bringing hands across bellies. They both sighed and shook their heads.

"That was some good shit," Darryl said. "Mm!"

"Bet you didn't know you could cook, huh?" Socrates asked.

"Shit no!" the boy said.

"Keep your mouth clean, li'l brother. You keep it clean an' then they know you mean business when you say sumpin' strong."

Darryl was about to say something but decided against it. He looked over at the door, and then back at Socrates.

"Could I go now?" he asked, a boy talking to his elder at last.

"Not yet."

"How come?" There was an edge of fear in the boy's voice. Socrates remembered many times reveling in the fear he brought to young men in their cells. Back then he enjoyed the company of fear.

"Not till I hear it. You cain't go till then."

"Hear what?"

"You know what. So don't be playin' stupid. Don't be playin' stupid an' you just et my friend."

Darryl made to push himself up but abandoned that idea when he saw those hands rise from the table.

"You should be afraid, Darryl," Socrates said, reading the boy's eyes. "I kilt men with these hands. Choked an' broke 'em. I could crush yo' head wit' one hand." Socrates held out his left palm.

"I ain't afraid'a you," Darryl said.

"Yes you are. I know you are 'cause you ain't no fool. You seen some bad things out there but I'm the worst. I'm the worst you ever seen."

Darryl looked at the door again.

"Ain't nobody gonna come save you, li'l brother. Ain't nobody gonna come. If you wanna make it outta here then you better give me what I want."

Socrates knew just when the tears would come. He had seen it a hundred times. In prison it made him want to laugh; but now he was sad. He wanted to reach out to the blubbering child and tell him that it was okay; that everything was all right. But it wasn't all right, might not ever be.

"Stop cryin' now, son. Stop cryin' an' tell me about it."

" 'Bout what?" Darryl said, his words vibrating like a hummingbird's wings.

" 'Bout who you killed, that's what."

"I ain't killed nobody," Darryl said in a monotone.

"Yes you did. Either that or you saw sumpin'. I heard it in your deny when you didn't know I was talkin' 'bout Billy. I know when a man is guilty, Darryl. I know that down in my soul."

Darryl looked away and set his mouth shut.

"I ain't a cop, li'l brother. I ain't gonna turn you in. But you kilt my friend out there an' we just et him down. I owe t'Billy an' to you too. So tell me about it. You tell me an' then you could go."

They stared at each other for a long time. Socrates grinned to put the boy at ease but he didn't look benevolent. He looked hungry.

Darryl felt like the meal.


**Four**


He didn't want to say it but he didn't feel bad either. Why should he feel bad? It wasn't even his idea. Wasn't anybody's plan. It was just him and Jamal and Norris out in the oil fields above Baldwin Hills. Sometimes dudes went there with their old ladies. And if you were fast enough you could see some pussy and then get away with their pants.

They also said that the army was once up there and that there were old bullets and even hand grenades just lying around to be found.

But then this retarded boy showed up. He said he was with his brother but that his brother left him and now he wanted to be friends with Darryl and his boys.

"At first we was just playin'," Darryl told Socrates. "You know—pushin' 'im an' stuff."

But when he kept on following them—when he squealed every time they saw somebody—they hit him and pushed him down. Norris even threw a rock at his head. But the retard kept on coming. He was running after them and crying that they had hurt him. He cried louder and louder. And when they hit him, to shut him up, he yelled so loud that it made them scared right inside their chests.

"You know I always practice with my knife," Darryl said. "You know you got to be able to get it out quick if somebody on you."

Socrates nodded. He still practiced himself.

"'I'ont know how it got in my hand. I swear I didn't mean t'cut 'im."

"You kill'im?" Socrates asked.

Darryl couldn't talk but he opened his mouth and nodded.

They all swore never to tell anybody. They would kill the one who told about it—they swore on blood and went home.

"Anybody find 'im?" Socrates asked.

"'I'ont know."

The red spider danced while the woman in red kept her arms folded and stared her disapproval of all men—especially those two men. Darryl had to go to the bathroom. He had the runs after that big meal—and, Socrates thought, from telling his tale.

When he came out he looked ashy, his lips were ashen.

He slumped back in Socrates' cheap chair—drowsy but not tired. He was sick and forlorn.

For a long time they just sat there. The minutes went by but there was no clock to measure them. Socrates learned how to do without a timepiece in prison.

He counted the time while Darryl sat hopelessly by.


Five

"What you gonna do, li'l brother?"

"What?"

"How you gonna make it right?"

"Make what right? He dead. I cain't raise him back here."

When Socrates stared at the boy there was no telling what he thought. But what he was thinking didn't matter. Darryl looked away and back again. He shifted in his chair. Licked his dry lips.

"What?" he asked at last.

"You murdered a poor boy couldn't stand up to you. You killed your little brother an' he wasn't no threat; an' he didn't have no money that you couldn't take wit'out killin' 'im. You did wrong, Darryl. You did wrong."

"How the fuck you know?" Darryl yelled. He would have said more but Socrates raised his hand, not in violence but to point out the truth to his dinner guest.

Darryl went quiet and listened.

"I ain't your warden, li'l brother. I ain't gonna show you to no jail. I'm just talkin' to ya—one black man to another one. If you don't hear me there ain't nuthin' I could do."

"So I could go now?"

"Yeah, you could go. I ain't yo' warden. I just ask you to tell me how you didn't do wrong. Tell me how a healthy boy ain't wrong when he kills his black brother who sick."

Darryl stared at Socrates, at his eyes now—not his hands.

"You ain't gonna do nuthin'?"

"Boy is dead now. Rooster's dead too. We cain't change that. But you got to figure out where you stand."

"I ain't goin' t'no fuckin' jail if that's what you mean."

Socrates smiled. "Shoo'. I don't blame you for that. Jail ain't gonna help a damn thing. Better shoot yo'self than go to jail."

"I ain't gonna shoot myself neither. Uh-uh."

"If you learn you wrong then maybe you get to be a man."

"What's that s'posed t'mean?"

"Ain't nobody here, Darryl. Just you'n me. I'm sayin' that I think you was wrong for killin' that boy. I know you killed'im. I know you couldn't help it. But you was wrong anyway. An' if that's the truth, an' if you could say it, then maybe you'll learn sumpin'. Maybe you'll laugh in the morning sometimes again."

Darryl stared at the red spider. She was still now. He didn't say anything, didn't move at all.

"We all got to be our own judge, li'l brother. 'Cause if you don't know when you wrong then yo' life ain't worf a damn."

Darryl waited as long as he could. And then he asked, "I could go?"

"You done et Billy. So I guess that much is through."

"So it ain't wrong that I killed'im 'cause I et him?"

"It's still wrong. It's always gonna be wrong. But you know more now. You ain't gonna kill no more chickens," Socrates said. Then he grunted out a harsh laugh. "At least not around here."

Darryl stood up. He watched Socrates to see what he'd do.

"Yo' momma cook at home, Darryl?"

"Sometimes. Not too much."

"You come over here anytime an' I teach ya how t'cook. We eat pretty good too."

"Uh-huh," Darryl answered. He took a step away from his chair.

Socrates stayed seated on his trash can.

Darryl made it all the way to the door. He grabbed the wire handle that took the place of a long-ago knob.

"What they put you in jail for?" Darryl asked.

"I killed a man an' raped his woman."

"White man?"

"No."

"Well . . . bye."

"See ya, li'l brother."

"I'm sorry . . .'bout yo' chicken."

"Billy wasn't none'a mine. He belonged to a old lady 'cross the alley."

"Well . . . bye."

"Darryl."

"Yeah."

"If you get inta trouble you could come here. It don't matter what it is— you could come here to me."


## Six

Socrates stared at the door a long time after the boy was gone; for hours. The night came on and the cool desert air of Los Angeles came in under the door and through the cracks in his small shack of an apartment.

A cricket was calling out for love from somewhere in the wall.

Socrates looked at the woman, sun shining on her head. Her red sun hat threw a hot crimson shadow across her face. There was no respite for her but she still stood defiant. He tried to remember what Theresa looked like but it had been too long now. All he had left was the picture of a painting—and that wasn't even her. All he had left from her were the words she never said. *You are dead to me, Socrates. Dead as that poor boy and that poor girl you killed.*

He wondered if Darryl would ever come back.

He hoped so.

SOCRATES WENT THROUGH THE DOORLESS doorway into his other room. He lay down on the couch and just before he was asleep he thought of how he'd wake up alone. The rooster was hoarse in his old age, his crow no more than a whisper.

*But at least that motherfucker tried.*

# BIBLIOGRAPHY
## A 1997 Yearbook, compiled by
## Edward D. Hoch

## I. COLLECTIONS AND SINGLE STORIES

Andrews, Val. *Sherlock Holmes and the Baker Street Dozen*. London: Breese Books. Thirteen new Sherlockian stories.

Bradbury, Ray. *Driving Blind*. New York: Avon Books. A mixed collection of twenty-one stories, all but four new, a few criminous, two from *EQMM*.

Browne, Howard. *Carbon-Copy Killer* and *Twelve Times Zero*. Brooklyn: Gryphon. Two science fiction detective stories, the first originally published as by "Alexander Blade."

———. *Incredible Ink,* Tucson, AZ: Dennis McMillan Publications. Limited edition of sixteen stories and novelettes from the pulps, with a brief memoir by the author.

Burke, Jan. *A Fine Set of Teeth*. Mission Viejo, CA: A.S.A.P. Publishing. A single new short story in a limited edition. Introduction by Michael Connelly, afterword by the author.

Burrage, A. M. *The Occult Files of Francis Chard: Some Ghost Stories*. Penyffordd, Chester, England: Ash-Tree Press. Ten previously uncollected stories about an occult detective, from *Blue Magazine* (British), 1927, plus sixteen ghost stories, thirteen of them collected as *Some Ghost Stories* (1927). Edited and introduced by Jack Adrian.

Cave, Hugh B. *The Dagger of Tsiang*. Chicago: Tattered Pages Press. Adventure stories from the pulps, set in Borneo.

———. *Escapades of the Eel*. Chicago: Tattered Pages Press. Fifteen stories from the pulps, about an adventurer and occasional private eye.

Chesterton, G. K. *Father Brown of the Church of Rome*. San Francisco, CA: Ignatius Press. Edited with an introduction and footnotes by John Peterson. Ten Father Brown mysteries, chosen for their insights into the Catholic faith (1996).

Christie, Agatha. *The Harlequin Tea Set*. New York: Putnam. Nine stories previously uncollected in America, including six romances from the 1920s and three mysteries from 1930, 1939 and 1971.

Coel, Margaret. *Dead End*. Mission Viejo, CA: A.S.A.P. Publishing. A single short story in a limited edition.

Cross, Amanda. *The Collected Stories*. New York: Ballantine. One new story

391

and seven reprints, three from *EQMM*, about academic sleuth Kate Fansler, with an additional nonseries mystery tale.

Ellison, Harlan. *Slippage.* New York: Houghton Mifflin. A mixed collection of twenty-one stories, some criminous, from *EQMM* and elsewhere. Includes the MWA Edgar-nominated mystery-fantasy novelette "Mefisto in Onyx."

Gilbert, Michael. *The Man Who Hated Banks and Other Mysteries.* Norfolk, VA: Crippen & Landru. Eighteen stories and novelettes, 1948–79, eight published for the first time in America.

Gorman, Ed & Richard Chizmar. *Dirty Coppers.* Springfield, PA: Gauntlet Publications. A novelette and a long short story, both new.

Hoch, Edward D. *Five Rings in Reno.* Norfolk, VA: Crippen & Landru. A single short story from *EQMM* (7/76, as by "R. L. Stevens") in a separately printed pamphlet included with the limited edition of *The Ripper of Storyville.*

———. *The Ripper of Storyville and Other Ben Snow Tales.* Norfolk, VA: Crippen & Landru. Fourteen historical mysteries from The Saint Magazine and *EQMM*, 1961–86. Afterword and chronology by Marvin Lachman.

Keating, H. R. F. *In Kensington Gardens Once . . .* Norfolk, VA: Crippen & Landru. Ten stories, 1972–97, three new, mainly criminous, set around the monuments and locations of London's Kensington Gardens.

Lovisi, Gary. *Hellbent on Homicide.* London: The Do-Not Press. A 1996 hardboiled short novel with two short stories about the same characters added for this British edition.

Manasek, F. J. *Under Cover: Death Stalks the Book Dealer: Twelve Tales of the Intrigue, Murder and Mayhem that Infect the Rare Book World.* Norwich, VT: Museum Street Press. Twelve new stories, supposedly based on fact.

Maron, Margaret. *Shoveling Smoke: Selected Mystery Stories.* Norfolk, VA: Crippen & Landru. Twenty-two stories (1968–97), one new, including some cases solved by series characters Sigrid Harald and Deborah Knott.

McCrumb, Sharyn. *Foggy Mountain Breakdown and Other Stories.* New York: Ballantine Books. Twenty-four stories, two new, mainly criminous.

McDermid, Val. *The Writing on the Wall and Other Stories.* London: Revolver. Six stories, 1989–96, in a 47-page limited edition chapbook.

Mosley, Walter. *Always Outnumbered, Always Outgunned.* New York: Norton. Connected short stories about an ex-convict living in the Watts area of Los Angeles.

Nolan, William F. *The Pop-Op Caper with A Long Time Dying* and *The Pulpcon Kill.* Brooklyn: Gryphon. Two stories about private eye Bart Challis, and a third about his half-brother Nick Challis.

Rankin, Ian. *Herbert in Motion and Other Stories.* London: Revolver. Four stories, two new, in a 64-page limited edition chapbook. The title story won the 1996 CWA Gold Dagger.

Rhea, Nicholas. *Constable at the Gate*. London: Robert Hale. Eight new stories in a continuing series.

Saylor, Steven. *The House of the Vestals*. New York: St. Martin's. Nine stories about Gordainus the Finder, set in ancient Rome, eight from *EQMM*.

Spark, Muriel. *Open to the Public: New & Collected Stories*. New York: New Directions. Thirty-seven stories, ten previously uncollected. A few criminous.

Starrett, Vincent. *The Return of Jimmy Lavender*. Toronto: Metropolitan Toronto Reference Library. Edited by Peter Ruber. Thirteen previously uncollected stories.

———. *Wayside Tales*. Toronto: Metropolitan Toronto Reference Library. Edited by Peter Ruber. Eleven stories, three previously published in *The Blue Door* (1930).

Theroux, Paul. *The Collected Stories*. New York: Viking. Sixty-eight stories, four previously uncollected. A few criminous.

Thomson, June. *The Secret Documents of Sherlock Holmes*. London: Constable. Seven new Sherlockian pastiches in the fourth volume of the series.

Van de Wetering, Janwillem. *Judge Dee Plays His Lute, A Play and Selected Mystery Stories*. Bar Harbor, ME: Wonderly Press. A radio play and nine short stories, one previously collected in a slightly different version.

Wandrei, Howard. *The Last Pin*. Minneapolis: Fedogan & Bremer. A small-press collection of stories by a little-known pulp writer.

Wishnia, K. J. A. *Flat Rate and Other Tales*. East Setauket, NY: The Imaginary Press. A crime novella and short story, along with two brief science fiction tales.

Yaffe, James. *My Mother, the Detective: The Complete "Mom" Short Stories*. Norfolk, VA: Crippen *and* Landru. Eight stories from *EQMM*, 1952–68.

———. *The Problem of the Emperor's Mushrooms*. Norfolk, VA: Crippen and Landru. A single short story from *EQMM* (9/45) in a separately printed pamphlet included with the limited edition of *My Mother, the Detective*.

# II. ANTHOLOGIES

Ashley, Mike, ed. *The Mammoth Book of New Sherlock Holmes Adventures*. New York: Carroll & Graf. Twenty-six Holmes cases by various authors, all but four new.

———, ed. *Shakespearean Whodunnits*. New York: Carroll & Graf. Twenty-five stories, all but one new, based on Shakespeare's plays.

Belbin, David, ed. *City of Crime*. Nottingham, England: Five Leaves Publications. Fifteen new stories, set in and around Nottingham.

Cameron, Vicki & Linda Wiken, eds. *Cottage Country Killers*. Burnstown, Ontario, Canada: General Store Publishing House. Twenty-four new stories and poems by Canadian women crime writers loosely organized as the Ladies' Killing Circle.

Chizmar, Richard, ed. *Screamplays*. New York: Ballantine/Del Rey. A mixed collection of seven unproduced screenplays, some fantasy. Introduction by Dean Koontz.

Clark, Mary Higgins, presenter. *The Plot Thickens*. New York: Pocket Books. Eleven new stories in a volume for Literacy Partners. Introduction by Liz Smith.

Datlow, Ellen, ed. *Lethal Kisses: 19 Stories of Sex, Horror & Revenge*. London: Orion. Eighteen new stories and a reprint by Ruth Rendell. Some fantasy.

Douglas, Carole Nelson, ed. *Marilyn: Shades of Blonde*. A mixed collection of twenty-one new stories, mainly by mystery and fantasy writers, based upon the life and legend of Marilyn Monroe.

Edwards, Martin, ed. *Whydunit?: Perfectly Criminal 2*. Sutton, England & New York: Severn House. Seventeen stories, all but one new, in the annual anthology from England's Crime Writers' Association. (Bibliographic note: On the dust jacket the title appears as *Perfectly Criminal 2: Whydunit?*)

English, Priscilla; Lisa Seidman & Mae Woods, eds. *Murder by Thirteen*. Acton, CA: Crown Valley Press. Thirteen new stories by members of the Los Angeles chapter of Sisters in Crime.

Foxwell, Elizabeth & Martin H. Greenberg, eds. *Malice Domestic 6*. New York: Pocket Books. Presented by Anne Perry. Seventeen new traditional mysteries in an annual series.

Gorman, Ed & Martin H. Greenberg, eds. *The Fatal Frontier*. New York: Carroll & Graf. Twenty-three western crime stories, seven new. Introduction by Bill Pronzini.

———, eds. *Love Kills*. New York: Carroll & Graf. Thirty-one crime and suspense stories, four new.

Gorman, Ed, Bill Pronzini & Martin H. Greenberg, eds. *American Pulp*. New York: Carroll & Graf. Thirty-five stories and novelettes, one new, mainly from the mystery magazines, 1937–97.

Greenberg, Martin H., ed. *Legends of the Batman*. New York: MJF Books. Fifteen stories from previous anthologies, plus two new tales about Poison Ivy and Mr. Freeze.

Greenberg, Martin H. & Elizabeth Foxwell, eds. *Murder, They Wrote*. New York: Boulevard Books/Berkley. Eighteen new stories by women writers.

Greenberg, Martin H., Ed Gorman & Larry Segriff, eds. *Cat Crimes for the*

*Holidays.* New York: Donald J. Fine. Nineteen new stories set on various holidays throughout the year.

Greene, Douglas G., ed. *Detection by Gaslight.* Mineola, NY: Dover Thrift Editions. Fourteen Victorian detective stories, with introduction and headnotes by Greene.

Haining, Peter, ed. *Crime Movies 2.* London: Severn House. Twelve stories that have inspired popular television crime series.

Hess, Joan, ed. *Funny Bones.* New York: Signet. Fifteen new humorous mysteries and one reprint.

Hess, Joan, Ed Gorman & Martin H. Greenberg, eds. *The Year's 25 Finest Crime and Mystery Stories: Sixth Annual Edition.* New York: Carroll & Graf. Introduction by Jon L. Breen, bibliography and necrology by Edward D. Hoch. Stories from various sources.

Hoch, Edward D., ed. *Twelve American Detective Stories.* Oxford & New York: Oxford University Press. A dozen stories, 1844–1962.

Hutchings, Janet, ed. *Simply the Best Mysteries.* New York: Carroll & Graf. Sixteen Edgar-winner stories and six nominees from *EQMM.*

Koster, Elaine & Joseph Pittman, eds. *The Best of the Best.* New York: Signet. A mixed collection of eighteen new stories, nearly half criminous, to celebrate the publisher's fiftieth anniversary (1/98).

Manson, Cynthia, ed. *Canine Crimes II.* New York: Berkley Prime Crime. Thirteen stories about dogs from *EQMM* and *AHMM.*

———, ed. *Law and Order.* New York: Berkley Prime Crime. Fourteen stories of cops, lawyers and prisons from *EQMM* & *AHMM.*

Manson, Cynthia & Kathleen Halligan, eds. *Murder to Music.* New York: Carroll & Graf. Fifteen stories mainly from *EQMM* and *AHMM,* 1947–93.

Marcus, Laura, ed. *Twelve Women Detective Stories.* Oxford & New York: Oxford University Press. A dozen stories featuring women sleuths, 1861–1950.

Monfredo, Miriam Grace & Sharan Newman, eds. *Crime Through Time.* New York: Berkley Prime Crime. Twenty-one new historical mysteries in the first of a proposed annual series.

Mosiman, Billie Sue & Martin H. Greenberg, eds. *Death in Dixie.* Nashville: Rutledge Hill Press. Fifteen mystery and crime stories set in southern states, from various sources.

Muller, Marcia & Bill Pronzini, eds. *Detective Duos.* New York: Oxford University Press. Twenty-five stories, one new, featuring crime-solving twosomes.

Mystery Scene, Staff of, eds. *Mystery's Most Wanted: The Year's Finest Crime and Mystery Stories.* New York: St. Martin's. Sixteen stories from the 1996 edition of *The Year's 25 Finest Crime and Mystery Stories.*

Polito, Robert, ed. *Crime Novels: American Noir of the 1930s & 40s.* Crime

*Novels: American Noir of the 1950s.* New York: The Library of America. A two-volume anthology of eleven novels and novellas.

Randisi, Robert J., ed. *First Cases, Volume 2: First Appearances of Classic American Sleuths.* Fifteen stories by modern authors, 1966–95.

Ripley, Mike & Maxim Jakubowski, eds. *Fresh Blood 2.* London: The Do-Not Press. Fifteen new stories by British writers.

Skene-Melvin, David, ed. *Bloody York: Tales of Mayhem, Murder and Mystery in Toronto.* Toronto: Simon & Pierre. Thirteen stories, two new, some fantasy, with a bibliography of crime novels set in Toronto (1996).

Slung, Michele, ed. *Murder & Other Acts of Literature.* New York: Dunne/St. Martin's. Twenty-four stories of murder and sudden death by celebrated mainstream writers, past and present. Some fantasy.

Spillane, Mickey & Max Allan Collins, eds. *Private Eyes.* Sixteen stories, all but two new, with an introduction by Collins (1/98).

———, eds. *Vengeance Is Hers.* New York: Signet. Sixteen stories by women mystery writers, all but one new, plus a reprint by Spillane and an introduction by Collins.

Wallace, Marilyn, ed. *The Best of Sisters in Crime.* New York: Berkley Prime Crime. Twenty-two stories chosen from the five previous volumes of the popular paperback series.

Waugh, Charles G. & Martin H. Greenberg, eds. *Sci-Fi Private Eye.* New York: Roc Books. Nine crime stories from leading science fiction authors.

Weinberg, Robert, Stefan Dziemianowicz & Martin H. Greenberg, eds. *100 Sneaky Little Sleuth Stories.* New York: Barnes & Noble Books. One hundred stories, mainly short-shorts, from various sources.

# III. NONFICTION

Assouline, Pierre. *Simenon. A Biography.* New York: Knopf. A new life of Maigret's creator.

Bachelder, Frances H. *Mary Roberts Rinehart, Mistress of Mystery.* San Bernardino, CA: Brownstone Books/Borgo Press. A detailed study of ten of Rinehart's major mystery novels.

Carraze, Alain & Jean-Luc Putheaud. *The Avengers Companion.* London: Titan Books. First English translation of a 1990 French guide to the popular 1960s television series, including interviews with stars and writers, an episode guide, and detailed synopses of thirteen classic episodes. More than 200 illustrations.

Corvasce, Mauro V. & Joseph R. Paglino. *Murder One: A Writer's Guide to*

*Homicide.* Cincinnati: Writer's Digest Books. A volume in the continuing "Howdunit Series" for mystery writers.

Deeck, William F., compiler. *CADS: An Index to Issues 1–30.* South Benfleet, Essex, England: CADS. A 70-page index to the first thirty issues of the popular British fanzine *Crime and Detective Stories.*

Diemart, Brian. *Graham Greene's Thrillers and the 1930s.* Montreal: McGill-Queen's University Press. A study of Green's early thrillers and his other novels of the period (1996).

Dove, George N. *The Reader and the Detective Story.* Bowling Green, OH: Popular Press. An analysis of how detective fiction is read.

Ewell, Barbara C. & Mary A. McCay, eds. *Performance for a Lifetime: A Festschrift Honoring Dorothy Harrell Brown. Essays on Women, Religion, and the Renaissance.* New Orleans: Loyola University. Seventeen essays including Joe R. Christopher's "The Pride of Sister Ursula," about the Sister Ursula mysteries of Anthony Boucher.

Faron, Fay. *Missing Persons: A Writer's Guide to Finding the Lost, the Abducted and the Escaped.* Cincinnati: Writer's Digest Press. A volume in the continuing "Howdunit Series" for mystery writers.

Glassman, Steve & Maurice O'Sullivan, eds. *Crime Fiction and Film in the Sunshine State: Florida Noir.* Bowling Green, OH: Popular Press. A survey of authors, films and books associated with Florida.

Grape, Jan, Dean James & Ellen Nehr, eds. *Deadly Women.* New York: Carroll & Graf. Nearly one hundred essays, interviews and checklists celebrating women's contributions to crime fiction.

Green, Joseph & Jim Finch. *Sleuths, Sidekicks and Stooges.* Aldershot, Hants, England: Scolar Press. An annotated bibliography of over 7,000 detectives, their assistants and their rivals in mystery, crime and adventure fiction, 1795–1995.

Hershenson, Bruce. *Crime Movie Posters.* West Plains, MO: Bruce Hershenson. Reproductions of full-color movie posters, lobby cards, etc., 1913–1996.

Hiney, Tom. *Raymond Chandler.* Boston: Atlantic Monthly. A new biography of Philip Marlowe's creator.

Hunter, Evan. *Me and Hitch.* London: Faber and Faber. A 91-page memoir of Hunter's work with Hitchcock on the screenplays for *The Birds* and *Marnie.*

Inness, Sherrie A., ed. *Nancy Drew and Company: Culture, Gender, and Girls' Series.* Bowling Green, OH: Popular Press. An anthology of essays on girls' series fiction,

Kaufman, Natalie Hevener & Carol McGinnis Kay. *"G" Is for Grafton: The World of Kinsey Millhone.* New York: Henry Holt. A guide to the first thirteen novels in the best-selling series about a woman private eye.

King, Nina, with Robin Winks. *Crimes of the Scene: A Mystery Novel Guide for the International Traveler.* New York: St. Martin's. Notes on hundreds of novels set outside the United States, grouped by country or region.

Margolies, Edward & Michel Fabre. *The Several Lives of Chester Himes.* University, MS: University of Mississippi Press. A biography of the creator of black detectives Coffin Ed Johnson and Grave Digger Jones.

Melling, John Kennedy. *Murder Done to Death: Parody and Pastiche in Detective Fiction.* Metuchen, NJ: The Scarecrow Press. A wide-ranging look at the subject.

Morelius, Iwan & Margareta. *Meeting With Authors and Other People in the Book World.* Alicante, Spain: Iwan Morelius. A privately printed memoir (in English) by a well-known Swedish mystery fan, editor of *Dast* Magazine, and his wife. Indexed and illustrated with more than two hundred photographs of British and American crime writers.

Ousby, Ian. *Guilty Parties: A Mystery Lover's Companion.* New York: Thames and Hudson. An illustrated history and guide to mystery fiction. British title: *The Crime and Mystery Book.*

Peters, Barbara & Susan Malling, eds. *AZ Murder Goes . . . Classic.* Scottsdale, AZ: The Poisoned Pen Press. Fourteen papers of an annual mystery writer's conference held in Scottsdale in February 1996, discussing classic authors of the genre.

Pronzini, Bill. *Six-Gun in Cheek: An Affectionate Guide to the "Worst" in Western Fiction.* Minneapolis: Crossover Press. Though the emphasis is on western fiction, the author's commentary includes some mentions of mystery pulp magazines and authors.

Randisi, Robert J., ed. *Writing the Private Eye Novel.* Cincinnati: Writer's Digest Books. Twenty-three new articles by members of the Private Eye Writers of America.

Redmond, Christopher, ed. *Canadian Holmes: The First Twenty-Five Years.* Ashcroft, B. C., Canada: Calabash Press. Seventy Sherlockian essays and stories from *Canadian Holmes,* a journal of the Bootmakers of Toronto.

Riviere, Francois. *In the Footsteps of Agatha Christie.* North Pomfret, VT: Trafalgar Square. Text and illustrations following Christie's life in England through the settings of her books.

Sennett, Ted. *Murder on Tape.* New York: Billboard Books. A guide to over one thousand mystery and murder movies on videotape.

Snow, Marshall W. *A Comprehensive Price List of Crime, Mystery, Thriller, Detective and Horror Fiction, 1997 Edition.* South Grafton, MA: Mostly Murder, Mystery and Mayhem Publications. A two-volume spiral-bound listing of used book prices. Published annually for the past three years.

Taylor, Thomas F. *The Golf Murders.* Westland, MI: Golf Mystery Press. A limited-edition study of more than 150 crime and detective stories with a golf background.

Weber, Ronald. *Hired Pens: Professional Writers in America's Golden Age of Print*. Athens, OH: Ohio University Press. A study of freelance writers, including Mary Roberts Rinehart, James M. Cain and more than a dozen others, some criminous.

West, W. J. *The Quest for Graham Greene*. London: Weidenfeld & Nicolson. A new one-volume biography of Greene. U.S. edition: St. Martin's Press, 1998.

Willett, Ralph. *The Naked City: Urban Crime Fiction in the USA*. Manchester, England: Manchester University Press. A study of mystery writers identified with six major American cities.

# IV. NECROLOGY

James Robert Baker (1947?–1997). Satirical novelist who authored at least two crime novels, *Fuel-Injected Dreams* (1986) and *Adrenaline* (1985), the latter as by "James Dillinger."

Samm Sinclair Baker (1909–1997). Co-author of diet books who published two paperback mysteries in the 1950s.

Donald R. Bensen (1927–1997). Editor and author who published two Sherlockian novels, notably *Irene, Good Night* (1982), as well as six romantic suspense novels as by "Julia Thatcher."

Edwin Brock (1927–1997). British poet and former policeman who authored a single crime novel, *The Little White God* (1962).

William Burroughs (1914–1997). Well known "beat" writer whose works included a few crime novels.

Martin Caidin (1927–1997). Author of adventure thrillers who published more than twenty crime and suspense novels, notably *Cyborg* (1972).

Matthew F. Christopher (1917–1997). Author of children's sports books who published a single mystery novel, *Look for the Body* (1952).

Matthew Coady (1923–1997). British book reviewer who published a number of mystery short stories in the London *Daily Mirror*.

Ellen Dearmore (1936–1996). Pseudonym of Erlene Hubly, author of two short stories featuring a detective collaboration between Gertrude Stein and Alice B. Toklas.

Kit Denton (1928–1997). Australian writer whose works included at least one crime novel, *Fiddler's Bridge* (1986).

James Dickey (1923–1997). Well-known poet who authored a single best-selling suspense novel, *Deliverance* (1970).

Dame Jean Conan Doyle (1912–1997). Daughter of Sherlock Holmes' creator, who played an important part in preserving and expanding the popularity of the noted sleuth.

William DuBois (1903–1997). Playwright and novelist who published three mystery novels in 1940–41, all featuring sleuth Jack Jordan.

Harman Grisewood (1906–1997). British radio pioneer who authored a trio of crime novels beginning with *The Recess* (1963).

George Hardinge (1921–1997). British author and publisher who edited eleven volumes of the annual *Winter's Crimes* anthology, and under the pseudonym of George Milner also published eight mystery novels of his own, 1953–85.

Leo Harris (?–1997). Mystery reviewer for *Punch* and other British publications, and long-time editor of "Red Herrings," monthly bulletin of the Crime Writers' Association.

Robert Hoskins (1933–1993). Fantasy editor who also authored a film novelization, *Survival Run* (1980) and other crime novels as by "Grace Corren, Susan Jennifer and Michael Kerr." (Reportedly died 6/1/93 near Albany, NY.)

Elspeth Huxley (1907–1997). Well-known British author whose works included a half-dozen mystery novels, notably *The African Poison Murders* (1939).

Carl Jacobi (1908–1997). Long-time author of short stories, mainly weird fantasy. At least one of his collections, *South of Samarinda* (1990), consists mostly of crime and adventure tales.

Velda Johnston (1911?–1997). Author of thirty-five Gothic mysteries, 1967–91, including one under the pseudonym of "Veronica Jason."

Marie Joseph (1920?–1997). British romance writer who published one suspense novel, *Footsteps in the Park* (1978).

Mary Jane Latsis (1927–1997). Co-author, with Martha Henissart, of the popular "Emma Lathen" series about banker John Putnam Thatcher. Beginning with *Banking on Death* (1961), the collaborators published some two dozen novels under the Lathen name and another eight under a second pseudonym, "R. B. Dominic." They were honored with the first Ellery Queen Award from Mystery Writers of America in 1983.

Frank Launder (1906?–1997). British director and screenwriter who collaborated with Sidney Gilliat on a mystery play *Meet a Body* (1955), filmed as *The Green Man*.

Cecil Lewis (1898–1997). British pioneer of radio drama whose many books included one crime novel, *The Gospel According to Judas* (1989).

J. G. Links (1904–1997). Collaborator with Dennis Weatley on the crime dossier series, beginning with *Murder Off Miami* (1936).

W. O. G. Lofts (1923–1997). British bibliographer who co-authored (with Derek Adley) *The Saint and Leslie Charteris: A Biography* (1970).

William H. Lyles (?–1996). An expert on early Dell paperbacks who authored two 1983 studies, *Putting Dell on the Map: A History of the Dell Paperbacks* and *Dell Paperbacks 1942 to Mid-1962: A Catalog-Index.*

Richard Mason (1919–1997). Mainstream author who published a single crime novel *The Fever Tree* (1962) under his own name and two others as by "Richard Lakin."

Judith Merril (1923–1997). Well-known science fiction editor, reviewer and writer who also wrote as "Cyril Judd." She published three mysteries in *The Saint Mystery Magazine* and The Saint Mystery Library, 1960–63.

Sam Moskowitz (1920?–1997). Legendary science fiction fan and historian, who published one science-fiction mystery "Death of an Asteroid" in *The Saint Mystery Magazine* (4/67).

Carl Noone (1913?–1997). Pseudonym of British radio comedian Charlie Chester, who published at least three paperback thrillers in England during the 1970s.

Samuel A. Peeples (1917–1997). Western writer who authored a single mystery novel, *The Man Who Died Twice* (1976).

Dudley Pope (1925–1997). British historical novelist who authored suspense novels about World War II, including *Convoy* (1979) and *Decoy* (1983).

Herbert Resnicow (1921–1997). Author of fifteen mystery novels beginning with *The Gold Solution* (1983), plus collaborations with well-known personalities Fran Tarkenton, Tom Seaver, Pele, and Edward I. Koch.

Harold Robbins (1916–1997). Best-selling mainstream author whose novels, beginning with *Never Love a Stranger* (1948), often contained criminous elements.

Leo Rosten (1908–1997). Author and humorist who published three mystery novels, beginning with *A Most Private Intrigue* (1967).

William Rotsler (1926–1997). Author and artist whose works included four mystery novels, 1982–84.

Kenneth Royce (1920–1997). Pen name of Kenneth Royce Gandley, British author of some three dozen mystery thrillers, including three as "Oliver Jacks." Some feature reformed burglar Spider Scott, beginning with *The XYY Man* (1970).

William Rushton (1937?–1996). British humorist who authored two crime fantasies unpublished in America, notably *W. G. Grace's Last Case* (1984).

Don Sandstrom (1921–1997). Mystery reviewer long active in fan circles.

David Shahar (1926–1997). Israeli author of a single suspense novel, *His Majesty's Agent* (1980).

Sheldon Stark (1909?–1997). Radio and television writer who authored a single paperback mystery, *Too Many Sinners* (1954).

James M. Ullman (1926?–1997). Author of four suspense novels, 1963–68, and more than thirty short stories for *EQMM*, *AHMM*, and other publications, a few under the pseudonym of "Martin Ivory."

Penelope (Penny) Wallace (1923–1997). Daughter of British mystery novelist Edgar Wallace, founder of the Edgar Wallace Society and past chairman of CWA, she published more than a dozen short stories in *EQMM*, *AHMM*, *Edgar Wallace Mystery Magazine*, and various anthologies.

Lael Tucker Wertenbaker (1909?–1997). Journalist and novelist who authored a novel about the spy Mata Hari, *The Eye of the Lion* (1964).

Ira Wolfert (1908?–1997). Best-selling writer who authored a single crime novel, *Tucker's People* (1943), basis for the film *Force of Evil*.